P9-DHT-167

G·L·O·B·E
LITERATURE

Alvin Granowsky · Eden Force Eskin · John Dawkins

Globe Book Company
Englewood Cliffs, New Jersey

RED LEVEL

CONSULTANTS

Barbara Benson
English Teacher
Watauga High School
Boone, North Carolina

Suzanne Chavez
Teacher
Palos Verdes Unified School District
Palos Verdes Estates, California

Mariann Cholakis
Reading Specialist
New York City Board of Education
New York, New York

Mary Contreras
Fellow of UCLA Writing Project
Rancho Buena Vista High School
Vista, California

Patricia Devaney
Reading Resource Teacher
Board of Education
City of New York
New York, New York

Ellen Flanagan
Principal
St. Brigid School
Brooklyn, New York

Josephine Gemake
Associate Professor
School of Education
St. John's University
Jamaica, New York

Francine Guastello
Assistant Principal
P.S. 312K
New York, New York

Margaret Haley
Reading Specialist/
Special Programs Instructor
St. John's University
Staten Island, New York

Nelda Hobbs
ECIA Coordinator/Language Arts
Social Studies Coordinator
High Schools of North Chicago Public Schools
Chicago, Illinois

Barbara Milhorn
Los Angeles Unified School District
Los Angeles, California

Mary M. O'Brien
Reading Specialist
Head of Reading Department
Hazelwood West Junior and Senior High Schools
Hazelwood, Missouri

Anthony V. Patti
Full Professor and
Chairman of Secondary
Adult, and Business Education
Herbert H. Lehman College
City University of New York
New York, New York

Evelyn Pittman
Supervisor of Language Arts
Paterson Board of Education
Paterson, New Jersey

Judy Rios
Secondary Language Arts and Resource Teacher
West Allis—West Milwaukee School District
West Allis, Wisconsin

Robert J. Scaffardi
English Department Chair
Area Coordinator (K–12)
Cranston High School East
Cranston, Rhode Island

Richard Sinatra
Director, Reading Clinic
St. John's University
Jamaica, New York

Beth Craddock Smith
Reading Specialist
Durham County Schools
Durham, North Carolina

Sheila Byrd Smith
Language Arts/Reading Teacher
St. Paul School
Staten Island, New York

Benjamin Stewart
English Teacher
Pine Forest Senior High School
Fayetteville, North Carolina

Judith E. Torres
Coordinator/Limited English Proficiency Programs
Yonkers Public Schools
Yonkers, New York

Paula Travis
Language Arts
Department Head
Newton County High School
Covington, Georgia

O. Paul Wielan
Associate Professor
School of Education
St. John's University
Jamaica, New York

G·L·O·B·E

LITERATURE

BLUE LEVEL

Annotated Teacher's Edition
Teacher's Resource Binder

RED LEVEL

Annotated Teacher's Edition
Teacher's Resource Binder

PURPLE LEVEL

Annotated Teacher's Edition
Teacher's Resource Binder

GREEN LEVEL

Annotated Teacher's Edition
Teacher's Resource Binder

SILVER LEVEL

Annotated Teacher's Edition
Teacher's Resource Binder

GOLD LEVEL

Annotated Teacher's Edition
Teacher's Resource Binder

CONTRIBUTING WRITERS

Barbara Keeler
Nicholas Singman
Linda Schechet Tucker

PHOTO RESEARCH

Cover: Lisa Kirchner
Unit Openers and Text interior: Rhoda Sidney

COVER DESIGN

Marek Antoniak

FRONTISPIECE

Adirondack Guide, Winslow Homer.
Bettmann Archive

COVER PHOTO

Behind the Wave off Kanagawa, Katsushika Hokusai. The Bettmann Archive

ABOUT THE COVER

Behind the Wave off Kanagawa, Katsushika Hokusai (1790–1849). The treatment of perspective in Japanese painting is unique, and Hokusai's print is a classic example. This picture consists solely of vividly contrasting foreground and background. The tiny shape of Mount Fujiyama in the background is barely visible behind the foreground's enormous crashing wave. This picture has no middle ground. This type of representation is alien to standard Western representation of perspective, but typical of Japanese painting.

Published simultaneously in Canada by Globe/Modern Curriculum Press.

Printed in the United States of America. 10 9 8 7 6 5 4 3

ISBN: 1-55675-169-9

GLOBE BOOK COMPANY
A Division of Simon & Schuster

CONTENTS

UNIT 1 American Portraits 1

UNIT INTRODUCTION 2

Learn About Narrative and Lyric Poems 4
POETRY A Lesson in Sharing *Sia Indian* 5
POETRY Let Our Children Live and Be Happy *Inuit Indian* 6
POETRY Illinois: At Night, Black Hawk's Statue Broods *J.W. Rivers* 7
Learn About Description 10
NONFICTION The Pony Express *Mark Twain* 11
BIOGRAPHY Mark Twain 13
Learn About Narration 16
NONFICTION Prairie Fire *Laura Ingalls Wilder* 17
BIOGRAPHY Laura Ingalls Wilder 21
Learn About Third Person Point of View 24
NONFICTION Amelia's Bloomers *Linda Schechet Tucker* 25
Learn About Biographies 32
NONFICTION Harriet Tubman, Liberator *Langston Hughes* 33
BIOGRAPHY Langston Hughes 39

FOCUS ON NONFICTION 42

NONFICTION The Pathway from Slavery to Freedom *Frederick Douglass* 45
Learn About First Person Point of View 52
NONFICTION The First Day *George and Helen Papashvily* 53
Learn About Speaker 60
POETRY I Am an American *Elias Lieberman* 61
POETRY Western Wagons *Rosemary and Stephen Vincent Benét* 63
POETRY Grudnow *Linda Pastan* 64
POETRY When I First Saw Snow *Gregory Djanikian* 66
POETRY from the New Colossus *Emma Lazarus* 67
Learn About Characterization 70
FICTION Split Cherry Tree *Jesse Stuart* 71

UNIT 1 REVIEW 84

UNIT 2 Inner Space 89

UNIT INTRODUCTION 90

Learn About Fables 92
FOLKTALE The Donkey Who Did Not Want to Be Himself *Aesop* 93
Learn About Plot: Climax and Resolution 98
FICTION The Speckled Hen's Egg *Natalie Savage* 99
Learn About Character: Actions 108
FICTION The Kind of Man She Could Love *O. Henry* 109
Learn About Theme 118
POETRY The Butterfly and the Caterpillar *Joseph Lauren* 119
FICTION The Parable of the Eagle *James Aggrey Carlson* 120
Learn About Simile 124
FICTION The Confidence Game *Pat Carr* 125
Learn About Symbolism 134
POETRY The Day Millicent Found the World *William Stafford* 135
POETRY maggie and millie and molly and may *E. E. Cummings* 136
BIOGRAPHY E. E. Cummings 137

FOCUS ON POETRY 140

POETRY Thumbprint *Eve Merriam* 142
POETRY Advice to Travelers *Walter Gibson* 144
POETRY The Rest of My Life *May Swenson* 145
POETRY You *Nikki Giovanni* 146
BIOGRAPHY Eve Merriam 147
Learn About First Person Point of View 150
FICTION Aquí Se Habla Español *Leslie Jill Sokolow* 151
Learn About Connotation and Denotation 160
DRAMA Blind Sunday *Arthur Barron* 161

UNIT 2 REVIEW 190

UNIT 3 Monsters 195

UNIT INTRODUCTION 196

Learn About Character Traits 198
FICTION Staley Fleming's Hallucination *Ambrose Bierce* 199
Learn About Myths 204
MYTH Perseus and Medusa 205
MYTH Theseus and the Minotaur 211
Learn About Rhyme 216
POETRY Medusa at Her Vanity *Tom Disch* 217
POETRY The Bat *Theodore Roethke* 218
Learn About Humorous Tone 222
FICTION Mr. Dexter's Dragon *Robert Arthur* 223

FOCUS ON FICTION 234

FICTION The Fog Horn *Ray Bradbury* 237
Learn About Articles 248
NONFICTION The Ten-Armed Monster of Newfoundland *Elma Schemenauer* 249
Learn About Theme 258
DRAMA The Monsters Are Due on Maple Street *Rod Serling* 259

UNIT 3 REVIEW 282

UNIT 4 Success 287

UNIT INTRODUCTION 288

Learn About Conflict 290

FICTION The Finish of Patsy Barnes *Paul Laurence Dunbar* 291

Learn About Theme 300

FICTION The Kick *Elizabeth Van Steenwyk* 301

Learn About Narrative Poetry 308

POETRY Casey at the Bat *Ernest L. Thayer* 309

Learn About Imagery 316

POETRY Success *Emily Dickinson* 317

POETRY "Hope" Is the Thing with Feathers *Emily Dickinson* 318

POETRY If I Can Stop One Heart from Breaking *Emily Dickinson* 318

BIOGRAPHY Emily Dickinson 319

FOCUS ON POETRY 322

POETRY A Psalm of Life *Henry Wadsworth Longfellow* 324

BIOGRAPHY Henry Wadsworth Longfellow 326

POETRY This Day Is Over *Calvin O'John* 327

POETRY Factory Work *Deborah Boe* 328

Learn About Irony 332

FICTION The Wolf of Thunder Mountain *Dion Henderson* 333

Learn About Third Person Point of View 344

FICTION The Pot of Gold *Salvador Salazar Arrué* 345

UNIT 4 REVIEW 352

UNIT 5 Faces of Nature 357

UNIT INTRODUCTION 358

Learn About Setting 360
FICTION The Man Who Was a Horse *Julius Lester* 361
Learn About Irony 372
FICTION The Tiger's Heart *Jim Kjelgaard* 373
Learn About Connotation 384
POETRY Who Has Seen the Wind? *Christina Rossetti* 385
BIOGRAPHY Christina Rossetti 386
POETRY The Storm *William Carlos Williams* 387
POETRY Clouds *Gregory Djanikian* 388

FOCUS ON DRAMA 392

DRAMA The Big Wave *Pearl Buck* 395
BIOGRAPHY Pearl Buck 417
Learn About Parables 420
FICTION The Black Box: A Science Parable *Albert B. Carr* 421
Learn About Images 428
POETRY Three Haiku *Matsuo Basho* 429
BIOGRAPHY Matsuo Basho 430
POETRY The Bare Tree *William Carlos Williams* 431
POETRY Winter *Nikki Giovanni* 432
BIOGRAPHY Nikki Giovanni 433

UNIT 5 REVIEW 436

UNIT 6 Family Matters 441

UNIT INTRODUCTION 442

Learn About Imagery 444
POETRY The Family Album *Jane O. Wayne* 445
POETRY Lineage *Margaret Walker* 446
POETRY The Last Words of My English Grandmother *William Carlos Williams* 447
Learn About Characters 450
FICTION The Richer, the Poorer *Dorothy West* 451
Learn About Tone 460
FICTION Mama and Papa *Kathryn Forbes* 461
Learn About Character 468
POETRY Mother to Son *Langston Hughes* 469
POETRY While I Slept *Robert Francis* 471
POETRY These Are the Gifts *Gregory Djanikian* 472
Learn About Plot 476
FICTION Charles *Shirley Jackson* 477
BIOGRAPHY Shirley Jackson 483
Learn About Point of View 486
FICTION A Mother in Mannville *Marjorie Kinnan Rawlings* 487
BIOGRAPHY Marjorie Kinnan Rawlings 495

FOCUS ON FICTION 498

FICTION Sweet Potato Pie *Eugenia Collier* 501
BIOGRAPHY Eugenia Collier 511
Learn About Theme 514
NONFICTION Fifth Chinese Daughter *Jade Snow Wong* 515
BIOGRAPHY Jade Snow Wong 527
Learn About Ideas and Values 530
FICTION The Circuit *Francisco Jimenez* 531

UNIT 6 REVIEW 540

Make literature a part of your life.

The Unit Openers will start you thinking.

Discover the theme or time period in the exciting unit opener.

Fine art suggests the theme or period of the literature illustrations.

See how the quotation relates the theme to your life.

Set the Stage...

Enjoy reading the best in classic and contemporary literature.

Explore ideas about the theme or period.

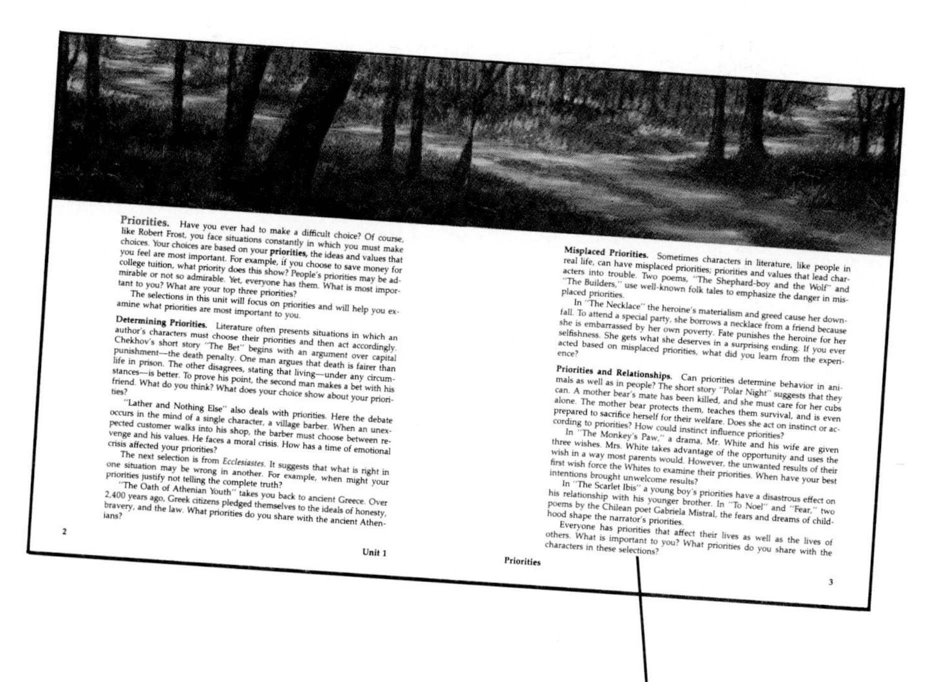

Priorities. Have you ever had to make a difficult choice? Of course, like Robert Frost, you face situations constantly in which you must make choices. Your choices are based on your **priorities,** the ideas and values that you feel are most important. For example, if you choose to save money for college tuition, what priority does this show? People's priorities may be admirable or not so admirable. Yet, everyone has them. What is most important to you? What are your top three priorities?

The selections in this unit will focus on priorities and will help you examine what priorities are most important to you.

Determining Priorities. Literature often presents situations in which an author's characters must choose their priorities and then act accordingly. Chekhov's short story "The Bet" begins with an argument over capital punishment—the death penalty. One man argues that death is fairer than life in prison. The other disagrees, stating that living—under any circumstances—is better. To prove his point, the second man makes a bet with his friend. What do you think? What does your choice show about your priorities?

"Lather and Nothing Else" also deals with priorities. Here the debate occurs in the mind of a single character, a village barber. When an unexpected customer walks into his shop, the barber must choose between revenge and his values. He faces a moral crisis. How has a time of emotional crisis affected your priorities?

The next selection is from *Ecclesiastes*. It suggests that what is right in one situation may be wrong in another. For example, when might your priorities justify not telling the complete truth?

"The Oath of Athenian Youth" takes you back to ancient Greece. Over 2,400 years ago, Greek citizens pledged themselves to the ideals of honesty, bravery, and the law. What priorities do you share with the ancient Athenians?

Misplaced Priorities. Sometimes characters in literature, like people in real life, can have misplaced priorities; priorities and values that lead characters into trouble. Two poems, "The Shephard-boy and the Wolf" and "The Builders," use well-known folk tales to emphasize the danger in misplaced priorities.

In "The Necklace" the heroine's materialism and greed cause her downfall. To attend a special party, she borrows a necklace from a friend because she is embarrassed by her own poverty. Fate punishes the heroine for her selfishness. She gets what she deserves in a surprising ending. If you ever acted based on misplaced priorities, what did you learn from the experience?

Priorities and Relationships. Can priorities determine behavior in animals as well as in people? The short story "Polar Night" suggests that they can. A mother bear's mate has been killed, and she must care for her cubs alone. The mother bear protects them, teaches them survival, and is even prepared to sacrifice herself for their welfare. Does she act on instinct or according to priorities? How could instinct influence priorities?

In "The Monkey's Paw," a drama, Mr. White and his wife are given three wishes. Mrs. White takes advantage of the opportunity and uses the wish in a way most parents would. However, the unwanted results of their first wish force the Whites to examine their priorities. When have your best intentions brought unwelcome results?

In "The Scarlet Ibis" a young boy's priorities have a disastrous effect on his relationship with his younger brother. In "To Noel" and "Fear," two poems by the Chilean poet Gabriela Mistral, the fears and dreams of childhood shape the narrator's priorities.

Everyone has priorities that affect their lives as well as the lives of others. What is important to you? What priorities do you share with the characters in these selections?

Preview the selections to see how they relate to the theme.

...For Active Reading

Develop Appreciation...

Read actively with the help of skills instruction.

Discover the characteristics of literature by studying the lesson before you read.

Relate the literary skill to your own experience by using the Skill Builder activity.

LEARN ABOUT

Setting

Every story must take place somewhere. That place might be a fantasy world in fiction, a romantic scene in a poem, or an urban site in a piece of journalism. In literature, the **setting** is the place where the events of a story, play, or poem take place. The setting also includes time, since people and places may change greatly from one time period to another. The setting can also contain natural events. In many stories, for instance, weather is an important element.

Setting can be a very important part of writing because it can affect the people and the events of the story.

You can tell what the setting is by looking for words that tell where and when. You need to be aware of the time and the place because settings in stories can change. For instance, in "The Bet" fifteen years pass from the beginning to the end of the story.

As you read "The Bet," ask yourself:

1. What is Chekhov's setting?
2. How does he make it believable?

SKILL BUILDER

Writers use vivid words and phrases to create settings. Write a description that tells where you are now—in a classroom, in the kitchen, on the job.

4 Unit 1

THE BET

by Anton Chekhov

It was a dark autumn night. The old banker was pacing fretfully from corner to corner in his room, recalling to his mind the party he had given in the autumn 15 years before.

There had been many clever people at that party, and there was much good talk. They talked among other things of capital punishment. The guests for the most part disapproved of it. They found it old-fashioned and evil as a form of punishment. They thought it had no place in a country that called itself Christian. Some of them thought that capital punishment should be replaced right away with life in prison.

"I don't agree with you," said the host. "In my opinion, capital punishment is really kinder than life in prison. Execution kills instantly; prison kills by degrees. Now, which is better? To kill you in a few seconds, or to draw the life out of you for years and years?"

"One's as bad as the other," said one of the guests. "Their purpose is the same, to take away life. The government is not God. It has no right to take a human life. It should not take away what it cannot give back."

Among the company was a young lawyer, a man about 25. "Both are evil," he stated. "But if offered the choice between them, I would definitely take prison. It's better to live somehow than not to live at all."

"Nonsense!"

"It is so!"

"No!"

"Yes!"

The banker, who was then younger and more nervous, suddenly lost his temper. He banged his fist on the table. Turning to the young lawyer, he cried out:

"It's a lie! I bet you two million you couldn't stay in a prison cell, even for five years."

"Do you mean that?" asked the lawyer.

The banker nodded eagerly, his face red.

"Then I accept your bet," the lawyer said simply. "But I'll stay not five years but 15."

capital (KAP i tul) involving loss of life
fretfully (FRET ful ee) in an anxious, worried way
degrees (di GREEZ) small stages or steps

Priorities 5

Motivational questions relate literature to skills.

Learn unfamiliar vocabulary from footnotes at the bottom of the page.

...While Building Skills

Develop your skills with creative activities.

Exercise all your thinking skills with comprehension questions.

Explore the selection's meaning by writing about it.

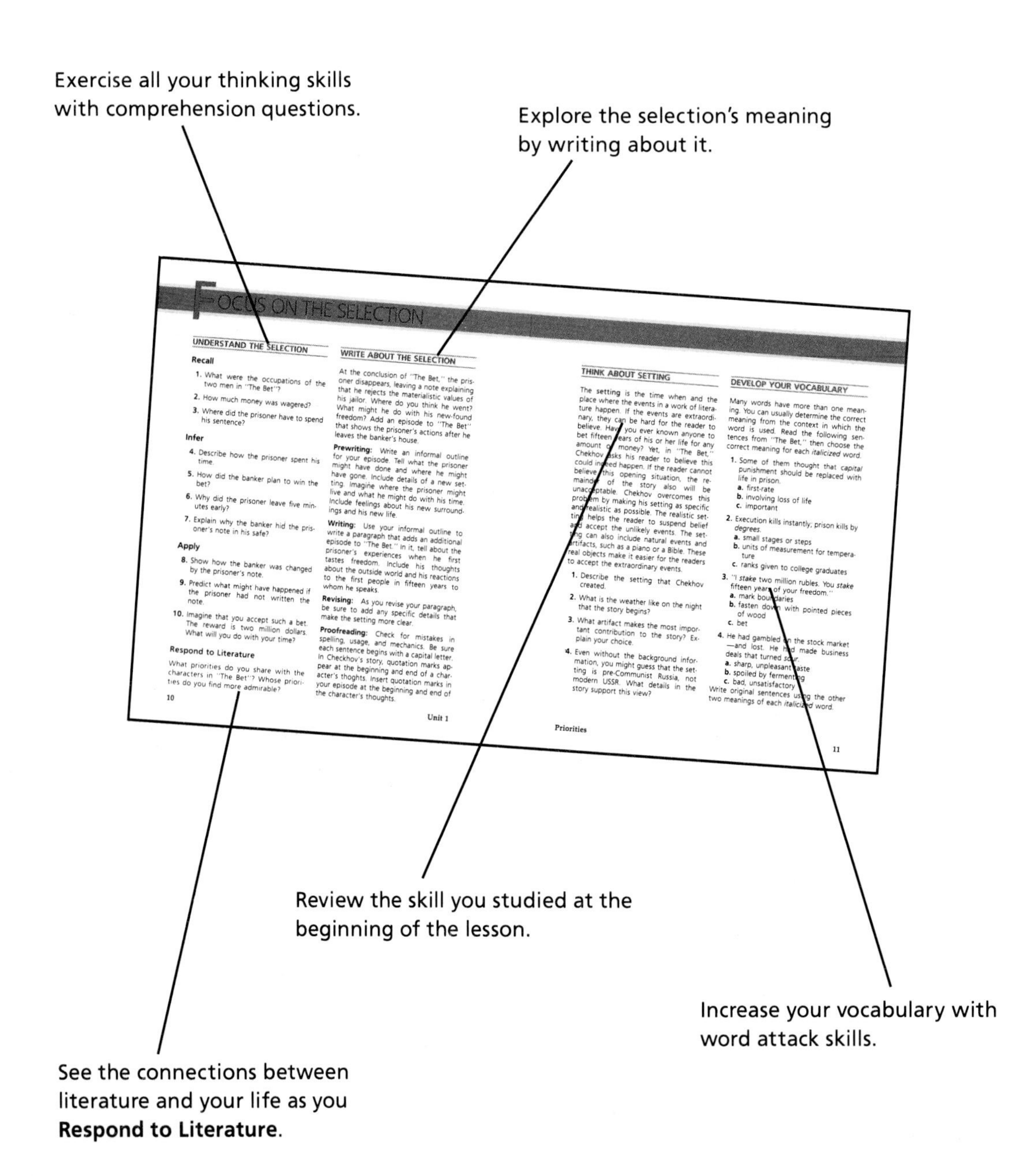

FOCUS ON THE SELECTION

UNDERSTAND THE SELECTION

Recall

1. What were the occupations of the two men in "The Bet"?
2. How much money was wagered?
3. Where did the prisoner have to spend his sentence?

Infer

4. Describe how the prisoner spent his time.
5. How did the banker plan to win the bet?
6. Why did the prisoner leave five minutes early?
7. Explain why the banker hid the prisoner's note in his safe?

Apply

8. Show how the banker was changed by the prisoner's note.
9. Predict what might have happened if the prisoner had not written the note.
10. Imagine that you accept such a bet. The reward is two million dollars. What will you do with your time?

Respond to Literature

What priorities do you share with the characters in "The Bet"? Whose priorities do you find more admirable?

10

WRITE ABOUT THE SELECTION

At the conclusion of "The Bet," the prisoner disappears, leaving a note explaining that he rejects the materialistic values of his jailor. Where do you think he went? What might he do with his new-found freedom? Add an episode to "The Bet" that shows the prisoner's actions after he leaves the banker's house.

Prewriting: Write an informal outline for your episode. Tell what the prisoner might have done and where he might have gone. Include details of a new setting. Imagine where the prisoner might live and what he might do with his time. Include feelings about his new surroundings and his new life.

Writing: Use your informal outline to write a paragraph that adds an additional episode to "The Bet." In it, tell about the prisoner's experiences when he first tastes freedom. Include his thoughts about the outside world and his reactions to the first people in fifteen years to whom he speaks.

Revising: As you revise your paragraph, be sure to add any specific details that make the setting more clear.

Proofreading: Check for mistakes in spelling, usage, and mechanics. Be sure each sentence begins with a capital letter. In Checkhov's story, quotation marks appear at the beginning and end of a character's thoghts. Insert quotation marks in your episode at the beginning and end of the character's thoughts.

Unit 1

THINK ABOUT SETTING

The **setting** is the time when and the place where the events in a work of literature happen. If the events are extraordinary, they can be hard for the reader to believe. Have you ever known anyone to bet fifteen years of his or her life for any amount of money? Yet, in "The Bet," Chekhov asks his reader to believe this could indeed happen. If the reader cannot believe this opening situation, the remainder of the story also will be unacceptable. Chekhov overcomes this problem by making his setting as specific and realistic as possible. The realistic setting helps the reader to suspend belief and accept the unlikely events. The setting can also include natural events and artifacts, such as a piano or a Bible. These real objects make it easier for the readers to accept the extraordinary events.

1. Describe the setting that Chekhov created.
2. What is the weather like on the night that the story begins?
3. What artifact makes the most important contribution to the story? Explain your choice.
4. Even without the background information, you might guess that the setting is pre-Communist Russia, not modern USSR. What details in the story support this view?

Priorities

DEVELOP YOUR VOCABULARY

Many words have more than one meaning. You can usually determine the correct meaning from the context in which the word is used. Read the following sentences from "The Bet," then choose the correct meaning for each *italicized* word.

1. Some of them thought that *capital* punishment should be replaced with life in prison.
   a. first-rate
   b. involving loss of life
   c. important
2. Execution kills instantly; prison kills by *degrees*.
   a. small stages or steps
   b. units of measurement for temperature
   c. ranks given to college graduates
3. "I *stake* two million rubles. You *stake* fifteen years of your freedom."
   a. mark boundaries
   b. fasten down with pointed pieces of wood
   c. bet
4. He had gambled on the stock market—and lost. He had made business deals that turned *sour*.
   a. sharp, unpleasant taste
   b. spoiled by fermenting
   c. bad, unsatisfactory

Write original sentences using the other two meanings of each *italicized* word.

11

Review the skill you studied at the beginning of the lesson.

Increase your vocabulary with word attack skills.

See the connections between literature and your life as you **Respond to Literature**.

Explore Genres...

Explore the elements of fine literature as you focus on the genre.

Learn about elements of fiction, nonfiction, poetry, and drama.

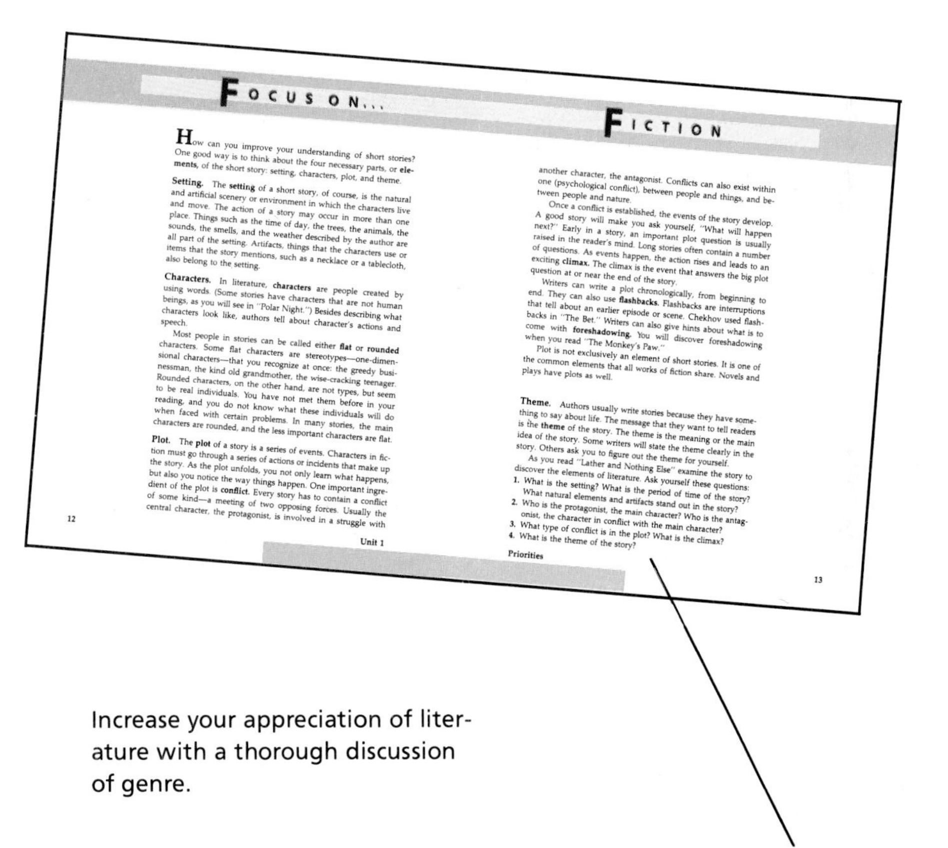

FOCUS ON... FICTION

How can you improve your understanding of short stories? One good way is to think about the four necessary parts, or **elements,** of the short story: setting, characters, plot, and theme.

Setting. The **setting** of a short story, of course, is the natural and artificial scenery or environment in which the characters live and move. The action of a story may occur in more than one place. Things such as the time of day, the trees, the animals, the sounds, the smells, and the weather described by the author are all part of the setting. Artifacts, things that the characters use or items that the story mentions, such as a necklace or a tablecloth, also belong to the setting.

Characters. In literature, **characters** are people created by using words. (Some stories have characters that are not human beings, as you will see in "Polar Night.") Besides describing what characters look like, authors tell about character's actions and speech.

Most people in stories can be called either **flat** or **rounded** characters. Some flat characters are stereotypes—one-dimensional characters—that you recognize at once: the greedy businessman, the kind old grandmother, the wise-cracking teenager. Rounded characters, on the other hand, are not types, but seem to be real individuals. You have not met them before in your reading, and you do not know what these individuals will do when faced with certain problems. In many stories, the main characters are rounded, and the less important characters are flat.

Plot. The **plot** of a story is a series of events. Characters in fiction must go through a series of actions or incidents that make up the story. As the plot unfolds, you not only learn what happens, but also you notice the way things happen. One important ingredient of the plot is **conflict.** Every story has to contain a conflict of some kind—a meeting of two opposing forces. Usually the central character, the protagonist, is involved in a struggle with

12

Unit 1

another character, the antagonist. Conflicts can also exist within one (psychological conflict), between people and things, and between people and nature.

Once a conflict is established, the events of the story develop. A good story will make you ask yourself, "What will happen next?" Early in a story, an important plot question is usually raised in the reader's mind. Long stories often contain a number of questions. As events happen, the action rises and leads to an exciting **climax.** The climax is the event that answers the big plot question at or near the end of the story.

Writers can write a plot chronologically, from beginning to end. They can also use **flashbacks.** Flashbacks are interruptions that tell about an earlier episode or scene. Chekhov used flashbacks in "The Bet." Writers can also give hints about what is to come with **foreshadowing.** You will discover foreshadowing when you read "The Monkey's Paw."

Plot is not exclusively an element of short stories. It is one of the common elements that all works of fiction share. Novels and plays have plots as well.

Theme. Authors usually write stories because they have something to say about life. The message that they want to tell readers is the **theme** of the story. The theme is the meaning or the main idea of the story. Some writers will state the theme clearly in the story. Others ask you to figure out the theme for yourself.

As you read "Lather and Nothing Else" examine the story to discover the elements of literature. Ask yourself these questions:

1. What is the setting? What is the period of time of the story? What natural elements and artifacts stand out in the story?
2. Who is the protagonist, the main character? Who is the antagonist, the character in conflict with the main character?
3. What type of conflict is in the plot? What is the climax?
4. What is the theme of the story?

Priorities

13

Increase your appreciation of literature with a thorough discussion of genre.

Test your new knowledge with thought-provoking questions.

...Develop Literary Skills

Develop your reading skills
with study hints.

Master the steps in active reading
as you read the annotated
selection.

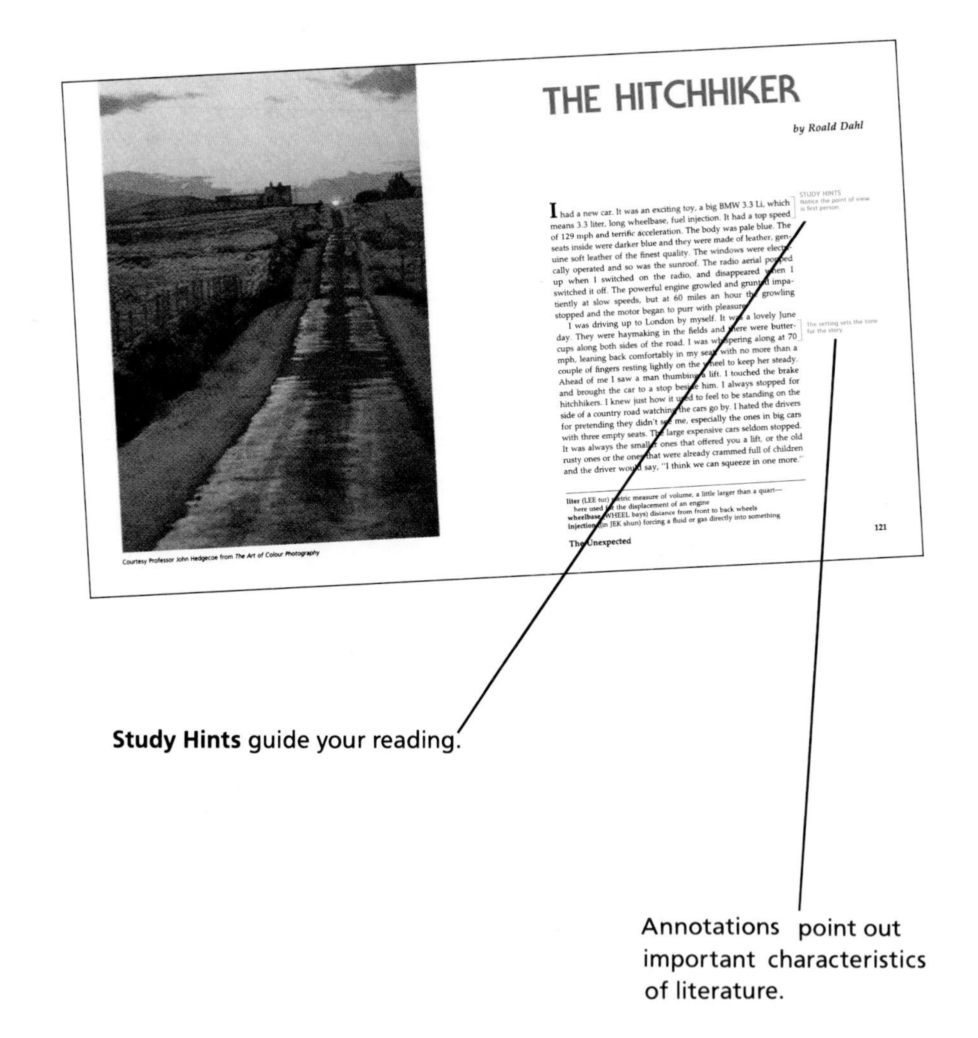

THE HITCHHIKER

by Roald Dahl

I had a new car. It was an exciting toy, a big BMW 3.3 Li, which means 3.3 liter, long wheelbase, fuel injection. It had a top speed of 129 mph and terrific acceleration. The body was pale blue. The seats inside were darker blue and they were made of leather, genuine soft leather of the finest quality. The windows were electrically operated and so was the sunroof. The radio aerial popped up when I switched on the radio, and disappeared when I switched it off. The powerful engine growled and grunted impatiently at slow speeds, but at 60 miles an hour the growling stopped and the motor began to purr with pleasure.

I was driving up to London by myself. It was a lovely June day. They were haymaking in the fields and there were buttercups along both sides of the road. I was whispering along at 70 mph, leaning back comfortably in my seat with no more than a couple of fingers resting lightly on the wheel to keep her steady. Ahead of me I saw a man thumbing a lift. I touched the brake and brought the car to a stop beside him. I always stopped for hitchhikers. I knew just how it used to feel to be standing on the side of a country road watching the cars go by. I hated the drivers for pretending they didn't see me, especially the ones in big cars with three empty seats. The large expensive cars seldom stopped. It was always the smaller ones that offered you a lift, or the old rusty ones or the ones that were already crammed full of children and the driver would say, "I think we can squeeze in one more."

STUDY HINTS
Notice the point of view is first person.

The setting sets the tone for the story.

liter (LEE tur) metric measure of volume, a little larger than a quart—here used for the displacement of an engine
wheelbase (WHEEL bays) distance from front to back wheels
injection (in JEK shun) forcing a fluid or gas directly into something

121

The Unexpected

Courtesy Professor John Hedgecoe from *The Art of Colour Photography*

Study Hints guide your reading.

Annotations point out important characteristics of literature.

Review, Enrich...

Improve your language skills with literature-based activities.

Make language connections through the Unit Review.

Explore themes and relationships.

Use the writing process.

Enrich your vocabulary.

Practice writing correctly.

UNIT 1 REVIEW

LITERATURE-BASED WRITING

BUILDING LANGUAGE SKILLS

Vocabulary

Usage and Mechanics

UNIT 1 REVIEW

SPEAKING AND LISTENING

CRITICAL THINKING

EFFECTIVE STUDYING

Learn with others in collaborative activities.

Analyze literature through oral interpretation.

...Extend, Express

Improve your critical thinking, speaking and listening, and study skills.

Apply higher-level thinking skills to literature.

Practical suggestions help you study effectively.

MIRROR BARBER

American Portraits

I hear America singing,
the varied carols I hear. . . .

—Walt Whitman

The Block, detail, Romare Bearden, 1971.
The Metropolitan Museum of Art. Gift of
Mr. and Mrs. Samuel Shore.

American Portraits. If you grew up in the United States of America, you probably call yourself an American. Suppose you grew up in another country. What would you think of when you thought of Americans? How would an American look? What language would an American speak?

It might not be easy to picture an American. Americans and their ancestors have come from all over the world. They came speaking different languages and bringing with them different customs. You or your ancestors may have come from Africa, Asia, Europe, Central or South America, Australia, or from the Caribbean. You may speak Spanish, French, Cantonese, or another language better than you speak English.

What do all the Americans have in common? All Americans or their ancestors originally came from another continent. Many took great risks and endured bitter hardships to come to America. Why did they come to the United States?

The selections in this unit will focus on Americans. They will help you to think about what being American means to you and other Americans.

The First Americans. The first Americans were Native Americans and Eskimos, who migrated from Asia thousands of years ago. These Native Americans were hunters, gatherers, and farmers. Their way of life depended on their ability to search large areas of unsettled land for their food.

The first three poems in this unit are about Native Americans. The first, "Let Our Children Be Happy," is an Eskimo story that expresses some values of this early American culture. The second, a poem of the Sia people, teaches a lesson in sharing. When Native Americans' lands were taken by other groups of Americans, the old way of life was lost. The third poem, "Illinois: At Night, Black Hawk's Statue Broods," expresses a Native American's sorrow over this loss.

American Pioneers. No sooner had the thirteen original colonies become free from Great Britain than many of these settlers began to seek new homes on the western frontier. Usually when you say "pioneers," you mean those Americans who first migrated west. In the selection "Pony Express," Mark Twain describes the swift riders who carried mail from the Middle West to California. "Prairie Fire" by Laura Ingalls Wilder is about one of the many dangers facing a family of pioneers. Why do you suppose pioneers left home and friends to face hardship and danger?

"With Liberty and Justice for All." Americans live in a country founded on the beliefs that people should govern themselves and that all should be free and equal under the law. However, long after the United States became independent, some groups of Americans continued to struggle for freedom and equality.

The Constitution guarantees rights and freedom to all men. "Men" is exactly what the founding fathers meant. Women, like a number of other groups of Americans, had to fight for freedom and equality.

"Amelia's Bloomers" is about some women in the 1850s who refused to dress as they were expected to. Would you wear something unusual if your friends disapproved?

African Americans have also had to fight for equality and freedom. "Harriet Tubman, Liberator" tells of an African American woman who escaped from slavery. She then risked her life to lead other slaves to freedom.

Even the freedom to learn to read and write was denied African American slaves. Frederick Douglass, a slave, saw reading and writing as "The Pathway from Slavery to Freedom." Why might he hold this view?

More People Become Americans. Since the birth of the United States, millions of people have left other countries to come here, often with no money, no friends, and no knowledge of the language. "The First Day" is about the experiences of a man from Russia.

The next group of poems is about why some Americans came here.

Americans have always wanted their children's lives to be better than their own. However, it is not always easy for parents to accept new ways. In "Split Cherry Tree," a father discovers that modern classes are different from the ones he attended as a child.

What does being American mean to you? Think about what the Americans in these selections have in common with you and with each other.

Learn About

Narrative and Lyric Poems

Most poems have special characteristics. Their form is different from that of a story or an article. They are written in lines rather than paragraphs. They may or may not rhyme. Their rhythm, flow, and sound are as important as their ideas. There are different forms of poetry.

A **narrative poem** tells a story. It has a main character and tells about events and actions.

A **lyric poem** is one that communicates feelings and impressions. It may paint a picture, share an experience, or show something in a new light.

You will appreciate a poem more if you know what the poet means to communicate. A narrative poem tells a story. A lyric poem communicates feelings.

As you read each poem, ask yourself:

1. Is this a narrative or a lyric poem?
2. What elements in the poem identify it as narrative or lyric?

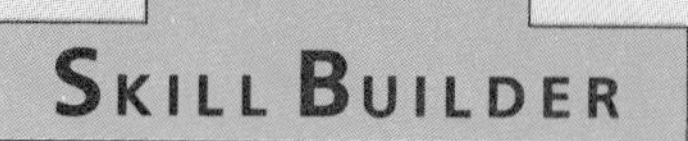

Skill Builder

Poets use vivid words to describe how something looks, sounds, feels, tastes, or smells. They also use words to describe their feelings. Write a few lines of poetry describing a familiar object. Then, write a few lines describing your feelings about it.

A LESSON IN SHARING

by the Sia

A lame man asked Kaluarsuk to move in with him
and be his hunting mate.
This lame man wasn't able to walk
but he was good at paddling a kayak
5 so Kaluarsuk teamed up with him
and during the caribou season they shared the meat.

But when winter came, Kaluarsuk figured
that the lame one was not good for much
when it came to hunting at the breathing holes.
10 He couldn't get there over the ice with his bad legs, could he?
So when Kaluarsuk went out and caught seal
he did not share any with his lame buddy at home
and never gave him a bite to eat.

15 Two brothers next door saw the poor cripple dying of hunger
and took pity on him
and brought him into their house
telling their wives to feed him dried salmon to revive him.
And when the lame man was no longer weak from hunger
20 they took him with them to the breathing holes
by driving him there on a sled
and he turned out to be a good shot with a harpoon.
In fact he caught seals right away
which he shared with his old sharing partner,
25 Kaluarsuk, who had come along.

Kaluarsuk who had caught nothing himself that day
took his share of seal
and said, "How good to have a hunting companion."
The two brothers spoke right up:
30 "You like having hunting mates now?
Then why didn't you think of your hunting mate
when you were the one catching seals!"

---

caribou (KAR uh boo) a kind of large reindeer
breathing holes places in the ice where water animals come up to get air
revive (rih VYV) to bring back to health or life

LET OUR CHILDREN LIVE AND BE HAPPY

by the Inuit

Whale Dance, Rie Munoz.

Let our children live and be happy.

Send us the good south winds.

Send us your breath over the lakes
that our great world may be made
5 beautiful and our people may live.

There, far off, my Sun Father arises,
ascends the ladder, comes forth from
his place.

May all complete the road of life,
10 may all grow old.

May the children inhale more of the
sacred breath of life.

May all my children have corn that
they may complete the road of life.

15 Here sit down; here remain; we give
you our best thoughts.

Hasten over the meal road; we are
jealous of you.

We inhale the sacred breath through
our prayer plumes.

---

ascend (uh SEND) go up, rise
plume (PLOOM) large feather, used in some Native American ceremonies.

ILLINOIS: AT NIGHT, BLACK HAWK'S STATUE BROODS

by J. W. Rivers

For Robt. D. Sutherland

The forests I believed in,
Where pathways were open,
Come to this:
Duck decoys,
5 Picnic tables,
Oak furniture,
Faces in mirrors.

Where is my father,
Who thrived
10 On a trickle of water,
Could feast
On skunk or buzzard?

My mother, whose hands,
Weaving like sand in the wind,
15 Took in birds
To mend their broken wings?

The land is old and tired,
It sleeps in its own shadow.

I cannot kneel
20 To touch the soil.
The wind in my ears
Makes everywhere
And nowhere
My home.

---

decoys (DEE koiz) wooden ducks used as lures by hunters.
thrived (THRYVD) prospered or flourished
trickle (TRIK ul) to flow slowly in a thin stream or fall in drops
buzzard (BUZ urd) a kind of hawk

FOCUS ON THE SELECTION

UNDERSTAND THE SELECTION

Recall

1. What did the lame man hunt when he went out with the two brothers?
2. The Sia people pray for what food for their children?
3. Whose statue broods in Illinois?

Infer

4. What kind of person was Kaluarsuk?
5. What do the Sia people believe will enable their children to live happily?
6. Where is Black Hawk's statue?
7. Why is Black Hawk's statue unhappy?

Apply

8. Imagine that someone who had refused to help you is now in need. Would you help that person? Why or why not?
9. Predict what would happen to the children of the Sia people if the warm weather did not come.
10. Imagine that you were a Native American when the white man settled in your lands. Would you keep the tribal ways?

Respond to Literature

Would Black Hawk believe that a poem about him might belong in a unit called "American Portraits"?

WRITE ABOUT THE SELECTION

At the end of "A Lesson in Sharing," the lame man has shared his seal with Kaluarsuk. Earlier, Kaluarsuk had allowed the lame man to go hungry rather than give him some of his seal. Write a narrative episode in which Kaluarsuk meets another hungry man with no seal. What will Kaluarsuk do this time? Did he learn the lesson in sharing? You may write your episode either in lines of poetry or in a paragraph.

Prewriting: List the events and actions that take place. The following questions may help you plan: Why was the man hungry and without any food? How does Kaluarsuk meet him? What does Kaluarsuk do?

Writing: Use the list of events to write a story or poem that adds an episode to "A Lesson in Sharing." Have the hungry man meet Kaluarsuk. Describe the hungry man's situation. Tell how Kaluarsuk and the two brothers treat the hungry man. Then tell what Kaluarsuk does after the two brothers have spoken. Describe his situation, and tell what Kaluarsuk does.

Revising: When you revise your episode, be sure that you describe each event and action so that the reader knows what happened. Make the order of events clear.

Proofreading: Read your episode to check for errors. Be sure all your sentences begin with capital letters and end with periods, question marks, or exclamation marks.

THINK ABOUT KINDS OF POEMS

Both narrative and lyric poems may use words to paint a picture. A narrative poem paints pictures of events and sometimes characters. A lyric poem paints pictures that show how someone is feeling or a new way of looking at something.

Reread each poem. Answer these questions about each poem:

1. Is the poem describing mostly events or how someone feels?
2. Is the poem a lyric poem or a narrative poem?
3. If the poem is a narrative poem, what events are described?
4. If the poem is a lyric poem, what feelings or wishes are being expressed?
5. Which poem paints the most vivid pictures?

DEVELOP YOUR VOCABULARY

You can better understand new words if you notice how they are used in the selections you read. Does the author use them to tell about the events, the setting, the characters, or a character's problem or goal?

Review the way the words below were used in "A Lesson in Sharing," "Let Our Children Live and Be Happy," or "Illinois: At Night, Black Hawk's Statue Broods." Write a very short story using all these words. You may change the form of a word to make it plural or to change the tense. For example, you may write *kayaks,* or *ascended.*

1. kayak
2. revive
3. plume
4. inhale
5. lame
6. caribou
7. harpoon
8. ascend
9. decoy
10. brood

Learn About

Description

When you tell someone about a city you visited, you want your listeners to be able to picture it in their minds. How do you talk about something so that other people can picture it? You describe it by giving details about it.

Writers use details that help readers to picture the characters, the scene, the subject matter, or the action. Sometimes they make a general description and follow it with details.

In "Pony Express," Mark Twain describes this exciting express mail service. He presents details that allow the reader to picture the Pony Express as Twain saw it.

As you read "The Pony Express," ask yourself the following questions:

1. Can you picture what Mark Twain is describing?
2. What details has Mark Twain supplied that help you picture the scene or the action?

Skill Builder

When writers describe something, they use words that paint a picture. They tell you how something looks, sounds, feels, tastes, or smells. Write a paragraph describing your classroom for someone who has never seen it.

THE PONY EXPRESS

by Mark Twain

In a little while, all interest was taken up in stretching our necks and watching for the "pony-rider." This was the speedy messenger who carried letters nineteen hundred miles in eight days! Think of that for horse and human flesh and blood to do!

The pony-rider was usually a little bit of a man, full of spirit and endurance. It didn't matter what time of the day or night his turn came. It didn't matter whether it was winter or summer, raining, snowing, hailing, or sleeting. It didn't matter whether he had a level, straight road or a crazy trail over mountains. It didn't matter whether it led through peaceful regions or regions with many dangers. He must be always ready to leap into the saddle and be off like the wind!

There was no idle time for a pony-rider on duty. He rode fifty miles without stopping, by daylight, moonlight, starlight, or through the blackness of darkness. He rode a splendid horse that was born for a racer and fed and treated like a gentleman. The pony-rider kept the horse at his utmost speed for ten miles. Then he came crashing up to the station where two men stood holding a fresh, impatient steed. The transfer of rider and mailbag was made in the twinkling of an eye. Away flew the eager pair and were out of sight before the spectator could get hardly the ghost of a look.

Both rider and horse traveled light. The rider's dress was thin and fitted close. He wore a short, tight jacket and a snug cap without a brim. He tucked his pants into his boot tops like a race rider. He carried no arms. He carried nothing that was not absolutely necessary. Because postage was *five dollars a letter* very

---

endurance (en DUUR uns) patience; power to last and keep on going
utmost (UT mohst) greatest amount possible
steed (STEED) fine horse

The Overland Pony Express, engraving. The Granger Collection.

little foolish mail was carried. His bag had business letters in it, mostly.

His horse was stripped of all unnecessary weight, too. He wore a little wafer of a racing saddle and no visible blanket. He wore light shoes or none at all. The little flat mail pockets strapped under the rider's thighs would each hold about the thickness of a child's first reader. They held many an important business and newspaper letter. These were written on paper nearly as airy and thin as a leaf. In that way, thickness and weight were economized.

The stagecoach traveled about a hundred to a hundred and twenty-five miles in a twenty-four hour day. The pony-rider covered about two hundred and fifty miles. There were about eighty pony-riders in the saddle all the time, night and day, stretching from Missouri to California. Forty flew eastward, and forty toward the west. Among them they made four hundred gallant horses earn a stirring living and see a deal of scenery every single day in the year.

We had had a great desire, from the beginning, to see a pony-rider. But somehow or other, all that passed us and all that met us managed to streak by in the night. So we heard only a whiz and a shout. The swift phantom of the desert was gone before we could get our heads out of the windows. But now we were expecting one along every moment. We would see him in broad daylight.

Before long, the driver exclaims, "Here he comes!"

Every neck is stretched further, and every eye strained wider. Away across the endless level of the prairie, a black speck appears against the sky. It is plain that it moves. Well, I should think so! In a second or two it becomes a horse and rider, rising and falling, rising and falling—sweeping toward us nearer and nearer—growing more and more clear, more and more sharp—nearer and still nearer. The sound of the hooves comes faintly to ear. Another instant a whoop and a hurrah from our stagecoach top, a wave of the rider's hand, but no reply. A man and horse burst past our excited faces and go winging away like a late fragment of a storm!

So sudden is it all, and so like a flash of unreal fancy, that except for the flake of white foam left quivering on a mail sack after the vision had flashed by and disappeared, we might have doubted whether we had seen any actual horse and man at all, maybe.

Mark Twain (1835-1910)

If everything had gone as he had planned, America might never have known one of its greatest writers. After working as a printer for several years, the young man set out to seek his fortune in Brazil. Instead, he landed in New Orleans and learned how to be a Mississippi riverboat pilot. As a pilot he earned a good salary. Then the Civil War interrupted travel on the river.

It was on the river that the man who was born with the name Samuel Langhorne Clemens first heard the cry, "mark twain." This river expression meant that the boat was in safe water for sailing.

In 1861, his older brother Orion Clemens was named Secretary of the Nevada Territory. Samuel joined him in a trip west. During the journey, Samuel started to write newspaper articles about their experiences. People enjoyed reading them. After a while, he took the name Mark Twain, the name by which the world knows him today.

Mark Twain's first books were travel books. His descriptions had lots of interesting detail in addition to good humor. Humor and good descriptions became two important parts of Twain's writing.

Today, Twain's two best-known books are *The Adventures of Tom Sawyer* and *The Adventures of Huckleberry Finn.*

---

strain (STRAYN) to stretch beyond usual limits
fragment (FRAG munt) small piece

FOCUS ON THE SELECTION

UNDERSTAND THE SELECTION

Recall

1. How much did it cost to send a letter by Pony Express?
2. How far did a rider ride one horse?
3. How far did a Pony Express rider ride in a day?

Infer

4. Why were most Pony Express riders small?
5. Why did the rider change horses often?
6. Was five dollars worth more, less, or the same in the days of the Pony Express?
7. Why did the rider have to ride even if the weather was bad?

Apply

8. Imagine that you lived in the West in 1860. Tell why you might want to send mail as quickly as possible?
9. Use the facts given in the selection to determine how long a stagecoach took to travel 1,900 miles.
10. Compare the Pony Express with Express Mail today.

Respond to Literature

Why might Americans need a Pony Express more than the English would?

WRITE ABOUT THE SELECTION

The selection "Pony Express" tells you something about Pony Express riders. It also tells you about the demands of the job and the dangers riders faced. What qualities and skills would a person need to meet these demands and face these dangers? What physical characteristics should a rider have? Imagine that you must hire a Pony Express rider. Write a want ad to appear in a newspaper. In the ad, describe the qualities and abilities a Pony Express rider must have.

Prewriting: List the duties, dangers, and challenges a Pony Express rider must face. Then list the qualities or abilities these duties, dangers, and challenges would require of a rider. Try to be as specific as possible about the hardships of the job and the qualities a rider would need to handle it.

Writing: Use your list to write a want ad for a rider. First explain to the reader the special hardships of the job. Be sure to include all of the major difficulties. Then explain to the reader what qualifications a person must possess in order to get the job.

Revising: When you revise your ad, use details and descriptive words to tell the reader what kind of person you will hire. Try to include the most important details. Use vivid but accurate descriptive words.

Proofreading: Read your ad to check for errors. Be sure all your sentences begin with capital letters and end with periods, question marks, or exclamation marks.

THINK ABOUT DESCRIPTION

Description is a technique authors use to help you picture something in the selection. Sometimes the author will use **adjectives,** or words that describe things, to help create the picture. The words *little, black,* and *flat* are adjectives. Use descriptive details from the selection to answer the following questions.

1. Describe the Pony Express service.
2. How would it feel to be a Pony Express rider?
3. What makes a rider's job particularly challenging?
4. What makes a rider's job tiring?
5. What makes a rider's job so dangerous?
6. What details help you picture Mark Twain's experience on the stagecoach?

DEVELOP YOUR VOCABULARY

A **thesaurus** is a dictionary of synonyms. When you look up a word in a thesaurus, you will find a list of words that have meanings that are similar to the meaning of that word.

The words that you find in a thesaurus can be very helpful when writing a poem, story, or essay. For example, suppose you are writing an advertisement and you need a one-syllable word that means little. If you look up the word *little* in a thesaurus, you will find the word *small*—which is exactly the word that you need.

Look up the following words in a thesaurus, and find at least two synonyms for each word. Then use each word in an original sentence.

1. endurance
2. spectator
3. visible
4. fragment
5. utmost
6. economized
7. phantom
8. vision

Learn About

Narration

When you write about something that happened, you use narration. **Narration,** or narrative, tells about an event or series of events. It tells about actions. In narration, authors often use words or phrases that make time order clear. Such expressions include *that night, next, before, after, then, when, while,* or *until.*

Usually the author writes about the events in the order in which they occurred. However, sometimes authors interrupt the sequence of events to write about something that happened earlier. In a work of fiction, this is called a **flashback.** Sometimes the author of a nonfiction selection will also interrupt the sequence to give you some background to help you better understand what is happening. The background information may be about an event that happened earlier.

As you read "Prairie Fire," ask yourself:

1. What steps did the Ingalls family take to protect their home from the fire?
2. How does the author make the order of events clear?

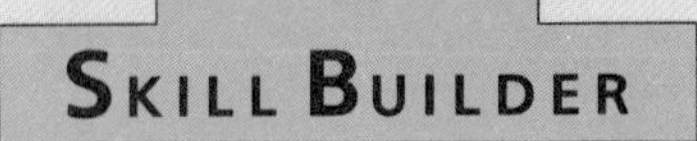

Write a paragraph about what you did in school today. Describe the events in the order in which they happened.

Prairie Fire

by Laura Ingalls Wilder

One day Mary and Laura were helping Ma get dinner. Baby Carrie was playing on the floor in the sunshine, and suddenly the sunshine was gone.

"I do believe it is going to storm," Ma said, looking out of the window. Laura looked, too, and great black clouds were billowing up in the south, across the sun.

Pet and Patty, the horses, were coming running from the field, Pa holding to the heavy plow and bounding in long leaps behind it.

"Prairie fire!" he shouted. "Get the tub full of water! Put sacks in it! Hurry!"

Ma ran to the well, Laura ran to tug the tub to it. Pa tied Pet to the house. He brought the cow and calf from the picket-line and shut them in the stable. Ma was pulling up buckets of water as fast as she could. Laura ran to get the sacks that Pa had flung out of the stable.

Pa was plowing, shouting at Pet and Patty to make them hurry. The sky was black now, the air was as dark as if the sun had set. Pa plowed a long furrow west of the house and south of the house, and back again east of the house. Rabbits came bounding past him as if he wasn't there.

Pet and Patty came galloping, the plow and Pa bounding behind them. Pa tied them to the north corner of the house. The tub was full of water. Laura helped Ma push the sacks under the water to soak them.

"I couldn't plow but one furrow; there isn't time," Pa said.

---

billow (BIL oh) rise in waves, swell up
bound (BOUND) jump, leap
picket-line (PIK it LYN) rope attached to a thick stick in the ground, used for keeping animals from wandering
furrow (FUR oh) long, narrow trench that a plow makes in the earth

"Hurry, Caroline. That fire's coming faster than a horse can run."

A big rabbit bounded right over the tub while Pa and Ma were lifting it. Ma told Laura to stay at the house. Pa and Ma ran staggering to the furrow with the tub.

Laura stayed close to the house. She could see the red fire coming under the billows of smoke. More rabbits went leaping by. They paid no attention to Jack, the dog, and he didn't think about them. He stared at the red undersides of the rolling smoke and shivered and whined while he crowded close to Laura.

The wind was rising and wildly screaming. Thousands of birds flew before the fire, thousands of rabbits were running.

Pa was going along the furrow, setting fire to the grass on the other side of it. Ma followed with a wet sack, beating at the flames that tried to cross the furrow. The whole prairie was hopping with rabbits. Snakes rippled across the yard. Prairie hens ran silently, their necks outstretched and their wings spread. Birds screamed in the screaming wind.

Pa's little fire was all round the house now, and he helped Ma fight it with the wet sacks. The fire blew wildly, snatching at the dry grass inside the furrow. Pa and Ma thrashed at it with the sacks, when it got across the furrow they stamped it with their feet. They ran back and forth in the smoke, fighting that fire.

The prairie fire was roaring now, roaring louder and louder in the screaming wind. Great flames came roaring, flaring and twisting high. Twists of flame broke loose and came down on the wind to blaze up in the grasses far ahead of the roaring wall of fire. A red light came from the rolling black clouds of smoke overhead.

Mary and Laura stood against the house and held hands and trembled. Baby Carrie was in the house. Laura wanted to do something, but inside her head was a roaring and whirling like the fire. Her middle shook, and tears poured out of her stinging eyes. Her eyes and her nose and her throat stung with smoke.

Jack howled. Pet and Patty were jerking at the ropes and squealing horribly. The orange, yellow, terrible flames were coming faster than horses can run, and their quivering light danced over everything.

Pa's little fire had made a burned black strip. The little fire

---

stagger (STAG ur) walk in an unsteady way

went backing slowly away against the wind. It went slowly crawling to meet the racing furious big fire. And suddenly the big fire swallowed the little one.

The wind rose to a high, crackling, rushing shriek, flames climbed into the crackling air. Fire was all around the house.

Then it was over. The fire went roaring past and away.

Pa and Ma were beating out little fires here and there in the yard. When they were all out, Ma came to the house to wash her hands and face. She was all streaked with smoke and sweat, and she was trembling.

She said there was nothing to worry about. "The back-fire saved us," she said, "and all's well that ends well."

The air smelled scorched. And to the very edge of the sky, the prairie was burned naked and black. Threads of smoke rose from it. Ashes blew on the wind. Everything felt different and miserable. But Pa and Ma were cheerful because the fire was gone and it had not done any harm.

Pa said that the fire had not missed them far, but a miss is as good as a mile. He asked Ma, "If it had come while I was in Independence, what would you have done?"

"We would have gone to the creek with the birds and the rabbits, of course," Ma said.

All the wild things on the prairie had known what to do. They ran and flew and hopped and crawled as fast as they could go, to the water that would keep them safe from fire. Only the little soft striped gophers had gone down deep into their holes, and they were the first to come up and look around at the bare, smoking prairie.

Then out of the creek bottoms the birds came flying over it, and a rabbit cautiously hopped and looked. It was a long, long time before the snakes crawled out of the bottoms and the prairie hens came walking.

The fire had gone out among the bluffs. It had never reached the creek bottoms or the Indian camps.

That night Mr. Edwards and Mr. Scott came to see Pa. They were worried because they thought that perhaps the Indians had

---

back-fire (BAK fyr) fire started to stop an approaching fire by burning out all the grass and other things that can burn
cautiously (KAW shus lee) carefully, trying to avoid danger
bluff (BLUF) cliff; high, steep land

started that fire on purpose to burn out the white settlers.

Pa didn't believe it. He said the Indians had always burned the prairie to make green grass grow more quickly and traveling easier. Their ponies couldn't gallop through the thick, tall, dead grass. Now the ground was clear. And he was glad of it, because plowing would be easier.

Pa said he figured that Indians would be as peaceable as anybody else if they were let alone. On the other hand, they had been moved west so many times that naturally they hated white folks. With soldiers at Fort Gibson and Fort Dodge, Pa didn't believe these Indians would make any trouble.

"As to why they are congregating in these camps, Scott, I can tell you that," he said. "They're getting ready for their big spring buffalo hunt."

He said there were half a dozen tribes down in those camps. Usually the tribes were fighting each other, but every spring they made peace and all came together for the big hunt.

"They're sworn to peace among themselves," he said, "and they're thinking about hunting the buffalo. So it's not likely they'll start on the warpath against us. They'll have their talks and their feasts, and then one day they'll a hit the trail after the buffalo herds. The buffalo will be working their way north pretty soon, following the green grass. By George! I'd like to go on a hunt like that, myself. It must be a sight to see."

"Well, maybe you're right about it, Ingalls," Mr. Scott said, slowly. "Anyway, I'll be glad to tell Mrs. Scott what you say."

---

congregate (KONG gruh gayt) gather together, meet

Laura Ingalls Wilder (1867-1957)

When Laura Ingalls Wilder was growing up, her family lived in the frontier country west of the Mississippi River. Thus Wilder experienced all the trials of pioneer life. The family moved from place to place in search of fertile land to farm. Droughts, unfriendly Indians, and illness all threatened their existence.

Yet there were wonders in that life, as well. Wilder often wrote of the beauty of the land. She was amazed when she thought about being the first to settle the land. And she thrived in the closeness of her family as they set about building a new life.

Long after, Wilder would tell about this time in her beloved *Little House on the Prairie* series of books. But her early writing appeared in western newspapers. She wrote columns on farming for the *Missouri Ruralist* and was poultry editor for the *St. Louis Star.*

It wasn't until Wilder was in her sixties that she got the idea for the *Little House* books. In fact, it was her daughter Rose who sold the first manuscript—"When Grandma Was a Little Girl"—to a publisher. To this day, the series remains popular. The stories are filled with life—excitement, danger, love, and sorrow. The characters and settings are real and interesting. And Wilder's style almost brings the reader back to pioneer times.

Long after Wilder died, her stories were made into a television series entitled *Little House on the Prairie.* The show starred Michael Landon, and can still be seen in reruns. Besides good acting, the show owes its popularity to the strong, sensitive writing of Laura Ingalls Wilder.

FOCUS ON THE SELECTION

UNDERSTAND THE SELECTION

Recall

1. What did the wild animals do when the fire came toward them?
2. How did Ma and Pa keep the fire from jumping across the plowed furrow?
3. Why was Pa glad about the prairie fire?

Infer

4. Why did Pa plow a strip of ground between the fire and the house?
5. How did starting a fire save the house?
6. How did Mr. Scott and Mr. Edwards feel about Pa? Explain your answer.
7. Why did Ma say that if Pa had not been there they would have gone to the creek with the animals instead of saving the house?

Apply

8. Predict what will happen on the prairie following the fire.
9. Imagine that your home was in danger from a fire. What would you do?
10. Contrast Mr. Edwards' opinion of the Indians with Pa's.

Respond to Literature

What does this story illustrate about the Americans who settled this country?

WRITE ABOUT THE SELECTION

Imagine that you are a reporter for a radio news program. Write a short news report about the fire. Remember, most radio news stories report only the main ideas, events, and actions. They tell you who, what, where, when, and sometimes why. Sometimes they include comments and opinions from the people involved.

Prewriting: Divide your paper into five columns. Use the following headings for each column. In the "who" column, list the people involved. In the "what" column, list the most important events and actions. List events in the order they happened. In the "where" column, list the place where the fire occurred. In the "when" column, pick a day of the week. In the "why" column, list possible causes of the fire.

Writing: Write a news report about the fire. Focus on the events and actions that actually happened.

Revising: When you revise your story, check to be sure that you have made the order of events clear. Use time order words where they are helpful. Remember that some useful time order words are *first, before, after, then,* and *when.*

Proofreading: Read your news report to check for errors. Be sure all your sentences begin with capital letters and end with periods, question marks, or exclamation marks. Have you used correct forms of verbs?

THINK ABOUT NARRATION

Narration tells what happened. It focuses on events and on actions. Usually events are told in the order in which they occurred.

Description in a narrative is there to help you picture better what happened. Descriptive words make the events and actions vivid and colorful. They help you picture yourself in the story.

1. Tell what happened in "Prairie Fire."
2. In what order are the events related?
3. What elements keep the order of events clear?
4. How does the description help you follow the narration of events?
5. What descriptions were especially helpful in understanding what happened?

DEVELOP YOUR VOCABULARY

You have often read words to which the endings *s, es, ed,* and *ing* have been added. The word to which the ending is added is called the **base word.**

When you look up a word in the dictionary, usually you will find an entry and a definition for only the base word. For example, when you look up *billowing,* you will find only the word *billow.* After you read the definition of *billow,* you should also understand the word *billowing.*

Look up each word in the dictionary. Use the base word in an original sentence. Then write a second sentence using the form of each word as it is presented below.

1. billowing
2. congregating
3. cracking
4. scorched
5. whirling
6. thrashed
7. quivering
8. hopped
9. ashes
10. rippled

Susan B. Anthony and Elizabeth Cady Stanton, engraving. The Granger Collection

LEARN ABOUT

Third Person Point of View

Every piece of writing has a point of view. Some stories are told as though one of the characters were telling the story, using the pronouns *I* and *me.* This is called the **first person point of view.**

In the **third person point of view,** the story is told by a narrator who is not a character. A story in the third person refers to all the characters as *he* or *she.* A story told in the third person often tells more than any of the characters know.

Nonfiction selections are often written from the third person point of view.

You can tell the point of view by the words that refer to the people in the selection. As you read the nonfiction selection "Amelia's Bloomers," ask yourself:

1. What words show that the selection was written from the third person point of view?
2. What extra information do you have because of the third person point of view?

SKILL BUILDER

Write a few sentences about something you did this morning. First write about it in the first person. Then rewrite it in the third person.

Amelia's Bloomers

by Linda Schechet Tucker

It was spring in the year 1850, and Elizabeth Smith Miller was working in her garden. She was not thinking about the weeds she was pulling out or the flowers she was transplanting. She was thinking about how awful she felt.

"I don't know why I continue to wear these horrid clothes when they make me so uncomfortable," she said to herself. Elizabeth was wearing long underwear trimmed with lace, a stiff petticoat that stood out like a bell, a flannel petticoat with a scalloped hem, another flannel petticoat, a plain white petticoat, a fancy white petticoat, and finally a huge skirt that went down to the ground.

Around her middle, under her dress, she wore stays, whalebone strips that were pulled in tight to make her waist look small. Over that she wore a camisole which protected her dress from the stays. Unfortunately, nothing protected Elizabeth's body from the stays, and her ribs hurt her where the stays were pressing against them. Elizabeth panted. It was hard for her to breathe in her tightly laced stays, and it was always difficult for her to stand up straight with the pieces of whalebone jabbing into her back.

This was Elizabeth's gardening outfit. In 1850, it was the outfit women wore all the time. They cooked in it, cleaned in it, and even took care of their babies in it. When they were at home, they didn't always pull their stays quite as tight as they did in public. Sometimes they also took off one or two petticoats, but they always wore their long dresses. Elizabeth had just been married, and she was quickly learning how impossible it was to keep house in such cumbersome clothing.

Elizabeth was angry. "I simply cannot go on wearing clothes that I know are ridiculous. I don't care what the fashion is." She got up from her garden and went

---

bloomers (BLOO murz) loose-fitting pants that are gathered below the knee
scalloped (SKAHL upt) cut along the edge in half-circles
stays (STAYZ) corset; a close-fitting undergarment worn around the waist and hips
camisole (KAM ih sohl) a woman's undergarment that looks like the top part of a slip
cumbersome (KUM bur sum) clumsy; difficult to manage

into the house. She went right to her sewing room and took out some fabric she had bought to make a new dress. She took out her pins, needle, thread, and scissors. Elizabeth was soon busily working. She was not making just another dress.

Earlier, Elizabeth had visited a rest home where women were recuperating from the effects of tightly laced stays. They had welts on their bodies and cracked ribs. Some of them even had hurt the inside parts of their bodies because of lacing the outside too tightly. Their waists had looked tiny, but their bodies were not healthy.

While they were recovering, the women wore special outfits given to them at the rest home. They wore loose-fitting pants that were tied closed at the ankle. Over the pants they wore dresses that did not go down to the floor but stopped about four inches below the knee. They were the first outfits Elizabeth had ever seen where you could actually tell that a woman had legs.

The dresses were not pulled in at the waist, and, of course, the women wore no stays. These outfits were called Turkish outfits because people in Turkey wore this style of pants. Elizabeth had decided to make herself a Turkish outfit.

The next morning Elizabeth came downstairs wearing her new clothes. Her pants were full and were gathered in with an elastic band at the ankle. Her dress was loose at the waist and reached a little below her knee. She wore no petticoats. Elizabeth felt comfortable. Her husband looked astonished. "What-ever are you wearing, Elizabeth?" he asked her.

"I'm sick and tired of wearing stays and petticoats. I don't see why I have to be uncomfortable all the time. This is my new outfit, and I don't care what you or anybody else thinks of it!"

"Just a minute, Elizabeth," he said. "In fact, I think your outfit is very sensible and looks much more comfortable than what you usually wear. I only asked you what it was."

Elizabeth was embarrassed that she had jumped down Charles's throat. Of course, she should have realized that he would approve of her new clothes. It was just that she was so worried about what people would say.

Elizabeth knew that her father would be very pleased when he saw her. He had often said that women would never win their rights until they started wearing clothes they could move in. When she was a child, Elizabeth had been the only girl in Peterboro, New York, who wore comfortable play clothes as the boys did. Her father had refused to dress her in long proper skirts.

Unfortunately, Elizabeth's neighbors did not find her outfit as sensible as her husband and father did. They could not believe that Elizabeth would walk out of her house in such clothes. Mrs. Williams in her stays and petticoats and long dress said to Mrs. Johnson in her stays and petticoats and long dress, "Have you seen Mrs. Miller?"

"I have indeed," said Mrs. Johnson to Mrs. Williams as their skirts dragged through the mud. "Imagine a woman

Bloomer Costume, 1851, anonymous, Culver Pictures.

wearing pants. Who does she think she is—a man?"

But Elizabeth continued to wear her Turkish outfit. She had worn the fashionable clothes long enough. Now she was determined to be comfortable. She made herself more Turkish outfits and began to wear them every day. She wore them at home and, despite disapproving glares of her neighbors, wore them into town as well.

It wasn't long after Elizabeth began wearing her new clothes that she decided to pay a visit to Elizabeth Cady Stanton. Besides being cousins, the two Elizabeths had been friends for many years. Elizabeth was sure that Lizzie would approve of her Turkish outfit. They had both long agreed that women could never expect to be able to do all the things that men could do as long as they could hardly move in their stays and petticoats.

Elizabeth arrived at Lizzie's house in Seneca Falls wearing full Turkish pants, a short dress, and a Spanish cloak all made of black broadcloth. She also wore dark furs and a beaver hat with feathers. Lizzie was astonished.

"How wonderful!" she said. "You must feel so comfortable and free. I've never seen such an outfit."

"You should make yourself one, Lizzie," Elizabeth said. "I've never felt so good. Look at how I can move." Elizabeth twirled around to show her cousin her freedom, as well as to show her how the outfit looked from the back.

"Oh, I don't know if I could wear such clothes in Seneca Falls," answered Lizzie.

The two women walked toward the house together, one with a tight waist and long dress, the other walking more briskly with her loose waist and Turkish pants. As soon as they entered the house, Lizzie heard her baby crying upstairs. She gathered up her skirts and climbed the stairs. She came down a few minutes later holding little Theodore in one arm and her skirt and petticoats in the other. It was late in the day, and it was difficult to see on the stairway.

"Lizzie, you should carry a candle. You could fall and hurt yourself and your baby walking downstairs in the dark like that."

---

glare (GLAIR) angry look

Lizzie laughed. "Now how am I going to do that?" One hand was busy with skirts and petticoats, and the other was busy with a baby. "I only have two hands."

Elizabeth took Theodore out of his mother's arms and picked up a candle with her free hand. She walked up the stairs quickly and easily. When she reached the landing, she turned and looked at Lizzie at the foot of the stairs. "It's really quite simple," she said.

Lizzie was convinced. The next day she sat down and made herself a Turkish outfit of black satin. The two women could now be seen walking through Seneca Falls together in their loose pants and short skirts. They had never enjoyed walking so much. The disapproving looks of Lizzie's neighbors did not bother them. With no long skirts to get in their way and no stays to hamper their breathing, the cousins could walk for miles.

One day they stopped at the post office. Amelia Bloomer, the postmaster's wife, was busily working in a room next to the post office. She was the publisher of a monthly newspaper called *The Lily.* Amelia claimed that *The Lily* was the first paper in the United States that was owned, edited, and published by a woman. When Lizzie and Elizabeth arrived at the post office, Amelia was wrapping and addressing her newspapers for mailing. She had already written many of the articles for the new issue, edited the articles that other people had written, and arranged for the paper to be printed.

Just by coincidence, in this issue of *The Lily,* Amelia had written an article on how much women needed more comfortable clothing than the stays and petticoats that she was wearing. Imagine her surprise when Lizzie and Elizabeth walked into the post office wearing their Turkish pants and short skirts! "Excuse me for not bothering with pleasantries, but please tell me all about your outfits. It just happens that I have been writing in my newspaper about the need for a change in women's dress. I must describe your clothing in *The Lily.*"

Elizabeth gladly told Amelia all about how she had come to wear the Turkish outfit. Amelia realized the time had come to put into practice what she had been writing about. At home that night, she made herself a Turkish outfit.

Now Mrs. Miller, Mrs. Stanton, and Mrs. Bloomer could all be seen walking through Seneca Falls breathing deeply and moving briskly. The town talked of nothing else. Young boys taunted them as they walked.

Heigh! ho!
Thro' sleet and snow.
Mrs. Bloomer's all the go.
Twenty tailors take the stitches,
Mrs. Stanton wears the breeches.
Heigh! ho!
The carrion crow.

Mrs. Stanton's own son, who was away at boarding school, wrote to his mother to ask her please not to visit him

---

taunt (TAWNT) mock; laugh at

in her new clothes. She wrote back to him.

"Now suppose you and I were taking a long walk in the fields and I had on three long petticoats. Then suppose a bull should take after us. You with your arms and legs free could run like a shot, but I, alas, should fall a victim to my graceful flowing drapery. My petticoats would be caught by the stumps and the briars, and what could I do at the fences? Then you in your agony, when you saw the bull gaining on me, would say, 'Oh, I wish Mother could use her legs as I can.'

"Now why do you wish me to wear what is uncomfortable, inconvenient, and many times dangerous? I'll tell you why. You want me to be like other people. You do not like to have me laughed at. You must learn not to care for what foolish people say."

It was hard for a young boy to learn, but the three women truly did not care what foolish people said. They did what they wanted to do no matter who laughed at them.

Elizabeth went home to Peterboro and continued to wear her Turkish outfit in spite of her neighbors' stares and comments. Her husband, Charles, and her father always supported her decision to wear the new clothes. Elizabeth even wore her outfit to Washington, D.C., where her father was a congressman.

Lizzie also continued to wear her Turkish outfit. She carried her baby safely and comfortably up and down the stairs in her house. She wore her new clothes all over New York State, where she traveled to talk to people about rights for women.

And in the next issue of *The Lily,* Amelia wrote about the Turkish outfit and announced to her readers that she was now wearing it herself. Hundreds of women wrote to her asking for sewing patterns so that they could make their own Turkish outfits. But thousands of people were still shocked at the very idea of women wearing pants and short skirts.

Articles began to appear in other newspapers about the Turkish outfit. Most of them said that it was terrible for women to wear pants. Amelia wrote back to one newspaper saying, "If gentlemen really think they would be comfortable in long, heavy skirts, well, let them wear them." More and more women began to wear Turkish outfits.

Since the other newspapers had first learned about the Turkish outfit from Mrs. Bloomer's articles, they called it "Mrs. Bloomer's outfit." Then they began to call it "the Bloomer outfit," and finally just "bloomers." The women who wore bloomers were called "bloomerites," and the whole idea of wearing the new clothes was called "bloomerism." Amelia insisted over and over again that it was Mrs. Miller who had first worn the outfit in public and that she should be given credit for her idea and her courage.

"They should be called 'millers,' not 'bloomers,'" said Amelia. But nobody listened. The name "bloomers" stuck. There was nothing that anybody could do about it.

---

inconvenient (in kun VEEN yunt) troublesome; not easy to do

FOCUS ON THE SELECTION

UNDERSTAND THE SELECTION

Recall

1. Why did women wear stays?
2. What did most women wear in 1850?
3. What did Elizabeth's husband think of the Turkish outfit?

Infer

4. Why did women continue to wear uncomfortable clothing?
5. What kind of person was Elizabeth's husband? Explain.
6. Why did Lizzie's son ask her not to visit his school in her Turkish outfit?
7. Why did Lizzie decide to wear Turkish outfits?

Apply

8. If a friend's mother did something that improved her life but caused people to disapprove, would you discourage her? Why?
9. Would you risk being considered odd for doing something unusual but practical? Why or why not?
10. Predict what Elizabeth would wear if she were alive today.

Respond to Literature

How were the women in this story like many other Americans?

WRITE ABOUT THE SELECTION

Imagine that you are one of Amelia Bloomer's readers. Write her a letter explaining why women should or should not wear pants. You may have more fun if you write an opinion that is the opposite of what you really think. Give reasons for your opinion. Remember, the reasons do not have to make sense by today's standards.

Remember also that newspapers sometimes get letters from people who have strange reasons for thinking as they do. Decide what kind of a person you are going to pretend to be. Make what you say consistent with that person's point of view. You may want to be a "crank."

Prewriting: List the reasons why a person in Amelia's time would approve or disapprove of women wearing pants. Create two columns. Label one *approve* and the other *disapprove*. List your reasons under the appropriate heading.

Writing: Write your letter. Be sure to write it as a person in Amelia's time would write it. Whether you are writing to approve or disapprove, include some reasons from the opposite view.

Revising: When you revise your letter, think about the way people react to something new and different. Try to write what people would really think and say.

Proofreading: Read your letter to check for errors. Check your capitalization of the heading, greeting, and closing.

THINK ABOUT POINT OF VIEW

When you read a selection written in the third person, you may get information from more than one character's point of view. You may have access to the knowledge, thoughts, and feelings of more than one character. Sometimes you find out more than any of the characters know.

1. What point of view did the author use in "Amelia's Bloomers"? Give two examples from the selection that show the point of view the author used.
2. What characters' thoughts and feelings did you learn about?
3. How did the point of view determine what you learned in the selection?
4. Suppose the selection were written in the first person. How could the author tell you what was happening with more than one person?

DEVELOP YOUR VOCABULARY

Sometimes you can determine the meaning of the word from the way it is used in a sentence. Read the following .

> Earlier, Elizabeth had visited a rest home where women were *recuperating* from the effects of tightly laced stays. They had welts on their bodies and cracked ribs.

The second sentence mentions injuries from the stays. The first sentence says women are in a rest home. You can guess that recuperating must mean "recovering."

Find the following words in the selection. Look for clues to determine the meaning of the word. Write any clues you find. Then use each word in a sentence.

1. camisole
2. cumbersome
3. hanger
4. petticoat
5. scalloped
6. pleasantries

The Misses Cookes' Schoolroom in the Freedman's Bureau, Richmond Virginia. Engraving. The Granger Collection.

LEARN ABOUT

Biographies

Do you like true stories about real people? The true story of all or part of a real person's life is called a **biography.** The person about whom the selection is written is called the **subject.** The person who writes the biography is called the **biographer.** An **autobiography** is a work a person writes about his or her own life.

Who are some people whose lives interest you? Some people like to read about film stars or musicians. Others like to read about those who made outstanding contributions in other ways.

Usually the subject of a biography has done something very important or made a significant contribution to society.

As you read "Harriet Tubman, Liberator," ask yourself:

1. What did Harriet Tubman do that made the author want to write her biography?
2. How did Harriet Tubman change the lives of other Americans?

SKILL BUILDER

Biographers look for interesting events in the lives of their subjects. Write a few lines about something that happened to someone you know. Write it in the third person.

Harriet Tubman, Liberator

by Langston Hughes

Some forty years before Abraham Lincoln signed the Emancipation Proclamation, Harriet Tubman was born on the eastern shore of Maryland, a slave, the property of the Broadas Plantation. One of 11 brothers and sisters, she was a homely child, moody and willful as well. Harriet was not cut out at all for slavery.

When Harriet was nine or ten years old, she was ordered into the Big House to assist the servants there. On her very first day, her mistress whipped her four times. Soon the white lady grew impatient with the seemingly stupid girl so she sent her to work in the fields. This Harriet liked better than washing pots, emptying garbage, and making kitchen fires. Even a slave out under the sky could look up at the sun and sometimes listen to birds singing in the bright air. But in her early teens a cruel thing happened to Harriet. From the slavemaster's point of view, it was her own fault.

One evening about dusk a slave boy wandered away from the corn husking to which he had been assigned and went down the road to a country store. An overseer pursued him, intending to whip him for leaving the place without permission. When he grabbed the boy in the store, the youth resisted. The white man then called upon other slaves standing about to help him. No one moved to do so. Then the boy started to run and the overseer called to Harriet who was standing in the door to stop him. Harriet did not stop him nor did she move out of the door so that the overseer could get by. This made the white man so angry that he picked up an iron weight used on the scales and threw it at Harriet. The weight struck her in the head, making a deep gash and knocking her unconscious in the doorway. As she lay there bleeding, everyone thought she was dead, and she did not come to her senses again for days.

---

liberator (LIB ur ayt ur) person who sets others free
Emancipation Proclamation (ih man suh PAY shun prok luh MAY shun) the announcement of freedom for slaves in the South, made by President Lincoln on January 1, 1863
moody (MOO dee) having many changes of feelings or mood
willful (WIL ful) wanting things one's own way
seemingly (SEEM ing lee) the way things appear to be
overseer (OH vur sir) person in charge of slaves on a plantation

Tossing and turning on the floor of her mother's cabin, talking strange talk, Harriet caused the others in the family to conclude that she might be insane for life. Indeed, when she finally recovered, her master believed her to be half-crazy. Harriet did nothing to change his opinion—but she was not crazy. From the blow on her head there did result, though, an unusual condition. From that time on, all her life, Harriet could not prevent herself at times from unexpectedly blacking out, suddenly falling asleep no matter where she was. Then, after a spell, just as suddenly, she would come to herself again. And the deep dent that the iron weight made in her head remained until her death.

When Harriet grew to be a young woman she determined to escape from slavery. She had never learned to read or write, she had never seen a map, and she had no idea where the North—that place of freedom—was. But, nevertheless, she made up her mind to find it. Meanwhile, she had married. She urged her husband to come North with her but he refused. She also asked some of her brothers and sisters if they would go with her. Only two of them, Henry and Robert, agreed, but at the last moment, they turned back. But with company or without, Harriet had made up her mind to risk the dangerous trek to freedom.

Before dawn one morning the young slave girl gathered her necessities into a bundle and started out. For fear that her mother and others would be greatly worried upon finding her missing, perhaps even thinking that slave-catchers had kidnapped her to sell into the Deep South, Harriet wanted in some way to tell them good-bye. But to do this was dangerous, both to them and to herself. So instead, in the early evening of the night she planned to leave, Harriet walked slowly through the slave quarters singing. She knew that all the slaves would understand her song—if not then, soon:

When dat old chariot comes,
I's gwine to leave you.
I's bound for de Promised Land.
Friends, I's gwine to leave you.
Farewell! Oh, farewell!
I's sorry friends to leave you.
Farewell! Oh, farewell!
But I'll meet you in de mornin'
On de other side of Jordan. . . .
Farewell! Oh, farewell!

That night Harriet stole away across the dark fields and through the woods, guided only by the North Star, heading for freedom. When she reached the Choptank River, she trudged hour after hour upstream, for by walking in water bloodhounds trained to scent runaways could not trail her. Eventually she found a sheltering place with kindly Quakers whom she knew to be friendly to escaping slaves. There she was rested and fed

---

pursue (pur SOO) chase, follow after
determine (dih TUR min) decide, make up one's mind
trek (TREK) journey, difficult trip

Harriet Tubman, oil-painted photograph, 1860. The Granger Collection.

and given directions for crossing into Delaware. Finally Harriet reached Philadelphia where she found work, and was no longer anybody's slave. But to Harriet, the North was not heaven so long as her friends and kinfolks remained in the slave country. Almost immediately she began to make plans to go back South to lead others along the hazardous road to freedom. In the years to come, it was as a liberator of slaves that Harriet Tubman became famous. She became one of the most successful conductors in the Underground Railroad, noted for her courage and her cunning. At one time a reward of $40,000 was offered for her capture.

The Underground Railroad was a widespread system of aiding escaped slaves that the Quakers and other friends of freedom had established. Such friends set up way stations along several routes from South to North at which runaways could be sure of assistance. Along these routes slaves were hidden in barns, corncribs, attics, cellars, sometimes even churches. They were provided with hot food, warm clothing, perhaps a little money, and information as to where to find the next friendly family. Passwords, or the correct number of raps on a door in the night, were given. Above all from such friends came the knowledge that not all whites were out to harass and endanger those who sought escape from bondage.

It was dangerous, and eventually illegal, for whites to engage in such activities. But it was doubly dangerous for a Negro to do so, and especially for an escaped slave such as Harriet Tubman. But Harriet did not let fear stand in her way. Most former slaves, once having escaped, never ventured back into slave territory again. But Harriet returned to the South more than 19 times, and each time she brought back with her to the North a band of fugitives. None were ever captured. As a conductor on the Underground Railroad she once said, "I never run my train off de track, and I never lost a passenger." It is estimated that she brought more than 300 slaves to freedom in the ten years between 1850 and 1860.

To earn money, Harriet worked between trips as a servant or hotel maid in Pennsylvania and New Jersey. After the cruel Fugitive Slave Law was passed in 1850, which permitted escaped slaves (and even free Negroes falsely charged as slaves) to be seized in the North and sent back in chains to the South, Harriet had to accumulate enough money to buy train tickets for her fugitives all the way through the Free States to Canada. In Canada slave catchers did not operate. But from Maryland to the Canadian border was almost 500 miles—a long journey for a man or a woman with nothing. Her tales of adventure are beyond

---

cunning (KUN ing) cleverness; sly, clever behavior
harass (huh RAS) give trouble to; bother a lot
bondage (BON dij) slavery
venture (VEN chur) to dare going; take a risk
fugitive (FYOO jih tiv) runaway, one who escapes

anything in fiction. . . . The slaves called her Moses.

Numerous examples of Harriet Tubman's heroism have been recorded. One example is in Troy, New York. There, one day in 1859 while on her way to an antislavery meeting in New England, she heard that a runaway slave named Charles Nalle was that very afternoon in federal court for return to slavery. Immediately Harriet sprang into action, organized a rescue party of free Negroes and whites and arranged to have a boat ready to take Nalle across the river to Albany as soon as he could be kidnapped from the court. She had no difficulty in getting followers for this daring attempt. The abolitionists believed that whether a rescue attempt failed or not, it got headlines in all the papers, served to keep antislavery sentiment alive, and was worth a hundred speeches.

By pretending to be a crippled old woman of no importance, Harriet hobbled into the courtroom to watch and wait for the proper moment to give a signal to the crowd outside. When they prepared to move the prisoner, Harriet seized the astonished slave and the crowd in the street immediately gathered about them. Harriet and Nalle made for the river but officers overtook them. A battle went on for hours between officers and abolitionists that day and both Harriet and Nalle were injured in the struggle. But finally the police were bested and the boat with the fugitive started for Albany. There, another battle with the authorities took place but eventually Nalle got away. That night he was safely hidden in a wagon bound for Canada. But Harriet Tubman had to go into hiding, for the next day her name made headlines throughout the nation. She had taken a prisoner away from government marshals.

Most of Harriet's rescues from slavery, however, were made without the help of crowds. They began in slave territory itself and were therefore full of danger. One of these dangers was betrayal. All who went North with her were, of course, sworn to secrecy but some grew weak and weary on the way. Frightened, cold and tired, they wanted to turn back. Once back on the plantation they could be beaten until they disclosed all they knew and the names of the other runaways as well as their leader. This Harriet could not permit. For weak-kneed freedom seekers she had a remedy. That remedy was a pistol that she carried in the folds of her dress. And weary ones who wanted to turn back were faced with this pistol and advised that they would either go on or be shot. They always found the strength to go on. In this way no one who started out for freedom with

---

Moses (MOH zuz) in the old Testament, Moses led his people out of slavery in Egypt into the promised land
Abolitionist (ab uh LISH un ist) person working to put an end to slavery
sentiment (SEN tuh munt) feeling, emotion
bested (BEST id) defeated

Harriet Tubman ever failed to become free. Her bands of runaways were never betrayed.

Because of her qualities as a leader, when the slave problem split the nation and the war between the North and South broke out, Harriet Tubman went into the service of the Union Army. She became the only woman in American military history ever to plan and conduct an armed expedition against enemy forces.

Harriet Tubman lived for a half-century after the Emancipation Proclamation was signed by President Lincoln and those for whom she cared so greatly were freed. Eventually the government granted her a very small pension of $20 a month. And from the book, *Harriet, the Moses of Her People,* which Sarah H. Bradford wrote, came a little money. But, ever generous to a fault, Harriet Tubman died poor at the age of nearly a hundred. Poor but remembered—for the whole city of Auburn, New York, where she died, went into mourning. And quite appropriately, her last rites as a soldier of liberation, were military. At her funeral the local post of the army presented the colors.

One of the most beautiful of tributes ever paid her came, however, from that other great fighter for the freedom of the slave, Frederick Douglass. In a letter to her years before she died, he wrote:

"The difference between us is very marked. Most that I have done and suffered in the service of our cause has been in public and I have received much encouragement at every step of the way. You, on the other hand, have labored in a private way. I have wrought in the day—you in the night. I have had the applause of the crowd and the satisfaction that comes of being approved by the multitude, while the most that you have done has been witnessed by a few trembling, scared, and footsore bondsmen and women whom you have led out of the house of bondage and whose heartfelt, *God bless you,* has been your only reward. The midnight sky and the silent stars have been the witnesses of your devotion to freedom and of your heroism."

---

appropriately (uh PROH pree it lee) fitting the purpose, properly
last rites one of the last ceremonies performed for a dead or dying person
colors (KUL urz) a nation's flag
tribute (TRIB yoot) words of praise
marked (MAHRKT) noticeable, easy to see
wrought (RAWT) worked, made
multitude (MUL tuh tood) crowds of people
heartfelt (HAHRT felt) sincere, honest

Langston Hughes (1902-1967)

If you wanted to find an American writer who wrote almost every kind of work possible, you would not have to look much further than Langston Hughes. He wrote poems, stories, novels, biographies, an autobiography, plays, children's stories, words for songs, newspaper and magazine articles, and even ideas for movies. His works have been translated into almost every major language. Hughes's writing is known for its jazz rhythms, a sense of humor, and a concern for black people.

He was born in Joplin, Missouri, but his family moved several times. He graduated from high school in Cleveland, Ohio. Like many other American writers, he traveled and did many kinds of work before he settled down to write full time. In 1921, his poem, "The Negro Speaks of Rivers" was published. That helped him get a scholarship to Lincoln University in Pennsylvania. After graduation, he settled in Harlem, a section of New York City.

At the time, Harlem was a great center of writing, music, and art. Langston Hughes became one of the most important Americans in this exciting time for the arts. In addition to his own work, he put together collections of works by and about other black people. The story "Harriet Tubman, Liberator" is from a book of his biographies of great black people.

FOCUS ON THE SELECTION

UNDERSTAND THE SELECTION

Recall

1. Why did an overseer throw an iron weight at Harriet Tubman's head?
2. How did Harriet let the other slaves know that she was planning to escape?
3. What was the underground railroad?

Infer

4. Why did Harriet's husband and brothers not join her plan to escape?
5. Why didn't Harriet tell her friends directly that she was escaping that night?
6. Who might have offered a $40,000 reward for Harriet Tubman's capture? Explain your answer.
7. Why did Harriet Tubman die poor?

Apply

8. What facts in the story illustrate Harriet Tubman's bravery?
9. Do you approve of Harriet Tubman's threatening to shoot slaves?
10. Do you think Harriet Tubman would really have shot a slave?

Respond to Literature

Harriet Tubman was stealing someone else's property when she freed slaves. Is it ever acceptable to break the law for something you believe in?

WRITE ABOUT THE SELECTION

Harriet Tubman must have cared deeply about other slaves in order to risk her life for them. She spent her own money helping them escape. Yet she threatened to shoot escaping slaves who were too tired or frightened to go on. How would she explain this?

Write a dialogue between Tubman and a person who disapproves of her reasons. Have the person question Tubman's behavior. Write what Tubman would say to explain or defend her actions.

Prewriting: List Tubman's reasons for threatening to shoot those who wanted to turn back. Refer to the selection for ideas.

Writing: Write the dialogue. Include what someone who disapproved of Tubman's actions would say or ask. Make Tubman explain why she threatened to shoot slaves who wanted to turn back. Show who is speaking by writing the speaker's name, followed by a colon, and then write the speaker's exact words.

Revising: When you revise your dialogue, try to add historical facts about dangers to escaping slaves. Choose facts that would explain Tubman's behavior with the gun.

Proofreading: Read your dialogue to check for errors. Be sure all the characters' lines begin with capital letters and end with periods, question marks, or exclamation marks. Make sure you have used a colon to separate the speaker's name from the speaker's words.

THINK ABOUT BIOGRAPHIES

How would you find out facts about a person for a biography? If the subject is alive, you might ask him or her. If the subject is not alive, there may be people still living who knew the subject. You could also read historical accounts, letters, diaries, and journals.

What details would you want to know? Most biographers write about the person's important contributions. They would describe exciting or interesting events in the subject's life, and the personal qualities that make the subject interesting.

1. What contributions make Harriet Tubman a good subject for a biography?
2. Which events in her life make exciting or interesting reading?
3. What personal qualities would make people want to read about her?
4. Where might the author, Langston Hughes, have found information about Harriet Tubman?
5. If you had not been told that this biography was not written by Harriet Tubman, how could you have guessed?

DEVELOP YOUR VOCABULARY

Sometimes in reading you see words you do not know. Have you ever discovered that you really did know a word once you have heard it pronounced? Sometimes if you figure out how to pronounce an unfamiliar word, you will recognize it.

Breaking a word into syllables can help you pronounce it. A **syllable** is a word part with one vowel sound. The dictionary breaks words into syllables for you by separating them with hyphens or dots.

Look up six of the following words in the dictionary and break them into syllables.

Study the definition of each word. Put a check by any word that you already knew. Use each word in an original sentence. Try to include other words in each sentence that gives clues to the meaning of the word.

1. accumulate
2. determine
3. emancipation
4. hazardous
5. fugitive
6. kinfolk
7. liberator
8. marked
9. necessities
10. overseer
11. plantation
12. unconscious

FOCUS ON...

If you read the selection "Harriet Tubman, Liberator," you read a biography. The subject of this biography was Harriet Tubman, because the story was about her life. The biographer was Langston Hughes.

Biography. The true story of a real person's life is a biography. Some biographies tell about the person's entire life, while others tell only a part of the subject's life or only an incident in the subject's life. Did the last selection tell the story of Harriet Tubman's whole life, or only a part of it? It begins with her birth and ends with her death, so it tells the story of her whole life.

The biography did not tell you everything that happened to Harriet Tubman. Nobody could write every fact about her, and you would not be interested in everything that ever happened to her. Good biographies are based on fact. They should be interesting to read as well. The biographer will select the parts of a person's life that are important and that will be interesting to the reader.

People living today may be the subjects of biographies. Biographers may also write about people who lived a long time ago. These biographers need to know something about the historical periods in which their subjects lived. How does a biographer find out the facts about a person who lived long ago? Sometimes they may get information from public records or history textbooks. Articles in magazines and newspapers written at the time the subject lived can also be a source of information.

Diaries and letters which the subject wrote can give some idea of the subject's personal thoughts and feelings. Even so, biographers are limited in what they can know about the thoughts, the feelings, and the opinions of the subject. Sometimes they will guess at their subject's thoughts, or describe the subject's experiences the way they imagine them to be.

Autobiography. The true story of a person's life written by the person who lived it is an autobiography. Auto- in this case means *self.* Being written by the subject, an autobiography can present a complete and accurate picture of the subject's thoughts, feelings and opinions. Very often you will not get a very objective view of history from an autobiography. You will view events and issues through the subject's own thoughts and opinions.

Autobiographies are often good sources of information for biographers who are researching the subject's life. Some autobiographies, however, present the subject's life the way the subject wants other people to see it, and this creates a false picture of their actions and their lives.

If you read the selection "Harriet Tubman, Liberator," you read many facts about Harriet Tubman's life. Where could Langston Hughes have found these facts? Besides the sources previously mentioned, he could have read one biography that was written about Harriet Tubman while she was still living. Do you remember the title of this book from the selection? If Harriet Tubman had written this book, it would be called an autobiography. How might it be different from the biography that Langston Hughes wrote?

Harriet Tubman's biography ends with a beautiful tribute to her heroism in a letter written to her by Frederick Douglass, another black person born in slavery. The next selection, "The Pathway from Slavery to Freedom," is from Frederick Douglass's autobiography. Because it is an autobiography, you know that it was written by Frederick Douglass about himself. This autobiography tells only part of the story of his life. As you read "The Pathway from Slavery to Freedom," look for the elements of an autobiography. Ask yourself these questions:

1. During what historical period did this take place?
2. Why are these facts important?
3. What are some facts or thoughts that only Frederick Douglass himself could know?
4. What other elements show that this is Douglass's own story of his life?

Frederick Douglass. Painting, attritubed to E. Hammond, 1844. The Granger Collection.

The Pathway from Slavery to Freedom

by Frederick Douglass

Mrs. Auld, my new mistress, had never before had a slave under her control. And before her marriage, she had to earn her own living. For these reasons, I believe, she had been in a good degree saved from the dehumanizing effects of slavery. In the simplicity of her soul, she began to treat me as she supposed one human being ought to treat another. In entering upon the duties of a slaveholder, she did not seem to understand that I was a mere slave, a non-human being, a creature to be treated like any other piece of property, no better than a cow or pig. She was a pious, warm, and tender-hearted woman. There was no sorrow or suffering for which she had not a tear. She had bread for the hungry, clothes for the naked, and comfort for every mourner that came within her reach.

I was utterly astonished at the goodness of Mrs. Auld. I scarcely knew how to behave towards her. She was entirely unlike any other white woman I had ever seen. I could not approach her as I had learned to approach other white ladies. The crouching dog-like behavior, usually so acceptable in a slave, did not gain her favor. Indeed, she seemed to be disturbed by it. She did not think it bold or improper for a slave to look her in the face. The meanest slave was put fully at ease in her presence, and

STUDY HINTS

You can tell this is an autobiography. It is a true story of the subject's life. Notice that the words *I* and *me* refer to the subject.

Note that you view Mrs. Auld through the subject's eyes. You get his opinion of her character.

Because the subject wrote this autobiography, you learn only what the subject learns or guesses of Mrs. Auld's thoughts.

---

mistress (MIS tris) woman who is head of a household or institution
dehumanizing (dee HYOO muh nyz ing) depriving of human qualities, as pity, kindness, or personality
mourner (MAWRN er) someone who shows sadness or respect for someone who has died
astonished (uh STON isht) filled with sudden wonder or great surprise
crouching (KROWCH ing) bending low with the limbs close to the body

none left without feeling better for having seen her. Her face was made of heavenly smiles, and her voice of gentle music.

But, alas! this kind heart had but a short time to remain such. Slavery soon proved its ability to steal from her these heavenly qualities. Under its influence, the tender heart became stone, and the lamb-like character gave way to one of tiger-like fierceness. The fatal poison of irresponsible power began its infernal work. That cheerful eye, under the influence of slavery, soon became red with rage. That voice, made all of sweet harmony, changed to one of harsh and horrid discord. And that angelic face gave place to that of a demon.

Thus slavery proved to be as injurious to her as to me. Very soon after I went to live with Mr. and Mrs. Auld, she very kindly began to teach me the ABC's. After I had learned this, she assisted me in learning to spell words of three or four letters. Just at this point of my progress, Mr. Auld found out what was going on. He at once forbade Mrs. Auld to instruct me further. He told her to let well enough alone. And he explained to her that it was unlawful to teach a slave to read. "If you give a slave an inch, he will take an ell. A slave should know nothing but to obey his master—to do as he is told to do. Learning would *spoil* the best slave in the world. Now," said he, "if you teach this new slave of yours how to read, there would be no keeping him. It would forever unfit him to be a slave. He would at once become unmanageable, and of no value to his master. As for himself, reading would do no good, but a great deal of harm. It would make him discontented and unhappy."

Here the subject gives you information you probably could not learn if this were a biography. Only Douglass could know his own thoughts.

These words sank deep into my heart. They stirred up sentiments that lay slumbering and called into existence an entirely new train of thought. It was a new and special revelation, explaining dark and mysterious things with which my youthful understanding had hopelessly struggled. I now understood what had been to me a most perplexing difficulty—I mean, the white

---

fatal (FAYT ul) resulting in death
irresponsible (ir ih SPON suh bul) unreliable; lacking a sense of responsibility
infernal (in FUR nul) of or relating to hell
furbade (for BAD) to prevent; a command against
ell (EL) unit of length
slumbering (SLUM bur ing) sleeping
perplexing (pur PLEKS ing) confusing; puzzling

man's power to enslave the black man. From that moment, I understood that the pathway from slavery to freedom was books. It was just what I wanted, and I got it at a time when I the least expected it. Whilst I was saddened by the thought of losing the aid of my kind mistress, I was gladdened by the precious instruction which, by the merest accident, I had gained from my master. Though conscious of the difficulty of learning without a teacher, I set out with high hope, at whatever cost, to learn how to read. The very decided manner with which he spoke about the evil consequences of giving me instruction served to convince me of the absolute truth of his words. What he most dreaded, that I most desired. What he most loved, that I most hated. That which to him was a great evil, to be avoided at all costs, was to me a great good, to be sought at all costs. In learning to read, I owe almost as much to the bitter opposition of my master as to the kindly aid of my mistress. I acknowledge the benefit of both.

My mistress soon began to follow her husband's advice. In time she became even more violent in her opposition than her husband himself. She was not satisfied with simply doing as well as he had suggested. She seemed anxious to do better. Nothing seemed to make her more angry than to see me with a newspaper. She seemed to think that here lay the danger. I have had her rush at me with a face made all up of fury, and snatch from me a newspaper, in a manner that fully revealed her concern. She was an intelligent woman; and a little experience soon demonstrated to her that education and slavery were incompatible.

The word *seemed* tells you that the author is guessing at the thoughts of people around him.

From that time on I was most closely watched. If I was in a separate room any length of time, I was sure to be suspected of having a book. And I was at once told to give an account of myself. All this, however, was too late. The first step had been taken. Mistress, in teaching me the alphabet, had given me the *inch,* and nothing could then prevent me from taking the *ell.*

The plan which I adopted, and the one by which I was most successful, was that of making friends of all the little white boys whom I met in the street. As many of these as I could, I turned

You can tell this is an autobiography. Subject is telling events in his life from his point of view, using *I* and *me.*

---

merest (MIR ist) nothing more than
sought (SAWT) searched for; looked for
anxious (ANK shus) worried; uneasy in mind

into teachers. With their kindly aid, obtained at different times and in different places, I finally succeeded in learning to read. When I was sent on errands, I always took my book with me. Then, by doing one part of my errand quickly, I found time to get a lesson before my return. I used also to carry bread with me, enough of which was always in the house and to which I was always welcome. As for food, I was much better off than many of the poor white children in our neighborhood. This bread I used to give to the hungry little boys. They, in return, would give me that more valuable bread of knowledge. I am strongly tempted to give the names of two or three of those little boys, as an expression of the gratitude and affection I bear them. But it might not be wise. It would not injure me, but it might embarrass them, for it is almost an unpardonable offense to teach slaves to read in this Christian country.

I used to talk this matter of slavery over with them. I would sometimes say to them, I wished I could be as free as they would be when they got to be men. "You will be free as soon as you are 21, *but I am a slave for life!* Have not I as good a right to be free as you have?" These words used to trouble them. They would express genuine sympathy and comfort me with the hope that something would happen that would make me free.

What elements of an autobiography can you find in this paragraph?

I was eager to hear any one speak of slavery. I was a ready listener. Every little while, I could hear something about the abolitionists. It was some time before I found what the word meant. It was always used in such connections as to make it an interesting word to me. If a slave ran away and succeeded in getting clear, or if a slave killed his master, set fire to a barn, or did any thing very wrong in the mind of a slaveholder, it was spoken of as the fruit of *abolition.* Hearing the word in this connection very often, I set about learning what it meant. The dictionary afforded me little or no help. I found it was "the act of abolishing," but then I did not know what was to be abolished. Here I was. I did not dare to ask any one about its meaning, for I was satisfied that it was something they wanted me to know very

---

errand (ER und) a short trip to do some business, often for another person

sympathy (SIM puh thee) sameness of feeling between persons or of one person for another

little about. Finally, I got one of our city papers containing an account of the number of petitions from the north praying for the abolition of slavery. From this time I understood the words *abolition* and *abolitionist.* I always drew near when that word was spoken, expecting to hear something of importance to myself and fellowslaves.

I went one day down to the wharf where two Irishmen were unloading stone. I went, unasked, and helped them. When we had finished, one of them came to me and asked me if I were a slave. I told him I was. He asked, "Are ye a slave for life?" I told him that I was. The good Irishman seemed to be deeply affected by the statement. He said to the other that it was a pity so fine a little fellow should be a slave for life. He said it was a shame to hold me. They both advised me to run away to the north. They said I should find friends there, and that I should be free. I pretended not to be interested in what they said, acting as if I did not understand them. You see, I feared they might be treacherous. White men have been known to encourage slaves to escape, and then, to get the reward, catch them and return them to their masters. I was afraid that these seemingly good men might use me so; but I nevertheless remembered their advice. From that time I resolved to run away. I looked forward to a time at which it would be safe for me to escape. I was too young to think of doing so immediately. Besides, I wished to learn how to write, as I might need to write my own pass. I comforted myself with the hope that I should one day find a good chance. Meanwhile, I would learn to write.

Like a biography, an autobiography can tell the story of all or part of a subject's life. Notice that this autobiography tells part of Douglass's life.

---

petitions (puh TISH uns) serious requests to a superior
wharf (HWAWRF) a structure built at the shore of a harbor for unloading ships
treacherous (TRECH ur us), unreliable; likely to betray trust; disloyal
encourage (en KUR ij) to give hope or confidence
resolved (rih ZOLVD) firm and fixed in purpose

FOCUS ON THE SELECTION

UNDERSTAND THE SELECTION

Recall

1. What convinced Douglass that it was important to learn to read?
2. How did Mrs. Auld react to Douglass's reading after talking to her husband?
3. Who taught Douglass to read after Mrs. Auld stopped teaching him?

Infer

4. Why were the slaveholders afraid of having slaves read?
5. Why did the word "abolition" interest Douglass?
6. Why did Mr. Auld say that reading would make Douglass "unhappy"?
7. Why was Douglass afraid to trust the Irishmen who urged him to run away?

Apply

8. Were reading and writing the pathway from slavery to freedom? Explain.
9. How would you feel if you were a slave and not allowed to read? Explain your answer.
10. What parts of the story show that some Americans did not like slavery?

Respond to Literature

Why do you think the law requires all Americans to go to school?

WRITE ABOUT THE SELECTION

In the selection, Douglass was forbidden to learn to read and write. He is determined to learn. Imagine that you could not read or write a word. Write a narrative about a day in your life. Show how activities such as shopping, looking for streets, choosing television programs, and other activities, would be affected. If you have younger brothers or sisters who cannot yet read, think about things they cannot do by themselves.

Prewriting: List the ways in which you use reading and the times when you *must* read at least a word or two. You can also include those times when you have the opportunity to read a short story, magazine article, or newspaper, and decide not to because you do not have time.

Try to decide if you might have saved yourself some trouble or extra work by taking the time to read something, such as a "how-to" article. Think about how you would need to change what you do if you could not read.

Writing: Write your narrative. Include events that show how your activities would be affected by your not being able to read.

Revising: When your revise your narrative, be sure you have described the events clearly.

Proofreading: Read your report to check for errors. Be sure all your sentences begin with capital letters and end with periods, question marks, or exclamation marks. Have you used correct forms of verbs?

THINK ABOUT AUTOBIOGRAPHY

An autobiography is told in the first person. When you read an autobiography, you learn everything from the subject's point of view. You learn much that only the subject could know about his or her thoughts, feelings, opinions, intentions and motives.

1. Why would people be interested in reading about Frederick Douglass's life?
2. How could you tell this selection was an autobiography if you had not been told?
3. What did you learn from this selection that you could not have learned from a biography?
4. What might a biography have included that this autobiography did not?
5. What did you find most interesting about Douglass's thoughts and feelings?

DEVELOP YOUR VOCABULARY

Frederick Douglass figured out the meaning of the word *abolition* from its context in a newspaper article. Before that, he looked the word up in a dictionary. When you look up a word in a glossary or a dictionary, how do you find the word? The entries for words are in alphabetical order.

You will find guide words at the top of every dictionary or glossary page. They help you to find the page containing the word you want. They tell you that, in alphabetical order, the words on the page come between the two guide words.

Write the following words. Circle the ones that would come between the two guide words *destructive* and *elm*. Then look up each word in a dictionary. Write the guide words from the top of the page on which the word is listed.

1. dehumanizing
2. discord
3. ell
4. injurious
5. revelation
6. treacherous

Learn About
First Person Point of View

When you tell someone about something that happened to you, you probably tell it from the **first person point of view.** You use words like *I, me, we, my,* and *us.*

Many stories are written from the first person point of view. A story written in the **first person** is told as if one of the characters were telling it. The words *I* and *me* are used to refer to the character telling the story.

Nonfiction selections may also be written in the first person. An autobiography is always written in the first person. "The Pathway from Slavery to Freedom," for example, is in the first person. When you read it, you learn only what Frederick Douglass does, observes, thinks, feels, or knows.

Point of view is important in a selection, because it determines who is interpreting the facts and events. As you read "The First Day," ask yourself:

1. From whose point of view is the story told?
2. How does the point of view affect the way the story is told?

Write a few lines about something that happened today. Use the first person point of view. Use words like *I* and *we.*

The First Day

by George and Helen Papashvily

At five in the morning the engine stopped, and after 37 days the boat was quiet.

We were in America.

I got up and stepped over the other men and looked out the porthole. Water and fog. We were anchoring off an island. I dressed and went on deck.

Now began my troubles. What to do? This was a Greek boat and I was steerage, so of course by the time we were halfway out I had spent all my landing money for extra food.

Hassan, the Turk, one of the six who slept in the cabin with me, came up the ladder.

"I told you so," he said as soon as he saw me. "Now we are in America and you have no money to land. They send you home. No money, no going ashore. What a disgrace. In your position, frankly, I would kill myself."

Hassan had been satisfied to starve on black olives and salt cheese all the way from Gibraltar. He begrudged every piece of lamb I bribed away from the first-cabin steward.

We went down the gangplank into the big room. Passengers with pictures in their hands were rushing around to match them to a relative. Before their tables the inspectors were busy with long lines of people.

The visitors' door opened and a fellow with a big pile of caps, striped blue and white cotton caps with visors and a top button, came in. He went first to an old man with a fur hat near the window, then to a Russian in the line. At last he came to me.

"Look," he said in Russian, "look at your hat. You want to be a greenhorn all your life? A fur hat! Do you expect to see anybody in the U.S.A. still with a fur hat? The inspector, the doctor, the captain—are they wearing fur hats? Certainly not."

I didn't say anything.

"Look," he said. "I'm sorry for you. I was a greenhorn once myself. I wouldn't want to see anybody make my mistakes.

---

steerage (STIR ij) least expensive way to travel in a ship
begrudge (bih GRUJ) feel angry at something another person has
gangplank (GANG plangk) movable board for going on or off a ship
visor (VY zur) front part of a cap that shades the eyes from sun
greenhorn (GREEN hawrn) person who is new in a country

Look, I have caps. See, from such rich striped materials. Like railroad engineers wear, and house painters, and coal miners." He spun one around on his finger. "Don't be afraid. It's a cap in real American style. With this cap on your head, they couldn't tell you from a citizen. I'm positively guaranteeing. And I'm trading you this cap even for your old fur hat. Trading even. You don't have to give me one penny."

Now it is true I bought my fur hat new for the trip. It was a fine skin, a silver lamb, and in Georgia it would have lasted me a lifetime. Still—

"I'll tell you," the cap man said. "So you can remember all your life you made money the first hour you were in America, I give you a cap and a dollar besides. Done?"

I took off my fur hat and put on his cap. It was small and sat well up on my head, but then in America one dresses like an American and it is a satisfaction always to be in the best style. So I got my first dollar.

Ysaacs, a Syrian, sat on the bench and smoked brown paper cigarettes and watched all through the bargain. He was from our cabin, too. He knew I was worried about the money to show the examiners. But now, as soon as the cap man went on to the next customer, Ysaacs explained a way to get me by the examiners—a good way.

Such a very good way, in fact, that when the inspector looked over my passport and entry permit I was ready.

"Do you have friends meeting you?" he asked me. "Do you have money to support yourself?"

I pulled out a round fat roll of green American money—tens, twenties—a nice thick pile with a rubber band around.

"Okay," he said. "Go ahead." He stamped my papers.

I got my baggage and took the money roll back again to Ysaac's friend, Arapouleopolus, the moneylender, so he could rent it over again to another man. One dollar was all he charged to use it for each landing. Really a bargain.

On the outer platform I met Zurabeg, who had been down in steerage, too. But Zurabeg was no greenhorn coming for the first time. Zurabeg was an American citizen with papers to prove it, and a friend of Buffalo Bill besides. This Zurabeg first came to America 20 years before as a trick show rider. Later he was boss cook on the road with Buffalo Bill.

"Can't land?" he asked me.

"No, I can land," I said, "but I have no money to pay the little boat to carry me to shore."

"Listen, donkey-head," Zurabeg said, "this is America. The carrying boat is free. It belongs to my government. They take us for nothing. Come on."

So we got to the shore.

And there—the streets, the people, the noise! The faces flashing by—and by again.

---

guarantee (gar un TEE) promise that something is true
Georgia (JAWR juh) a part of the Soviet Union

We walked a few blocks through this before I remembered my landing cards and passport. I took them out and tore them into little pieces and threw them all in an ash can. "They can't prove I'm not a citizen, now," I said. "What we do next?"

"We get jobs," Zurabeg told me. "I show you."

We went to an employment agency. Conveniently, the man spoke Russian. He gave Zurabeg a ticket right away to start in a Russian restaurant as first cook.

"Now, your friend? What can you do?" he asked me.

"I," I said, "am a worker in decorative leathers, particularly specializing in the ornamenting of whip handles according to the traditional designs."

"My goodness!" the man said. "This is the U.S.A. No horses. Automobiles. What else can you do?"

Fortunately my father was a man of great foresight and I have two trades. His idea was that in the days when a man starves with one, by the other he may eat.

"I am also," I said, "a swordmaker. Short blades or long."

"A whip maker—a swordmaker. You better take him along for a dishwasher," he said to Zurabeg. "They can always use another dishwasher."

The restaurant was on a side street and the lady-owner spoke kindly. "I remember you from the tearoom," she said to Zurabeg. "I congratulate myself on getting you. You are excellent on the *piroshkis,* isn't it?"

"On everything, Madame," Zurabeg said grandly. "On everything. Buffalo Bill, an old friend of mine, has eaten thirty of my *piroshkis* at a meal. My friend"—he waved toward me—"will be a dishwasher."

I made a bow.

The kitchen was small and hot and fat—like inside of a pig's stomach. Zurabeg unpacked his knives, put on his cap, and, at home at once, started to dice celery.

"You can wash these," the owner said to me. "At four we have party."

It was a trayful of glasses. And such glasses—thin bubbles that would hardly hold a sip—set on stems. The first one snapped in my hand, the second dissolved, the third to tenth I got washed, the eleventh was already cracked, the twelfth rang once on the pan edge and was silent.

Perhaps I might be there yet, but just as I carried the first trayful to the service slot, the restaurant cat ran between my feet.

When I got all the glass swept up, I told Zurabeg, "Now, we have to eat. I'ts noon. I watch the customers eat. It makes me hungry. Prepare lamb and some cucumbers, and we enjoy our first meal for good luck in the New World."

"This is a restaurant with very strict organization," Zurabeg said. "We get to eat when the customers go, and you get

---

conveniently (kun VEEN yunt lee) making it easy
traditional (truh DISH uh nul) according to customs passed on from parents to children
piroshki (pih ROSH kee) meat dumpling

what the customers leave. Try again with the glasses and remember my reputation. Please."

I found a quart of sour cream and went into the back alley and ate that and some bread and a jar of caviar, which was very salty—packed for export, no doubt.

The owner found me. I stood up. "Please," she said, "please go on. Eat sour cream. But after, could you go away? Far away? With no hard feelings. The glasses—the caviar—it's expensive for me—and at the same time I don't want to make your friend mad. I need a good cook. If you could just go away? Quietly? Just disappear, so to speak? I give you five dollars."

"I didn't do anything," I said, "so you don't have to pay me. All in all, a restaurant probably isn't my fate. You can tell Zurabeg afterward."

She brought my cap and a paper bag. I walked for hours. I couldn't even be sure it was the same day. I tried some English on a few men that passed.

"What watch?" I said. But they pushed by me so I knew I had it wrong.

I tried another man. "How many clock?" He showed me on his wrist. Four-thirty.

A wonderful place. Rapidly, if one applies oneself, one speaks the English.

I came to a park and went in and found a place under a tree and took off my shoes and lay down. I looked in the bag the owner gave me. A bologna sandwich and a nickel—to begin in America with.

What to do? While I decided, I slept.

A policeman was waking me up. He spoke. I shook my head I can't understand. Then with motions, with gestures (really he was as good as puppets I saw once), he showed me to lie on the grass is forbidden. But one is welcome to the seats instead. All free seats in this park. No charge for anybody. What a country!

But I was puzzled. There were iron armrests every two feet along the benches. How could I distribute myself under them? I tried one leg. Then the other. But when I was under, how could I turn around? Then, whatever way I got in, my chin was always caught by the hoop. While I thought this over, I walked and bought peanuts for my nickel and fed the squirrels.

Lights began to come on in the towers around the park. It was almost dark. I found a sandy patch under a rock and went to sleep. I was tired from America and I slept some hours. It must have been almost midnight when the light flashed in my face. I sat up. It was from the headlight of a touring car choking along on the road below me. While I watched, the engine coughed and died. A man got out. For more than an hour he knocked with tools and opened the hood and closed it again.

---

reputation (rep yuh TAY shun) idea that most people have of a person
caviar (KAV ee ahr) tiny eggs of certain fish, usually very expensive
gesture (JES chur) motion, hand signal
touring car (TUUR ing KAHR) old car with a top that folds down and a crank to start it moving

Then I slid down the bank. In the war there were airplanes. Of course cars are much the same except, naturally, for the wings. I showed him with my hands and feet and head, like the policeman: "Give me the tools and let me try." He handed them over and sat down on the bench.

I checked the spark plugs and the distributor, the timer, and the coils. I looked at the fuel line, at the ignition, at the gas. In between, I cranked. I cranked until I cranked my heart out onto the ground. Still the car wouldn't move.

I got mad. I cursed it. Then I kicked the radiator as hard as I could. The motor started with a snort that shook the car like a leaf.

The man came running up. He was laughing and he shook my hands and talked to me and asked questions. But the policeman's method didn't work. Signs weren't enough. I remembered my dictionary—English-Russian, Russian-English—it went both ways. I took it from my blouse pocket and showed the man. Holding it under the headlights, he thumbed through.

"Work?" he found in English.

I looked at the Russian word beside it and shook my head.

"Home?" he turned to that.

"No," again.

I took the dictionary. "Boat. Today."

"Come home"—he showed me the words—"with me"—he pointed to himself. "Eat. Sleep. Job." It took him quite a time between words. "Job. Tomorrow."

"Automobiles?" I said. We have the same word in Georgian.

"Automobiles!" He was pleased we found one word together.

We got in his car, and he took me through miles and miles of streets with houses on both sides of every one of them until we came to his own. We went in and we ate and we drank and ate and drank again. For that, fortunately, you need no words.

Then his wife showed me a room and I went to bed. As I fell asleep, I thought to myself: Well, now, I have lived one whole day in America and—just like they say—America is a country where anything, anything at all can happen.

And in 20 years—about this—I never changed my mind.

---

distributor (dih STRIB yuh tur) part of a car's engine

FOCUS ON THE SELECTION

UNDERSTAND THE SELECTION

Recall

1. Why did the friend Hassan have more money than the main character?
2. How did the main character get ashore even though he had no money?
3. How did the main character find a job?

Infer

4. Why do you suppose the people on the boat were not allowed to enter the United States without money?
5. Why did the man trade the cotton hat for the fur hat?
6. Why did the main character ask people "what watch" and "how many clock"?
7. How did he learn to work on engines?

Apply

8. What do his two occupations tell you about Russia at that time?
9. Do you think most immigrants have been as lucky on their first day as the main character in this story? Why?
10. How could the main character have kept his first job in the restaurant?

Respond to Literature

What does being an American mean to this character?

WRITE ABOUT THE SELECTION

At the end of "The First Day," the main character has gone home with a stranger. The stranger has fed him, given him a place to sleep, and offered him a job working with automobiles. Write a story called "The Second Day." What will this character's second day be like? What will his job be? Where will he live? Will he make other friends? Will he keep his job, or will he make mistakes like he did on the last job?

Prewriting: Think about what is most likely to happen. Start by making a list of questions about what might happen, and then decide what you want the answers to be. List the answers beside your listed questions.

Writing: Use the answers to your questions to write a paragraph about the character's second day. In it give more information about what the character's new life in America is going to be like.

Revising: When you revise your story, decide whether the details you have provided are believable. Think about what you know of the character, the man who offered him this job, and what has already happened in the story.

Proofreading: Read your paragraph to check for errors. Be sure all your sentences begin with capital letters and end with periods, question marks, or exclamation marks.

THINK ABOUT POINT OF VIEW

A selection with a first person point of view is written as though one of the characters in it were telling the story. A selection in the first person tells you only what is known to the character telling the story. It often shares much of the thoughts, feelings, and opinions of the narrator.

1. What elements identify the point of view in "The First Day"?
2. How would this story be different if it were told in the third person?
3. How did the first person point of view contribute humor to the story?
4. Why did you not find out what happened to Hassan and Zurabeg?
5. How do you know what others thought of the main character?
6. Did you disagree with anything the story stated as a fact? How do you explain this?

DEVELOP YOUR VOCABULARY

What kinds of clues have you used to figure out the meaning of a new word? Sometimes writers want to use a word that will be unfamiliar to many of their readers. They will give very specific clues to its meaning. They may include a definition, an example, or a word that means the same or the opposite. Sometimes the clue will be between two commas immediately following the unfamiliar word.

Write the following sentence. Circle the word or group of words that gives clues to the meaning of the word in boldface.

1. Our hostess **begrudged**, or resented, every mouthful of food we ate.
2. The new waitress was a **greenhorn**. She had never waited on tables before.
3. We ordered **piroshkis**—Russian fillings enclosed in a crust of dough.
4. We traveled **steerage**—the least expensive class of travel on the ship.

Learn About

The Speaker

When you read a poem written in the first person, do you ever wonder to whom the "I" refers? The person to whom the "I" refers is called the **speaker.** Sometimes the speaker may be the poet. Other times the speaker may be an identified or unidentified fictional character. At other times the poet is pretending that a very famous person, living or dead, is saying or writing the poem.

In the first poem, "I Am an American," by Elias Lieberman, there are two different speakers. In the poem "Western Wagons," by Rosemary and Stephen Vincent Benét, the speakers are characters in the poem. The poem "Grudnow," by Linda Pastan, is really about someone other than the speaker.

Identifying the speaker will help you interpret the content of the selection. As you read these poems, ask yourself these questions:

1. Who is the speaker?
2. Is the speaker a person?
3. Does the speaker change? Where?

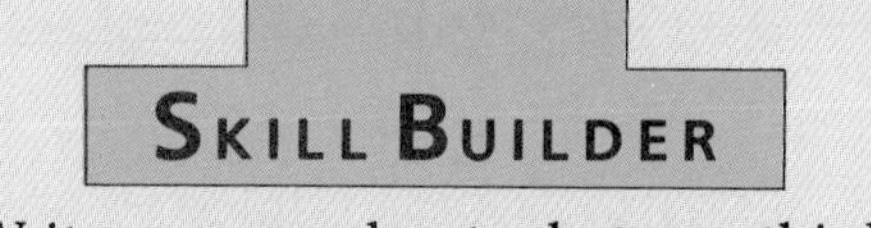

Write a poem about what you think a family member, a classmate, or a teacher might have to say about something that happened today.

I Am an American

by Elias Lieberman

I am an American.
My father belongs to the Sons of the Revolution;
My mother, to the Colonial Dames.

One of my ancestors pitched tea overboard in Boston Harbor;
5 Another stood his ground with Warren;
Another hungered with Washington at Valley Forge.
My forefathers were Americans in the making:
They spoke in her council halls;
They died on her battle-fields;
10 They commanded her troop-ships;
They cleared her forests.
Dawns reddened and paled.
Staunch hearts of mine beat fast at each new star
In the nation's flag.
15 Keen eyes of mine foresaw her greater glory:
The sweep of her seas,
The plenty of her plains,
The man-hives in her billion-wired cities.
Every drop of blood in me holds a heritage of patriotism.
20 I am proud of my past.
I am an AMERICAN.

I am an American.
My father was an atom of dust,
My mother a straw in the wind,

Warren general at the Battle of Bunker Hill
staunch (STAWNCH) steady and true
heritage (HER ih tij) things we inherit from our ancestors
atom (AT um) tiny bit

25 To His Serene Majesty.
One of my ancestors died in the mines of Siberia;
Another was crippled for life by twenty blows of the knout.
Another was killed defending his home during the massacres.
The history of my ancestors is a trail of blood
30 To the palace-gate of the Great White Czar.
But then the dream came—
The dream of America.
In the light of the Liberty torch
The atom of dust became a man
35 And the straw in the wind became a woman
For the first time.
"See," said my father, pointing to the flag that fluttered near,
"That flag of stars and stripes is yours;
It is the emblem of the promised land.
40 It means, my son, the hope of humanity.
Live for it—die for it!"
Under the open sky of my new country I swore to do so;
And every drop of blood in me will keep that vow.
I am proud of my future.
45 I am an AMERICAN.

---

serene (suh REEN) very calm; "Serene Majesty" is a title used by some kings, queens, emperors, and empresses.
Siberia (sy BIR ee uh) cold northern part of the Soviet Union, used as a place of punishment
knout (NOUT) leather whip used in Russia
humanity (hyoo MAN uh tee) all people

Western Wagons

by Rosemary and Stephen Vincent Benét

They went with axe and rifle
when the trail was still to blaze,
They went with wife and children
in the prairie schooner days,
5 With banjo and with frying pan—
Susanna, don't you cry!
For I'm off to California
to get rich out there or die!

We've broken land and cleared it,
10 but we're tired of where we are,
They say that wild Nebraska
is a better place by far.
There's gold in far Wyoming,
there's black earth in Ioway,
15 So pack up the kids and blankets,
for we're moving out today.

The cowards never started
and the weak died on the road,
And all across the continent
20 the endless campfires glowed.
We'd taken land and settled—
but a traveler passes by—
And we're going West tomorrow—
Lordy, never ask us why!

25 We're going West tomorrow,
where the promises can't fail.
O'er the hills in legions, boys,
and crowd the dusty trail!
We shall starve and freeze and suffer.
30 We shall die, and tame the lands.
But we're going West tomorrow
with our fortune in our hands.

West Bound Wagon Train on the Salt Lake Trail, O. E. Berninghaus, c. 1840s. Painting. Three Lions.

GRUDNOW

by Linda Pastan

When he spoke of where he came from,
my grandfather could have been
clearing his throat
of that name, that town
5 sometimes Poland, sometimes Russia,
the borders pencilled in
with a hand as shaky as his.
He left, I heard him say,
because there was nothing there.

10 I understood what he meant
when I saw the photograph
of his people standing
against a landscape emptied
of crops and trees, scraped raw
15 by winter. Everything
was in sepia, as if the brown earth
had stained the faces,
stained even the air.

I would have died there, I think
20 in childhood maybe
of some fever,
my face pressed for warmth
against a cow with flanks
like those of the great aunts

---

borders (BAWR durz) dividing lines between two countries, states, etc., or the land along it
pencilled (PEN suld) marked, written or drawn with or as with a pencil
landscape (LAND skayp) a picture representing a section of natural, inland scenery, as of a prairie, woodland, mountain, etc.
sepia (SEE pee uh) a dark, reddish-brown color

25 in the picture. Or later
I would have died of history
like the others, who dug

their stubborn heels into that earth,
heels as hard as the heels
30 of the bread my grandfather tore
from the loaf at supper. He always
sipped his tea through a cube of sugar
clenched in his teeth, the way
he sipped his life here, noisily,
35 through all he remembered
that might have been sweet in Grudnow.

I and the Village,
Marc Chagall. 1911.
Collection, The Museum
of Modern Art, New York,
Mrs. Simon Guggenheim
Fund.

When I First Saw Snow

by Gregory Djanikian

Bing Crosby was singing "White Christmas"
  on the radio, we were staying at my aunt's house
  waiting for papers, my father was looking for a job.
We had trimmed the tree the night before,
5 sap had run on my fingers and for the first time
  I was smelling pine wherever I went.
Anais, my cousin, was upstairs in her room
  listening to Danny and the Juniors.
Haigo was playing Monopoly with Lucy, his sister,
10 Buzzy, the boy next door, had eyes for her
  and there was a rattle of dice, a shuffling
  of Boardwalk, Park Place, Marvin Gardens.
There were red bows on the Christmas tree.

It had snowed all night.
15 My boot buckles were clinking like small bells
  as I thumped to the door and out
  onto the grey planks of the porch dusted with snow.
The world was immaculate, new,
  even the trees had changed color,
20 and when I touched the snow on the railing
  I didn't know what I had touched, ice or fire.

I heard, "I'm dreaming. . . ."
I heard, "At the hop, hop, hop . . . oh, baby."
I heard "B&O" and the train in my imagination
25 was whistling through the great plains.
And I was stepping off,
I was falling deeply into America.

---

clinking (KLINGK ing) making or causing to make a slight, sharp sound, as of glasses striking together
thumped (THUMPD) made a dull, heavy sound; pounded, throbbed
planks (PLANGKS) long, broad, thick boards
immaculate (ih MAK yuh lit) perfectly clean; without a spot or stain; unsoiled

From The New Colossus

by Emma Lazarus

"Give me your tired, your poor,
Your huddled masses yearning to breathe free,
The wretched refuse of your teeming shore.
Send these, the homeless, tempest-tossed to me—
I lift my lamp beside the golden door!"

---

wretched (RECH id) very unhappy, miserable
refuse (REF yoos) things thrown away
teeming (TEEM ing) crowded and moving
tempest (TEM pist) big storm

FOCUS ON THE SELECTION

UNDERSTAND THE SELECTION

Recall

1. In "I Am an American," what did the ancestors of the first speaker do?
2. In "I Am an American," what did the father point out near the liberty torch?
3. In "Grudnow," why had the grandfather left his homelands?

Infer

4. What does Linda Pastan think about who was an American?
5. In "Grudnow," what did the poet mean by ". . . or later I would have died of history like the others who dug their stubborn heels into that earth."?
6. Who speaks in "The New Colossus"?
7. What kind of climate is the speaker in "When I First Saw Snow" used to?

Apply

8. Do you think most of these Americans were happy in their new homes? Support your answer with examples.
9. How is American history illustrated by the words from "The New Colossus?"
10. What might make you want to go to a strange and distant land?

Respond to Literature

What do these poems tell you about how people became Americans?

WRITE ABOUT THE SELECTION

All but one of the Americans in the poems you have read left their homes for distant lands. They had different reasons for leaving and different feelings about leaving. Choose two of the Americans or groups of Americans in these poems. Write one paragraph telling how they are alike. Write another paragraph telling how they are different. Be sure to consider why these Americans left their original homelands in the first place.

Prewriting: Make a chart with three columns. In the left hand column, write facts about one American. In the right hand column, write facts about the other American. In the middle, write facts that apply to both of them.

Writing: Write your paragraphs. Focus on how these people became Americans and their reasons for leaving their original homes.

Revising: Revise your paper. Be sure that you have written the ways these Americans are alike in the first paragraph, and the ways they are different in the second. Be sure each paragraph has a topic sentence. Check your paragraph further for organization. Consider adding, deleting, substituting or rearranging your sentences to make your writing clearer and more effective.

Proofreading: Check your paper for errors in spelling, capitalization, usage, and punctuation. When you are writing about people with unfamiliar names, be careful to spell them correctly. Be sure you have indented each paragraph.

THINK ABOUT THE SPEAKER

Sometimes the speaker is identified for you. Other times you have to identify the speaker yourself. The speaker may be a type of person rather than a specific individual. Sometimes you need to identify the speaker in order to understand fully the content and message of the selection.

1. What is the difference between the two speakers in "I Am an American"?
2. Where does the speaker change in "I Am an American"?
3. How did changing the speaker in "I Am an American" contribute to the theme, or central idea, of the poem?
4. In which poems was the poem about the speaker?
5. In which poems were the speakers someone other than the main character of the poem?

DEVELOP YOUR VOCABULARY

The dictionary is the best source for definitions of unfamiliar words. However, even if you know the meaning of a word, a dictionary has other valuable information. You can use a dictionary to find spelling, proper pronunciation, or part of speech. Some dictionaries tell you the origin of the word. Dictionaries sometimes include sentences to show you how a word is used correctly. They will tell you how to write the plural and the past tense of a word. Studying all of the elements in a dictionary entry will help you add the word to your working vocabulary.

Review the meanings of these words from the poems you just read. Use each in an original sentence to show that you understand not only their meaning, but how to use them correctly in writing.

1. ancestors
2. foresaw
3. heritage
4. legion
5. refuse
6. immaculate

Learn About

Characterization

Characters are the actors in a story. They may be people, animals, or sometimes even objects or machines.

How can you get to know a character? **Character traits,** or qualities, include a character's appearance and personality. Sometimes authors describe a character's traits directly. Other times you can tell what story characters are like by how they behave and what they say. Sometimes you can learn a great deal about a character from what other characters say or think about him or her.

As you read "Split Cherry Tree," ask yourself these questions:

1. What is the father like?
2. How does the author reveal the father's character?
3. What parts of the story make you like or dislike this character?

Authors help you learn about characters by describing their traits. They also tell you what the characters say, do, think, and feel. Write a paragraph about a character. It can be a real person that you know, or it can be a character that you make up. Someone should be able to tell from the paragraph what the character is like.

SPLIT CHERRY TREE

by Jesse Stuart

"I don't mind staying after school," I says to Professor Herbert, "but I'd rather you'd whip me with a switch and let me go home early. Pa will whip me anyway for getting home two hours late."

"You are too big to whip," says Professor Herbert, "and I have to punish you for climbing up in the cherry tree. You boys knew better than that! The other five boys have paid their dollar each. You have been the only one who has not helped pay for the tree. Can't you borrow a dollar?"

"I can't," I says. "I'll have to take the punishment. I wish it would be quicker punishment. I wouldn't mind."

Professor Herbert stood and looked at me. He was a big man. He wore a gray suit of clothes. The suit matched his gray hair.

"You don't know my father," I says to Professor Herbert. "He might be called a little old-fashioned. He makes us mind him until we're twenty-one years old. I'll never be able to make him understand about the cherry tree. I'm the first of my people to go to high school."

"You must take the punishment," says Professor Herbert. "You must stay two hours after school today and two hours after school tomorrow. I am allowing you twenty-five cents an hour. That is good money for a high school student. You can sweep the schoolhouse floor, wash the blackboards, and clean windows. I'll pay the dollar for you."

I couldn't ask Professor Herbert to loan me a dollar. He never offered to loan it to me. I had to stay and help the janitor and work out my fine at a quarter an hour.

I thought as I swept the floor: "What will Pa do to me? What lie can I tell him when I go home? Why did we ever climb that cherry tree and break it down for anyway? Why did we run crazy over the hills away from the crowd? Why did we do all of this? Six of us climbed up in a little cherry tree after one little lizard! Why did the tree split and fall with us? It should have been a stronger tree! Why did Eif Crabtree just happen to be below us plowing and catch us in his cherry tree? Why wasn't he a better man than to charge us six dollars for the tree?"

It was six o'clock when I left the schoolhouse. I had six miles to walk home. It would be after seven when I got home. I had all my work to do when I got home. It took Pa and me both to do the work. Seven cows to milk. Nineteen head of cattle to feed, four mules, twenty-five hogs. Firewood and stovewood to cut and water to draw from the well. He would be doing it when I got home. He would be mad and wondering what was keeping me!

I hurried home. I would run under the dark leafless trees. I would walk fast uphill. I would run down the hill. The ground was freezing. I had to hurry. I had to run. I reached the long ridge that led to our cow pasture. I ran along this ridge. The wind dried the sweat on my face. I ran across the pasture to the house.

I threw down my books in the chip-yard. I ran to the barn to spread fodder on the ground for the cattle. I didn't take time to change my clean school clothes for my old work clothes. I ran out to the barn. I saw Pa spreading fodder on the ground to the cattle. That was my job. I ran up to the fence. I says: "Leave that for me, Pa. I'll do it. I'm just a little late."

"I see you are," says Pa. He turned and looked at me. His eyes danced fire. "What in th' world has kept you so? Why ain't you been here to help me with this work? Make a gentleman out'n one boy in th' family and this is what you get! Send you to high school and you get too onery fer th' buzzards to smell!"

I never said anything. I didn't want to tell why I was late from school. Pa stopped scattering the bundles of fodder. He looked at me. He says: "Why are you gettin' in here this time o' night? You tell me or I'll take a hickory switch to you right here on th' spot!"

I says: "I had to stay after school." I couldn't lie to Pa. He'd go to school and find out why I had to stay. If I lied to him it would be too bad for me.

"Why did you haf to stay after school?" says Pa.

I says: "Our biology class went on a field trip today. Six of us boys broke down a cherry tree. We had to give a dollar apiece to pay for the tree. I didn't have the dollar. Professor Herbert is making me work out my dollar. He gives me twenty-five cents an hour. I had to stay in this afternoon. I'll have to stay in tomorrow afternoon!"

"Are you telling me th' truth?" says Pa.

"I'm telling you the truth," I says. "Go and see for yourself."

"That's just what I'll do in th' mornin'," says Pa. "Jist whose cherry tree

---

biology (by OL uh jee) the study of living things
fodder (FOD ur) food for cattle
onery (AWN uh ree) ornery, mean and stubborn

did you break down?"

"Eif Crabtree's cherry tree!"

"What was you doin' clear out in Eif Crabtree's place?" says Pa. "He lives four miles from th' County High School. Don't they teach you no books at that high school? Do they jist let you get out and gad over th' hillsides? If that's all they do I'll keep you at home, Dave. I've got work here fer you to do!"

"Pa," I says, "spring is just getting here. We take a subject in school where we have to have bugs, snakes, flowers, lizards, frogs, and plants. It is biology. It was a pretty day today. We went out to find a few of these. Six of us boys saw a lizard at the same time sunning on a cherry tree. We all went up the tree to get it. We broke the tree down. It split at the forks. Eif Crabtree was plowing down below us. He ran up the hill and got our names. The other boys gave their dollar apiece. I didn't have mine. Professor Herbert put mine in for me. I have to work it out at school."

"Poor man's son, huh," says Pa. "I'll attend to that myself in th' mornin'. I'll take keer o' 'im. He ain't from this country nohow. I'll go down there in th' mornin' and see 'im. Lettin' you leave your books and galavant all over th' hills. What kind of a school is it nohow! Didn't do that, my son, when I's in school. All fared alike, too."

"Pa, please don't go down there," I says. "Just let me have fifty cents and pay the rest of my fine. I don't want you to go down there! I don't want you to start anything with Professor Herbert!"

"Ashamed of your old Pap, are you, Dave," says Pa, "atter the way I've worked to raise you! Tryin' to send you to school so you can make a better livin' than I've made."

I thought once I'd run through the woods above the barn just as hard as I could go. I thought I'd leave high school and home forever! Pa could not catch me! I'd get away! I couldn't go back to school with him. He'd have a gun and maybe he'd shoot Professor Herbert. It was hard to tell what he would do. I could tell Pa that school had changed in the hills from the way it was when he was a boy, but he wouldn't understand. I could tell him we studied frogs, birds, snakes, lizards, flowers, insects. But Pa wouldn't understand. If I did run away from home it wouldn't matter to Pa. He would see Professor Herbert anyway. He would think that high school and Professor Herbert had run me away from home. There was no need to run away. I'd just have to stay, finish foddering the cattle and go to school with Pa the next morning.

The moon shone bright in the cold March sky. I finished my work by moonlight. Professor Herbert really didn't know how much work I had to do at home. If he had known he would not have kept me after school. He would have loaned me a dollar to have paid my part on the cherry tree. He had never lived in the hills. He didn't know the way the hill boys had to work so that they could go to school. Now he was teaching in a County High School where all the boys who attended were from hill farms.

After I'd finished doing my work I went to the house and ate my supper. Pa and Mom had eaten. My supper was getting cold. I heard Pa and Mom talking in the front room. Pa was telling Mom about me staying in after school.

"I had to do all th' milkin' tonight, chop th' wood myself. It's too hard on me atter I've turned ground all day. I'm goin' to take a day off tomorrow and see if I

---

galavant (GAL ih vant) gallivant, run about having fun

can't remedy things a little. I'll go down to the high school tomorrow. I won't be a very good scholar fer Professor Herbert nohow. He won't keep me in atter school. I'll take a different kind of lesson down there and make 'im acquainted with it."

"Now, Luster," says Mom, "you jist stay away from there. Don't cause a lot o' trouble. You can be jailed fer a trick like that. You'll get th' Law atter you. You'll jist go down there and show off and plague your own boy Dave to death in front o' all th' scholars!"

"Plague or no plague," says Pa, "he don't take into consideration what all I haf to do here, does he? I'll show 'im it ain't right to keep one boy in and let the rest go scot-free. My boy is good as th' rest, ain't he? A bullet will make a hole in a schoolteacher same as it will anybody else. He can't do me that way and get by with it. I'll plug 'im first. I aim to go down there bright and early in th' mornin' and get all this straight! I am to see about bug learnin' and this runnin' all over God's creation huntin' snakes, lizards, and frogs. Ransackin' th' country and goin' through cherry orchards and breakin' th' trees down atter lizards! Old Eif Crabtree ought to a-poured th' hot lead into 'em instead o' chargin' six dollars fer th' tree! He ought to a-got old Herbert the first one!"

I ate my supper. I slipped upstairs and lit the lamp. I tried to forget the whole thing. I studied plane geometry. Then I studied my biology lesson. I could hardly study for thinking about Pa. "He'll go to school with me in the morning. He'll take a gun for Professor Herbert! What will Professor Herbert think of me! I'll tell him when Pa leaves that I couldn't help it. But Pa might shoot him. I hate to go with Pa. Maybe he'll cool off about it tonight and not go in the morning."

Pa got up at four o'clock. He built a fire in the stove. Then he built a fire in the fireplace. He got Mom up to get breakfast. Then he got me up to help feed and milk. By the time we had our work done at the barn, Mom had breakfast ready for us. We ate our breakfast. Daylight came and we could see the bare oak trees covered white with frost. The hills were white with frost.

"Now, Dave," says Pa, "let's get ready fer school. I aim to go with you this mornin' and look into bug larnin', frog larnin', lizard and snake larnin', and breakin' down cherry trees! I don't like no sicha foolish way o' larnin' myself!"

Pa hadn't forgot. I'd have to take him to school with me. He would take me to school with him. I was glad we were going early. If Pa pulled a gun on Professor Herbert there wouldn't be so many of my classmates there to see him.

I knew that Pa wouldn't be at home in the high school. He wore overalls, big boots, a blue shirt and a sheepskin coat, and a slouched black hat gone to seed at

---

plague (PLAYG) pester, give trouble to
ransack (RAN sak) search through
plane geometry (PLAYN jee OM uh tree) branch of mathematics that studies flat shapes

the top. He put his gun in its holster. We started trudging toward the high school across the hill.

It was early when we got to the County High School. Professor Herbert had just got there. I just thought as we walked up the steps into the schoolhouse: "Maybe Pa will find out Professor Herbert is a good man. He just doesn't know him. Just like I felt toward the Lambert boys across the hill. I didn't like them until I'd seen them and talked to them, then I liked them and we were friends. It's a lot in knowing the other fellow."

"You're th' Professor here, ain't you?" says Pa.

"Yes," says Professor Herbert, "and you are Dave's father?"

"Yes," says Pa, pulling out his gun and laying it on the seat in Professor Herbert's office. Professor Herbert's eyes got big behind his black-rimmed glasses when he saw Pa's gun. Color came into his pale cheeks.

"Jist a few things about this school I want to know," says Pa. "I'm tryin' to make a scholar out'n Dave. He's the only one out'n eleven youngins I've sent to high school. Here he comes in late and leaves me all th' work to do! He said you's all out bug huntin' yesterday and broke a cherry tree down. He had to stay two hours after school yesterday and work out money to pay on that cherry tree! Is that right?"

"W-w-why," says Professor Herbert, "I guess it is."

He looked at Pa's gun.

"Well," says Pa, "this ain't no high school. It's a bug school, a lizard school, a snake school! It ain't no school nohow!"

"Why did you bring that gun?" says Professor Herbert to Pa.

"You see that little hole," says Pa as he picked up the long blue forty-four and put his finger on the end of the barrel. "A bullet can come out'n that hole that will kill a schoolteacher same as it will any other man. It will kill a rich man same as a poor man. It will kill a man. But after I come in and saw you, I know'd I wouldn't need it. This maul o' mine could do you up in a few minutes."

Pa stood there, big, hard, brown-skinned, and mighty beside Professor Herbert. I didn't know Pa was so much bigger and harder. I'd never seen Pa in a schoolhouse before. I'd seen Professor Herbert. He always looked big before to me. He didn't look big standing beside Pa.

"I was only doing my duty," says Professor Herbert, "Mr. Sexton, and following the course of study the state provided us with."

"Course o' study!" says Pa. "What study? Bug study? Takin' youngins to th' woods. Boys and girls all out there together a-galavantin' in the brush and kickin' up their heels and their poor old Mas and Pas at home a-slavin' to keep 'em in school and give 'em a education!"

Students are coming into the schoolhouse now. Professor Herbert says: "Close the door, Dave, so others won't hear."

I walked over and closed the door. I was shaking like a leaf in the wind. I thought Pa was going to hit Professor Herbert every minute. He was doing all the talking. His face was getting red. The red color was coming through the brown, weather-beaten skin on Pa's face.

"It jist don't look good to me," says Pa, "a-takin' all this swarm of youngins out to pillage th' whole deestrict. Breakin' down cherry trees. Keepin' boys in atter school."

"What else could I have done with Dave, Mr. Sexton?" says Professor Herbert. "The boys didn't have any business all climbing that cherry tree after one lizard. One boy could have gone up the tree and got it. The farmer charged us six dollars. It was a little steep, I think, but we had it to pay. Must I make five boys pay and let your boy off? He said he didn't have the dollar and couldn't get it. So I put it in for him. I'm letting him work it out. He's not working for me. He's working for the school!"

"I jist don't know what you could a-done with 'im," says Pa, "only a-larruped 'im with a withe! That's what he

---

pillage (PIL ij) rob and destroy
steep (STEEP) very expensive; costly
larrup (LAR up) whip; beat
withe (WITH) thin, strong twig

needed!"

"He's too big to whip," says Professor Herbert, pointing at me. "He's a man in size."

"He's not too big fer me to whip," says Pa. "They ain't too big until they're over twenty-one! It jist didn't look fair to me! Work one and let th' rest out because they got th' money. I don't see what bugs has got to do with a high school! It don't look good to me nohow!"

Pa picked up his gun and put it back in its holster. The red color left Professor Herbert's face. He talked more to Pa. Pa softened a little. It looked funny to see Pa in the high school building. It was the first time he'd ever been there.

"We're not only hunting snakes, toads, flowers, butterflies, lizards," says Professor Herbert, "but, Mr. Sexton, I was hunting dry grass to put in an incubator and raise some protozoa."

"I don't know what that is," says Pa. "Th' incubator is th' new-fangled way o' cheatin' th' hens and raisin' chickens. I ain't so sure about th' breed o' chickens you mentioned."

"You've heard of germs, Mr. Sexton, haven't you?" says Professor Herbert.

"Jist call me Luster if you don't mind," says Pa, very casual like.

"All right, Luster, you've heard of germs, haven't you?"

"Yes," says Pa, "but I don't believe in germs. I'm sixty-five years old and I ain't seen one yet!"

"You can't see them with your naked eye," says Professor Herbert. "Just keep that gun in the holster and stay with me in the high school today. I have a few things I want to show you. That scum on your teeth has germs in it."

"What," says Pa, "you mean to tell me I've got germs on my teeth!"

"Yes," says Professor Herbert. "The same kind as we might be able to find in a living black snake if we dissect it!"

"I don't mean to dispute your word," says Pa, "but danged if I believe it. I don't believe I have germs on my teeth!"

"Stay with me today and I'll show you. I want to take you through the school anyway. School has changed a lot in the hills since you went to school. I don't guess we had high schools in this country when you went to school."

"No," says Pa, "jist readin', writin', and cipherin'. We didn't have all this bug larnin', and findin' germs on your teeth and in the middle o' black snakes! Th' world's changin'."

"It is," says Professor Herbert, "and we hope all for the better. Boys like your own there are going to help change it. He's your boy. He knows all of what I've told you. You stay with me today."

"I'll shore stay with you," says Pa. "I want to see th' germs off'n my teeth. I jist want to see a germ. I've never seen one in my life. 'Seein' is believin',' Pap allus told me."

Pa walks out of the office with Profes-

---

protozoa (proht uh ZOH uh) one-celled animals that can be seen only under a microscope
dissect (dih SEKT) cut open and examine
cipherin' (SY fur un) ciphering; arithmetic

sor Herbert. I just hoped Professor Herbert didn't have Pa arrested for pulling his gun. Pa's gun has always been a friend to him when he goes to settle disputes.

The bell rang. School took up. I saw the students when they marched in the schoolhouse look at Pa. They would grin and punch each other. Pa just stood and watched them pass in at the schoolhouse door. Two long lines marched in the house. The boys and girls were clean and well dressed. Pa stood over in the schoolyard under a leafless elm, in his sheepskin coat, his big boots laced in front with buckskin and his heavy socks stuck above his boot tops. Pa's overalls legs were baggy and wrinkled between his coat and boot tops. His blue work shirt showed at the collar. His big black hat showed his gray-streaked black hair. His face was hard and weather-tanned to the color of a ripe fodder blade. His hands were big and gnarled like the roots of the elm tree he stood beside.

When I went to my first class I saw Pa and Professor Herbert going around over the schoolhouse. I was in my geometry class when Pa and Professor Herbert came in the room. We were explaining our propositions on the blackboard. Professor Herbert and Pa just quietly came in and sat down awhile. I heard Fred Wurts whisper to Glenn Armstrong: "Who is that old man? Lord, he's a rough-looking scamp." Glenn whispered back: "I think he's Dave's Pap." The students in geometry looked at Pa. They must have wondered what he was doing in school. Before the class was over, Pa and Professor Herbert got up and went out. I saw them together down on the playground. Professor Herbert was explaining to Pa. I could see the outline of Pa's gun under his coat when he'd walk around.

At noon in the high school cafeteria Pa and Professor Herbert sat together at the little table where Professor Herbert always ate by himself. They ate together. The students watched the way Pa ate. He ate with his knife instead of his fork. A lot of the students felt sorry for me after they found out he was my father. They didn't have to feel sorry for me. I wasn't ashamed of Pa after I found out he wasn't going to shoot Professor Herbert. I was glad they had made friends. I wasn't ashamed of Pa. I wouldn't be as long as he behaved.

In the afternoon when we went to biology Pa was in the class. He was sitting on one of the high stools beside the microscope. We went ahead with our work just as if Pa wasn't in the class. I saw Pa take his knife and scrape one of his teeth. Professor Herbert put it under the lens and adjusted the microscope for Pa. He adjusted it and worked awhile. Then he says: "Now, Luster, look! Put your eye right down to the light. Squint the other eye!"

Pa put his head down and did as Professor Herbert said: "I see 'im," says Pa. "Who'd a ever thought that? Right on

---

gnarled (NAHRLD) twisted
proposition (prop uh ZISH un) geometry problem to be solved

a body's teeth! Right in a body's mouth! You're right certain they ain't no fake to this, Professor Herbert?"

"No, Luster," says Professor Herbert. "It's there. That's the germ. Germs live in a world we cannot see with the naked eye. We must use the microscope. There are millions of them in our bodies. Some are harmful. Others are helpful."

Pa holds his face down and looks through the microscope. We stop and watch Pa. He sits upon the tall stool. His knees are against the table. His legs are long. His coat slips up behind when he bends over. The handle of his gun shows. Professor Herbert quickly pulls his coat down.

"Oh, yes," says Pa. He gets up and pulls his coat down. Pa's face gets a little red. He knows about his gun and he knows he doesn't have any use for it in high school.

"We have a big black snake over here we caught yesterday," says Professor Herbert. "We'll chloroform him and dissect him and show you he has germs in his body, too."

"Don't do it," says Pa. "I believe you. I jist don't want to see you kill the black snake. I never kill one. They are good mousers and a lot o' help to us on the farm. I like black snakes. I jist hate to see people kill 'em. I don't allow 'em killed on my place."

The students look at Pa. They seem to like him better after he said that. Pa with a gun in his pocket but a tender heart beneath his ribs for snakes, but not for man! Pa won't whip a mule at home. He won't whip his cattle.

Professor Herbert took Pa through the laboratory. He showed him the different kinds of work we were doing. He showed him our equipment. They stood and talked while we worked. Then they walked out together. They talked louder when they got in the hall.

When our biology class was over I walked out of the room. It was our last class for the day. I would have to take my broom and sweep two hours to finish paying for the split cherry tree. I just wondered if Pa would want me to stay. He was standing in the hallway watching the students march out. He looked lost among us. He looked like a leaf turned brown on the tree among the treetop filled with growing leaves.

I got my broom and started to sweep. Professor Herbert walked up and says: "I'm going to let you do that some other time. You can go home with your father. He is waiting out there."

I laid my broom down, got my books, and went down the steps.

Pa says: "Ain't you got two hours o' sweepin' yet to do?"

I says: "Professor Herbert said I could do it some other time. He said for me to go home with you."

"No," says Pa. "You are goin' to do as he says. He's a good man. School has changed from my day and time. I'm a dead leaf, Dave. I'm behind. I don't belong here. If he'll let me I'll get a broom and we'll both sweep one hour. That

---

chloroform (KLAWR uh fawrm) use a chemical that produces sleep

pays your debt. I'll help you pay it. I'll ast 'im and see if he won't let me hep you."

"I'm going to cancel the debt," says Professor Herbert. "I just wanted you to understand, Luster."

"I understand," says Pa, "and since I understand he must pay his debt fer th' tree and I'm goin' to hep him."

"Don't do that," says Professor Herbert. "It's all on me."

"We don't do things like that," says Pa; "we're just and honest people. We don't want somethin' fer nothin'. Professor Herbert, you're wrong now and I'm right. You'll haf to listen to me. I've learned a lot from you. My boy must go on. Th' world has left me. It changed while I've raised my family and plowed th' hills. I'm a just and honest man. I don't skip debts. I ain't larned 'em to do that. I ain't got much larnin' myself but I do know right from wrong after I see through a thing."

Professor Herbert went home. Pa and I stayed and swept one hour. It looked funny to see Pa use a broom. He never used one at home. Mom used the broom. Pa used the plow. Pa did hard work. Pa says: "I can't sweep. Durned if I can. Look at th' streaks o' dirt I leave on th' floor! Seems like no work a-tall fer me. Brooms is too light 'r somethin'. I'll jist do th' best I can, Dave. I've been wrong about th' school."

I says: "Did you know Professor Herbert can get a warrant out for you for bringing your pistol to school and showing it in his office! They can railroad you for that!"

"That's all made right," says Pa. "I've made that right. Professor Herbert ain't goin' to take it to court. He likes me. I like 'im. We jist had to get together. He had the remedies. He showed me. You must go on to school. I am as strong a man as ever come out'n th' hills fer my years and th' hard work I've done. But I'm behind, Dave. I'm a little man. Your hands will be softer than mine. Your clothes will be better. You'll allus look cleaner than your old Pap. Jist remember, Dave, to pay your debts and be honest. Jist be kind to animals and don't bother th' snakes. That's all I got agin th' school. Puttin' black snakes to sleep and cuttin' 'em open."

It was late when we got home. Stars were in the sky. The moon was up. The ground was frozen. Pa took his time going home. I couldn't run like I did the night before. It was ten o'clock before we got the work finished, our suppers eaten. Pa sat before the fire and told Mom he was going to take her and show her a germ some time. Mom hadn't seen one either. Pa told her about the high school and the fine man Professor Herbert was. He told Mom about the strange school across the hill and how different it was from the school in their day and time.

FOCUS ON THE SELECTION

UNDERSTAND THE SELECTION

Recall

1. Why did Dave have to stay after school?
2. Why didn't the other boys have to stay?
3. What did Pa do at the school?

Infer

4. Why did Pa respond to conflict with threats of force?
5. Why did Professor Herbert pay Dave's dollar personally, even though Dave was working for the school?
6. Why did Pa put the gun on Professor Herbert's chair?
7. Why did Pa's attitude toward new methods change after he saw the germs?

Apply

8. What parts of the story show Pa to be kind in some ways?
9. How does Pa show that he has a strong sense of right and wrong?
10. If you asked Pa how he justified using guns, threats, and force to settle disagreements, what would he say?

Respond to Literature

What does Dave's father have in common with many other Americans?

WRITE ABOUT THE SELECTION

At the end of "Split Cherry Tree" Dave's father has accepted the new knowledge and methods in Dave's school. He has deepened his awareness of the importance of Dave's education. However, Pa still believes his children should obey him until age twenty-one, and Pa is set in his ways.

Imagine that Dave wins a scholarship. He wants to leave home at age eighteen to go to college and major in psychology. Psychology is the study of the mind, emotions, and behavior. Write the conversation Dave and his father would have on this subject. Be sure to keep them both in character. This means each should say what that character would really say.

Prewriting: List the points each character might make, and the other's reactions. Consider how each would feel about Dave's leaving home and about the study of psychology.

Writing: Write your conversation. Make sure that the character's speak as only they would. Remember that in real conversation, people usually speak one sentence at a time unless they are explaining or describing something.

Revising: When you revise your paper, decide whether each character's lines are what that character would really say.

Proofreading: Be sure you have enclosed each speaker's exact words in quotation marks. Use commas to separate the quotes from the rest of the sentence.

THINK ABOUT CHARACTERIZATION

Some stories have both major characters and minor characters. The major characters are the ones that are really important to the story. There may be minor characters in the story, too, but the story is not about them. Usually you do not learn much about the minor character's traits.

The problem, or conflict, in a story is often caused by the traits of the major characters.

1. Who are the major characters in "Split Cherry Tree"?
2. What are some traits of these characters?
3. What traits of a major character caused the problem in this story?
4. How did the author reveal these traits to you?
5. Why was there so little information about the minor characters' traits?

DEVELOP YOUR VOCABULARY

Sometimes a word you know will not make sense in the sentence in which it is used. The word may have another meaning that you do not know. You can find additional meanings in your dictionary. Sometimes the dictionary will illustrate in sentences the different meanings of the word.

If you look up a word and cannot decide which meaning is intended in a particular sentence, try substituting one of the definitions for the word in the sentence. When one of the definitions seems to make sense, that is probably the intended meaning.

Look up each of the following words in your dictionary. Note the different meanings. Then find the word in the selection. Write a sentence in which the word has the same meaning as it does in the selection.

1. fodder
2. maul
3. plague
4. proposition

UNIT 1 REVIEW

LITERATURE-BASED WRITING

1. All of the main characters in this unit are Americans, or became Americans later. Choose characters from two different selections. Imagine that they meet at a Fourth of July celebration. Write a dialogue for them. What do they say about the ways in which they and other Americans are alike? How do they describe the differences between Americans and people who live in other countries? Tell the reader which character is speaking by writing the character's name followed by a colon in front of his or her exact words.

Prewriting: Think about the selections you have read and the characters in them. Choose two characters who are very different. List some of their similarities and their differences.

Writing: Use the lists of the characters' similarities and differences to write the dialogue. Have them describe their differences as well as what they have in common with each other and with other Americans.

Revising: As you revise your dialogue, be sure that what each character is saying is true for that character. Think about any general statements about Americans and whether or not they apply to all Americans in this unit.

Proofreading: Read over your dialogue to check for errors. Make sure your sentences end with periods, question marks, or exclamation marks.

2. Write a paragraph about a part of your life that was very important to you. It may be a single incident. First, write it as an autobiography. Then write it as a biography, as though someone else were writing it. Remember what you have learned about point of view, narrative technique, and use of description in narration.

Prewriting: Think about the part of your life or the incident that you want to share. List the facts, statements, or events that you are going to include. Put a star beside those that you think will require some description. Then, think about the ways that the two paragraphs will differ. What will you write in the autobiography that only you could know? When you write it as a biography, what you say will have to be limited to what someone else would be able to find out.

Writing: Write about the incident or the part of your life that you have chosen. Write the events and actions in order. Write descriptions of persons, places, things, or actions that the reader will want to picture.

Revising: Check your paragraph to see if you need time-order words to make the order of events clear. See if there are places where you need to add description.

Proofreading: Read over your paragraph to check for errors. Make sure that your sentences end with periods, question marks, or exclamation marks.

BUILDING LANGUAGE SKILLS

Vocabulary

Many of the words you have read in these selections are words that have had suffixes added to them. A **suffix** is a word part added to the end of a word. It changes the meaning of the word to which it was added. Read these two sentences from "Prairie Fire": *Suddenly the sunshine was gone. The wind was rising and wildly screaming.* In the first sentence *suddenly* means "in a sudden manner." In the second sentence, *wildly* means "in a wild manner." Therefore, *-ly* added to a word changes the meaning to "in a ______ manner." It means in the manner described by the word to which *-ly* was added. Read the following sentences from selections you have read. In the selection *-ly* was added to at least one word in each sentence. Rewrite each sentence, adding *-ly* to one of the words to make it describe the manner in which something was done.

1. Prairie hens ran silent.
2. The little fire went backing slow away against the wind.
3. A rabbit cautious hopped and looked.
4. She walked up the stairs quick.
5. Elizabeth glad told Amelia all about how she had come to wear the Turkish outfit.

Usage and Mechanics

Adjectives are words that describe a noun. A **noun** is the name of a person, place or thing. Mark Twain called the Pony Express rider "a speedy messenger." *Messenger* is a noun, and *speedy* is an adjective describing the noun.

Sometimes an author will use more than one adjective to describe a noun. If two or more adjectives come before a noun that they both describe, they are usually separated by commas, as in this sentence from "Pony Express": "Then he came crashing up to the station where two men stood holding a fresh, impatient steed."

The following sentences are from selections in this unit. Each is missing at least one comma between two adjectives. Some sentences have more than two adjectives coming before a noun. Rewrite the sentences, adding commas between the adjectives that come before nouns.

1. He wore a short tight jacket and a snug cap without a brim.
2. It didn't matter whether he had a level straight road or a crazy trail over mountains.
3. The orange yellow terrible flames were coming faster than horses can run.
4. The wind rose to a high crackling rushing shriek.

UNIT 1 REVIEW

SPEAKING AND LISTENING

It is sometimes fun to pretend that stories are real happenings that might be reported in a newspaper. When a story is reported in a newspaper, there are certain questions that a reporter asks to help him cover the story. Those questions are who, what, where, when, why and how.

When you read a selection, you often think of the same questions as you become involved in the story. Answering questions such as those the reporter asks helps you to understand basic story elements.

Select a story from this unit. As you read the story, think of yourself as a reporter. Try to get the basic who, what, where, when, why and how out of the story. If you practice the following steps it will seem quite easy.

1. Think about the "who," the main character, of the story. Get to know him and the minor characters. Pay attention to the names of characters and any peculiar traits they might have that make them unique. Imagine them as real people with real personalities and problems.

2. Think about the "when" and "where," the setting of the story. Determine if it is essential to the plot and the development of the story. Picture the setting in your mind.

3. Consider the "what," "why," and "how," the plot, of the story. Determine the conflict that the main character is involved in. Decide at what point your interest was the highest as you were reading the story.

4. Finally, consider the final outcome of the story. Think about the resolution. Decide whether the main character resolved his conflict. What did the main character do to resolve his conflict?

5. Take notes as you read. Any good reporter is never without his notebook. Let your notes fall under the headings of who, what, where, when, why and how. Use these notes when you are "reporting" to the class.

Now, pretend you are a newspaper reporter and describe a story you have selected from this unit as a reporter might describe it. Give the story a pertinent headline. Summarize the principal parts by following the steps above. Since any good reporter takes notes, feel free to jot a few down on notecards. They'll be helpful during your presentation.

CRITICAL THINKING

When you read a nonfiction selection, it is important to distinguish fact from opinion. A **fact** is information that can be checked, observed, or proved. An **opinion** is what someone thinks about something.

Sometimes opinions are signalled by words like *I think, I believe, in my opinion,* or *according to.* However, many times people state opinions as though they were facts. Then you have to decide if what they have said is something that can be observed, checked, or proved.

Think about the following sentences from "The Pathway from Slavery to Freedom." Mr. Auld had just caught Mrs. Auld teaching Frederick Douglass to read. He explained to her that it was unlawful to teach a slave to read. "It was unlawful to teach a slave to read" is a fact. This is something that you can prove by checking the laws at that time.

Next Mr. Auld says, "If you give a slave an inch, he will take an ell." (An ell is a measure of 45 inches.) This is an opinion. It is what Mr. Auld thinks and cannot be proved.

Choose a nonfiction selection. List five statements from it. Ask the following questions about each one:

1. Can this statement be checked, observed, or proved?
2. Are there any clue words like *should, think, believe, opinion, ought to?*
3. Is this statement a fact or an opinion?

EFFECTIVE STUDYING

When you read nonfiction selections, you may want to take notes so that you can remember the information, organize it so that it is easy to understand, or use it in a report you plan to write.

Organize your note-taking and it will be easy to do. Your notes should be clear, so that you will understand them when you read them later.

Before you begin to take notes, preview your selection to see how it is structured. Usually the structure of the selection will suggest how to take notes. For example, if the main ideas are listed as subheadings, you may wish to list the subheadings and the main points under each.

If the selection does not have subheadings, examine the paragraphs. Many paragraphs begin with a topic sentence that states the main idea. The topic sentence is followed by supporting details, reasons, or examples. You can sometimes take notes on one paragraph at a time. Write the main idea and list the important supporting details.

You do not have to use complete sentences in your notes. Use key words and phrases that give you information quickly.

Turn to "Pony Express" and take notes by listing the main ideas. Under each main idea, list important supporting details. Take notes on one paragraph at a time. (Some paragraphs will not contain any of the important ideas in a selection.)

UNIT 2

Inner Space

The unexamined life is not worth living.

—Plato

The False Mirror, René Magritte, 1928. Oil on canvas, 21¼ x 31⅞". Collection, The Museum of Modern Art, New York.

Inner Space. You are someone important that nobody else can ever be—you. You occupy a place that nobody else can ever enter—your own inner space. Nobody else sees the world in quite the same way you do.

As you look out at the world from your inner space, it is easy to think of others entirely in terms of how their actions affect you and your world. Sometimes it is hard to remember that from within their own inner spaces, people feel joy, sorrow, hope, pride, and pain as strongly as you do.

Although you cannot enter another person's inner space, you can try to imagine how your actions appear to another person. In doing this, you will learn to understand and respect other people. Imagine how the world would be if everyone could see and feel the world from another person's inner space. For example, do you think people would murder, rob, or even make fun of others? Would they be hostile to people of a different race, nationality, or religion?

Being who you are. In literature, as in life, a character sometimes wants to be someone else who is better liked or more successful. In "The Donkey Who Did Not Want to Be Himself," a donkey hopes that if he behaves like a dog, he will be better treated. Have you ever tried to act like another person? If so, what did you learn from that experience?

What makes you who you are? Some people believe that ancestry is important. In "The Speckled Hen's Egg," a woman believes that her ancestors were important people. She begins to see herself as better than her neighbors. Why would someone think a person from an important family is better than a person from an ordinary family?

Often people pretend in order to impress others. In O.Henry's "The Kind of Man She Could Love," a young man pretends to be wealthy to impress a young girl. In doing so, he fails to show her his true best self.

Everyone grows and changes, but nobody becomes a different person. In "The Butterfly and the Caterpillar" by Joseph Lauren, a butterfly insults a caterpillar, forgetting that he used to be one, too. Are you ever impatient with very young children? Does it sometimes seem that they are a nuisance to have around?

We are influenced by the people around us. How would you be different if you grew up in a different family and culture? In "The Parable of the Eagle" by James Aggrey Carlson, an eagle is raised as a chicken. He behaves like a chicken. However, one man believes that with the heart of an eagle it will discover itself for what it is—an eagle.

The view from another's inner space. Sometimes you must step out of your inner space to view a situation fairly. In "The Confidence Game" by Pat Carr, a swimmer is unable to consider the welfare of her teammates from within her inner space. It is only when she gets a glimpse of another swimmer's inner space that she is able to think of others and inspire confidence.

Exploring your own inner space. Sometimes you must get away from other people or your everyday surroundings to discover yourself. This is demonstrated in the next two poems.

The occupant of your inner space. In Eve Herriam's poem "Thumbprint," the speaker marvels at the uniqueness and the potential of the self. In "Advice to Travelers" by Walker Gibson, the poet discusses the importance of identifying yourself. In May Swenson's "The Rest of My Life," the poet reminds us that we must live in our inner space for the rest of our lives. In the poem "You" by Nikki Giovanni, the speaker discovers a very special friend with whom to share inner space.

Learning about another's inner space. Sometimes in order to understand other people you must learn something about their lives. In Leslie Jill Sokolow's story "Aquí Se Habla Español," a boy learns the language of his girlfriend's family. In "Blind Sunday," a play by Arthur Barrow, a boy spends a day blindfolded in order to learn what life is like for his blind girlfriend.

Learn About

Fables

Where did we get the idea of the "moral of the story is"? Some short stories were written to teach a lesson. They are called **fables.** The lesson, or moral, will be given in a separate line at the end of the story or it will be obvious from the story. The best known fables are those originally told by Aesop, who was a slave living in Greece in about 600 B.C. Have you read the Aesop fable "The Tortoise and the Hare"? What is the moral?

Many fables have animals as main characters—animals who talk and behave like human beings. The author wants you to see your behavior and that behavior of people you know in the form of animals. Moreover, the author wants the reader to learn a lesson from what happens to the animals.

As you read "The Donkey Who Did Not Want to Be Himself," ask yourself the following questions:

1. What is the moral of the story?
2. How is the moral illustrated?
3. What does the moral have to do with inner space?

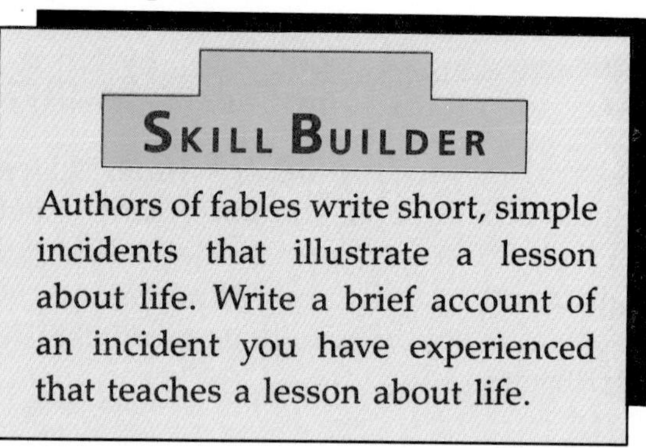

Skill Builder

Authors of fables write short, simple incidents that illustrate a lesson about life. Write a brief account of an incident you have experienced that teaches a lesson about life.

THE DONKEY WHO DID NOT WANT TO BE HIMSELF

ADAPTED *from Aesop*

There once was a donkey who led a tough life. His work never ended. His food was nothing but old hay. He slept on the hard ground, and the only blanket he ever had was the snow on a winter night. Only this and not even a "thank you" from his owner.

Then one day the donkey noticed how happy Fido the dog was. "Fido has an easy life," the donkey thought. "His work never even begins! His food is meat, corn-on-the-cob, fresh cookies, everything! He lives inside the house and has a soft bed and wool blanket with 'Fido' embroidered on a corner. He even naps on our owner's lap."

The donkey's eyes grew wider and wider as his thoughts went on and on. "Our owner seems to favor Fido. She's always hugging and petting him. She lets him in the house. She bought him a pretty collar just to show her affection." The more the donkey thought, the more he realized how lucky Fido was. Yes indeed! A dog's life would be good enough for him!

So the donkey studied Fido's ways. Fido barked for joy when their owner came home. He licked her face. He sat up and begged for food. He rolled over. He shook hands to get a bite of cookie. And the owner loved it all.

"Maybe I can't bark," the donkey thought, "but I can sure bray! So that's what I'll do. I'll bray when she comes home, just

---

embroidered (em BROI durd) decorated with fancy needlework
favor (FAY vur) give special treatment
affection (uh FEK shun) caring; love
bray (BRAY) make the sound a donkey makes

like that dog barks." The donkey was sure he had hit on a grand idea. "Why didn't I think of this a long time ago? If I want to lead a dog's life, I should act like a dog."

So the donkey did. When their owner came home, the donkey sat down and held out his hoof to shake hands, all the time braying a loud "Hello!" Then he rolled over and waved his legs in the air. "Just like a dog," he told himself. He brayed joyfully, trying to say, "Pat me. Put a collar on me. Call me cute names, if you want."

But his owner didn't understand. "What's gotten into you, you dumb donkey?" she asked. "Have you lost your mind? Who do you think you are?"

This made the donkey try harder. He put his front feet on her shoulders and licked her face.

"Fool!" she screamed. "What do you think you are—a dog? Stop it! Shoo! Get away from me!" She picked up a stick and chased the poor donkey out of the yard and into the barn. Then she locked him in.

All night the donkey tried hard to understand. He was sure his tricks were as good as Fido's. Why didn't their owner like him the way she liked Fido? Back at work the next day, he thought about it and thought about it. Gradually, an idea crossed his mind: *Be yourself or you will be nobody.*

FOCUS ON THE SELECTION

UNDERSTAND THE SELECTION

Recall

1. What was tough about the donkey's life?
2. What did he envy about Fido's life?
3. What did the donkey notice about Fido's behavior?

Infer

4. Why did the donkey bray at the owner, try to shake hands, and lick her face?
5. Why was the owner upset when the donkey did these things?
6. Why did the owner pick up a stick and chase the donkey into the barn?
7. Why did the owner treat two animals so differently when both of them were being themselves?

Apply

8. Would you act like someone else to get people to like you?
9. Predict what will happen in the donkey's life. Explain your answer.
10. How did this story illustrate the moral "Be yourself or you will be nobody?"

Respond to Literature

Why would this story be in a unit called "Inner Space"?

WRITE ABOUT THE SELECTION

In the well-known Aesop Fable, "The Donkey Who Did Not Want to Be Himself," the donkey tried to be like Fido. He thought if he could be like Fido he would be liked and treated as well as Fido was. Have you known people who behave in a similar manner? Write a short imaginary incident about someone your age who tries to behave like somebody else who is very popular. Give details that show how that person changes in personality and appearance to be more like the popular person.

Prewriting: Think of a situation in which someone your age might notice that somebody else is well liked and well treated. Then think of ways he or she might try to be like the other person. Be specific about the behavior they copy in their quest for approval and recognition.

Writing: Use your ideas to write a very short incident. Describe your main character's efforts to be like somebody else, and what the result is. The conclusion should include the moral or lesson that you can only be yourself.

Revising: Revise your incident. Make it clear to the reader what the main character is doing to be like the other person.

Proofreading: Read your incident to check for errors. Be sure that all your sentences begin with capital letters and end with periods, question marks, exclamation marks, or quotation marks set off by commas, if you have used conversation.

THINK ABOUT FABLES

A **fable** is a story written to teach a lesson. Many fables have animals as main characters. In some fables, an animal is the main character and a person is a minor character. The best fables were written by Aesop, a slave living in Greece in the sixth century, B.C.

1. What is the moral of this fable?
2. What elements in the fable might teach this lesson?
3. How did having an animal main character make the lesson more dramatic?
4. How did the donkey show he needed to learn this lesson?
5. What happened to teach him this lesson?
6. If you had not been told this was a fable, how could you have known that it was?

DEVELOP YOUR VOCABULARY

Sometimes in reading you may find a word you do not know. You can often determine the meaning from the way it is used in the sentence. You can use **context clues,** which are words or groups of words that come before or after a word that give clues to its meaning. Read the following sentence from the selection: *When their owner came home, the donkey sat down and held out his hoof to shake hands.*

Suppose you did not know what a hoof was. The sentence says the donkey held out a hoof to shake hands. You can guess that a donkey would have only a foot, not hands, to hold out. So a hoof must be a donkey's foot. Find the following words in the selection. Look for words that might have helped you determine the meaning of the word. Write any context clues you find. Then use each word in a sentence.

1. embroidered
2. favor
3. affection
4. bray

Learn About

Plot: Climax and Resolution

Plot is the planned arrangement of events or incidents in a story. All stories have: characters, plot, and setting. The setting is crucial in establishing the time, place, and mood. Fully developed characters create excitement.

The important part of the plot is the conflict. The **conflict** is the problem that the characters must try to solve. Other incidents in the story can complicate the problem or even add to the conflict.

The turning point in the story is called the **climax.** At this point you begin to know how the problem will be resolved. The climax is often the most exciting part of the story. After that, suspense and action begin to fall. The last event in the story, when the problem is solved, is called the resolution.

As you read "The Speckled Hen's Egg" ask yourself:

1. What is the climax of the story?
2. How is the conflict resolved?

Skill Builder

Novels, short stories, plays, television stories, and movies have climaxes and resolutions. Think of a story you know from television, movies, or novels. Write a paragraph describing the climax and the resolution.

The Speckled Hen's Egg

by Natalie Savage Carlson

Once in another time, a very strange thing happened to Madame Roberge.

Madame took very good care of her chickens. They produced many eggs, and she sold their eggs at the store for a good price.

She was miserly with her egg money and hoarded it in the closet in a silver bowl. The bowl was shaped something like a fan, and it was said to have been brought from Quebec in the long ago by her great-grandfather, Lazare Proutte.

Madame was very proud of the bowl. She was also proud of all the coins that her eggs made for her. So it was fitting that the coins should be saved in the silver bowl.

One day when Madame went out to her henhouse to gather the eggs, the scrawny old speckled hen was on the nest. Madame shooed her with her lips and a swing of her skirts. The hen jumped off the nest and ran away, flapping her wings and cackling.

---

miserly (MY zur lee) stingy
hoarded (HAWRD id) saved; stored up
scrawny (SKRAW nee) thin; skinny

Madame was displeased to see that there was only one egg in the nest.

"That worthless creature!" said Madame Roberge. "This is the first egg she has laid in a week. She is no longer worth her feed. I will put her in my stewpot on Sunday."

Madame was about to drop the egg into her apron when she noticed a strange thing about it. There was a picture on the egg, just as surely as if it had been painted there. She studied it carefully. Yes, the picture on the egg was certainly of something. But what?

The next time Madame went to the store in the village with her eggs, she took the unusual one with her.

"This one is not for sale," Madame told Henri Dupuis, the storekeeper. "It is a very strange egg laid by my old speckled hen. See, there is a picture on it. What would you say it is?"

Henri Dupuis looked at the egg closely. Others who were in the store gathered around.

"Perhaps you aren't feeding your hens the right food," said Henri. "Now I have a new kind of chicken feed that—"

But André Drouillard, who had taken the egg in his own hands, interrupted.

"It is surely some omen," he said. "See these long lines that curve like feathers—like an Indian war bonnet?"

"Perhaps there will be an Indian uprising," cried Angéline Meloche in terror.

But the pop-eyed Eusible Latrop had to have his say.

"You are all wrong," he said. "This is a crown on the egg. See! A royal crown. Perhaps it means that Madame Roberge has noble blood in her veins and does not know it."

Madame immediately believed this explanation because it sounded closer to the truth.

"My great-grandfather, Lazare Proutte, was a rich man," she remembered, "but everyone thought it strange that he had nothing to say of his life before he came here. Perhaps he was a *compte* or a *duc* in disguise. No doubt the King was displeased with him over some matter and he had to hide in the New World.

---

omen (OH mun) sign of what is to come
noble (NOH bul) related to royalty
comte (KAWNT) the French word for count (a nobleman)
duc (DOOK) the French word for duke (highest ranking nobleman)

Yes, I am sure of it. One said he always seemed a little uneasy when strangers were around."

Madame proudly went home and put the wonderful egg in a prominent place on her parlor table. Instead of stewing the speckled hen, she made a special pet of her and built her a runway all for herself. She planted flowers in it and saw that the water dish and feed bowl were always full.

Then a great change came over Madame. She no longer sold eggs at the store because she said that was quite beneath a noblewoman. She took in an orphan girl to do her work so that she would have more time for her embroidery, which was a pastime of the rich. She even began to call herself Madame *de* Roberge, which had a more aristocratic sound, even though the crown on the egg had nothing to do with her husband's family.

She took to walking about with the wart on her nose so high she no longer could see many of her old friends. She walked about with a la-la-de-da air and carried her handkerchief, so!

Sometimes her needle would snag in the fancy handkerchief she was embroidering and her eyes would have a faraway look.

"Perhaps I am really a *comtesse* or a *marquise* or even a *princesse,*" she would dream to herself. "If only Great-grandpère Proutte had not made such a secret of his life before he came here!"

She began to wonder why the egg with the crown had been laid on that certain day—no sooner, no later. It was an omen all right. But what did it mean?

Omens often had to do with death. Perhaps the death of some important person back in old France. Death in noble families meant money and castles and titles changing hands.

Perhaps—could it be—was it possible? Yes, that was it! Some high and rich relative in France had died. The crown on the egg

---

prominent (PROM uh nunt) standing out; easy to see
aristocratic (uh ris tuh KRAT ik) belonging to the upper classes
snag (SNAG) catch on something
comtesse (kawn TES) the French word for countess (a noblewoman)
marquise (mahr KEEZ) a noblewoman ranking just below a duchess or countess
title (TYT ul) an inherited name, such as Duke, Countess, or Prince, showing rank among nobility
inheritance (in HER ih tuns) money and belongings that are passed down from parent to child

meant that it was time for her to claim her inheritance.

She puzzled over this for a few days. Then she made up her mind. She would take her egg money and make the long trip to the big church in Quebec where the old priest kept the documents and records of the past. She would learn the secret of her noble blood.

She hitched Coquin, the wheezy horse, to the two-wheeled cart and set forth on the trip to Quebec. She would go to the old

---

wheezy (HWEE zee) breathing with difficulty

priest and have him look up the family record of the Prouttes. Her egg money would be spent for food and lodging along the way.

Madame de Roberge set off in high spirit. She sat straight on the edge of the hard seat, with the reins in her hands and her wart in the air, so!

It was as if the two-wheeled cart pulled by the wheezy Coquin had become a fine coach drawn by four spirited white horses. And Madame the Marquise rode forth in silks and brocades and jewels.

From time to time, she passed people on the road. To them she gave a stiff little bow of the head and half a smile, as if saluting her humble peasants.

At night Madame sought shelter in farmhouses, where the owners were overcome with awe and hospitality when they learned that their guest was a distinguished noblewoman riding to Quebec to claim an inheritance across the sea. They would not even accept payment for food and lodging, so honored were they. And the Marquise still had enough of the peasant left in her to be glad that she could hold fast to her egg money.

When Madame drove Coquin down the cobbled streets of Quebec to the big church, she had no feeling of the country bumpkin come to the city. Rather she sat proudly erect, with her la-la-de-da air and her wart high in the air, so!

She twirled her embroidered handkerchief daintily as she told the priest that she had come to seek records of the noble Proutte family so that she could rightfully claim an inheritance in France.

The priest led her into a cellar beneath the church where all the old papers and records were kept. He pulled out drawers, fussed through yellow papers and adjusted his spectacles. So old were most of the documents that fine, dry dust blew from the drawers and Madame from time to time had to use her fancy handkerchief with a vigor that was not so la-la-de-da.

"Proutte, Proutte, Proutte," chanted the priest. "Ah, here we

---

brocades (broh KAYDZ) clothing made of expensive cloth with pretty raised designs
awe (AW) respect and admiration
cobbled (KOB uld) paved with rounded stones
bumpkin (BUMP kin) awkward, simple person
embroidered (em BROI durd) decorated with fancy needlework
documents (DOK yuh munts) important papers

have him. Guillaume Proutte, who came to the New World with Champlain."

"Yes, yes," cried Madame impatiently, "that must be the one. Was he a *duc* or a *marquis?*"

The priest pinched his eyebrows together and popped the tip of his tongue out of his lips. He studied the fine handwriting. He shook his head sadly.

"Alas!" he said. "This Guillaume Proutte was released from a Paris prison on condition that he sail to the New World and turn over a new leaf."

Madame hastily leaned over his shoulder and strained her own eyes on the handwriting.

"Tut! Tut!" said the priest. "It seems that Guillaume did not turn his leaf over, for he was up before the council three times for stealing skins. And you must know, my daughter, that skins were the coin of the country in those days."

"How disgusting!" exclaimed Madame. "That must be some other family of Prouttes. Look further, my father. What about Lazare Proutte?"

The priest dug through some more documents.

"Here is another Proutte," he said. "Yes, it is your Lazare."

"That's the one!" exclaimed Madame. "He was my great-grandfather."

The priest slowly and laboriously read the document. He mumbled from time to time. Certain phrases crawled into Madame's ears like stinging ants.

"Baptized but never confirmed. Apprenticed to Marc Nadie, the silversmith. Disappeared from Quebec at the same time as the silver bowl of the Sieur de Mare, which had been left with the smith for polishing."

"But—but there must be some mistake," Madame stammered.

Then she told the priest about the wonderful egg with the crown on it which her speckled hen had laid.

"I have it here in my bag," she said, "wrapped in a piece of

New World North and South America
laboriously (luh BAWR ee us lee) with great effort
confirmed (kun FURMD) made a full member of a church or synagogue
apprenticed (uh PREN tist) taken on to learn a job

musquash fur."

She carefully took it out of the fur and held it up.

"See," she said, "a distinct crown. It must mean something."

The priest pinched his brows together again and pushed his glasses higher on his nose.

"But Madame is looking at it upside down," he said. "Turn it around—like this! Now what does it look like to you?"

"It—it looks like the silver bowl my great-grandfather, Lazare—er—ah—the bowl I keep my egg money in."

"There, you have it, my daughter," said the priest with a twinkle in his eye. "The sign on the egg is a warning that one of Proutte blood should never let money get too strong a hold on her."

So when Madame drove back to her village, the two-wheeled cart was no longer a coach and Coquin no longer divided himself into four prancing white steeds. And Madame the Marquise had been left behind in the dusty church cellar. The return trip dug quite deeply into the egg money, too. For while it is a rare privilege to entertain a *marquise,* it is nothing but a nuisance to have ordinary persons turning in from the road to crowd one's table and beds.

Madame Roberge's wart came down, her la-la-de-da manner was gone and her handkerchief had been left where it fell in the cellar of the big church in Quebec. She found a husband for the orphan girl and went back to her own scrubbing and cooking.

She began to sell eggs at the store again, and spoke in a friendly manner to everyone. The priest noticed that she became a bit more generous with her Sunday offerings, and she no longer took pleasure in hoarding money. Perhaps this was because she no longer had a fine bowl to save it in, since the silver one was turned into a water pan for the chickens. And the old speckled hen disappeared from the fancy runway only to find herself in the stewpot one Sunday.

So you see, my friends, it is not a good thing to hold one's nose high and go about with a la-la-de-da air, for a turn of the egg can easily change a crown into a stolen bowl.

---

musquash (MUS kwahsh) North-American Indian word for muskrat
distinct (dih STINGKT) clear; unmistakable
prancing (PRANS ing) moving with a light step
privilege (PRIV uh lij) special right
nuisance (NOO suns) bother

FOCUS ON THE SELECTION

UNDERSTAND THE SELECTION

Recall

1. How did Madame Roberge earn her living?
2. What was unusual about the egg?
3. Why did the first Proutte come to the New World with Champlain?

Infer

4. Why was Madame Roberge so quick to believe Latrop's theory on the picture?
5. Why did Madame Roberge begin to behave differently after finding the crown on the egg?
6. Why did Madame Roberge decide that an inheritance was waiting for her?
7. Why did the farmhouse owners refuse to charge Madame Roberge?

Apply

8. What might the reaction of Madame Roberge's friends be to her la-la-de-da airs?
9. Why did Madame Roberge stop hoarding money?
10. Would Madame Roberge be better off if she had found an inheritance?

Respond to Literature

In this story, how did the world within Madame Roberge's inner space change?

WRITE ABOUT THE SELECTION

In "The Speckled Hen's Egg," Madame Roberge began to believe she had noble blood in her veins. She walked about with her nose in the air and a la-la-de-da manner. What do you suppose her neighbors and friends thought of her unusual behavior? What would they say to each other? Write a conversation that Madame Roberge's neighbors might have had in which they discussed her behavior.

Prewriting: List the changes that came over Madame Roberge, including some things that her neighbors might think or say about them. Think about how your friends sound when they are gossiping about someone who seems "stuck up."

Writing: Write your conversation. Write what Madame Roberge's friends and neighbors would say to each other about her behavior.

Revising: When you revise your conversation, be sure that it sounds like what real people would say about Madame Roberge.

Proofreading: Read your conversation to check for errors. Be sure that you have enclosed each speaker's exact words in quotation marks. Use commas or other punctuation to separate the quotes from the rest of the sentence. Be sure that all your sentences end with periods, question marks, or exclamation marks.

THINK ABOUT PLOT

After the climax of the story, you can guess how the conflict is going to be resolved. Sometimes at the climax the mystery is solved or new facts are discovered or presented. The **resolution** tells you the final outcome of the story and how the conflict is resolved.

1. In what part of "The Speckled Hen's Egg" did the climax occur?
2. How did this incident tell you what the resolution was likely to be?
3. At what point did the suspense stop building and the action begin to "wind down?"
4. If the story had continued much beyond this point, would the rest of the story have been interesting?
5. How did the climax determine the outcome?

DEVELOP YOUR VOCABULARY

You are more likely to include words in your working vocabulary if you deepen your understanding of them by noticing how they relate to each other. For example, a person who does not want to spend or share money would be miserly. What would this person do with money? Perhaps the miser would *hoard* it.

Seven of the words from the list below are closely related. List the seven words and tell how they are related. Study each definition carefully.

1. apprenticed
2. aristocratic
3. awe
4. brocades
5. comte
6. comtesse
7. distinct
8. duc
9. embroidered
10. hoarded
11. marquise
12. miserly
13. musquash
14. New World
15. noble
16. privilege
17. prominent
18. title

Street Light, Giacomo Balla. Collection, The Museum of Modern Art, New York.

Learn About

Character: Actions

The **characters** are the people or animals in a story, a play or a novel. Sometimes the author will directly describe the character's traits. More often, an author will indirectly reveal a character's personality through actions and words. For example, you know that Snow White's stepmother is a cruel person when she orders a hunter to kill Snow White. Ask yourself, "What does this action tell me about this character?"

As you read "The Kind of Man She Could Love," ask yourself these questions:

1. What kind of person is Mr. Chandler?
2. What do Mr. Chandler's decisions and actions tell you about his traits?
3. What kind of person is Miss Marian?
4. What do Miss Marian's actions tell you about her?

Skill Builder

Authors help you to know a character by telling you what they say, do, think, and feel. Write a paragraph about a person you know, or it can be a character you make up. Describe something the character did that would tell a reader what the character is like.

THE KIND OF MAN SHE COULD LOVE

by O. Henry

Mr. Owen Chandler is first seen in his rented room. He is pushing an iron back and forth, pressing into the pants the straight creases that will form two straight lines, front and back, from his polished shoes to the edge of his low-cut vest. Mr. Chandler, you see, lives in genteel poverty; that is, he tries not to *look* poor.

We next see Mr. Chandler as he descends the steps of his apartment. He is correctly clothed. He is calm, assured, handsome. He looks to be the typical New York up-and-coming young man-about-town, slightly bored, as he sets out to enjoy the pleasures of the evening.

Young Mr. Chandler was employed in the office of an architect. His pay was 18 dollars a week. He considered architecture to be the highest form of art, and he felt it an honor to be so employed.

Out of each week's earnings Chandler set aside one dollar. At the end of each ten weeks he took the ten dollars thus saved and had himself a gentleman's evening on the town. In his freshly pressed suit he felt like a millionaire, and he took himself where life was brightest and showiest and most expensive. There he dined among the wealthy. With ten dollars, a man may play the part of one who belongs to the upper crust of society—for an evening. For the next 69 evenings he would eat at lunch counters or cook for himself on the one-burner stove in his room. Chandler was willing to pay the price. Truly here was a son of the

---

genteel (jen TEEL) polite; well-mannered

The Café Royal, Charles Ginner. The Granger Collection.

great city of razzle-dazzle. One evening in the limelight made up for seventy minus one in the lamplight of his room.

Even on this wintry night young Mr. Chandler walked slowly in order to lengthen the pleasure of his evening. Suddenly, then, from around a corner came a girl. She stopped, to avoid bumping into him. Then she slipped on a patch of ice and fell to the sidewalk.

Chandler, always the gentleman, helped her to her feet. The girl hobbled to the wall of the building, leaned against it, and thanked him.

"I think my ankle is hurt," she said. "It twisted when I fell."

"Does it pain you much?" asked Chandler.

"Only when I rest my weight on it. I think I will be able to walk in a minute or two."

"Can I be of any further help?" suggested the young man. "I will call a cab or—"

"Thank you," said the girl softly but heartily. "I am sure you need not trouble yourself any further. It was so awkward of me."

Chandler looked at the girl and found her swiftly drawing his interest. She was pretty in a proper way. Her eyes were merry and kind. She was clothed in a plain black dress that suggested a sort of uniform such as shop girls wear. Her dark brown hair showed its curls beneath a cheap hat of black straw whose only ornament was a velvet ribbon and bow. She could have posed as a model for the self-respecting working girl of the best type.

A sudden idea came into the head of the young architect. He would ask this girl to dine with him. Here was something that had before been absent from his evenings out. Here was something that would double the pleasure of this long-awaited night on the town.

"I think," he offered, "that your foot needs more rest than you are ready to admit. So please allow me to suggest something that will allow you to rest it and that will, at the same time, do me a favor. I was on my way to dine by myself when you fell, so to speak, at my feet. So why don't you come with me? We can have a warm dinner and pleasant talk. By that time your ankle will

---

razzle-dazzle (RAZ ul DAZ ul) glamour
limelight (LYM lyt) center of attention
heartily (HAHRT ul ee) with spirit; with enthusiasm

carry you home very nicely, I am sure."

The girl looked quickly up into Chandler's clear, pleasant face. Her eyes twinkled once very brightly, then she smiled. "But we don't know each other. It wouldn't be right, would it?" she said innocently.

"There is nothing wrong about it," said the young man. "I'll introduce myself—permit me—Mr. Owen Chandler. After our dinner, which I will try to make as pleasant as possible, I will bid you good evening or attend you safely to your door, whichever you prefer."

"But dear me!" said the girl, with a glance at Chandler's quite proper coat and scarf. "In this old dress and hat!"

"Never mind that," said Chandler cheerfully. "I'm sure you look more charming in them than anyone else we might see in the finest restaurant in town."

"My ankle does hurt yet," admitted the girl, trying a step or two. "I think I will accept your invitation, Mr. Chandler. You may call me—Miss Marian."

"Come then, Miss Marian," said the young architect, with perfect manners. "You will not have far to walk. There is a very respectable and good restaurant in the next block. You will have to lean on my arm—so—and walk slowly. It is lonely dining all by oneself. I'm just a little bit glad that you slipped on the ice."

When the two were seated at a candle-lit table, Chandler began to experience the real joy that his regular outings always brought to him. The restaurant was not so showy as one farther down Broadway, which he preferred, but it was nearly so. The tables were well filled with prosperous looking diners. There was an orchestra playing softly enough to make conversation a pleasure. The lighting, and the menu too, were perfect. The young girl, even in her cheap hat and dress, held herself with an air that added distinction to the natural beauty of her face and figure. And it is certain that she looked at Chandler, with his calm manner and his warm dark eyes, with something not far from admiration.

Then it happened. The Madness of Manhattan, the Phony Fuss of the Fashionable, the Bug of Broadway bit our hero. There he was on the World's stage, so to speak. All eyes were on him.

---

distinction (dih STINGK shun) special quality

Yes, and he was dressed for the part. All his good angels had not the power to prevent him from acting out his role.

So he began to brag to Miss Marian about his clubs, his golf, his polo, his horses, his tours abroad. He even threw out hints of a yacht lying at Larchmont. He could see that she was impressed by this talk, and it egged him on. He spoke of great wealth. He mentioned familiarly a few names that he had read about on the society pages of the newspaper.

"This way of living you speak of," she said, "sounds so useless and purposeless. Haven't you any work to do in the world that might interest you more?"

For a moment, then, Chandler saw the pure gold of this girl shine through the mist that his bragging had raised. But, alas, he went on: "Why my dear Miss Marian—work! Think of dressing every day for dinner, of making half a dozen calls in the afternoon. Think of having to play polo two evenings a week, of golf several whole afternoons, of having to take tea with the Rockefellers or Whitneys, if they so desire. We do-nothings are the hardest workers in the land."

The dinner was ended, the waiter generously tipped, and the two walked out to the corner where they had met. Miss Marian walked very well now. Her limp was hardly noticeable.

"Thank you for a nice time," she said. "I must run home now. I liked the dinner very much, Mr. Chandler."

He shook hands with her, smiling politely, saying something about a game of bridge at his club. He watched her walk rather rapidly eastward. Then he slowly walked homeward.

In his chilly bedroom, Chandler put away his evening clothes for a sixty-nine days' rest. He went about it thoughtfully. "That was a stunning girl," he said to himself. "She's all right, too, even if she is a working girl. Perhaps if I had told her the truth instead of all that razzle-dazzle, we might—but, confound it, I had to play up to my clothes."

Thus spoke the young architect who hoped, in his innocent way, to become one of the "best" in the great town of Manhattan.

As for the girl, she sped swiftly across town until she arrived at a handsome mansion. Here she entered and hurried up the stairs to a room where a young lady was looking anxiously out the window.

"Oh, you silly, reckless girl!" exclaimed the older girl. "When

will you quit frightening us this way? It's two hours since you ran out in that rag of an old dress and Marie's hat. Mama has been so alarmed. She sent Louis in the auto to try to find you. You are a bad, thoughtless thing."

The older girl touched a button and, in a moment, a maid came in.

"Marie, tell Mama that Miss Marian has returned."

"Don't scold, Sister. I only ran down to Madame Theo's to discuss the dress she is making for me. My costume and Marie's hat were just what I needed. Everyone thought I was a shop girl, I am sure."

"Dinner is over, dear. You stayed so late."

"I know. I slipped on the sidewalk and turned my ankle. I could not walk, so I hobbled into a restaurant and sat there until I was better. That is why I took so long."

The two girls sat in the window seat, looking out at the lights and the steady stream of vehicles hurrying by. The younger one grew serious.

"We will have to marry someday," she said, dreamily. "We have so much money that we will not be allowed to disappoint the public. Do you want me to tell you the kind of man I could love, Sis?"

"Go on, you scatterbrain," smiled the other.

"I could love a man with dark and kind eyes, a man who is gentle and respectful to poor girls. I don't object to a handsome man so long as he is good and does not try to flirt. But I could love him only if he had an ambition, a goal in life, some work to do in this world. I would not care how poor he was if I could help him work his way up. But, dear Sister, the kind of man we always meet, the man who lives an idle life between society and his clubs, this kind of man I could not love even if his eyes were dark, even if he were kind to poor girls whom he met on the street."

FOCUS ON THE SELECTION

UNDERSTAND THE SELECTION

Recall

1. Where did Mr. Owen Chandler work?
2. How did he and the girl meet?
3. Where did Miss Marian get the cheap-looking clothes she was wearing?

Infer

4. Why did Miss Marian agree to have dinner with the young man even though she didn't know him?
5. Why did Chandler tell Miss Marian that he was wealthy and didn't work?
6. Why did Miss Marian bid Mr. Chandler good night without having him see her home?
7. Why did Miss Marian borrow her maid's hat and costume?

Apply

8. Decide whether Mr. Chandler was the kind of man Miss Marian could love.
9. Predict what would have happened if Mr. Chandler had told Miss Marian honestly about his life.
10. Do some people you know pretend to be what they are not?

Respond to Literature

What might have happened if Miss Marian and Mr. Chandler had stepped inside each other's inner spaces?

WRITE ABOUT THE SELECTION

In "The Kind of Man She Could Love,' Mr. Chandler loses his chance to win Miss Marian's love. He tells her that he is wealthy and idle. If he had told her the truth about his life, what do you think would have happened? Write a different ending to the story. Begin the story at dinner, and have Mr. Chandler tell Miss Marian the truth. Write the story the way you think it would have ended. How will Miss Marian react to Mr. Chandler's honesty?

Prewriting: Make a list of all of the facts that Mr. Chandler would have told Miss Marian if he had told the truth. Then, prepare a detailed outline of what you think Miss Marian would have done when she heard these statements.

Writing: Use your notes to write a different ending to the story. Use your imagination to make the story end the way you think it would have ended if Mr. Chandler had told the truth.

Revising: When you revise your story ending, be sure that it builds to an exciting climax. Make sure the end of the story completely describes the resolution of the conflict.

Proofreading: Read your story ending carefully to check for errors. Then, check your capitalization and punctuation. In conversations, be sure to remember to use quotation marks to enclose a speaker's exact words. Separate quotes from the rest of the sentence with commas or other appropriate punctuation.

THINK ABOUT CHARACTERIZATION

The problem, or conflict, in a story is often caused by the traits of the major characters. The actions the characters take to resolve the conflict in the story tell you much about the personality traits of Miss Marian and Mr. Chandler.

1. What are some traits of the characters in this story?
2. What actions revealed these traits to you?
3. What traits of the main character caused the problem in this story?
4. How did the characters respond to this conflict?
5. What did their response to the conflict tell you about them?

DEVELOP YOUR VOCABULARY

The dictionary is most often used as a source of definitions for unfamiliar words. You can also find spelling, pronunciation, and parts of speech in a dictionary. It will also tell how to form the plural and the past tense of a word. Some dictionaries include the foreign word from which the word was derived. Dictionaries sometimes include sentences to show you how a word is used correctly in a sentence.

In a dictionary, look up all these words from "The Kind of Man She Could Love." Use each in an original sentence to show that you understand not only their meaning, but how to use them correctly in writing.

1. genteel
2. razzle-dazzle
3. limelight
4. heartily
5. distinction

Learn About

Theme

The **theme** is the underlying message or the major point the author is making. Some writers will state the theme directly, while others want you to figure out the theme for yourself. Often the theme is expressed in what the conflict is and how it is resolved. You can also learn about the theme by how the characters grow or change. The characters in "The Donkey Who Did Not Want to Be Himself," and in "The Speckled Hen's Egg" all learned something or had changed by the end of the story. Often a theme will be expressed in a character's thoughts or words. The character may state it specifically or express it in different parts of the story.

As you read "The Butterfly and the Caterpillar" and "The Parable of the Eagle" ask yourself:

1. What point is the author making in writing this story?
2. How is this idea expressed?
3. Do you agree with the themes in these stories?

Skill Builder

Authors often write about incidents that show us what they think about life. Write about a brief episode that illustrates an aspect of what you think about life.

The Butterfly and the Caterpillar

by Joseph Lauren

A butterfly, one summer morn,
Sat on a spray of blossoming thorn
And, as he sipped and drank his share
Of honey from the flowered air,
5 Below, upon the garden wall,
A caterpillar chanced to crawl.
"Horrors!" the butterfly exclaimed,
"This must be stopped! I am ashamed
That such as I should have to be

10 In the same world with such as he.
Protect me from such ugly things!
Disgusting shape! Where are his wings!
Fuzzy and gray! Eater of clay!
Won't someone take the worm away!"

15 The caterpillar crawled ahead,
But, as he munched a leaf, he said,
"Eight days ago, young butterfly,
You wormed about the same as I.
Just wait—a few weeks from today
20 Two wings will bear me far away
To brighter blooms and lovelier lures,
With colors that outrival yours.
So, flutter-flit, be not so proud;
Each caterpillar is endowed
25 With power to make it by and by
A bright and merry butterfly.
Remember, you who scorn me so,
Yes you who make so loud a show,
That you and other moths and millers
30 Are only dressed up caterpillars."

---

lure (LUUR) attraction
endow (en DOU) enrich
scorn (SKAWRN) have a low opinion of
miller (MIL ur) a kind of moth

THE PARABLE OF THE EAGLE

by James Aggrey

One day not so very long ago a man caught an eagle in a trap. He brought it home to his chicken farm and put it in a cage with his chickens. Although he knew it was an eagle, the king of birds, he fed it chicken food. After a while the eagle was walking around in the cage and eating off the ground just like the chickens.

When the eagle was fully grown, a naturalist visited the farm. He saw the eagle and said, "Why do you treat that eagle like a chicken?"

"You may think it's an eagle," said the chicken farmer, "but I have trained it to be a chicken. Its wings measure ten feet across, but it is no longer an eagle. It is just a big chicken."

"Oh, no!" said the naturalist. "If it has the heart of an eagle, it is an eagle. Give it a chance and it will soar above the clouds."

"You are wrong," said the chicken farmer. "It is a chicken. It will only hop along the ground."

Each man swore he was right, so they agreed to give the eagle a test.

The naturalist held up the eagle and spoke to it. "You are an eagle, the greatest of birds," he said. "Spread your wings and fly."

The eagle's head turned to the right and left. Then, looking down at the chickens, it hopped to the ground and began eating the chicken food.

"There," said the chicken farmer. "Just as I told you, it's a chicken."

"Give the eagle another chance," said the naturalist. "If it has the heart of an eagle, it must be an eagle."

---

naturalist (NACH ur uh list) a person who studies plants and animals

The next day the two men took the eagle to the roof of the house. There the naturalist spoke to it and said, "Eagle, listen. You are an eagle. Spread your wings and fly."

But the eagle didn't fly. Seeing the chickens on the ground, it hopped down from the roof and began eating the chicken food.

"Now do you see that I am right?" said the chicken farmer.

"No," said the naturalist. "Give it one more chance. It has the heart of an eagle, so it must be an eagle."

The next morning at sunrise, the naturalist and chicken farmer took the eagle to a hilltop. Over the distant mountains the sun was rising, spreading its golden glory across the land.

The naturalist once again picked up the eagle and spoke. "You are an eagle," he said. "Go and live with the wind on the mountains. Spread your wings and fly."

The eagle looked to the right and left. Its body began to tremble. It did not jump down, but it did not fly either.

"Eagle," said the naturalist, "behold the sun!"

And the eagle saw the sun. It lifted its head and spread its wings. Then up, up into the sky it soared. Higher and higher, on and on it went, screaming like an eagle.

The eagle never returned. It may have been trained to be a chicken, but it was an eagle.

---

behold (bih HOHLD) see; look at

FOCUS ON THE SELECTION

UNDERSTAND THE SELECTION

Recall

1. What did the butterfly think about the caterpillar?
2. What was the eagle's behavior at first?
3. What did the eagle do at the end?

Infer

4. What is meant by the phrase, "You and other moths and millers are only dressed up caterpillars?"
5. What lesson did the poet want to teach in "The Butterfly and the Caterpillar"?
6. Why did the eagle behave like a chicken in "The Parable of the Eagle"?
7. Why did the eagle fly away at the end?

Apply

8. Does the author of "The Parable of the Eagle" believe that people are a product of their environment? Explain.
9. Compare the behavior of the butterfly with the behavior of people you know.
10. Predict what would have happened if the naturalist had never come to visit the farmer.

Respond to Literature

What did the naturalist believe about the eagle's inner space?

WRITE ABOUT THE SELECTION

In "The Butterfly and the Caterpillar," the butterfly forgets that it began life as a caterpillar and speaks with disgust of the caterpillar. The caterpillar reminds the butterfly that he is still the same individual who used to be a caterpillar. Think of someone whom you knew as a very young child, who is now several years older. Write about this person in a paragraph of comparison and in a paragraph of contrast between then and now.

Prewriting: Make a chart with three columns. In the left-hand column list the qualities the person had in childhood. In the right-hand column list the qualities the person has now. In the middle column list the qualities that remained the same at both ages.

Writing: Use your chart to write a paragraph of comparison and a paragraph of contrast. Tell your readers how this person is the same, or how this person is different, at both ages.

Revising: When you revise your paragraph make sure you have used the similarities in the first paragraph and differences in the second. Remember that you are not trying to make either the similarities or the differences more important. You are simply showing both.

Proofreading: Read your paragraphs to check for errors. Be sure that all your sentences begin with capital letters and end with periods, question marks, or exclamation marks.

THINK ABOUT THEME

You will understand a story better if you look for and identify the theme. The events in the story will be more meaningful if you think about how they relate to the theme.

1. What is the theme of each selection?
2. What is similar about the message in both selections?
3. How do the themes of the selections differ?
4. Which event in "The Parable of the Eagle" best reveals the story's theme?
5. What does the theme of these selections have to do with the theme of the unit, "Inner Space"?

DEVELOP YOUR VOCABULARY

Sometimes writers want to use a word that may be unfamiliar to some readers. They may give clues to its meaning—a definition, an example, or a word that means the same or the opposite. Sometimes the clue will be between two commas immediately following the unfamiliar word.

Write the following sentences. Circle the word or group of words that give clues about the meaning of the italicized word.

1. Max could not resist the *lure,* or attraction, of the sea.
2. Nature *endowed* the puppy with her mother's coloring. She was born white with brown and black patches.
3. She did not respect their opinion. She *scorned* it.
4. A *miller,* or moth, is attracted to light.
5. Joan wants to be a *naturalist* and study plants and animals.

Learn About

Simile

Authors create visual images by comparing something in the selection with something familiar to you, often through **simile**, a figure of speech that compares two unlike things. Usually it will use the words *like* or *as.*

The following simile appears in "The Speckled Hen's Egg": *Certain phrases crawled into Madame's ears like stinging ants.* How does this comparison help you picture how Madame Roberge felt? What other similes do you recall reading? Do you ever use similes in conversation?

Authors often use similes to help you understand how a character in the story feels about another character or situation.

As you read "The Confidence Game" ask yourself:

1. What similes does the author use?
2. What is being compared?
3. How are the things that are being compared alike?
4. What is the author trying to tell you with this comparison?

Skill Builder

Authors use words such as "like" and "as" to compare two unlike things. They do this to give you a better picture of something they want to describe. Write a few similes that describe something familiar.

THE CONFIDENCE GAME

by Pat Carr

My confidence started draining out my toes the day Angela Brady showed up at the pool for workout. I even started to chew the inside of my cheek, a nervous habit I usually reserve for fighting the fear that clutches at me just before a race. In a way, I guess I knew it *was* a race between Angela and me for the backstroke position on our team relay for the National Championship.

I hadn't even seen her swim yet, but the whole team knew she had been swimming for a famous club in California. We were just a small city team, only two years old. But we had a coach whose middle name was motivation. He'd motivated me into swimming a killing three miles a day, and now I was actually in the running to compete at the Nationals. Or I was until Angela showed up.

"Okay, swim freaks, hit the water for an 800-meter freestyle warm-up!" barked Coach. Then he added in a more human voice, "Angela, why don't you try lane four today?"

Lane four was the fast lane, my lane. I'd had to earn my place in that lane by swimming 400 meters in less than five minutes. Now all Angela had to do was jump in. It wasn't fair.

I didn't think I could pretend friendliness, so I started the 800 before Angela hit the water. But I didn't even have time to settle into my pace when I felt the water churning behind me. I stroked harder, but I could still feel the churning water of someone closing in on me. I soon felt a light touch on my foot.

In swim workouts, it's one of the rules that when a teammate taps your foot, you move to the right to let that swimmer go ahead of you. I knew that, and I also knew that I was interfering with Angela's pace by not letting her pass me. My conscience told me to move over, but something stubborn kept my body in the middle of the lane.

At the end of the 800, I glanced up and saw Coach staring at me. Realizing that he had seen me refuse to let Angela pass, I took a deep breath and ducked underwater.

When the workout was over, everyone crowded around Angela, asking her if she knew any Olympic swimmers and stuff like that. Finding a quiet corner for

---

motivate (MOHT uh VAYT) cause to act

myself, I slipped on my warm-up suit, draped a towel over my head and hurried toward my bike.

"Hey, Tobi! Where are you going?" someone shouted.

I didn't answer, just hopped on my bike and pedaled fast.

It was like that for the next two weeks. At every workout Angela was the star of the show. I was an invisible stagehand. Even worse, during time trials she beat me in all four strokes and took my place as lane leader.

I was miserable. And I was scared, too. I was scared that Angela was taking away my chance at the Nationals, a chance I had earned by a lot of hard work.

I started to show up late to workouts so that I wouldn't have to talk to anyone. I even walked on the bottom of the pool and faked my stroke, a swimmer's cheating trick I'd never used before. It was easy to catch up to Angela that way. And I always managed to be underwater when she gave our lane instructions.

I'll admit I wasn't very happy with my actions. But my jealous feelings were like a current I couldn't swim against.

The day before the Riverdale Meet, Coach called me over. At that moment I would rather have tried to talk to King Kong.

"Tobi, I want to talk to you about sportsmanship," he began.

"Sportswomanship, in this case, Coach," I quipped, hoping to distract him.

"Okay, sportswomanship," he said, taking me seriously. "Or whatever you want to call it when one athlete accepts a better athlete in a spirit of friendly competition."

"Maybe the so-called better athlete is not as good as everyone thinks," I mumbled.

Coach left a big silence for my statement to fall into. I started to chew the inside of my cheek again.

"Let's stop talking about this athlete and that athlete," he said softly, "and talk instead about Tobi and Angela. She has made better time than you, Tobi. And that is an obvious fact, not something everyone thinks."

He paused. I stared at my toes, which were curling under my feet as if trying to hide.

"The worst of it, Tobi, is that your attitude is hurting your performance. Do you know that your times have become worse in the last two weeks? Maybe showing up late and walking on the bottom have something to do with that," he said. My face felt as if it had been splashed with hot pink paint.

"Do you have anything you want to say?" he asked. I shook my head. "That's all then, Tobi. I'll see you tomorrow at the Riverdale Meet."

The next morning I was too nervous to eat my special breakfast of steak and eggs. This meet would decide who was going to the Nationals.

---

quip (KWIP) make a witty remark
obvious (OB vee us) easily seen; clear

Inner Space

The early skies were still gray when I arrived at the Riverdale pool for the warm-up session. The other swimmers were screeching greetings at each other like a flock of gulls. I jumped into the water to cut off the sound and mechanically began my stroke.

Half an hour later, I shuddered as the public address system squealed. The meet was about to start. After climbing out of the pool, I quickly searched the heat sheet for my name. Disappointed, I saw that I had just missed making it into the last, and fastest, qualifying heat. Angela's name, of course, was there. She'd taken my place just as she had at the trials.

Better not to think about Angela at all, I told myself, recalling Coach's words. Better to concentrate on my own race. Carefully, I went over Coach's instructions in my mind, shutting out the noisy crowd around me. In my mind I was swimming my race perfectly, over and over again, always perfectly.

"Would you like an orange?"

Without looking, I knew whose voice it was. "It's good for quick energy," continued Angela, holding the orange out to me.

"No thanks," I said. "I've got all I need." I saw that she was about to sit down next to me, so I added, "I don't like to talk before a race."

She nodded sympathetically. "I get uptight, too. The butterflies are free," she said with a nervous laugh.

For a moment I felt a little better toward her, knowing that she had the jitters, too. Then I remembered that she didn't have to worry.

"You'll be an easy winner," I said.

"You never know about that," she replied uncertainly.

My heat was called. Up on the blocks, I willed my muscles into obedience, alert for the starter's commands. At the gun, I cut into the top of the water smoothly.

I swam exactly as I had been imagining it before the race, acting out the pictures in my mind. I felt the water stream past me, smooth, steady and swift. When I finished, I was certain I had done my best in that heat.

Overwhelmed by exhaustion, I sat on the deck for several minutes, eyes closed, totally spent. I knew I was missing Angela's heat, but I was too tired to care.

The sound of the announcer's voice was like a crackling firecracker of hope bursting through my fatigue. Then I heard my name. I'd made it!

I also heard Angela's name, but it was several minutes before I realized that my name had been called last. That meant my time had been better. Figuring there must have been a mistake, I checked the official postings, but there were our times with mine four seconds faster.

Heading for the gym, where all the swimmers rest and wait for the heats to be called, I saw Angela sitting alone with her back against the wall. Her shoulders were rounded in a slump.

It could be me, I whispered to myself, remembering what it feels like to mess up a race. There's no worse anger than the kind you feel toward yourself when you've ruined something you care about. I knew how she felt, and I also knew

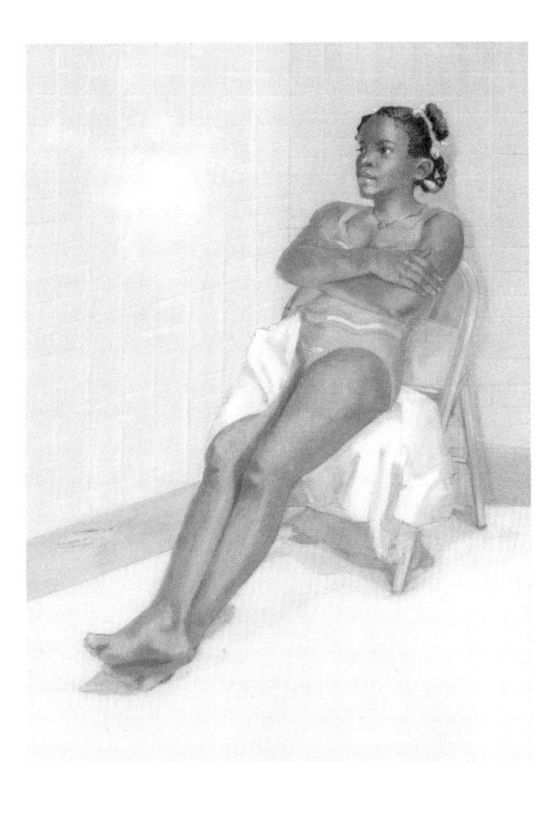

there was no way I could make up for the way I had acted. But I just had to try.

"I don't talk before races, but I do talk after them. Sometimes it helps," I said, knowing Angela had every right to tell me to go drown myself.

"Talk if you want to," she murmured.

"Well, I will, but I was hoping you'd talk, too."

She hesitated, and I saw her trying to swallow. "I will as soon as I'm sure I'm not going to cry," she whispered.

So I babbled on for a few minutes about the meet, some of the other swimmers, the team standings, anything. I knew it didn't matter what I said as long as I kept talking.

All at once Angela interrupted my opinion of the snack bar's hamburgers. "I do this all the time," she burst out. "I do great at workouts, then comes a meet, and something happens. I just can't do it."

"Maybe you don't know how to play the confidence game," I said. She looked at me suspiciously, but I went on. "How do you psych yourself up for a race?"

"I don't exactly." She was twisting the ends of the towel into tiny corkscrews. "I just try to block it out, not think about it."

"What about during a race?"

"I concentrate on not making mistakes."

"Very negative methods," I commented.

"What do you mean?"

"Well, take my positive approach. First, I think about all the good things I've done in previous races. Then I plan my upcoming race carefully, going over each detail in my mind, picturing myself the perfect swimmer. Then when I'm in the water, I tell myself to do it again, only this time for real."

"And you win," Angela added with a smile. Now I really felt bad, remembering how I had acted when Angela had done better than I in workouts.

"Listen, I have an idea," I said. Maybe I *could* make it up to her. "You swim faster than me, right?" Angela looked doubtful.

"Yes, you do, that's an obvious fact," I insisted. "Now, my idea is that you use me as a pacer in the backstroke final this afternoon."

At first Angela wasn't sure, but I soon

had her convinced, and we were planning our strategy when Coach showed up.

"What's going on here?" He gave me an accusing look.

"We've got it all settled," Angela spoke up. "Tobi and I are going to be a team from now on."

"All right!" he said, giving us a smile usually reserved for winners.

As Angela and I sat together on the ready bench, I had conflicting thoughts about helping her. What was I doing anyway? Handing her my relay position on a silver platter, that's what.

I hadn't time to get worked up over it, though, because the whistle blew, and we stepped up to the blocks. At the sound of the gun I was into the water with barely a splash, skimming the surface like a water bug.

As I reached the wall, I pretended all my strength was in my legs as I flipped and pushed off. Pull hard, hard, hard, I told myself, muscles aching from the effort. Then on the last lap, I concentrated on a single word. Win! I shot through the water and strained for the finish.

Immediately, I looked to Angela's lane. She was there, but it was too close to tell who had won. She gave me the thumbs-up sign, and I returned it.

I stared at the electronic scoreboard. Usually it didn't take long for the times to appear, but now it remained blank for so long I was beginning to worry that a fuse had blown.

Please, please let me be the winner, I whispered over and over. Finally, the winning times flashed on. I blinked away the chlorine haze, or maybe tears. Angela had won. I managed to give her a congratulatory hug.

"I couldn't have done it without you, Tobi," she bubbled.

"You did it, girls!" Coach couldn't keep himself from shouting, he was so excited. "You've just raced yourself to the Nationals!"

I had never felt so left out, so disappointed, in my whole life. "Well, at least Angela has," I said, struggling to smile.

Coach looked startled. "And you did, too, Tobi."

What was he talking about? "I saw that Angela won the place on our relay team."

"That's right, but you missed something. You both swam so fast that you made qualifying times for the *individual* backstroke event!"

I was stunned. I had concentrated so hard on the relay place I hadn't even thought about the individual events.

"So you'll both go to the Nationals!" Coach couldn't resist doing a couple of dance steps, and I was so ecstatic, I joined him. But a wet concrete swim deck is not an ideal dance floor.

"Look out!" yelled Angela, as we just missed falling into the water. "I don't want my partner to break a leg. We've got a long way to go before the Olympics."

"What?" I gasped.

"Just doing some positive mental rehearsing." She grinned.

"A little confidence sure goes a long way," I laughed.

Still, maybe that *is* something to think about!

FOCUS ON THE SELECTION

UNDERSTAND THE SELECTION

Recall

1. What effect did Angela Brady's arrival have on Tobi?
2. How did Tobi "cheat" in the pool?
3. What was the coach's definition of sportsmanship?

Infer

4. Why wasn't Tobi glad when an excellent swimmer joined their team?
5. Tobi compares her jealous feelings to ". . . a current I couldn't swim against." What does this simile tell you about Tobi's struggle with her jealousy?
6. What made Tobi change her attitude toward Angela?
7. What did Angela mean by "positive mental rehearsing"?

Apply

8. How did Tobi show that she had changed after the race was over?
9. Which do you think is more important, winning or sportsmanship?
10. Compare Angela and Tobi.

Respond to Literature

What did Tobi share from her inner space which helped Angela?

WRITE ABOUT THE SELECTION

At the end of "The Confidence Game," Tobi learns that she will go to the Nationals to compete in the individual backstroke event. Imagine that you are a sportscaster for a radio station. You are covering the national swim meet in which Tobi and Angela are racing. Write a sportscast about the individual backstroke event. Decide what will happen and describe it in as much detail as possible for your radio audience. Listen to some radio sportscasts to pick up the style.

Prewriting: Decide what will happen in the race. Write an informal outline listing the actions and events you will need to describe.

Writing: Use your list to write a sportscast. Describe the race for your radio audience, using colorful details about the athletes, how they look, the spectators, the setting, the weather, etc.

Revising: Revise your sportscast. Be sure you have written the details in a way that will help your listeners picture the race. You may wish to add similes to paint a better picture.

Proofreading: Read your sportscast carefully to check for errors in spelling and punctuation. Be sure that all your sentences begin with capital letters and end with periods, question marks, or exclamation marks. Also check for correct use of commas.

THINK ABOUT SIMILE

Writers use similes to help you picture something clearly by comparing it to something else. You can usually recognize a simile by the use of words such as *like* or *as* to introduce the second element in the comparison.

1. What words or features helped you to identify the similes in "The Confidence Game"?
2. To what does the narrator compare the way Tobi skimmed the surface of the water?
3. In what way does this simile help you to picture clearly the action in "The Confidence Game"?
4. What does the narrator compare to a flock of gulls?
5. How does this simile help you picture the scene?

DEVELOP YOUR VOCABULARY

There are probably many words that you understand in your reading but do not use yourself. You are more likely to include words in your working vocabulary if you think about how they relate to other words. For example, you could think about how the words *quip* and *obvious* relate to each other. Perhaps one person makes a *quip.* It is *obvious* from that quip that the person is not being serious.

Review the meanings of these words from "The Confidence Game." Find them in the selection. Think about how you could relate one word to another. Then write five original sentences using at least two of these words in each sentence.

1. motivate
2. quip
3. obvious
4. negative
5. positive
6. pacer
7. strategy
8. conflict
9. ecstatic

Learn About

Symbolism

Sometimes a writer will use one thing to stand for something else. You may have noticed symbolism in American political cartoons. For example, the figure of Uncle Sam is a symbol. The flag and the bald eagle are also used as political symbols. What do these symbols represent or stand for?

Poems often contain many symbols. To understand fully what the poet wants to say, you must think about the symbols in the poem. The speakers in "I Am an American" can symbolize whole groups of American people. In this way, the poem has a broader and deeper meaning. You will understand the message in a poem better if you know what each symbol stands for.

As you read the two poems that follow, "The Day Millicent Found the World" and "Maggie and Milly and Molly and May," ask yourself:

1. What symbols has the poet used?
2. What do these symbols stand for?
3. What is the poet telling you with the use of these symbols?

Skill Builder

Writers often use objects or characters as symbols. Make a list of such objects or characters that might be symbols for something else.

The Day Millicent Found the World

by William Stafford

Every morning Millicent ventured farther
into the woods. At first she stayed
near light, the edge where bushes grew, where
her way back appeared in glimpses among
5 dark trunks behind her. Then by farther paths
or openings where giant pines had fallen
she explored ever deeper into the dim
interior, until one day she stood under a great
dome among columns, the heart of the forest, and knew:
10 Lost. She had achieved a mysterious world
where any direction would yield only surprise.
And now not only the giant trees were strange
but the ground under her feet had a velvet nearness;
intricate lines on bark wove messages all
15 around her. Long strokes of golden sunlight
shifted over her feet and hands. She felt
caught up and breathing in a great powerful embrace.
A birdcall wandered forth at leisurely intervals
from an opening to her right: "Come away, Come away."
20 Never before had she let herself realize
that she was part of the world and that it would follow
wherever she went. She was part of its breath.

Aunt Dolbee called her back that time, a high
voice tapering faintly among the farthest trees,
25 "Milli-cent! Milli-cent!" And that time she returned,
but slowly, her dress fluttering along pressing
back branches, her feet stirring up the dark smell
of moss, and her face floating forward, a stranger's
face now, with a new depth in it, into the light.

---

ventured (VEN churd) took a risk
glimpse (GLIMPS) a brief, incomplete view
interior (in TIR ee ur) inner part
intricate (IN trih kit) having many parts, complicated
leisurely (LEE zhur lee) without hurry
intervals (IN tur vulz) time or space between
taper (TAY pur) make or become gradually smaller at one end

maggie and milly and molly and may

by E.E. Cummings

maggie and milly and molly and may
went down to the beach (to play one day)

and maggie discovered a shell that sang
so sweetly she couldn't remember her troubles, and

5 milly befriended a stranded star
whose rays five languid fingers were;

and molly was chased by a horrible thing
which raced sideways while blowing bubbles: and

may came home with a smooth round stone
10 as small as a world and as large as alone.

For whatever we lose (like a you or a me)
it's always ourselves we find in the sea

---

languid (LANG gwid) lazy; weak; slow-moving

E. E. Cummings (1894-1962)

E. E. Cummings wrote possibly the most unusual poetry of the 20th century. Cummings is well known for his unusual punctuation and phrasing. He didn't like capital letters at the beginning of sentences. Often, he experimented with word use, as in one of his poems that begins, "what if a much of a which of a wind." Even punctuation marks were written in his own way. In one of his poems, he wrote the word *thrushes* as t,h;r:u;s,h;e:s. That was his way of showing birds on a branch in the moonlight.

Cummings was born in Cambridge, Massachusetts. He attended Harvard University and was graduated with honors. In 1917 he volunteered to drive an ambulance in France during World War I. There, he was imprisoned because he refused to say he hated the Germans. He would only say "I like the French." All his life he believed that love was the only hope for a peaceful world. He also thought people are too easily bogged down by a need to own things. The curse of owning things and the need for love are themes in much of his poetry.

His book *The Enormous Room* (1922) relates his prison experience in France. It has been called the best book to come out of World War I. Cummings was a playwright and painter as well as a poet, but his plays and paintings are of minor importance compared with his poetry.

FOCUS ON THE SELECTION

UNDERSTAND THE SELECTION

Recall

1. Where did Millicent take her walks?
2. Why does Millicent leave the woods?
3. What happened to Molly at the beach?

Infer

4. Why had Millicent never realized before that she was part of the world and it would follow her wherever she went?
5. Why did Millicent feel changed at the end of the poem?
6. What horrible thing chased Molly?
7. What does Cummings mean by "it's always ourselves we find in the sea"?

Apply

8. Imagine that a person is suddenly in a completely different place where he has never been before, away from everyone he knows. How might he feel differently about himself?
9. What do you think E. E. Cummings would say to people who did not like what they were getting out of life?
10. For what might the sea be a symbol in "maggie and milly and molly and may?"

Respond to Literature

Why did Millicent need to get away to find her inner space?

WRITE ABOUT THE SELECTION

In "maggie and milly and molly and may," each girl has a very different experience at the beach. Why do you think their impressions are so different? Write diary entries for each girl. Tell in detail about the day at the beach from each girl's point of view. Describe the trip as you think each girl would describe it.

Prewriting: Make four columns on a sheet of paper. Label the columns Maggie, Milly, Molly, and May. Think about what the poem tells you about each girl. In each column, list details that you think each girl would use in describing the day at the beach.

Writing: Use your chart to write diary entries Maggie, Milly, Molly and May. Write each girl's entry as the girl herself would write it.

Revising: Revise your entries, adding specific details that capture the precise mood and personalities of the characters. Make sure each entry is written as the girl herself would write it.

Proofreading: Read your entries to check for errors. Be sure that all your sentences begin with capital letters and end with periods, question marks, or exclamation marks. Be certain to check your internal punctuation as well.

THINK ABOUT SYMBOLISM

Symbolism is the representation of one thing by the use of another thing that stands for or suggests it, especially an object used to represent something abstract. Poets hope that by using symbolism in their poetry you will gain new understanding of the objects or ideas the symbols represent.

1. What symbols did you identify in "The Day Millicent Found the World"?
2. What symbols did you find in "maggie and millie and molly and may"?
3. Why did E.E. Cummings use these symbols instead of directly stating the message?
4. What did the symbols tell you about the characters in the poem?
5. Why did each girl find something different?

DEVELOP YOUR VOCABULARY

When you look up a word in a glossary or dictionary, how do you find the word? The entries for words are in alphabetical order. As you look through the dictionary, you want to be able to find the page on which the word you want is listed. You will find guide words, in alphabetical order, at the top of every dictionary or glossary page that help you find the page containing the word you want.

Write the following words under the set of guide words that would appear at the top of the page where they are listed.

Guide words:

glance–intervene　　intervention–lap

lapel–near　　suspect–wax

1. ventured
2. glimpses
3. interior
4. intricate
5. leisurely
6. intervals
7. tapering
8. languid

FOCUS ON...

When you read a poem, the poet is sharing an experience, a feeling, a picture, or a new way for you to look at something. Most poetry comes from the poet's emotions and imagination. Several features set poetry apart from other forms of literature.

The Forms of Poetry. You can usually tell that a selection is a poem by looking at it. It is written in lines instead of paragraphs. You may have noticed in "Millicent Finds the World" that a sentence does not necessarily end at the end of a line. The lines may be arranged in groups called **stanzas.**

You can often tell a selection is a poem when you hear it spoken aloud. The language of poetry is chosen for its sound as well as for its meaning. Poetry is written in lines that have **rhythm.** Some poems have a very regular, measured rhythm called **meter.** Meter in poetry is like the beat you hear in music. Other poems are written in **free verse,** which is poetry written without regular meter, rhyme or stanzas.

The words in poems may also **rhyme,** as they do in "maggie and milly and molly and may." In free verse poems like "The Day Millicent Found the World," the words do not rhyme.

Repetition of sounds is common in poetry. What sound is repeated in this line from "The Raven" by Edgar Allen Poe: "Doubting, dreaming dreams no mortal ever dared to dream before?" This kind of repetition is called **alliteration.** Words, phrases, and lines may be repeated as well.

The Content of Poetry. Have you noticed that many poems are very short? Yet they seem to express as much feeling as a longer work. They may contain as many ideas. Poems usually express much more in far fewer words than do other forms of literature. The next three poems will have a **theme,** or message, very similar to the message in the other selections in this unit. However, they are much shorter than the other selections. Poets achieve this partly by choosing language for its power to suggest.

POETRY

The content of poetry is often emotional. Even **narrative** poems, which tell a story, describe something about which the poet feels strongly.

Poetry usually paints pictures and creates images. The poet may want you to see, hear, feel, smell, and taste what is being described.

Techniques of Poetry. Using language to create pictures in the mind is called **imagery.** Often poets will paint pictures for you using **figures of speech.** They may, for example, use **similes** and **metaphors** to compare something in the poem with something familiar to you. You have learned that a simile says that one thing is like another. A metaphor says one thing *is* another or speaks of it as though it were something else. The comparison is implied rather than stated. "He is a gem" is a metaphor.

Poems often use **symbols,** or objects that stand for something else. You will understand poetry better if you understand the use of symbols in literature, a practice that is called **symbolism.**

The Purpose of Poetry. You have read some poems that tell stories and others that made you laugh. These are purposes that poets may share with other writers. Most poetry is written to express an idea or a feeling. The poet may want you to feel or understand an emotion, or to look at something differently. Poets share feelings, impressions, and experiences by painting pictures and choosing language for its sound and its power to suggest.

As you read the next three poems, examine each to discover the elements of poetry that are present. Ask yourself:

1. What elements of form identify the selection as a poem?
2. Which of the following techniques of poetry are present: meter, rhyme, symbolism, similes, metaphors, or repetition?
3. How does the poet use elements of poetry to help you look at something in a new way?

by Eve Merriam

STUDY HINTS

Notice the repetition of sound.

This poem has rhythm, but it is not regular. Therefore it is not meter.

Thumbprints are symbols. What do they symbolize?

Some words rhyme, but the rhyme pattern is not regular.

Notice the figure of speech.

In the heel of my thumb
are whorls, whirls, wheels
in a unique design:
mine alone.
What a treasure to own!
My own flesh, my own feelings.
No other, however grand or base,
can ever attain the same.
My signature,
thumbing the pages of my time.
My universe key,
my singularity.
Impress, implant,
I am myself,
of all my atom parts I am the sum.
And out of my blood and my brain
I make my own interior weather,
my own sun and rain.
Imprint my mark upon the world,
whatever I shall become.

---

whorl (HWURL) a circle, as made by petals around the center of a flower or by the turns of a shell
unique (yoo NEEK) one of a kind
base (BAYS) of low value
attain (uh TAYN) reach; gain
singularity (sing gyuh LAR uh tee) uniqueness
impress (IM pres) mark; stamp
implant (IM plant) something deeply planted
imprint (im PRINT) make a mark

Advice to Travelers

by Walker Gibson

Notice the rhyme pattern. Every other line rhymes.

A burro once, sent by express,
His shipping ticket on his bridle,
Ate up his name and his address,
And in some warehouse, standing idle,

This poem has meter, a regular rhythm.

He waited till he like to died.
The moral hardly needs the showing:

The theme is stated. What is it?

Don't keep things locked up deep inside
Say who you are and where you're going.

burro (BUR oh) a small donkey
bridle (BRY dul) the part of a horse's harness that fits on its head

The Rest of My Life

by May Swenson

I'm the one
who'll be with me
for the rest of my life.

This poem is written in free verse. It has no rhyme or meter.

I'm the one
5 who'll enjoy myself,
take care of myself,
be loveable, so as to love
myself for the rest
of my life.

What is the theme of this poem?

10 Arms, be strong to hold me.
Eyes, be with me.
Will you be with me
for the rest of my life?

I'm the one,
15 the only one,
the one who won't leave me
for the rest of my life.

What words or phrases are repeated in this poem? How does repetition contribute to the meaning?

YOU

by Nikki Giovanni

What words or phrases are repeated in this poem? How does the repetition add to the meaning?

Notice the change in rhythm. It helps contrast the crowd with "you."

What is the theme of this poem? How does the poet use the techniques of poetry to communicate the theme?

I came to the crowd seeking friends
I came to the crowd seeking love
I came to the crowd for understanding

I found you

5 I came to the crowd to weep
I came to the crowd to laugh

You dried my tears
You shared my happiness

I went from the crowd seeking you
10 I went from the crowd seeking me
I went from the crowd forever

You came, too

---

seeking (SEEK ing) tracing down, trying to find out; searching for

Eve Merriam (1916-Present)

Perhaps the reason that Eve Merriam became a writer was because she is so fascinated by words. She loves puns and is constantly finding extra meanings in the most commonplace words. Her delight in words can be seen in the titles of some of her books: *What's in the Middle of a Riddle, It Doesn't Always Have to Rhyme,* and *What Can You Do With a Pocket?*

Although Merriam writes novels, nonfiction, and biographies, her favorite form of writing is poetry. This is because poetry fits her joy with words. The words in a poem are chosen not only for their meanings, but for their sounds. Merriam also thinks of poetry as "immediate." The sensations and emotions are transmitted directly to the reader. That is, nothing has to be explained—the reader experiences sensations and emotions for himself or herself.

Merriam writes many of her books for young readers, and young people appreciate her work. Some of her poems are almost like riddles. For example, in "There Is No Rhyme for Silver," Merriam tries to find a rhyme for *silver.* Is there such a rhyme? If you play with words, as Merriam does, you will find one.

Merriam grew up in Philadelphia and lives in New York City. Although she loves to travel, she says she will never move from the city, even if she is the last person living there. As she says, even in the winter, the city is her "delight."

FOCUS ON THE SELECTION

UNDERSTAND THE SELECTION

Recall

1. According to the poem "Thumbprint," what is special about a thumbprint?
2. What happened in "Advice to Travelers"?
3. In the poem "You," what did the speaker want from the crowd?

Infer

4. In "Thumbprint," what does a thumbprint symbolize?
5. In "Advice to Travelers" what does the burro's address symbolize?
6. What is the theme in "The Rest of My Life?"
7. Why did the speaker "You" leave?

Apply

8. Judging by the poems, what do all of these poets think you should value?
9. Would the speaker in "The Rest of My Life" advise doing what you think is right or what others think is right?
10. According to the speaker in "You," what is more valuable than a group?

Respond to Literature

According to the speaker, is it easier to share one's inner space with a crowd or with one person?

WRITE ABOUT THE SELECTION

The "you" addressed in the poem "You" must have been a very special friend indeed. What would such a person be like? Think about a person who could be that important a friend to you. Write a description of this person. Tell what qualities the person has that are important in a good friend. Or, if you don't know such a person in your own life, try to imagine what such a friend should be like.

Prewriting: First, write an informal outline of qualities your good friends have or that you would like them to have. Then, list the qualities you think a good friend should have.

Writing: Use your outline and your list to write a description of the person who is or could be a good friend to you. Also include enough details about the person so that he or she emerges as a realistic personality.

Revising: Revise your description. Make sure you have painted a clear picture of this person by adding very specific details. Consider rearranging your sentences to make your description as vivid and powerful as possible.

Proofreading: Read your description to check for errors. Be sure that all your sentences begin with capital letters and end with periods, question marks, or exclamation marks. Check your internal punctuation as well.

THINK ABOUT POETRY

Poems are written in rhythmic lines. They usually use fewer words to express an idea or feeling than most other forms of literature. The content of a poem is often emotional and imaginative. The sound of a poem is usually as important as the ideas it contains. Poems are more likely to paint pictures and convey feelings than present facts.

1. Which poems contain rhyme?
2. What techniques does each poem use to paint pictures?
3. What symbols did you find in these poems?
4. How did the symbols help convey the message? Which symbols seemed most effective to you?
5. What themes were expressed in the poems? Which do you think were stated most directly?

DEVELOP YOUR VOCABULARY

A **prefix** is a word part added to the beginning of a word. It changes the meaning of that word. Some of the words listed below have prefixes. The word to which the prefix is added is called the **root word.** If you know the meaning of the root word and the prefix, you can determine the meaning of the whole word.

Several of the listed words begin with the prefix *im-*. If you look up the word *implant,* you will see that it means "to plant within." This tells you that the prefix *im-* must mean "within."

Look up each word in the dictionary. If the word has a prefix, think about what the prefix adds to the meaning of the word. Use each word in a sentence of your own.

1. whorl
2. unique
3. base
4. attain
5. singularity
6. impress
7. implant
8. imprint
9. burro
10. bridle

LEARN ABOUT

First Person Point of View

A story written in the **first person** is told as if one of the characters were narrating it. Words such as *I* and *me* are used to refer to the character telling the story.

When you read a story written in the first person, you learn only what the narrator does, observes, thinks, feels, or knows. In "The Confidence Game," you learned only what Tobi knew, thought, or felt. You learned about other people's thoughts only when these thoughts were expressed to Tobi.

Point of view affects the kind of information you receive as you read a selection. You can tell a selection is written in the first person because the words *I* and *me* refer to one of the people or characters.

As you read "Aquí Se Habla Español" ask yourself:

1. Is the story told in the first or third person?
2. How does the point of view affect the way the story is told?

SKILL BUILDER

Write a few lines about something that has happened to you or someone you know. Use the first person point of view. Use words like *I* and *we*.

AQUÍ SE HABLA ESPAÑOL

by Leslie Jill Sokolow

The pool had just opened for the summer, so there were plenty of new girls around. But it was Marina who caught my eye.

It took most of the morning before I got up the nerve to make a move. It just sort of happened. She was swimming lazily back and forth, so I dove in and made a long, slow ascent and bumped smack into her. When I surfaced, I started talking wildly so she wouldn't swim away.

"Gee! I'm sorry. I wasn't looking. Are you okay? Boy, for a little thing like you, you sure gave me a knock." I hated myself for talking so stupidly, but I couldn't collect my thoughts.

She smiled but said nothing. I tried again.

"How long have you been bumping guys at this pool? I bet all the guys go around black-and-blue 'cause of you!"

"I—I don't understand," she said, smiling faintly.

"Oh, of course. What a crazy fool I am. You know, *loco.* I don't know too much Spanish, you know. *No hablo español.* You *comprenda* me, huh?"

"Oh, yes," she replied. "I know the English, it's just the idioms that I have trouble in. Black-and-blue?"

The sun shone through her gleaming wet black hair. Tossing her head, she smiled up at me, her face shining like bright sunlight.

"My name's Andy. What's yours?"

She hesitated—that must have been the longest minute in my life—then she decided. "My name is Marina."

From then on, it was every Saturday night for the whole

summer. But don't think we didn't have troubles. It was her parents. She was associating with me so much that she began to speak English, and it became a habit with her. I thought it was a good habit. Her mother didn't.

A month after I had met her, Marina invited me to her house for supper.

"Andy," she said, with that cute little accent of hers, "I did not ask my parents, you know, but please come to have supper tonight with me."

I must have looked startled, because right off she started saying how poor her home was and how they didn't have big meals like our family.

"Mari," I finally managed to answer when I'd gotten over my surprise, "that'd be great. I'd love to meet your family. I really would."

"Sure, Andy, at eight o'clock tonight, okay? We eat late."

"Sure, eight. That's fine, honey. I'll be there with bells on." I gave her a peck good-bye.

The subway ride was long, hot, stuffy. I was slammed in between a pole and the door, facing a heavy woman. Sweat was pouring from everyone. The train lurched to a sudden stop—something was wrong; it would probably take a few minutes to get fixed. I couldn't stand it. There wasn't any fan, any draft, or any breeze. I had to stare at all those people jammed together, unsmiling, unhappy, staring ahead with eyes that refused to say anything. If the train hadn't started just then, I think I would have screamed.

At last I was there. I straightened my sky-blue-pink shirt, smoothed my hair, and knocked on the door. I started to shake.

A big mean-looking kid about my age stood at the door. He was the kind I was always too proud to admit I was afraid of at school.

"I'm Andrew Redina," I offered. "Marina invited me to supper tonight, you know."

"Oh, yeah." He broke into a big smile. "Come in. I'm Marina's brother, José. I got quite a sister, ain't I? Like my father was telling us," he said, ushering me to an easy chair. "Marina's got it over any girl on this here block."

---

usher (USH ur) lead someone into a place

AVAILABLE
265-3405
EL ESPEC

He seemed pleasant, but I was relieved when Marina walked into the room. As always, she looked like something out of a story book, but then her mother was calling her. Marina turned and left, answering in rapid Spanish. Soon the living room was swarming with all the Chavez kids, ranging from seven to seventeen. An older guy who looked about twenty-two, with a little curly mustache, came over to me and smiled.

"I am Richie. Nice shirt you got there. You goin' with Carmen?"

"He's goin' with Marina, Richie."

"Wrong sister," he grinned. I felt good about his liking my shirt.

Soon we sat down to supper. Mrs. Chavez was a nice-looking woman, but her hair was unkempt. She was sweating from the stuffy room. Mr. Chavez was a rather short, stocky man who looked like an outcast sitting at the table. He spoke to no one and ate the little he did quickly.

José and Marina were speaking English. I think José did it for my sake; he was having great difficulty.

Then the trouble began. I think I must have symbolized America to the Chavezes. It started unnoticeably and ended with all the kids speaking English except little Johnny.

Then Johnny piped up, "'Ey, don't call me Juanito no more. Call me Johnny."

José laughed, "Sure we call you Johnny. Okay, everybody repeat Johnny. Carmen, say you Johnny. Marina, say you Johnny. Chico—" and so he went down the line.

Suddenly Mrs. Chavez turned a sickly greenish-purple, matching her housedress, and started screaming in Spanish. She directed most of her accusations at José. He didn't act surprised. I guess he expected it.

"Aquí se habla español," Mrs. Chavez screamed. Here you speak Spanish. It was horrible—she kept on repeating it until my ears rang and the chills ran up my spine. All the children kept their heads bent except José. Marina stole a glance at me, then she looked down, too.

---

unkempt (un KEMPT) neglected; untidy
symbolize (SIM bul yz) be a sign or symbol of
accusation (ak yoo ZAY shun) a charge of wrongdoing

Finally, in a low voice, the father uttered a command. Mrs. Chavez looked around the table and then marched into the kitchen. José, Marina, and I rose and went downstairs to the back alley. We stood there silently. José looked angry, Marina looked frightened, and I was bewildered.

"José—" Marina pleaded in a small, timid voice. He peered at us, his stern dark eyes narrowed.

"I'm sorry," he mumbled finally, his head bowed and his feet shifting. "I'm sorry." He turned to go.

"That's okay, that's okay," I said softly, but he was already gone.

After that evening it was hard to see Mari. But in our few meetings I learned the only thing that mattered—she loved me, I loved her. I had to do something about it.

I went to see José. I knew where to find him. He looked as if he'd been through a lot, real punchy.

"Hi, José. How've you been?" I said. He didn't seem to know me.

"I'm Marina's boyfriend, remember? I was up the house and—" He walked right past me. His face was blank.

"Hey, listen kid, what's the matter? Are you all right? I've gotta talk to you, José." I took a friendly but firm grip on his collar.

"Hey, 'ey—" He started shouting in Spanish that I should get off his coat collar, then stopped suddenly.

"Oh, you Marina's sweetheart, eh? What you want outta me?"

"Your sister and I want to go steady, Joe. We can't 'cause—"

"I know. I understand, Andy. But so what? What you wan' me to do, huh? It's hard makin' friends, you know, learnin' to speak American an' all. I bring friends, she won't like them. So say it short and quick."

"I wanna learn to speak Spanish. Mari is so upset—your old lady won't accept me. I mean, I understand Spanish okay, but I can't speak it."

"Why the world don't you go to some school? You loaded?" he bit off.

"Me?" I laughed. "I've got no more dough than you do."

---

bewilder (bih WIL dur) puzzle; confuse

He stared at me in disbelief.

"Listen," I went on, "at least your old lady cares who you go out with and all that. That's good. All parents should do that. Only in your mama's case, she's just—you know—a little mixed up."

"Okay! Okay, okay, okay. You know where to find me, it seems. Meet me after my work is out. Tomorrow," he mumbled abruptly.

We became pretty friendly. José took a lot of pleasure in expecting to knock his mother off her feet with my Spanish. I wasn't bad in grammar and things like that, but when José snapped a fast question at me I was at a loss for words.

I progressed, though, slowly but surely, and one day at the end of August, José and I, dressed in those sky-blue-pink Italian shirts, marched into the Chavez house. Marina nearly flipped when she saw us together. "José!" she exclaimed, surprise in her voice like a Fourth of July skyrocket.

José's eyes softened for a split-second and then he was back to his cool self. "Where's the ol' lady?" he asked, copying me.

"Don't do anything stupid, José, don't—she's in the kitchen."

"Good mornin', Mama. What's up? How's life down on the farm?"

Mrs. Chavez turned to him, wondering what he was up to now. He gave her a quick peck and whispered in Spanish too fast for me to catch. Then he began to talk very slowly.

"You remember Mr. Andrew Redina, don't you, Mama? Mr. Redina, this is my mother."

"I'm very glad to know you, Mrs. Chavez," I said in Spanish. "I didn't realize that Marina had such a nice mother and so pretty." I felt like a fool. José had made me say that. But Mrs. Chavez seemed pleased.

"Mr. Redina has taken pains to learn Spanish. He thinks it so beautiful," José added. "Even more than his own Italian." I choked. About all my Italian was "yes" and "no."

José went on and on. He had a good tongue—he was a natural-born flatterer.

Then came the big surprise. "Mr. Redina," said Mrs. Chavez—yes, in English. It wasn't perfect English by any means, but it was English all right. "Mr. Redina," she repeated, "please, we like you to come to dinner sometime."

I don't know who was more surprised, José, Marina, or me. We all smiled. Then José and Marina laughed and patted their mother on the back.

"Soon," said Mrs. Chavez.

So I came back for dinner the next night. Afterwards, Mari and I went downstairs to the alley. We both refused to give in—she spoke English, I spoke Spanish. We kissed under our mutual-speaking moon.

FOCUS ON THE SELECTION

UNDERSTAND THE SELECTION

Recall

1. How did Andy manage to meet Marina?
2. What happened at the Chavez's dinner table?
3. How did Andy learn Spanish?

Infer

4. Why might Mrs. Chavez want the children to speak Spanish?
5. Why did Andy decide to learn Spanish?
6. Why did José imply to his mother that Andy spoke Italian?
7. Why did Mrs. Chavez invite Andy to dinner at the end of the story?

Apply

8. In a foreigh land, would you want your children to speak English at home, or the language of the country in which they lived?
9. What is your opinion of José's behavior at the table?
10. Predict what would have happened if Andy had not learned Spanish.

Respond to Literature

What problems were created by the character's inability to view situations from another's inner space?

WRITE ABOUT THE SELECTION

In "Aquí Se Habla Español," you read the story from Andy's point of view. You looked into Andy's inner space and were able to understand his personal thoughts and feelings. What do you think was happening in Marina's inner space during the course of the story? Write an incident in the story from Marina's point of view. Use the first person and tell the story as you imagine Marina would have told it.

Prewriting: Choose an incident in the story that especially appeals to you. Imagine how that incident would appear from Marina's inner space. Make an informal outline of what you think she would say.

Writing: Use your outline and your notes to write your incident from Marina's point of view.

Revising: When you revise your incident, be sure that everything you say is something Marina could know. Use the setting and mood of the story to get yourself started but try to be as imaginative as you can.

Proofreading: Read your incident to check for errors. Be sure that all your sentences begin with capital letters and end with correct punctuation. If you have written conversation, be sure you have enclosed the speaker's exact words in quotation marks. Check your internal punctuation as well.

THINK ABOUT POINT OF VIEW

A story told in the first person tells you only what is known to the character telling the story. When you read "Aquí Se Habla Español," you did not learn about Marina's family until Andy visited them.

1. What elements identified the point of view in the story "Aquí Se Habla Español?"
2. How would this story be different if it were told in the third person?
3. How would the story be different if Marina were telling it?
4. How did you learn about the thoughts and feelings of characters other than Andy?
5. Would you feel that you knew Andy as well if the story were told in the third person? Explain your answer.

DEVELOP YOUR VOCABULARY

Have you ever read a word you thought was unfamiliar and discovered that you really did know it once you heard it pronounced? Sometimes if you figure out how to pronounce an unfamiliar word, you will recognize it.

You can pronounce an unfamiliar word more easily if you break it down into syllables. A **syllable** is a word part with one vowel sound. The dictionary breaks words into syllables for you by separating them with hyphens or dots.

Review the meanings of these words from the story in your dictionary. Then use each in an original sentence to show that you understand not only the meaning but how they are used correctly.

1. usher
2. unkempt
3. symbolize
4. accusation
5. bewilder

Learn About
Connotation and Denotation

You can have a positive response to one word and a negative response to another word that has the same meaning, such as *inexpensive* and *cheap.*

The literal meaning, or dictionary definition, of a word is its **denotation.** What the word suggests to you is its **connotation.** The way you feel about a word is also part of its connotation.

You probably need to understand the connotation as well as the denotation of the words your friends use. Otherwise you would not understand what they are saying to you.

Connotation is as important as denotation in understanding a word. The connotation tells you as much about what a writer is saying as the denotation does.

As you read "Blind Sunday," ask yourself:

1. What words have a connotation in addition to their literal meanings?
2. How do you respond to these words?

Skill Builder

Writers often choose words that suggest a meaning or create a feeling beyond the literal meaning of the word. Write a few statements that contain words with a strong positive or negative connotation.

Blind Sunday

by Arthur Barron

CHARACTERS

EILEEN, *a teenager*
JEFF, *a teenager*
MRS. HAYS, *a woman who works with blind people*
DAD, *Jeff's father*
MARGE, *Eileen's friend*
ERIC, *Marge's friend*
WAITER
LIFEGUARD
CABDRIVER
MAN
TICKET TAKER

SCENE 1

Early June, late afternoon, at a public swimming pool. EILEEN *is swimming.* MRS. HAYS *is sitting at the side of the pool.* JEFF *tests the diving board, then executes a rather good jackknife. In a moment, he emerges from underwater.*

EILEEN: Hey, neat dive!
JEFF: Thanks.
EILEEN: What do you call that?
JEFF: Jackknife.
EILEEN: Oh—right. Can you do a half gainer?
JEFF: No. That's outta my class.

(There is a pause as EILEEN *waits for more conversation, but* JEFF *is shy. He nods at* EILEEN*, swims over to the side of the pool, and gets out. As he dries himself,* EILEEN *swims over to him and speaks from the edge of the pool.*

---

executes (EK sih kyoots) carries out; does

EILEEN: I'm Eileen.

JEFF: Uh, I'm Jeff.

(EILEEN *feels in front of her, then pushes herself out of the pool. She smiles.* JEFF *returns the smile but is confused and doesn't know what to say.)*

EILEEN: Where do you go to school?

JEFF: Western.

EILEEN: I go to Eastern.

(At this moment, MRS. HAYS *appears.)*

MRS. HAYS: Lee, hi! How's the water today?

EILEEN: Great. Warmer than yesterday. Mrs. Hays, this is Jeff. He goes to Western. Jeff, this is Mrs. Hays. She's the librarian at Eastern—and my friend.

JEFF: Hi.

MRS. HAYS: Hello, Jeff. *(pause)* Well, this water looks terrific. I'm going to get some exercise. Nice to meet you, Jeff.

(JEFF *nods.)*

EILEEN: Lee's my nickname. (JEFF *does not know what to say.)* Hey, you're the strong silent type, huh?

JEFF: Yeah, I guess so. *(trying to think of anything to say)* Hey, you want some peanuts?

EILEEN: Why not?

JEFF: I've got some in my jacket. *(He stands, goes for the bag of peanuts and returns, setting the bag in front of* EILEEN*)* Help yourself.

EILEEN: Thanks. *(She doesn't know where the bag is, of course, and has to feel for it.* JEFF *notices, watching intently. He is perplexed and shocked. Finally, he pushes the bag under her hand. She takes a handful.)* Unsalted, huh? (JEFF *can't speak.)* What's the matter? (JEFF *can't find the right words.)* So didn't you ever eat peanuts with a blind girl before? (JEFF *stares, his lips trying to say something.)* Hey, are you okay?

JEFF: Uh—yeah.

EILEEN: Relax, will you?

JEFF: Sure.

EILEEN: You're funny.

JEFF: I am?

EILEEN: *(laughing)* You should see yourself.

JEFF: *(smiling finally)* Yeah, I guess so.

EILEEN: Well now that you're okay again, hold the peanuts for me. I feel a half gainer coming on.

(She walks to the diving board, climbs the ladder, walks to the edge of the board. JEFF *stares at her. The lifeguard watches.* MRS. HAYS, *just out of the water, watches with a smile.)*

MRS. HAYS: Okay, Lee, it's all clear.

EILEEN *gets set, takes a breath, executes a nice half gainer, and breaks from under the water with a smile.)*

EILEEN: Like it?

JEFF: That was fantastic!

SCENE 2

Breakfast. JEFF *is eating as his father enters.*

DAD: Hi, Jeff.

JEFF: *(without enthusiasm)* Hiya, Dad.

DAD: How are you doing?

JEFF: Okay.

DAD: *(pouring himself a glass of orange juice)* You don't look any too terrific.

JEFF: I've been thinking. You know—wondering. How do you talk to somebody?

DAD: What?

JEFF: I mean, how do you make conversation? You know, when you just want to be friendly?

DAD: Oh—you mean like small talk?

JEFF: Yeah, that's it.

DAD: Maybe you try too hard.

JEFF: Yeah, I get tongue-tied. Nothing comes out.

DAD: I suppose you know that everything you say doesn't have to be earthshaking or super-ha-ha funny. Just relax. Be yourself.

JEFF: You know this school dance that's coming up, after the game?

DAD: Yes?

JEFF: I'd kinda like to go. You know—but if I did, what would I

talk about?

DAD: Anything.

JEFF: Did you ever know a blind person?

DAD: *(pause)* I see you do.

JEFF: Yeah.

DAD: And this blind person's a girl?

JEFF: Yeah.

DAD: And you don't know how to talk to her?

JEFF: No.

DAD: But you kind of like her?

JEFF: *(pause)* Yeah. Guess so.

SCENE 3

It is the end of the school day. Students are mixing outside school on the street. EILEEN, *using her cane, enters with* MARGE. ERIC *joins them.*

MARGE: Hi, Eric.

ERIC: Hi, Marge. Hi, Lee.

EILEEN: Hi.

(They stroll along the sidewalk.)

ERIC: So how'd the French test go?

MARGE: Awful!

ERIC: Yeah?

MARGE: If I made a D, I'm lucky.

ERIC: Man, and your French is better than my English.

(They reach a corner. MARGE *and* EILEEN *start to turn left, but* ERIC *taps* MARGE *on the shoulder and silently indicates she should stop.)*

ERIC: I got a history final tomorrow.

(While talking, he points to another boy and girl standing a few feet away to the right. In pantomime he indicates that MARGE *should leave* EILEEN *and join him and the other couple.* MARGE *shakes her head no, indicating she can't leave* EILEEN.

MARGE: Oh, well. I guess you'll have to hit the books tonight.

ERIC: *(insisting she come, in pantomime)* Yeah, and there's this great movie on TV, too.

MARGE: *(beginning to weaken)* Well, uh—well, I guess you'll have to miss it.

ERIC: Yeah. *(He smiles as* MARGE *shakes her head "yes.")* Yeah, it's too bad. *(He winks at* MARGE.*)* Well, see you.

MARGE: Okay, see you.

(MARGE *turns to* EILEEN, *who has been listening to this encounter and sensing what's going on.* ERIC *walks away and joins the other couple to wait for* MARGE *to join them.* MARGE *and* EILEEN *walk a few steps along the sidewalk.)*

MARGE: Oh, gee—

EILEEN: What's the matter?

MARGE: I gotta go back, Lee. I forgot something.

EILEEN: Okay. I'll wait here.

MARGE: No! No—uh—I'll be awhile. I gotta find something.

EILEEN: Hey, listen, Marge. If you want to go off with Eric, it's okay with me. Really.

MARGE: *(feeling guilty)* What?

EILEEN: I mean, don't you think I heard all that "signing" going on? He did everything but send smoke signals.

MARGE: What do you mean, Lee?

EILEEN: I mean it's perfectly okay if you want to be alone. I know three's a crowd—only don't be hypocrites.

MARGE: *(feeling bad)* Oh, gee, Lee. I—

EILEEN: Hey, go on, willya. I'll get home all right. *(smiling)* I could do it in the dark.

MARGE: *(turning to look at* ERIC, *who waves impatiently)* Lee, I'm sorry. I didn't mean anything.

EILEEN: Sure, I know. Look, I'll see you tomorrow. *(touching* MARGE'S *arm)* Have fun. Okay?

(MARGE *walks off and joins the other couple.* EILEEN *stands alone for a moment. Her face shows how she feels, but not for long.*

Across the street, JEFF *appears. He has been hurrying. He stops, looks, and notices* EILEEN. EILEEN *prepares to cross the street, sweeping her cane in front of her.* JEFF *quickly crosses the street and joins her.)*

JEFF: Uh—hi.

---

encounter (en KOUN tur) a meeting

EILEEN: Hi.

JEFF: Remember me?

EILEEN: I think so. Say some more.

JEFF: Gee—uh—what should I say? Uh—the light changed. Can I help you cross?

EILEEN: *(nicely)* No, thanks. I can manage.

(She crosses with JEFF *following along. She comes to the opposite curb.)*

JEFF: You're at the curb.

EILEEN: Now I know who you are. You're Fido, the guide dog.

JEFF: *(hurt)* Oh.

EILEEN: I'm sorry. You see, I like to manage myself. You're the guy I met at the pool, right?

JEFF: Yeah.

EILEEN: You go to Western.

JEFF: Right.

EILEEN: What are you doing over here?

JEFF: I had an errand to do.

EILEEN: Well—it was nice seeing you.

(She starts to walk on. He pauses, then catches up with her.)

JEFF: My errand's done. I'm going this way. Maybe I can join you.

EILEEN: Sure—it seems you already have.

JEFF: *(trying to relax)* I'm kinda hungry. Do you want a hamburger or something?

EILEEN: *(pleased)* Why not? May I take your arm?

(Dissolve to: A restaurant. JEFF *and* EILEEN *enter. Among the kids crowding the place are* MARGE *and* ERIC. MARGE *notices* EILEEN *and looks uncomfortable as* EILEEN *walks by.* JEFF *and* EILEEN *sit in a booth,* EILEEN *feeling her way in.)*

JEFF: *(making conversation)* Well, here we are.

EILEEN: Yeah.

JEFF: Nice place.

EILEEN: Uh-huh.

(Another silence is relieved by the waiter, who approaches, puts down glasses of water in front of them, and notices Eileen is blind.)

WAITER: *(to* JEFF*)* What'll you have?

JEFF: Uh, a burger—and a shake and—uh—fries.

WAITER: What's she gonna have?

EILEEN: *(angry) She* will have a cheeseburger, a vanilla shake, and french fries.

(Waiter shrugs, gives JEFF *a look, and leaves.)*

EILEEN: *That* makes me mad.

JEFF: I noticed.

EILEEN: Blind people aren't supposed to know what they want. *(pause)* Sometimes people ask me the dumbest things.

JEFF: Like what?

EILEEN: Like—how do you find your mouth with your fork? A lady asked me that once. Or—do you sleep with your eyes open or closed? That's another.

JEFF: Dumb is hardly the word for it. *(He is still uncomfortable.)* You know—

EILEEN: In case you're wondering—I can't remember ever being able to see.

(The waiter returns and puts their order on the table.)

JEFF: Thanks. *(He watches as* EILEEN *carefully arranges her dishes.)* Can I help?

EILEEN: No, thanks. I can manage.

JEFF: Sorry.

EILEEN: You don't have to be sorry. Look, I just want to be treated like everybody else. You see that girl over there? The one with the long hair?

JEFF: Uh-huh.

EILEEN: Well, that's my girlfriend Marge. Now would you ask her if she wanted help with her food?

JEFF: No. Hey, how'd you know she was there?

EILEEN: I heard her when we passed by. Now here's how I manage my food. My plate's a clock.

JEFF: A clock.

EILEEN: Uh-huh. And my cheeseburger's here at twelve o'clock. My french fries are at seven. And my pickles are at eleven. *(Pauses while* JEFF *studies.)* Now where's my shake?

JEFF: *(twisting his head around to see from her point of view)* Three o'clock.

EILEEN: Thanks. *(She picks up the shake and pretends to pour it on her*

french fries.) That's the way blind people eat french fries, right? (JEFF *laughs, then looks at her with appreciation and pleasure.)*

SCENE 4

JEFF *and* EILEEN *are walking to* EILEEN'S *house.*

EILEEN: What color are your eyes?

JEFF: Blue.

EILEEN: Color's the hardest thing.

JEFF: What do you mean?

EILEEN: I mean the hardest thing to visualize. What's blue, for example?

JEFF: The sky—

EILEEN: No. I mean, what *is* blue? I know what *things* are blue. But what does blue look like? (JEFF *doesn't answer.)* Stumped, huh?

JEFF: Guess so.

EILEEN: Color's the thing I miss most—I guess.

(Dissolve to: Another street scene as they approach EILEEN'S *house.)*

JEFF: I don't know. I like working with my hands. An engineer maybe. What about you?

EILEEN: A lawyer. Or maybe a model—the kind that just stands around looking glamorous, and they take pictures of you and you make hundreds of thousands. Hey, this is where I live. Want to come in?

JEFF: Uh, no thanks. I better get home.

EILEEN: Okay. I had fun.

JEFF: Me too. Well—so long.

EILEEN: Bye.

JEFF: Do you want to go to the park tomorrow?

EILEEN: Oh, sure! Why not? That would be fun.

JEFF: Great! See you tomorrow.

SCENE 5

The park. JEFF *and* EILEEN *walk past someone sitting on a bench listening to a portable radio.*

EILEEN: Do you like to dance?
JEFF: Well, I'm not very good at it.
EILEEN: I love it. I love music. All kinds.
JEFF: Yeah?

(Dissolve to: The zoo. They are standing in front of a lion cage. The lion provides them with a roar.)

EILEEN: Hey, there's a lion.
JEFF: It sure is.
EILEEN: When I hear that, I expect a movie to start.

(They laugh. They wander past other cages. JEFF *is holding a bag of peanuts.* EILEEN *helps herself from time to time.)*

(Dissolve to: Another zoo scene. Some people are feeding an elephant, whose trunk reaches through the bars. EILEEN *feeds the elephant some peanuts.)*

EILEEN: That's a vacuum cleaner, right?
JEFF: *(laughs)* Yeah—with big ears.

(They wander on, passing an area with gorillas.)

JEFF: Gee, they look sad.
EILEEN: Who?
JEFF: Oh, I'm sorry!
EILEEN: Don't be. Who looks sad?
JEFF: The gorillas. I hate seeing them penned up. Come on, let's go.

SCENE 6

Another day, another park. JEFF *and* EILEEN *are riding a two-seater bicycle.* JEFF *is sitting in front and steering. They come down a hill, picking up speed.* JEFF *begins to brake.*

EILEEN: Don't brake! Come on, faster!
JEFF: Okay.
EILEEN: Wow! I love it! Love it! Love it!

(Her hair is blowing. Her head is back as she enjoys the sensation of speed. Suddenly JEFF *has to swerve to avoid hitting someone.)*

JEFF: Oh, no! *(He slows, braking hard.)*
EILEEN: What's wrong?
JEFF: I'm stopping.
EILEEN: How come?

(JEFF *gets off the seat, standing astride the bar.)*

EILEEN: Why'd you stop? That was some fantastic ride!
JEFF: It was dangerous.
EILEEN: You were worried about me. Look, I told you, just treat me like everybody else. Can't you understand?
JEFF: Now wait a minute. I was worried about myself. *(After pause, he chuckles.)* And you, too.
EILEEN: Chicken!
JEFF: I'm not kidding, Eileen. I just—
EILEEN: Hey, call me Lee.
JEFF: Okay, Lee. But you're changing the subject.
EILEEN: Yeah, that's because nicknames are more interesting. What's yours?
JEFF: I don't have one.
EILEEN: Well then I'll just have to think one up. *(pause)* So how about "chicken"?

(They laugh and ride off.)

SCENE 7

JEFF'S *house, in the driveway. His father is washing the car as* JEFF *enters.*

JEFF: *(cheerful)* Hi, Dad.
DAD: What's happening?
JEFF: Not much.
DAD: Hey, grab a rag, will you?
JEFF: Okay. *(He starts to work.)* You know that dance I was telling you about the other day?
DAD: Dance? Oh, yeah.
JEFF: *(Pause)* Well, it's a pretty important one. It's a dance sponsored by Western and Eastern. I've been thinking about taking somebody.

---

astride (uh STRYD) with one leg on each side

DAD: That nice girl you've been seeing?

JEFF: But I feel funny about it. I mean, everyone would be staring at us. They'd think I was desperate for a date or something.

DAD: You like being with her, don't you? You must have fun together. *(pause while they continue working)* And—uh—is she pretty?

JEFF: Yeah.

DAD: *(long pause)* Well, I guess you don't think too highly of yourself. Is that it?

JEFF: *(surprised)* What do you mean?

DAD: It seems to me you care more about what other people think than what you think.

JEFF: Oh, I don't know about that.

DAD: Well, let's face it. If you worry too much about what other people think, it means you lack self-confidence.

JEFF: *(starts working hard)* I'll have to think about that.

SCENE 8

The school library. MRS. HAYS *and* EILEEN *are working quietly. After a moment,* EILEEN *speaks.*

EILEEN: You know what I'd want more than anything if I could see just one thing?

MRS. HAYS: What?

EILEEN: My face.

MRS. HAYS: You have a very nice face.

EILEEN: I don't think so.

MRS. HAYS: Why not?

EILEEN: I don't have dates. I mean, I have friends and all. People like me. But boys don't ask me out.

MRS. HAYS: What about Jeff?

EILEEN: We have fun together. *(pause)* But I think he's more like a friend.

MRS. HAYS: Maybe it will develop into something else.

EILEEN: But suppose I *am* ugly?

MRS. HAYS: But you're not. You're very attractive. What is all this, anyway? You know it's the person inside you that counts.

EILEEN: I guess so.

SCENE 9

The swimming pool. It is crowded. EILEEN *sits with* MARGE *and* ERIC. MRS. HAYS *is in the background, talking to a friend. The lifeguard is standing and yelling at some kids in the water to stop horsing around.* ERIC *jumps in the water and yells to* MARGE.

ERIC: Hey, Marge, hurry up.

MARGE: Okay.

EILEEN: *(to Marge)* You know that guy I've been seeing?

MARGE: Jeff?

EILEEN: Yeah. I was thinking of inviting him—to the dance. I mean—

MARGE: That'd be neat, Lee.

EILEEN: But you know—it was just a thought.

MARGE: It sounds like a good idea to me.

ERIC: *(from the water)* Hey, you guys, you coming in?

EILEEN: Yeah, in a second.

*(*MARGE *jumps into the pool.* JEFF *walks over to* EILEEN.

JEFF: Hi, Lee.
EILEEN: Hi. Crowded today, huh?
JEFF: Yeah.

(There is a lot of activity, a lot of horseplay. A couple of boys are trying to throw girls into the pool. The girls are shrieking with mock fright, but really enjoying themselves. Soon ERIC *and* MARGE *are out of the pool and joining the horseplay.* JEFF *watches as* ERIC *throws* MARGE *in.* MARGE *shrieks with delight and swims away.)*

JEFF: There goes Marge. She just got thrown in.
EILEEN: Yeah. *(She sounds as if she is missing out on the fun.* JEFF *notices her tone of voice. He stares at her, looks at all the kids having a good time and makes up his mind.)*
JEFF: *(grabbing* EILEEN*)* You're next. *(And he pushes her in.)*

*(*EILEEN *screams, and she isn't kidding. She's startled and frightened. She hits the water and goes under. After a moment, she comes to the top, but seems confused. She opens her mouth to yell, swallows a mouthful of water. She coughs, chokes, and becomes even more alarmed. The lifeguard dives into the pool. He tries to help* EILEEN *but this only infuriates her and she tries to push him away.* JEFF *has seen all this with horror. Kids rush to the side of the pool.* MARGE *and* MRS. HAYS *join* JEFF *there.)*

JEFF: Here, take my hand, Lee.
EILEEN: I'm okay.

*(*EILEEN *climbs out herself. She slips on a wet tile, losing her balance, but she does not fall. She feels that all eyes are on her, and she is humiliated.* MRS. HAYS *offers her a towel, but* LEE *doesn't take it. She wants to be left alone.)*

JEFF: Lee, I'm sorry. I'm awfully sorry.
EILEEN: *(trying to hide her embarrassment)* It's okay. I'm fine.
JEFF: You said it seemed like fun. You know, I thought you wanted to be treated like everybody else. I didn't mean it like this.

---

infuriates (in FYUUR ee ayts) makes angry

EILEEN: *(softly, pleadingly)* Please, I just want to get out of here. I've got to get out of here.

(She walks away quickly but with dignity. JEFF *looks confused.* MRS. HAYS *walks over to him and puts her hand on his arm.)*

MRS. HAYS: Jeff, let's have a talk, okay?

(Dissolve to: JEFF *and* MRS. HAYS *off to one side, the pool and the noises in the background.)*

JEFF: I feel terrible.

MRS. HAYS: I know you must feel bad about it.

JEFF: I mean, she's angry with me.

MRS. HAYS: I don't know about angry. She's embarrassed. She doesn't want her embarrassment to be the center of attention.

JEFF: I tried to understand what it means to be blind. I mean, *really* understand. It's like being in a different world—I mean, I can't imagine what it would be like.

MRS. HAYS: Shut your eyes, Jeff.

JEFF: Huh?

MRS. HAYS: Shut them. Keep them shut.

SCENE 10

Sunday noon. JEFF *is sitting in the back of a taxi. He is wearing dark patches over his eyes and dark sunglasses. The cab pulls up to* EILEEN'S *house.* JEFF *gets out, and walks to the front of the cab, feeling his way with a cane and his hands.*

JEFF: How much?

DRIVER: Three-fifty.

JEFF: Thanks. Keep the change. *(gives the driver four bills)*

DRIVER: Thank you. Can I give you a hand, buddy?

JEFF: No, but you can put me in the direction of the front door.

DRIVER: Straight ahead up the driveway. Then up the steps to the right. Okay?

JEFF: Thanks.

(The cab pulls away. JEFF *turns in the direction of the house. He taps carefully with his cane, making agonizing progress. He comes to the steps, feels with his cane, and gently kicks the bottom step with his toe. It seems like Mt. Everest to him.*

He takes the steps one at a time, planting both feet solidly on the first, before going on to the second. He continues slowly. A truck passes on the street, grinding gears. JEFF *tenses, freezing until it passes.*

There is a slight concrete rise, not high enough to be called a step but high enough to create a raised level in front of the door. JEFF'S *cane passes over it without his noticing. He stumbles as his right foot hits it. He falls awkwardly, banging against the door. He fumbles for his cane, gets up, and searches for the bell. He feels everywhere but can't find it. He gives up and knocks on the door. No one comes. He knocks harder and harder until he is pounding.)*

JEFF: It's me! Hello!

(Someone comes to the door. JEFF *hears the knob turning and steps back a bit as the door opens. It's* EILEEN.

EILEEN: Jeff!
JEFF: It's me—Jeff.
EILEEN: Why didn't you ring the doorbell?
JEFF: I couldn't find it.
EILEEN: Why not?
JEFF: I'm blind.

(Dissolve to: Total blackness.)

SCENE 11

(A park where JEFF *and* EILEEN *are walking. He is holding onto her elbow. She is guiding him.)*

JEFF: So I decided I wanted to know how it felt to be blind. I mean, I've done so many dumb things.
EILEEN: That's great.
JEFF: I mean, I felt real bad about making mistakes all the time. (EILEEN *giggles.)* What are you laughing about?
EILEEN: You're shouting.
JEFF: *(loudly)* I am? *(much quieter)* I am?
EILEEN: That's one of the tricky things about being blind—learning just how loud to talk.

JEFF: I didn't know that.

EILEEN: It's true.

(Dissolves to: Another area of the park. A hot dog stand is in the background. EILEEN *and* JEFF *are each eating a hot dog and holding a soda.* EILEEN *eats with practiced ease.* JEFF *is having difficulty.)*

JEFF: Do people cheat you with change and stuff?

EILEEN: No. See, I always fold my bills differently so I know how much I'm giving. Like I fold fives in half and tens lengthwise and ones I don't fold at all. And of course I can feel change. Anyway, I think most people are pretty honest, don't you?

JEFF: Sure.

EILEEN: I guess I'm a pretty positive person. I think life is great. *(Pause. Then she begins to giggle.)*

JEFF: What's so funny now?

EILEEN: At this place for the blind where I trained they also train sighted people, like Mrs. Hays. And those people have to go around for a time like you—with goggles and stuff on. And once I went out with this man and we had lunch, right? And he asked me to order for both of us. So I ordered spaghetti for him. *(She laughs.)* What a time he had with that stuff. It was sliding all over the place.

JEFF: You're mean, you know that?

EILEEN: *(laughing)* I know.

JEFF: *(smiling)* Like I probably have mustard all over me. *(He feels around on his shirt and touches something sloppy.)* Oh! oh! I feel something. *(They both laugh.)*

(Dissolve to: One of the tunnels in the park. It leads to the zoo. As they walk through the tunnel the camera and sound effects create the experience as JEFF *undergoes it. The screen grows black. Sounds are loud, echoing. There are strange noises. The black screen wavers.*

Dissolve to: A bear cage. EILEEN *and* JEFF *pass by.)*

JEFF: What's that?

EILEEN: A bear.

JEFF: How can you tell?

EILEEN: He smells like a bear.

JEFF: What does a bear smell like?

EILEEN: Like a bear.

JEFF: Do I have a smell?
EILEEN: Sure!
JEFF: *(nervous)* What do I smell like?
EILEEN: *(smiling)* Like a Jeff.

(Dissolve to: The bird house. JEFF *and* EILEEN *appear. Then we slowly move to* JEFF'S *point of view—the screen goes black. We hear the weird, strange, frightening screams of birds—trills, caws, yelps, whistles, etc. Slowly, then, the screen grows light and we see* JEFF *and* EILEEN *walking through the bird house.* JEFF *is growing nervous.)*

EILEEN: It's all right.
JEFF: Let's get out of here.
EILEEN: Okay.

(They exit. Outside JEFF *stops and* EILEEN *turns to him.)*

JEFF: Those noises were like a nightmare—if nightmares have noises. I'm not sure of anything. I mean, I feel disoriented—like I'm in space or something. I'm afraid if I take a step, I'll fall a million miles. Lee, I'm scared.
EILEEN: It's okay, Jeff. Honest.
JEFF: Do you ever feel like this?
EILEEN: No. You get over those things. You get your confidence.
JEFF: How long does it take?

EILEEN: Well, see—I've been this way as long as I can remember. I've never known anything different. It's harder for people who lose their sight. They're much more scared. *(She takes his arm and they walk on.)* Hey, I just thought of something funny.

JEFF: What?

EILEEN: The blind leading the blind.

JEFF: How do you know your way around so well?

EILEEN: Oh, I've been here lots of times. When you're blind, you get maps in your head. I know exactly where I am right now. There's a phone booth right about here. *(She feels it with her cane.)* Excuse me. I promised to call Mom.

(She steps in and closes the door. There is a man sitting across the walk from JEFF. *He has a dog with him, off the leash. It is a tiny dog, a toy poodle. The dog runs over to* JEFF *and begins barking. To* JEFF, *this tiny creature sounds like the Hound of the Baskervilles.)*

JEFF: Go 'way. *(The dog barks louder.)* Hey, go away! *(The dog barks louder.* JEFF *begins to edge back and poke out with his cane. The dog snaps at the cane.)* Get out of here! *(Almost terrified,* JEFF *gets into the phone booth with* EILEEN.*)*

EILEEN: Hey, what's wrong?

JEFF: There's a ferocious dog after me.

EILEEN: Huh?

JEFF: He tried to attack me.

(The man walks over to retrieve the dog.)

MAN: Fluff! Come on, Fluff!

EILEEN: Fluff?

JEFF: Yeah—

EILEEN: That's a funny name for a monster.

(The man walks away with the dog on a leash. JEFF *and* EILEEN *wait inside for a moment.)*

EILEEN: Look, I think it's all right now. Come on.

(They leave the booth and start on their way. Dissolve to: Another area of the park. It is peaceful as they stroll by a pond. Across the way there appears an ice cream man riding a bicycle with attached

---

ferocious (fuh ROH shus) savage; vicious

freezer. As he pedals, the bells on the bar of the bicycle tinkle.)

JEFF: Wait—listen. *(They pause as* JEFF *listens.)*

EILEEN: What?

JEFF: Sh-h! *(He holds his finger to his lips. We become very aware of the tinkling bells as they fade away.)* What a nice sound. I never realized how nice a sound that was before.

EILEEN: Yeah.

JEFF: You really hear things like this.

*(*EILEEN *smiles and they stroll on. In the pond two ducks begin a dialogue in the chatty almost whispering way of contented ducks.)*

EILEEN: Hear the ducks.

JEFF: Yeah. *(pause)* It's as if I never heard ducks before.

EILEEN: Hey, do me a favor, huh?

JEFF: Sure.

EILEEN: I want to feel what you look like. *(She holds her hand up in front of his face.)* Okay? *(She runs her hand over his face, down his nose, across his forehead, and so on.)*

JEFF: *(trying to be casual)* Well?

EILEEN: Well, your nose is kinda big.

JEFF: Thanks a lot.

EILEEN: And your ears stick out.

JEFF: They do not.

EILEEN: A little.

JEFF: Okay—a little. But not so's you'd notice. *(He smiles.)*

EILEEN: That's a nice smile.

JEFF: I'm glad you like something.

EILEEN: All in all, it's a nice face.

JEFF: You think so?

EILEEN: Yeah, it's a really nice face.

JEFF: *(smiling)* You had me worried there for a minute.

(There is an embarrassed pause. EILEEN *lets her hand drop from* JEFF'S *face.)*

EILEEN: Hey, come on, Nice Face.

(Dissolve to: Music and a colorful moving merry-go-round. JEFF *and* EILEEN *are standing beside it. The ticket taker is standing on the moving merry-go-round, holding onto a horse. As the horses pass by, we see a few teenagers riding on them and, of course, some*

kids with their parents. The machine slowly stops and the music runs down.)

EILEEN: There's a step here, kinda high.

JEFF: Okay.

EILEEN: You got it.

(They climb on. The ticket taker, a burly man, notices them and comes over.)

TICKET TAKER: Hey—you there.

JEFF: What?

TICKET TAKER: You've got to get off.

JEFF: What do you mean?

TICKET TAKER: I said you've got to get off. I can't take you people.

JEFF: What people? We just want a ride.

TICKET TAKER: It ain't allowed. I can't have blind people on the horses.

EILEEN: Come on, Jeff. It's no big deal.

JEFF: No, wait a minute. We're all right. I've been on this ride a million times.

TICKET TAKER: Not with me here, buddy. I ain't covered.

Jeff: Huh?

TICKET TAKER: I don't have insurance for your kind. Now look, I don't want to be mean. So come on. Let me help you off.

JEFF: Get your hands off me.

TICKET TAKER: *(takes* JEFF'S *arm)* My customers want to ride.

EILEEN: Come on, Jeff. It's all right. It's okay.

TICKET TAKER: Thanks, lady. Thanks.

JEFF: No, wait! It's not okay. Nothing's gonna happen. We just want a crummy ride, that's all.

(A kid sitting on a horse yells "Hey, mister, let's go" and is joined by a few other kids.)

EILEEN: Come on, Jeff. Please.

(They go. JEFF *stumbles, almost falling. The ticket taker walks to the lever on the merry-go-round. It begins to move. The music blares. The kids smile, laugh, wave.* JEFF *and* EILEEN *stand helplessly on the side.*

---

burly (BUR lee) excellent, noble, big and strong

Dissolve to: A street in the park. JEFF *and* EILEEN *are standing on the curb, waiting to cross to the other side. Cars are whizzing by. The traffic light is green, but then there is a click. It turns to yellow, then red.)*

EILEEN: Hey, it's red.

(They begin to cross. JEFF *moves slowly. He has trouble getting down the curb.)*

JEFF: It's okay?

EILEEN: Yeah, come on. They don't give you a lot of time.

(They move across. The engines seem to be running too loudly. One of them revs up as if readying for a race. A couple of drivers in back begin to honk.)

JEFF: *(angry and nervous)* Hold your horses!

(A driver beside JEFF *suddenly revs his engine.* JEFF *jumps.)*

JEFF: What's wrong with those guys?

EILEEN: It's okay.

JEFF: *(The traffic light has just clicked.)* We're not even half way. *(He stumbles.)*

EILEEN: It's all right. Come on.

JEFF: Don't they know we're blind?

EILEEN: They'll wait.

JEFF: *(He has heard another click.)* It turned green!

(The cars in the lane behind them begin to move, taking off with a screech. The car nearest JEFF *revs its engine.)*

JEFF: *(turns to the car and waves his cane)* Shut up!

(Again the screen goes black, giving us JEFF'S *point of view. We hear the noise of the horns, tires, traffic becomes a roar. Then the picture gradually returns and we see* JEFF *frantically begin to take off his glasses, clawing at his face.)*

EILEEN: What are you doing?

JEFF: Taking this junk off!

EILEEN: No! *(She takes his arm, firmly leading him on.)* Not yet! *(They are at the other side now.* JEFF *is breathing deeply.)* It's okay. Take it easy.

JEFF: I'm sorry. I panicked.
EILEEN: Listen, it's all right. Just rest a minute.
JEFF: Such a coward. I'm sorry. *(Pause.* EILEEN *takes his arm.)* How do you do it?
EILEEN: You get used to it.
JEFF: Do you? Do you really?
EILEEN: Hey, let's go.

(Dissolve to: Another part of the park. They are alone and pass a flowering lilac bush.)

EILEEN: Hey, wait a minute. *(She stops at the bush.)*
JEFF: What?
EILEEN: Come here. *(*JEFF *returns.)* Smell that. *(*JEFF *inhales.)* Feel. *(They both feel the same puff of flowers.)* Some kind of flowers.
JEFF: There's a big puff of them. And soft.
EILEEN: What kind are they?
JEFF: I don't know.
EILEEN: They're beautiful. I'd like to know.
JEFF: I'll ask somebody.
EILEEN: There's no one around.
JEFF: Oh.
EILEEN: Do me a favor.
JEFF: Okay.
EILEEN: Take that stuff off your eyes.
JEFF: Now?

EILEEN: Yes. Now.

(He hesitates, then begins to remove the glasses and the picture fades to JEFF'S *point of view. It is black and quiet. Then, as the last patch comes off, we see the lilac bush. The purple flowers are gorgeous.)*

JEFF: *(showing surprise, pleasure)* Oh!

EILEEN: Tell me. . . .

JEFF: Well, they're purple. Dark purple. Lots of little flowers on a stem. Four or five little petals on a flower. They're beautiful. . . . *(He turns around, slowly, with appreciation.)* Everything's beautiful. The sky . . . the trees . . . the grass. . . . *(laughs with pleasure)* It's like a fairy tale. I never realized—look, Eileen—*(He suddenly realizes with stunning clarity that she can never take off patches and see.)* I'm sorry.

EILEEN: It's okay, Jeff. I can feel how nice it is from your voice.

JEFF: You can? *(He stares at her for a long moment.)* You know what's beautiful?

EILEEN: What?

JEFF: You're beautiful.

EILEEN: You mean that?

JEFF: I mean it. *(There is a long moment as she returns his stare by taking his arm. Then, embarrassed, they turn and start on their way.)* Hey, wait a minute. *(He goes back and picks a sprig from the lilac bush.)*

EILEEN: What are you doing?

JEFF: I'm taking one of these. They'll forgive me just this once. *(He takes her hand and puts the sprig of flowers into it.)*

EILEEN: Thank you. *(She smells it.)* Um-m-m. *(She puts it in her hair, takes his arm, and they walk on.)*

JEFF: *(casual, happy)* You know, I heard about this dance our two schools are having, after the game.

EILEEN: *(casual and happy too)* Yeah, I've heard about it.

JEFF: Want to go with me?

EILEEN: Why not?

JEFF: *(laughing)* Why not?

(The screen slowly fades to black.)

---

clarity (CLAR uh tee) the condition or state of being clear

FOCUS ON THE SELECTION

UNDERSTAND THE SELECTION

Recall

1. How does Jeff first discover that Eileen is blind?
2. What does Eileen tell Mrs. Hayes she would like to see more than anything?
3. How does Eileen know whether she is paying someone with a five dollar bill or a ten dollar bill?

Infer

4. Why is color the hardest thing for a blind person to imagine?
5. Why does Jeff throw Eileen in the pool?
6. Why does Jeff put dark patches and sun glasses over his eyes?
7. Why won't Eileen let Jeff take his patches off when he panics?

Apply

8. What parts of the story show that Eileen is sensitive about being blind?
9. How does Jeff show that he is not comfortable with Eileen's blindness?
10. What could Eileen do to make people more comfortable around her?

Respond to Literature

What does Jeff learn about Eileen's inner space?

WRITE ABOUT THE SELECTION

In ''Blind Sunday,'' Jeff finds that he sometimes needs verbal directions from sighted people in order to find his way. An example of this is the scene in which he has just gotten out of a taxi in front of Eileen's house and asks the cab driver to point him in the direction of the front door. Imagine you are telling a blind person how to go from your desk to the door of the classroom. Write a set of directions that would allow the person to go from your desk to the door without help.

Prewriting: Walk to the door from your chair. Notice what you are doing. Think about how you would describe it. Draw a rough diagram of your classroom, showing the route to the door. Make a note of approximate distances and what objects and people you pass along the way.

Writing: Use your diagram to write directions. Write the directions so that a person could get to the door without being able to see.

Revising: Follow your directions exactly to see if they get you to the door. Revise them as necessary.

Proofreading: Read your directions to check for errors. Be sure that all your sentences begin with capital letters and end with periods, question marks, or exclamation marks. Check your internal punctuation as well.

THINK ABOUT WORD MEANINGS

Words have literal meanings. Some words also suggest meanings or associations. Words may have a positive or negative connotation.

1. What did Eileen mean to suggest by calling Andy "Fido, the guide dog"?
2. How does her suggested meaning differ from the literal meaning of her words?
3. Why does Eileen use this expression to suggest a meaning rather than stating literally what she means?
4. In "Blind Sunday," what other expressions have a connotation different from their denotation?
5. Suppose you understood only the literal meanings of these words and expressions. What might you misunderstand in the story?

DEVELOP YOUR VOCABULARY

When you find new words in a story, you will gain understanding of the words if you notice how they are used. Are they used to describe the setting, the characters, or the character's problems or goals?

Think about the words listed below. Do you remember what the author used them to describe? Find each word in the story. Decide which of the following ways the author used each word.

1. To describe the setting.
2. To describe a character.
3. To tell what a character wanted.
4. To explain or illustrate a character's problem.
5. To show how the problem was solved.
6. To describe a character's feelings.
7. To be part of or describe the action.

Review the meanings of these words from "Blind Sunday." Write a very short story using all of these words.

1. execute
2. encounter
3. astride
4. infuriate
5. ferocious
6. burly
7. clarity

UNIT 2 REVIEW

LITERATURE-BASED WRITING

1. All the characters in the selections in this unit have learned something about themselves. Imagine that two of the characters meet each other and begin to discuss what they have learned about their own or other people's inner space through the experiences in their stories? Write the conversation as a dialogue for a short story.

Prewriting: Before you begin to write, choose two characters that learned the lessons that are the most interesting to you. Then think about what each character should have learned in the selection. For each character make a column and list the points that the character would make.

Writing: Use your list to write your dialogue. Have the characters say their lines the way they talked in the story.

Revising: Revise the conversation. Make sure that each character behaves and talks as that character really would behave and talk. Cross out anything that seems wrong for the character. Add details that would make the characters more real.

Proofreading: Read your conversation to check for errors. Be sure that you have enclosed each speaker's exact words in quotation marks. Use commas or other punctuation to separate the quotes from the rest of the sentence.

2. You have studied the elements of poetry—its forms, its content, its techniques, and its purpose. You have learned about specific techniques such as imagery, symbolism, and figures of speech such as similes and metaphors. Choose a poem that you liked or disliked. Write a review of the poem, commenting on its form, its content, the specific techniques used, and its purpose.

Prewriting: Review the work you did for the "Learn About" sections in this unit. Reread the section called "Elements of Poetry." Then make a chart that has four columns. Label one column *form,* one *content,* another *techniques,* and another *purpose.* In each of the columns make specific notes about the selection.

Writing: Write a review of the poem, commenting on its form, content, techniques, and purpose. You may comment on these elements in any order that you wish.

Revising: Revise your review. Make it clear to the reader when you are commenting on the form, content, techniques, or purpose of the poem.

Proofreading: Read your review to check for errors. Be sure that all your sentences begin with capital letters and end with periods, question marks, or exclamation marks.

BUILDING LANGUAGE SKILLS

Vocabulary

Sometimes you can use context clues to understand the meaning of a word you don't know. A **context clue** is a word or group of words near the unfamiliar word that gives clues about its meaning. The context clues may be in the same sentence, or in the sentences before or after the one in which the word appears.

Sometimes there will be a word in the same sentence, or a nearby sentence, that means the opposite. Such a word is an **antonym.** In the poem "Thumbprint," the line "No other, however grand or base . . ." contains the two words *grand* and *base.* The word *or* tells us that they are probably opposites, so *base* must mean the opposite of *grand.* A context clue may also be a **synonym,** or word that means nearly the same as the unfamiliar word.

Read the following sentences. Underline the context clues that suggest the meaning of the *italicized* word, and label them *synonym, antonym, definition,* or *example.*

1. Madame Roberge was *miserly,* not generous.
2. In a story a character tries to *attain,* or reach, a goal.
3. Every team needs a *strategy,* a well-thought out plan of action, for each game.
4. The cat was a *nuisance.* It ate food off the plates on the table and shed hair over everything.

Usage and Mechanics

When you write names, dates, and addresses, you can save space by using abbreviations. An **abbreviation** is a form of a word that has been shortened.

When you write names you may abbreviate titles. For example, in "Aquí se Habla Español" the following are examples of titles and their abbreviations.

- The author writes Mr. Chavez instead of Mister Chavez.
- The author writes Mrs. Chavez instead of Mistress Chavez.

Many women today prefer the title Ms., whether or not they are married. Other examples of abbreviated titles include *Dr.* for *Doctor, Jr.* for *Junior, Sr.* for *Senior, Lt.* for *Lieutenant, Hon.* for *Honorable,* and *Rev.* for *Reverend.*

Write a very short letter. Include your address and the date in the heading. Use the person's last name and a title of respect in the greeting. Abbreviate titles, names of states and streets, and names of months. Use the dictionary to find the correct abbreviation. If you are writing a letter to someone who lives outside the United States, be sure to include the abbreviation, if any, for the foreign country.

UNIT 2 REVIEW

SPEAKING AND LISTENING

Do you remember the children's rhyme "The Itsy Bitsy Spider" and the pantomime that accompanied it? If you do, then you are familiar with narrative pantomime. **Narrative pantomime** is a kind of creative drama. Using creative drama to extend a story allows you to interpret characters and understand their actions. In narrative pantomime the leader narrates the story while other participants act out the words.

There are some simple guidelines to follow when you want to adjust a story or a poem to the technique of narrative pantomime. Read them over and try to imagine a selection in this unit that may be suitable for this type of creative drama.

1. Look for a story or an episode in a story with lots of action, a fairly simple plot, and little or no dialogue.

2. Edit the selection or the part of the selection so that the action of the narrative pantomime is speeded up. Take out "talky" sections, condense the time span if necessary, and cut or add additional description to make the action flow more logically and sequentially.

3. Discuss what gestures and movements will accompany the narrator.

4. Rehearse with dialogue and gestures a couple of times. Make suggestions for improvements—no personal comments—just some new ideas on which to focus. Consider what would be more visual for your audience and what might improve your narrative pantomime.

5. Understand that no character development occurs in simple narrative pantomime; it is just a literal interpretation of a story or poem. What this technique will focus upon is action, setting and sequence.

6. Do not make your production too complex. That would take longer than the time available to you. Keep it simple and you will find the activity easy to complete.

Now, with a small group of your classmates choose a story or a poem, or a section of a story or poem from this unit. Read the selection together, round-robin style, so you have a clear idea of what it is about. Then, put your heads together to create a narrative pantomime. Try to keep it between five and seven minutes. Follow the guidelines above. They will give you a basis from which to work. Enjoy working out this idea and presenting it to your class. Who knows, you may even take your show on the road!

CRITICAL THINKING

Sometimes when you think about two people or things you think about how they are alike. When you describe the ways in which two things are alike you are making a **comparison** between them. You may notice that your dog and cat are both furry and like to be petted. Both seem to be thinking about food all the time. When you discuss these similarities, or ways that they are the same, you are comparing them.

On the other hand, you may notice that your dog barks noisily when people come to the door, and your cat runs and hides. Your dog may gulp down everything you give him. The cat may sniff everything suspiciously. When you discuss the differences between them you are **contrasting** them. Almost any two people, animals, objects or ideas that you can think of are alike in some ways and different in others. Choose two characters from any of the selections that you have read.

1. **Compare** the two characters by telling how they are alike.
2. **Contrast** the two characters by telling how they are different.

EFFECTIVE STUDYING

After reading a chapter in a book, many people are unable to remember what they have read. When you look up something in a dictionary or an encyclopedia, however, you usually remember what you have read because you are seeking the answer to a question you have in your mind.

You can set your own purpose when you read by asking yourself some questions. One easy way to do this is to make a question out of the title. For example, if you read the title "The Confidence Game," you could ask yourself, "What was the confidence game?" What are some questions you could make out of "The Donkey Who Did Not Want to Be Himself"?

To ask questions, you need to know what a selection is about. You can get this information from titles, subheadings, or pictures.

In reading fiction, a good question to ask is, "What will happen next?"

Choose five selections and write questions that a reader could keep in mind while reading them. Make questions out of the title, or ask questions about what will happen next.

UNIT 3

Monsters

The person who fights monsters should be careful that he doesn't become a monster himself.

—Friedrich Nietzsche

Ming noble's badge, 17th century.
Art Resource, New York.

Monsters. When you were a young child, did you ever think there might have been monsters under your bed or in your closet? Do you remember any of your friends thinking there might have been monsters somewhere in their homes? When you or your friends thought of a monster, what sort of creature did you picture? The word *monster* has many meanings. For example, it can mean a creature that is enormous. It can also mean something frightening, regardless of its size; and it can mean any animal or plant with an abnormal shape or structure. For example, a dog with two tails could be called a monster. However, when you think of a monster, you probably think of a more frightening-looking creature.

Monsters are usually viewed with more fear than are very dangerous, real life animals such as tigers or grizzly bears. Sometimes monsters are believed to possess terrifying supernatural powers.

Monsters are common in folklore and myths. If you have read *The Hobbit* by J.R.R. Tolkien you have read about terrible monsters. If you have read fairy tales you have probably read about monsters such as dragons and trolls. People usually assume that monsters intend to harm them.

The selections in this unit will help you focus on the nature of a monster. You will also see what appear to be monsters to the characters.

Whose Monster? Sometimes the same creature can be a monster to one person and not to another. In "Staley Fleming's Hallucination" by Ambrose Bierce, Staley Fleming has nightmares about a Newfoundland dog that belonged to a murder victim.

Mythical Monsters. Monsters in folklore and myths often have forms with both human and animal characteristics. Many are partly human in form, while others resemble animals that really exist. Why do you suppose people imagined monsters that resembled real animals?

Many myths are about the efforts of great heroes to kill or overcome a mythical monster. In Eden Force Eskin's retelling of the myth "Perseus and Medusa" Perseus undertakes the dangerous task of killing Medusa, a

monster so ugly that one sight of her turns men to stone. In "Theseus and the Minotaur," also retold by Eden Force Eskin, Theseus promises to save many countrymen by slaying the Minotaur, a people-eating monster.

The next two selections are poems. In "Medusa at Her Vanity" by Tom Ditch, we learn more about Medusa. In "The Bat" by Theodore Roethke, we explore how an animal may appear as a monster.

One well-known mythical monster is the dragon. In Robert Arthur's "Mr. Dexter's Dragon," Waldo Dexter buys an old book which contains a picture of a dragon. The first page bears a warning that the book should not be opened at night. Unfortunately Mr. Dexter ignores the warning.

Monsters and Real Animals. Over the years, people have reported seeing monsters that are very similar to real animals, both present-day and prehistoric. The enormous monster in "The Fog Horn" by Ray Bradbury resembles a dinosaur. It is drawn to the lighthouse by the cry of the horn. For many years, a large ten-armed monster was reported seen by fishermen. Then, when science discovered the giant squid these stories were finally explained. "The Ten-Armed Monster of Newfoundland" by Elma Schemenauer tells the story of this discovery.

The Monster in Human Beings. Certain qualities in human beings can be as dangerous as those of any monster. "The Monsters Are Due on Maple Street" by Rod Serling, is a play taken from the series *The Twilight Zone.* The residents of Maple Street are expecting monsters from outer space. Instead they discover a more terrifying monster within.

We are all keenly aware of people abuse, mass murder of innocent people, war, and terrorism. Could any monsters be more terrifying or destructive than the monster that lurks in human beings?

Which of the creatures in these selections seem like real monsters? Which monsters exist only in the imagination of the characters? How would you deal with the monsters facing these characters?

Learn About

Character Traits

A story is about characters and their efforts to resolve a problem or conflict, or reach a goal. Characters can be people, animals, or objects.

When you are reading a story, are the characters so real to you that they seem like friends? If they do, the author has allowed you to get to know the characters well. Well-drawn characters are often based on people the author knows well.

How do you get to know characters in a story? Sometimes the author will describe their physical traits or will sometimes allude to other traits, such as greediness, shyness, or generosity.

In life you learn about character traits by seeing what people say or do or listening to what people tell you about others. You can also tell what story characters are like by how they behave and what they say.

As you read "Staley Fleming's Hallucination," ask yourself these questions:

1. What were Staley Fleming's traits?
2. How were his traits revealed?

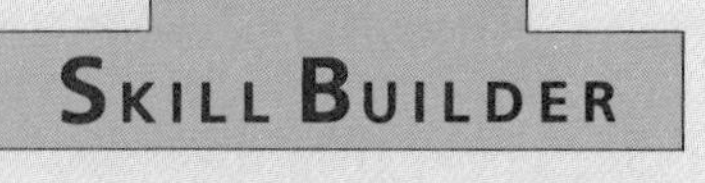

Skill Builder

Write a paragraph about a character, either a real person that you know, or a character that you make up. Describe the character's traits.

STALEY FLEMING'S HALLUCINATION

by Ambrose Bierce

Two men were talking. One was a doctor.

"I sent for you, Doctor," said the other. "But I don't think you can do me any good. Maybe you can recommend a specialist in psychiatry. I think I'm a bit loony."

"You look all right," the doctor said.

"You shall judge—I have hallucinations," said Staley Fleming. "I wake every night and see in my room—watching me—a big black Newfoundland dog with a white forefoot."

"You say you wake," replied the doctor. "Are you sure about that? Hallucinations are sometimes only dreams."

"Oh, I wake, all right. Sometimes I lie still a long time, looking at the dog as hard as he looks at me. I always leave the light going. When I can't stand it any longer I sit up in bed—and nothing is there!"

"Hmm, hmm . . . What's the beast's expression?" asked the doctor.

"It seems evil to me. Of course I know that an animal's face always has the same expression—except in art. But this is not a real animal. Newfoundland dogs are pretty gentle looking, you know. What's the matter with this one?"

"Really, I can't give a diagnosis. I'm not going to treat the dog."

The doctor laughed at his own joke. But he watched his patient from the corner of his eye. Presently he said, "Fleming, your description of the beast fits the dog of the late Atwell Barton."

---

recommend (rek uh MEND) suggest someone who would be good for a job

hallucination (huh loo sin AY shun) seeing something that does not really exist

Newfoundland dog (NOO fun lund DOG) a kind of large, strong dog with a thick black coat

diagnosis (dy ug NOH sis) a decision about the kind of illness a person has

Fleming half rose from his chair. Then he sat again and tried not to look interested. "I remember Barton," he said. "I believe he was—it was reported that—wasn't there something suspicious in his death?"

Looking right into the eyes of his patient, the doctor said, "Three years ago, the body of your old enemy, Atwell Barton, was found in the woods near his home and yours. He had been stabbed to death. There have been no arrests. There was no clue. Some of us had theories. I have one. Have you?"

"I? Why, what could I know about it?" Fleming said. "You remember that I left for Europe almost immediately afterward—quite a while afterward. In the few weeks since my return, you could not expect me to come up with a theory. In fact, I have not given the matter a thought. What about his dog?"

"It was the first to find the body. It died of starvation on his grave."

We do not know much about the law of coincidences. Staley Fleming did not either. Or perhaps he would not have sprung to his feet as the night wind brought in through the open window the long wailing howl of a distant dog. He strode several times across the room in the steady gaze of the doctor. Then, suddenly facing him, Fleming almost shouted, "What has all this to do with my trouble, Dr. Halderman? You forget why you were sent for."

Rising, the doctor laid his hand on his patient's arm and said gently, "Pardon me. I cannot diagnose your problem without giving it more time. Tomorrow, perhaps. Please go to bed. Leave your door unlocked. I will pass the night here with your books. Can you call me without getting up?"

"Yes, there is an electric bell."

"Good. If anything disturbs you, push the button without sitting up. Good night."

Comfortably settled in an armchair, the doctor stared into the glowing coals and thought deeply for a long time. But he frequently rose and opened a door leading to the staircase. He listened carefully. Then he went back to his seat. Presently,

---

theory (THEE uh ree) idea that is used to explain an event
coincidence (koh IN suh duns) two or more things that happen at the same time, by accident
strode (STROHD) walked; past tense of stride

Animals,
Rufino Tamayo.
Collection, The Museum
of Modern Art, New York
Inter-American Fund

however, he fell asleep. When he woke, it was past midnight. He stirred the fire and lifted a book from the table at his side. He opened it at random and began to read.

"All flesh has spirit," the book said. "Flesh can take on the power of spirit. Also, the spirit can take on the power of the flesh. And there are those who say that beasts as well as humans can do this, and . . ."

The reading was interrupted by a shaking of the house, as if a heavy object had fallen. The doctor flung down the book, rushed from the room, and mounted the stairs to Fleming's bedroom. He tried the door, but it was locked—against his orders. He set his shoulder against it with such force that it gave way. On the floor near the disordered bed, in his nightclothes, lay Staley Fleming gasping away his life.

The doctor raised the dying man's head from the floor and observed a wound in the throat. "I should have thought of this," he said. The doctor believed it was suicide.

When the man was dead, an examination showed the unmistakable marks of an animal's fangs deeply sunken into the neck.

But no animal was to be found.

---

at random (at RAN dum) happening by chance, with no plan
unmistakable (un mih STAYK uh bul) clear; without being able to make a mistake about something

FOCUS ON THE SELECTION

UNDERSTAND THE SELECTION

Recall

1. What hallucination did Staley Fleming describe to the doctor?
2. What fits that description?
3. How did Atwell Barton's dog die?

Infer

4. Why did Fleming half rise from his chair and then try not to look interested when Atwell Barton was mentioned?
5. What do you think was the doctor's theory about Barton's death?
6. Why was Staley Fleming seeing the dog at night?
7. How did Staley Fleming die?

Apply

8. What facts make it appear likely that Staley Fleming killed Atwell Barton?
9. Predict what would have happened if the doctor had stayed with Fleming.
10. At the beginning of the story Staley Fleming says he thinks he is a bit loony. Do you agree? Explain your answer.

Respond to Literature

Who was the monster in this selection?

WRITE ABOUT THE SELECTION

At the end of "Staley Fleming's Hallucination," Fleming is found dead under mysterious circumstances and the police are called. Imagine you are a policeman called to Fleming's home. Write a police report describing what you find when you arrive. Report the facts and the statements of witnesses.

A police report gives detailed descriptions and facts. The police must be, however, careful to leave opinions out of their reports.

Prewriting: Imagine Fleming's bedroom. You will need to invent some details. Draw a diagram showing the room, the bed, and the body. Show the marks on Fleming's throat.

Writing: Use your diagram to write your report. Include details about when Fleming was last seen alive. Report what the doctor said.

Revising: Revise your report. Add facts and details to give a clear picture of what happened. Cross out anything that is opinion.

Proofreading: Read your report to check for errors. Be sure all your sentences begin with capital letters and end with periods, question marks, or exclamation marks. Use the dictionary to check your spelling.

THINK ABOUT CHARACTER TRAITS

A character's traits can be inferred from their words and actions. Sometimes all of the actions are not directly described in the selection. You must infer, or figure out, the character's actions.

1. What were Staley Fleming's character traits?
2. How did his words reveal his traits?
3. How did his actions reveal his traits?
4. What actions did you have to infer?
5. Did another person's thoughts tell you anything about Fleming's traits? If so, what were these thoughts and what did they tell you?

DEVELOP YOUR VOCABULARY

Usually you use the dictionary to look up definitions for unfamiliar words. However, even if you know the meaning of a word, a dictionary can give you other important information. You can find spelling, pronunciation, or the part of speech in a dictionary. The dictionary will also provide information on how to form the plural, past tense, or the comparative forms of a word. Some dictionaries also include the origin of a word. A dictionary will sometimes include sentences to show how a word is used correctly. Studying all the parts in a dictionary entry will help you add the word to your working vocabulary.

In a dictionary, look up these words from "Staley Fleming's Nightmare." Use each in an original sentence to show that you understand not only the meaning, but how to use it correctly in writing.

1. recommend
2. hallucination
3. diagnosis
4. presently
5. coincidence
6. strode
7. random
8. unmistakable

Perseus Slaying Medusa, Anonymous. Northwind Picture Archive

LEARN ABOUT

Myths

Suppose you were born in a time before scientists understood much about the world. **Myths** are stories which were created in ancient times to explain events in the world, especially in nature. They also attempt to explain human behavior and conditions of life. In myths much is explained by the actions and decisions of gods who possessed supernatural powers.

Myths describe the important beliefs of a specific culture or group of people. However, the events in myths did not really happen.

In some cultures, myths were used to give reasons for rules and customs. For example, a king might say that his ancestor was appointed by the gods to rule the people.

Many of the best known myths originated in ancient Greece. The next two selections are Greek myths.

As you read each myth, ask yourself:

1. What characteristics of a myth do you find in these stories?
2. What elements tell you the story is not true?

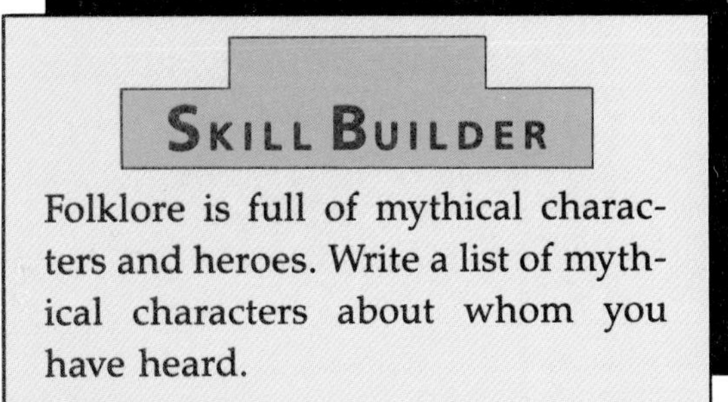

SKILL BUILDER

Folklore is full of mythical characters and heroes. Write a list of mythical characters about whom you have heard.

PERSEUS AND MEDUSA

Retold by Eden Force Eskin

Medusa! Even her name made people shrink with terror. She was a hideous monster with long pointed teeth, claws of brass, golden scales like those of a fish or a dragon, and a pair of wings. The most frightening thing about Medusa's appearance, however, was the living serpents that grew out of her head instead of hair. One look at this ugly creature could turn people to stone—and many brave heroes were now just stone statues.

Medusa was one of three sisters called the Gorgons. They lived in the Hall of the Gorgons, a huge cave with a strange glow but very little light to see by. All around the cave were stone statues of men and beasts. These were once real people and animals, until they looked at Medusa. Except for these statues, little else could be seen in the dim and smoky hall. Although two of these sisters were immortal, the third one, Medusa, was not. She could be killed if someone could find a way to do it and remain alive.

Despite the great danger, a young man named Perseus had promised to kill Medusa—and now he had to keep his promise. Perseus was the son of a princess named Danaë, and he and his mother lived far from their own land, Argos. Danaë's father, the king of Argos, had sent them to sea in a great wooden chest because he was afraid for his life. A prophecy had warned the king that Danaë would have a son who would one day kill his

---

Medusa (muh DOOS uh)
hideous (HID ee us) very ugly; horrible to look at
serpent (SUR punt) snake
Perseus (PUR see us)
Danaë (DAN uh ee)
prophecy (PROF ih see) statement telling what will happen in the future

grandfather. To keep the prophecy from coming true, the king forced Danaë and Perseus to leave Argos.

So the king sent a great wooden chest carrying Danaë and Perseus to sea. It landed on an island ruled by a man named Polydectes. Although Polydectes was not always kind to Danaë and Perseus, he did allow them to live on his island. On this island, the baby Perseus grew into a handsome young man, and it was to Polydectes that he made the promise to kill Medusa. If he did not keep his promise, he and his mother would be in serious trouble.

Polydectes was about to be married, and he demanded that Perseus bring him Medusa's head as a wedding present. Perseus was glad to promise almost anything, especially since Polydectes had stopped trying to marry Danaë, who disliked him. Nevertheless, this promise was more than he had planned on, and it was going to be very difficult to keep.

Perseus said good-bye to his mother and set out to find Medusa. He was not sure how to go about it, but help soon came to him in the form of the god Hermes and the goddess Athena. Hermes was the guide and the swift messenger of the gods. He gave Perseus a helmet of darkness that would make the wearer invisible, a curved sword of the strongest metal known, and a magic pouch. Then Hermes removed his own winged sandals and lent them to Perseus. Hermes told Perseus that he must first find the Gray Sisters; they were the only ones who knew how to find Medusa.

Athena, the goddess of wisdom, appeared to Perseus in a dream. She gave him her bright shield that shone like a mirror. She told him to look only at Medusa's image in the shield and never at the creature herself. If he did not look directly at her, he would be safe. Then she told him where to find the Gray Sisters.

Perseus awoke and went in search of the Gray Sisters. He found them in a damp cave filled with cobwebs and insects. There was a smell of seawater and seaweed in their cave. The walls felt moist and chilly. The Gray Sisters were strange creatures with the bodies of swans and heads and hands that

---

Polydectes (pol ih DEK teez)
Hermes (HUR meez) guide and messenger of the Greek gods
Athena (uh THEE nuh) Greek goddess of wisdom

Medusa, Caravaggio. Scala/Art Resource

were almost human. Among them, the Gray Sisters had only one eye and one tooth, which they shared. They kept passing these treasures back and forth to each other.

As they were passing the eye, Perseus grabbed it and held it away from them. They screamed and tried to get it back, but he said he would return it only when they gave him directions for finding Medusa. They had no choice and soon told him that Medusa was in the Hall of the Gorgons. He returned the eye, but before the Gray Sisters had a chance to use it, he escaped quickly from the moldy cave.

When Perseus arrived at the Hall of the Gorgons, he found the hideous Medusa asleep in the strangely lit cave. Statues of long-lost heroes stood everywhere. They were caught in poses of action, and the expressions on their faces looked lifelike. Perseus put on the helmet and became invisible. He was very much tempted to look at the monster, but he thought of Athena's words and kept his eyes on his bright shield as he carefully approached the sleeping Medusa. She and her sisters did not stir, but some of the serpents in her hair hissed in warning as Perseus came near. Then, still not looking at the creature except in the shield, he rushed forward and sliced off her head with one sweep of his super-strong sword.

While the serpents on the head still hissed and writhed, Perseus grabbed the head and put it quickly into the magic pouch. He knew that the head itself still had the power to turn people to stone, but the pouch would keep it safely out of sight.

Wearing Hermes' winged sandals, Perseus started to fly toward the island where he lived. As he flew over the country of Ethiopia, he saw a beautiful girl chained to a cliff near the sea. The sea waters were rough and often struck at her. A hideous sea monster swam below trying to devour her. The girl was Andromeda, the daughter of the king of Ethiopia. Like Perseus, she had been punished because of a prophecy although she had done no wrong. The prophecy had warned her father that chaining her to the rock was the only way to save his country from disaster.

Having seen Andromeda, Perseus fell in love with her beauty and decided to save her. He swooped down to fight the sea monster, whose body was covered with scales of iron. Perseus

---

writhe (RY*TH*) twist and turn

tried to find a place between the monster's scales to plunge his sword. Again and again they attacked each other. They fought hard and long until the cliff and waters were red with blood. Finally, Perseus gave the monster the final blow with his sword and freed Andromeda.

The princess fell in love with her brave and handsome rescuer, and her parents agreed to let them marry. Everyone was preparing to celebrate the wedding in the royal hall when another man came to claim her as his rightful bride. Andromeda had been promised in marriage to him earlier, but since he had never tried to rescue her from the sea monster, she did not think much of him. Nevertheless, now he was trying to stop her marriage to Perseus on her wedding day, and he had brought his soldiers with him. They began to attack Perseus and the wedding party. Perseus shouted to his friends to hide their eyes. Quickly he drew Medusa's head out of the magic pouch and showed it to his enemies. They all turned to stone where they stood.

At last Perseus returned with his bride to his mother. There he learned that Polydectes had not married after all. Instead, with Perseus away, he had been causing trouble for Danaë by trying to persuade her to marry him. So Perseus decided to give Polydectes the gift.

"Here," said Perseus. "I have brought you the wedding gift I promised." Saying that, he drew Medusa's head out of the pouch and held it high. Polydectes and his evil followers all turned to stone.

It was now time for Perseus to return the sandals, sword, and helmet to Hermes and to thank him for his help. He returned Athena's bright shield to her, and as a present he added Medusa's head, which could not kill an immortal like Athena. Since that time, Medusa's head has often been shown on the shield in pictures and statues of Athena.

Shortly afterward, Perseus went to compete in a great sports contest in Larissa. One contest that he entered was the discus throw. As he threw the discus high into the air, the wind caught it and shifted its direction. The discus landed on the foot of an old man who was standing there. It killed him. That man was the king of Argos, Danaë's father. The prophecy had come true.

---

plunge (PLUNJ) jab
discus (DIS kus) disk thrown for distance in athletic contests

Black-figured Greek Amphora, 6th Century B.C. The Metropolitan Museum of Art. Purchase, Joseph Pulitzer Bequest.

THESEUS AND THE MINOTAUR

Retold by Eden Force Eskin

The only son of Minos, the ruler of the island of Crete, had died when visiting the city of Athens. Minos's grief was more than he could bear, and he blamed Athens and its ruler for his son's death. Revenge was all that Minos could think of, so he invaded the city of Athens and threatened to burn it to the ground unless the Athenians followed his orders. And his orders were cruel! Every nine years, Athens would have to send seven young women and seven young men to Crete. There, they would be shut in the Labyrinth to meet their death.

The Labyrinth was a huge place—a kind of prison with winding paths that twisted and turned so that nobody could find the way out. It had been built by one of the great architects of the time. To those who were shut within its rough, rocky walls, it was dark, gloomy, and frightening. Sooner or later, anyone in the Labyrinth would run into the Minotaur. And meeting the Minotaur meant meeting death.

Minos had had the Labyrinth built to hold the Minotaur, a monster with the head of a bull and the body of a human. When

---

Theseus (THEE see us)
Minotaur (MIN uh tawr)
Labyrinth (LAB uh rinth)
Minos (MY nus)
Crete (KREET) an island in the Mediterranean Sea
Athens (ATH unz) a city in Greece
Athenian (uh THEE nee un) person from Athens, Greece
architect (AHR kuh tekt) person who designs buildings

the Minotaur found people inside the Labyrinth, it devoured them.

It was once again time for Athens to send seven young men and seven young women to Crete. And now the choice had to be made. One young man stepped forward to offer to go. It was Theseus, son of King Aegeus of Athens.

Theseus had been raised away from Athens and had grown up strong and courageous. He reached his father's home just before the time to send the young people off to their doom. The king did not want him to go. Father and son had known each other such a short time. But when Theseus explained that he intended to try to kill the Minotaur, King Aegeus had to agree.

Theseus promised his father that if he was successful, he would send a signal from the boat when it returned to Athens. The boat from Crete usually carried a black sail to show mourning for the victims of the Minotaur. Theseus promised that he would lower the black sail and raise a white sail as the ship approached Athens to show that he was still alive.

So Theseus and the others set sail for Crete. He still did not know how he would defeat the Minotaur and escape from the Labyrinth. But luck would surely be on his side.

When the Athenians reached Crete, they were paraded through the streets. Ariadne, who was Minos's daughter, saw Theseus—so strong, handsome, and brave looking. She fell in love with him and decided to help him. She found a way to meet Theseus secretly and told him that she would help him escape. In return he promised to take her back to Athens where they would marry.

Ariadne gave Theseus a spool of thread that she had gotten from the man who designed the Labyrinth. If Theseus would tie one end of the thread to the door at the entrance, he could unwind it as he made his way through the confusing paths. Then all he would have to do to find his way out was to follow the thread back to the entrance.

The thread would help Theseus escape from the Labyrinth,

---

devour (dih VOUR) eat up quickly
Aegeus (uh JEE us)
mourning (MAWRN ing) showing and feeling sorrow after someone's death
Ariadne (ar ee AD nee)

but he would have to fight the Minotaur on his own. Theseus strode boldly into the Labyrinth searching for the Minotaur. He made his way carefully among the rocky, winding paths. Suddenly, he found himself looking straight at the sleeping monster.

Theseus realized he had no weapon, but he had to act quickly before the Minotaur awoke. He prayed for strength. Then he looked at his fists—they would have to be his weapons. Quickly, he pinned the Minotaur to the ground and began to attack him with his fists. The monster stirred and snorted, but it had been caught off guard. Theseus kept attacking with his fists as the Minotaur tried to stab him with its horns. The man kept attacking the beast with crushing blows. The Minotaur tried to get to its feet to fight back, but it was already weakened by the ironlike fists. It placed its four feet on the hard rock, staggered to a standing position, and lowered its head to attack. Theseus aimed one final blow at the weak spot in the Minotaur's neck, and the beast stumbled and collapsed. The life had gone out of this creature that had caused so much terror. Theseus had won.

Then he went searching for the other Athenians in the Labyrinth and found them all safe. He gathered them together and led them out of the dark gloom of the Labyrinth into the sunlight by following the spool of thread that Ariadne had given him.

Quickly, Theseus and the Athenians took Ariadne, fled to the ship that was waiting in the harbor, and started out for Athens. On the way, Ariadne became seasick, so Theseus set her on shore while he went back to the ship to make some repairs. But a storm carried the ship out to sea. Theseus remained on board and Ariadne still lingered on land. When the storm was over, he returned and found that Ariadne had died. He was heartbroken.

Perhaps it was his sadness that made Theseus forget to change the black sail for the white as they headed into Athens. King Aegeus saw the black sail and plunged into the sea in his grief. The sea was named the Aegean Sea after the king. It is still called by that name.

After his father's death, Theseus ruled Athens as a wise and good king. Finally, he decided that the people should rule themselves. Athens became a city of liberty and democracy.

Aegean (uh JEE un)

FOCUS ON THE SELECTION

UNDERSTAND THE SELECTION

Recall

1. Describe the monsters in the stories.
2. Both heroes needed help from someone else in order to accomplish their mission. Who helped them, and how?
3. What was the prophecy in Perseus and Medusa, and how did it come true?

Infer

4. Was Athens stronger, or Crete?
5. Why did King Aegeus allow his only son to risk his life by going to Crete?
6. How did the gods feel about Medusa?
7. Why didn't the old man recognize the man who was supposed to kill him?

Apply

8. Compare the heroes in these two selections. How were they alike?
9. Do you think it was right for Perseus to use the head of Medusa to turn his enemies to stone? Explain your answer.
10. Imagine that you are the king of Athens. Minos threatens to burn Athens unless you send fourteen people to be killed each year. What will you do?

Respond to Literature

Which of the monsters in these selections seemed more frightening? Why?

WRITE ABOUT THE SELECTION

When Theseus returned to Athens many people must have been very interested in how he slew the Minotaur and managed to find his way out of the Labyrinth. Imagine that you are a newspaper reporter interviewing Theseus about his adventures on Crete. Write a series of interview questions about Theseus's adventures. Write Theseus's answers as you imagine they might have been. Identify each question with a *Q* followed by a colon, and each answer with an *A* followed by a colon:

Prewriting: List the questions you will ask Theseus about his experience with the Minotaur and his escape from the Labyrinth. Refer to the selection for ideas about the answers he might give.

Writing: Use your questions to write the interview. Write the answers that you think Theseus would give.

Revising: Revise your interview. Be sure you have organized the interview so that it is easy for readers to follow. Consider changing the order of the questions or even adding or deleting questions and answers to improve the interview.

Proofreading: Read your interview to check for errors. Be sure all your sentences begin with capital letters and end with periods, question marks, or exclamation marks. Make sure that a *Q* followed by a colon appears before each question and an *A* followed by a colon appears before each answer.

THINK ABOUT MYTHS

Myths are stories about the beliefs of a particular culture. Some myths are about the history of a people or civilization. The people who created them felt no need to distinguish between scientific facts, historical facts, and fiction. Therefore myths are often a blend of fact and fiction.

1. What characteristics of a myth did you find in these stories?
2. Which gods and goddesses played roles in these myths?
3. Which characters could have existed?
4. Which characters were imaginary?
5. How was historical fact and fiction blended in these myths?

DEVELOP YOUR VOCABULARY

There are probably many words that you recognize and understand in your reading but do not use very often. You are more likely to include words in your working vocabulary if you think about how they relate to other words. For example, you could think about what the words *devoured, architect,* and *mourning* might have to do with each other. Someone might say, "The lion devoured the architect, and his family is in mourning."

Review the meanings of these words from the two myths you read. Find them in the selections. Think about how one word might relate to another. Then write five original sentences using at least two of these words in each sentence.

1. serpent
2. prophecy
3. writhe
4. plunge
5. compete
6. discus
7. architect
8. devour
9. mourning

Learn About

Rhyme

Many poems have different rhyme patterns. In some poems, the second line rhymes with the first line. When one line rhymes with the line that follows it, the two lines are called a **couplet.** However, in another kind of poetry, known as **free verse,** the lines do not rhyme. They do not have meter nor a stanza form.

The rhyme pattern of poetry is important because it affects the flow of the language. When read aloud, rhymed poetry sounds different from free verse. A poem written in one rhyme pattern will have a very different sound and rhythm from a poem written with another rhyme pattern. Poets use the different rhyme patterns or lack of rhyme to express images differently or create special moods or feelings.

As you read each of the next two poems try to answer the following questions:

1. Does the poem contain rhyme?
2. What is the pattern of the rhyme?
3. Is the poem written in free verse?

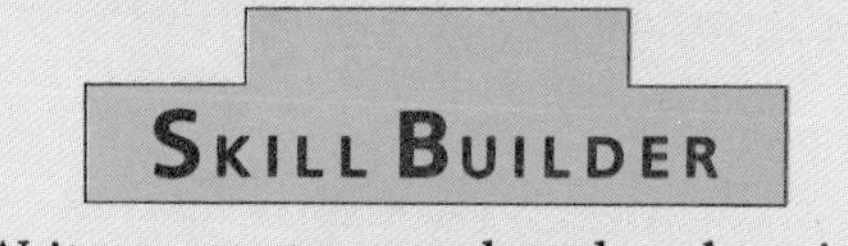

Writers create couplets by rhyming the last word in the second line with the last word in the first line. Write a couplet.

MEDUSA AT HER VANITY

by Tom Disch

Her hair, not having breakfasted,
Coils restlessly, like anxious thoughts.
She daubs some blood into her cheeks
And smears her lips with gore.
5 Deaths flutter round her and alight,
Crisping their wings on her despair.
The night drags on. She tries to read.
She feeds the snakes. She yawns
Over an abyss. It's such a bore—
10 The books, the snakes—and it will be
Like this forever, or until the dreamt-of day
A mirror appears, to die upon her kiss.

daubs (DAWBZ) coat or cover with, apply, smear
gore (GAWR) blood that is shed from a wound; usually clotted blood
abyss (uh BIS) deep, bottomless pit or gulf

THE BAT

by Theodore Roethke

By day the bat is cousin to the mouse.
He likes the attic of an aging house.

His fingers make a house about his head.
His pulse beat is so slow we think him dead.

He loops in crazy figures half the night.
Among the trees that face the corner light.

---

pulse (PULS) beat of the heart
crazy (KRAY zee) wild and excited

But when he brushes up against a screen,
We are afraid of what our eyes have seen;

For something is amiss or out of place
When mice with wings can wear a human face.

---

amiss (uh MIS) wrong; not correct

FOCUS ON THE SELECTION

UNDERSTAND THE SELECTION

Recall

1. What does Medusa put on her cheeks?
2. What does the face of a bat look like, according to the poem?
3. Describe a bat's pulse during the day.

Infer

4. What will end Medusa's boredom?
5. What is a mouse with wings?
6. Tell what is being described in the first two lines of "Medusa at her Vanity": Her hair, not having breakfasted, coils restlessly like anxious thoughts.
7. Why is the speaker afraid of the bat?

Apply

8. Suppose you had not read "Perseus and Medusa." What parts of "Medusa at her Vanity" might be hard to understand?
9. Why does the poem say that the bat is cousin to the mouse?
10. Compare and contrast "Medusa at her Vanity" with "Perseus and Medusa."

Respond to Literature

Why is the poem, "The Bat," in a unit about monsters?

WRITE ABOUT THE SELECTION

"Medusa at Her Vanity" describes Medusa, the mythical monster that Perseus slew. You will enjoy monster stories more if you can picture the monster in your mind. Use your imagination to invent a new kind of monster. Write a description of it, outlining the strange or special features that make it a monster. Include enough detail so that someone else could draw the monster from your written description.

Prewriting: Picture the monster carefully in your mind. Draw a rough sketch of what you think the monster should look like, but include all of its special details.

Writing: Looking at your sketch, write a description of your imagined monster. Give the readers enough detail so that they are then able to picture the monster in their minds. You may want your monster to be humorous, frightening, magical, or any other quality you feel is appropriate.

Revising: When you revise your description be sure to add specific details to paint a picture that your readers clearly can see. Consider adding or deleting details to make your description more effective.

Proofreading: Read your description to check for errors. Be sure all your sentences begin with capital letters and end with periods, question marks, or exclamation marks.

THINK ABOUT RHYME

Free verse has no regular rhythm nor rhyme or stanza pattern. Rhyme may occur in a number of different patterns. In a **couplet** a line follows immediately after the line with which it rhymes.

1. Which poem or poems were written in free verse?
2. Which poem or poems have rhyme?
3. What is the rhyme pattern in the poems that have rhyme?
4. How does the rhyme contribute to the feeling the poem conveys?
5. If the poem had been written in free verse, how might the feeling have been different?

DEVELOP YOUR VOCABULARY

Sometimes poems contain a word or words you do not know. However, you can often determine the meaning from the way in which it is used in the line. You can use **context clues** which are words or groups of words that come before or after a word and that give clues to its meaning. They may be in the same line or in a line before or after the one containing the unfamiliar word. Read the following line from "The Bat": "For something is amiss or out of place."

This line contains a definition of the word *amiss.* Sometimes writers use words they do not expect their readers to know, but they will supply clues about the words' meanings. Such clues may include a definition, a synonym, an antonym, an example, or some other helpful information.

Find the following words in the poems. Look for words that might have helped you determine the meaning of the word. Write any context clues you find. Then use each word in a sentence. Include in each sentence a clue such as a definition, a synonym, an antonym, or an example.

1. daubs
2. gore
3. abyss
4. pulse
5. amiss

Learn About

Humorous Tone

Have you heard people describe an incident in a way that told you they were making fun of the situation? Something about their attitude and their choice of words revealed that they knew they were describing something funny. **Tone** is what you call the attitude of speakers or writers toward their subject. You may have read some selections and noticed that the author seemed to be laughing at the characters. Some authors do make fun of their characters. It is important to notice the tone an author uses in writing a story and describing the characters. The tone adds shades of meaning to the author's words.

As you read "Mr. Dexter's Dragon," ask yourself the following questions:

1. What is the author's tone?
2. In what ways does the author show his tone?
3. What sentences make the tone obvious?

Skill Builder

When writers use a humorous tone, they usually do not need to tell the reader that they think the subject matter is funny. Write a few lines about a subject or an incident. Use a tone that implies the subject is amusing.

Mr. Dexter's Dragon

by Robert Arthur

Waldo Dexter found the book in the most ordinary of places—a secondhand shop. Not even a good secondhand shop. Just a dingy hole in the wall on Canal Street, east of Broadway. It was a region as commonplace as Manhattan has to offer.

It was a shop devoted chiefly to secondhand luggage and old clothes of the most depressing appearance. Mr. Dexter entered it in the first place only because a high wind had blown away his hat. It then whisked it in a series of eccentric leaps out of sight into a dark alley well supplied with puddles.

Waldo Dexter watched the hat vanish without emotion. He was accustomed to losing things. His hats blew away. He left his umbrellas on trains and in subways, and his glasses frequently dropped and broke. He was a smallish man, going bald. He had an eager glitter in his eye that denoted the passionate hobbyist—which he was. His specialty was the collection of books and manuscripts devoted to magic and witchcraft.

It was to stave off a cold in the head rather than because he cared how he looked that Mr. Dexter turned into the little secondhand store. There were some caps in the window, and he intended to buy one. A cap would keep his skull warm, be cheap, and wouldn't blow off. Mr. Dexter was not an impractical man, for all his eager absorption in his hobby.

It was very easy to buy a cap. The only difficulty was to avoid buying half the contents of the store. If Waldo Dexter had been a fraction more suggestible, or the small, talkative shopowner a trifle more persuasive, he might have indeed done so. Mr. Dexter, however, was firm enough to avoid this sorry consequence of his slight mishap. But he could not very well refuse the shopowner's last impassioned plea. The plea was that he at least look around to see if there positively wasn't anything else he could use.

Mr. Dexter let his glance run swiftly over the shelves, counters, and racks. Then, as if some magnetic quality in the volume had drawn his eyes to it, he saw the book on a low shelf, gathering dust.

The volume was not thick. In height

---

mishap (MIS hap) accident

and breadth it was about the shape of an old-fashioned ledger. It was bound in leather. The leather had an unusual purplish-black color and a fine, unfamiliar texture. There was no title or inscription. There was, however—and Waldo Dexter's small, gray mustache quivered with interest—an inch-wide iron strap running completely about the book. The strap kept the book not only shut but locked. For a small, rusty iron padlock of antique design was hooked through a hasp where the ends of the iron strap overlapped.

With a murmur indicating an interest so slight as to be almost nonexistent, and a gesture so casual that a word might have stopped it, Mr. Dexter reached for the book. He brought it forth and blew a fine film of dust from it.

"Hmmm," he commented, and turning a lackluster eye upon the shopowner, shook the book slightly. "What is it?" he sighed.

It was, he gathered from the instant reply, a volume of the utmost rarity. It was the personal diary of a European nobleman of note, an intimate friend of Napoleon's. It had been found in a suitcase bought by the proprietor himself at a sale of unclaimed luggage from the various hotels. It had belonged to a European gentleman who had been so uncouth as to run out on his hotel bill. At least, he had vanished from his room and never been seen again. And so the book had come into the shopowner's possession with the utmost legality. He was holding it for a collector who had offered him a hundred dollars for it. However, if Mr. Dexter cared to make a better offer—

Waldo Dexter sighed, and yawned politely. He restrained the itch that quivered in every fiber of him to see what lay behind that suggestively locked iron strap.

"If it's worth so much," he inquired, raising one eyebrow, "why did the owner have to beat his hotel bill? Why didn't he just sell the book?"

Then, not waiting for an answer, he fumbled at the small padlock. It proved to be not locked—the shopowner had picked it. Mr. Dexter swung back the cover, the iron hinge at the back moving with some difficulty. As his eye fell upon the first page, his heart pounded so with excitement that it was with the greatest effort he kept his hands steady.

The book was not a printed volume. It was handwritten in ink, with flowing letters so ornate as to be almost unreadable, upon ruled pages. The writing seemed to be a mixture of bad French and Italian, with some Latin thrown in for good measure.

It was not a diary at all, though the fact of its being handwritten might have misled an ignorant buyer.

At the top of the page, in the bold, flowing script, was written in Italian: *Recipes and Conjurations.* And beneath that a few lines of verse. Mr. Dexter, because of the complicated mixture of languages, was not able to puzzle them out. Beneath the verse was the single

---

lackluster (LAK lust ur) dull

capital letter: C.

Waldo Dexter's pulse was hammering as he flipped rapidly through the pages of the volume. He dared not inspect it more closely, lest he reveal his interest. But his gratified eye made out, at the top of several of the pages, such tantalizing headings as *To Be Invisible,* and *To Make a Demon Bring Three Bags of Gold.*

There were others, equally promising. But his scholarship was not great enough to untangle the language mixture of their wording in such a brief time. He did, however, pause to study with gleaming eyes the picture which some hand had inset into the exact center of the book.

The picture had been painted by a skilled artist upon the finest of parchment. The parchment was a trifle yellowed, but the brilliant colors of the small, hungry-looking dragon upon it were undimmed.

It was a quite repulsive little creature. It squatted upon the flagstoned floor, staring out from the page with bright yellow eyes. At a slight distance behind the dragon, the unknown artist had added a touch of artistic detail by putting in a cluttered heap of bones. Mr. Dexter did not try to make out more.

He closed the volume, yawned again, and shook his head.

"You lied to me," he accused the shopowner, looking him in the eye. "This isn't a diary at all. It's just a lot of nonsense. It's either an old copybook that some child did compositions in, or something similar. The picture's obviously a child's drawing. The whole thing isn't worth a dollar, except for the binding and clasp. If this was a real book, I might buy it, but just to put in my library as a curiosity. Even then I wouldn't give more than ten dollars for it."

He shrugged and started to put the book back. The shopowner brought forth a hasty torrent of words. Ultimately Mr. Dexter allowed himself to be persuaded. Having set his own price, he was eventually talked out of ten dollars. Presently, shaking so with suppressed eagerness he could hardly hold the paper-wrapped book in his hands, he emerged from the shop. After one quick gulp of fresh air, he dived into a taxi to be taken to Pennsylvania Station. From there he went by train to Bayside, Long Island. There he lived comfortably in a small house close to the water, tended by an aged couple.

Arriving home, Waldo Dexter popped directly into his study. There, with trembling fingers, he unwrapped his treasure. He leafed through it, at first quickly, then giving close attention to some of the pages. He spent perhaps an hour in this preliminary survey. After that, because he simply had to tell someone of his find, he took enough time out to dash off a quick letter to his nearest crony. This was one McKenzie Muir, whose residence was in the Bay Ridge section of Brooklyn.

It is (wrote Waldo Dexter) a handwritten volume of recipes and conjurations dating at least to the early eighteenth century. It is bound in, I am positive, human skin; a Senegambian's, I would

---

conjuration (con jur AY shun) magic spell

wager. An iron band serves as part of the binding, and this locks with an iron padlock. Within, upon the first page, is a bit of doggerel verse which I have finally translated as

Ope' not this book
'Twixt dusk and dawn
Lest you let loose
The devil's spawn.

Beneath that is the single letter, an ornate capital *C.*

The warning I take to be intended to scare off unauthorized persons who might wish to make use of the volume. For—I have no proof, but hope to discover some—I am convinced that this was Cagliostro's own personal volume of magical charms and conjurations!

The whole thing is written in a hash of Latin, French, and Italian. This I take to have been an additional precaution against unauthorized use. Only a very well educated person could possibly have read it. It will take considerable digging to make the necessary translations. However, I have already partially translated two of the conjurations. One is simply called, *To Be Invisible.* The other, *To Make a Demon Bring Three Bags of Gold.*

If the ingredients were available, I would most certainly try the charms out! But one of the necessary articles for the first, for instance, is fat melted from the hand of a man hanged upon a gibbet. This imposes some difficulty in using the recipes! But I have no doubt I will find others which are simpler. Then I shall positively experiment to discover their effectiveness.

The most noteworthy item in the volume, though, is an inset parchment. It contains the brilliantly colored picture of a dragon. The monster has green scales, long blue claws, blue fangs in a crimson mouth, and a scarlet tail. Scarlet filaments or antennae dangle from its head and spine like seaweed. Its eyes are bright yellow shot through with scarlet. They gleam from its head with an almost living brilliance.

The dragon seems to be squatting upon a tiled floor of stone, looking directly at you, jaws slightly agape, and a ravenous expression plain upon its features. Its scaled flanks are lean and sunken. Its bones show through everywhere. A leaner, hungrier, more sinister monster I have never seen pictured. I have, accordingly, decided to nickname it Cassius.

Behind the dragon, partially obscured, is a pile of bones—a pleasantly gruesome touch! For they are human bones. I have examined the picture through the glass, and there are visible thirteen human skulls. They are so skillfully done by the artist that under magnification every detail of them is accurate. There is even discoloration showing some to be older than the others. Mingled with them are a mass of other bones and shreds of cloth. The whole is startling and almost upsetting in its vivid accuracy.

More than this I cannot tell you now.

---

doggerel (DAWG ur l) trivial or bad poetry

I have only had a few minutes in which to examine my find. Mrs. Studley is calling me for dinner, and I shall resume my examination after I have eaten.

You must come over and see it—today (as you get this) if possible. Please bring your collection of Cagliostro's letters. A handwriting comparison will tell us instantly whether this volume was written by him or not. Don't try to buy it from me, though. Perhaps I'll leave it to you in my will, but you will never get it away from me sooner!

Cordially,
Waldo Dexter

Mr. Dexter then sealed the letter, stamped and addressed it. Upon going downstairs to dinner, he gave it to Mrs. Studley to mail later. He ate rapidly, gulping down a really excellent meal, as Mrs. Studley testified later. Then he dashed back to his study to resume his examination of his odd volume.

The Studleys, having cleaned up the dinner dishes, left for their own home several blocks distant. Mr. Dexter was so engrossed he did not even respond to their good nights—a fact which somehow greatly upset Mrs. Studley the next day.

For when, the next morning, she sent Studley up to call Mr. Dexter to breakfast, Waldo Dexter was not to be found. He was not in his bedroom. He was not in his study. He was nowhere in the house. He was simply gone.

When the police arrived, they found no explanation for the mystery of Waldo Dexter's disappearance. He was just gone, with nothing to show for his going save a slight disturbance of his study. Some books had been knocked off his desk, as if swept off by a careless arm. Mr. Dexter's glasses had fallen to the floor and broken.

Beyond this there was no trace of him. The disturbance was not enough to suggest a fight. Waldo Dexter was not wealthy enough to warrant his having been kidnapped. The police finally decided that Mr. Dexter had either deliberately vanished for reasons of his own, or wandered off in a state of amnesia.

Neither of these suggestions could be improved upon by Mr. McKenzie Muir, who arrived during the latter part of the afternoon.

Mr. Muir, a lanky Scotsman, was not so interested in discovering the whereabouts of Waldo Dexter. He was more interested in getting hold of the volume Dexter had written him about. Quickly learning the facts, he did not think it necessary to show the police Waldo Dexter's note to him. Neither, in fact, did he discuss the handwritten volume which they found opened upon Mr. Dexter's desk. The police gave a casual scrutiny to it, and put it aside.

Muir favored the amnesia theory himself. He had small doubt that Dexter would reappear shortly. Before he did, Mr. Muir intended to see that the volume Waldo Dexter had stumbled upon was in his possession. And possession he inter-

engrossed (en GROHST) having all one's attention focused

preted as nine points of the law.

Accordingly, he awaited a favorable opportunity. He opened the purple leather-bound book and quickly slapped upon the inside cover one of his own bookmarks. He carried a supply of them in his wallet. Then, having given the glue time to dry, he took the book to the lieutenant in charge of the case. Convincingly, he explained that his chief reason for calling that day had been to get back the volume. He said that it was borrowed from him by Dexter. He showed the bookmark, and was presently allowed to depart with the ledger.

He left, filled with the exultation of the collector, and returned by bus and subway to his home. It was a trip of several hours, so that it was after dark when he arrived. In studying the volume on the way, all thought of Waldo Dexter passed from his mind.

Arrived at his own residence, however, Mr. Muir was forced for a time to abandon his examination of his newly acquired treasure. First, he had to eat the dinner his butler had kept waiting for him. Then, a neighbor dropped in and sat gossiping the rest of the evening.

Mr. Muir picked up the book again. He found himself fascinated, as Waldo Dexter had been, by the repulsive little dragon.

After a moment he reached for a glass to study it more carefully. And doing so, he snorted. For he perceived that Dexter had been guilty of a distinct inaccuracy in describing the beast.

"'Lean and hungry!'" he sniffed aloud.

"'Bones showing through everywhere.' Gross overstatement. The beastie is not fat, to be sure, but his bones don't show through. And though one might say his expression was hungry, I'd not call it ravenous. There's even a bit of bulge to the belly, which is not an indication of starvation." Muir peered more closely through the glass. "And there are fourteen skulls, not thirteen, in the heap behind the beastie. Ha! It's not like old Dexter to be so careless. No doubt he did wander off somewhere with amnesia. Must have been slipping in his mind to make so many mistakes!"

Noting that it was now close to midnight, McKenzie Muir hastily turned out his study light. He strode into his bedroom. He found he still held the purplish volume in his hand, and set it down upon a bureau. He put the reading glass on top of the picture of the hungry little dragon.

Then, having extinguished the light, he did not give the thing another thought.

Even the crash of the reading glass falling to the floor some time later did not disturb him.

The disappearance of McKenzie Muir was really a delightful sensation for the newspapers.

There was very little disarray. A broken reading glass was on the floor. The bedclothes were tossed in a heap into a

---

disarray (dis uh RAY) disorder; confusion
exultation (eg zul TAY shun) triumph or rejoicing

corner. The disappearance was most mysterious, especially as the door and all windows were locked. Resorting to the vague statement that they were working on clues, the police presently found it convenient to forget about the whole affair.

So the house was put in order, and

the servants dismissed. It was Johnson, the butler, performing his last duties, who slipped the odd volume that his master had stolen from Waldo Dexter onto a shelf. Then he made everything neat.

As he handled the volume, it fell open in his hands at the picture of a small dragon. Johnson gazed at it for a moment with passing interest.

"Jolly fat little beast," he commented to Dora, the maid, who was pulling down the window shades. "Got a grin on him from ear to ear." Then, closing the book and putting it away, they left the study to gather dust.

The house remained tightly locked for some months. Meanwhile some distant cousins sought to prove that McKenzie Muir was dead so that they might inherit it. Then one winter night a defective wire started a fire. Before morning it had reduced the entire structure to a heap of charred beams and powdery ashes fallen into the cellar hole.

And once again the newspapers received an unexpected godsend. It was the discovery of bones constituting the mortal remains of no less than fifteen human beings. Nearby were some larger bones whose origin was obscure. This discovery pleasantly titillated several million newspaper readers for almost a week.

The scientists to whom the unidentifiable bones were taken were more than titillated, however. They were at first interested, and then vexed. They found themselves unable to come to any agreement about the creature to whom those skeletal remains had once belonged. Eventually, however, they were able to save their professional pride. They announced that the bones belonged to some previously unknown species of the saber-toothed tiger.

So that, except for one small point, the authorities in the end were able to explain the whole affair rather neatly. The bones, they concluded, represented the victims of McKenzie Muir. Muir was a homicidal maniac who lured people to his residence, killed them, and buried them in the cellar. Undoubtedly he had so treated his unfortunate friend, Waldo Dexter. Then Muir, becoming frightened, had cleverly vanished.

Later he had returned to the locked house to burn it and destroy the evidence of his crimes. He himself had perished in the flames. Easily recognizable among the grisly relics dug forth by the searchers had been McKenzie Muir's dentures.

Thus almost all the loose ends were cleverly tied up. There was only one point for which the authorities never were able to offer any plausible explanation. That was the question of what, exactly, a saber-toothed tiger was doing in the house.

---

godsend (GOD send) something needed and unexpected
titillate (TIT ul ayt) excite pleasantly
grisly (GRIZ lee) horrible
relic (REL ik) something that has survived from the past

FOCUS ON THE SELECTION

UNDERSTAND THE SELECTION

Recall

1. Where was the book before it was in a secondhand shop.
2. Why did Mr. Muir decide that Dexter had described the dragon inaccurately?
3. How did the police explain the disappearance of the two men?

Infer

4. Why did the owner sell the book to Mr. Dexter for ten dollars instead of holding it for the collector?
5. If the dragon had eaten thirteen people, why did it look so skinny and hungry?
6. Why had the European man vanished?
7. When did the dragon eat Mr. Dexter, before or after the Studleys had left?

Apply

8. What warning did Dexter and Muir have? What was it?
9. What facts should have warned Mr. Muir about the danger?
10. Was McKenzie Muir a very good friend to Waldo Dexter? Explain your answer.

Respond to Literature

Why wasn't the shopowner eaten by the monster?

WRITE ABOUT THE SELECTION

The selection "Mr. Dexter's Dragon" is about two of the dragon's victims. There were thirteen skulls in the picture. The dragon must have eaten thirteen people between the time the picture was drawn and Mr. Dexter's purchase of the book. Write a short story. The story should tell about one of the other thirteen victims. Include how the book came into the victim's possession and then describe what happened. You may choose the European gentleman who disappeared in the hotel, or you may invent a character who could have been one of the other victims.

Prewriting: Decide which victim you want to write about. Remember that the book is very old. You will need to choose the time period in which the story will be set. Make some informal notes telling how the victim gained possession of the book. Add notes that tell what happened.

Writing: Use your notes to write your story. Tell a little about the character, how he happened to have the book, and what he did that made him the dragon's victim.

Revising: Revise your paper. You may want to add language that gives your story a humorous tone, as did the author of "Mr. Dexter's Dragon."

Proofreading: Read your story to check for errors. Be sure that all your sentences begin with capital letters and end with periods, question marks, or exclamation marks.

THINK ABOUT HUMOROUS TONE

It is important to notice the tone an author uses in writing a story and describing the characters. The tone adds shades of meaning to the author's words.

1. What is the author's tone, or attitude, toward the incident in this story?
2. What is the author's attitude toward the characters?
3. Which characters does the author find particularly amusing?
4. Which parts of the story does the author think are especially funny?
5. This could have been a dreadful and frightening story. How could the author have written it to make it less amusing and more of a horror story?

DEVELOP YOUR VOCABULARY

Sometimes you will find that you know a word once you have heard it pronounced, even though you did not recognize it in print. If you figure out how to pronounce an unfamiliar word, you will be able to recognize it.

Breaking a word into syllables can help you pronounce it. A **syllable** is a word part with one vowel sound. The dictionary breaks words into syllables by separating them with hyphens or dots.

Look up the following words in the dictionary and break them into syllables.

1. mishap
2. lackluster
3. doggerel
4. conjuration
5. engrossed
6. exultation
7. disarray
8. godsend
9. titillate
10. grisly
11. relic

FOCUS ON...

Any story that you read about imaginary characters and incidents is a work of fiction. Novels, short stories, mysteries, fantasies, science fiction, fables, folktales, legends, and myths are works of fiction. What types of fiction do you like best?

You will understand fiction better if you think about the four necessary elements of fiction writing: setting, character, plot, and theme. These four elements always operate together and can be studied together in connection with a single story.

Setting. It is important to remember that the setting is the time, place, environment, and surrounding circumstances of a story. Place and environment are important elements of the setting, and these may change over the course of the story. The setting may include several places and times. For example, the story may take place over a period of fifty years. The scene of the action may change from one place to another within the story. Elements such as the time of day, scenery, sounds, smells, and weather are all part of the setting. In addition, setting is important because it can affect the characters as well as the events. It can even create the conflict in the story.

Characters. Character is the most important element in a work of fiction. Characters are the ones about whom the story is written. Most characters are human beings, but they may also be animals, imaginary creatures, or even things. Most novels and short stories are about a character's efforts to reach a goal, deal with a problem, or resolve a conflict.

A story usually has a main character. Major characters include the main character and other characters who play roles which are almost as important. For example, a character who opposes the main character is usually considered a major character. A story often has several minor characters as well.

You will enjoy a story more if you get to know the characters. You can learn about the characters' traits mainly from their actions and words, and from the author's direct description. You may also learn about characters from what other people think and say about them.

Plot. A work of fiction usually has a plot. The plot is a planned series of events, related by conflict in a story.

Conflict can exist between the main character and another character, or characters, and it can also exist within one character. Conflict may also occur between people and things or between people and nature. Sometimes, conflict develops because the character has a goal and is prevented from reaching it, or because a mystery exists that can not be solved. Novels and longer short stories often contain more than one conflict.

Once the conflict is introduced the reader is drawn into the story and begins to wonder what will happen next. Early in a story an important plot question is usually raised. The action that follows and answers this question can either end the story, or lead to still another question. Long stories, such as novels, often contain a number of questions. The rising action in such a story leads finally to an exciting climax. The **climax** is the action that answers the big plot question, at or near the end of the story. After the climax you can guess how the conflict will be resolved.

Theme. Authors usually write fiction because they want to say something about an aspect of life. Their message is called the theme of the story, or the main idea. Some writers state the theme very clearly. Others will state it indirectly in different parts of the story. Some writers want you to figure out the theme for yourself.

As you read "The Fog Horn," examine it to discover the elements of fiction that are present. Ask yourself these questions:

1. What is the setting? What is the time span of the story? What natural elements in the setting are important to the plot?
2. Who are the characters?
3. What type of conflict is in the plot? What happens at the climax?
4. What is the theme? How is the theme resolved?

THE FOG HORN

by Ray Bradbury

Out there in the cold water, far from land, we waited every night for the coming of the fog. It came, and we oiled the brass machinery and lit the fog light up in the stone tower. Feeling like two birds in the gray sky, McDunn and I sent the light touching out, red, then white, then red again, to eye the lonely ships. And if they did not see our light, then there was always our Voice. The great deep cry of our Fog Horn shuddered through the rags of mist. It startled the gulls away like decks of scattered cards and made the waves turn high and foam.

STUDY HINTS
These clues tell you where the story is set. Where are McDunn and the narrator?

"It's a lonely life, but you're used to it now, aren't you?" asked McDunn.

"Yes," I said. "You're a good talker, thank the Lord."

"Well, it's your turn on land tomorrow," he said, smiling, "to dance the ladies and drink gin."

"What do you think, McDunn, when I leave you out here alone?"

The author is telling you something about the characters through their dialogue.

"On the mysteries of the sea." McDunn lit his pipe. It was a quarter past seven of a cold November evening. The heat was on, the light switching its tail in two hundred directions, the Fog Horn bumbling in the high throat of the tower. There wasn't a town for a hundred miles down the coast. Just a road came lonely through dead country to the sea, with few cars on it. There was a stretch of two miles of cold water out to our rock, and rare few ships.

Here are more details about the setting. What clues give you the approximate time period? How could this setting be important to a plot?

"The mysteries of the sea," said McDunn thoughtfully. "You know, the ocean's the most confounded big snowflake ever? It rolls and swells a thousand shapes and colors, no two alike. Strange."

I shivered. I looked out at the long gray lawn of the sea stretching away into nothing and nowhere.

"Oh, the sea's full." McDunn puffed his pipe nervously, blinking. He had been nervous all day and hadn't said why.

This is the first hint about the conflict. Probably what McDunn tells Johnny will introduce the conflict.

"Come on. I got something special I been saving up to tell you."

We ascended the eighty steps, talking and taking our time. At the top, McDunn switched off the room lights so there'd be no reflection in the plate glass. The great eye of the light was humming, turning easily in its oiled socket. The Fog Horn was blowing steadily, once every fifteen seconds.

The character is telling you that the fog horn is an important part of the plot.

"Sounds like an animal, don't it?" McDunn nodded to himself. "A big lonely animal crying in the night. Sitting here on the edge of ten billion years called out to the Deeps, I'm here, I'm here, I'm here. And the Deeps do answer, yes, they do. You been here now for three months, Johnny, so I better prepare you.

This line introduces the conflict.

About this time of year," he said, studying the murk and fog, "something comes to visit the lighthouse."

"The swarms of fish like you said?"

"No, this is something else. I've put off telling you because you might think I'm daft. But tonight's the latest I can put it off. For if my calendar's marked right from last year, tonight's the night it comes. I won't go into detail, you'll have to see it yourself.

This section tells you that the other character, the "something" that visits, is extremely frightening.

Just sit down there. If you want, tomorrow you can pack your duffel and take the motorboat in to land. You can get your car parked there at the dinghy pier on the cape. Then you can drive on back to some little inland town and keep your lights burning nights. I won't question or blame you. It's happened, three years now, and this is the only time anyone's been here with me to verify it. You wait and watch."

Half an hour passed with only a few whispers between us. When he grew tired waiting, McDunn began describing some of his ideas to me. He had some theories about the Fog Horn itself.

Again, McDunn is telling you that the fog horn is important to the plot. It has something to do with the motives of one character, the "thing" that visits the lighthouse.

"One day many years ago, a man walked along and stood in the sound of the ocean on a cold sunless shore. He said, 'We need a voice to call across the water, to warn ships. I'll make one. I'll make a voice like all of time and all of that fog that ever was. I'll make a voice that is like an empty bed beside you all night long. It will be like an empty house when you open the door, and like trees in autumn with no leaves. A sound like the birds flying south, crying. And a sound like November wind and the sea on the hard, cold shore. I'll make a sound that's so alone that no one can miss it. Whoever hears it will weep in their souls. Hearths will seem warmer, and being inside will seem better to all who hear it in the distant towns. I'll make me a sound and an apparatus and they'll call it a Fog Horn. Whoever hears it will know the sadness of eternity and the briefness of life.'"

The Fog Horn blew.

"I made up that story," said McDunn quietly, "to try to explain why this thing keeps coming back to the lighthouse every year. The Fog Horn calls it, I think, and it comes. . . ."

"But—" I said.

"Sssst!" said McDunn. "There!" He nodded out to the Deeps.

Something was swimming toward the lighthouse tower.

It was a cold night, as I have said. The high tower was cold, the light coming and going, and the Fog Horn calling and calling through the mist. You couldn't see far and you couldn't see plain. But there was the deep sea moving on its way about the night earth. It was flat and quiet, the color of gray mud. Here were the two of us alone in the high tower. And there, far out at first, was a ripple, followed by a wave, a rising, a bubble, a bit of froth. And then, from the surface of the cold sea came a head, a large head, dark-colored, with immense eyes, and then a neck. And then—not a body—but more neck and more! The head rose a full forty feet above the water on a slender and beautiful dark neck. Only then did the body, like a little island of black coral and shells and crayfish, drip up from the subterranean. There was a flicker of tail. In all, from head to tip of tail, I estimated the monster at ninety or a hundred feet.

Can you see why this setting is so important to this plot?

Another character is introduced, and the plot is further developed.

I don't know what I said. I said something.

"Steady, boy, steady," whispered McDunn.

"It's impossible!" I said.

"No, Johnny, *we're* impossible. *It's* like it always was ten million years ago. *It* hasn't changed. It's *us* and the land that've changed, become impossible. *Us!*"

It swam slowly and with a great dark majesty out in the icy waters, far away. The fog came and went about it, momentarily erasing its shape. One of the monster eyes caught and held and flashed back our immense light, red, white, red, white, like a disk

---

subterranean (sub tuh RAY nee un) below the earth's surface

Sea Serpent, Hans Egidius. North Wind Picture Archive.

held high and sending a message in primeval code. It was as silent as the fog through which it swam.

"It's a dinosaur of some sort!" I crouched down, holding to the stair rail.

"Yes, one of the tribe."

"But they died out!"

"No, only hid away in the Deeps. Deep, deep, down in the deepest Deeps. Isn't *that* a word now, Johnny, a real word. It says so much: the Deeps. There's all the coldness and darkness and deepness in the world in a word like that."

"What'll we do?"

"Do? We got our job, we can't leave. Besides, we're safer here than in any boat trying to get to land. That thing's as big as a destroyer and almost as swift."

"But here, why does it come here?"

The next moment I had my answer.

The Fog Horn blew.

And the monster answered.

A cry came across a million years of water and mist. A cry so anguished and alone that it shuddered in my head and my body. The monster cried out at the tower. The Fog Horn blew. The monster roared again. The Fog Horn blew. The monster opened its great toothed mouth and the sound that came from it was the sound of the Fog Horn itself. Lonely and vast and far away. The sound of isolation, a viewless sea, a cold night, apartness. That was the sound.

"Now," whispered McDunn, "do you know why it comes here?"

I nodded.

"All year long, Johnny, that poor monster there lying far out. It's a thousand miles at sea, and twenty miles deep maybe, biding its time. Perhaps it's a million years old, this one creature. Think of it, waiting a million years. Could you wait that long? Maybe it's the last of its kind. I sort of think that's true. Anyway, here come men on land and build this lighthouse, five years ago. And set up their Fog Horn and sound it. They sound it out toward the place where you bury yourself in sleep and sea memories of a

---

primeval (pry MEE vul) prehistoric; the earliest times
anguished (ANG gwisht) in great pain, grief, or distress

world where there were thousands like yourself. But now you're alone, all alone in a world not made for you, a world where you have to hide.

What action does this character take to solve its problem?

"But the sound of the Fog Horn comes and goes, comes and goes. You stir from the muddy bottom of the Deeps, and your eyes open like the lenses of two-foot cameras. And you move, slow, slow, for you have the ocean sea on your shoulders, heavy. But that Fog Horn comes through a thousand miles of water, faint and familiar. The furnace in your belly stokes up, and you begin to rise, slow, slow. You feed yourself on great satisfying meals of cod and minnow, on rivers of jellyfish. You rise slow through the autumn months, through September when the fogs started, through October with more fog. The horn still calls you on. And then, late in November, after pressurizing yourself day by day, a few feet higher every hour, you are near the surface and still alive. You've got to go slow. If you surfaced all at once you'd explode. So it takes you all of three months to surface. And then it takes a number of days to swim through the cold waters to the lighthouse. And there you are, out there, in the night, Johnny, the biggest monster in creation. And here's the lighthouse calling to you. It has a long neck like your neck sticking way up out of the water, and a body like your body, and, most important of all, a voice like your voice. Do you understand now, Johnny, do you understand?"

Notice that while the monster is frightening and dangerous, the other characters do not think of it as a "bad guy." The author has done a masterful job of helping the reader understand and sympathize with the monster's feelings.

The Fog Horn blew.

The monster answered.

I saw it all, I knew it all—the million years of waiting alone, for someone to come back who never came back. The million years of isolation at the bottom of the sea. The insanity of time there, while the skies cleared of reptile-birds. The swamps dried on the continental lands, the sloths and sabertooths had their day and sank in tar pits, and men ran like white ants upon the hills.

The Fog Horn blew.

This kind of information is often given as part of a flashback. Because it is described in the dialogue, no flashback is necessary.

"Last year," said McDunn, "that creature swam round and round, round and round, all night. Not coming too near, puzzled, I'd say. Afraid, maybe. And a bit angry after coming all this way. But the next day, unexpectedly, the fog lifted. The sun came out

---

sloth (SLAWTH) a slow-moving mammal that lives in trees; also laziness; idleness

fresh. The sky was as blue as a painting. And the monster swam off away from the heat and the silence and didn't come back. I suppose it's been brooding on it for a year now, thinking it over from every which way."

The monster was only a hundred yards off now, it and the Fog Horn crying at each other. As the lights hit them, the monster's eyes were fire and ice, fire and ice.

"That's life for you," said McDunn. "Someone always waiting for someone who never comes home. Always someone loving some thing more than that thing loves them. And after a while, you want to destroy whatever that thing is, so it can't hurt you no more."

These are some hints about the theme.

The monster was rushing at the lighthouse.

The climax begins here.

The Fog Horn blew.

"Let's see what happens," said McDunn.

Notice the action rise as McDunn takes action to solve the problem.

He switched the Fog Horn off.

The ensuing minute of silence was so intense that we could hear our hearts pounding in the glassed area of the tower. We could hear the slow greased turn of the light.

Suspense builds. What action will the monster take in response to McDunn's turning off the fog horn?

The monster stopped and froze. Its great lantern eyes blinked. Its mouth gaped. It gave a sort of rumble, like a volcano. It twitched its head this way and that, as if to seek the sounds now dwindled off into the fog. It peered at the lighthouse. It rumbled again. Then its eyes caught fire. It reared up, threshed the water, and rushed at the tower. Its eyes were filled with angry torment.

"McDunn!" I cried. "Switch on the horn!"

McDunn fumbled with the switch. But even as he flicked it on, the monster was rearing up. I had a glimpse of its gigantic paws, fishskin glittering in webs between the finger-like projections, clawing at the tower. The huge eyes on the right side of its anguished head glittered before me like a caldron into which I might drop, screaming. The tower shook. The Fog Horn cried; the monster cried. It seized the tower and gnashed at the glass, which shattered in upon us.

This is the climax. Will all the characters survive?

McDunn seized my arm. "Downstairs!"

The tower rocked, trembled, and started to give. The Fog Horn and the monster roared. We stumbled and half fell down

---

ensuing (en SOO ing) following
gnash (NASH) strike or grind the teeth together

the stairs. "Quick!"

We reached the bottom as the tower buckled down toward us. We ducked under the stairs into the small stone cellar. There were a thousand concussions as the rocks rained down. The Fog Horn stopped abruptly. The monster crashed upon the tower. The tower fell. We knelt together, McDunn and I, holding tight, while our world exploded.

Then it was over, and there was nothing but darkness and the wash of the sea on the raw stones.

That and the other sound.

"Listen," said McDunn quietly. "Listen."

We waited a moment. And then I began to hear it. First a great vacuumed sucking of air. And then the lament, the bewilderment, the loneliness of the great monster. It folded over and upon us, above us. The sickening reek of its body filled the air, a stone's thickness away from our cellar. The monster gasped and cried. The tower was gone. The light was gone. The thing that had called to it across a million years was gone. And the monster was opening its mouth and sending out great sounds. The sounds of a Fog Horn, again and again. And ships far at sea, not finding the light, not seeing anything, but passing and hearing late that night, must've thought: There it is, the lonely sound, the Lonesome Bay horn. All's well. We've rounded the cape.

And so it went for the rest of that night.

The sun was hot and yellow the next afternoon when the rescuers came out to dig us from our stoned-under cellar.

"It fell apart, is all," said Mr. McDunn gravely. "We had a few bad knocks from the waves and it just crumbled." He pinched my arm.

There was nothing to see. The ocean was calm, the sky blue. The only thing was a great algaic stink from the green matter that covered the fallen towerstones and the shore rocks. Flies buzzed about. The ocean washed empty on the shore.

The next year they built a new lighthouse. But by that time I had a job in the little town, and a wife. I had a good small, warm house that glowed yellow on autumn nights, the doors locked, the chimney puffing smoke. As for McDunn, he was master of the new lighthouse. It was built to his own specifications, out of still-reinforced [sic] concrete. "Just in case," he said.

The new lighthouse was ready in November. I drove down alone one evening late. I parked my car and looked across the gray waters. I listened to the new horn sounding, once, twice, three, four times a minute far out there, by itself.

The monster?

It never came back.

"It's gone away," said McDunn. "It's gone back to the Deeps. It's learned you can't love anything too much in this world. It's gone into the deepest Deeps to wait another million years. Ah, the poor thing! Waiting out there, and waiting out there, while man comes and goes on this pitiful little planet. Waiting and waiting."

I sat in my car, listening. I couldn't see the lighthouse or the light standing out in Lonesome Bay. I could only hear the Horn, the Horn, the Horn. It sounded like the monster calling.

I sat there wishing there was something I could say.

---

specifications (spes uh fih KAY shunz) detailed, precise list of measurements and materials for a structure.

FOCUS ON THE SELECTION

UNDERSTAND THE SELECTION

Recall

1. What was it that McDunn had been waiting to tell the main character?
2. How did McDunn know when the monster was going to come?
3. What happened to the lighthouse?

Infer

4. What was McDunn's job?
5. Why had McDunn not told anyone about the monster before?
6. Why did the monster return?
7. Why didn't McDunn tell the rescuers what really happened?

Apply

8. What would have happened if McDunn hadn't switched off the fog horn?
9. Predict what would have happened to the ships if the monster had not continued to cry after leveling the lighthouse.
10. Do you agree with the following? "Always someone loving something more than that thing loves them, and after a while, you want to destroy whatever that thing is . . ."

Respond to Literature

Would this dinosaur be surprised to find its story in a unit called "Monsters"?

WRITE ABOUT THE SELECTION

Imagine you were a newspaper reporter and you happened to be on the waterfront the night the incident of the attack on the lighthouse occurred. Write an eyewitness account of the incident for your newspaper. Remember, a newspaper article usually answers the following questions: *Who? What? When? Where?* It may also answer the questions *How?* or *Why?* or it may include some guesses about the answers based on the information obtained.

Prewriting: Divide your paper into five columns. Label the columns *Who, What, Where, When, Why.* Under each question write the appropriate answer. If you do not know the answers to all of these questions, make an educated guess.

Writing: Use the information from your chart to write an eyewitness account of the lighthouse incident for the newspaper. Include all the information you have gathered and present it in the order of the "5W" questions.

Revising: Revise your article. Be sure that you have described the incident clearly. Your reader should be able to answer each of the five listed questions after reading the article.

Proofreading: Read over your newspaper report to check for errors. Be sure all your sentences begin with capital letters and end with periods, question marks, or exclamation marks.

THINK ABOUT FICTION ELEMENTS

Elements of fiction are characters, plot, theme and setting. All of these elements are closely related. For example, the setting may play an important role in the story's plot.

1. Describe the setting. What elements of the setting were necessary to understand the plot?
2. Why couldn't this story have taken place in the mountains, in a desert or in a large city?
3. Describe the characters in the selection. Which characters did you get to know best?
4. What conflict did you find in the story? Was there more than one?
5. Describe what happened during the climax of the story.
6. What do you think was the theme of the story?

DEVELOP YOUR VOCABULARY

As you learned earlier, when you are reading you can often find the meaning of words you do not know by using context clues. Context clues may be formed in the same sentence as the unknown word. They may also be in a sentence before or after the one containing the unfamiliar word. Read the following line from the selection: "A cry so anguished and alone that it shuddered in my head and my body."

The word *cry* is usually used to describe a noise someone makes when they are expressing strong feelings. The words *alone* and *shuddered* suggest that it sounds like a sad or pained cry. Anguished might mean "expressing or feeling deep suffering." Find the following words in the selection. Look for context clues that might have helped you determine the meaning of the word. Use each word in a sentence. Try to write sentences with context clues that would be helpful to someone unfamiliar with the word.

1. primeval
2. subterranean
3. anguished
4. sloth
5. ensuing
6. gnashed
7. specifications

Kraken Attacking a Ship, 19th century. The Granger Collection.

Learn About

Articles

Most of the selections you have read in this unit are fiction. They tell a story that is not true. The next selection will be an **informational article.** The purpose of such an article is to inform or to explain. It is organized in a way to help you get the information easily.

If an article tells about an incident, such as a news story does, it will usually tell *who, what, where, when,* and sometimes *how* and *why.* Often it presents a series of events in the order in which they occurred. An article that explains a particular subject will state the main idea. It will then explain the idea further with details, examples, or reasons. An article about a problem may explain the problem, and then suggest a solution.

As you read the selection, ask yourself the following:

1. How is this article organized?
2. About what does the article give information?

Skill Builder

Writers of articles want to inform the writer about something. Think of a subject which you know well—your hobby, for example. Write a few sentences about the subject.

The Ten-Armed Monster Of Newfoundland

by Elma Schemenauer

The mighty kraken floats quietly beneath the surface of the water like an underwater island," said the Norwegian storyteller. "Fishing people may row their boats to and fro in the shallow water above it. They will catch many fish. For the monster's strong smell draws the smaller sea creatures, who gather about it in great numbers.

"But the fishermen must always be watchful. If the water under their boats suddenly becomes shallower, they know that the powerful monster is raising itself out of the deep. They must then get away as fast as they can. For the terrible kraken has long arms that can reach as high as the mast of any ship. It can easily drag a fishing boat to the bottom, together with all those who are on board. . . ."

It's an old story—the legend of the kraken. Long before the Norwegian writer recorded it in 1752, sailors were telling tales of the long-armed monster.

"Ridiculous!" said most of the scientists who heard their reports. "We have no record of any such creature."

"But we saw it," protested the sailors. "Actually, it looked very much like the little squids that we sometimes catch in our nets. But it was much bigger. Could it be that the kraken is really a very large squid—bigger than anything you scientists have yet discovered?"

---

kraken (KRAH kun) sea monster in legends from Norway
Norwegian (nawr WEE jun) from Norway, a country in Europe
squid (SKWID) a kind of sea animal with ten arms

Over the years more and more people began to think this might be. But scientists continued to reject the theory. Until proof was offered, they preferred to regard the kraken as a legend.

Perhaps the kraken would have remained a legend forever, in the same class as mermaids, man-eating sea serpents, and other mysterious creatures of the deep. But in the 1870s a number of gigantic ten-armed bodies began to be washed up on the rocky shores of Newfoundland and Labrador.

Local fishing people who came upon the rubbery-looking giants often just hacked them up. They used the meat to bait their hooks or to feed their dogs. Maybe the fishermen simply didn't realize the importance of what they had found. Or maybe they thought people would laugh at them if they dared to suggest that there might be some connection between these monsters and the legendary kraken.

It was left to a twelve-year-old boy from Newfoundland to bring forward evidence proving that the giant squid did exist.

The boy's name was Thomas Piccot. On October 26, 1873, he and his father and another man named Daniel Squires went out fishing. The three set off very early, in the cold gray light before dawn. Thick fog still blanketed the little cove. Young Tom shivered in spite of his heavy coat. But he felt excited and happy. For this was the first time his father had ever taken him out for a full day's fishing.

He settled himself comfortably on a pile of nets in the big flat-bottomed, high-sided dory. Then he watched the fog slowly swallow up the little village as his father and Mr. Squires rowed the boat out into the bay. After a while, they stopped and let down the nets.

The morning passed quickly. By the time the noonday sun stood directly overhead, the three fishermen had netted a good catch of herring. They stopped to eat the lunch that they had brought along. Just as they were finishing, Tom's father hap-

---

regard (rih GAHRD) think about; consider
Newfoundland (NOO fun land) province and island in eastern Canada, on the Atlantic Ocean
Labrador (LAB ruh dawr) section of northeastern Canada, on the Atlantic Ocean, part of the province of Newfoundland
legendary (LEJ un deh ree) found in legends

pened to notice a flat, dark mass of something floating and bobbing in the choppy water not far from the dory. "Looks like a raft of seaweed," he said.

"Yes, or it could be part of a wrecked ship, I suppose," said Daniel Squires. "Let's go over and have a look."

As they rowed the dory closer, they saw that the floating mass in the water was reddish brown. It was covered with a sort of shiny skin. And it was very, very big—nearly three times as large as the boat! "It almost looks like some kind of animal," said Mr. Squires.

"It's lying awfully still, if it is an animal," said Tom's father.

"Maybe it's dead," suggested Tom.

"We'll soon see," said his father. "Hand me that boat hook, will you, son?"

Grasping one end of the long pole, Mr. Piccot got up on his knees and leaned out over the water. Then, with a sudden quick movement, he jabbed the jellylike blob with the hook.

A great shudder rippled through the floating mass. Then a huge ugly beak raised itself straight up out of the water. Long arms like giant snakes began to thrash about wildly. The boat rocked and tipped dangerously. "Look out!" yelled Tom's father. He and Mr. Squires seized the oars. They turned the dory and started rowing furiously away.

But they weren't quick enough. A dark snakelike tentacle rose high in the air. It hovered there for a moment and then slithered down—right into the boat! Tom leaped back, gazing in wild-eyed horror at the thick rubbery arm with its rows and rows of sharp crown-shaped suckers. Suddenly the dory tipped to one side. The creature had wrapped another long arm around the outside of the boat and was beginning to draw it down into the water. At the same time it lifted its parrotlike beak once again and started to gnaw at the upper edge of the boat.

---

dory (DAWR ee) small boat with a flat bottom
blob (BLOB) small lump or shapeless object
shudder (SHUD ur) tremble, shake
tentacle (TEN tuh kul) long, thin part of an animal, somewhat like an arm, used for feeling and touching
hover (HUV ur) hang in the air
slither (SLI*TH* ur) slide and move as a snake does

Kraken Attacking a Ship, 19th century. The Granger Collection.

Tom's father and Daniel Squires raised their oars. They began pounding on the creature's long arms, desperately trying to force it to slacken its grip. As the waves sloshed over into the sinking dory, Tom's father seized a bucket and started bailing frantically.

Tom was about to snatch up the oar that his father had laid down. But suddenly his eyes fell on a hatchet lying in the bottom of the dory. It made him think of an old story he'd heard. Some Norwegian fishermen in a small boat had once been attacked by one of the dreaded krakens that haunt their cold waters. They had managed to save themselves by chopping off the creature's arms with an axe.

Tom crept as close as he dared to the long, sharp-suckered arm that clung to the inside of the dory. Clutching the hatchet in both hands, he raised it high. He paused for a second. Then he brought the sharp blade down with all his might on the tough, rubbery tentacle. Again he raised the hatchet and again he brought it down. Again and again and again! Like a madman he hacked at the arm until at last it was dangling by a mere thread of dark red flesh. The grip of its suckers loosened. And then the whole arm slowly slithered, lifeless, into the bottom of the boat.

But the creature's other arm was still trying to drag the boat down into the water. Tom's father and Mr. Squires were both bailing furiously, barely managing to keep the dory afloat.

Tom leaned out over the gunwale, and raising the hatchet once more, he began hacking at the arm that was wrapped around the outside of the boat. This one was harder to reach. But it wasn't quite as thick as the first. He finally managed to cut it off as well. His father turned and helped him heave it up over the gunwale into the boat. They flung it down beside the other one. Then they both wheeled around and prepared to meet the monster's next attack.

But the huge creature now seemed confused. It began to dart about in circles around and under the dory. It gave out great clouds of black ink that spread and colored the water for some distance around. At last it raised its great beak just once more,

---

sucker (SUK ur) part of an animal that can attach itself to objects by sucking and creating a vacuum between itself and the object
bail (BAYL) dip water out of
gunwale (GUN ul) upper edge of the side of a boat
wheel (HWEEL) turn quickly and suddenly

gasped, and then slowly sank from view beneath the dark waves.

Mr. Piccot's hands were shaking. Slowly and carefully he laid down the hatchet, which he had picked up waiting for fresh attack from the creature. He threw his arms around his son. "You did well, my boy," he said in a choked voice. . . .

All three were completely exhausted from their struggle. But they realized that they might still be in danger. As quickly as they could, they rowed the dory back towards the little village. "These will make good bait, Dan," said Tom's father as they were approaching the shore. He pointed at the two long suckered arms lying, coiled up, in the bottom of the boat.

"No, don't cut them up!" cried Tom in horror. "I'm going to keep them."

"Well, they're yours, I guess," said Mr. Squires with a smile. "You earned them, that's for sure. But you won't be able to keep them long anyway. They'll soon spoil, even in this cool weather."

The two men tied the boat to the dock. Then they set off into the village to tell their neighbors what had happened. They left Tom sitting in the dory with the souvenirs of the adventure.

The boy tossed the shorter arm up on the shore. As he sat in the boat examining the longer one, several hungry dogs came along. They snatched up the arm that was lying on the beach and trotted off with it. Tom leaped out of the boat and raced across the rocks after them. But he was too late. By the time he caught up with the dogs, they had torn the rubbery arm to shreds. Deeply disappointed, Tom slowly made his way back towards the dock where the dory was tied.

By this time his father and Daniel Squires had told a number of the villagers about their experience. But nobody believed them. The tale seemed too strange to be true.

It wasn't until the villagers came down to the dock and actually saw the gigantic snakelike arm that they began to take the men's story seriously. "If that's the size of its arm, just think how big the whole creature must have been," someone remarked.

"How many arms did you say it had, Dan?" asked someone else.

"Ten altogether," replied Mr. Squires. "Of course, thanks to young Tom here, it's missing a couple of them at the moment."

"I wonder what Reverend Harvey would make of it," said

Tom's father suddenly. The Reverend Moses Harvey lived not far away, in the city of St. John's. He had spent years studying marine life. Local people often called upon him to identify sea creatures that were unknown to them.

When Reverend Harvey saw the huge tentacle, he became very excited. He had studied the stories of the legendary kraken and the giant squid. He felt sure that the two were actually one and the same. But he had never before had any really solid proof of the existence of either one.

The tentacle was carefully preserved in alcohol. The scientists who saw it had to admit that it definitely pointed to the existence of a giant squid. It corresponded exactly with the tentacles of the ordinary small squids that the fishermen often caught. But it was much, much larger! In the months that followed, several other Newfoundlanders came forward with parts or complete bodies of giant squids that they had either captured or found.

With this evidence, scientists all over the world finally changed their minds. They added the giant squid to their list of known sea creatures. At least part of the credit for the discovery belongs to a boy named Thomas Piccot. He showed great courage during his meeting with the dangerous creature. And he was curious enough and far-sighted enough to recognize the importance of keeping the proof of what he had experienced.

What about other mysterious creatures of the deep? Are they simply products of people's imagination? Or could some of them turn out to be just as real as the kraken? Perhaps the day will come when scientists will have solid proof of the existence of "Nessie," the monster who is said to lurk in the depths of Scotland's Loch Ness. And perhaps someday we'll know the true identity of other legendary monsters.

Some scientists claim that, even today, about half the existing forms of underwater life are still unknown to them. No wonder people still tell tales of mysterious creatures, just as our ancestors did in the past. In future years many of these legendary creatures of the deep may well prove to be just as real as the terrible kraken, or giant squid.

---

correspond (kawr uh SPOND) agree; match
far-sighted (FAHR syt id) smart enough to see what will be needed later
ancestors (AN ses turz) people from whom one is descended

FOCUS ON THE SELECTION

UNDERSTAND THE SELECTION

Recall

1. How did science come to recognize that giant squids really existed?
2. Why did the squid attack the boat?
3. What did Reverend Harvey study?

Infer

4. Why did scientists reject the reports about a kraken or giant squid?
5. Why had scientists never seen a giant squid?
6. Why did the squid stop attacking?
7. Why did Tom want to keep the arms?

Imply

8. What would have happened had Tom not cut the tentacles off the squid?
9. Do you think people may have seen real creatures whose existence is not now known to science? Why?
10. Suppose Big Foot, the Loch Ness Monster, or other mythical creatures were real. What would it take to get their existence accepted by science?

Respond to Literature

Why is an article about squid in a unit called "Monsters"?

WRITE ABOUT THE SELECTION

At the end of "The Ten-Armed Monster of Newfoundland," scientists had accepted the giant squid as real. Suppose, however, that Tom Piccot had not managed to save the arms of the squid. Imagine a conversation that he might have held with Reverend Moses Harvey. Would Reverend Moses Harvey have believed him? Write a conversation between Tom Piccot and Reverend Moses Harvey. Have Tom try to convince the Reverend that the squid is real without the proof of the arm.

Prewriting: Think about what Tom Piccot might say to Reverend Harvey to convince him that the giant squid really does exist. Think about Reverend Harvey's reaction. Freewrite their conversation.

Writing: Use your prewriting to write a conversation between Tom Piccot and Reverend Harvey. Write it as you would a dialogue for a short story, using quotation marks.

Revising: Revise your conversation. Add the information that you think Tom Piccot will want Reverend Harvey to have about his experience.

Proofreading: Read your conversation to check for errors. Be sure all the characters' lines begin with capital letters and end with periods, question marks, or exclamation marks. Be sure you have enclosed each speaker's exact words in quotation marks. Use commas to separate the quotes from the rest of the sentence.

THINK ABOUT ARTICLES

In reading an informational article it is important to know the difference between facts and theories. Sometimes scientists, for example, will have an idea that might possibly explain something in nature. If the idea has not been proved, it is called a **theory.** **Facts** are pieces of information that are known to be true. "People have reported seeing a huge creature in Loch Ness" (a lake in Scotland) is a fact. "There is a very huge, monster-like creature living in Loch Ness" is a theory.

1. What kind of information does this article give?
2. What facts are presented in this article?
3. What theories are presented?
4. What character had a theory in this story?
5. What theory was later proven true?

DEVELOP YOUR VOCABULARY

How do you find a particular word in a glossary or dictionary? The entries for words are in alphabetical order. As you look through the dictionary, you want to be able to find the page on which the word is listed.

Guide words appear at the top of every dictionary or glossary page. They help you find the page containing the word you want. They tell you that the words listed in alphabetical order on the page come between the two guide words.

Locate the following words in a dictionary or glossary. Write the guide words that appear at the top of the page where they are listed.

1. regard
2. legendary
3. blob
4. shudder
5. hover
6. bail
7. wheel
8. correspond
9. far-sighted

Learn About

Theme

Authors often use fiction to describe some aspect of life. The message in the story is the **theme.** Sometimes the theme will be directly stated by a character or the narrator. At other times, you have to figure out the theme for yourself as the plot develops.

The theme of the story may be expressed in the nature of the conflict and how the conflict is resolved. Imagine a story with a friendly but ugly monster as the main character. The monster is hunted down and killed by human beings. What would an author be trying to tell you by writing this story?

Theme is important in a story because it allows you to see the meaning behind the actions in a story, and it explains why the characters are created as they are.

As you read "The Monsters Are Due on Maple Street," ask yourself:

1. What is the theme of the story?
2. How did you identify the theme?

Skill Builder

Writers usually choose themes that apply to a large number of people and situations. Write a few ideas that might make good themes for a story.

The Monsters Are Due on Maple Street

by Rod Serling

CHARACTERS

NARRATOR	CHARLIE'S WIFE
FIGURE ONE	TOMMY
FIGURE TWO	SALLY, *Tommy's mother*
DON MARTIN	LES GOODMAN
STEVE BRAND	ETHEL GOODMAN, *Les's wife*
MYRA BRAND, *Steve's wife*	MAN ONE
PETE VAN HORN	WOMAN ONE
CHARLIE	WOMAN TWO

ACT I/SCENE 1

(Fade in on shot of the night sky. The various heavenly bodies stand out in sharp, sparkling relief. As the camera begins a SLOW PAN across the heavens, we hear the narrator.)

NARRATOR *(offstage):* There is a fifth dimension beyond that which is known to man. It is a dimension as vast as space, and as timeless as infinity. It is the middle ground between light and shadow—between science and superstition. And it lies between the pit of man's fears and the summit of his knowledge. This is the dimension of imagination. It is an area which we call the Twilight Zone.

SCENE 2

(The camera begins to pan down until it passes the horizon and stops on a sign which reads "Maple Street." It is daytime. Then we see the street below. It is a quiet, tree-lined, small-town American street. The houses have front porches on which people sit and swing on gliders, talking across from house to house. STEVE BRAND *is polishing his car, which is parked in front of his house. His neighbor,* DON MARTIN, *leans against the fender watching him. A Good Humor man riding a bicycle is just in the process of stopping to sell some ice cream to a couple of kids. Two women gossip on the front lawn. Another man is watering his lawn with a garden hose.*

At this moment TOMMY, *one of the two boys buying ice cream from the vendor, looks up to listen to a tremendous screeching roar from overhead. A flash of light plays on the faces of both boys and then moves down the street and disappears.*

Various people leave their porches or stop what they are doing to stare up at the sky.

STEVE BRAND, *the man who has been polishing his car, stands there transfixed, staring upwards. He looks at* DON MARTIN, *his neighbor from across the street.)*

STEVE: What was that? A meteor?

DON: That's what it looked like. I didn't hear any crash though, did you?

STEVE: Nope. I didn't hear anything except a roar.

MYRA *(from her porch):* Steve? What was that?

STEVE *(raising his voice and looking toward the porch):* Guess it was a meteor, honey. Came awful close, didn't it?

MYRA: Too close for my money! Much too close.

(The camera pans across the various porches to people who stand there watching and talking in low conversing tones.)

NARRATOR: Maple Street. Six-forty-four P.M. on a late September evening. *(A pause)* Maple Street in the last calm and reflective moment . . . before the monsters came!

(The camera takes us across the porches again. A man is replacing a light bulb on a front porch. He gets down off his stool to flick the

---

transfixed (trans FIKST) made motionless

switch and finds that nothing happens.

Another man is working on an electric power mower. He plugs in the plug, flicks the switch of the mower off and on; but nothing happens.

Through a window we see a woman pushing her finger back and forth on the dial hook of a telephone. Her voice sounds far away.)

WOMAN ONE: Operator, operator, something's wrong on the phone, operator!

(MYRA BRAND *comes out on the porch and calls to* STEVE.*)*

MYRA *(calling):* Steve, the power's off. I had the soup on the stove and the stove just stopped working.

WOMAN ONE: Same thing over here. I can't get anybody on the phone either. The phone seems to be dead.

(We look down again on the street. Small, mildly disturbed voices creep up from below.)

VOICE ONE: Electricity's off.

VOICE TWO: Phone won't work.

VOICE THREE: Can't get a thing on the radio.

VOICE FOUR: My power mower won't move, won't work at all.

VOICE FIVE: Radio's gone dead!

*(*PETE VAN HORN, *a tall, thin man, is seen standing in front of his house.)*

PETE: I'll cut through the back yard . . . see if the power's still on, on Floral Street. I'll be right back!

(He walks past the side of his house and disappears into the back yard.

The camera pans down slowly until we are looking at ten or eleven people standing around the street and overflowing to the curb and sidewalk. In the background is STEVE BRAND*'s car.)*

STEVE: Doesn't make sense. Why should the power go off all of a sudden and the phone line?

DON: Maybe some kind of an electrical storm or something.

CHARLIE: That don't seem likely. Sky's just as blue as anything. Not a cloud. No lightning. No thunder. No nothing. How could it be a storm?

MAPL

WOMAN ONE: I can't get a thing on the radio. Not even the portable.

(The people again murmur softly in wonderment.)

CHARLIE: Well, why don't you go downtown and check with the police, though they'll probably think we're crazy or something. A little power failure and right away we get all flustered and everything—

STEVE: It isn't just the power failure, Charlie. If it was, we'd still be able to get a broadcast on the portable.

(There is a murmur of reaction to this.
STEVE *looks from face to face and then over to his car.)*

STEVE: I'll run downtown. We'll get this all straightened out.

(He walks over to the car, gets in, and turns the key.
Looking through the open car door, we see the crowd watching STEVE *from the other side. He starts the engine. It turns over sluggishly and then stops dead. He tries it again, and this time he can't get it to turn over. Then very slowly he turns the key back to "off" and gets out of the car.*
The people stare at STEVE. *He stands for a moment by the car and then walks toward them.)*

STEVE: I don't understand it. It was working fine before—

DON: Out of gas?

STEVE *(shakes his head):* I just had it filled up.

WOMAN ONE: What's it mean?

CHARLIE: It's just as if . . . as if everything had stopped. *(Then he turns toward* STEVE.*)* We'd better walk downtown.

(Another murmur of assent to this.)

STEVE: The two of us can go, Charlie. *(He turns to look back at the car.)* It couldn't be the meteor. A meteor couldn't do *this.*

(He and CHARLIE *exchange a look. Then they start to walk away from the group.*
TOMMY *comes into view. He is a serious-faced young boy in spectacles. He stands halfway between the group and the two men who start to walk down the sidewalk.)*

---

assent (uh SENT) agreement

TOMMY: Mr. Brand . . . you'd better not!
STEVE: Why not?
TOMMY: They don't want you to.

*(*STEVE *and* CHARLIE *exchange a grin and* STEVE *looks back toward the boy.)*

STEVE: Who doesn't want us to?
TOMMY *(jerks his head in the general direction of the distant horizon):* Them!
STEVE: Them?
CHARLIE: Who are *them*?
TOMMY *(intently):* Whoever was in that thing that came by overhead.

*(*STEVE *knits his brows for a moment, cocking his head questioningly. His voice is intense.)*

STEVE: What?
TOMMY: Whoever was in that thing that came over. I don't think they want us to leave here.

*(*STEVE *leaves* CHARLIE, *walks over to the boy, and puts his hand on the boy's shoulder. He forces his voice to remain gentle.)*

STEVE: What do you mean? What are you talking about?
TOMMY: They don't want us to leave. That's why they shut everything off.
STEVE: What makes you say that? Whatever gave you *that* idea?
WOMAN ONE *(from the crowd):* Now isn't that the craziest thing you ever heard?
TOMMY *(persistent but a little frightened):* It's always that way, in every story I ever read about a ship landing from outer space.
WOMAN ONE *(to the boy's mother,* SALLY, *who stands on the fringe of the crowd):* From outer space yet! Sally, you better get that boy of yours up to bed. He's been reading too many comic books or seeing too many movies or something!
SALLY: Tommy, come over here and stop that kind of talk.
STEVE: Go ahead, Tommy. We'll be right back. And you'll see. That wasn't any ship or anything like it. That was just a . . . a meteor or something. Likely as not—*(He turns to the group, now trying very hard to sound more optimistic than he feels.)* No doubt it did have something to do with all this power failure

and the rest of it. Meteors can do some crazy things, like sunspots.

DON *(picking up the cue):* Sure. That's the kind of thing—like sunspots. They raise Cain with radio reception all over the world. And this thing being so close—why, there's no telling the sort of stuff it can do. *(He wets his lips, smiles nervously.)* Go ahead, Charlie. You and Steve go into town and see if that isn't what's causing it all.

*(*STEVE *and* CHARLIE *walk away from the group down the sidewalk, as the people watch silently.*

TOMMY *stares at them, biting his lips, and finally calls out again.)*

TOMMY: Mr. Brand!

(The two men stop. TOMMY *takes a step toward them.)*

TOMMY: Mr. Brand . . . please don't leave here.

*(*STEVE *and* CHARLIE *stop once again and turn toward the boy. In the crowd there is a murmur of irritation and concern, as if the boy's words—even though they didn't make sense—were bringing up fears that shouldn't be brought up.*

TOMMY *is partly frightened and partly defiant.)*

TOMMY: You might not even be able to get to town. It was that way in the story. *Nobody* could leave. Nobody except—

STEVE: Except who?

TOMMY: Except the people they'd sent down ahead of them. They looked just like humans. And it wasn't until the ship landed that—*(The boy suddenly stops, conscious of the people staring at him and his mother, and of the sudden hush of the crowd.)*

SALLY *(in a whisper, sensing the antagonism of the crowd):* Tommy, please son . . . honey, don't talk that way—

MAN ONE: That kid shouldn't talk that way . . . and we shouldn't stand here listening to him. Why, this is the craziest thing I ever heard of. The kid tells us a comic book plot and here we stand listening—

*(*STEVE *walks toward the camera, and stops beside the boy.)*

STEVE: Go ahead, Tommy. What kind of story was this? What about the people they sent out ahead?

TOMMY: That was the way they prepared things for the landing.

They sent four people. A mother and a father and two kids who looked just like humans . . . but they weren't.

(There is another silence as STEVE *looks toward the crowd and then toward* TOMMY. *He wears a tight grin.)*

STEVE: Well, I guess what we'd better do then is to run a check on the neighborhood and see which ones of us are really human.

(There is laughter at this; but it's a laughter that comes from a desperate attempt to lighten the atmosphere. The people look at one another in the middle of their laughter.)

CHARLIE *(rubs his jaw nervously):* I wonder if Floral Street's got the same deal we got. *(He looks past the houses.)* Where is Pete Van Horn anyway? Didn't he get back yet?

(Suddenly there is the sound of a car's engine starting to turn over. We look across the street toward the driveway of LES GOODMAN*'s house. He is at the wheel trying to start the car.)*

SALLY: Can you get started, Les?

(LES GOODMAN *gets out of the car, shaking his head.)*

LES: No dice.

(He walks toward the group. He stops suddenly as, behind him, the car engine starts up all by itself. LES *whirls around to stare at it.*

The car idles roughly, smoke coming from the exhaust, the frame shaking gently.

LES*'s eyes go wide, and he runs over to his car.*

The people stare at the car.)

MAN ONE: He got the car started somehow. He got his car started!

(The people continue to stare, caught up by this revelation and wildly frightened.)

WOMAN ONE: How come his car just up and started like that?

SALLY: All by itself. He wasn't anywhere near it. It started all by itself.

(DON MARTIN *approaches the group, stops a few feet away to look toward* LES*'s car and then back toward the group.)*

DON: And he never did come out to look at that thing that flew overhead. He wasn't even interested. *(He turns to the group, his*

face taut and serious.) Why? Why didn't he come out with the rest of us to look?

CHARLIE: He always was an oddball. Him and his whole family. Real oddball.

DON: What do you say we ask him?

(The group start toward the house. In this brief fraction of a moment, they take the first step toward a metamorphosis that changes people from a group into a mob. They begin to head purposefully across the street toward the house. STEVE *stands in front of them. For a moment their fear almost turns their walk into a wild stampede; but* STEVE's *voice, loud, incisive, and commanding, makes them stop.)*

STEVE: Wait a minute . . . wait a minute! Let's not be a mob!

(The people stop, pause for a moment, and then, much more quietly and slowly, start to walk across the street.
LES *stands alone facing the people.)*

LES: I just don't understand it. I tried to start it and it wouldn't start. You saw me. All of you saw me.

(And now, just as suddenly as the engine started, it stops, and there is a long silence that is gradually intruded upon by the frightened murmuring of the people.)

LES: I don't understand. I swear . . . I don't understand. What's happening?

DON: Maybe you better tell us. Nothing's working on this street. Nothing. No lights, no power, no radio. *(Then meaningfully)* Nothing except one car—yours!

(The people's murmuring becomes a loud chant filling the air with accusations and demands for action. Two of the men pass DON *and head toward* LES, *who backs away from them against his car. He is cornered.)*

LES: Wait a minute now. You keep your distance—all of you. So I've got a car that starts by itself—well, that's a freak thing—I admit it. But does that make me some kind of a criminal or something? I don't know why the car works—it just does!

---

taut (TAWT) tense; drawn tightly
incisive (in SY siv) penetrating or sharp

(This stops the crowd momentarily and LES, *still backing away, goes toward his front porch. He goes up the steps and then stops, facing the mob.)*

LES: What's it all about, Steve?

STEVE *(quietly):* We're all on a monster kick, Les. Seems that the general impression holds that maybe one family isn't what we think they are. Monsters from outer space or something. Different from us. Fifth columnists[1] from the vast beyond. *(He chuckles.)* You know anybody that might fit that description around here on Maple Street?

LES: What is this, a gag? *(He looks around the group again.)* This a practical joke or something?

(Suddenly the car engine starts all by itself, runs for a moment, and stops. One woman begins to cry. The eyes of the crowd are cold and accusing.)

LES: Now that's supposed to incriminate me, huh? The car engine goes on and off; and that really does it, doesn't it? *(He looks around the faces of the people.)* I just don't understand it . . . any more than any of you do! *(He wets his lips, looking from face to face.)* Look, you all know me. We've lived here five years. Right in this house. We're no different from any of the rest of you! We're no different at all. . . . Really . . . this whole thing is just . . . just weird—

WOMAN ONE: Well, if that's the case, Les Goodman, explain why—*(She stops suddenly, clamping her mouth shut.)*

LES *(softly):* Explain what?

STEVE *(interjecting):* Look, let's forget this—

CHARLIE *(overlapping him):* Go ahead, let her talk. What about it? Explain what?

WOMAN ONE *(a little reluctantly):* Well . . . sometimes I go to bed late at night. A couple of times . . . a couple of times I'd come out here on the porch and I'd see Mr. Goodman here in the wee hours of the morning standing out in front of his house . . . looking up at the sky. *(She looks around the circle of*

---

incriminate (in KRIM uh nayt) cause to appear guilty

[1] **fifth columnists:** A secret group of people working within their own country for the enemy.

faces.) That's right, looking up at the sky as if . . . as if he were waiting for something. *(A pause)* As if he were looking for something.

(There's a murmur of reaction from the crowd again as LES *backs away.)*

LES: She's crazy. Look, I can explain that. Please . . . I can really explain that. . . . She's making it up anyway. *(Then he shouts.)* I tell you she's making it up!

(He takes a step toward the crowd, and they back away from him. He walks down the steps after them, and they continue to back away. Suddenly he is left completely alone; and he looks like a man caught in the middle of a menacing circle as the scene slowly fades to black.)

ACT II/SCENE 1

(Fade in on Maple Street at night. On the sidewalk, little knots of people stand around talking in low voices. At the end of each conversation, they look toward LES GOODMAN*'s house. From the various houses we can see candlelight but no electricity. The quiet which blankets the whole area is disturbed only by the almost whispered voices of the people standing around. In one group,* CHARLIE *stands staring across at the Goodman's house. Two men stand across the street from it in almost sentry-like poses.)*

SALLY *(in a small, hesitant voice):* It just doesn't seem right, though, keeping watch on them. Why . . . he was right when he said he was one of our neighbors. Why, I've known Ethel Goodman ever since they moved in. We've been good friends—

CHARLIE: That doesn't prove a thing. Any guy who'd spend his time lookin' up at the sky early in the morning—well, there's something wrong with that kind of person. There's something that isn't legitimate. Maybe under normal circumstances we could let it go by; but these aren't normal circumstances. Why, look at this street! Nothin' but candles. Why, it's like goin' back into the Dark Ages or somethin'!

*(*STEVE *walks down the steps of his porch, down the street to the Goodmans' house, and then stops at the foot of the steps.* LES *is*

standing there; ETHEL GOODMAN *behind him is very frightened.)*

LES: Just stay right where you are, Steve. We don't want any trouble; but this time if anybody sets foot on my porch—that's what they're going to get—trouble!

STEVE: Look, Les—

LES: I've already explained to you people. I don't sleep very well at night sometimes. I get up and I take a walk and I look up at the sky. I look at the stars!

ETHEL: That's exactly what he does. Why, this whole thing, it's . . . it's some kind of madness or something.

STEVE *(nods grimly):* That's exactly what it is—some kind of madness.

CHARLIE'S VOICE *(shrill, from across the street):* You best watch who you're seen with, Steve! Until we get this all straightened out, you aren't exactly above suspicion yourself.

STEVE *(whirling around toward him):* Or you, Charlie. Or any of us, it seems. From age eight on up!

WOMAN ONE: What I'd like to know is—what are we gonna do? Just stand around here all night?

CHARLIE: There's nothin' else we can do! *(He turns back, looking toward* STEVE *and* LES *again.)* One of 'em'll tip their hand. They *got* to.

STEVE *(raising his voice):* There's something you can do, Charlie. You can go home and keep your mouth shut. You can quit strutting around like a self-appointed hanging judge. Just climb into bed and forget it.

CHARLIE: You sound real anxious to have that happen, Steve. I think we better keep our eye on you, too!

DON *(as if he were taking the bit in his teeth, takes a hesitant step to the front):* I think everything might as well come out now. *(He turns toward* STEVE.*)* Your wife's done plenty of talking, Steve, about how odd you are!

CHARLIE *(picking this up, his eyes widening):* Go ahead, tell us what she's said.

*(*STEVE *walks toward them from across the street.)*

STEVE: Go ahead, what's my wife said? Let's get it *all* out. Let's pick out every idiosyncrasy of every single man, woman, and

---

idiosyncracy (id ee oh SING kruh see) unusual trait, habit, or practice

child on the street. And then we might as well set up some kind of kangaroo court.[2] How about a firing squad at dawn, Charlie, so we can get rid of all the suspects? Narrow them down. Make it easier for you.

DON: There's no need gettin' so upset, Steve. It's just that . . . well . . . Myra's talked about how there's been plenty of nights you spent hours down in your basement workin' on some kind of radio or something. Well, none of us have ever seen that radio—

(By this time STEVE *has reached the group. He stands there defiantly.)*

CHARLIE: Go ahead, Steve. What kind of "radio set" you workin' on? I never seen it. Neither has anyone else. Who do you talk to on that radio set? And who talks to you?

STEVE: I'm surprised at you, Charlie. How come you're so dense all of a sudden? *(A pause)* Who do I talk to? I talk to monsters from outer space. I talk to three-headed green men who fly over here in what look like meteors.

*(*MYRA BRAND *steps down from the porch, bites her lip, calls out.)*

MYRA: Steve! Steve, please. *(Then looking around, frightened, she walks toward the group.)* It's just a ham radio set, that's all. I bought him a book on it myself. It's just a ham radio set. A lot of people have them. I can show it to you. It's right down in the basement.

STEVE *(whirls around toward her):* Show them nothing! If they want to look inside our house—let them get a search warrant.

CHARLIE: Look, buddy, you can't afford to—

STEVE *(interrupting him):* Charlie, don't start telling me who's dangerous and who isn't, and who's safe, and who's a menace. *(He turns to the group and shouts.)* And you're with him, too—all of you! You're standing here all set to crucify—all set to find a scapegoat—all desperate to point some kind of a finger at a neighbor! Well now, look, friends, the only thing that's gonna happen is that we'll eat each other up alive—

(He stops abruptly as CHARLIE *suddenly grabs his arm.)*

---

[2] **kangaroo court:** An unauthorized court that does not follow normal, legal procedures.

CHARLIE *(in a hushed voice):* That's not the only thing that can happen to us.

(Down the street, a figure has suddenly materialized in the gloom, and in the silence we hear the clickety-clack of slow, measured footsteps on concrete as the figure walks slowly toward them. One of the women lets out a stifled cry. SALLY *grabs her boy, as do a couple of other mothers.)*

TOMMY *(shouting, frightened):* It's the monster! It's the monster!

(Another woman lets out a wail and the people fall back in a group staring toward the darkness and the approaching figure.

The people stand in the shadows watching. DON MARTIN *joins them, carrying a shotgun. He holds it up.)*

DON: We may need this.

STEVE: A shotgun? *(He pulls it out of* DON's *hand.)* No! Will anybody think a thought around here? Will you people wise up. What good would a shotgun do against—

(The dark figure continues to walk toward them as the people stand there, fearful, mothers clutching children, men standing in front of their wives.)

CHARLIE *(pulling the gun from* STEVE'*s hands):* No more talk, Steve. You're going to talk us into a grave! You'd let whatever's out there walk right over us, wouldn't yuh? Well, some of us won't!

*(*CHARLIE *swings around, raises the gun, and suddenly pulls the trigger. The sound of the shot explodes in the stillness.*

The figure suddenly lets out a small cry, stumbles forward onto his knees, and then falls forward on his face. DON, CHARLIE, *and* STEVE *race forward to him.* STEVE *is there first and turns the man over. The crowd gathers around them.)*

STEVE *(slowly looks up):* It's Pete Van Horn.

DON *(in a hushed voice):* Pete Van Horn! He was just gonna go over to the next block to see if the power was on—

WOMAN ONE: You killed him, Charlie. You shot him dead!

CHARLIE *(looks around at the circle of faces, his eyes frightened, his face contorted):* But . . . but I didn't know who he was. I certainly didn't know who he was. He comes walkin' out of the darkness—how am I supposed to know who he was? *(He grabs* STEVE.*)* Steve—you know why I shot! How was I supposed to know he wasn't a monster or something? *(He grabs* DON.*)* We're all scared of the same thing. I was just tryin' to . . . tryin' to protect my home, that's all! Look, all of you, that's all I was tryin' to do. *(He looks down wildly at the body.)* I didn't know it was somebody we knew! I didn't know—

(There's a sudden hush and then an intake of breath in the group. Across the street all the lights go on in one of the houses.)

WOMAN ONE *(in a hushed voice):* Charlie . . . Charlie . . . the lights just went on in your house. Why did the lights just go on?

DON: What about it, Charlie? How come you're the only one with lights now?

LES: That's what I'd like to know.

(A pause as they all stare toward CHARLIE.*)*

LES: You were so quick to kill, Charlie, and you were so quick to tell us who we had to be careful of. Well, maybe you had to kill. Maybe Pete there was trying to tell us something. Maybe he'd found out something and came back to tell us who there was amongst us we should watch out for—

(CHARLIE *backs away from the group, his eyes wide with fright.)*

CHARLIE: No . . . no . . . it's nothing of the sort! I don't know why the lights are on. I swear I don't. Somebody's pulling a gag or something.

(He bumps against STEVE, *who grabs him and whirls him around.)*

STEVE: A *gag?* A gag? Charlie, there's a dead man on the sidewalk and you killed him! Does this thing look like a gag to you?

(CHARLIE *breaks away and screams as he runs toward his house.)*

CHARLIE: No! No! Please!

(A man breaks away from the crowd to chase CHARLIE.

As the man tackles him and lands on top of him, the other people start to run toward them. CHARLIE *gets up, breaks away from the other man's grasp, lands a couple of desperate punches that push the man aside. Then he forces his way, fighting, through the crowd, and jumps up on his front porch.*

CHARLIE *is on his porch as a rock thrown from the group smashes a window beside him, the broken glass flying past him. A couple of pieces cut him. He stands there perspiring, rumpled, blood running down from a cut on the cheek. His wife breaks away from the group to throw herself into his arms. He buries his face against her. We can see the crowd converging on the porch.)*

VOICE ONE: It must have been him.
VOICE TWO: He's the one.
VOICE THREE: We got to get Charlie.

(Another rock lands on the porch. CHARLIE *pushes his wife behind him, facing the group.)*

CHARLIE: Look, look I swear to you . . . it isn't me . . . but I do know who it is . . . I swear to you, I do know who it is. I know who the monster is here. I know who it is that doesn't belong. I swear to you I know.

DON *(pushing his way to the front of the crowd):* All right, Charlie, let's hear it!

(CHARLIE's *eyes dart around wildly.)*

CHARLIE: It's . . . it's . . .
MAN TWO *(screaming):* Go ahead, Charlie, tell us.
CHARLIE: It's . . . it's the kid. It's Tommy. He's the one!

(There's a gasp from the crowd as we see SALLY *holding the boy.* TOMMY *at first doesn't understand and then, realizing the eyes are all on him, buries his face against his mother.)*

SALLY *(backs away):* That's crazy! He's only a boy.
WOMAN ONE: But he knew! He was the only one who knew! He told us all about it. Well, how did he know? How *could* he have known?

(Various people take this up and repeat the question.)

VOICE ONE: How could he know?
VOICE TWO: Who told him?
VOICE THREE: Make the kid answer.

(The crowd starts to converge around the mother, who grabs TOMMY *and starts to run with him. The crowd starts to follow, at first walking fast, and then running after him.*

Suddenly CHARLIE*'s lights go off and the lights in other houses go on, then off.)*

MAN ONE *(shouting):* It isn't the kid . . . it's Bob Weaver's house.
WOMAN ONE: It isn't Bob Weaver's house, it's Don Martin's place.
CHARLIE: I tell you it's the kid.
DON: It's Charlie. He's the one.

(People shout, accuse, and scream as the lights go on and off. Then, slowly, in the middle of this nightmarish confusion of sight and sound, the camera starts to pull away until once again we have reached the opening shot looking at the Maple Street sign from high above.)

SCENE 2

(The camera continues to move away while gradually bringing into focus a field. We see the metal side of a spacecraft which sits shrouded in darkness. An open door throws out a beam of light from the illuminated interior. Two figures appear, silhouetted against the bright lights. We get only a vague feeling of form.)

FIGURE ONE: Understand the procedure now? Just stop a few of their machines and radios and telephones and lawn mowers . . . throw them into darkness for a few hours, and then just sit back and watch the pattern.

FIGURE TWO: And this pattern is always the same?

FIGURE ONE: With few variations. They pick the most dangerous enemy they can find . . . and it's themselves. And all we need do is sit back . . . and watch.

FIGURE TWO: Then I take it this place . . . this Maple Street . . . is not unique.

FIGURE ONE *(shaking his head):* By no means. Their world is full of Maple Streets. And we'll go from one to the other and let them destroy themselves. One to the other . . . one to the other . . . one to the other—

SCENE 3

(The camera pans up for a shot of the starry sky; and over this we hear the NARRATOR's *voice.)*

NARRATOR: The tools of conquest do not necessarily come with bombs and explosions and fallout. There are weapons that are simply thoughts, attitudes, prejudices—to be found only in the minds of people. For the record, prejudices can kill, and suspicion can destroy, and a thoughtless, frightened search for a scapegoat has a fallout all its own for the children . . . and the children yet unborn. *(A pause)* And the pity of it is . . . that these things cannot be confined to . . . The Twilight Zone!

(Fade to black.)

FOCUS ON THE SELECTION

UNDERSTAND THE SELECTION

Recall

1. What happened after the flying object went over?
2. What did Tommy say that made the neighbors suspicious of each other?
3. What was unusual about Les's car?

Infer

4. Why did people suspect Les of being an alien?
5. Why did the neighbors start looking for an enemy?
6. Why did some neighbors think that Pete was a monster?
7. Did the neighbors forget that Pete had left the group?

Apply

8. What did the spaceman mean by the following statement: "They pick the most dangerous enemy they can find . . . and it's themselves."?
9. What did he mean when he said: "Their world is full of Maple Streets."?
10. Predict what will happen now.

Respond to Literature

Would Steve Brand agree that this selection belongs in a unit called "Monsters"?

WRITE ABOUT THE SELECTION

At the end of "Monsters Are Due on Maple Street" we do not know what is going to happen next, or how the conflict is going to be resolved. Will the aliens turn the power back on? If they do, what will happen? If they leave it off, what will happen? Add an episode to this play. In it, tell the final outcome and the fate of the people on Maple Street. Write it in the form of a play. Put the actions in parentheses. Use the person's name, followed by a colon, to show who is speaking.

Prewriting: Decide first what the aliens will do. Will they turn on the power, or not? Then decide what the people on Maple Street will do. Will they fight among themselves or against the aliens? Make an informal outline of the ending and the actions leading up to it.

Writing: Use your notes and outline to write another scene for this play. Show what happens to the people on Maple Street.

Revising: When you revise your scene be sure the readers will be able to picture the action in their minds. Make it clear who is speaking to whom.

Proofreading: Read your scene to check for errors. Be sure that you have used the speaker's name followed by a colon to show which character is speaking. Also check to be sure that you have enclosed your description of the characters' actions in parentheses.

THINK ABOUT THEME

The events in some stories express a theme. A character may state the theme in one sentence. Sometimes the theme is expressed throughout the story in the words or thoughts of one or more of the characters.

1. What is the theme of "The Monsters Are Due on Maple Street"?
2. Which character or characters do you think come closest to stating the theme?
3. Which of the neighbors on Maple Street seems to show some understanding of the play's theme?
4. Read the quotation on page 193 at the beginning of this unit. How could you relate that quotation to the theme of this play?
5. In your opinion why is this selection in a unit that has "Monsters" as the theme?

DEVELOP YOUR VOCABULARY

You are more likely to add words to your working vocabulary if you notice how others use them. When you read a story, notice how new words are used in the story. For example, does the author use them to tell about the setting, the characters and the character's problem or goal?

Think about the following words. Do you remember how the playwright used them to describe? Find each word in the play. Is it in the dialogue or in the directions? Decide which of the following ways the playwright used each word.

1. To describe the setting.
2. To describe a character.
3. To tell what a character wanted.
4. To explain or illustrate a character's problem.
5. To show how the problem was solved.
6. To describe a character's feelings.
7. To be part of or describe the action.

Review the meanings of these words from "The Monsters Are Due on Maple Street." Use each word in an original sentence.

1. transfixed
2. assent
3. taut
4. incisive
5. incriminate
6. idiosyncracy

UNIT 3 REVIEW

LITERATURE-BASED WRITING

1. All of the selections in this unit have been about a monster of some kind. Some selections were about terrifying creatures. Others were about creatures that were terrifying under some circumstances, while other selections dealt with monster tendencies in human beings. Decide which monster in this unit was the most frightening. Write an opinion paragraph giving your reasons.

Prewriting: Write the name of the monster you think is the most frightening. Then list some frightening qualities this monster possesses. List some of the reasons it is more frightening than the other monsters.

Writing: Use your notes to help you write your opinion paragraph. Describe the frightening traits of the monster. Tell why it is more frightening than the other monsters.

Revising: Revise your paragraph. Be sure that you have given frightening details about your monster, and reasons why it is more frightening than the other monsters.

Proofreading: Read your paragraph to check for errors. Be sure all your sentences begin with capital letters and end with periods, question marks, or exclamation marks.

2. You have been studying the elements of fiction in this unit. You have studied setting, characters, plot, and theme. Choose a short story or play from this unit. Describe the elements of fiction in the story.

Prewriting: Review the work you did for the "Thinking About the—" sections in this unit. Then make a chart that has the name of the selection you have chosen at the top, and the four literary elements down the side. Fill in the spaces on the chart with details about each element of fiction from the story.

Writing: Use your chart to write a description of each of the elements of fiction found in the short story or the play you have chosen.

Revising: Revise your paper. Be sure you have finished discussing one element of fiction before moving on to the next. Consider deleting or adding to your descriptions to make them as clear and accurate as possible.

Proofreading: Read your report to check for errors. Be sure all your sentences begin with capital letters and end with periods, question marks, or exclamation marks.

BUILDING LANGUAGE SKILLS

Vocabulary

You know that a noun names a person, place, or thing. You also know that an adjective describes a noun. Adding a suffix can change the part of speech of the word to which it is added. A **suffix** is a word part added to the end of a base word.

The word *silky* means "having the quality of silk." You can figure out from this that the suffix *y* can mean "full of, covered with, or having the quality of." Did you notice that when this suffix was added an adjective was formed?

When you add *y* to a word that has a short vowel followed by a single consonant, you double the consonant *(fog-foggy)*. When you add *y* to a word ending in *e*, you drop the *e (slime-slimy)*.

Write the following sentences. An adjective ending in *y* has been replaced by a noun in parentheses. Turn the word back into an adjective by adding *y*.

1. Little else could be seen in the dim and *(smoke)* hall.
2. A heap of charred beams and *(powder)* ashes had fallen into the cellar hole.
3. It swam slowly and with great dark majesty out in the *(ice)* waters.
4. A number of gigantic ten-armed bodies began to be washed up on the *(rock)* shores of Newfoundland and Labrador.

Usage and Mechanics

When you are speaking with someone, you sometimes call that person by name. In story dialogue, characters sometimes say the name of the person to whom they are speaking. When speakers name the person they are addressing, the person's name is called a **noun of direct address.**

Writers use commas to separate a noun of direct address from the rest of the sentence. If the noun of direct address comes at the beginning or the end of the sentence, only one comma is needed. Read the following example from "The Monsters Are Due on Maple Street." "Steve, the power's off." If the noun of direct address comes in the middle of the sentence, then two commas are needed: "Look, buddy, you can't afford to—." The speaker didn't finish the sentence. *Buddy* is a noun of direct address in the middle of the sentence fragment, and it is set off by two commas. Write the following sentences from "The Monsters Are Due on Maple Street." Add the commas where they are needed:

1. Tommy come over here and stop that kind of talk.
2. Go ahead Tommy.
3. We're all on a monster kick Les.
4. Go ahead Charlie tell us.
5. No more talk Steve.

UNIT 3 REVIEW

SPEAKING AND LISTENING

On one hand, reading poetry can be a wonderful experience. On the other hand, it can be frustrating because sometimes a poet's meaning is difficult to grasp. One way to approach and understand a poem is to read it with the idea that the poet is telling a story.

Many poems, like stories, have characters, a setting, and a theme or main idea. Of course, the poet uses fewer words and these things may not be as clearly defined; nonetheless, they are there if only in skeleton form.

In order to find these elements in a poem, you must be a "poem sleuth" and concentrate on certain things. When you begin reading a poem practice the following steps. The poem's meaning will certainly become clear because you have brought the poem to life.

1. Read the entire poem two or three times. Enjoy what it says!
2. Focus on certain words and try to identify the poet's message. Is he or she attempting to entertain you, does the poet want to give you a point of view, teach you something, or is the poet just making a statement?
3. Has the poet used words that help you to know the time and place of the poem? Is there a certain tone that is obvious because of the words used by the poet? Is the language used of present day or does it seem from another time?
4. Look at the title of the poem. Does it make the meaning of the poem more clear? Does it tell you anything about the main idea of the poem?
5. Who is speaking in the poem? Is it the poet or another person? Are they young or old? Are they happy, sad, angry or confused? What words in the poem help you to know something about the main "character"?

When you are thoroughly familiar with the poem you have selected, go back and read it again. Before long you will discover that although you are reading a poem, a story is being told. You will find that you understand the poem's meaning.

Practice in your mind how you would tell this poem if it were a story. Then prepare to present this "story" to a small group or your class. In two or three minutes, help your audience to understand the poem by describing its "characters", "setting", and "theme". After you have finished your talk, recite or read the poem so your classmates can appreciate the words of the poet.

CRITICAL THINKING

What do José Feliciano, Diana Ross, Bruce Springsteen, and Beverly Sills have in common? All of them have made their living singing professionally. A class is a group of people, things, or ideas that have something in common. The name of a class that could include all of these people would be "singers." We could not name the class "pop singers" because that would not include Beverly Sills, a former opera singer.

Who else could you put into a class called singers? When you put people, things, or ideas into a class or group, you are **classifying** them. You decide in what class something belongs by knowing what characteristics or features the members of a class have in common. If you call the class "pop singers," Beverly Sills, an opera singer, does not belong. If you call the class "women singers," Sills and Ross do belong.

The selections in this unit are classified for you. The title of the theme tells you the name of the class. All of the stories in the first unit were about Americans. All of the stories in this unit were about monsters.

Make two headings on your paper. Under the heading "monsters" list all the characters in this unit that were monsters. Under the heading "heroes" list all characters who were heroes. Remember that a hero is more than a main character. Some stories have no heroes. A hero has to do a great and important deed. Make another heading called "the monster in human beings." In this column, list characters whose actions and personalities showed some of the characteristics of a monster.

EFFECTIVE STUDYING

When you write a report, how do you organize the information for your report? One method you can use is to make an outline. An **outline** is the bare bones of a report. It organizes information into main ideas and supporting ideas and details.

When you make an outline follow these steps:

I. Identify the main ideas. Make each main idea a main topic.

II. List the main topics and label them with Roman numerals followed by a period.

   A. Within each main topic identify the supporting ideas and details.

   B. List the supporting details under the correct main topic.

   C. Indent the subtopics or supporting ideas. Label them with capital letters followed by a period.

      1. If you want to give further details about one of the subtopics, list them under the subtopic.

      2. Indent the further details and label them with Arabic numerals followed by a period.

Outlining is important because it shows you how the facts fit together and how to relate one fact to another. Make an outline of "The Ten-Armed Monster of Newfoundland." Identify the main topics, and follow the steps listed above.

UNIT 4

Success

To travel hopefully is a better thing than
to arrive, and the true
success is to labor.

—Robert Louis Stevenson

New School Mural, Thomas Hart Benton.
Art Resource

Success. How do you define success? When you look up "success" in a dictionary you will find words like *goal, objective, achieve,* and *accomplish.* When you explore your own ideas about success, you may discover that its true meaning is more difficult to pin down. Success often depends on an individual's experiences and attitudes toward life. Some people believe that striving for a goal brings its own success. They feel that working toward a goal is more important than actually achieving it. Other people believe that reaching a specific goal is the only true measure of success. Which idea about success do you agree with?

The selections in this unit will focus on the different ideas people have about success and will help you examine and understand your own personal definition of success.

Setting Goals for Success. Establishing goals is a key element in success. What goals do you have about school, friends, or career? Do you have a strategy for reaching these goals? In "The Finish of Patsy Barnes" by Paul Laurence Dunbar, a courageous boy realizes that he alone can help his sick mother. He sets a difficult goal for himself. He must conquer his fears and win the most important race of his life.

The next two selections examine the goals that athletes set for themselves. In "The Kick" by Elizabeth van Steenwyk, a young woman seeks to demonstrate that she can compete successfully in track events with boys—and learns something quite new about the meaning of success. Ernest Thayer's "Casey at the Bat" focuses on a gifted baseball player who has a very specific goal. Many people depend upon his success. However, the poem points out the dangers that come from being distracted from your goals. What techniques do you use to keep focused on your goals?

Determining Attitudes About Success. In literature, as in life, a person's attitude often determines his or her idea about success. Emily Dickinson shares her most private thoughts and attitude about success in three incisive poems, "Success," "'Hope' Is the Thing with Feathers," and "If I Can Stop One Heart from Breaking."

Henry Wadsworth Longfellow's "A Psalm of Life" makes a convincing argument that success is within every person's grasp. In "This Day Is Over," Calvin O'John discusses the choices that people have in life, and explains how a positive attitude can insure success. How important is the proper attitude in achieving success? Deborah Boe's "Factory Life" focuses on another, more complicated attitude about success. In this poem, the main character is successful at work, yet feels unsuccessful in life. Have you ever been torn by two opposing feelings about success?

The Lessons of Success. Can success cause unplanned results? Two stories in this unit suggest that success often teaches unexpected lessons. In "The Wolf of Thunder Mountain" Dion Henderson describes a boy's visit to his grandfather who lives on a mountain, far from civilization. The boy's wilderness experiences completely change his ideas about success. Has a single, important experience ever changed your ideas about success?

The last story in this unit is a folktale that shows the unplanned rewards of success. In "The Pot of Gold," Salvador Salazar Arrué describes a lazy man who works extremely hard to find buried treasure. What he fails to learn in his search focuses on yet another meaning of success.

How many definitions of success can you identify? As you read the selections in this unit, think about what each reveals about success. Ask yourself if you agree or disagree with these different interpretations.

Learn About

Conflict

Imagine a story in which the main character achieves his or her goal without having to overcome any obstacles. The absence of a struggle, or problem, would probably make the story very dull.

Conflict is the element that makes a story interesting and exciting. It is the struggle between two opposing forces.

In literature, as in life, there are three basic kinds of conflict. The first involves a person's struggle against another person. The second concerns a person's struggle against outside forces or objects. For example, an outside force may be a natural event, like a hurricane.

The third kind of conflict takes place within a person. In this type of conflict, persons struggle with their opposing thoughts, desires or feelings.

As you read "The Finish of Patsy Barnes" ask yourself:

1. What kinds of conflict occur in this story?
2. How are these conflicts resolved?

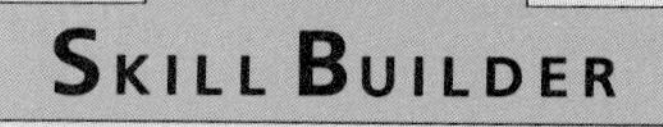

Skill Builder

Think of a conflict in your life. Write a brief passage that describes the type of conflict you are experiencing right now.

THE FINISH OF PATSY BARNES

by Paul Laurence Dunbar

His name was Patsy Barnes, and he lived in Little Africa. In fact, he lived on Douglass Street. By all the laws governing people and their names, he should have been Irish. But he was not. He was black, and very much so. That was the reason he lived on Douglass Street. Patsy's mother had found her way to Little Africa when she had come North from Kentucky.

Patsy was beyond reform. The truant officer and the terrible penalty of the compulsory education law had come into Little Africa. Time and time again, poor Eliza Barnes had been brought up on account of that son of hers. She was a hard-working, honest woman. Day by day, she bent over her tub, scrubbing away to keep Patsy in shoes and jackets that would wear out so much faster than they could be bought. But she never murmured, for she loved the boy with a deep affection, though his behavior was a sore thorn in her side.

She wanted him to go to school. She wanted him to learn. She had the idea that he might become something better, something higher than she had been. But for him, school had no charms. His school was the cool stalls in the big livery stable nearby. The arena of his activity was its sawdust floor. The height of his ambition was to be a horseman. Either here or in the racing stables at the Fairgrounds he spent his truant hours. It was a school that taught much, and Patsy was as good a pupil as he was a constant visitor. He learned strange things about horses though he had only turned into his fourteenth year.

A man goes where he is appreciated. Then could this slim black boy be blamed for doing the same thing? He was a great favorite with the horsemen. He picked up

---

truant (TROO unt) person who plays hooky from school, who stays away from school without permission

compulsory (kum PUL suh ree) required (by the government, for example)

livery (LIV ur ee) stable where horses are kept for hire

many a dime or nickel for dancing or singing, or even a quarter for warming up a horse for its owner. He was not to be blamed for this. First of all, he was born in Kentucky. He had spent his baby days about the paddocks near Lexington where his father had lost his life on account of his love for horses. The little fellow had shed no tears when he looked at his father's bleeding body, bruised and broken by the wild young two-year-old horse he was trying to tame. Patsy did not sob or whimper, though his heart ached. Along with all his feelings of grief was a mad, burning desire to ride that horse.

His tears were shed, however, when they moved to Dalesford with the idea that times would be easier up North. Then, when he learned that he must leave his old friends, the horses and their masters whom he had known, he wept. The rather simple Fairgrounds at Dalesford proved a poor exchange for what he had known. For the first few weeks Patsy had dreams of running away—back to Kentucky and the horses and stables. Then after a while he settled himself to make the best of what he had. With a mighty effort, he took up the burden of life away from his beloved home.

Eliza Barnes, older and more experienced though she was, took up her burden less cheerfully than her son. She worked hard and made a scanty living, it is true. But she did not make the best of what she had. Her complainings were loud in the land. Her wailings for her old home struck the ears of any who would listen to her.

They had been living in Dalesford for a year nearly, when hard work and exposure brought the woman down to bed with pneumonia. They were very poor, too poor even to call in a regular doctor. There was nothing to do but to call in the city physician. Now this medical man had too many calls into Little Africa, and he did not like to go there. So he was very rough when anyone called him. It was even said that he was careless of his patients.

Patsy's heart bled as he heard the doctor talking to his mother.

"Now, there can't be any foolishness about this," he said. "You've got to stay in bed and not get yourself damp."

"How long you think I got to lay hyeah, doctah?" she asked.

"I'm a doctor, not a fortune-teller," was the reply. "You'll lie there as long as the disease holds you."

"But I can't lay hyeah long, doctah, case I ain't got nuffin' to go on."

"Well, take your choice—the bed or the boneyard."

Eliza began to cry.

"You needn't sniffle," said the doctor.

---

paddock (PAD uk) fenced-in area where horses are saddled and exercised
burden (BURD un) heavy weight; great load
scanty (SKAN tee) very small; hardly enough for what is needed
exposure (ik SPOH zhur) being outside in bad weather; being in a helpless position
boneyard (BOHN yahrd) slang term for cemetery

"I don't see what you wanted to come up North for anyhow. Why didn't you stay down South where you belong?"

There was an angry being in the room, and that was Patsy. His eyes were full of tears that scorched him and would not fall. He dared not let his mother hear him swear. Oh! to have a stone, to be across the street from that man!

When the physician walked out, Patsy went to the bed, took his mother's hand, and bent over to kiss her. The little mark of affection comforted Eliza greatly. The mother-feeling overwhelmed her in one burst of tears. Then she dried her eyes and smiled at him.

"Honey," she said, "mammy ain' gwine lay hyeah long. She be all right putty soon."

"Nevah you min'," said Patsy with a choke in his voice. "I can do somep'n', an' we'll have anothah doctah."

"La, listen at de chile. What kin you do?"

"I'm goin' down to McCarthy's stable and see if I kin git some horses to exercise."

A sad look came into Eliza's eyes as she said, "You'd bettah not go, Patsy. Dem hosses'll kill you yit, des like dey did yo' pappy."

But the boy, used to doing pretty much as he pleased, was stubborn. Even while she was talking, he put on his ragged jacket and left the room.

Patsy was not wise enough to be diplomatic. He got right to the point with McCarthy, the stable man.

The big red-faced fellow slapped him until he spun round and round. Then he said, "Ye little devil, ye! I've a mind to knock the whole head off o' ye. Ye want harses to exercise, do ye? Well, git on that 'un an' see what ye kin do with him."

The boy's honest desire to be helpful had tickled the big, generous Irishman's peculiar sense of humor. From now on, instead of giving Patsy a horse to ride now and then as he had formerly done, he put into his charge all the animals that needed exercise.

It was with a king's pride that Patsy marched home with his first considerable earnings.

They were small yet, and would go for food rather than a doctor, but Eliza was very proud of him. It was this pride that gave her strength and the desire of life to carry her through the coming days of the crisis of her disease.

Patsy saw his mother growing worse. He saw her gasping for breath. He heard the rattling as she drew in the little air that kept going through her clogged lungs. He felt the heat of her burning hands. He saw the pitiful appeal in her poor eyes. Soon he became convinced that the city doctor was not helping her. She must have another. But the money?

That afternoon, after his work with

---

diplomatic (dip luh MAT ik) careful and wise in dealing with people
considerable (kun SID ur uh bul) fairly large
crisis (KRY sis) dangerous time when an illness or other problem can either get better or worse

McCarthy, he was at the Fairgrounds. The spring races were on. He thought he might get a job warming up the horse of some independent jockey. He hung around the stables, listening to the talk of men he knew and some he had never seen before. One of those he had not seen before was a tall, thin man, speaking to a group of men.

"No, suh," he was saying to them. "I'm goin' to withdraw my hoss, because thaih ain't nobody to ride him as he ought to be rode. I haven't brought a jockey along with me, so I've got to depend on pick-ups. Now, people are set again my hoss, Black Boy, because he's been losin' regular. But that hoss has lost for the want of ridin', that's all."

The crowd looked in at the slim-legged, bony horse, and walked away laughing.

"The fools!" muttered the stranger. "If I could ride myself I'd show 'em!"

Patsy was gazing into the stall at the horse.

"What are you doing thaih?" called the owner to him.

"Look hyeah, mistah," said Patsy, "ain't that a bluegrass hoss?"

"Of co'se it is, an' one o' the fastest that evah grazed."

"I'll ride that hoss, mistah."

"What do you know 'bout ridin'?"

"I used to be roun' Mistah Boone's paddock in Lexington, an'—"

"Aroun' Boone's paddock—what!

---

bluegrass (BLOO gras) a type of bluish-green grass grown especially in Kentucky and used as feed for horses

Look here, if you can ride that hoss to a winnin' I'll give you more money than you ever seen before."

"I'll ride him."

Patsy's heart was beating very wildly beneath his jacket. That horse. He knew that glossy coat. He knew that bony body and those flashing nostrils. That black horse there owed something to the orphan he had made.

The horse was to ride in the race before the last. Somehow out of odds and ends, his owner scraped together a suit and racing colors for Patsy. The colors were maroon and green, a curious combination. But then it was a curious horse, a curious rider, and a more curious combination that brought the two together. Long before the time for the race, Patsy went into the stall to become better acquainted with his horse. The animal turned its wild eyes upon him and neighed. He patted the long, slender head and grinned as the horse stepped aside as gently as a lady.

"He sholy is full o' spirit," he said to the owner, whose name he had found to be Brackett.

"He'll show 'em a thing or two," laughed Brackett.

"His dam was a fast one," said Patsy, without thinking.

Brackett whirled on him in a flash. "What do you know about his dam?" he asked.

The boy would have taken it back, but it was too late. Stammering, he told the story of his father's death and the horse's connection with him.

"Well," said Brackett, "if you don't turn out to be a hoodoo, you're a winner for sure. I'll be blessed if this don't sound like a story! But I've heard that story before. The man I got Black Boy from told it to me."

When the bell sounded and Patsy went to warm up, he felt as if he were riding on air. Some of the jockeys laughed at his outfit. But there was something in him—or under him, maybe—that made him rise above their laughter. He saw a sea of faces about him, then saw no more. Only a shining white track appeared ahead of him. A restless steed was running with him around the curve. Then the bell called him back to the stand.

They did not get away at first, and back they trooped. A second start was also a failure. But at the third, they were off in a line as straight as a chalk mark. There were Essex and Firefly, Queen Bess and Mosquito, galloping away side by side, and Black Boy a neck ahead. Patsy knew the family reputation his horse had for endurance as well as fire. He began

---

curious (KYUUR ee us) very strange; odd
dam (DAM) mother, said of animals
stammering (STAM ur ing) speaking with involuntary stops and repetition
hoodoo (HOO doo) a person or thing that brings bad luck
steed (STEED) fine, high-spirited riding horse
endurance (en DUUR runs) the ability to withstand hardship, misfortune, or stress

riding the race from the first. Black Boy came of blood that would not be passed. To this his rider trusted. At the eighth, the line was hardly broken. But as the quarter was reached, Black Boy had moved a length ahead, and Mosquito was at his flank. Then, like a flash, Essex shot out ahead under whip and spur, his jockey standing straight in the stirrups.

The crowd in the stands screamed. But Patsy smiled as he lay low over his horse's neck. He saw that Essex had made her best move. His only fear was for Mosquito, who hugged and hugged his flank. They were nearing the three-quarter post. He was tightening his grip on the black. Essex fell back; his move was over. The spurs dug him in vain.

Black Boy's breath touches the leader's ear. They are neck and neck—nose to nose. The black stallion passes him.

Another cheer from the stands. Again Patsy smiles as they turn into the stretch. Mosquito has gained a head. The black boy flashes one glance at the horse and rider who are so surely gaining upon him. His lips close in a firm line. They are halfway down the stretch, and Mosquito's head is at the stallion's neck.

For a single moment Patsy thinks of the sick woman at home and what that race will mean to her. Then his knees

---

flank (FLANGK) side near the back leg; hip
spur (SPUR) metal piece attached to a rider's shoe used to make the horse go faster

close against the horse's sides with a firmer dig. The spurs shoot deeper into the steaming flanks. Black Boy shall win. He must win! The horse that has taken away his father shall give him back his mother. The stallion leaps away like a flash and goes under the finish wire—a length ahead.

Then the band thundered. Patsy was off his horse. Very warm and very happy, he followed his mount to the stable. There, a little later, Brackett found him. He rushed to him and flung his arms around him.

"You little devil," he cried. "You rode like you were kin to that hoss! We've won! We've won!" And he began sticking money at the boy. At first Patsy's eyes bulged. Then he seized the money and got into his clothes.

"Goin' out to spend it?" asked Brackett.

"I'm goin' for a doctah fu' my mother," said Patsy, "She's sick."

"Don't let me lose sight of you."

"Oh, I'll see you again. So long," said the boy.

An hour later, he walked into his mother's room with a very big doctor, the greatest the druggist could direct him to. The doctor left his medicines and his orders. But, when Patsy told his story, it was Eliza's pride that started her on the road to recovery. Patsy did not tell her his horse's name.

FOCUS ON THE SELECTION

UNDERSTAND THE SELECTION

Recall

1. Where is Patsy originally from?
2. How old is Patsy?
3. How many false starts occur at the beginning of the race?

Infer

4. Explain how Patsy's father died.
5. What does Patsy think about the doctor's attitude toward Mrs. Barnes?
6. After his first glance, what does Patsy know immediately about Black Boy?
7. During the race, Patsy hopes that "the horse that has taken away his father shall give him back his mother." Does this desire come true?

Apply

8. Describe what Mrs. Barnes is like.
9. Two different kinds of school are mentioned in this story. Can you name them? What elements do they share in common? What makes them different?
10. Predict what kind of career Patsy will probably have. Will he be successful?

Respond to Literature

Motivation is often the key to a person's success. What do you think motivates Patsy to achieve success in his life?

WRITE ABOUT THE SELECTION

In this story, Patsy Barnes conquers his fears to win the most important race of his life. Throughout the story, he demonstrates intelligence, determination, and most of all, courage. What do you think courage really means? Is courage limited to physical deeds? Or does courage also include mental and spiritual strength? Write a paragraph in which you explain your own definition of courage.

Prewriting: Before you write your paragraph, think about courageous people you have known in your own life or read about. Make a list of the characteristics you associate with courage.

Writing: Use your list to write a paragraph that explains your definition of courage. In it, include examples of courageous people and courageous actions that you have read about in this, or other books.

Revising: When you revise your paragraph, make sure that it begins with a clear, convincing statement of your definition. Reread your sentences to see if each one includes specific details that support your definition. Consider rearranging your sentences to make your writing clearer or more effective.

Proofreading: When you proofread your paragraph check to see that you have indented the first word in the paragraph, and that the first word in each sentence is capitalized. Reread your paragraph to check for errors in spelling and punctuation.

THINK ABOUT CONFLICT

As was previously mentioned, there are three principal kinds of **conflict.** Conflict can be a physical or an emotional struggle between people. It can also be a contest between a person and an object, or force, such as nature. Sometimes conflict can take place within a person's mind. When this happens, the person feels divided between opposing ideas or feelings. Understanding conflict gives you insights into people's inner thoughts and feelings.

1. What is Patsy's main conflict?
2. What conflict does Patsy experience when he sees his father's body?
3. What opposing thoughts or feelings does Patsy have about Black Boy?
4. What conflicts does Mrs. Barnes experience throughout the story?
5. A conflict is resolved when one side wins the struggle. At the end of the story, what gives you the feeling that Patsy has won his struggle?

DEVELOP YOUR VOCABULARY

Nouns are words that name people, places, objects, ideas, or actions. In the sentence, "The statue was beautiful," *statue* is a noun. **Verbs** are words that express action or a state of being. In the sentence, "She jogged across the field," *jogged* is a verb.

Read the sentences below. Then tell whether each *italicized* word is used as a noun or a verb. You may use a dictionary to learn how each word is used in the sentence.

1. We were hit by a *blast* of cold air. The workers prepared to *blast* the boulder.
2. Good friends *stand* by each other. The band played a two-night *stand.*
3. *Credit* 20 dollars to my account. We received *credit* for our project.
4. That action helped to *seal* her fate. Water spilled from the broken *seal.*

Learn About

Theme

Most authors try to express a message about some aspect of human experience in their stories. This special message, or insight, is called the **theme.**

Sometimes a writer may state the theme directly. More often though, the theme is developed indirectly. In such stories, you must figure out the author's message, or theme. To determine the theme of a story, pay attention to what the characters do and say, and what happens to them.

As you think about the theme, ask yourself the following questions. What is the main character's goal? What steps does he or she take to achieve this goal? How do other characters react to the main character? Finally, what is the end result of the main character's actions?

After you figure out the theme of a story, express it using a complete sentence, or several sentences.

As you read "The Kick," ask yourself:

1. How does the main character achieve her goal?
2. Does the author try to communicate a message about life?

Skill Builder

Write the following topics on a piece of paper: friendship, competition, winning. For each topic, write two possible insights, or themes. Be sure to write complete sentences.

THE KICK

by Elizabeth Van Steenwyk

The announcer's voice boomed over the loudspeaker, "Last call for frosh-soph milers." The moment she stepped on the track with the guys, she heard the snickering start again. Why couldn't the spectators get used to her presence, too? Why couldn't people understand that girls loved to run as much as boys?

The starter called out their names and assigned lanes; she was seeded in the fifth.

"Boys," he began, then looking at her, "I mean, boys and girl, this is the mile run, four laps around the track. Stay in your lanes until you come to the red markers down there." He pointed to the far turn. "Then you can cut for the pole. There will be two commands to start, the whistle and the gun. Have a good race, boys, I mean, boys and girl."

She assumed the beginning stance and tried to wash her mind of everything but the race before her. Today was no ordinary meet, but League prelims, and she was the first girl ever to be entered from any school. Sure she felt nervous, but she had a good feeling about the meet. Maybe today was her day.

The starter blew the whistle; she tensed. He fired the gun. They were off. For a couple of glorious moments, she ran ahead of the pack because of her advantage in the fifth lane, but it didn't last. The kid from Springdale passed her, but she'd expected this.

---

frosh (FROSH) freshman, person in first year of high school or college
soph (SOF) sophomore, person in the second year of high school or college
seeded (SEED id) in sports, placed or arranged in order of ability
stance (STANS) way of standing
prelims (PREE limz) sports event you must pass to enter the main event
advantage (ad VAN tij) something that gives a person a better chance, a more favorable position

He was a real hotshot; he'd probably be a class runner by this time next year. She stayed with the other three boys until the first stretch. Then gradually, two more pulled away and she was left with the Crown City boy.

"You're doing fine, Mary Beth," she heard someone shout from the infield and recognized the voice of her friend, Bones, the varsity two-miler. He was a senior and captain of the team. She'd been so proud and grateful when he took a special interest in her, a lowly freshman.

"Keep those arms down," he called again.

She tried to think about form. She knew its importance as a part of the training strategy she'd practiced for so many months. Milers had to have a good combination of stamina and speed and all the training had been directed to that. Would it pay off for her?

Fortunately, speed came naturally. Dad had been a sprinter on his college team and her three brothers lettered in track before her. Bill, now a senior and a class runner in the mile, discovered her speed last summer when he clocked her running the junior high track and suggested she go out as a freshman. Then, when she did, he had acted like a total stranger. If it hadn't been for Bones, she might have quit. He was the only one on the team who acknowledged her membership in the human race.

She and the Crown City kid rounded the far turn on the first lap and crossed their lanes. She felt a prickly sensation on her legs and knew it to be a spray of fine gravel he'd kicked up as he pulled away from her. Now, as they passed the grandstand, she heard voices but no words, and she hoped it would stay that way. If she heard Mom shouting, she'd just die.

The next lap seemed easier and she felt light, almost airborne, hardly feeling the ground when her feet touched it. That was a bad sign, and fearing that sort of self-hypnosis most of all, she shook it off. Then she heard Bones calling again, "Keep him in sight, Mary Beth. Hang in there." Good, she needed that. She

---

varsity (VAHR suh tee) belonging to a school's best team
stamina (STAM uh nuh) strength and ability to last
sprinter (SPRINT ur) one who runs quickly for a short distance
acknowledge (ak NOL ij) admit that something is true
prickly (PRIK lee) full of sharp points; tingling
self-hypnosis (SELF hip NOH sis) putting oneself in a condition resembling a trance

pulled closer to the Crown City kid, but they had nearly two more laps to go and she had to hold something back for the kick.

What was a kick anyway? Jim Ryun talked about it, so did Francie Larrieu and the rest of the running world, but no one ever could define it exactly. Oh, she knew a kick was that last hard sprint at the finish line, but it was more than that. Was it courage, strength, competitiveness, or just plain guts? The coach said he didn't know for sure, she'd have to find it out for herself.

They passed the grandstand for the third time and then she heard it, Mom's voice shouting, "Come on, Honey Bunch."

Crumb, she thought. Why does she have to call me that? For a minute she thought she'd broken her rhythm she got so upset, but then she retrieved it and held the Crown City kid in tight. The lead boy from Springdale was a half lap ahead of them, he was really kicking and the other two boys were fighting for second and third.

She made up her mind. I'm not going to be last, she thought. I won't be last. She picked up her speed, but the Crown City kid sensed it ahead and kept the distance between them.

She wondered what his nickname was, or if he had one. Nicknames were a status symbol, or at least they were on her team. It was a sign that you'd really arrived when the boys bestowed a special name on you. Well, she was still Mary Beth and probably always would be, except to Mom. *"Honey bunch," Ugh!*

But she should be concentrating on the event. She closed the gap on the Crown City kid at the final turn. This was the moment she'd trained for, hoped for, and yes, prayed for. Did she have the will to win? Could she at least beat a boy? A sudden thought grabbed her. Did the Crown City kid have a good kick? She couldn't remember from their dual meet.

She heard Bones yelling again, "Kick it on home, Mary Beth."

Now she knew it was now or never. Would she have it, that kick, when she wanted it? Her mouth was parched and dry as a

---

competitiveness (kum PET uh tiv nis) trying hard to win against others
retrieve (rih TREEV) get something back
status symbol (STAYT us SIM bul) something used to show how important a person is
concentrate (KON sun trayt) give all one's attention to
parched (PAHRCHT) dried out

day-old sandwich. She was afraid that her kick wouldn't be there when she needed it most.

She ran even with the Crown City kid now. Neck and neck. Was it his breathing or hers that she heard?

Then she reached way back in her brain and told every cell in her body, every screaming tendon, every breath, every pounding beat of her heart to kick and soon, slowly, then quickly, it washed over her with a flood of strength and desire and sweat. She was kicking it on home and the spectators saw it and knew magic was in the air. They rose as one and roared and shouted their approval. The girl, she felt them thinking, the girl was going to beat that boy, actually beat a boy for the first time in the history of the league.

Then she heard Bill's voice shouting at her from the infield. "You've got him, Honey Bunch."

Crumb, she thought. Why that name, now at a time like this?

---

tendon (TEN dun) part of the body that connects a muscle to a bone

Then she knew and just the knowing enveloped her like a soft garment. They'd given her a special nickname, like everyone else, just like Bones and Brick and Spider and Zap. She'd been accepted.

She pulled away for good then, and crossed the finish line two steps ahead of the Crown City kid, kept her lane for another 20 feet, stopped, and leaned over to gasp and catch her breath. Sweat dripped from her, her hair felt like a soggy mop hanging down her back but she didn't care. Victory was sweet.

The team surrounded her. She gloried in their praise, and listened intently as the announcer spoke her name.

"Mary Beth Barkley of Walnut Hill, fourth place in the time of 5:21.04."

She walked out to the center of the track and waved to the grandstand just like Olga Korbut.

Finally, the magic softened to a warm glow within her, the cheering stopped, and she couldn't wait to drink some tea, that super honey tea the mothers provided for every meet. Set up on an old bench at the grandstand's far corner, cups and jugs were ready and waiting. She walked over, grateful to be alone, and poured herself a cup.

Then she saw him. At first she glimpsed only a pair of legs sticking out from under the grandstand. But when she bent over and looked underneath, she recognized the kid from Crown City in his green and orange uniform. His shoulders heaved with dry sobs and he pounded the dirt with his fists in frustration and rage.

She knew, of course. She knew what he felt, because she'd been last so many times herself. But it was more than that with him. He'd been beaten by a girl and somehow, he'd have to live with it for a long time.

She put her tea down so suddenly, it sloshed out of the cup. Crumb, she thought. Why didn't someone tell her there's more to a victory than winning? She kicked off her spikes and walked barefoot back to the dressing room.

---

envelop (en VEL up) wrap; surround
intently (in TENT lee) with sharp attention
frustration (frus TRAY shun) disappointment people feel when they cannot get what they had hoped for

FOCUS ON THE SELECTION

UNDERSTAND THE SELECTION

Recall

1. In which lane does Mary Beth run?
2. Throughout the race, who gives Mary Beth encouragement?
3. In what place in the race does Mary Beth finish?

Infer

4. Explain why Mary Beth's brother, Bill, "acted like a total stranger" when she made the freshman track team.
5. Explain what decision Mary Beth makes after she passes the grandstand for the third time.
6. Why is having a runner's nickname so important to Mary Beth?
7. Explain the elements that contribute to a successful kick.

Apply

8. If you had been Mary Beth, how would you have reacted to the starter's instructions?
9. What kind of person is Mary Beth?
10. Agree or disagree with the following: "Girls and boys should be allowed to compete on the same sports teams."

Respond to Literature

Mary Beth makes an unexpected discovery about winning. Have you ever regretted winning something? Explain.

WRITE ABOUT THE SELECTION

Sportswriters frequently interview athletes after a sporting event. What kinds of questions do these writers usually ask? Imagine that you are a sportswriter who has just watched Mary Beth's historic performance. Write an interview with her.

Prewriting: Before you write your interview make an informal list of questions that you, a sportswriter, would like to ask Mary Beth. To gain information about a person's thoughts and feelings, interviewers generally ask *who? what? when? why? how?* and *where?* questions.

Writing: Use your informal list of questions to write an interview with Mary Beth. In it, write three questions, and three answers you think Mary Beth might give. If necessary, include any follow-up questions you might have.

Revising: When you revise your interview, reread Mary Beth's responses. Think carefully about whether Mary Beth would really speak this way. Ask yourself if her answers tell something important about her inner thoughts and emotions about the race.

Proofreading: When you proofread your interview, circle any words whose spelling you are unsure of. When you have proofread your entire interview, use a dictionary to check the correct spelling of your circled words. Also check to make sure that all your sentences begin with capital letters and end with correct punctuation.

THINK ABOUT THEME

The **theme** of a story is its important point, or message. The theme is what the story tells about people in general, not just the main character. Often, you can figure out the theme by thinking about what the characters do and say. Sometimes a character may perform an important action which gives a hint about the theme. Think about how the main character's changes during the story may also help you understand the theme.

1. What is Mary Beth's goal?
2. After the race, how does Mary Beth feel? How do you know her feelings?
3. Although Mary Beth doesn't win the race, her teammates still praise her. Explain why they are so proud.
4. Do Mary Beth's feelings about her victory change at all?
5. State the theme of the story, using complete sentences.

DEVELOP YOUR VOCABULARY

A **synonym** is a word that has the same or almost the same meaning as another word. Authors often choose between similar words, or synonyms, to find the perfect word for a sentence. For example, during the race, Mary Beth's mouth is *parched*—dried out—rather than *dry, hot,* or *thirsty.*

Read the sentences below. Choose the best synonym for each *italicized* word.

1. The sportswriters *badgered* the athlete with questions.
   a. surrounded **c.** swamped
   b. annoyed **d.** involved
2. After our fifth straight victory, we knew we could *attain* the championship.
   a. follow **c.** achieve
   b. repeat **d.** control
3. The coach *devised* a new training schedule for our next track meet.
   a. talked about **c.** invented
   b. planned **d.** added

Learn About
Narrative Poetry

Sometimes a poet feels that a particular topic, or subject, deserves special attention. When a poet decides to focus more closely on a certain character or event he or she will write a type of poetry that tells a story, called **narrative poetry.**

Narrative poems are usually longer than other forms of poetry. This gives the poet the opportunity to tell more fully about people, events, and experiences. In a narrative poem, you will find more in-depth information.

As you might expect, the story in a narrative poem is told by a narrator. Narrative poems however, also contain words that other characters speak.

Many narrative poems contain rhyme. Rhyme captures your attention and helps you remember important words and actions.

As you read "Casey at the Bat," think about:

1. What story is told in this poem?
2. How is this poem different from other poems you have read?

Skill Builder

Think of a famous athlete you have seen, or read about. Write a brief passage about that athlete's greatest sports performance. Could this story be told in a narrative poem?

Casey at the Bat

by Ernest L. Thayer

The outlook wasn't brilliant for the Mudville nine
that day;
The score stood two to four, with but an inning
left to play.
So, when Cooney died at second, and Burrows
did the same,
A sickly silence fell upon the patrons of the
game.

5 A straggling few got up to go, leaving there the
rest,
With that hope that springs eternal within the
human breast,
For they thought, "If only Casey could get a
whack at that,"
They'd put up even money now, with Casey at
the bat.

But Flynn preceded Casey, and likewise so did
Blake,
10 And the former was a puddin', and the latter was
a fake,

---

brilliant (BRIL yunt) remarkably fine
sickly (SIK lee) feeble
straggle (STRAG ul) wander from the main group
put up bet
even money (EE vun MUN ee) equal amounts of money, for and against
puddin' (PUUD un) slang term of disrespect

So on that stricken multitude the deathlike
  silence sat,
For there seemed but little chance of Casey's
  getting to the bat.

But Flynn let drive a "single," to the
  wonderment of all,
And the much-despisèd Blakey "tore the cover
  off the ball."
15 And when the dust had lifted and they saw what
  had occurred,
There was Blakey safe at second, and Flynn a-
  huggin' third.

Then from the gladdened multitude went up a
  joyous yell,
It rumbled in the mountain-tops, it rattled in the
  dell;
It struck upon the hillside and rebounded on the
  flat;
20 For Casey, mighty Casey, was advancing to the
  bat.

There was ease in Casey's manner as he stepped
  into his place;
There was pride in Casey's bearing, and a smile
  on Casey's face.
And when, responding to the cheers, he lightly
  doffed his hat,
No stranger in the crowd could doubt 'twas
  Casey at the bat.

25 Ten thousand eyes were on him as he rubbed
  his hands with dirt,
Five thousand tongues applauded when he wiped
  them on his shirt;

---

stricken (STRIK un) affected by something painful or upsetting
multitude (MUL tuh tood) a large number of persons gathered together
dell (DEL) small valley, usually wooded
bearing (BAIR ing) way of carrying oneself
doff (DOF) take off

THULSTRUP

Then while the New York pitcher ground the ball
into his hip,
Defiance gleamed in Casey's eye, a sneer curled
Casey's lip.

And now the leather-covered sphere came
whirling through the air,
30 And Casey stood a-watching it in haughty
grandeur there.
Close by the sturdy batsman the ball unheeded
sped—
"That ain't my style," said Casey. "Strike one!"
the umpire said.

From the benches, black with people, there went
up a muffled roar,
Like the beating of storm waves on a stern and
distant shore.
35 "Kill him! Kill the umpire!" shouted someone on
the stand.
And it's likely they'd have killed him had not
Casey raised a hand.

With a smile of Christian charity great Casey's
visage shone;
He stilled the rising tumult; he bade the game go
on;
He signaled to the pitcher, once more the
spheroid flew;
40 But Casey still ignored it, and the umpire said:
"Strike two!"

"Fraud!" cried the maddened thousands, and
echo answered "Fraud!"

---

sphere (SFIR) ball
haughty (HAWT ee) overly proud of oneself
visage (VIZ ij) face
tumult (TOO mult) noisy uproar
bade (BAD) asked that
spheroid (SFIR oid) nearly round object
fraud (FRAWD) cheat

But one scornful look from Casey and the
audience was awed.
They saw his face grow stern and cold, they saw
his muscles strain,
And they knew that Casey wouldn't let that ball
go by again.

45 The sneer is gone from Casey's lip, his teeth are
clenched in hate;
He pounds with cruel violence his bat upon the
plate.
And now the pitcher holds the ball, and now he
lets it go,
And now the air is shattered by the force of
Casey's blow.

Ah, somewhere in this favored land the sun is
shining bright;
50 The band is playing somewhere, and somewhere
hearts are light.
And somewhere men are laughing, and
somewhere children shout:
But there is no joy in Mudville—mighty Casey
has struck out.

---

awed (AWD) full of respect or wonder

FOCUS ON THE SELECTION

UNDERSTAND THE SELECTION

Recall

1. When the poem begins, by how many runs are the "Mudville nine" losing?
2. Tell how many people are watching this baseball game?
3. Do the "Mudville nine" win this particular baseball game?

Infer

4. What does the name of the town suggest about the town and its team?
5. In line 3, you learn that Cooney and Burrows "died at second." Explain the meaning of this figurative expression.
6. Explain whether the crowd expected Flynn and Blake to get any hits.
7. Were you surprised by the ending? Why?

Apply

8. Choose two new titles for the poem.
9. Imagine that you are the manager of the "Mudville nine." How would you react to Casey's batting performance?
10. Briefly describe Casey's character.

Respond to Literature

An important ingredient in success is having a positive attitude. Does Casey demonstrate such an attitude? Would you want Casey on your sports team?

WRITE ABOUT THE SELECTION

When Casey first stepped to the plate, most of the baseball fans assumed that he would win the game. Casey, however, turned out to be a different from what he seemed to be. Write the opening of a narrative poem that tells about a person who is not what he or she seems. Think about the events in the entire poem, but only write the first eight lines.

Prewriting: Think about a person who behaves differently from what you might expect. For example, an airplane pilot who is afraid to fly or a doctor who is scared by the sight of blood. Then create a character cluster to describe your character. What does he or she look like? How does he or she behave? Think about the kind of story that will best demonstrate your character's real personality.

Writing: Use your character cluster to write the first eight lines of a narrative poem. In it, show a difference between what the character seems to be, and what he or she is really like.

Revising: When you revise your poem think about your character's conflict. Have you included enough specific details that show what your character really believes and how he or she behaves?

Proofreading: When you proofread your poem you may find that certain letters or words are out of order. To change the order of words or letters, use this proofreading mark: ∩∪. *Example:* The cuatious cat.

THINK ABOUT NARRATIVE POETRY

Narrative poetry is poetry that tells a story. Therefore it shares certain elements with other forms of literature including the short story, the novel and the play. For example, narrative poems focus on characters. When you read a narrative poem you learn what kind of person the main character is. Every narrative poem has a plot, or sequence of events. Narrative poems also describe specific settings. The setting of a narrative poem may influence the behavior of the poem's characters. Finally, narrative poems express a theme, or central message.

1. Who is this poem about?
2. Is a whole story told about the main character, or does the poet concentrate on a few specific things?
3. What specific events are related in this poem?
4. "Casey at the Bat" is one of the most popular American narrative poems. Why do you think it is so well liked?
5. Does this poem teach a lesson about how people should or shouldn't behave? Explain your thinking.

DEVELOP YOUR VOCABULARY

Jargon is the term for special words and phrases used by a group of people who share the same job, hobby, profession or interest. You may think of jargon as a special language with its own vocabulary. For example, when baseball players refer to a *ball,* or talk about a *shoestring catch,* they are using jargon to speak about a pitch that is outside the strike zone, and a ball caught just before it touches the ground.

Jargon is easily understood by members of the group. People outside the group however, may be unfamiliar with the different words and phrases.

Use a dictionary or reference book to find the meaning of each of the following jargon words in baseball. Write original sentences using four of these words or phrases. You may suggest additional baseball jargon words.

1. chatter
2. balk
3. save
4. dugout
5. pennant
6. perfect game
7. skipper
8. diamond
9. sacrifice
10. pill
11. RBI
12. rookie
13. K
14. rundown

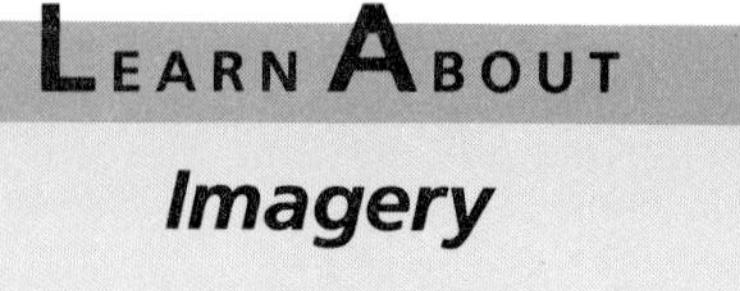

Learn About

Imagery

In literature, **imagery** is the creative use of words or phrases that appeal to one of the five senses. Imagery appeals to the senses of sight, hearing, smell, taste, and touch. Often, a writer will use images to help you really experience what is being described. A visual image, for instance, helps you form a mental picture of a particular person, object, or event.

With imagery, you not only hear or see something, you actually feel part of the description. For example, think about the difference between these two sentences. "It was a cold, windy day." "The flag snapped in the sharp, bitter wind." Notice how the second sentence helps you hear, see, and actually experience the weather.

As you read the following poems by Emily Dickinson, think about:

1. Which words or phrases appeal to your five senses?
2. What mental pictures do these words help you form?

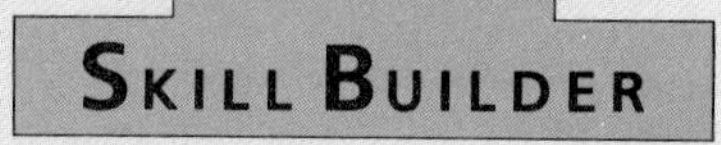

Skill Builder

Write your own vivid descriptions of these subjects, using the sensory words in parentheses. Thunderstorm: (sight, sound). Lemon peel: (smell, taste, touch).

SUCCESS

by Emily Dickinson

Success is counted sweetest
By those who ne'er succeed.
To comprehend a nectar
Requires sorest need.

5 Not one of all the purple host
Who took the flag today
Can tell the definition
So clear of victory

As he defeated, dying,
10 On whose forbidden ear
The distant strains of triumph
Burst agonized and clear.

---

ne'er (NAIR) never
comprehend (kom prih HEND) understand
nectar (NEK tur) delicious, heavenly drink
sorest need (SAWR ist NEED) great desire
host (HOHST) great number of people; army
strains (STRAYNZ) sounds or songs
agonized (AG uh nyzd) suffering greatly;
in great pain

"HOPE" Is the Thing with Feathers

by Emily Dickinson

"Hope" is the thing with feathers
That perches in the soul,
And sings the tune without the words,
And never stops at all.

5 And sweetest in the gale is heard.
And sore must be the storm
That could abash the little bird
That kept so many warm.

I've heard it in the chillest land,
10 And on the strangest sea.
Yet, never, in extremity,
It asked a crumb of me.

If I Can Stop One Heart from Breaking

by Emily Dickinson

If I can stop one heart from breaking
I shall not live in vain.
If I can ease one life the aching
Or cool one pain

Or help one fainting robin
Unto his nest again
I shall not live in vain.

---

abash (uh BASH) make uneasy
in vain (in VAYN) without success

Mount Holyoke Female Seminary, engraving, The Granger Collection. (inset) *Emily Elizabeth Dickinson*, daguerreotype, 1848, The Granger Collection

Emily Dickinson (1830-1886)

If no one had looked through Emily Dickinson's dresser drawers after her death, America would have lost one of its greatest poets. Emily Dickinson wrote more than a thousand poems in her lifetime but she published only a handful. Her sister Lavinia discovered all the poems in Emily's dresser. The first two books of poetry were not published until 1900.

The daughter of a lawyer, Emily Dickinson grew up in the town of Amherst, Massachusetts. She was better educated than most girls at the time. As a young woman, she enjoyed the life of the village and the companionship of her school friends. But during her thirties, Emily began to go out less and less. She continued to see people, however, because her father was an important man in the town, and many interesting people came to the house.

Some people believe there may have been a secret love in her life. They think that she fell in love with a man she met while on a trip with her parents. There are other people who say that she wanted to marry another man but her father refused to allow the marriage. No one is really sure, since Emily Dickinson led a very private life, and we know her mainly through her poetry.

FOCUS ON THE SELECTION

UNDERSTAND THE SELECTION

Recall

1. In "'Hope' Is the Thing with Feathers," what kind of tune does hope sing?
2. Identify the setting of "Success."
3. In "If I Can Stop One Heart from Breaking," what kind of bird is mentioned?

Infer

4. In "'Hope' Is the Thing with Feathers" what is hope compared with?
5. In the same person, do people pay a price for hope? Explain.
6. In "Success," what kind of people best appreciate the meaning of success?
7. According to "If I Can Stop One Heart from Breaking," what is most valuable about life?

Apply

8. Predict what the speaker of "If I Can Stop One Heart from Breaking" might do if he or she found a lost puppy.
9. In "Success" do you agree with the speaker's definition of success?
10. The speaker of "Hope" compares hope to a particular animal. Do you agree?

Respond to Literature

The speaker of "If I Can Stop . . ." feels that great achievements come from small deeds. Do you agree?

WRITE ABOUT THE SELECTION

A good way to achieve success is to set specific goals for yourself. These goals may involve school, sports, and personal relationships, among many others. Do your goals always remain the same? Or, do some goals change over a period of time? Write two paragraphs that explain how the goals you want to achieve today are different from those when you were younger.

Prewriting: Make an informal outline of the goals, or objectives, you want to achieve today. Then, think about how these goals have changed over time. For instance, is choosing a career a new goal? Make an informal outline of these different goals.

Writing: Use your informal outline to write two paragraphs that tell how your ideas about success have changed over time. In it, compare your current goals with those you had in the lower grades.

Revising: When you revise your paragraphs ask yourself if you have fully explained how your perceptions, or insights, about goals have changed over time. Decide if you have included opinions and feelings that make your passage lively and colorful.

Proofreading: If you have written compound sentences in your paragraph, make sure you have placed a comma between the two main clauses, or different ideas. In compound sentences, the comma goes just before the words *and, but,* or *or.*

THINK ABOUT IMAGERY

Imagery is the specific, colorful use of descriptive words that appeal to one of the five senses: sight, hearing, smell, taste, and touch. Effective imagery has a powerful effect on the imagination. While reading, think about the mental pictures, or images, that help you really experience a work of literature.

1. In the poem "If I Can Stop One Heart from Breaking," what does the expression "stop one heart from breaking" mean?
2. In the same poem, how does the poet make you experience the idea of pain?
3. In the poem "Success," the speaker compares triumph to a special sound. What is that sound? What instrument might make that sound?
4. In " 'Hope' is the Thing with Feathers," which images appeal to your sense of sound?
5. In the same poem, which sensory image tells how hope comforts people?

DEVELOP YOUR VOCABULARY

A **figurative expression** is a vivid and creative way of saying something in which the individual words have a meaning that is different from their usual definition. For instance, imagine that two people are having a serious argument. To describe their actions, you might say that they are *locking horns.* You don't mean that these two people are fighting with horns. The figurative expression helps you visualize the fierce way that they are arguing.

Read the sentences below. Write the meaning of each *italicized* figurative expression.

1. Our poor behavior made the substitute teacher *fly off the handle.*
2. The cool lemonade helped to *drown my thirst.*
3. After running three events in the track meet, she went home and *slept like a log.*
4. His *heart sank* when he found out about the pop quiz.

FOCUS ON...

Poetry is creative writing that combines words, sounds, and images to create a powerful, emotional effect. Each word in a poem is chosen to create vivid pictures, feelings, and thoughts. Poetry can tell stories, describe people and objects, and express thoughts, emotions, and moods. It is important to understand the essential elements that make poetry unique.

Rhythm. Rhythm is what gives a poem its sense of flow, or movement. Rhythm is a poem's pattern of repeated words, sounds, and phrases. It may help to think of rhythm as a poem's special beat.

Each line of a poem usually has a rhythm, or **beat.** To figure out the beat, you should pay attention to the syllables in each word. Reading a poem aloud often helps you determine if a syllable is **accented**—pronounced strongly, or **unaccented**—pronounced less strongly.

Read the following line of poetry. "She did not wear her gorgeous dress." Did you pronounce the syllables *did, wear, gor,* and *dress* more strongly? If you clapped the beat, you would hear this rhythm:

She did/not wear/her gor/geous dress
and ONE/and TWO/and THREE/and FOUR

Rhyme. In a poem, certain words may contain the same, or identical, sounds. These words are said to rhyme. For example, *up* rhymes with *cup* and *dove* rhymes with *love.* When rhyming words are found at the end of a line of poetry, they are called **end rhymes.** An **internal rhyme** occurs in the middle of a line.

The pattern of rhymes in a poem is called the **rhyme scheme.** To determine the rhyme scheme of a poem, label the word at the end of the first line *a.* Then label the other lines that end with the same sound *a.* Find the next rhyming sound and label it *b.* Continue this pattern by labeling all the other lines that end with this rhyme, *b.* When you have labeled all of the rhymes, write the letters in the order that they appear in the poem.

POETRY

Alliteration. Alliteration occurs when several words in a line of poetry start with the same sound. For example, "the ruined, red rug," or "the beautiful sound of the babbling brook." While looking for alliteration in a poem, think about how certain consonants sound when they are spoken aloud. Some consonants, such as *l, m, n, r,* and *s* will produce smooth, pleasing sounds when spoken aloud. Other consonants, like *b, d, k, p,* and *t* will produce quick, sharp sounds when you say them aloud.

Onomatopoeia. Onomatopoeia (ON uh mat uh PEA uh) is the use of words that make their own special sounds. These can be animal sounds, such as the *buzzing* of a bee or the *tweeting* of a bird. Onomatopoeia can also imitate other natural sounds, such as the *hissing* of steam or the *honking* of a horn.

Free Verse. Sometimes poetry doesn't have a regular rhythm or contain any rhymes. When saying the poem aloud, you don't pronounce certain syllables more strongly than others. This type of poetry is called free verse because it is free of any rhythm or rhyme. Free verse sounds more like the way you naturally speak. Words and images are combined and repeated for emotional effect.

Persona. When you read a poem, listen carefully to certain voices. Sometimes, you may hear the voice of the characters. You always hear the voice of the speaker, the person who is telling the poem. Persona is another word for the speaker. The persona of a poem does not always represent the voice of the poet. You can figure out the persona, or speaker, of a poem by looking at word clues that suggest the speaker's age, gender, and attitude about life.

As you read "A Psalm of Life," "This Day Is Over," and "Factory Work," ask yourself:

1. Does the poem have a regular rhythm, or beat?
2. What feeling does this rhythm give you?
3. Does this poem have a rhyme scheme?
4. Who is the speaker of this poem?

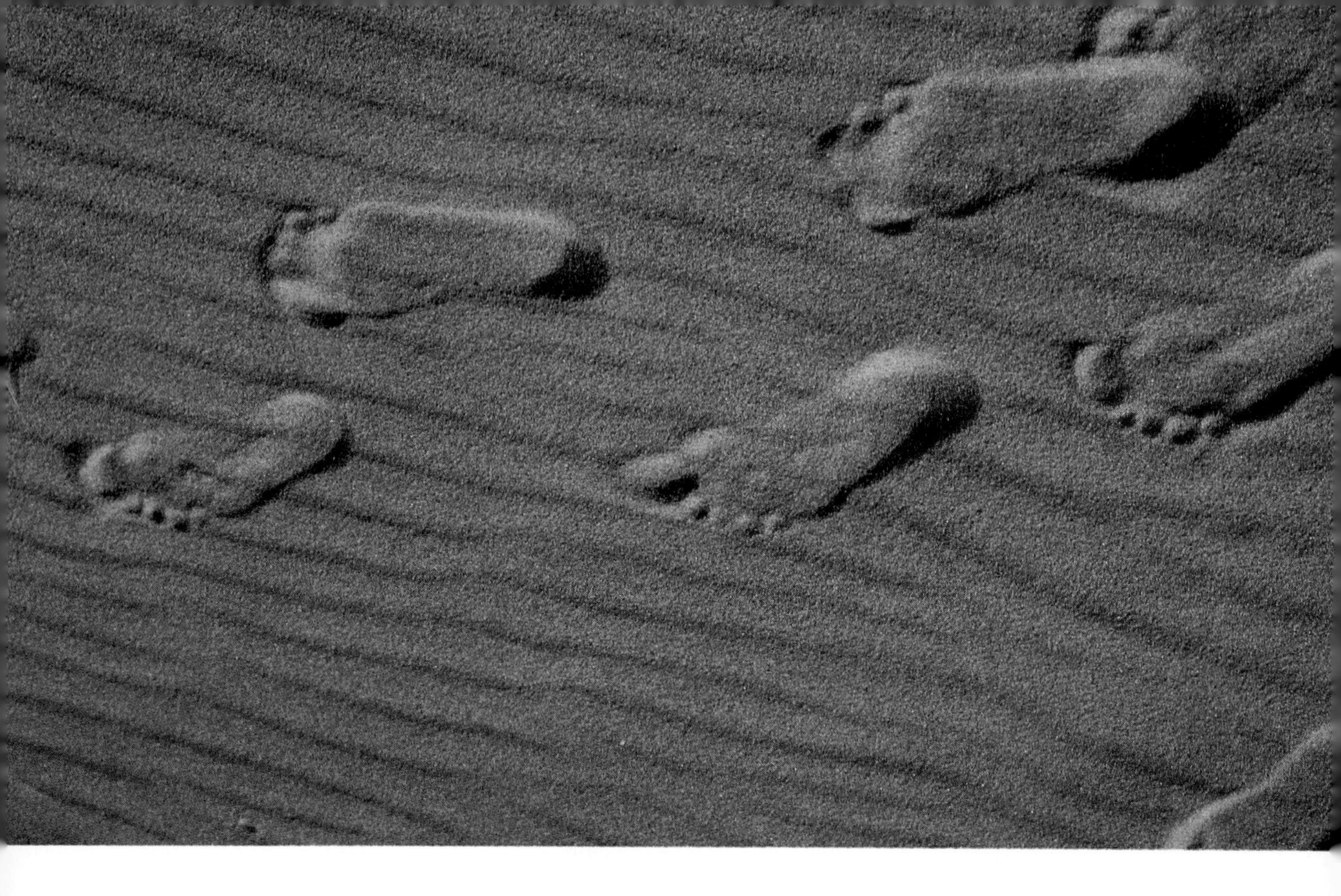

A Psalm of Life

by Henry Wadsworth Longfellow

STUDY HINTS
Here, the poem's rhythm is introduced. Can you clap out the beat of each line in this stanza?
Think about the rhyme scheme in this stanza.

Tell me not, in mournful numbers,
 Life is but an empty dream!—
For the soul is dead that slumbers,
 And things are not what they seem.

Life is real! Life is earnest! 5
 And the grave is not its goal;
Dust thou art, to dust returnest,
 Was not spoken of the soul.

---

mournful (MAWRN ful) sad; sorrowful
slumbers (SLUM burz) sleeps; is inactive
earnest (UR nist) serious; sincere

Not enjoyment, and not sorrow,
10 Is our destined end or way;
But to act, that each to-morrow
Find us farther than to-day.

Here, the speaker gives you a clue about the central idea of the poem.

Art is long, and Time is fleeting,
And our hearts, though stout and brave,
15 Still, like muffled drums, are beating
Funeral marches to the grave.

In the world's broad field of battle,
In the bivouac of Life,
Be not like dumb, driven cattle!
20 Be a hero in the strife!

To what object or idea does the poet compare life. Is life peaceful?

Trust no Future, howe'er pleasant!
Let the dead Past bury its dead!
Act—act in the living Present!
Heart within, and God o'erhead!

25 Lives of great men all remind us
We can make our lives sublime,
And, departing, leave behind us
Footprints on the sands of time;

Think about the meaning of this phrase. What picture, or image, does it help you visualize?

Footprints, that perhaps another,
30 Sailing o'er life's solemn main,
A forlorn and shipwrecked brother,
Seeing, shall take heart again.

Let us, then, be up and doing,
With a heart for any fate;
35 Still achieving, still pursuing,
Learn to labor and to wait.

Notice the repeated words. Think about what the poet is trying to accomplish by using repetition.

---

destined (DES tind) something that is bound to happen
fleeting (FLEET ing) soon gone; fast disappearing
stout (STOUT) bold; strong
bivouac (BIV wak) temporary shelter or camp
strife (STRYF) contest; struggle
o'erhead (awr HED) poetic spelling of overhead
sublime (suh BLYM) grand; on a high level
solemn (SOL um) dark; gloomy
main (MAYN) open sea
forlorn (fur LAWRN) very unhappy; hopeless

(inset) *Henry Wadsworth Longfellow,* engraving, The Granger Collection

Henry Wadsworth Longfellow

(1807-1882)

At the time of his death, and for many years after, Henry Wadsworth Longfellow had no rival as America's best-loved poet. His poetry often appeared in magazines and his books were in constant demand. Schoolchildren read dozens of his poems, and often memorized them.

Longfellow's popularity is easy to understand. He saw beauty everywhere—in an old ship against the moon in Boston Harbor, in the forests, in the fields. He was interested in the common life of the common people, from the village blacksmith to the well-traveled sailor. He usually wrote rather simple, melodious poems that nearly everyone could understand. But most of all, he calmed the nerves of the nation. In an age when life was often hard, Longfellow told his American readers to work hard and to accept whatever fate had to offer.

Longfellow's life was mostly a comfortable one. He grew up in Maine, sailed through college at an early age, and went to Europe for further study. After that he managed to keep two careers going at the same time—first as a poet, and second as a professor of foreign languages. He had money, friends, and fame. He lived to see his poetry translated into 24 languages. But as he told his readers, "Into each life some rain must fall." In 1861 his wife burned to death when her dress accidentally caught fire. Longfellow's own struggle out of sorrow is reflected in some of his best poems.

This Day Is Over

by Calvin O'John (Ute-Navajo)

When the day is over,
I think of all I did.
Did I goof off,
Or did I accomplish something?
5 Did I make a new friend,
Or did I make an enemy?
Was I mad at everybody,
Or was I nice?
Anyway, what I did today is over.
10 While I sleep,
The world will be shining up
A new day for me to use,
Or goof up,
Or whatever I decide
15 To do with it.
Tonight, I pick out
"Nice," and
"Friendly," and
"Accomplish something."

STUDY HINTS
Here, the speaker talks about certain choices in life.

Does the speaker believe that people are forced to make certain decisions?

Notice the use of repeated words and phrases throughout the poem.

---

goof up (GOOF UP) slang for make a mistake

FACTORY WORK

by Deborah Boe

STUDY HINTS

Here are descriptive clues about the speaker's job. Think about how the speaker "talks."

All day I stand here, like this,
over the hot-glue machine,
not too close to the wheel
that brings up the glue,
and I take those metal shanks, 5
slide the backs of them in glue
and make them lie down
on the shoe-bottoms, before the sole
goes on. It's simple, but the lasts
weigh, give you big arms. 10
If I hit my boyfriend now,
in the supermarket parking lot,
he knows I hit him.

Notice the clues that help you figure out the poet's persona.

Phyllis, who stands next to me,
had long hair before the glue machine 15
got it. My machine ate up my shirt once.
I tried to get it out, the wheel
spinning on me, until someone with a brain
turned it off. It's not bad
here, people leave you alone, 20
don't ask you what you're thinking.

Notice the indirect way the speaker shows you her attitude towards factory work.

It's a good thing, too, because all this morning
I was remembering last night,
when I really thought my grandpa's soul
had moved into the apartment, 25
the way the eggs fell, and the lamp
broke, like someone was trying
to communicate to me, and he
just dead this week. I wouldn't

Here, you learn what is troubling the speaker.

---

shanks (SHANGKS) metal reinforcement glued in the sole of a shoe
lasts (LASTS) a special form shaped like a person's foot on which shoes are made or repaired

Woman in Green Dress, Pablo Picasso, 1954, Phototheque SPADEM/ Art Resource.

30 blame him. That man in the next aisle
reminds me of him, a little.

It's late October now, and Eastland
needs to lay some people off.
Last week they ran a contest
35 to see which shankers shanked fastest.
I'm not embarassed to say
I beat them all. It's all
in economy of motion, all the moves
on automatic. I almost
40 don't need to look at what
I'm doing. I'm thinking of the way
the leaves turn red when the cold
gets near them. They fall until
you're wading in red leaves up to your knees,
45 and the air snaps
in the tree-knuckles, and you begin
to see your breath rise
out of you like your own ghost
each morning you come here.

Here are more clues about the speaker's attitude towards factory work.

Notice the sensory words that help you experience the season of year.

---

lay some people off slang for putting people out of work for a short time
economy (ih KON uh mee) orderly, efficient use of time and effort
automatic (awt uh MAT ik) done without thinking
wading (WAYD ing) walk, as if through water or mud

FOCUS ON THE SELECTION

UNDERSTAND THE SELECTION

Recall

1. In "A Psalm of Life" what animal does the speaker warn people not to be like?
2. What is the time in "This Day is Over"?
3. In "Factory Work," where does the speaker work? What is his job?

Infer

4. In "A Psalm of Life," explain what the speaker believes the goal of life to be.
5. In "This Day Is Over," the speaker believes that people are given what choices in their lives?
6. In "Factory Work," is the speaker's job dangerous?
7. Explain what kind of a loss the speaker in "Factory Work" has experienced.

Apply

8. In "A Psalm of Life," what effect do the lives of great men have on the troubled?
9. Predict how the speaker of "This Day Is Over" might behave tomorrow.
10. In "Factory Work," the speaker says, "It's not bad here." Is this the whole truth?

Respond to Literature

These three poets have different backgrounds. Do you think the speakers, or personas, in their poems reveal any clues about the poets?

WRITE ABOUT THE SELECTION

In both "A Psalm of Life" and "This Day is Over," the speakers suggest that people have control over their lives. People, they believe, are free to make positive choices, and then act upon these choices. Does the speaker in "Factory Work" seem to be in control of her life? Write a paragraph in which you explain two new goals that the speaker in "Factory Work" could develop in order to take charge of her life.

Prewriting: Before writing your paragraph, think about the speaker's personality. Is she happy with factory work? Is the speaker smart, or especially perceptive? Next, brainstorm several goals that the speaker could set for herself, such as finding a new job.

Writing: Use your brainstorming to write a paragraph. In it, recommend two goals that the speaker of "Factory Work" might set to gain more control over her life.

Revising: When you revise your paragraph, make sure the goals that you suggested are well-suited to the speaker's personality. Then, decide whether you should include a process, or method, that shows how these goals can be achieved.

Proofreading: When you proofread your paragraph, check to see if you have placed periods and commas where they belong. Use this proofreading mark [⊙] to add a period at the end of a sentence. Use this proofreading mark [‸] to show where a comma should be added.

THINK ABOUT POETRY

Thinking about how the elements of poetry work together can give you insights into the meaning of a poem.

Rhythm is a poem's pattern of repeated sounds, words, and phrases. **Rhyme** is produced by words that have identical sounds. A **rhyme scheme** is the specific pattern of rhymes in a poem. A **stanza** is a group of lines in a poem that shares the same rhyme scheme. Unlike most poetry, **free verse** lacks any rhyme or rhythm, and therefore, is more like everyday speech. Finally, **persona** is the "voice" that tells the poem. The persona, however, does not always "speak" in the poet's actual voice.

1. Does "A Psalm of Life" contain any rhymes? Identify three end rhymes.
2. Is there a rhyme scheme in "A Psalm of Life"?
3. In "This Day Is Over" what words are repeated? What effect does this repetition have on the meaning of the poem?
4. Does "Factory Work" have a regular beat or rhyme? What kind of poem is "Factory Work?"
5. Who is the speaker of "Factory Work?"

DEVELOP YOUR VOCABULARY

A **syllable** is the part of a word that contains only one vowel sound. Certain words, such as *run, talk,* and *class* have only one syllable. However, many words, like *passion, confidence,* and *charity* contain more than one syllable.

Breaking words into their syllable parts serves two important purposes. It helps you determine the rhythm, or beat, in a line of poetry. When reading, it also helps you recognize a word that you have heard before. By dividing a word into its syllable parts, you can first pronounce the word, and then recognize it.

Divide each of the following words into syllables. Write the word and capitalize the accented syllables. Then, write an original sentence using four of these words. Use a dictionary to check your work.

1. amplify
2. distribution
3. prejudice
4. resourceful
5. situation
6. temporary
7. victorious
8. wretched

Learn About

Irony

When people speak with irony, they say something quite different from what they really mean. Have you ever said something that was the exact opposite of what you really meant?

For example, if you said, "We certainly needed this snowstorm today," you might really mean that "we didn't need this snowstorm at all." Or, perhaps you observed a friend's new outfit, and said, "Interesting looking sweater." You might really mean that it is an unattractive sweater.

In a story, **irony** is the contrast between what is expected to happen and what really happens. An ironic situation is one that turns out completely different from what a character, or even a reader, expects.

As you read "The Wolf of Thunder Mountain," ask yourself:

1. What is ironic about the way events turn out in the story?
2. Why does the author use irony in this story?

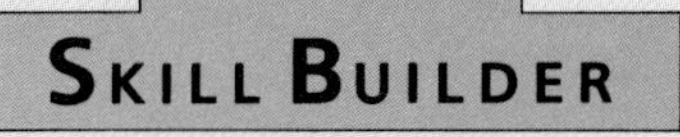

Think of three situations that might turn out the opposite of what you would expect. Briefly explain what makes each situation ironic.

THE WOLF OF THUNDER MOUNTAIN

by Dion Henderson

All the way to the station my mother kept giving me the same instructions she'd been giving me for a week. This was the first time I was allowed to take the train up north by myself to see Grandpa. Finally I reminded her how old I was. Then she said a funny thing. Growing up or growing old, my mother said, it doesn't make much difference how many birthdays you have. And all the way up north on the train I tried to figure out whether she was talking about me or Grandpa.

At the Settlement, the train stopped just long enough to let me off. The conductor helped me with the duffel bag. It was so heavy I could hardly lift it. I looked around for Grandpa, but he wasn't there yet. It wasn't hard to tell. Grandpa was about nine feet tall.

The lumberjacks sitting on the bench in front of the general store watched me. When I got close, one of them said did I figure I could stay overnight without any more gear than that. I put the duffel bag down and said politely that I figured I had enough gear to spend a year on Thunder Mountain. "Thunder Mountain," one of the other ones said. He was kind of polite, too, all of a sudden. He said, "You the boy that goes up there to see the wolf?"

I said, "That's the boy I am, all right."

Later on it turned out we meant different things when we talked about the wolf of Thunder Mountain. I meant the

---

duffel bag (DUF ul BAG) large canvas bag, shaped like a closed tube, used for carrying clothing

lumberjack (LUM bur jak) logger; worker who cuts down trees and prepares them for the sawmill

old gray wolf who got the moonlight in his eyes. The people in the Settlement meant Grandpa.

Just then there was a commotion up at the end of the street, and the people on the sidewalk started to go indoors. The street was empty, and then I heard Grandpa. He was singing a Chippewa war song.

Pretty quick he came in sight, driving the red horse on the dog cart. He never bothered with a car, because the first thing you had to cross on the way up the mountain was the Little Warrior. He said he'd stick with the red horse until he found a car that could swim.

Right in front of me he stopped and looked at me and finished the last couple whoops of the song. Then he reached down smiling and picked up me and the duffel bag together and put us on the seat.

I said, "I'm glad to see you aren't real puny yet."

"How's that?" Grandpa said.

"My mother said you ought to come back down to the city with me this fall, because you're getting too old and puny to stay on the mountain all winter."

"Might have known it," Grandpa said. "Your mother's been saying that for 30 years."

"Well," I said, "how's the wolf?"

"He's like me, boy. Gets older and maybe even a mite smarter, but no punier."

"Has he got a family this year?"

"No," Grandpa said, a little sadly. "Not anymore."

"Did you catch them?"

"I didn't fix to catch them, boy. But wolves are something like people. You fix to catch the smartest one of all, you have to catch all the young ones and the foolish ones and the ignorant ones first. That's what it is."

"Did you catch the puppies, too?"

"No." He sounded disappointed that I'd asked. "I ain't caught a pup since that first one, and that was an accident. I caught the she-wolf before there were any pups."

"I suppose you had to."

"Yes," Grandpa said. "I had to. He brought her down last year, and he showed me to her. Got so I knew they were following me and watching me. The old wolf was saying to his mate, 'See the way he does and learn all about him.'"

"So you had to catch her, all right."

"Yes." Grandpa felt better because I understood. "The old wolf knew it and I knew it."

"Does he know you're going to catch him, too?"

"I couldn't rightly say," Grandpa said. "I reckon he figures there's some question about that."

"But you will."

---

commotion (kuh MOH shun) noisy disturbance
Chippewa (CHIP uh waw) a Native American group that lives in the northern United States and southern Canada
puny (PYOO nee) small and weak
mite (MYT) little bit

"Yes," Grandpa said. "I got to."

While we were talking, the red horse was picking his way up the logging road that led through the Norway pine and spruce trees.

"They wanted to build a road up Thunder Mountain." Grandpa said.

He meant the forestry people from the Settlement.

"What'd you tell them?"

Grandpa looked over at me, and the dark blue eyes twinkled and he smiled. "I told 'em that if any of them needed any toothpicks, they could come up and whittle them, one at a time."

Now we were across the stream, and the red horse was working hard, up the trail on Thunder Mountain.

Grandpa said, "You can't change a place like this a little bit. Either you don't change it at all, or you change it altogether."

"Maybe," I said, "maybe they'll build the road while you're down in the city spending the winter."

"That'll be the day," Grandpa said. "When I go down to the city to spend the winter, they're welcome to build the road."

It appeared I said the wrong thing again. So I asked him to tell me about how he and the wolf first met.

Of course, that was five or six years ago, when it started. The old wolf was a young wolf then, just another wolf. That was the spring there was no snow in the North country. The deer ranged widely from the yards where ordinarily they gathered in a herd. And the wolf came down early, following the deer.

Although Grandpa didn't trap much anymore, he saw the wolf's sign beside the body of a fawn and put out a trap, just to keep in practice. Because in the days when he trapped seriously, he was the kind of trapper that some violin players are musicians. The next day when he came back to the place where the trap was, he saw the wolf sitting there quietly.

Wolves are very intelligent. When a wolf like that is caught in a trap and he knows that he can't escape, he won't struggle. Instead, he will sit quietly full of hate and wait to see the man who has brought him to the end of his splendid journey. Grandpa said he understood this very well. The wolf, he said, looked at him while he prepared his revolver. Then Grandpa looked at the wolf for the first time as an individual, and the wolf looked back at him fiercely.

But suddenly, the wolf came smoothly to his feet and with the magical wolf grace bounded beautifully and rapidly into nowhere, and he was gone. He wasn't caught in the trap after all. But he

---

whittle (HWIT ul) cut thin slices, or shavings, of wood using a knife
ordinarily (AWRD un ER uh lee) usually
fawn (FAWN) young deer
splendid (SPLEN did) grand; excellent; worthy of high praise
revolver (rih VOL vur) certain type of handgun; pistol
grace (GRAYS) special beauty; ease of movement
bound (BOUND) leap; jump

had been, Grandpa said. The wolf had stepped in the trap and two toes of his forefoot were still there.

The wolf had waited at the trap for him, to see the man so that he could recognize him again. And that was fair enough, Grandpa said, because the footprint with the toes missing let him recognize the wolf. But they did not meet again, face to face, for a long time, although they came close.

In the spring, the wolf brought a bride down while there still was snow. On the cold nights of late spring Grandpa would lie in his cabin and hear the signal yelps of the two wolves hunting.

Maybe he would not have trapped anymore for this wolf if it had not been for the people of the Settlement. There was a terrible situation, they said. A wolf pack had descended on the community. The people of the Settlement said, "Will you catch them?"

Grandpa put out his traps for the wolves. The pup was caught accidentally in a weasel set and drowned. Grandpa felt so bad about that, that he stopped trapping for that year. The next year he caught the she-wolf before she had pups. But he did not meet the old wolf face to face again until the night I remembered.

Grandpa did not have to tell me about that again. Maybe I was pretty young then, but I remembered all right. I was in my bunk in the cabin. Suddenly I was not asleep anymore. I was wide awake, straining my ears to hear something, and there was nothing. That was the trouble, there was no sound at all. There was silence all around.

I got out of my bunk and went to the door of the cabin. I went out on the porch and put my bare feet against fur. When I bent over to look, I saw it was Grandpa's cat. Dead. I looked around the clearing, and there at the edge the heifer was lying, and I walked over there. The heifer was dead, too. And in their yard, the geese too—dead, dead, dead. I turned, suddenly frightened then, more frightened than I'd ever been, to run back to the cabin. But out of nowhere the wolf was

---

set (SET) trap placed to catch wild animals
strain (STRAYN) cause to work as hard as possible; injure or weaken by force
clearing (KLIR ing) piece of land from which trees have been removed
heifer (HEF ur) young cow

there, in the yard, sitting between me and the cabin. I stood still. The wolf sat there, and the moon was in his eyes.

I don't know what would have happened then because by the wolf's reckoning I belonged to Grandpa, too. But it did not come to that. Suddenly my grandfather spoke from the cabin. The wolf turned smoothly and swiftly. Then the carbine crashed from the porch, and crashed again. The wolf fell heavily, and Grandpa came off the porch running. I tell you he was nine feet tall in the moonlight. But the wolf was gone.

Grandpa said, "I touched him that time, boy."

Now, riding up into the clearing behind the red horse, I recalled how frightened I had been. I felt that I must be very strong and brave to make up for it.

Grandpa went and sat on the porch. I unhitched the red horse and put him in the barn and rubbed him down. Then I said, "How about a trout for supper?"

"That's fine," Grandpa said.

"You want to catch him?"

"I believe I'll let you do it," Grandpa said.

I found a cricket and went down to the pool. I put the cricket on the hook and tied a little stick on the line a foot above it. Then I let it into the pool gently. Suddenly the rod bent and the line hummed, and I had a trout hooked.

When I went back up to the cabin, Grandpa still was sitting on the porch. He looked kind of tired. He said he'd let me fix supper, too. So I cleaned the trout, rolled it in cornmeal, and fried it in bacon grease. I fixed some beans in the skillet. For dessert I opened a can of peaches.

Right after we ate, Grandpa said he believed he'd go to bed, if I could clean things up.

"That'll be fine," I said. "I believe I'll sit up awhile."

The red horse had to be fed and turned out, but there weren't any other chores outside. When I was through, I built up the fire and sat down on the bearskin and looked around at the things in the cabin.

Next thing I knew it was morning and the fire was out. Grandpa was still sleeping. That was kind of funny. When I stopped to think, I didn't remember ever seeing Grandpa asleep before. But by the time I had the fire built up and breakfast ready, he was sitting on the edge of the bunk. He still looked tired.

"Reckon I won't eat any breakfast just now," he said. I must have had some sort of expression on my face, because he said, "Well, maybe just a mite."

He didn't eat much. When I finished he said, "I believe you'll have to go out and look at a couple of traps this morning."

"Yes, sir," I said. "Where are they?"

"Well, I'll draw you a kind of map," Grandpa said.

"Wolf traps?" I asked eagerly.

---

reckoning (REK un ing) way of thinking; calculated guessing
carbine (KAHR byn) short, lightweight rifle
unhitched (un HICHT) untied; unfastened

"Yes. Wolf traps." Grandpa smiled at me. "I calculate the old wolf was going to cross that way last night, and he won't cross there again for a year."

"He won't?"

"No," Grandpa said. "I understand him. To understand a wolf, you need only to think like a wolf. I have had more experience than the wolf has. That is my advantage."

"All right," I said. "If you will draw me the map."

"Be careful," Grandpa said. "You haven't had hardly any experience thinking like a wolf. One trap is in the trail, and you may find a hare in it. But there is another set, above the first, where a wolf might go in order to inspect the trap in the trail. You must be careful not to step in that yourself."

"Yes, sir," I said. "I'll bring them back."

"No," Grandpa said. "Spring them and leave them."

That was when I realized that Grandpa was sick. "Leave them?"

---

calculate (KAL kyuh layt) figure out by reasoning; to determine by using mathematics
advantage (ad VAN tij) something that helps one person win or succeed against another
hare (HAIR) wild rabbit
spring (SPRING) release a trap so that it cannot work

"Yes," Grandpa said. "If I have not caught him now, I will not try again. The wolf and I are both growing old. And maybe"—he smiled at me—"maybe as your mother says, puny."

I said, "Before I go to the traps, I could ride up and find Doc Champion."

"First the traps," Grandpa said.

He was very firm. I took the map and saddled the red horse. Then I came back into the house for the carbine. Grandpa was lying down again. I paused, worried, and he did not open his eyes, but he said, "First the traps."

So I went to the traps. It was a good thing I was leading the horse when we got close to the traps, because suddenly he snorted and reared and almost pulled the reins out of my hand. I tied him to a tree and went on to the crossing place.

And there was the wolf, waiting, the old gray wolf with the white streak across the top of his head that must have been from Grandpa's bullet. He looked at me the same way he had looked that night when the moon was in his eyes. But he looked surprised to see me. His foreleg was caught deeply in the trap. There was no use struggling and he hadn't struggled.

I looked at the wolf and my hands were sweating so I almost dropped the carbine. When I brought it up I could not hold the barrel steady until I braced it against a tree. The old wolf sat there with his leg in the trap, looking at me with that strange expression, surprised at seeing me instead of someone else. He did not believe it when I brought the barrel steady on him. He did not believe any of it, not the trap nor the gun nor me nor the shot either. He did not believe any of it at all, and then he was dead.

I saw him lying there and smelled the powder smoke, and I did not believe it either. I went over and touched him with my foot and turned his head. Then I saw his eyes and I believed it. The eyes did not hate anymore.

Afterward I went back for the red horse. I took the rope from the saddle and tied it to the wolf and tied the other end to the saddle. I could not get the red horse any closer than that to the wolf, even if the wolf was dead. The red horse did not believe it either. That was how we got back to the cabin.

Grandpa still was lying down. Without opening his eyes, he said, "Was there a rabbit in the lower set?"

"Yes," I said. "And the wolf was in the other."

"Yes," Grandpa said. "To be sure."

"Really," I said. "The wolf."

"A wolf," Grandpa said, opening his eyes. "Some wolf."

"No," I said. "The old wolf. With the two toes missing and the bullet mark on his head."

"No," Grandpa said. He sat up suddenly on his bunk. "No. Not after all this time."

---

reared (RIRD) rise up suddenly
foreleg (FAWR leg) front leg
brace (BRAYS) make steady; hold firm

"Yes," I said. "It was just the way you said. He was caught in the trap when he went to look at the place where you put the other trap."

"Where is he now?" Grandpa said, looking hard at me.

"He's out in the yard. I had to drag him behind the red horse. I thought you would want to see him."

"Drag him," Grandpa said, the beginning of a strange expression on his face. "He is not dead?"

"He is dead all right," I said. "He did not believe and the horse did not believe it and you do not believe it, but he is dead all right."

"No," Grandpa said. "He can't be dead."

The expression was getting clear on his face now.

"He is dead as anything. If you will come outside you can see him."

"No," Grandpa said.

I started to say something, then I saw quite suddenly the expression on Grandpa's face. He was not looking at me now. He was looking beyond me.

"I'm sorry," I said to my grandfather, without knowing why. "Did I do something wrong?"

"No," Grandpa said. "No."

"Maybe I could have let him go."

Grandpa said, "He did not ask you to."

"No," I said. "He looked at me with his teeth showing, he looked surprised."

"Yes," Grandpa said. "All right. He was old then, but not too old."

I didn't understand him.

"You must not worry," Grandpa said. "But neither a man nor a wolf should get too old."

"I didn't mean to do wrong."

"You did very well," Grandpa said. "You mustn't worry. But perhaps you will bury him now."

"All right," I said. "But shouldn't I go for Doc first?"

"No," Grandpa said. "Maybe after you bury the wolf, you will hitch up the red horse, and we will go down to the Settlement. I believe maybe your mother knows best."

"You mean about how you're getting—" I couldn't say it.

"Maybe she does," Grandpa said. "Maybe I ought to go back to the city with you, after all."

For a little while I didn't say anything. Then I said, "She didn't really think you'd come. She didn't think you'd leave the mountain."

Grandpa lay back on the bunk. He was smiling. "Things change, boy."

He looked at the ceiling, still smiling. "You come back here, boy, when you're grown up. There'll be a road. And the pine'll be gone. And you know what? There won't hardly be a mountain anymore."

He lay there. I went out and buried the wolf and hitched up the red horse. Afterward I went back and helped Grandpa out of the cabin and into the dogcart. He wasn't really nine feet tall. All the way to the Settlement I kept one arm around him and did my best not to cry.

FOCUS ON THE SELECTION

UNDERSTAND THE SELECTION

Recall

1. Identify the Little Warrior.
2. In what season, and how many years ago, did Grandpa meet the wolf?
3. What allows Grandpa to recognize it?

Infer

4. Explain why Grandpa stopped trapping.
5. Explain the meaning of the sentence: "He was the kind of trapper that some violin players are musicians."
6. Explain why the wolf killed all of Grandpa's animals and threatened the boy.
7. What is the first clue that Grandpa has changed his mind about leaving?

Apply

8. At the beginning of the story, the boy thinks Grandpa is nine feet tall. What event(s) causes this attitude to change?
9. Briefly explain the relationship between Grandpa and the wolf.
10. In your opinion, can there be more than one "Wolf of Thunder Mountain"?

Respond to Literature

Sometimes, we try to help other people by fighting their battles for them. Do you think this is always a good idea? Explain.

WRITE ABOUT THE SELECTION

At the end of the story, the boy has difficulty keeping back his tears. Why do you think he is crying? Is it possible that he has learned an important lesson about growing up? Imagine that you are the boy, several weeks after you have returned with Grandpa to the Settlement. Write a personal letter to Grandpa that explains what your experiences on Thunder Mountain taught you about growing up.

Prewriting: You may find it helpful to think about the specific experiences on Thunder Mountain as causes, and what the boy learned about growing up, as the effect of these causes. Make an informal cause-and-effect chart by listing the boy's experiences, and then the changes they caused.

Writing: Use your cause and effect chart to write a personal letter. In it, imagine that you are the boy, and are telling Grandpa what lessons about growing up you learned on Thunder Mountain.

Revising: When you revise your letter, make sure your first sentence identifies the main effect—what you learned about growing up. Decide if you have included enough details from the story to explain this effect.

Proofreading: When you proofread your letter, make sure that your indirect quotations are not surrounded, or enclosed, by quotation marks. An indirect quotation does not need quotation marks because it does not record a person's exact words.

THINK ABOUT IRONY

In a story, a character may expect a situation to have a certain outcome. Irony occurs when that situation turns out quite differently, or the opposite, from what the character expects. Learning about irony can help you to understand a deeper meaning in a story. For instance, irony often suggests that life is more complicated than it seems. Often, irony expresses certain truths about human nature.

1. At the end of the story, the trapped wolf reacts strangely when he sees the boy. Explain the wolf's attitude. Who did the wolf expect to see?
2. What is ironic about the way things turned out for the boy?
3. Why is this ironic?
4. Were you surprised by the ending of the story? Explain your answer.
5. Why do you think the author uses irony in this story?

DEVELOP YOUR VOCABULARY

Sometimes, you can figure out the meaning of an unfamiliar word by looking closely at the words that surround it. These surrounding words are called **context clues.** For example, you may be unfamiliar with the meaning of *modify* in the following sentence. "The discovery of a mountain on Mars caused scientists to *modify* their views about that planet's structure." By examining the words that surround *modify,* you can make an educated guess that it means "make a change."

Use context clues to determine the meaning of the *italicized* words below. On a piece of paper, circle the context clues that helped you figure out the word's meaning.

1. He looked *absurd* wearing his dungaree shorts to school in the middle of winter.
2. Strong and sturdy, the *hardy* oak tree survived the hurricane winds.
3. The *colossal* skyscraper was the tallest building in the world.
4. By the end of the race his heart was pounding in a fast, *irregular* beat.

Learn About
Third Person Point of View

In literature, **point of view** is the position, or perspective, from which a particular story is told. Point of view refers to the person telling the story. Sometimes, the story is told by a story character.

When a story is told in the **third person,** the storyteller, or narrator, is not a character in the story. The narrator uses third-person pronouns, such as *he, she,* and *it* to tell about other characters.

In the third person, everything you learn about a story and its characters is told by the narrator. He or she can enter the minds of any characters, at any time in the story. You learn what the characters in the story think and feel from information provided by the third-person narrator.

As you read "The Pot of Gold," ask yourself:

1. Who is telling this story?
2. What do you learn about the characters' thoughts and feelings?

Skill Builder

Write a brief, honest description of your best friend, using the third-person point of view. Do not use this person's real name.

THE POT of GOLD

by Salvador Salazar Arrué

José Pashaca was a body that had been tossed into a skin. The skin had been tossed into a shanty. The shanty was a *rancho* tossed on to the side of a hill.

Petrona Pelunto was the mother of that body.

"Son, open your eyes. I've even forgotten what color they are."

José Pashaca wriggled. Sometimes, he even stretched a leg.

"What you want, Mamma?"

"Son, you've got to find some work to do. You're just bone-lazy."

But the good-for-nothing showed only a slight improvement. From sleeping, he moved to sitting around, frowning, and yawning.

One day, Ulogio Isho came by. He carried something he had found. It was made of stone and shaped like a toad. He had turned it up while plowing. It had a chain of round pebbles around its neck. There were three holes in its head, one for the mouth and two for the eyes.

---

shanty (SHAN tee) small shabby shack or hut
rancho (RAN choh) Spanish for a hut for ranch workers
wriggle (RIG ul) twist and turn; squirm

"Did you ever see anything so ugly?" he said with a guffaw. "It looks just like one-eyed Cande."

And he left it for María Elena's children to play with.

Two days later, old Bashuto happened by. When he saw the toad, he said:

"These things were made long ago, in the days of our grandparents. You turn a lot of them up while plowing. And pots of gold, too."

That made José Pashaca stir. He wrinkled the skin between his eyes, where other people have a forehead.

"What's that you say, *Ño* Bashuto?"

Bashuto took his homemade cigar out of his mouth and spat.

"Just luck, my boy. You're going along plowing. All of a sudden—*plocosh*—you turn up a buried pot. And there you are, rich as cream.

"Really? You mean it, *Ño* Bashuto?"

"Just as sure as I'm sitting here."

Bashuto puffed at his cigar and became a cloud of smoke. Why he'd seen people find pots of gold thousands of times. When he left, he never realized he had planted a seed in the mind of José Pashaca.

It so happened that Petrona Pelunto died about this time. José opened his mouth and carried it all around town. But no one gave him food. He lived on bananas he managed to steal. So he decided he would look for buried pots of gold.

To do this, he got behind a plow and pushed. His eyes and his plow dug into the earth. In this way, José Pashaca became both the laziest and the hardest-working person in the neighborhood. He worked without working, without realizing he was working. He worked into the dark hours. Night always found him with his eyes on the ground and his hands on the plow handle.

Like an insect of the hillside, he crawled up and down the black loam. He watched the ground carefully. It seemed he was planting his soul in the soil. Of course, only laziness would have grown from such planting. Pashaca knew he was the most worthless person in the valley. He was not working. He was

---

guffaw (guh FAW) loud laugh
ÑO (NYAW) probably short for *señor* (Mr.)
loam (LOHM) rich soil

looking for pots full of golden coins. The pots went *plocosh* when the plow hit against them. Then they vomited forth silver and gold.

As he grew, so did his obsession. Ambition had done what hunger could not do. It had straightened him up in his skin. It had driven him to the slopes of the hills. There he plowed and plowed.

Pashaca shaved the hillsides clean. The *patrón* was awed by this miracle. Pashaca was now the best renter he had. The *patrón* gladly gave him as much land as he wanted to plow. And the renter kept thinking about the buried gold. He dug the earth with his eye always alert for the pot of gold.

And Pashaca also had to plant the fields. The owner expected crops from all this plowing. For the same reason, Pashaca had to harvest and sell the grain on all the land he plowed. He was careless with his own share of the money. He tucked it into a hole in the floor of his house, "just in case."

No other renter was the equal of José. "He's made of iron," people said. "Look how he settled down, once he decided to earn money. He must have a nice little pile put aside."

But José Pashaca never realized that he had a nice little pile. He was looking for that pot of gold. The pots were supposed to be buried in the fields. Sooner or later, he would find one.

He had not only become a hard worker. His neighbors said he had even become generous. Some days he had no land of his own to plow. Then he would help out the others. He would tell them to go off and rest while he did their plowing. And he did a good job. He always plowed deep, straight lines. It was a pleasure to look at them.

He would talk to the gold while he worked. "Now, where the devil are you hiding? I'm going to find you, whether you like it or not. I'll find you even if I kill myself in these fields."

And that was just what happened. Not that he found the buried treasure. But that he killed himself.

It happened one day at the hour when the sky turns a tender green. It was that time when the rivers are white stripes upon the plains. José Pashaca realized that for him there would be no pots

---

obsession (ub SESH un) overpowering desire or idea
patrón (pah TRON) Spanish for landowner

of gold. His first warning was a fainting spell. He fell forward over the plow handle. The oxen came to a halt, as though the plowshare had caught in the roots of darkness.

José Pashaca was a sick man. But he did not want anyone to take care of him. Ever since Petrona died, he had lived all alone.

One night, he gathered up his strength and slipped out of the house. He was carrying all his money in an old jug. With his grubbing machete, he began to dig a hole. Whenever he heard a noise, he would slink behind the bushes. Every now and then he had to stop because of the pain. But then he would go back to work with renewed zeal.

He set the pot in the hole. Then he covered it carefully and patted down the dirt over it. He erased all traces of his digging. Then he raised his arms, which were old before their time. He uttered these words in a deep sigh:

"Now nobody can say there are no more pots of gold to be found in the fields."

---

plowshare (PLOU shair) blade of a plow
grubbing (GRUB ing) digging; clearing land of roots, stumps and so on
machete (muh SHET ee) kind of large, heavy-bladed knife
zeal (ZEEL) eager desire

FOCUS ON THE SELECTION

UNDERSTAND THE SELECTION

Recall

1. Identify what Ulogio Isho found.
2. Where does José hide the money?
3. What was José Pashaca's first warning that he was sick?

Infer

4. Explain these phrases:
   Bashuto "had scattered the seeds of what he had said behind him."
   "Both his eyes and the plow furrowed the earth."
5. What effect does the death of his mother have on José Pashaca?
6. Explain how José's goals are different from the goals of other farmers.
7. Explain whether José Pashaca's farming success is planned or unplanned.

Apply

8. What kind of man is José Pashaca?
9. Why does José Pashaca bury his money?
10. José never finds his "pot of gold." Or, does he? Evaluate what the expression "pot of gold" can also mean here.

Respond to Literature

Have you ever experienced a kind of success that was accidental, or unplanned? Explain what you learned from it.

WRITE ABOUT THE SELECTION

Do you think that José Pashaca behaves properly in this story? How does his behavior contribute to his final ending? Imagine that you are a biographer writing the story of José Pashaca's life. Select two events from "The Pot of Gold" and write a passage that explains how they show José Pashaca's attitude toward life.

Prewriting: Before writing your passage, reread the sections of the story that tell you what kind of person José is. Create an informal outline of José's character traits, or personality, based upon what you learn in these story sections.

Writing: Use your informal outline to write an exerpt, or special part, from José Pashaca's biography. In it, explain José's attitude about life, and how this attitude contributes to José Pashaca's misfortune.

Revising: When you revise your passage, decide if the sentences accurately explain José's attitude toward life. Have you evaluated how this attitude makes José behave? You might want to include story quotes that show José's chief ambition.

Proofreading: When you proofread your passage, decide if you want to include, or remove, certain words to make your writing more effective. If you wish to insert a word in a line, use this proofreading mark [^] and write the new word above it. Use this proofreading mark [ ] if you wish to remove, or delete, a word.

THINK ABOUT POINT OF VIEW

In **third-person point of view,** you learn about events and characters from the narrator's viewpoint. Sometimes, the narrator chooses to enter the minds of every character in the story. Other times, though, the narrator focuses on a single character. You experience the world through this character's eyes. You may often understand more about this character than do other characters in the story.

1. Who is telling this story?
2. From what point of view is this story told? How do you know?
3. Does the person telling this story describe different characters, or does he or she focus on a single character?
4. Does José Pashaca think he is working hard? What story details help you understand José's inner thoughts and feelings?
5. What do you know about José Pashaca that other characters in the story do not know?

DEVELOP YOUR VOCABULARY

An **adjective** is a word that modifies, or describes, a noun or pronoun. For instance, *excellent* teacher, *difficult* homework, *correct* answer. An **adverb** is a word that modifies an adjective, a verb, even another adverb. For example, wrote *clearly,* spoke *smoothly, certainly* correct.

You can often form adverbs from adjectives by adding the suffix *-ly*. For example, "He was *calm* and controlled." "*Calmly,* he walked to the blackboard."

Copy six of the adjectives below on a piece of paper. Use a dictionary to find the meaning of each word. Then, add *-ly* to each word. Write a sentence that shows your understanding of each new adverb.

1. accurate
2. bare
3. furious
4. fluid
5. large
6. quick
7. worthless
8. deep
9. careless
10. direct
11. generous
12. tender

UNIT 4 REVIEW

LITERATURE-BASED WRITING

1. Many of the characters in this unit have struggled to accomplish specific goals. Some set objectives for themselves, while others achieved unplanned success. Each character however, learned an important lesson about success during his or her experiences. Imagine that two of the characters from this unit meet on a bus trip, and share their definitions of success. Write their conversation as a dialogue, as it might really occur.

Prewriting: Before you begin to write, select the two characters you understand most clearly. Then, think about what each character's experiences have taught him or her about success. Reread certain story sections and evaluate how each character really speaks. Then, begin to freewrite their conversation.

Writing: Use your freewriting to write a conversation between two characters from this unit. In it, have them discuss what they have learned about the meaning of success.

Revising: When you revise your conversation, makes sure that each character speaks "in character," according to his or her personality. Think about adding a description of the characters' expressions and actions during the conversation.

Proofreading: When you proofread your conversation, make sure that a new paragraph signals each new speaker. Use this proofreading mark [¶] to show where a paragraph should begin.

2. You have studied rhythm, rhyme, word sounds, free verse, and persona, which you can use to help you to evaluate the poems that you have read in this unit. Choose two poems and compare and contrast three literary elements, or essential parts, in a brief essay.

Prewriting: Briefly review the work you did for the "Think About ______" sections in this unit. Make an informal outline that lists the name of the two poems you have chosen. For each poem, include three literary elements as main topics, then list supporting details about each element from the poems. You may choose to analyze each poem's plot, theme, or imagery, as well, in your essay.

Writing: Use your informal outline to write a brief essay that compares and contrasts two literary elements in two poems appearing this unit. In your essay, explain which poem you think combines these literary elements in the most effective and pleasing way.

Revising: Reread your essay carefully and check for overused words. Try to substitute more vivid and effective words for repeated words, such as *like, because, very,* and *really.*

Proofreading: When you proofread your essay, use a comma to separate the two parts of a compound sentence. Correct any comma errors with these proofreading marks. Add comma [;], take out [ ].

BUILDING LANGUAGE SKILLS

Vocabulary

A **simile** is a direct comparison in which one thing is said to be similar, or like, something else. A simile uses the words *like* or *as.* The sentence, "The ocean was *as* calm *as* a puddle," uses a simile. To help you understand how calm the ocean is, it is compared to a puddle.

A **metaphor** is another kind of comparison. A metaphor is more direct than a simile. In a metaphor, one thing is said *to be* something else. Metaphors use words such as *is, are, was,* or *were.* The sentence, "Her brain *was* a computer," uses a metaphor. The metaphor compares the person's brain to a computer to help you realize how smart she is.

Each of the following sentences contains a simile or a metaphor. For each sentence, write *S* or *M* on your paper. Then, tell which two things are being compared.

1. The lemonade was as cold as an icy winter stream.
2. Like a glowing lantern, the campfire burned brightly through the night.
3. The sunset was an explosion of colors.
4. He ran like the wind to catch the school bus.
5. The substitute teacher assigned us a mountain of homework.
6. A curtain of rain prevented us from seeing across the street.

Usage and Mechanics

Whenever you write a person's or character's exact words, you must enclose what they say in a pair of quotation marks. You do not however, use quotation marks when you are only reporting or paraphrasing someone else's words.

If there is an introductory expression in the direct quote *(Casey said,* or *Mary Beth answered),* place a comma after it. When an expression is interrupted, surround it with commas. Always place concluding question marks, periods, and exclamation points within the quotation mark.

Example:

"Yes, sir," I said. "Where are they?"
"Well, I'll draw you a kind of map," Grandpa said."
"Wolf traps?" I asked eagerly.

Add commas, end marks, and quotation marks to these quotations. One of the sentences is an indirect quote.

1. Hold on she said I'll answer the door
2. Then I went to check the other traps he said
3. The teacher responded by telling us we would have a test tomorrow
4. I can't believe it he said rubbing his forehead
5. There's a message for you he said to the shop clerk

UNIT 4 REVIEW

SPEAKING AND LISTENING

There are several interesting ways you can get to know a character in a story. One of the most interesting ways to ponder the intricacies of a character's personality is to hold a mock trial. Of course, in order to prepare for a court trial, there are certain procedures you will want to follow that will help ensure a successful day in court. The day of the assignment do the following:

1. Think about the logistics of the courtroom. Discuss how the court will operate. Also, decide if the teacher or a student will act as judge. It will be the duty of the judge to supervise and add comments or advice as needed.
2. Appoint counsels for the defense and prosecution of the accused. You may decide to have one or two per side.
3. Decide who will play other parts such as the accused, witnesses for the prosecution and the defense, and so forth.
4. Permit each side time to discuss the case and develop questions. The questions asked by the lawyers should require a range of responses from simple one-word answers to those that entail thought and ingenuity. The questions should reveal the character's personality and motives for his behavior throughout the story.
5. During the trial, lawyers may call certain characters as witnesses, so each side should discuss the characters that they feel will be favorable witnesses for their side. Talk about the questions you will want to ask.
6. Practice your questioning technique. Also practice your mannerisms. Think about how and where you will stand as you question certain witnesses. Your voice and your "courtroom" manner will give your role more dimension. It will also add dramatic interest for the audience.

Right now, think about the story selections in this unit. Recall a character you think would be a good candidate to stand trial. You may want to re-read or skim the selection to confirm your choice. Then, meet with others in your class and begin to prepare for trial by following the steps above.

CRITICAL THINKING

It is 7:15 on a hot summer night. A large crowd waits in line for an eight o'clock movie. Suddenly, people pour out of the movie theater. They are complaining loudly about something. Why are these people leaving the theater?

Often, writers give you only partial or incomplete information. By thinking carefully about certain clues, you can fill in the missing information and draw a conclusion. A conclusion is an understanding of something that is not stated directly.

To draw a conclusion, read the passage above and look for story clues: *people walking out of a theater, before the show is over.* Think about what you know from past experience about these clues: *People may leave a theater when a movie is particularly bad or boring.* Combine your experience clues with story clues to draw a logical conclusion: *The movie was so bad that the audience decided to leave early.*

Sometimes, you discover new information that may cause you to modify your conclusion. For example, you observe that most of the people are sweating. Also, the theater manager is giving them back their money. Your modified conclusion might be: *The movie projector, or air conditioner broke, and the audience was forced to leave the theater.*

Draw a different conclusion about an event, cause, or result of an event, in two of the selections in this unit. Explain the process you used to draw your conclusion.

EFFECTIVE STUDYING

To prepare for a test, you should do more than simply review and study your notes. There are effective techniques that you can use to improve your test-taking skills. One of the most common types of test is the multiple-choice test. You can prepare for this kind of test by following this strategy.

1. Preview the test
- **a.** Write your name on the test.
- **b.** Decide how much time you should spend on each section.
- **c.** Read the test directions carefully.
- **d.** Determine if you should draw a line around an answer, underline an answer, or fill in a circle.

2. Answer the questions
- **a.** First answer the questions that you are most sure of.
- **b.** Go back to answer any question that caused you difficulty.
- **c.** Read all the answers for each question before choosing your answer.
- **d.** Eliminate the most unlikely answers first. You are then more likely to choose the correct answer.

3. Check your work
- **a.** Make sure that you followed the directions correctly.
- **b.** Check that you have answered all the questions.
- **c.** Proofread your answers. Make sure you only marked one answer for each question.

UNIT 5

Faces of Nature

Nature does nothing uselessly.

—Aristotle

The Starry Night, Vincent van Gogh, 1889.
Oil on canvas, 29 x 36¾". Collection, The Museum
of Modern Art. Lillie P. Bliss Bequest.

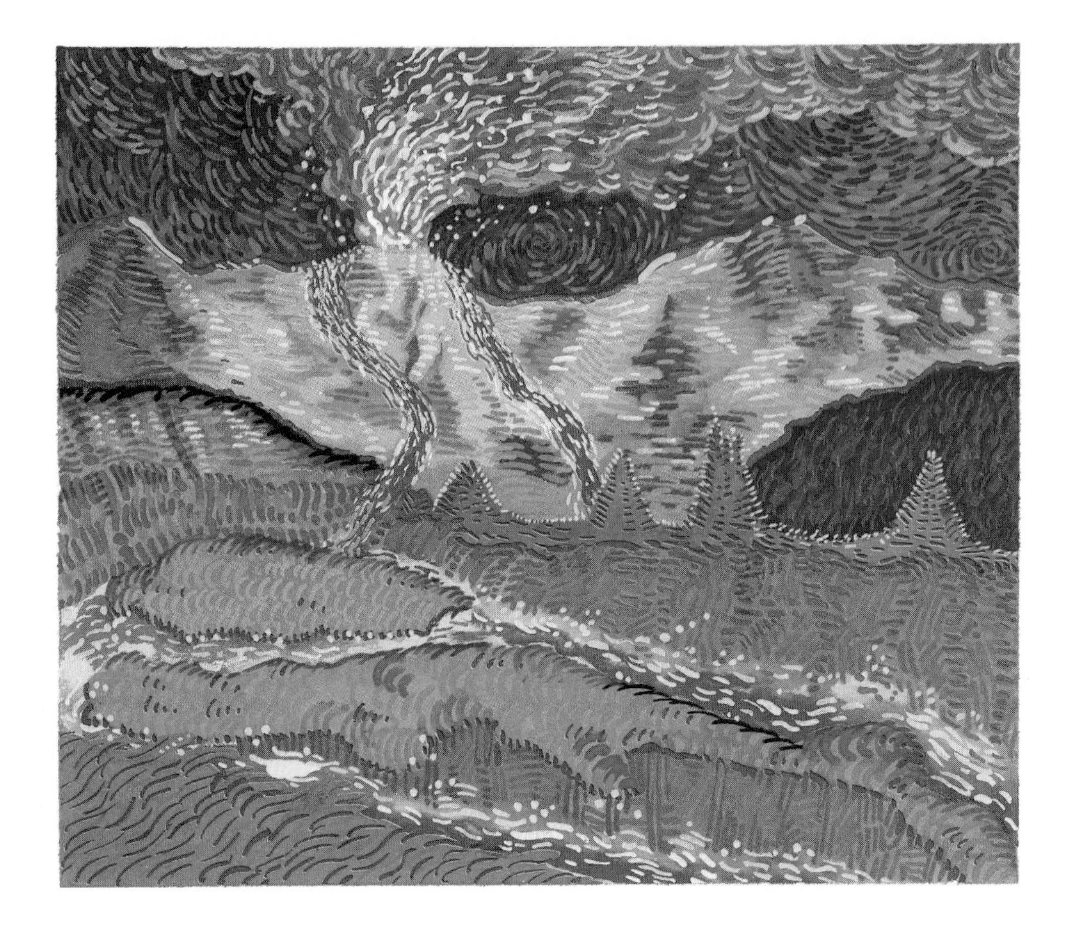

Faces of Nature. Nobody lives alone in the world. You live in a world with other people. You live in a world with animals, a world with trees and mountains and lakes and rivers. You live with the sun and the rain and the wind and the snow.

All of these aspects of nature in which you live are parts of your environment. They are parts of the world of nature, so you must learn how to live with them.

The selections in this unit are all about people and nature. Perhaps reading them will help you to think about how you relate to the world of nature around you.

Many stories tell about how people feel about their environments. You have certainly had experiences in your own life which relate to the world of nature around you. Have you ever been frightened by a terrible thunderstorm? Have you ever visited a beautiful lake that made you feel wonderful? Have you ever found yourself face to face with a wild animal?

People and Animals. The first story you will read is called "The Man Who Was a Horse," by Julius Laster. Of course, the man, Bob Lemmons, wasn't really a horse. However, he felt that he could understand things the way a horse does. He never told anybody how he felt because he was afraid people might think he was crazy. Bob Lemmons's way of relating to nature was unusual, but that is what makes his story interesting.

The second selection, "The Tiger's Heart," by Jim Kjelgaard, tells a very different story. The main character, Pepe, must kill a ferocious tiger. The story shows the relationship between Pepe and the tiger he kills as well as the relationship between Pepe and the people of his village.

Sky and Ocean. Next you will read three poems. One is about the wind ("Who Has Seen the Wind," by Christina Rossetti); one is about a storm ("The Storm," by William Carlos Williams); and the last is about clouds ("Clouds," by Gregory Djanikian). Wind, storms, and clouds are all parts of the environment you live in. Three different poets look at these parts of nature in three different ways.

The fourth selection is a play by Pearl Buck called *The Big Wave.* The big wave is so important to the play that it is almost a character itself. Every person in the play has a relationship with the big wave. Every person in the play has a relationship with the land and the sea. The environment in which people live truly shapes all aspects of their lives, as the play so successfully conveys.

Mysteries. "The Black Box: A Science Parable," by Albert B. Carr, is a short story that shows another way that people can react to their environment. Some children find a mysterious box on a beach. Of course, they want to find out what is inside it. They try to react to the box in the way they normally react to things. However, nothing they do seems to work. They cannot open the box. The children must find a whole new way to relate to the mysterious black box.

The last selection in the unit is another group of poems. You will find out about different poets' relationships with a silent pond in three haiku by Matsuo Basho, a bare tree in "The Bare Tree," by William Carlos Williams, and the changing of the seasons in "Winter," by Nikki Giovanni.

As you read each story in the unit, think about the effect the world of nature has on the characters. Sometimes nature is a friend. Sometimes nature is an enemy. Sometimes it is both.

As you read each poem in the unit, think about the effect the world of nature has on the poet.

Then think about the effect the world of nature has on you. How do you feel about the environment in which you live? Is the world around you comforting, or is it frightening? Does your world seem different to you at different times? How important do you think the world of nature really is in your life?

Cruising for Stock. North Wind Picture Archives.

LEARN ABOUT

Setting

The events of a story, whether fiction or nonfiction, happen in specific places at definite times. These times and places in a story are called **settings.** Writers often provide detailed descriptions of a setting so readers can easily picture where and when each event of the story takes place.

A story setting can be real even though the story itself is fictional. For example, a story about the American Civil War might happen in a real place at a specific time in history even though the characters and events are imaginary.

A story setting can also be totally imaginary. A writer might create a place that does not actually exist. He or she might write about a time that has never actually happened. A writer sometimes creates an especially fanciful setting by imagining both time and place.

As you read the story "The Man Who Was a Horse," ask yourself:

1. What is the setting of the story?
2. How does the setting make the story believable?

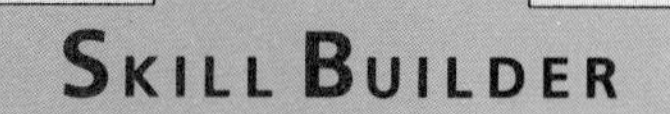

SKILL BUILDER

Think about where you are at this very minute. Write a short paragraph that describes your setting. Remember to make your writing very clear.

THE MAN WHO WAS A HORSE

by Julius Lester

It wasn't noon yet, but the sun had already made the Texas plains hotter than an oven. Bob Lemmons pulled his wide-brimmed hat tighter to his head and rode slowly away from the ranch.

"Good luck, Bob!" someone yelled.

Bob didn't respond. His mind was already on the weeks ahead. He walked his horse slowly, being in no particular hurry. That was one thing he had learned early. One didn't capture a herd of mustang horses in a hurry. For all he knew, a mustang stallion might have been watching him at that very moment. And if he were galloping, the stallion might get suspicious and take the herd miles away.

As far as Bob could see, the land was flat, stretching unbroken like the cloudless sky over his head until the two seemed to meet. Nothing appeared to be moving except him on his horse. But he knew that a herd of mustangs could be galloping near the horizon line at that moment and he would be unable to see it until it came much closer.

He rode north that day, seeing no sign of mustangs until close to evening, when he came across some tracks. He stopped and dismounted. For a long while he stared at the tracks until he was able to identify several of the horses. As far as he could determine, it seemed to be a small herd of a stallion, seven or eight mares, and a couple of colts. The tracks were no more than three days old, and he half expected to come in sight of the herd the next day or two. A herd didn't travel in a straight line, but ranged back and forth within what the stallion considered his territory. Of course, that could be the size of a county. But Bob knew he was in it, though he had not seen a horse.

He untied his blanket from behind the saddle and laid it out on the ground. Then he removed the saddle from the horse and hobbled the animal to a stake.

---

mustang (MUS tang) wild horse
dismount (dis MOUNT) get off a horse, bicycle, etc.
hobble (HOB ul) a horse is hobbled when two legs are tied loosely together so it cannot move freely

He didn't want a mustang stallion coming by during the night and stealing his horse. Stallions were good at that. Many times he had known them to see a herd of tame horses and, for who knew what reason, become attracted to one mare and cut her out of the herd.

He took his supper out of the saddlebags and ate slowly as the chilly night air seemed to rise from the very plains that a few short hours before had been too hot for a man to walk on. He threw the blanket around his shoulders, wishing he could make a fire. But if he had, the smell of wood-smoke in his clothes would have been detected by any herd he got close to.

After eating he laid his head back against his saddle and covered himself with his thick Mexican blanket. The chilliness of the night made the stars look to him like shining slivers of ice. Someone had once told him that the stars were balls of fire, like the sun. Bob didn't feel them that way. But he wasn't educated, so he wouldn't dispute with anybody about it. Just because you gave something a name didn't mean that that was what it actually was, though. The thing didn't know it had that name, so it just kept on being what it thought it was. And as far as he was concerned, people would be better off if they tried to know a thing like it knew itself. That was the only way he could ever explain to somebody how he was able to bring in a herd of wild horses by himself. The way other people did it was to go out in groups of two and three and run a herd until it almost dropped from exhaustion. He guessed that was all right. It worked. But he wouldn't want anybody running him to and fro for days on end, until he hardly knew up from down or left from right.

Even while he was still a slave, he'd felt that way about mustangs. Other horses, too. But he had never known anything except horses. Born and raised on a ranch, he had legally been a slave until 1865, when the slaves in Texas were freed. He had been 18 at the time and hadn't understood when Mr. Hunter had come and told him that he was free. That was another one of those words, Bob thought. Even as a child, when his father told him he was a slave, he'd wondered what he meant. What did a slave look like? What did a slave feel like? He didn't think he had ever known. He and his parents had been the only black people on the ranch and he guessed it wasn't until after he was "freed" that he saw another black person. He knew sometimes, from the names he heard the cowboys use, that his color somehow made him different. He heard them talking about "fighting a war over slavery," but it meant nothing to him. So when Mr. Hunter had told him he was free, that he could go wherever he wanted to, he nodded and got on his horse and went on out to the range to see after the cattle like he always had. He smiled to himself, wondering how Mr. Hunter had ever

---

dispute (dih SPYOOT) argue

gotten the notion that he couldn't have gone where he wanted.

A few months after that he brought in his first herd of mustangs. He had been seeing the wild horses since he could remember. The first time had been at dusk one day. He had been playing near the corral when he happened to look toward the mesa and there, standing on top of it, was a lone stallion. The wind blew against it, and its mane and tail flowed in the breeze like tiny ribbons. The horse stood there for a long while. Then, without warning, it suddenly wheeled and galloped away. Even now Bob remembered how seeing that horse had been like looking into a mirror. He'd never told anyone that, sensing how people might think him a little touched in the head. Many people thought it odd enough that he could bring in a herd of mustangs by himself. But, after that, whenever he saw one mustang or a herd, he felt like he was looking at himself.

One day several of the cowboys went out to capture a herd. The ranch was short of horses and no one ever thought of buying horses when there were so many wild ones. He had wanted to tell them that he would bring in the horses, but they would have laughed at him. Who'd ever heard of one man bringing in a herd? So he watched them ride out, saying nothing. A few days later they were back, tired and disgusted. They hadn't even been able to get close to a herd.

That evening Bob timidly suggested to Mr. Hunter that he be allowed to try. Everyone laughed. Bob reminded them that no one on the ranch could handle a horse like he could, that the horses came to him more than anyone else. The cowboys acknowledged that that was true, but it was impossible for one man to capture a herd. Bob said nothing else. Early the next morning he rode out alone, having asked the cook to leave food in a saddlebag for him on a tree in the north pasture every day. Three weeks later the cowboys were sitting around the corral one evening and looked up to see a herd of mustangs galloping toward them, led by Bob. Despite their amazement, they moved quickly to open the gate, and Bob led the horses in.

That had been some 20 years ago, and long after Bob left the Hunter Ranch he found that everywhere he went he was known. He never had trouble getting a job. But capturing mustangs was only a small part of what he did. Basically he was just a cowboy who worked from sunrise to sunset, building fences, herding cattle, branding calves, pitching hay, and doing everything else that needed to be done.

Most cowboys had married and settled down by the time they reached his age, but Bob had long ago relinquished any such dream. Once he'd been in love with a Mexican girl named Pilar, but her father didn't want her to marry a "colored" man. It was another lesson he had

---

mesa (MAY suh) a high, flat area with a sharp slope on one side
corral (kuh RAL) pen for horses and cattle
relinquish (ruh LING kwish) give up, abandon

to learn about people—or about some people. Some people thought that Bob's skin color somehow made a difference. It made a big enough difference to Pilar's father for him to stop Pilar from marrying Bob. After that, he decided not to be in love again. It was a decision he never regretted. Almost every morning when he got up and looked at the sky lying full and open and blue, stretching toward forever, he knew he was married to something. He wanted to say the sky, but it was more than that. He wanted to say everything, but he felt that it was more than that, too. How could there be more than everything? He didn't know, but there was.

The sun awakened him even before the first arc of its roundness showed over the horizon. He saddled his horse and rode off, following the tracks he had discovered the previous evening. He followed them west until he was certain they were leading him to the Pecos River. He smiled. Unless it was a herd traveling through, they would come to that river to drink every day. Mustangs never went too far from water, though they could go for days without a drop if necessary. The Pecos was still some distance ahead, but he felt his horse's body quiver slightly, and she began to strain forward against his tight hold on the reins. She smelled water.

"Sorry, honey. But that water's not for you," he told the horse. He wheeled around and galloped back in the direction of the ranch until he came to the outermost edge of what was called the west pasture. It was still some miles from the ranch house itself, and today Bob couldn't see any cattle grazing up there.

But on a tree at the outer edge of the ranch was a saddlebag filled with food. Each day one of the cowboys would bring a saddlebag of food up there and leave it for him. He transferred the food to his own saddlebags. He was hungry but would wait until evening to eat. The food had to have time to lose its human odor, an odor that mustangs could pick out of the slightest breeze. He himself would not venture too close to the horses for another few days, not until he was certain that his own odor had become that of his horse.

He rode southward from the pasture to the banks of the Nueces River. There he dismounted, took the saddle off his horse, and let her drink her fill and wade in the stream for a while. It would be a few days before she could drink from the Pecos. The mustangs would have noticed the strange odor of horse and man together, and any good stallion would have led his mares and colts away. The success of catching mustangs, as far as Bob was concerned, was never to hurry. If neces-

---

arc (ARK) any part of a circle
pasture (PAS chur) a grassy field or hillside
grazing (GRAYZ ing) feeding on growing grass
Nueces River (noo AY sus) a river in southern Texas flowing into the Gulf of Mexico

Watering the Herd (engraving), William M. Cary. North Wind Picture Archives

sary he would spend two weeks getting a herd accustomed to his distant presence once he was in sight of them.

He washed the dust from his face and filled his canteen. He lay down under a tree, but its shade didn't offer much relief from the heat of high noon. The day felt like it was on fire and Bob decided to stay where he was until the sun began its downward journey. He thought Texas was probably the hottest place in the world. He didn't know, not having traveled much. He had been to Oklahoma, Kansas, New Mexico, Arizona, and Wyoming on cattle drives. Of all the places, he liked Wyoming the most, because of the high mountains. He'd never seen anything so high. There were mountains in Texas, but nothing like that. Those mountains just went up and up and up until it seemed they would never stop. But they always did, with snow on the

---

canteen (kan TEEN) a small container for carrying water and other liquids

top. After a few days, though, he wasn't sure that he did like the mountains. Even now he wasn't sure. The mountains made him feel that he was penned in a corral, and he was used to spaces no smaller than the sky. Yet he remembered Wyoming with fondness and hoped that some year another cattle drive would take him there.

The heat was still intense when Bob decided to go north again and pick up his trail. He would camp close to the spot where his mare had first smelled the Pecos. That was close enough for now.

In the days following, Bob moved closer to the river until one evening he saw the herd come streaming out of the hills, across the plain, and to the river. He was some distance away, but he could see the stallion lift his head and sniff the breeze. Bob waited. Although he couldn't know for sure, he could feel the stallion looking at him, and for a tense moment Bob didn't know if the horse would turn and lead the herd away. But the stallion lowered his head and began to drink and the other horses came down to the river. Bob sighed. He had been accepted.

The following day he crossed the river and picked up the herd's trail. It was not long after sunrise before he saw them grazing. He went no closer, wanting only to keep them in sight and, most important, make them feel his presence. He was glad to see that after a moment's hesitation, the stallion went back to grazing.

Bob felt sorry for the male horse. It always had to be on guard against dangers. If it relaxed for one minute, that just might be the minute a nearby panther would choose to strike, or another stallion would challenge him for the lead of the herd, or some cowboys would throw out their ropes. He wondered why a stallion wanted the responsibility. Even while the horses were grazing, Bob noticed that the stallion was separate, over to one side, keeping a constant lookout. He would tear a few mouthfuls of grass from the earth, then raise his head high, looking and smelling for danger.

At various times throughout the day Bob moved a few hundred yards closer. He could see it clearly now. The stallion was brown, the color of the earth. The mares and colts were black and brown. No sorrels or duns in this herd. They were a little smaller than his horse. But all mustangs were. Their size, though, had nothing to do with their strength or endurance. There was no doubt that they were the best horses. He, however, had never taken one from the many herds he had brought in. It wasn't that he wouldn't have liked one. He would have, but for him to have actually ridden one would have been like taking a piece of

---

penned (PEND) shut in; confined
intense (in TENS) extreme
hesitation (hez uh TAY shun) failure to act promptly
sorrel (SAWR ul) reddish brown
dun (DUN) dull brown
endurance (en DUUR uns) ability to keep going

the sky and making a blanket. To ride with them when they were wild was all right. But he didn't think any man was really worthy of riding one, even though he brought them in for that purpose.

By the sixth day he had gotten close enough to the herd that his presence didn't attract notice. The following day he moved closer until he and his mare were in the herd itself. He galloped with the herd that day, across the plain, down to the river, up into the hills. He observed the stallion closely, noting that it was a good one. The best stallions led the herd from the rear. A mare always led from the front. But it was only at the rear that a stallion could guard the herd and keep a mare from running away. The stallion ran up and down alongside the herd, biting a slow mare on the rump or ramming another who threatened to run away or to bump a third. The stallion was king, Bob thought, but he worked. It didn't look like much fun.

He continued to run with the herd a few days more. Then came the critical moment when, slowly, he would begin to give directions of his own, to challenge the stallion in little ways until he had completely taken command of the herd and driven the stallion off. At first he would simply lead the herd in the direction away from the one the stallion wanted to go. Then, just before the stallion became enraged, he would put it back on course. He did this many times, getting the stallion confused as to whether or not there was a challenger in his midst. But enough days of it and the stallion gradually wore down, knowing that something was happening but unable to understand what. When Bob was sure the herd was in his command, he merely drove the stallion away.

Now came the fun. For two weeks Bob led the herd. Unlike the stallion, he chose to lead from the front, liking the sound and feel of the wild horses so close behind. He led them to the river and watched happily as they splashed and rolled in the water. Like the stallion, however, he kept his eyes and ears alert for any sign of danger. Sometimes he would pretend he heard something when he hadn't and would lead the herd quickly away simply as a test of their willingness to follow him.

At night he stopped, unsaddled his horse, and laid out his blanket. The herd grazed around him. During all this time he never spoke a word to the horses, not knowing what effect the sound of a voice might have on them. Sometimes he wondered what his own voice sounded like. And sometimes he even wondered if he would return to the ranch and find himself able only to snort and neigh, as these were the only sounds he heard. There were other sounds though, sounds that he couldn't reproduce, like the flaring nostrils of the horses when they were galloping, the dark, bulging eyes, the

---

critical (KRIT uh kul) at an important moment
reproduce (ree pruh DOOS) copy
flare (FLAIR) spread out

Head of a White Horse, Theodore Gericault. The Granger Collection

flesh quivering and shaking. He knew that he couldn't hear any of these things —not with his ears at least. But somewhere in his body he heard every ripple of muscles and bending of bones.

The longer he was with the herd, the less he thought. His mind slowly emptied itself of anything relating to his other life and refilled with sky, plain, grass, water, and shrubs. At these times he was more aware of the full-bodied animal beneath him. His own body seemed to take on a new life and he was aware of the wind against his chest, of the taut muscles in his strong legs and the strength of the muscles in his arms, which felt to him like the forelegs of his horses. The only thing he didn't feel he had was a tail to float in the wind behind him.

Finally, when he knew that the herd would follow him anywhere, it was time to take it in. It was a day he tried to keep away as long as possible. But even he began to tire of going back to the west pasture for food and sometimes having to chase a horse that had tried to run away from the herd. He had also begun to weary of sleeping under a blanket on the ground every night. So one day, almost a month after he had left, he rode back toward the ranch until he saw one of the cowhands and told him to get the corral ready. Tomorrow he was bringing them in.

The following morning he led the herd on what he imagined was the ride of their lives. Mustangs were made to run. All of his most vivid memories were of mustangs, and he remembered the day he had seen a herd of what must have been at least a thousand of them galloping across the plains. The earth was a dark ripple of movement, like the swollen Nueces River at floodtime. And though his herd was much smaller, they ran no less beautifully that day.

Then, toward evening, Bob led them east, galloping, galloping, across the plains. And as he led them toward the corral, he knew that no one could ever know these horses by riding on them. One had to ride with them, feeling their hooves pound and shake the earth, their bodies glistening so close by that you could see the thin straight hairs of their shining coats. He led them past the west pasture, down the slope, and just before

taut (TAWT) stretched tight

In With the Horse Herd, North Wind Picture Archives

the corral gate, he swerved to one side, letting the horses thunder inside. The cowboys leaped and shouted, but Bob didn't stay to hear their congratulations. He slowed his mare to a trot and then to a walk to cool her off. It was after dark when he returned to the ranch.

He took his horse to the stable, brushed her down, and put her in a stall for a well-earned meal of hay. Then he walked over to the corral, where the mustangs mingled restlessly. He sat on the rail for a long while, looking at them. They were only horses now. Just as he was only a man.

After a while he climbed down from the fence and went into the bunkhouse to go to sleep.

---

mingle (MING gul) mix together

FOCUS ON THE SELECTION

UNDERSTAND THE SELECTION

Recall

1. What kind of horses did Bob Lemmons capture?
2. When did Bob stop being a slave?
3. About how long did it take Bob to bring in a herd of horses?

Infer

4. In what state did Bob Lemmons live?
5. Why did Bob tie his horse to a stake?
6. How did Bob Lemmons go about capturing a herd of horses?
7. How did other people go about capturing a herd of horses?

Apply

8. What was unusual about Bob Lemmons's way of capturing horses?
9. How do you think Bob learned to capture a herd of horses in his special way?
10. Bob did not tell people that he could put himself in the place of a horse. He was afraid they might think he was crazy. What do you think about Bob's way of relating to horses?

Respond to Literature

How does the setting of "The Man Who Was a Horse" make the story more believable?

WRITE ABOUT THE SELECTION

You have just read a true story about a man named Bob Lemmons. Bob Lemmons was an unusual person. In the story he did something that no other person had ever done before.

Write a paragraph describing Bob Lemmons. Descriptive writing paints a picture of a person, a place, or a thing. Vivid language and details make descriptive writing come alive.

Prewriting: Write a list of details about Bob Lemmons. What do you think Bob Lemmons was really like? Which details on your list support the overall impression you want to give about Bob? Take out details that don't belong in your paragraph. Add new details that help show more of what Bob was like.

Writing: Write a topic sentence that tells your overall idea of what Bob Lemmons was like. Then write the details that support your topic sentence. Organize your paragraph in a way that makes sense to you.

Revising: Be sure that you have a topic sentence that states your overall idea of what Bob Lemmons was like. Then, look at your details to see if they support your topic sentence. Finally, check your paragraph for mistakes in spelling, grammar, and punctuation.

Proofreading: Read over your paragraph to check for errors. Be sure that all your sentences end with periods, question marks, or exclamation marks.

THINK ABOUT SETTING

The **setting** of a story is the time and place in which the action occurs. Details such as the time of day, the weather, the mountains, and even how the sky looks can all be parts of the setting.

1. Look at the first sentence of "The Man Who Was a Horse." What does it tell you about the setting of the story?
2. What is the land like where the story takes place?
3. Why is it important for you to know what the land is like?
4. Does the story take place in modern times? Explain your answer.
5. How does the setting make the story more believable?

DEVELOP YOUR VOCABULARY

A **contraction** is a word that is formed by combining two words into one, leaving out one or more letters. An apostrophe replaces the letter or letters that have been left out.

I + am = I'm
you + have = you've
we + will = we'll
who + had = who'd

is + not = isn't
were + not = weren't
does + not = doesn't
had + not = hadn't

Read the sentences below. Identify each contraction. Then write the two words that make up the contraction.

1. "It wasn't noon yet, but the sun had already made the Texas plains hotter than an oven."
2. "A herd didn't travel in a straight line, but ranged back and forth within what the stallion considered his territory."
3. "But he wasn't educated, so he wouldn't dispute with anybody about it."
4. "Even while he was a slave, he'd felt that way about mustangs."
5. "Who'd ever heard of one man bringing in a herd?"

Learn About

Irony

There is **irony** in a story when there is a difference between the way things seem and the way they really are. A situation is ironic when there is a difference between what is expected and what happens.

Suppose there was an elderly man living in your neighborhood who appeared to be very poor. He lived in a tiny apartment and always wore old, torn clothing. He never went anywhere and never seemed to have money to buy anything. Suppose when that man died, you read in the newspaper that he had had a million dollars hidden away in his apartment. You would be quite surprised, wouldn't you? It would be ironic that the man lived his life as though he had been poor when in reality he was wealthy.

As you read "The Tiger's Heart," ask yourself the following questions:

1. What is ironic about the way Pepe kills the tiger?
2. What will people think happened, and what really happened?

Skill Builder

Think of something that has happened to you that was ironic. Think of something that seemed to be one way but turned out to be quite different. Write a short paragraph that tells what happened.

THE TIGER'S HEART

by Jim Kjelgaard

The approaching jungle night was, in itself, a threat. As the night deepened, an eerie silence covered the village. People were silent. The cattle stood quiet, tied to their posts. Roosting chickens did not stir. Wise goats made no noise.

It had been this way for thousands of years. And it would continue to be this way. The brown-skinned inhabitants of the village knew the jungle. They had walked its dim paths and forded its rivers. They had endured its steaming heat. They knew its deer, tapir, crocodiles, screaming green parrots and countless other creatures.

That was the daytime jungle. They could see, feel, and hear it. But at night everything became different. When darkness came, the jungle was alive with strange and horrible things. No man had ever seen them, and no man could describe them. They were shadows with no substance. They struck and killed before you were even aware of them. With morning, they changed themselves back into the shape of familiar things. Night was a time of the unknown. That made it a time of fear.

Except to the man who owned a rifle, Pepe Garcia thought. As the night closed in, Pepe reached out to fondle his rifle. He would make sure it was close to him.

---

eerie (IR ee) mysterious or weird in such a way as to frighten
inhabitants (in HAB ih tantz) persons or animals that live in some specific region, dwelling, etc.
dim (DIM) not bright, somewhat dark; not clear or distinct in character
forded (FORD id) crossed at a passage
endured (en DUURD) held up under pain, fatigue, etc.; put up with
tapir (TAY pur) any of a family of large, hoofed, hoglike mammals inhabiting places with tropical climates
countless (COWNT lis) too many to count
substance (SUB stuns) the real or essential part of anything; reality; the physical matter of which anything consists
fondle (FON dul) to stroke or handle in a tender, loving way

As long as it was, he was king.

That was only fair, since the rifle had cost him dearly. Pepe had worked on a new road with eleven others from his village. They had used machetes, and they had worked hard. Unlike the others, Pepe had saved every peso he didn't need for living expenses. He then used the money for a rifle. He also bought a supply of powder and lead, and a mold for making bullets.

The rifle had cost him eighty pesos. But it was worth the price. No man with a rifle had to fear the jungle at night. The others had only machetes to guard themselves from the terrors of the dark. They were willing to pay well for protection. Pepe went peacefully to sleep.

He did not know what awakened him. He knew only that something was there. He listened intently. But there was no change in the jungle's monotonous night sounds. Still, something was not as it should be.

Then he heard a goat bleat from the far end of the village. Silence followed. The goat bleated again, louder and more fearful. There was a rush of small hoofs. Then he heard a frightened bleat cut short. Then silence.

Because he owned a rifle, Pepe did not need to imagine fantastic creatures in the night. He interpreted correctly what he had heard. A tiger—a jaguar—had come in the night. It had leaped the torn fence that surrounded the village. And it had made off with one of Juan Aria's goats.

Pepe went peacefully back to sleep. In the morning, Juan Aria would certainly come to him.

He did not awaken until the sun was up. He emerged from his hut and ate a papaya for breakfast. Then he waited for his visitor. They must always come to him. It was not proper for a man with a rifle to seek out anyone.

Soon Pepe saw Juan Aria and his brother coming up the path. Others stared curiously. But nobody else came because their flocks had not been raided. They did not want to pay a hunter.

---

dearly (DIR lee) much valued; costly

machetes (muh SHET eez) large, heavy-bladed knives used for cutting down sugar cane

peso (PAY soh) the basic monetary unit of several Central and South American countries

intently (in TENT lee) earnestly; firmly directed or fixed

monotonous (muh NOT un us) going on in the same tone without variation

interpreted (in TER prut id) explained the meaning of; made understandable; translated

papaya (puh PY uh) a tropical American tree bearing a large, oblong, yellowish-orange fruit like a melon

curiously (KYUUR ee us lee) carefully, arousing attention or interest because something is unusual or strange

Pepe waited until the two were near. Then he said, "*Buenos dias.*"

"*Buenos dias,*" they replied.

They sat down in the sun, looking at nothing in particular. They were not afraid now. The day was not a time of fear. Only now and then did a tiger come by daylight for a goat, a burro, or a cow.

Juan Aria said, "I brought my goats into the village last night. I thought they would be safe."

"And they were not?" Pepe said.

"They were not. Something came and killed one. It was my favorite, a fine black and white nanny. When the thing left, the goat went too."

"What killed your goat?" Pepe asked.

"A devil. But this morning, I saw only the tracks of a tiger."

"Did you hear it come?"

"I heard it."

"Then why did you not defend your flock?"

"It would be madness to attack a devil—or a tiger—with nothing but a machete."

"That is true," Pepe agreed. "Let us hope that the next time it is hungry, it will not come back for another goat."

"But it will!" Juan Aria said.

Pepe relaxed. Juan Aria's statement greatly improved Pepe's bargaining position. What Juan Aria said was true. Having had a taste of easy game, the tiger would come again. Only death would end its attacks.

"That is bad," Pepe said. "A man may lose many goats to a tiger."

"Unless a hunter kills him," Juan Aria said.

"Unless a hunter kills him," Pepe agreed.

"That is why I have come to you, Pepe," Juan Aria said. A troubled look spread over his face. "I hope you will follow and kill this tiger. You are the only man who can do so."

"It would give me great pleasure to kill him. But I cannot work for nothing."

"Nor do I expect you to. Even a tiger will not eat an entire goat. You are sure to find what is left of my favorite goat. Whatever the tiger has not eaten, you may have for your pay."

Pepe became angry. "You want me to put myself and my rifle to work for a corpse left by a tiger?"

"No, no!" Juan Aria protested. "In addition, I will give you one live goat!"

"Three goats."

"I am a poor man!" Juan Aria wailed. "You will bankrupt me!"

"No man with twenty-nine goats is poor. But he would be if a tiger raided his flock enough times."

"I will give you one goat and two kids."

"Two goats and one kid."

"You drive a hard bargain, Pepe. But I cannot say no. Kill the tiger."

Buenos dias (BWEH nos DEE ahs) good day or good morning in Spanish
nanny (NAN ee) nanny goat; a female goat
bankrupt (BANGK rupt) anyone unable to pay his or her debts

Pepe casually took his rifle from the fine blanket where he kept it. He examined his powder horn and his bullet pouch. He strapped on his machete and sauntered toward Juan Aria's hut.

A half-dozen worshipful children followed. Pepe chased them away. They fell behind, but continued to follow.

Pepe reached the place where Juan Aria's flock had spent the night. He saw the tiger's paw marks imprinted in the dust. It was a huge cat, lame in the right front paw.

Expertly, Pepe found the place where it had gone back over the thorn fence. The tiger had carried the sixty-pound goat in its jaws. Still, only a couple of thorns were disturbed at the place where it had leaped.

Though he did not look around, Pepe knew that the villagers were watching him with respect. Most of the men went into the jungle sometimes with their machetes. But none would work where tigers were known to be. Not one would dare to follow a tiger's trail. Only Pepe dared. Because he did, he must be revered.

Still being casual, Pepe sauntered through the gate. Behind him, he heard the villagers sigh with relief and admiration. A raiding tiger was a very real and terrible threat. Goats and cattle were hard to get. The man with a rifle could protect them. He must necessarily be a hero.

In the jungle, where the villagers could not see him, Pepe underwent a great change.

He lost his air of indifference. He became as alert as a doe. A rifle might be a symbol of power. But a rifle was no good unless a man was also a hunter. Impressing the villagers was one thing. Hunting a tiger was quite another.

Pepe knew the great cats were death in bodily form. They could move with incredible swiftness. They were strong enough to kill an ox. They feared nothing.

Pepe slipped along as softly as a jungle shadow. His machete slipped a little. He shifted it to a place where it would not bump his legs. From time to time, he glanced at the ground before him.

To trained eyes, there was a distinct trail. Pepe saw an occasional drop of

---

revered (rih VIRD) regarded with deep respect, love, and awe
sauntered (SAWN turd) strolled or walked about idly
indifference (in DIF ur uns) the state or quality of being indifferent; showing a lack of concern, interest, or feeling
alert (uh LERT) watchful and ready, as in facing danger; quick in thought or action
symbol (SIM bul) something that stands for or represents another thing; emblem
incredible (in KRED uh bul) not believable; seeming too unusual or improbable to be possible
swiftness (SWIFT nis) moving or capable of moving with great speed
distinct (dih STINGKT) not alike; different; separate; individual

A.FRANCO 88

blood from the dead goat. Then he would find a bent or broken twig. Next, there would be a few hairs where the tiger had squeezed between trees. Within a quarter of a mile, Pepe knew many things about this tiger.

He was not an ordinary beast. An ordinary beast would have gone only far enough so that he could not smell the village. He would have eaten what he wanted there. Then he would have covered the remainder of the goat with sticks and leaves.

The beast was also not old. His trail did not show the lagging step of an old cat. The proof of his strength was in the easy way he had leaped the fence with a goat in his jaws.

Pepe stopped to load his rifle. When he saw the tiger, he must shoot straight. He slowed his pace, warned by some super jungle sense. A moment later, he found his game.

He came upon it suddenly in a grove of scattered palm trees. He had not expected to see it there. So he did not see it until it was nearer than safety allowed.

The tiger crouched at the base of a fifty-foot palm tree. Its front paws were on what was left of the dead goat. It did not snarl or grimace, or even twitch its tail. But there was a lethal quality about the great cat. The tiger was bursting with raw anger that seemed to swell and grow.

Pepe stopped in his tracks. Cold fear crept up his spine. But he did not give way to fear. With careful slowness, he brought the rifle to his shoulder and aimed. He had only one bullet, and there would be no time to reload. But even a tiger could not withstand the smash of that enormous lead ball right between the eyes. Pepe steadied the rifle.

His finger tightened slowly on the trigger. He must not let nervousness spoil his aim. When the gun fired, Pepe's brain and body became momentarily numb.

There was no satisfying roar. There was no puff of black powder smoke. Instead, there was only a sudden hiss, as though cold water had spilled on a hot stone. Pepe himself had loaded the rifle. But he could not have done so correctly.

Anger exploded in the tiger's lithe and deadly body. He emitted a coughing snarl and began his charge. He was Lord of the Jungle. He would crush this puny man who dared to interfere with him.

---

lagging (LAG ing) falling, moving or staying behind
scattered (SKAT urd) thrown here and there or strewn loosely; sprinkled
snarl (SNAHRL) to growl fiercely, baring the teeth, as a threatening dog; to speak harshly or sharply
grimace (GRIM is) a twisting or distortion of the face, as in expressing pain, contempt, disgust
lethal (LEE thul) causing, or capable of causing, death
momentary (MOH mun teree) lasting for only a moment; passing; transitory
numb (NUM) weakened in, or deprived of, the power of feeling or moving
lithe (LY*TH*) flexible; bendable

A. FRANCO

Pepe jerked back to reality. But he took time to think of his rifle, leaning it lovingly against a tree. In the same motion, he pulled his machete from its sheath.

It was now a hopeless fight. In the memory of the village's oldest inhabitants, no one had ever killed a tiger with a machete. But it was better to fight hopelessly than to turn and run. If he ran, he would surely be killed. No tiger that attacked anything was ever known to turn aside.

With his machete in hand, Pepe studied the onrushing cat. He had read the tracks correctly. The tiger's right front foot was swollen to almost twice the size of the left. It must have stepped on a poisonous thorn or been bitten by a snake.

Even with such a handicap, it was a hopeless fight. The tiger was more than a match for a man armed only with a machete. But Pepe watched the right front paw carefully. If he had any advantage, it was there.

The tiger was a terrible, pitiless engine of destruction. It flung itself at Pepe. Pepe was ready for exactly this opening pounce. He swerved and bent his body outward. The great cat brushed past him. With all the strength in his powerful arm, Pepe swung the machete.

He stopped just short of the tiger's silken back. He knew suddenly that there was only one way to end this fight.

The tiger whirled. Hot spittle from its mouth splashed on the back of Pepe's left hand. Pepe held the machete before him, like a sword. He stepped back.

The tiger sprang, as though its rear legs were made of powerful steel springs. His left paw flashed at Pepe. It hooked in his shirt. The paw ripped the shirt away from Pepe's arm as though it were paper. Burning claws sank into the flesh. Red blood welled out.

Pepe did not try again to slash with the machete. Instead, he thrust, as he would with a knife or sword. The machete's point met the tiger's throat. Pepe put all his strength and weight behind it. The blade explored its way into living flesh. The tiger gasped. Blood bubbled over the machete.

With a powerful effort, the tiger pulled himself away. But blood was rushing from his throat now. He shook his head, then stumbled and fell. He pulled himself up. He looked at Pepe with glazing eyes and dragged himself toward him. There was a strangled snarl. The

---

emitted (ih MIT id) sent out; gave forth; discharged

handicap (HAN dih kap) something that hampers a person; difficulty; disadvantage

pitiless (PIT ee lis) without pity; unfeeling

destruction (dis TRUK shun) the act, or process, of destroying

pounce (POUNS) the act of pouncing, swoop, spring or leap

swerved (SWERVD) turned aside, or caused to turn aside, sharply or suddenly from a straight line or course

thrust (THRUST) to push with sudden force; shove; drive; to pierce; stab

tiger slumped to the ground. The top of his tail twitched. Then it was still.

Pepe stared. He barely saw the blood that flowed from his lacerated arm. He had done the impossible. He had killed a tiger with a machete. He brushed a hand across his eyes and took a trembling step forward.

He picked up his rifle and examined it. There seemed to be nothing wrong. Bracing one foot against the tiger's head, he drew the machete out.

Then he held the rifle barrel right next to the machete wound. He pulled the trigger. The wound became wider. It was now fringed with smoke-blackened fur. Pepe felt regret for a second. Then he steadied himself. This is the way it must be.

Everybody had a machete. In his village, the man who owned a rifle must remain supreme.

---

lacerated (LAS ur ayt id) torn jaggedly; mangled; wounded or hurt deeply
fringed (FRINJD) decorated with fringe; bordered; trimmed

FOCUS ON THE SELECTION

UNDERSTAND THE SELECTION

Recall

1. How much did Pepe's rifle cost?
2. What did Juan Aria finally agree to pay Pepe to kill the tiger?
3. What did Pepe use to kill the tiger?

Infer

4. Why did the villagers think the jungle was so different at night?
5. How did Pepe know that Juan Aria would come to him the morning after a goat had bleated in the night?
6. Why did the villagers think a man with a rifle must be a hero?
7. What happened when Pepe first tried to shoot the tiger?

Apply

8. How do you think you would feel about going into the jungle at night?
9. In the story it says, "It ill befitted a man with a rifle to seek out anyone at all." What does that sentence mean?
10. What should Pepe have told the villagers about how he killed the tiger?

Respond to Literature

What do you think the tiger really meant to Pepe?

WRITE ABOUT THE SELECTION

In "The Tiger's Heart," the jungle at night is described as a terrifying place. Many people find nighttime frightening no matter where they are. For some, darkness is something they must get through until morning comes. For others, the night is a quiet, comfortable time. Try to describe how you feel about the night.

Write a paragraph describing what nighttime is like for you. Use vivid language to give as clear a picture as possible of the sights and sounds of night.

Prewriting: Use sensory details that show how the night looks and sounds. Brainstorm by writing down as many details as you can think of. Then choose which details you want to use in your paragraph.

Writing: Begin your paragraph by writing a topic sentence. Then use details to support your overall idea of what the night is like. Use vivid language.

Revising: Look back to see if you have used vivid and colorful sensory details to describe the night. Will your reader have a clear picture of what the night is like for you? Check your paragraph to be sure there are no errors in spelling, grammar, or punctuation.

Proofreading: Read over your paragraph to check for errors. Check your internal punctuation and be sure that all your sentences end with periods, question marks, or exclamation marks.

THINK ABOUT IRONY

Irony is the difference between what seems to be and what is. Sometimes the reader knows something that the characters don't know. Sometimes one character knows more than another character.

1. Why does Juan Aria think Pepe is the only man in the village who can kill the tiger?
2. Why do the people of the village think a rifle is so important?
3. How important is the rifle to Pepe when he actually kills the tiger?
4. What do Pepe and the reader know that Juan Aria and the other people in the village will never find out?
5. What is the irony in the story "The Tiger's Heart"?

DEVELOP YOUR VOCABULARY

Synonyms are words that have similar meanings. For example, some synonyms for the word *cold* are: *freezing, chilly, frigid, frosty, cool, icy, wintry.* Although they have similar definitions, synonyms may differ considerably in the feelings they express. A *frigid wind* seems much colder than a *chilly wind.* By choosing carefully among synonyms, a writer can determine the feeling, or tone, of a story.

In "The Tiger's Heart," the author uses many descriptive words that express very strong feelings. Reread parts of the story. Try to imagine the story with a different, less dramatic tone. Using a thesaurus, rewrite the following phrases from the story, using less dramatic synonyms for the words in italics.

1. *horrible* things
2. *steaming* heat
3. *fantastic* creatures
4. *worshipful* children
5. *incredible* swiftness
6. *lethal* quality
7. *puny* man
8. *pitiless* engine

LEARN ABOUT

Connotation

The **denotation** of a word is its dictionary definition. However, a word's connotation goes beyond its dictionary meaning. **Connotations** are the images or pictures that words make you think of.

The words *thin* and *skinny* have similar meanings. They both mean the opposite of fat. When someone is described as thin, a pleasant picture comes to mind. When someone is described as skinny, the picture is not so pleasant. *Thin* and *skinny* have similar denotations, but different connotations.

When you write poetry, you must think about both the denotations and connotations of the words you use. You must think not only about what you want to say, but also what your words will make your readers think of.

As you read the following poems, ask yourself:

1. What do the words the poets use suggest to me?
2. What other words might have different connotations?

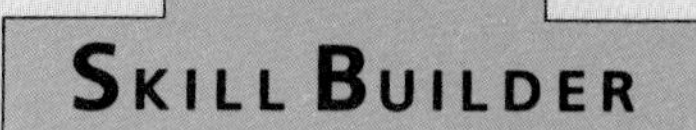

SKILL BUILDER

Think of two words that have the same denotation but different connotations. Write the words' dictionary definitions and their different connotations.

Who Has Seen the Wind?

by Christina Rossetti

Who has seen the wind?
    Neither I nor you:
But when the leaves hang trembling
    The wind is passing through.

Who has seen the wind?
    Neither you nor I:
But when the trees bow down their heads
    The wind is passing by.

---

trembling (TREM bling) shaking; shivering

Christina Rossetti (1830-1894)

You might see a painting of Christina Rossetti without realizing it. That is because her brother, Dante Gabriel Rossetti, and several other artists often used her as a model. Christina came from a very talented family. Her father was an Italian poet who escaped to England because of political differences with the Italian government. One brother, Dante, was a poet and painter and another brother, William Michael, wrote nonfiction.

Christina never went to school, but her mother taught her at home. She grew up speaking both Italian and English. A deeply religious person, many of her writings are about religious topics. She refused to marry the man she loved because they did not agree about religion.

Many people consider Christina Rossetti one of the greatest women poets of the English language.

The STORM

by William Carlos Williams

A perfect rainbow! a wide
arc low in the northern sky
spans the black lake

troubled by little waves
5 over which the sun
south of the city shines in

coldly from the bare hill
supine to the wind which
cannot waken anything

10 but drives the smoke from
a few lean chimneys streaming
violently southward

The Hollow of a Deep-Sea-Wave, Hokusai. The Granger Collection

---

spans (SPANZ) reaches from one side to the other
supine (SOO pyn) lying on the back

Clouds

by Gregory Djanikian

It was a test on clouds, Science 1,
Seventh grade, Mrs. Snyder, who,
I remember, always wore dark colors.
My fingers trembled, I couldn't keep
5 A point on my pencil, and in the next row,
John Carlson was getting all the answers.
Cumulus, altostratus, cirrus.

What was I dreaming of? Clouds,
They reminded me of Iowa or Kansas,
10 Or my notion of them, expanses of wheat,
Big skies somewhere west of where I was,
Somewhere with rural addresses, dogs
Named "Blue" or "Jake," and railroad crossings,
And a boy's river lazing through farm and pasture.

15 *Cirrus fibratus, cirrus uncinus,*
Altocumulus, cumulus congestus

I was losing time, my answer sheet
Was white as a cloud, and there was
A scratching of pencils on paper.
20 What was I after? Summer. A hillside.
A cumulus sky driven by the breezes.
Kites, and kite string humming in the air.
Shouts, laughter, in the distance only.

Cumulus humilis, cumulus fractus

25 Time was up and we were let go
And I reeled out to the playground lightened.
There was the bluest sky and I saw
Fibrous wisps converging into grey.

---

cumulus (KYOOM yuh lus) a thick type of cloud
expanses (ik SPANS iz) large open areas or unbroken surfaces

"Cirrus spissatus," John Carlson announced
30 From behind me, maybe to himself,
And skipped away at ease with the world.

All the way home, I spat out those names
I'd learned one by one, cirrostratus nebulosus,
Altocumulus undulatus, cirrocumulus, cumulonimbus,
35 Until I was left with just "cloud,"
Something vague and inexact, but prevailing,
Like some notion of happiness,
Or longings without name.

---

fibrous (FY brus) composed of slender, threadlike structures
wisps (WISPS) thin, filmy strands
converging (kun VERJ ing) coming together

FOCUS ON THE SELECTION

UNDERSTAND THE SELECTION

Recall

1. In "Who Has Seen the Wind?" how does the poet know that the wind is passing through?
2. What color is the lake in "The Storm"?
3. In "Clouds," who was the poet's seventh grade science teacher?

Infer

4. What does the poet Christina Rossetti mean when she says ". . . the trees bow down their heads"?
5. In "The Storm," what does "a wide arc low in the northern sky" describe?
6. In "Clouds," what are "cumulus, altostratus, and cirrus"?
7. How do you think the poet Gregory Djanikian felt about John Carlson?

Apply

8. Do you think anybody has ever actually seen the wind? Explain your answer.
9. How does the poem "The Storm" make you feel?
10. Why does Gregory Djanikian keep repeating the names of all the clouds?

Respond to Literature

Why do you think poets are interested in the weather?

WRITE ABOUT THE SELECTION

You have just read three poems. Choose one that you would like to write about. Then write a short paragraph in which you explain the meaning of the poem.

Poetry is a special kind of writing. It aims at expressing feelings or describing something that the poet has seen in a special way. Examine the poem you have chosen and explain what the poem makes you think of and how it makes you feel.

Prewriting: Read the poem aloud several times. Then write down your first thoughts about its meaning, how it makes you feel, and what images it evokes. Finally, write what you think is the main idea of the poem.

Writing: Begin your paragraph by writing a topic sentence. The topic sentence should state the main idea of the poem. Then write details that explain more fully what the poem means. Where you think it will help you to express your ideas, you may use quotes from the poem in your paragraph.

Revising: Look back to see if you have stated the meaning of the poem clearly. If you used quotations from the poem, be sure you copied them correctly and that you used quotation marks properly.

Proofreading: Read over your paragraph to check for errors. Check your internal punctuation and be sure that all your sentences end with periods, question marks, or exclamation marks.

THINK ABOUT CONNOTATION

You can easily find a word's denotation by looking it up in a dictionary. However, there is no place you can look up a word's connotation. You learn words' connotations by writing, reading, speaking, and listening. Just using the English language in these ways will help you learn to use the right word or words at the right time.

1. In "Who Has Seen the Wind?" what does the word "trembling" make you think of?
2. In "The Storm," why do you think the poet says the lake is black?
3. What does the "bare hill" suggest to you?
4. In "The Clouds," the poet says his teacher always wore dark colors. What does that make you think about the teacher?
5. The poet says he ". . . reeled out to the playground." What is the connotation of the word "reeled"?

DEVELOP YOUR VOCABULARY

Some words can be used either as nouns or verbs. A **noun** is a word that names a person, place, thing, or idea. A **verb** is a word that expresses an action or expresses a state of being.

Sometimes the meaning of a word is different if it is used as a noun or as a verb.

noun: A *duck* has webbed feet.
verb: *Duck* before the ball hits you.

Read the following sentences. Decide whether each *italicized* word is used as a noun or a verb. Then write the meaning of each *italicized* word. Notice the differences.

1. The *leaves* hang trembling from the branches of the tree.
2. The boy *leaves* for school every day at 8:00.
3. Anna *heads* for the soccer field to practice for the game.
4. The subjects bowed their *heads* before the king.
5. The baby *waves* goodbye to everybody.
6. The *waves* in the ocean are rough today.
7. It was the bluest sky I ever *saw.*
8. We used a *saw* to cut the wood.

FOCUS ON...

A drama is a story performed by actors. The story unfolds through **dialogue;** a conversation between the actors. Drama is more like real life than any other form of literature, because the scenes take place before your very eyes.

A drama can be a stage play, a movie, or a television play like *The Big Wave,* the selection you are going to read next. Drama has four necessary elements: characters, plot, setting, and theme.

Characters. The characters are the players in a drama. They are usually people but can also be animals or other non-human beings.

In a drama, everything you learn about the characters usually comes from what they say, what they do, and what others say about them. Sometimes there is a narrator as there is in *The Big Wave,* where the narrator's role is small but important.

The playwright uses stage directions to tell how he or she wants the characters to look and act and move. For example, the stage directions can tell about a character's age, size, clothing, or personality type. In the opening scene of *The Big Wave,* Kino is described as "a sturdy boy of about 13."

Plot. The plot of a drama is the series of events that make up the story. Each scene shows one or more events in the plot.

The plot grows out of a conflict between the characters in the drama. The **conflict** is the problem in the story. Often the main character has a problem with another character. However, conflict can also be inside a person. It can be between people and things, and it can be between people and nature. In *The Big Wave,* the conflict is inside a person and between people and nature.

The action of a drama develops as the characters try to solve their problems. The conflict must appear early in a drama in order to get the attention of the audience. The action continues until the drama reaches its climax. The **climax** is the high point in the story when the tension is the strongest. The climax points toward the final outcome of the drama.

The final outcome is called the **resolution.** It is the conclusion of the story. All loose ends must be settled as the drama comes to a believable and satisfying end.

Setting. The setting of a drama is where and when the action takes place. Each scene may have its own setting, or there may be one setting for the whole drama. The setting is described in the stage directions. Stage directions tell about scenery, costumes, and props.

The setting is a very important part of a drama. It helps to make the story believable. The scenery and costumes must be true to the time period and the setting of the drama. Props can also help to make the action more realistic. For example, *The Big Wave* is set in Japan a long time ago. All scenery, costumes, and props are true to this setting.

Theme. The theme of a drama goes beyond what happens to the characters. The theme is the main idea of the work; it is the message the writer wants to give to the audience. Sometimes a theme is clearly stated. At other times you must figure it out for yourself.

In *The Big Wave,* the playwright tells a story about a disaster. However, the play is really about much more than that one event. It is about people's relationships to nature. It is about growing up. It is about the importance of life.

As you read *The Big Wave,* ask yourself these questions:

1. Who are the characters in the drama? How do you learn about them?
2. What is the conflict in the plot? What is the climax? What is the resolution?
3. What is the setting? How important is the setting?
4. What is the theme? What is the playwright trying to say?

Mt. Fuji in the Background, Hiroshige. Three Lions.

The Big Wave

by Pearl Buck

STUDY HINTS
The title tells you something about one of the play's themes.

CHARACTERS

The characters are listed in the order of their appearance.

NARRATOR
KINO UCHIYAMA *(KEE noh oo chee YAH mah), A FARMER'S SON*
MOTHER
FATHER, *THE FARMER*
SETSU *(SET soo), KINO'S YOUNGER SISTER*
JIYA *(JEE yah), A FISHERMAN'S SON*
JIYA'S FATHER, *THE FISHERMAN*
OLD GENTLEMAN, *A WEALTHY LANDOWNER*
TWO SERVANTS
GARDENER
FIRST MAN
SECOND MAN
WOMAN
CHILD

ACT ONE

Open on: A scene in Japan, sea and mountainside, and in the distance Fuji.

The setting is described briefly here. It is crucial to the plot.

Dissolve to: A small farmhouse, built on top of terraces.

This, as the NARRATOR *speaks, dissolves to: The inside of the house, a room with the simplest of Japanese furniture.*

NARRATOR: Kino lives on a farm. The farm lies on the side of a mountain in Japan. The fields are terraced by walls of stone,

---

Fuji (FOO jee) a volcano that has been dormant for over 300 years. It is the highest mountain in Japan.

each one of them like a broad step up the mountain. Centuries ago, Kino's ancestors built the stone walls that hold up the fields. Above the fields stands this farmhouse, which is Kino's home.

(Dissolve to: KINO *comes into the room. He is a sturdy boy of about 13, dressed in shorts and a Japanese jacket.)*

KINO: Mother!

*(*MOTHER *hurries in. She is a small, serious-looking woman dressed in a kimono. She is carrying a jar of water.)*

MOTHER: Dinner is ready. Where's your father?
KINO: Coming. I ran up the terraces. I'm starving.
MOTHER: Call Setsu. She is playing outside.
KINO *(turning his head):* Setsu!
FATHER: Here she is. *(He comes in, holding by the hand a small playful girl.)* Getting so big! I can't lift her any more. *(But he does lift her so high that she touches the low rafters.)*
SETSU: Don't put me down. I want to eat my supper up here.
FATHER: And fall into the soup?
KINO: How that would taste!
SETSU *(willfully):* It would taste nice.
MOTHER: Come, come . . .

(They sit on the floor around the table. MOTHER *serves from a bucket of rice, a bowl of soup, a bowl of fish. She serves* FATHER *first, then* KINO, *then* SETSU, *and herself.)*

FATHER: Kino, don't eat so fast.
KINO: I have promised Jiya to swim in the sea with him.
MOTHER: Obey your father.
FATHER *(smiling):* Let him eat fast. *(He puts a bit of fish in* SETSU's *bowl.)* There—that's a good bit.
KINO: Father, why is it that Jiya's father's house has no window to the sea?
FATHER: No fisherman wants windows to the sea.
MOTHER: The sea is their enemy.

One of two important themes is introduced here. Although man depends on nature for survival, nature is beyond his control.

---

kimono (kuh MOH nuh) a robe with wide sleeves and a sash, worn by Japanese men and women.

KINO: Mother, how can you say so? Jiya's father catches fish from the sea and that is how their family lives.

FATHER: Do not argue with your mother. Ask Jiya your question. See what he says.

KINO: Then may I go?

FATHER: Go.

(Dissolve to: A sandy strip of seashore at the foot of the mountain. A few cottages stand there.

Dissolve to: A tall slender boy, JIYA. *He stands at the edge of the sea, looking up the mountain.)*

This is a change in setting. In a TV drama, "dissolve to" means the image on the screen fades and is replaced. In this case, the setting changes.

JIYA *(calling through his hands):* Kino!

KINO: Coming!

(He is running and catches JIYA'S *outstretched hand, so that they nearly fall down. They laugh and throw off their jackets.)*

KINO: Wait—I am out of breath. I ate too much.

JIYA *(looking up the mountain):* There's Old Gentleman standing at the gate of his castle.

KINO: He is watching to see whether we are going into the sea.

JIYA: He's always looking at the sea—at dawn, at sunset.

(Dissolve to: OLD GENTLEMAN, *standing on a rock, in front of his castle, halfway up the mountain. The wind is blowing his beard. Withdraw the cameras to the beach.)*

Stage directions give information about another character.

JIYA: He is afraid of the sea—always watching!

KINO: Have you ever been in his castle?

JIYA: Only once. Such beautiful gardens—like a dream in a fairy tale. The old pines are bent with the wind, and under them the moss is deep and green and so smooth. Every day men sweep the moss with brooms.

KINO: Why does he keep looking at the sea?

JIYA: He is afraid of it, I tell you.

KINO: Why?

JIYA: The sea is our enemy. We all know it.

KINO: Oh, how can you say it? When we have so much fun—

JIYA: It is our enemy. . . .

KINO: Not mine—let's swim to the island!

JIYA: No. I must find clams for my mother.

KINO: Then let's swim to the sand bar. There are millions of clams there!

JIYA: But the tide is ready to turn. . . .

KINO: It's slow—we'll have time.

(They plunge into the sea and swim to the sand bar. JIYA *has a small, short-handled hoe hanging from his waist. He digs into the sand.* KINO *kneels to help him. But* JIYA *digs only for a moment; then he pauses to look over the sea.)*

Kino's character begins to be revealed to the reader through his dialogue with Jiya. Also, we have the first hint of Jiya's coming conflict.

KINO: What are you looking for?

JIYA: To see if the sea is angry with us.

KINO *(laughing):* Silly—the sea can't be angry with people!

JIYA: Down there, a mile down, the old sea god lives. When he is angry he heaves and rolls, and the waves rush back and forth. Then he gets up and stamps his feet, and earth shakes at the bottom of the sea. . . . I wish I were a farmer's son.

KINO: And I wish I were a fisherman's son. It is stupid to plow and plant and harvest when I could just sit in a boat and reap fish from the sea!

JIYA: The earth is safe.

KINO: When the volcano is angry the earth shakes, too.

JIYA: The angry earth helps the angry sea.

KINO: They work together.

JIYA: But fire comes out of the volcano.

(Meanwhile, the tide is coming in and swirls about their feet.)

JIYA *(noticing):* Oh—we have not half-enough clams. . . .

(They fall to digging frantically.

Dissolve to: The empty seashore and the tide rushing in. A man paces at the water's edge. He wears shorts and a fisherman's jacket, open over his bare breast. It is JIYA'S FATHER. *He calls, his hands cupped at his mouth.)*

JIYA'S FATHER: Ji—ya!

(There is only the sound of the surf. He wades into the water, still calling. Suddenly he sees the boys, their heads out of water,

---

reap (REEP) gather in (as a farmer gathers wheat)

swimming, and he beckons fiercely. They come in, and he pulls them out of the surf.)

JIYA'S FATHER: Jiya! You have never been so late before!

JIYA: Father, we were on the sand bar, digging clams. We had to leave them.

JIYA'S FATHER *(shaking his shoulder):* Never be so late!

KINO *(wondering):* You are afraid of the sea, too.

JIYA'S FATHER: Go home, farmer's son! Your mother is calling you.

(In the distance a woman's voice is calling KINO*'s name. He hears and runs toward the mountain.)*

JIYA: Father, I have made you angry.

JIYA'S FATHER: I am not angry.

JIYA: Then why do you seem angry?

JIYA'S FATHER: Old Gentleman sent down word that a storm is rising behind the horizon. He sees the cloud through his telescope.

JIYA: Father, why do you let Old Gentleman make you afraid? Just because he is rich and lives in a castle, everybody listens to him.

JIYA'S FATHER: Not because he is rich—not because he lives in the castle, but because he is old and wise and he knows the sea. He doesn't want anybody to die. *(He looks over the sea, and he mutters as though to himself.)* Though all must die . . .

JIYA: Why must all die, Father?

JIYA'S FATHER: Who knows? Simply, it is so.

The play's second and more important theme is introduced: the mystery of death.

(They stand, looking over the sea.)

ACT TWO

Open on: The Japanese scene of sea and mountainside, with Fuji in the distance, as in Act One.

NARRATOR: Yet there was much in life to enjoy. Kino had a good time every day. In the winter he went to school in the fishing village, and he and Jiya shared a bench and a writing table. But in summer Kino had to work hard on the farm. On those days he could not run down the mountainside to find Jiya.

View of Mt. Fuji, Hokusai. Three Lions

There were days when Jiya, too, could not play. He and his father sailed their boats out to sea to cast their nets at dawn. If they were lucky, their nets came up so heavy with fish that it took all their strength to haul them in.

Sometimes, if it were not seedtime or harvest, Kino went with Jiya and his father. It was exciting to get up in the night and put on his warm jacket. Down the stone steps of the mountain path, Kino ran straight to the narrow dock where the fishing boats bobbed up and down with the tide. Jiya and his father were already there, and in a few minutes their boat was nosing its way past the sand bar toward the open sea. Kino crouched down in the bow, and his heart rose with joy and excitement. It was like flying into the sky. The winds were so mild, the sea lay so calm and blue, that it was hard to believe it could be cruel and angry. Actually it was the earth that brought the big wave.

One day, as Kino helped his father plant turnips, a cloud came over the sun.

(Dissolve to: A field, and KINO *and his* FATHER. *The volcano is in the background.)*

KINO: Look, Father, the volcano is burning again!

FATHER *(straightens and gazes anxiously at the sky):* It looks very angry. I shall not sleep tonight. We must hurry home.

KINO: Why should the volcano be angry, Father?

FATHER: Who knows? Simply, the inner fire burns. Come—make haste.

(They gather their tools.)

Dissolve to: Night, outside the farmhouse. KINO'S FATHER *sits on a bench outside the door. He gazes at the red sky above the volcano. The* MOTHER *comes to the door.)*

MOTHER: Can you put out the volcano fire by not sleeping?

FATHER: Look at the fishing village! Every house is lit. And the lamps are lit in the castle. Shall I sleep like a fool?

MOTHER *(silent, troubled, watching him):* I have taken the dishes from the shelves and put away our good clothes in boxes.

FATHER *(gazing at the village):* If only I knew whether it would be earth or sea! Both work evil. The fires rage under the sea, the rocks boil. The volcano is the vent unless the sea bottom breaks.

The theme of man and his weakness is the face of nature is developed.

KINO *(coming to the door):* Shall we have an earthquake, Father?

FATHER: I cannot tell.

MOTHER: How still it is! There's no wind. The sea is purple.

KINO: Why is the sea such a color?

FATHER: Sea mirrors sky. Sea and earth and sky—if they work against man, who can live?

KINO *(coming to his* FATHER'S *side):* Do the gods forget us?

FATHER: There are times when the gods leave men alone. They test us to see how able we are to save ourselves.

KINO: What if we are not able?

FATHER: We must be able. Fear makes us weak. If you are afraid, your hands tremble, your feet falter. Brain cannot tell hands what to do.

SETSU *(her voice calling from inside the house):* Mother, I'm afraid!

MOTHER: I am coming! *(She goes away.)*

FATHER: The sky is growing black. Go into the house, Kino.

KINO: Let me stay with you.

FATHER: The red flag is flying over the castle. Twice I've seen that red flag go up, both times before you were born. Old Gentleman wants everybody to be ready.

KINO *(frightened):* Ready for what?

FATHER: For whatever must be.

(A deep-toned bell tolls over the mountainside.)

KINO: What is that bell? I've never heard it before.

FATHER: It rang twice before you were born. It is the bell inside Old Gentleman's temple. He is calling to the people to come up out of the village and find shelter within his walls.

KINO: Will they come?

FATHER: Not all of them. Parents will try to make their children go, but the children will not want to leave their parents. Mothers will not want to leave fathers, and the fathers will stay by the boats. But some will want to be sure of life.

(The bell continues to ring. Soon from the village comes a straggling line of people, nearly all of them children.)

KINO *(gazing at them):* I wish Jiya would come. *(He takes off his white cloth girdle and waves it.)*

(Dissolve to: JIYA *and his* FATHER *by their house. Sea in the background, roaring.)*

JIYA'S FATHER: Jiya, you must go to the castle.

JIYA: I won't leave you . . . and Mother.

JIYA'S FATHER: We must divide ourselves. If we die, you must live after us.

JIYA: I don't want to live alone.

JIYA'S FATHER: It's your duty to obey me, as a good Japanese son.

JIYA: Let me go to Kino's House.

JIYA'S FATHER: Only go . . . go quickly.

*(*JIYA *and his* FATHER *embrace fiercely, and* JIYA *runs away, crying, to leap up the mountainside.*

Dissolve to: Terrace and farmhouse, and center on KINO *and his* FATHER, *who put out their hands to help* JIYA *up the last terrace. Suddenly* KINO *screams.)*

This is the climax of the play. The aftermath and resolution will be longer than usual.

KINO: Look . . . look at the sea!

FATHER: May the gods save us.

(The bell begins to toll, deep, pleading, incessant.)

JIYA *(shrieking):* I must go back . . . I must tell my father.

FATHER *(holding him):* It is too late . . .

(Dissolve to: The sea rushes up in a terrible wave and swallows the shore. The water roars about the foot of the mountain. JIYA, *held by* KINO *and his* FATHER, *stares and then sinks unconscious to the ground. The bell tolls on.)*

---

incessant (in SES unt) without interruption

ACT THREE

NARRATOR: So the big wave came, swelling out of the sea. It lifted the horizon while the people watched. The air was filled with its roar and shout. It rushed over the flat, still waters of the sea; it reached the village and covered it fathoms deep in swirling, wild water—green, laced with fierce white foam. The wave ran up the mountainside until the knoll upon which the castle stood was an island. All who were still climbing the path were swept away in the wicked waters. Then with a great sigh, the wave ebbed into the sea, dragging everything with it—trees, rocks, houses, people.

Upon the beach, where the village had stood, not a house remained. All that had been was now no more.

(Dissolve to: Inside the farmhouse. The farm family is gathered about the mattress on which JIYA *lies.* KINO *cannot stop crying, though silently.)*

SETSU *(coming to stare at* JIYA*):* Is Jiya dead?

FATHER: No, Jiya is living.

SETSU: Why doesn't he open his eyes?

FATHER: Soon he will open his eyes.

KINO: What will we say to Jiya when he wakes? How can we tell him?

FATHER: We will not talk. We will give him warm food and let him rest. We will help him to feel he still has a home.

KINO: Here?

FATHER: Here. As soon as he knows this is his home, we must help him to understand what has happened. Ah, here is Mother, with your hot rice soup. Eat it, my son—food for the body is food, too, for the heart, sometimes.

*(*KINO *takes the bowl from his* MOTHER *with both hands and drinks.* SETSU *leans her head against her* MOTHER.

Dissolve to: Evening. The same room, the same scene except that MOTHER *and* SETSU *are not there.* FATHER *sits beside* JIYA'S *bed.* KINO *is at the open door.)*

KINO: The sky is golden, Father, and the sea is smooth. How cruel—

The theme of the mystery of death and the acceptance of it is developed.

FATHER: No, it is wonderful that after the storm the sea grows calm again, and the sky is clear. It was not the sea or the sky that made the evil storm.

KINO *(not turning his head):* Who made it?

FATHER: Ah, no one knows who makes evil storms. We only know that they come. When they come we must live through them as bravely as we can, and after they are gone we must feel again how wonderful is life. Every day of life is more valuable now than it was before the storm.

KINO: But Jiya's father and mother . . . and the other fisherfolk . . . so good and kind . . . all of them . . . lost. *(He cannot go on.)*

FATHER: We must think of Jiya—who lives. *(He stops.* JIYA *has begun to sob softly.)* Quick, Kino—call your mother and Setsu. He will open his eyes at any moment, and we must all be here—you his brother, I his father, and the mother, the sister. . . .

(KINO *runs out.* FATHER *kneels beside* JIYA, *who stirs, still sobbing.* KINO *comes back with* MOTHER *and* SETSU. *They kneel on the floor beside the bed.* JIYA'S *eyelids flutter. He opens his eyes and looks from one face to the other. He stares at the beams of the roof, the walls of the room, the bed, his own hands. All are quiet except* SETSU, *who cannot keep from laughing. She claps her hands.)*

SETSU: Oh, Jiya has come back. Jiya, did you have a good dream?

JIYA *(faintly):* My father, my mother . . .

Kino and his family further reveal their characters through their treatment of Jiya.

MOTHER *(taking his hand in both hers):* I will be your mother now, dear Jiya.

FATHER: I will be your father.

KINO: I am your brother now, Jiya. *(He falters.)*

SETSU *(joyfully):* Oh, Jiya, you will live with us.

(JIYA *gets up slowly. He walks to the door, goes out, and looks down the hillside.*

Dissolve to: The peaceful empty beach. Then back to the farm-house and JIYA, *standing outside and looking at the sea.* SETSU *comes to him.)*

SETSU: I will give you my pet duck. He'll make you laugh.

MOTHER *(leaving the room):* We ought all to eat something, I have a fine chicken for dinner.

ACT FOUR

NARRATOR: The body heals first, and the body heals the mind and the soul. Jiya ate food, he got out of bed sometimes, but he did not want to think or remember. He only wanted to sleep.

All through these days Kino did not play about as once he had. He was no longer a child. He worked hard beside his father in the fields. They did not talk much, and neither of them wanted to look at the sea. It was enough to look at the earth, dark and rich beneath their feet.

One evening Kino climbed the mountain behind the house and looked up at the volcano. The heavy cloud of smoke had gone away, and the sky was clear. He was glad that the volcano was no longer angry, and he went down again to the house. On the threshold his father was smoking his usual evening pipe. In the house his mother was giving Setsu her evening bath.

KINO: Is Jiya asleep again?

FATHER: Yes, and it is a good thing for him. When he sleeps enough, he will wake and remember.

KINO: But should he remember?

FATHER: Only when he dares to remember his parents will he be happy again.

(A silence.)

KINO: Father, are we not very unfortunate people to live in Japan?

FATHER: Why do you think so?

KINO: The volcano is behind our house, and the sea is in front. When they work together to make earthquake and big wave, we are helpless. Always, many of us are lost.

FATHER: To live in the presence of death makes us brave and strong. That is why our people never fear death. We see it too often, and we do not fear it. To die a little sooner or a little later does not matter. But to live bravely, to love life, to see how beautiful the trees are and the mountains—yes, and even the sea—to enjoy work because it produces food—in these we are fortunate people. We love life because we live in danger. We do not fear death, for we understand that death and life are necessary to each other.

Kino's father helps him to understand the mystery of death.

KINO: What is death?

FATHER: Death is the great gateway.

KINO: The gateway . . . where?

FATHER: Can you remember when you were born?

KINO: I was too small.

FATHER *(smiling):* I remember very well. Oh, how hard you thought it was to be born. You cried and you screamed.

KINO *(much interested):* Didn't I want to be born?

FATHER: You did not. You wanted to stay just where you were, in the warm dark house of the unborn. But the time came to be born, and the gate of life opened.

KINO: Did I know it was the gate of life?

FATHER: You did not know anything about it, and so you were afraid. But see how foolish you were! Here we were waiting for you, your parents, already loving you and eager to welcome you. And you have been very happy, haven't you?

KINO: Until the big wave came. Now I am afraid again because of the death the big wave brought.

FATHER: You are only afraid because you don't know anything about death. But someday you will wonder why you were afraid, even as today you wonder why you once feared to be born.

KINO: I think I understand. . . . I begin to understand. . . .

FATHER: Do not hurry yourself. You have plenty of time. *(He rises to his feet.)* Now what do I see? A lantern coming up the hill.

KINO *(running to the edge of the threshold):* Who can be coming now? It is almost night.

FATHER: A visitor . . . ah, why, it's Old Gentleman!

*(*OLD GENTLEMAN *is climbing the hill. He is somewhat breathless in spite of his long staff. His* SERVANT *carries the lantern and, when they arrive, steps to one side.)*

OLD GENTLEMAN *(to* SERVANT*):* Is this the house of Uchiyama, the farmer?

SERVANT: It is—and this is the farmer himself and his son.

FATHER *(bowing):* Please, Honored Sir, what can I do for you?

OLD GENTLEMAN: Do you have a lad here by the name of Jiya?

---

threshold (THRESH ohld) entrance to a house or building

FATHER: He lies sleeping in my house.

OLD GENTLEMAN: I wish to see him.

FATHER: Sir, he suffered the loss of his parents when the big wave came. Now sleep heals him.

OLD GENTLEMAN: I will not wake him. I only wish to look at him.

FATHER: Please come in.

(Dissolve to: JIYA *asleep. The* SERVANT *holds the lantern so that the light does not fall on* JIYA'S *face directly.* OLD GENTLEMAN *looks at him carefully.)*

OLD GENTLEMAN: Tall and strong for his age—intelligent—handsome. Hmm . . . yes. *(He motions to the* SERVANT *to lead him away, and the scene returns to the dooryard. To* FATHER*)* It is my habit, when the big wave comes, to care for those who are orphaned by it. Thrice in my lifetime I have searched out the orphans, and I have fed them and sheltered them. But I have heard of this boy Jiya and wish to do more for him. If he is as good as he is handsome, I will take him for my own son.

Now Jiya's conflict becomes clear.

KINO: But Jiya is ours!

FATHER *(sternly):* Hush. We are only poor people. If Old Gentleman wants Jiya, we cannot say we will not give him up.

OLD GENTLEMAN: Exactly. I will give him fine clothes and send him to a school, and he may become a great man and an honor to our whole province and even to the nation.

KINO: But if he lives in the castle we can't be brothers!

FATHER: We must think of Jiya's good. *(He turns to* OLD GENTLEMAN.) Sir, it is very kind of you to propose this for Jiya. I had planned to take him for my own son, now that he has lost his birth parents; but I am only a poor farmer, and I cannot pretend that my house is as good as yours or that I can afford to send Jiya to a fine school. Tomorrow when he wakes I will tell him of your kind offer. He will decide.

OLD GENTLEMAN: Very well. But let him come and tell me himself.

FATHER *(proudly):* Certainly. Jiya must speak for himself.

*(*OLD GENTLEMAN *bows and prepares to depart.* FATHER *bows and taps* KINO *on the head to make him bow.* OLD GENTLEMAN *and his* SERVANT *return down the mountain.)*

KINO: If Jiya goes away, I shall never have a brother.

Landscape, Sasahide. Musee Guimet, Paris. Giraudon/Art Resource.

FATHER: Kino, don't be selfish. You must allow Jiya to make his own choice. It would be wrong to persuade him. I forbid you to speak to him of this matter. When he wakes, I will tell him myself.

(Dissolve to: KINO *working in the terrace, weeding. It is evident that he has worked for some time. He looks hot and dusty, and he has quite a pile of weeds. He stops to look up at the farmhouse, but he sees no one and resigns himself again to his task. Suddenly his name is called.)*

FATHER: Kino!
KINO: Shall I come?
FATHER: No, I am coming—with Jiya.

*(*KINO *stands, waiting.* FATHER *and* JIYA *come down the terraces.* JIYA *is very sad. When he sees* KINO, *he tries not to cry.)*

FATHER *(putting his arm about* JIYA's *shoulder):* Jiya, you must not mind that you cry easily. Until now you couldn't cry because you weren't fully alive. You had been hurt too much. But today you are beginning to live, and so your tears flow. It is good for you. Let your tears come—don't stop them. *(He turns to* KINO.*)* I have told Jiya that he must not decide where he will live until he has seen the inside of the castle. He must see all that Old Gentleman can give him. Jiya, you know how our house is—four small rooms, and the kitchen, this farm, upon which we have to work hard for our food. We have only what our hands earn for us. *(He holds out his two workworn hands.)* If you live in the castle, you need never have hands like these.

JIYA: I don't want to live in the castle.

FATHER: You don't know whether you do or not; you have never seen the castle inside. *(He turns to* KINO.) Kino, you are to go with Jiya, and when you reach the castle you must persuade him to stay there for his own sake.

*(*KINO *and* JIYA *go, reluctantly, and* FATHER *watches them.*

Dissolve to: The mountainside and the two boys nearing the gate of the castle. The gate is open, and inside an old GARDENER *is sweeping moss under pine trees. He sees them.)*

GARDENER: What do you want, boys?

KINO: My father sent us to see the honored Old Gentleman.

GARDENER: Are you the Uchiyama boy?

KINO: Yes, please, and this is Jiya, whom Old Gentleman wishes to come and live here.

GARDENER *(bowing to* JIYA*):* Follow me, young sir.

(They follow over a pebbled path under the leaning pine trees. In the distance the sun falls upon a flowering garden and a pool with a waterfall.)

KINO *(sadly):* How beautiful it is—of course you will want to live here. Who could blame you?

*(*JIYA *does not answer. He walks with his head held high. They come to a great door, where a* SERVANT *bids them take off their shoes. The* GARDENER *leaves them.)*

SERVANT: Follow me.

(They follow through passageways into a great room decorated in the finest Japanese fashion. In the distance at the end of the room, they see OLD GENTLEMAN *sitting beside a small table. Behind him the open panels reveal the garden.* OLD GENTLEMAN *is writing. He is*

carefully painting letters on a scroll, his silver-rimmed glasses sliding down his nose. When the two boys approach, the SERVANT *announces them.)*

SERVANT: Master, the two boys are here.

OLD GENTLEMAN *(to boys):* Would you two like to know what I have been writing?

(JIYA *looks at* KINO, *who is too awed to speak.)*

JIYA: Yes, Honored Sir, if you please.

OLD GENTLEMAN *(taking up the scroll):* It is not my own poem. It is the saying of a wise man of India, but I like it so much that I have painted it on this scroll to hang there in the alcove where I can see it every day. *(He reads clearly and slowly.)*

> "The children of God are much revered,
> But rather weird—
> Very nice, but very narrow."

(He looks up over his spectacles.) What do you think of it?

JIYA *(looking at* KINO, *who is too shy to speak):* We do not understand it, sir.

OLD GENTLEMAN *(shaking his head and laughing softly):* Ah, we are all children of God! *(He takes off his spectacles and looks hard at* JIYA.) Well? Will you be my son?

(JIYA, *too embarrassed to speak, looks away.)*

Jiya resolves the conflict by making his decision.

OLD GENTLEMAN: Say yes or no. Either word is not hard to speak.

JIYA: I will say . . . no. *(He feels this is too harsh, and he smiles apologetically.)* I thank you, sir, but I have a home . . . on a farm.

KINO *(trying to repress his joy and speaking very solemnly as a consequence):* Jiya, remember how poor we are.

OLD GENTLEMAN *(smiling, half sad):* They are certainly very poor and here, you know, you would have everything. You can even invite this farm boy to come and play, sometimes, if you like. And I am quite willing for you to give the family some money. It would be suitable as my son for you to help the poor.

---

alcove (AL kohv) small room opening out of a larger room

JIYA *(suddenly, as though he had not heard):* Where are the others who were saved from the big wave?

OLD GENTLEMAN: Some wanted to go away, and the ones who wanted to stay are out in the backyard with my servants.

JIYA: Why do you not invite them to come into this castle and be your sons and daughters?

OLD GENTLEMAN *(somewhat outraged by this):* Because I don't want them for my sons and daughters. You are a bright, handsome boy. They told me you were the best boy in the village.

JIYA: I am not better than the others. My father was a fisherman.

OLD GENTLEMAN *(taking up his spectacles and his brush):* Very well—I will do without a son.

(The SERVANT *motions to the boys to come away, and they follow.)*

SERVANT *(to* JIYA*):* How foolish you are! Our Old Gentleman is very kind. You would have everything here.

JIYA: Not everything . . .

KINO: Let's hurry home—let's hurry—hurry . . .

(They run down the mountain and up the hill to the farmhouse. SETSU *sees them and comes flying to meet them, the sleeves of her bright kimono like wings, and her feet clattering in their wooden sandals.)*

SETSU: Jiya has come home—Jiya, Jiya . . .

*(*JIYA *sees her happy face and opens his arms and gives her a great hug.)*

ACT FIVE

NARRATOR: Now happiness began to live in Jiya, though secretly and hidden inside him, in ways he did not understand. The good food warmed him, and the love of the four people who received him glowed like a warm and welcoming fire upon his heart.

Time passed. Eight years. Jiya grew up in the farmhouse to be a tall young man, and Kino grew at his side, solid and strong. Setsu grew, too, from a mischievous, laughing child into a willful, pretty girl.

In all these years no one returned to live on the empty beach. The tides rose and fell, sweeping the sands clear every day. Storms came and went, but there was never such a wave as the big one. At last people began to think that never again would there be such a big wave. The few fishermen who had listened to the tolling bell from the castle, and were saved with their wives and children, went to other shores to fish. Then, as time passed, they told themselves that no beach was quite as good as the old one. There, they said, the water was deep and great fish came close to the shore.

Jiya and Kino had not often gone to the beach, either. When they went to swim in the sea, they walked across the farm and over another fold of the mountains to the shore. The big wave had changed Jiya forever. He did not laugh easily or speak carelessly. In school he had earnestly learned all he could, and now he worked hard on the farm. Now, as a man, he valued deeply everything that was good. Since the big wave had been so cruel, he was never cruel, and he grew kind and gentle. Sometimes, in the morning, he went to the door of the farmhouse and looked at the empty beach below, searching as though something might one day come back. One day he did see something. . . .

JIYA: Kino, come here! (KINO *comes out, his shoes in his hand.)* Look—is someone building a house on the beach?

KINO: Two men—pounding posts into the sand—

JIYA: And a woman . . . yes, and even a child.

KINO: They can't be building a house.

JIYA: Let's go and see.

(Dissolve to: The beach. The two Men, JIYA *and* KINO, WOMAN *and* CHILD.*)*

JIYA *(out of breath):* Are you building a house?

FIRST MAN *(wiping sweat from his face):* Our father used to live here, and we with him. We are two brothers. During these years we have lived in the houses of the castle, and we have fished from other shores. Now we are tired of having no homes of our own. Besides, this is still the best beach for fishing.

KINO: What if the big wave comes again?

SECOND MAN *(shrugging his shoulders):* There was a big wave, too, in our great-grandfather's time. All the houses were swept

Ferry Crossing, Hiroshige. Scala, N.Y./Art Resource.

away. But our grandfather came back. In our father's time there was again the big wave. Now we return.

KINO *(soberly):* What of your children?

FIRST MAN: The big wave may never come back.

(The MEN *begin to dig again. The* WOMAN *takes the* CHILD *into her arms and gazes out to sea. Suddenly there is a sound of a voice calling. All look up the mountain.)*

FIRST MAN: Here comes our Old Gentleman.

SECOND MAN: He's very angry or he wouldn't have left the castle.

(Both throw down their shovels and stand waiting. The WOMAN *sinks to a kneeling position on the sand, still holding the* CHILD. OLD GENTLEMAN *shouts as he comes near, his voice high and thin. He is very old now, and is supported by two* SERVANTS. *His beard flies in the wind.)*

OLD GENTLEMAN: You foolish children! You leave the safety of my walls and come back to this dangerous shore, as your father did before you! The big wave will return and sweep you into the sea.

Here Jiya reveals that he has learned to accept both the good and bad sides of nature as well as the certainty of death.

FIRST MAN: It may not, Ancient Sir.

OLD GENTLEMAN: It will come. I have spent my whole life trying to save foolish people from the big wave. But you will not be saved.

JIYA *(stepping forward):* Sir, here is our home. Dangerous as it is, threatened by the volcano and sea, it is here we were born.

OLD GENTLEMAN *(looking at him):* Don't I know you?

JIYA: Sir, I was once in your castle.

OLD GENTLEMAN *(nodding):* I remember you. I wanted you for my son. Ah, you made a great mistake, young man. You could have lived safely in my castle all your life, and your children would have been safe there. The big wave never reaches me.

KINO: Sir, your castle is not safe, either. If the earth shakes hard enough, even your castle will crumble. There is no refuge for us who live on these islands. We are brave because we must be.

SECOND MAN: Ha—you are right.

(The two MEN *return to their building.)*

OLD GENTLEMAN *(rolling his eyes and wagging his beard):* Don't ask me to save you the next time the big wave comes!

JIYA *(gently):* But you will save us, because you are so good.

OLD GENTLEMAN *(looking at him and then smiling sadly):* What a pity you would not be my son! *(He turns and, leaning on his* SERVANTS, *climbs the mountain.)*

(Dissolve to: The field, where FATHER *and* JIYA *and* KINO *are working.)*

FATHER *(to* JIYA*):* Did you soak the seeds for the rice?

JIYA *(aghast):* I forgot.

KINO: I did it.

JIYA *(throwing down his hoe):* I forget everything these days.

FATHER: I know you are too good a son to be forgetful on purpose. Tell me what is on your mind.

JIYA: I want a boat. I want to go back to fishing.

*(*FATHER *does not pause in his hoeing; but* KINO *flings down his hoe.)*

KINO: You, too, are foolish!

JIYA *(stubbornly):* When I have a boat, I shall build my house on the beach.

KINO: Oh, fool, fool!

FATHER: Be quiet! Jiya is a man. You are both men. I shall pay you wages from this day.

JIYA: Wages! *(He falls to hoeing vigorously.)*

(Dissolve to: The beach where KINO *and* JIYA *are inspecting a boat.)*

JIYA: I knew all the time that I had to come back to the sea.

KINO: With this boat, you'll soon earn enough to build a house. But I'm glad I live on the mountain.

(They continue inspecting the boat, fitting the oars, etc., as they talk.)

JIYA *(abruptly):* Do you think Setsu would be afraid to live on the beach?

KINO *(surprised):* Why would Setsu live on the beach?

JIYA *(embarrassed but determined):* Because when I have my house built, I want Setsu to be my wife.

KINO *(astonished):* Setsu? You would be foolish to marry her.

JIYA *(smiling):* I don't agree with you.

KINO *(seriously):* But why . . . why do you want her?

JIYA: Because she makes me laugh. It is she who made me forget the big wave. For me, she is life.

KINO: But she is not a good cook. Think how she burns the rice when she runs outside to look at something.

JIYA: I don't mind burned rice, and I will run out with her to see what she sees.

KINO *(with gestures of astonishment):* I can't understand. . . .

(Dissolve to: The farmhouse, and FATHER, *who is looking over his seeds.)*

KINO *(coming in stealthily):* Do you know that Jiya wants to marry Setsu?

FATHER: I have seen some looks pass between them.

KINO: But Jiya is too good for Setsu.

FATHER: Setsu is very pretty.

KINO: With that silly nose?

FATHER *(calmly):* I believe that Jiya admires her nose.

KINO: Besides, she is such a tease.

FATHER: What makes you miserable will make him happy.

KINO: I don't understand that, either.

FATHER *(laughing):* Someday you will understand.

(Dissolve to: NARRATOR.*)*

The resolution ties up all the strands of the plot. We know what will happen to the characters.

NARRATOR: One day, one early summer, Jiya and Setsu were married. Kino still did not understand, for up to the last, Setsu was naughty and mischievous. Indeed on the very day of her wedding she hid Kino's hairbrush under his bed. "You are too silly to be married," Kino said, when he had found it. "I feel sorry for Jiya," he said. Setsu's big brown eyes laughed at him. "I shall always be nice to Jiya," she said.

But when the wedding was over and the family had taken the newly married pair down the hill to the new house on the beach, Kino felt sad. The farmhouse was very quiet without Setsu. Every day he could go to see Jiya, and many times he would go fishing with him. But Setsu would not be in the farmhouse or in the garden. He would miss even her teasing. And then he grew very grave. What if the big wave came again?

(Dissolve to: The new house. KINO, JIYA, FATHER, MOTHER, *and* SETSU *are standing outside.* KINO *turns to* JIYA.*)*

KINO: Jiya, it is all very pretty—very nice. But, Setsu—what if the big wave comes again?

JIYA: I have prepared for that. Come—all of you. *(He calls the family in.)* This is where we will sleep at night, and where we will live by day. But look—

(The family watches as JIYA *pushes back a long panel in the wall. Before their eyes is the sea, swelling and stirring under the evening wind. The sun is sinking into the water.)*

JIYA: I have opened my house to the sea. If ever the big wave comes back, I shall be ready. I face it, night and day. I am not afraid.

KINO: Tomorrow I'll go fishing with you, Jiya—shall I?

JIYA *(laughing):* Not tomorrow, brother!

FATHER: Come—come! *(*SETSU *comes to his side and leans against him, and he puts his arm around her.)* Yes, life is stronger than death. *(He turns to his family.)* Come, let us go home.

The main theme is restated in a single sentence. The characters must believe that life is stronger than death in order to live courageous lives.

*(*FATHER *and* MOTHER *and* KINO *bow and leave.* JIYA *and* SETSU *stand looking out to sea.)*

JIYA: Life is stronger than death—do you hear that, Setsu?

SETSU: Yes, I hear.

Pearl Buck (1892–1973)

The daughter of American missionaries, Pearl Sydenstricker grew up in China where she developed a love for the people and their traditional ways of life. She returned to the United States during her college years. Once back in China she taught at Nanking University and married John Buck. She intended to live her life in China, but those were years of great political and social change, and it became impossible for her to stay on while the China she loved was torn apart by violence. So in 1932 she returned to the United States.

The Far East was the focus of her writing. Most of her stories are about the people and places of the Orient. During her lifetime, Pearl Buck wrote and had published 85 volumes of novels, stories, and essays.

Her first full-length book, *East Wind, West Wind* (1930), attempted to explain Chinese culture to the West. *The Good Earth* (1931), her most famous book, is about a peasant family and their struggle for survival. In 1932 the book earned her the Pulitzer Prize for "rich and genuine portrayals of Chinese life . . . " In 1938 she was awarded the Nobel Prize for Literature, which is given each year to one writer for an overall contribution to literature.

Concern for the people of the Orient made up a nonwriting career as well. Pearl Buck adopted and raised nine children of Asian parentage. During the 1940s, she founded The East and West Association, Welcome House, and The Pearl Buck Foundation. All these organizations were founded to insure the care of Asian children and to promote better East-West relations.

FOCUS ON THE SELECTION

UNDERSTAND THE SELECTION

Recall

1. How old is Kino when the play begins?
2. Where does Jiya live after the big wave?
3. Whom does Jiya marry at the play's end?

Infer

4. Why does Jiya say he wishes he were a farmer's son?
5. Why does Kino say he wishes he were a fisherman's son?
6. What happens to Jiya's parents?
7. Why does the Old Gentleman think people are foolish to build houses by the sea?

Apply

8. In Act 5, Kino says to the Old Gentleman, "There is no refuge for us who live on these islands. We are brave because we must be." Explain what Kino means.
9. Describe Kino and Jiya's relationship.
10. If you were Jiya, do you think you would choose to live by the sea?

Respond to Literature

The sea and the big wave are so important to this story that they are almost characters. How do the sea and the big wave affect people's lives in the play?

WRITE ABOUT THE SELECTION

You have just read the script of a television play called *The Big Wave.* Imagine that you are a television reviewer for your local newspaper. You have just watched *The Big Wave* on TV and must write a review for tomorrow's paper. The purpose of the review is to tell your readers about the play you have seen and to give them your opinion of it's strengths and weaknesses.

Prewriting: Make a chart showing the four elements of a drama. Write down information about each element. This will give you a good idea of what the play was about. Then jot down what you thought of the play. What did you like or dislike? How was it successful or unsuccessful? Give your opinion about the quality of each of the elements.

Writing: Use your chart and your thoughts about the play to write a two-paragraph review. The first paragraph should tell what the play was about. The second should give your opinion.

Revising: Remember that each paragraph should have one main idea. Check to see that each paragraph has a topic sentence. Be sure you have backed up your topic sentences with details that support your ideas. Then check for errors in spelling, grammar, and punctuation.

Proofreading: Read the review to check for errors in internal punctuation. Be sure that all your sentences end with periods, question marks, or exclamation marks.

THINK ABOUT DRAMA

All dramas have certain common elements. Each has characters, a plot, a setting, and a theme.

The **characters** are the people in the drama. The **plot** is the series of events that occur in the story. The plot involves a conflict that the characters face. The **setting** is where and when the story takes place. Finally, the **theme** of a drama is the message that the author wants to give to the audience.

1. Who are the main characters in *The Big Wave*?
2. What is the major conflict that the characters must face?
3. What is the setting of *The Big Wave*? Where does it take place? When does it take place?
4. What do you see as the playwright's theme or themes?

DEVELOP YOUR VOCABULARY

When you are reading, you sometimes come across a word with a meaning that you do not know. If you cannot figure out the meaning, you should look up the word in a dictionary.

The words in a dictionary are arranged in alphabetical order. Most dictionaries have guide words at the top of each page to help you. The **guide words** are the first and last words on the page. You can figure out that any word that falls alphabetically between the two guide words will be found on that page. For example, the word *even* will be found on a page with the guide words *evasion* and *every*. The word *evil* will not.

Look up each of the following words from *The Big Wave* in a dictionary. Write the guide words that appear on the page where you find each word.

1. kimono
2. reap
3. incessant
4. threshold
5. alcove

Learn About

Parables

A **parable** is a short story that teaches a lesson. The characters in a parable may be everyday characters, and the plot an ordinary series of events. It is the theme that is most important in a parable. The characters and plot are just used by the writer as a way of teaching a lesson.

A parable is very much like a fable. You have probably read some of Aesop's fables like "The Tortoise and the Hare" and "The Fox and the Crow." **Fable** is also a short story that teaches a lesson. However, fables usually have animal characters.

There is another difference between fables and parables. In a fable, the lesson, or moral, is clearly stated at the end of the story. In a parable, the reader must figure out the meaning of the story for him or herself.

As you read "The Black Box: A Science Parable," ask yourself:

1. What is the lesson the story teaches?
2. Is the lesson clearly stated, or must I figure it out for myself?

Skill Builder

Find a copy of the fable "The Tortoise and the Hare." Read it and look for the lesson that it teaches. Write the lesson, or moral, in your own words.

THE BLACK BOX: A SCIENCE PARABLE

by Albert B. Carr

Once upon a time some boys and girls were walking on the beach, just looking for what there was to find. But their findings had not been very good. Except for a few shells, their pockets were empty. They had just about decided to give up their looking and go swimming when they saw it lying there on the sand. It was black, all black—a black box.

The boys and girls approached the box carefully, for they had never seen a box quite like it before. They wondered what it could be, what it was doing there, where it might have come from, and what it might contain. They looked at it, all six sides of it. It wasn't shiny; it wasn't dull. It wasn't heavy; it wasn't light. It wasn't rough; it wasn't smooth. It wasn't big; it wasn't small. It really wasn't anything special—just a black box.

The girls and boys picked up the box and tried to open it, but they couldn't. No matter how hard they tried, they could not open the black box. They used their hands. They used their feet. They shook it. They banged it with rocks. They soaked it in the ocean water. They threw it down hard on the sand. They even used their teeth and tried to bite it open. But no matter what they did, they could not open the black box.

Then one of them said: "Maybe it's not a box at all, and that's why it can't be opened! Maybe it's just a black block!" But they knew it wasn't a block. They knew it was a box because they heard something moving inside when they shook it. And the harder they shook, the more they were able to hear. And the more they heard, the more they wondered about what was inside the box.

They wondered out loud: "Maybe it's something valuable, like gold or jewelry."

"Maybe it's something dangerous, like poison or a bomb."

"Maybe it's something from outer space that no one has ever seen before."

"Maybe it's like a seed pod filled with seeds."

"Maybe it's filled with things to eat, like bars of candy." "Maybe . . . ," "Maybe . . . ," "Maybe . . . ." And the more "maybes" there were, the more the boys and girls wondered what was inside the black box.

They decided to take the black box home where there were tools they could use to open it. On the way, they stopped at the fire station. Perhaps a fireman could open the box, but he couldn't. No matter how hard he tried with his axe and other pieces of equipment, he could not open the black box. So they continued on their way, leaving behind a confused fireman with a bent and broken axe.

As the girls and boys passed along Main Street, they stopped several times to see if anyone could open the black box. But no one could. The policeman, the grocer, the pharmacist, and the others—none of them could open the box.

The dentist had a very good idea. He thought that he could use his X-ray machine and take a picture of the inside of the box. But he couldn't. The X-rays passed easily through the box in every direction—but produced no picture of what was inside the black box!

Even a stop at the library, with all its books, gave no clue to what might be inside the box.

When the boys and girls arrived home, they tried hammers, chisels, saws, and even power tools. But no matter what they used, they could not open the black box. That night they all talked with their parents, for parents were usually very good at solving problems. But this time their parents could not help. And the mystery of what was inside the black box became even more perplexing.

Since the next day was Sunday, one of them took the black box to church. Perhaps the minister could help with their

---

perplexing (pur PLEKS ing) puzzling; bewildering

Michael Bryant

problem. He had been helpful at times in the past. But the minister said: "I'm sorry, this is not a problem for a minister. It seems to me that what you have here is a scientific problem. Why not take your black box to the university? Show it to the scientists and see if they can help you."

So the next day, after school, the girls and boys took their black box to the university to see the scientists.

They went to a laboratory where some young scientists were working on an experiment. The scientists were intrigued by the black-box problem. They tried every approach they could think of to discover what was inside the black box. But they were unsuccessful. The young scientists could not pry into or open the box even with their most powerful scientific equipment. They finally said: "We cannot open the box. We cannot tell you what is inside. But perhaps the professor, our teacher, can answer your question." And so the boys and girls took their black box and went to see the professor.

The professor was very old. He had a beard, and it was obvious that he was very wise indeed. In his office he was surrounded by many books—some he had even written himself. The professor had studied for a very long time. In fact he said that he was still studying. He had been almost everywhere that there was to go. He had done almost everything that there was to do. The boys and girls felt very confident in his presence. They felt sure that the professor would answer their question about what was inside the black box.

The professor took the box in his hands and listened carefully as the girls and boys told their story about the black box. Finally the professor said: "It seems to me that your black box is similar to other scientific problems. There appear to be no sure answers to the question you have raised. But this does not mean that there are no answers. It means that you will need to invent an answer—or perhaps several answers to your question." The professor paused and looked at the boys and girls. They looked at one another, wondering if they understood what the professor had said.

Then the professor continued: "You must observe as much as possible—from the outside of the box. And then, on the basis of

---

intrigued (in TREEGD) to be very curious about something

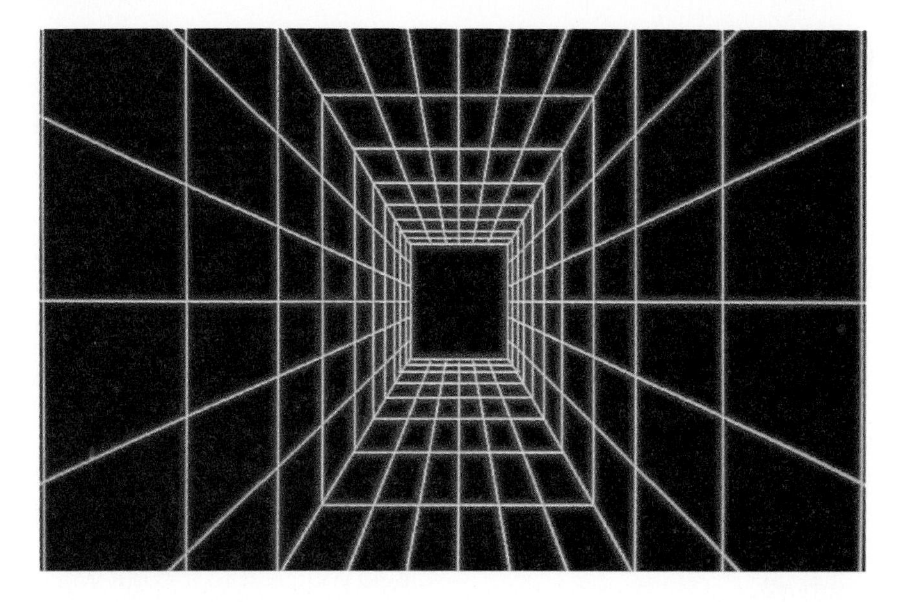

these observations, construct a model of what you think is inside. As you make more observations and gather more information, your model of what is inside may change. And this is good. It means your model is getting more and more like what really is inside the black box.

"This is the way it has always been in science and the way it will always be. We invent the best explanations we can on the basis of our best observations."

The girls and boys did not completely understand everything the professor said. They realized, however, that the absolute authority—someone with the right answer to their question—just did not exist in science.

And they managed to agree on the following model.

Inside the black box, there was a slightly smaller box
with a slightly smaller box inside of it
with a slightly smaller box inside of it
with a slightly smaller box inside of it
with a slightly smaller box inside of it
with a slightly smaller box inside of it
with a slightly smaller box inside of it
with a slightly smaller box inside of it
with a slightly smaller box inside of it
with a slightly smaller box inside of it

---

absolute (AB suh loot) complete; final; perfect

FOCUS ON THE SELECTION

UNDERSTAND THE SELECTION

Recall

1. Where did the children find the black box?
2. How did the children know the black box was a box and not a block?
3. What did X-rays show inside the box?

Infer

4. What was mysterious about the box?
5. Why did the children ask so many people to help them find out what was inside the box?
6. Why do you think the young scientists at the laboratory were interested in finding out what was inside the box?
7. Why was it clear to the children that the professor " . . . was very wise indeed"?

Apply

8. Could it have been dangerous to keep trying to open the box?
9. How do you think making a model helped solve the problem?
10. Does a scientific model always give an exact answer to a problem?

Respond to Literature

The children in the story learn about a new way to look at the world around them. What is this new way?

WRITE ABOUT THE SELECTION

You have just read "The Black Box: A Science Parable," a story about a group of children who find a mysterious black box lying on a beach.

Imagine that you found a mysterious sealed box that you could not open. What would you do to find out what was inside? Would you want to find out what was inside of it?

Write a short paragraph in which you tell what you would do if you found yourself in the same situation as the children in the story, "The Black Box: A Science Parable."

Prewriting: First think about whether you would want to find out what was inside the box. If you would not, write down three reasons why you would not. If you would, write down three things you would do to try to find out the answer.

Writing: Write a clear topic sentence for your paragraph. It should tell the reader what your paragraph will be about. Use the information you have already written down to support your topic sentence.

Revising: Look back to see that your supporting sentences all relate to your topic sentence. Then check spelling, grammar, and punctuation.

Proofreading: Read over your paragraph to check for errors. Check your internal punctuation and be sure that all your sentences end with periods, question marks, or exclamation marks.

THINK ABOUT PARABLES

Parables are stories that teach a lesson. Parables have been written throughout history. Ancient Greek and Roman writers used the parable as a form of short story. Perhaps the most famous parables are found in the Bible.

1. Is "The Black Box: A Science Parable" an ancient parable or a modern parable? How do you know?
2. What is the children's problem in the story?
3. How do the children go about solving their problem?
4. Do the children ever get an absolute answer to their problem? Why or why not?
5. What is the lesson that the parable teaches?

DEVELOP YOUR VOCABULARY

Antonyms are two words that have opposite meanings. Sometimes in your writing, you may want to contrast one word with another.

In "The Black Box: A Science Parable," the box is described in the following way: "It wasn't shiny; it wasn't dull. It wasn't heavy; it wasn't light. It wasn't rough; it wasn't smooth. It wasn't big; it wasn't small."

There are four pairs of antonyms used in the quote. The writer uses contrast to say that it was really just a very ordinary box. Of course, the rest of the story goes on to show that it was anything but ordinary.

The following words were all used in the story. Think of an antonym for each. Then write a sentence using the antonym. Your sentence should show that you understand the meaning of the new word.

1. carefully
2. valuable
3. perplexing
4. problem
5. confident

Images are mental pictures. Poets create images by using words that appeal to the senses. Although mental "pictures" make you first think of something you see, images can also be created by appealing to the senses of hearing, smelling, tasting, and touching.

Images are the sensory impressions that come to mind when you read a poem. If a poet writes about "crisp apples in the fall," you may think about an apple's color, the sound of biting into an apple, the smell of an orchard, the taste of the fruit, or the feeling of cooler weather approaching. "Crisp apples in the fall" is a concrete description that can bring to mind many different sensory images.

The use of words to create mental pictures is called **imagery.**

As you read the following poems, ask yourself:

1. What are the images that the poets created?
2. What sensory words did they use?

Skill Builder

Look at the following topics. What kinds of images can you create for each one? Use concrete language that appeals to the senses.

1. food **2.** weather **3.** anger

Three Haiku

by Matsuo Basho

An old silent pond . . .
into the pond a frog jumps
splash! silence again.

The still snow we watched
has it covered the same hill
again this winter?

So cold are the waves
the rocking gull can scarcely
fold itself to sleep.

Dolmen in the Snow, J. C. C. Dahl. Art Resource

Matsuo Basho (1644–1694)

At the time Matsuo Basho was born, Japan was at peace after many years of civil war. Basho was born into a family of samurai, or warriors. But since there were no wars to fight, he was sent to serve a lord in a castle.

He began writing haiku when he was a teenager. Basho was in his early 20s when the lord he worked for died. He left the castle to live among Buddhist monks, but he continued to write haiku. Later, he began to teach others to write haiku.

Basho is believed to have given the haiku form some of its rules. It was Basho who encouraged others to suggest pictures or ideas instead of describing them. Many people consider him the first of the great Japanese haiku poets.

The Bare Tree

by William Carlos Williams

The bare cherry tree
higher than the roof
last year produced
abundant fruit. But how
5 speak of fruit confronted
by that skeleton?
Though live it may be
there is no fruit on it.
Therefore chop it down
10 and use the wood
against this biting cold.

---

abundant (uh BUN dunt) well supplied, very plentiful
confronted (kun FRUNT id) met face to face boldly

WINTER

by Nikki Giovanni

Frogs burrow the mud
snails bury themselves
and I air my quilts
preparing for the cold
5 Dogs grow more hair
mothers make oatmeal
and little boys and girls
take Father John's Medicine

Bears store fat
10 chipmunks gather nuts
and I collect books
for the coming winter

burrow (BUR oh) to make a hole or tunnel by digging into the ground
snail (SNAYL) any of a large number of slow-moving creatures having straight or spiral shells

Nikki Giovanni (1943–Present)

When Nikki Giovanni was in college in the 1960s, she was part of a militant group working for civil rights. Her poetry of that time reflected her activities—demonstrations and protests. However, by the time she was in her thirties, her outlook had changed. Instead of being concerned with groups, she wrote more personal poetry. She wrote about black identity—not on a racial basis, but from a person-by-person standpoint.

Giovanni very often writes about love, life, and the fight to stay alive. Much of her work is drawn from her childhood, which was hard but happy, and her family. Other material comes from her present struggles: to raise a family by herself, to have a career, to care for her older relations, to give people hope.

Giovanni likes to be in front of people—in small groups, in classes, and at large readings. On paper, her poetry is inspiring. In person, her voice lends a power to the poems that the written word cannot give.

Wishing to give back to her community as much as she takes, Giovanni often gives free readings of her work. She gets joy from this because, as she says, "here you have some people who've never gotten what they asked for—nothing—and they ask for you, that you would make them feel better or help them understand, plus they give a lot to you. . . ."

FOCUS ON THE SELECTION

UNDERSTAND THE SELECTION

Recall

1. What are the waves like in the third haiku?
2. What type of tree is described in "The Bare Tree"?
3. What animals does the poet tell about in "Winter"?

Infer

4. What is the answer to the question in the second haiku? Is there an answer?
5. What is the wood going to be used for in "The Bare Tree"?
6. Why do the animals in the poem "Winter" prepare themselves in the way they do?
7. How are the people's activities similar to the animals'?

Apply

8. Where do you think the "old silent pond" in the first haiku might be?
9. Do you think "The Bare Tree" should be chopped down? Why or why not?
10. How do you prepare for winter?

Respond to Literature

Why do you think many poets choose to write about nature?

WRITE ABOUT THE SELECTION

You have just read five short poems about nature. Each poem has its own images. Each has its own rhythm and sound, but none of the poems rhyme.

You are going to write your own short poem now. It can be about a pond, the snow, a bird, a tree, a season, or anything else you choose. There is only one rule; your poem must not rhyme.

Prewriting: Think of a subject for your poem. You may use the same subject as one of the poems you read, or you may think of something different. Ask yourself how you feel when you think about your subject. What do you see or hear? Can you create images in your poem that will make other people remember their own experiences?

Writing: Introduce your subject. Use concrete descriptions that will appeal to the senses. Use words that go together well. Try to paint pictures with your words, but don't tell too much. Let your reader use his or her imagination.

Revising: Read your poem out loud. How does it sound to you? Have you used words and ideas that appeal to the senses? Does your poem say what you wanted it to say? How could you change the poem to make it exactly the way you want it to be?

Proofreading: Read over your poem to check for errors. Be sure that all your sentences end with periods, question marks, or exclamation marks.

THINK ABOUT IMAGES

When you read poetry, you often form a picture in your mind. A poet creates an image by appealing to your senses. The image the poet creates reminds you of experiences in your own life. The idea of a campfire makes you feel warm and cozy. It reminds you of how you felt when you sat outside by a fire late at night.

1. In the first haiku, which of your senses does the poet appeal to?
2. In the second haiku, which of your senses does the poet appeal to?
3. What kind of picture does "the rocking gull" in the third haiku bring to mind?
4. In "The Bare Tree," what does the word "skeleton" make you think of?
5. In "Winter," what does the line "mothers make oatmeal" make you think of?

DEVELOP YOUR VOCABULARY

You know that you can use a dictionary to find the meanings of words. You can also use a dictionary to find out how to pronounce words.

Dictionaries show words in parentheses the way they are spelled, using pronunciation symbols. There is a pronunciation key in the dictionary that tells you what each symbol means.

For example, the word "read" is spelled (rēd) in pronunciation symbols. The pronunciation key says the "e" is pronounced like the first "e" in "even."

Look up the following words in a dictionary. Write down the pronunciation symbols for each word. Look at the pronunciation key. Then say the word aloud. Next, write a sentence using each of the words. If you are not sure what a word means, look in the dictionary where the meaning of the word is listed.

1. scarcely
2. abundant
3. confront
4. burrow
5. quilt

UNIT 5 REVIEW

LITERATURE-BASED WRITING

1. Sometimes nature is a friend. Sometimes nature is an enemy. Sometimes it is both. Think about that idea. Then think about how it relates to the selections you have read.

Write an essay in which you discuss the quotation. Use examples from the selections. You may also use examples from your own experiences.

Prewriting: Make a chart that includes the name of each selection you read listed down the side. Along the top, write "Nature as a Friend" and "Nature as an Enemy." Think about how nature is viewed in each selection. Fill in the spaces in the chart with thoughts about each selection. Record examples that show nature as a friend and as an enemy.

Writing: First write several sentences explaining what the quotation means to you. Then extend your explanation by including examples from the reading selections. You may also wish to include examples from your own experiences.

Revising: Remember that this is an essay about a specific quotation. Check to be sure that everything you have written relates to the quotation. Then look for errors in spelling, grammar, and punctuation.

Proofreading: Read over your essay to check for errors. Check your internal punctuation and be sure that all your sentences end with periods, question marks, or exclamation marks.

2. You have learned that characters, plot, setting, and theme are the four main elements in a drama. They are also the main elements in a short story. Think about the three short stories you read in this unit. Each one had characters, a plot, a setting, and a theme.

Select one of the stories you have read. Think about how you could change it from a short story to a drama. Write the opening scene of the drama. Use stage directions to describe characters and setting.

Prewriting: Decide what the action will be in the opening scene. Which characters will be in the scene? Where is the scene set? How does the scene begin to develop the theme of the story?

Writing: Use stage directions to describe the setting. Where and when does the scene take place? What scenery and props should be used? Who are the characters in the scene? What do they look like? What costumes should they wear? Now you are ready to write the dialogue. Remember that in a drama you learn everything from the conversation between the characters.

Revising: Read the scene aloud to see if it makes sense. Is each character clearly identified? Does the action in the scene unfold through the dialogue?

Proofreading: Read over your scene to check for errors. Be sure that all your sentences end with periods, question marks, or exclamation marks.

BUILDING LANGUAGE SKILLS

Vocabulary

When you are reading, you sometimes come across a word with a meaning that you do not know. Of course, you could look up the word in the dictionary, but you can often figure out the meaning of the word for yourself by using context clues. You use **context clues** when you look at the other words in the sentence or paragraph to understand the meaning of the word you do not know. Sometimes only one meaning will make sense.

For example, read the following sentence: "Centuries ago, Kino's ancestors built the stone walls that hold up the fields." If you did not know the meaning of the word *ancestors,* you could figure out that they were people who lived long ago, people who came before Kino.

Use context clues to figure out the definitions of the words in *italics.*

1. "Then he removed the saddle from the horse and *hobbled* the animal to a stake."
2. "He listened intently, but there was no change in the jungle's *monotonous* night sounds."
3. "It is the bell inside the Old Gentleman's castle. He is calling to the people to come up out of the village and find *shelter* within his walls."
4. "Maybe it's something *valuable,* like gold or jewelry."

Usage and Mechanics

Every sentence must have a subject and a verb. In the present tense, the subject and verb must agree in number.

Singular Subject	Plural Subject
The bird sings.	The birds sing.

Only the singular verb ends in *-s.*

When your subject is a pronoun, the subject and verb must agree in person.

I sing	we sing
you sing	you sing
he, she, it sings	they sing

With the pronouns *he, she,* and *it,* the verb ends in *-s.*

Some verbs are irregular. They do not follow the same rules that most verbs do. The most common irregular verb is *to be.*

I am	we are
you are	you are
he, she, it is	they are

Write the correct present tense form of the verb in parentheses.

1. Kino ______ on a farm. *(live)*
2. The two boys ______ in the surf. *(swim)*
3. Jiya ______ overtaken by sadness. *(to be)*

Now write six present-tense sentences about one of the selections you read. Use singular subjects in three of your sentences. Use plural subjects in the other three.

UNIT 5 REVIEW

SPEAKING AND LISTENING

Reader's theatre is a kind of oral presentation with the emphasis on reading aloud rather than memorizing. Since there are no lines to memorize, this is something everyone can feel comfortable to perform.

There are no rules in Reader's theatre. The only requirements are a group of eager participants and something to read. You can add props if you like, but it doesn't take anything elaborate. Simplicity is the key!

Before you have a try at the fun of performing in Reader's theatre, follow the guidelines given below.

1. Silently read the selection that will be presented. Take your time with it. Read slowly and carefully so you understand what the selection is about. When you finish reading the selection, paraphrase it in your mind or ask a classmate to listen to your telling about it.
2. Read the selection round-robin style with others who will be part of Reader's theatre. This will give you a chance to test your "performance" voice and will give you confidence in your speaking ability.
3. Discuss each of the characters. Decide what they probably look like and how they might sound. Discuss what type of voice each character might have. Remember that a character who has a small part is just as important as one with a main role.
4. Review the pronunciation of any words that may be troublesome. Think about the words that you might want to emphasize in your presentation. Try saying them aloud for practice.
5. Next, decide what parts the participants of Reader's theatre will play. Remember, the narrator, the player who introduces the selection, sets the mood of the performance and provides narrative detail, is also a character.
6. Finally, read the selection through again. This time each player should read his part. Become somewhat familiar with your lines so you can comfortably glance at your audience throughout the reading.

Now you are ready to try your hand at Reader's theatre. With other "actors," choose a selection or a section of a selection from this unit that is conducive to Reader's theatre. Your choice may take as long as five minutes. Your group may be as small as two persons or as large as 20 or more. The key to a successful performance will be practice *and* following the steps above. Enjoy yourself and have fun entertaining others!

CRITICAL THINKING

There are many different ways to organize ideas and information when writing a paragraph. For example, suppose you are writing about a talent show in your school. You might choose to tell about the acts of the show in the order in which they were performed.

There are, however, other ways to report the same information. One other way is to decide which act was most exciting, which was least exciting, and rate those in between. Then, you can begin your paragraph by telling about the most exciting act followed by the other acts in order of their ratings. Or, you may want to begin with the least exciting act, saving the most exciting one as a strong finish to your paragraph.

Another way to organize your ideas is in the order of importance. Again, the most important idea could be first followed in order by your other ideas, or you might want to start with the least important idea building to and concluding with your most important one.

Choose one of the selections in this unit. State an opinion about the selection. Use that opinion as the topic sentence of a paragraph. Then write three ideas that support the topic sentence. List your supporting ideas in order of importance.

EFFECTIVE STUDYING

To do well on a test, you need to know the material. You should study your textbook and your class notes. You should also have good strategies for answering different kinds of test questions.

Very often you have to take objective tests in school. **Objective tests** ask for specific facts. Three kinds of questions you will find on objective tests are multiple-choice, fill-in-the-blank, and true-false.

Multiple-choice questions usually give you three or more answers to each question. You should carefully read the question and all three answers. If you are not sure of the right answer, you can eliminate the answers that you know are wrong.

In a fill-in-the-blank question, you must supply the answer yourself. If you do not know the answer, try to figure out something that makes sense. If you have no idea, leave the question blank.

True-false questions are really statements. You should read the statements very carefully. If any part of the statement is not true, your answer is false.

Answer the following questions:

1. To answer multiple-choice questions, you must ______
   - **a.** supply the answer yourself.
   - **b.** choose from several answers.
   - **c.** write true or false.
2. To answer a ______ question, you must supply the answer yourself.
3. True or False: If any part of a statement is not true, your answer is true.

UNIT 6

Family Matters

In my very own self,
I am part of my family.
—D.H. Lawrence

Family Portrait, II, Florine Stettheimer, 1933. Oil on canvas, 46¼ x 64⅝". Collection, The Museum of Modern Art. Gift of Miss Ettie Stettheimer

Family Matters. You are part of a family. So is everyone. Families are the basic building blocks of the world we live in. First, you learn to live in your family, then in your community, then in your nation, then in the world.

Think of your family as your first school. It was with your family that you learned to share, to laugh, to trust, and to be yourself. You carried these lessons with you as you started school and made new friends. Your family always remains a special place, the place you started from.

That is why there are so many stories, books, and plays about families. Often writers want to say something about how they were raised, as Eugenia Collier does in "Sweet Potato Pie." Or maybe they want to entertain with stories about the way things were done in their families, as Kathryn Forbes does in "Mama and Papa."

Each family is unique. Each family has its own traditions, jokes, and signs of love. You can again feel the love your own family gives you, and you can learn more about yourself and the world as you read these stories.

Grandmothers and Sisters. The first selection is a group of poems about a particular family member, a grandmother. Each poet is trying to touch feelings about grandmothers by remembering. What special feelings do you think people have about their grandparents, even grandparents they have never seen?

The next selection is a story of contrasts. In Dorothy West's "The Richer, the Poorer," two sisters have led very different lives. Each sister thinks the other has wasted her life. At the end of the story, in their old age, they both find that they have much to learn from the other.

Next you will read a chapter from a classic, *Mama's Bank Account.* Mama is a Norwegian immigrant who is kindly, wise, and careful with pennies. This story of immigrant life has universal appeal because it describes an experience immigrants share no matter where they came from.

Parents and Children. The next group of poems has to do with parents. Each of the first two is about a mother and her child. The third poem describes a father's view of his daughter. How do you think these poems will be alike and how will they be different?

Then you will read a humorous tale about growing up. In "Charles," by Shirley Jackson, a boy's first year at school is described in detail through the terrible behavior of a classmate named Charles. Do you remember your first school year? How did you feel about beginning school?

"A Mother in Mannville," by Margery Kinnan Rawlings, describes the author's experience with a very special boy in a rural mountain area. Have you ever wanted something so much that you pretended you had it until you began to believe it yourself?

Family Pride. "Sweet Potato Pie," by Eugenia Collier describes the joys and love of a poor farming family. You have heard that money isn't happiness, but as you read this story, you will be touched by the good things this hard-working family was able to share.

Old Worlds, New Worlds. The selection that follows, "Fifth Chinese Daughter," is part of an autobiographical novel by Jade Snow Wong. It describes her coming of age in America, with parents whose values were shaped half a world away in China. Her parents hold fast to traditional family values of obedience. Jade Snow discovers the American value of individuality in her high school classroom. This leads her and her parents through conflict to mutual respect.

The last selection is Francisco Jimenez's story about a family of migrant workers from Mexico. "The Circuit" takes place in California, where the family moves from place to place as the seasons change, in a continual search for work where crops are ready for harvest. The narrator is a young boy who attends school only when "picking seasons" permit. He discovers a new world in school, but quickly learns that the world of the circuit controls his life.

As you read the stories in this unit, look for the ways in which the families are alike and different. What does being part of a family mean to you?

LEARN ABOUT

Imagery

As you know, poetry is a special kind of writing. It doesn't even look like other kinds of writing. Poets express their ideas in groups of words that have a specific rhythm and arrangement of lines.

One of the ways poets express ideas is by using imagery. **Imagery** is creating pictures with words. When you read an example of imagery, you can picture something in your mind. This picture is called an image.

There are many kinds of imagery. Two of the most common are simile and metaphor. A **simile** uses *like* or *as* to make a comparison. *Old as the hills* and *dark as night* are examples of simile.

A **metaphor** makes a comparison by describing one object in terms of another. Calling the sun *a great golden eye* is an example of a metaphor.

As you read these poems, ask yourself:

1. What imagery do I find in these poems?
2. What words create this imagery in my mind?

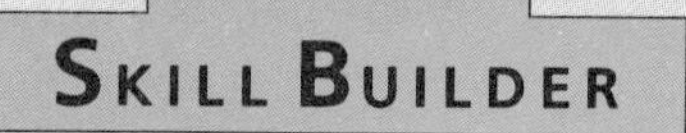

Choose an object you see every day. Study it carefully and then write a simile and a metaphor to describe the object.

The Family Album

by Jane O. Wayne

The spine creaks when you open it;
the thick pages flap
like black wings between your hands.
You don't stop
5 until you notice one of her
sitting on a wall, a girl your age
in braids, a school uniform—
white middy-blouse, dark tie,
dark stockings on her dangling legs.
10 You must be studying the mouth
they say you have,
the grandmother you never knew.
You even rub your hand
slowly over the shiny girl
15 the way I do a window
when I can't tell which side
the dust is on—
before you let the cover drop.

---

album (AL bum) a large book having blank pages and usually used for collecting photographs
spine (SPYN) the backbone of a bookcover, bearing the title, author's and publisher's name
middy-blouse (MID ee BLOUS) a loose-fitting blouse with a collar that is wide and square at the back

LINEAGE

by Margaret Walker

My grandmothers were strong.
They followed plows and bent to toil.
They moved through fields sowing seed.
They touched earth and grain grew.
5 They were full of sturdiness and singing.
My grandmothers were strong.

My grandmothers are full of memories.
Smelling of soap and onions and wet clay
With veins rolling roughly over quick hands
10 They have many clean words to say.
My grandmothers were strong.
Why am I not as they?

The Boch Family, Edvard Munch.
Three Lions.

---

lineage (LIN ee ij) a family line; parents, grandparents, and other relatives, directly descended from a common ancestor
toil (TOIL) work; chores
sow (SOH) plant; cast seed

The Last Words *of My* English Grandmother

by William Carlos Williams

There were some dirty plates
and a glass of milk
beside her on a small table
near the rank, disheveled bed—

5 Wrinkled and nearly blind
she lay and snored
rousing with anger in her tones
to cry for food,

Gimme something to eat—
10 They're starving me—
I'm all right I won't go
to the hospital. No, no, no

Give me something to eat
Let me take you
15 to the hospital, I said
and after you are well

you can do as you please.
She smiled, Yes
you do what you please first
20 then I can do what I please—

Oh, oh, oh! she cried
as the ambulance men lifted
her to the stretcher—
Is this what you call

25 making me comfortable?
By now her mind was clear—
Oh you think you're smart
you young people,

she said, but I'll tell you
30 you don't know anything.
Then we started.
On the way

we passed a long row
of elms. She looked at them
35 awhile out of
the ambulance window and said,

What are all those
fuzzy-looking things out there?
Trees? Well, I'm tired
40 of them and rolled her head away.

---

rank (RANGK) smelling bad
disheveled (dih SHEV uld) messy, untidy, disordered

FOCUS ON THE SELECTION

UNDERSTAND THE SELECTION

Recall

1. Whose picture does the poet study in "The Family Album?"
2. What kind of people were the poet's grandmothers in "Lineage?"
3. What was the grandmother tired of in William Carlos Williams's poem?

Infer

4. Why does the poet study the picture in "The Family Album"?
5. How is the poet different from her grandmothers in "Lineage"?
6. Why does the poet take his English grandmother to the hospital?
7. What does the title of William Carlos Williams's poem tell you?

Apply

8. Imagine that Jane O. Wayne wrote a letter to the grandmother in the photo. What do you think she might tell her?
9. Show that Margaret Walker's grandmothers were strong women.
10. Predict what will happen to Williams's grandmother at the hospital.

Respond to Literature

What do these poems say about families? Use examples from the poems.

WRITE ABOUT THE SELECTION

The poems you have just read are about a family relationship, that of younger people with grandmothers. Family relations have always provided writers with much of their material for stories and poems. Imagine that there is a contest to write a poem about *Family.* Your poem must describe what is special about family. You may use your own family or talk about families in general.

Prewriting: Make a list of the ideas you would like to include in your poem. Put your ideas in the order you will write about them. Make another list of images to include in your poem. If you are writing about your own family, remember that other people do not know them as well as you do. Some description of them will be necessary.

Writing: Write your poem. It may be short or it may contain many verses. Include the ideas from your lists.

Revising: Remember that poems should have rhythm and strong images. To get a better feeling for the rhythm of your poem, read it aloud to yourself. Replace words to improve the rhythm and to make more powerful images.

Proofreading: Remember that lines of poetry are divided by rhythm and imagery, and not by sentences. You can capitalize the letters at the beginning of each line. Put commas where they are needed and a period at the end of each sentence.

THINK ABOUT IMAGERY

Imagery makes it easier to understand and remember the ideas in a poem. Imagery helps us to picture the poet's ideas and to remember what the poet has to say.

1. What simile do you see in "The Family Album"?
2. Why does Jane Wayne make the image of looking for dust on a window?
3. What is the image of "They touched earth and grain grew" in "Lineage"?
4. What is the image of the grandmother's room with which Williams opens his poem?
5. What does Williams's grandmother mean when she says she is tired of trees?

DEVELOP YOUR VOCABULARY

A dictionary contains many kinds of information about words. Look up each listed word in a dictionary. Then answer the questions.

album	disheveled
middy-blouse	lineage
spine	sow
rank	toil

1. Which word is a compound word?
2. Which word means "to work hard" or "hard work"?
3. Which syllable is accented in *lineage?*
4. The word *sow* has two pronunciations. Write a sentence using the meaning of the word that does not appear in this story.
5. Which word identifies a kind of book?
6. Which word has a verb ending?

Learn About

Characters

There are several ways to learn about the characters in a story. The author may describe them, telling you exactly what kind of people they are.

In most cases, however, you have to decide for yourself what a character is like. You may study the character's words and actions. These will tell you if the character is generous or short-tempered or foolish.

You have to think about the characters. Imagine how you would feel if you were in that character's situation. What would you say and do? What do you think of the character as he or she acts and says things in the story? Do you like this person? Do you approve of the actions and words?

As you read, "The Richer, the Poorer," ask yourself:

1. What do I know about the kind of people these characters are?
2. How did I learn what I know about them?

Skill Builder

Describe a character in a story or book you have read recently. Tell what kind of person the character is and how you were able to form your opinion.

THE RICHER, THE POORER

by Dorothy West

Over the years, Lottie had urged Bess to prepare for her old age. Over the years, Bess had lived each day as if there were no other. Now they were both past sixty. It was time for summing up. Lottie had a bank account that had never grown lean. Bess had the clothes on her back. The rest of her possessions were in a battered suitcase.

Lottie had hated being a child. She had hated hearing her parents skimp and scrape. Bess had never seemed to notice. All she ever wanted was to go outside and play. She learned to skate on borrowed skates. She rode a borrowed bicycle. Lottie couldn't wait to grow up. She would have money. And she would buy herself the best of everything.

Lottie went to work as soon as anyone would hire her. She minded babies. She ran errands for old people.

She never touched a penny of her money. Her child's mouth watered for ice cream and candy. But she could not bear to share with Bess. Bess never had anything to share with her. Soon, her dimes began to add up to dollars. By then, she had lost her taste for sweets.

At twelve, she was a clerk in a small variety store. Saturdays she worked as long as she was needed. She decided to save her money for clothes. She would need them in high school. She

---

urge (URJ) encourage; persuade someone to do something
sum up (SUM UP) add up; look back at life
lean (LEEN) thin
battered (BAT urd) beaten up; well-used
skimp (SKIMP) do without; stretch to cover

Mrs. Eric Krans, Olaf Krans.

would have a wardrobe that no one would be able to match.

But in high school, she could not give in to such a frivolous idea. Her teachers admired her. They advised her to think seriously about college. No one in her family had ever gone to college. Bess certainly would never get there. She would show them all what she could do.

She began to bank her money. Her bank account became her most private and precious possession.

In her third year of high school, she found a restaurant job. She was a cashier from dinner until closing. In her last year, the business increased rapidly. Lottie was faced with a choice. She could stay in school or work full time.

She made her choice easily. A job now was worth two in the future.

Bess had a boyfriend in the school band. His only ambition was to play a horn. Lottie expected to be settled soon with a home and family. Bess would still be waiting for Harry to earn enough for a marriage license.

It was not surprising that Bess married Harry right after high school. It was not surprising either that Lottie never married. She was halfway persuaded two or three times. But she could not give up a job that paid well. Not for a homemaking job that paid nothing.

Lottie did not envy Bess's married life. Bess and Harry had no real home. He played in cheap bands all over the country. Once, they got stranded in Europe. They were often in rags. They were never in riches.

Bess was sad because she had no child. Lottie felt she was better off with no nieces and nephews to feel sorry for. Bess probably would have dumped them on her doorstep.

Lottie had a doorstep that she owned. Her boss had bought a second house. He offered Lottie his first house at a low price. Refusing the offer would have been like losing money.

---

wardrobe (WOR drohb) collection of clothes
frivolous (FRIV uh lus) silly; not serious; just for fun
precious (PRESH us) most valuable
ambition (am BISH un) desire to do something
persuade (pur SWAYD) talk someone into doing something
envy (EN vee) painful awareness that someone else has something you want
stranded (STRAND did) stuck; unable to go anywhere

She shut off the rooms that she didn't use. She let them get dusty and run-down. She had no food at home, because she always ate out. She did not encourage people to visit her. Visitors always expected a cup of tea.

Her way of life was mean and miserly. But she did not know it. She thought she was being thrifty so she could be comfortable later on.

After forty, the years began to race by. Suddenly, Lottie was sixty. Her boss's son forced her to retire. He had no sentimental feelings about her as a long-time employee.

She tried to find other work. But she looked older than she really was. For the first time in her life, Lottie would have gladly worked for nothing. She wanted someplace to go, something to do.

Harry died in Europe, in a cheap hotel. Bess cried as though he had left her a fortune. He had left her nothing but his horn. There wasn't even money for her trip home.

Lottie felt trapped by the blood relationship. She knew she would have to send for her sister. She knew she would have to take her in when she returned. It didn't seem fair. Bess would have the benefit of Lottie's lifetime of self-denial.

It took Lottie a week to get a bedroom ready. It was a week of hard work and hard cash. There was everything to do, everything to replace or paint. When she was done, the room looked fresh and new. Lottie felt she deserved it more than Bess.

She thought of giving Bess her old room. But the mattress was lumpy. The carpet was worn. The curtains were threadbare. Her conscience bothered her. She decided to redo that room, too. She went about doing it eagerly.

Finally, she was finished upstairs. Then she was shocked to see how dismal downstairs looked by comparison. She tried to ignore it. But she had nowhere to go to escape it. The contrast grew more intolerable.

---

mean (MEEN) stingy; cheap
miserly (MY zer lee) too careful with money
thrifty (THRIF tee) carefully managing money
sentimental (SENT ih men tul) full of feeling
self-denial (SELF de NY ul) sacrificing one's own desires or pleasures
threadbare (THRED bayr) worn out; falling apart
dismal (DIZ mul) dark and gloomy; bleak; run-down; sad
intolerable (in TAH ler uh bul) not to be put up with

She worked her way from kitchen to living room. She persuaded herself that she was doing it only to keep herself busy. At night, she slept like a child after a busy day of playing house. She was having more fun than she had ever had in her life. She was living each hour for itself.

There was only one more day before Bess would arrive. Lottie walked past the gleaming mirrors in her house. Suddenly, she saw herself as others saw her. She could not stand the sight.

She went on a spending spree. She visited specialty shops and a beauty salon. At the end, she was transformed into a woman who believes in miracles.

She was cooking a turkey when Bess rang the bell. Her heart raced. She wondered if it was because of the heat from the oven.

She went to the door, and Bess stood before her. Stiffly, she allowed Bess to hug her. Her heart was racing harder. The cold air hurt her eyes.

"Oh, Lottie, it's so good to see you," Bess said. But she said nothing about Lottie's splendid appearance.

Upstairs, Bess put her shabby suitcase down. "I'll sleep like a rock tonight," she said. But there was not a word of praise for her lovely room.

Lottie served the turkey on a lavish table. "I'll take light and dark meat both," Bess said. She did not marvel at the size of the bird. She was not even surprised that there was a turkey, even though she was too poor to buy bread.

With the glow of good food in her stomach, Bess began to spin stories rich with places and people. Most of them were poor or shabby. But they were all magnificent in Bess's stories. Her face reflected the joys and sorrows of her memories. Her love enhanced the poorest people and places.

Now Lottie knew why Bess had not mentioned her appearance, or the shining room, or the turkey. She had not even seen them. Tomorrow she would see everything as it really looked. Tonight she saw only what she had come looking for. She saw a place in her sister's home and heart.

---

spree (SPREE) a brief period of not holding back
lavish (LAV ish) generous; having huge amounts
marvel (MAHR vul) wonder; be astonished by
enhanced (en HANST) made greater or more attractive

"That's enough about me," Bess said. "How have the years treated you?"

"It was me who treated them badly," Lottie said sadly. "I saved for them. I forgot the best of them would go by without my ever enjoying them. That's my life story. It's been a life never lived. Now it's too near the end to try."

"No," Bess said. "Do you know how to begin to learn to live? First, you have to realize how much there is to know. Don't count the years that we have left. At this age, it's the days that count. You can't waste a minute feeling sorry for yourself. You have too much catching up to do."

Lottie grinned. It was a real, wide-open grin. "To tell the truth," she said, "I felt sorry for you. If I had any sense, maybe I would feel sorry for myself. I know I'm too old to kick up my heels. But I'm going to let you show me how. If I land on my head, it won't matter. I feel giddy already. And I like it."

---

giddy (GID ee) dizzy; excited with happiness

FOCUS ON THE SELECTION

UNDERSTAND THE SELECTION

Recall

1. Who are the main characters in Dorothy West's story?
2. What is the most important thing in Lottie's life?
3. What causes Bess to come to live with Lottie?

Infer

4. Why do you think Lottie has saved most of her money?
5. In your opinion, what has Bess learned from life?
6. Why does Lottie fix up her house and herself?
7. Finally, what important lesson does Bess teach Lottie?

Apply

8. Predict what Lottie will do with the rest of her life.
9. Imagine you were Bess. What would you feel as you came to stay with your sister?
10. Select details that show that, by the end of the story, Lottie is becoming a different person.

Respond to Literature

What do Lottie and Bess discover about being part of a family?

WRITE ABOUT THE SELECTION

Now that you have read "The Richer, the Poorer," you know both of the main characters well enough to imagine how they might act with people other than the ones in the story. Imagine that Bess is writing a letter to a friend in Europe. She wants to tell her friend how she feels about coming to live with Lottie. She also wants to describe what she has seen at Lottie's house. Remember the house as it is described in the story. Try to imagine how Bess would describe it.

Prewriting: Make an informal outline. Choose story details to include in your outline. One section of your outline will talk about feelings. The other section will describe what Bess has seen.

Writing: Write your letter. Use the details of your outline to complete your letter. Write a separate paragraph for each section of the outline. People write letters to entertain as well as to inform others. If you think Bess would find something funny in Lottie's house, you can use it in the letter.

Revising: Each paragraph should have a strong topic sentence, telling the main idea of the paragraph. Be sure your paragraphs begin with good topic sentences. Or, if you are leading up to a funny line, which is the topic sentence, the topic sentence may come at the end of the paragraph.

Proofreading: Remember that there are five parts to a friendly letter. Be sure your letter contains all five parts.

THINK ABOUT CHARACTERS

We learn about characters from what they say and do in a story. We have to think about their words and actions as we read. The author usually tells you some of the qualities that characters have, but in "The Richer, the Poorer," you learn everything from their thoughts and actions. Look for story details for clues to character.

1. How did Lottie feel about the way her parents lived?
2. How did Bess feel about the way her parents lived?
3. How did each woman feel about the fact that Bess had no children?
4. How did each woman feel about Bess's coming to live with Lottie?
5. What will the sisters' lives be like now that they are together?

DEVELOP YOUR VOCABULARY

We use phrases in English that do not mean exactly what the words in them say. They are called **figures of speech.** "Up the creek" is a figure of speech meaning helpless and in real trouble. Identify the figure of speech in each sentence below. Then tell what it means.

1. There will be an ambulance on hand in case of an emergency.
2. The castle had gone to rack and ruin, and ivy covered the collapsing walls.
3. I felt a blood-tie and agreed to care for my desperate nephew and niece.
4. Their heads were in the clouds when they heard they had won the contest.
5. They always manage to land on their feet no matter how serious their problems are.

Learn About

Tone

The feeling you get from a story is its *tone.* If a story makes you feel like laughing, it has a humorous tone. If you feel sad when you read a story, it has a serious tone. Other stories fill us with suspense and even fear.

There are many ways for authors to create the tone of a story. They may give characters silly names to make the readers laugh. They may write conversations between characters that are frightening and full of mystery. They may choose language which sets a serious or even sad tone.

As you read, think about how the selection makes you feel. Then look at the story again. What details and phrases created the tone that made you feel that way?

As you read "Mama and Papa," ask yourself:

1. What is the tone of this story?
2. What details create the tone of the story?

Skill Builder

Describe a place you know well. Use words and phrases which will set the tone for your description. Your tone may be humorous, serious, or even suspenseful.

MAMA AND PAPA

by Kathryn Forbes

The years that Christine and I spent at Lowell High were good years, for they all flew by so quickly. Our hair, by some miracle, had turned a passable golden color, and we discovered that we had nice complexions and attractive teeth. Clothes and school activities became interesting subjects, and boys were fun to know.

I was finally asked to join the Mummers' Club at school. I wrote plays—most of them tragic—which I insisted upon producing. Christine headed the debating team and the honor society, and Nels was in his fourth year of premedical studies at the university across the bay.

Our Baby Kaaren had become a solemn, lovable treasure of six, and sturdy Dagmar spent her days in collecting stray dogs and cats and her nights in caring for them.

Little by little, the foreignness had disappeared almost entirely from our family life. Only on special occasions did Mama make the *lutefisk* or *fladbröd,* and she and Papa seldom spoke Norwegian anymore. They had learned to play cards and went often to neighborhood card parties or to shows.

---

passable (PAS uh bul) good enough
complexion (kum PLEK shun) color and texture of skin
mummer (MUM ur) an actor
honor society (ON ur suh SY uh tee) group of excellent students
solemn (SOL um) very serious, not cheerful
lutefisk (LOO tuh fisk) Norwegian fishballs with sauce
fladbrod (FLAD brood) Norwegian bread pudding

But the Steiner Street house remained home in every sense of the word. We never even thought of it as a "boardinghouse," because although new boarders came, they stayed on and on to become part of the family.

Two little old ladies, the Misses Jane and Margaret Randolph, now had the sunny back bedroom upstairs. They told Mama shyly that they had never been so happy in their lives. They were real ladies, the Misses Randolph, and had been belles in the early days of San Francisco, before their dear father had been swindled out of his fortune. They had a tiny income, which they added to by doing fancy crocheting and beaded bags for the Woman's Exchange.

Then there was big, laughing Mr. Grady, who was a policeman and a widower. He had a fascinating Irish brogue, and every payday he brought Miss Margaret and Miss Jane a box of fancy peppermints from the Pig 'n Whistle. He never learned that the gentle ladies could not stand the flavor of peppermint, and we young ones never told, because we were the final and grateful consumers.

Papa enclosed the huge basement room in beaverboard, cut windows, and laid a smooth pine floor. Mr. Lewis and Mr. Clark and the Stanton brothers had a great time helping him paint it. Mrs. Sam Stanton made cushions for the benches Papa built along the wall, and the Misses Randolph sewed fancy shades for all the lamps.

Professor Jannough was able to get an old practice piano, and Mr. Grady contributed his big old-fashioned phonograph.

Nearly every evening the folks would congregate there to visit. They would listen to the phonograph or have the professor play for them, or beg Mrs. Jannough to sing her Polish lullabies.

There, too, Christine and Nels and I brought our friends and gave our parties. We considered ourselves blessed above all the

---

boarder (BAWR dur) person who regularly pays for a room and meals in someone else's home
belle (BEL) attractive and popular girl
swindle (SWIN dul) cheat; to get money or property from another under false pretenses; defraud
crochet (kroh SHAY) a form of needlework in which loops of thread are interwoven using a single needle
brogue (BROHG) a regional, usually Irish, pronunciation or dialect

Girls at the Piano, Auguste Renoir. Musee D'Orsay, Paris. SEF/Art Resource.

other young folk we knew, who had to entertain in small apartments or flats.

The newest addition to our group was Mr. Johnny Kenmore and his frail and lovely wife. Mr. Kenmore was that exciting thing, an aviator, and every Sunday he took people for airplane rides over the marina. Whenever he flew, Mrs. Kenmore would come out into the kitchen and sit with Mama until the telephone rang and Mr. Kenmore said he was on his way home.

Papa loved to talk of flying and of airplanes, and to hear Mr. Kenmore tell of his many adventures. Papa's eyes would sparkle and shine and he would shake his head in admiration.

"What a wonderful thing," he would marvel. "To fly. To *fly!*"

"It's a great feeling," Mr. Kenmore agreed.

"To fly," Papa said. "High up. Like a bird."

"I'll take you up sometime," Mr. Kenmore offered carelessly one evening. "Any time you say."

Papa sat up eagerly, and I heard Mama catch her breath.

I guess Papa heard her, too, because he sat back in his chair, and after a while he said, "N-n-no, no, I guess not."

"Oh, come on," Mr. Kenmore coaxed, "you'd love it."

"Would be wonderful," Papa said wistfully. "Just once—to fly."

He looked at Mama again, but her face was bent over her sewing. So Papa said, "Thank you for your offer, Mr. Kenmore, but no. Better, perhaps, that I stay on the ground."

Mr. Kenmore started to speak again, but Mrs. Kenmore stood up quickly and her usually quiet voice was shrill. "Stop urging, Johnny," she cried, "*please.*"

So nothing more was said about flying, and Papa didn't mention it again. But I could see that Mama was worried about something. Every once in a while she stole quick little glances at Papa's face, trying, perhaps, to read his thoughts.

One day as I helped her hang out the clothes, she looked up at the sky and said: "This flying, I do not understand it. It is a frightening thing."

When I didn't answer, she continued, as if she were thinking out loud, "To want to go so high. So far away."

---

aviator (AY vee ay tur) person who pilots a plane
shrill (SHRIL) high, sharp sound

Mama never served meals to the boarders on Sunday. That was the family's day. One Sunday, Papa and Nels had gone over to the bay to watch the fishermen. Aunt Sigrid and Uncle Peter had taken Dagmar and Kaaren to the park. Christine and I went down to the library to catch up on our homework.

But by five o'clock we had all returned and gathered in the kitchen to wonder why Mama wasn't home preparing our dinner for us.

Just as Papa had decided to telephone Aunt Jenny's to ask if Mama were there, we heard her quick step in the hall. She came into the kitchen in a rush, her cheeks pink and her eyes glowing.

"Papa," she said, "Papa, you must go flying. You must go with Mr. Kenmore next Sunday."

I had never seen Papa look more surprised. "You mean," he said, "that you would not mind?"

"So badly have you wanted to go," Mama said. "And you are right. It is wonderful."

"But how—"

"Oh," Mama said, "I go up today to see if it safe. Is all right now for you to go."

And Mama could not understand why Papa and the rest of us laughed until we cried.

FOCUS ON THE SELECTION

UNDERSTAND THE SELECTION

Recall

1. How old was the author when the events of this story took place?
2. What country did the author's family come from?
3. What did Papa want to do more than anything?

Infer

4. Why do you think the family took in boarders?
5. Why did the Misses Randolph live in the boardinghouse?
6. How did Papa get interested in going up in an airplane?
7. Why did Mama go up in the airplane before allowing Papa to go?

Apply

8. Predict what Papa will do after his first airplane flight.
9. Imagine you lived with the family. What would you like best about them?
10. Show that both Papa and Mama were adventurous people.

Respond to Literature

What is unusual about the family? It is clear that the family in this story is a very close one and that they all care a great deal for one another.

WRITE ABOUT THE SELECTION

At the end of the story, Mama says that it is safe and Papa can fly. Write a new story ending telling what happens the day Papa flies. Keep in mind that Mama has already had a good experience in flying. Consider the possibility that Papa's experience may not be so good. Feel free to make up details and conversation for your story ending.

Prewriting: Think about the characters. How do you think Mama and Papa will feel as Papa approaches his first experience in the air? Make a list of feelings for each character. Be sure to include notes about the feelings of the children.

Writing: Use your lists to write the new story ending. Remember to include the feelings of each of the main characters. You may make up conversation to add to your story ending if you wish. Remember that your story will be more interesting if there is a strong contrast between Papa's experience and the experience Mama had in "testing the air" for him.

Revising: Adverbs tell *how* and can make a sentence more interesting. Add adverbs telling *how* to your story ending. Try to choose adverbs that make your story interesting and exciting.

Proofreading: Make sure that you have used quotation marks correctly. Proper nouns, the names of people, and places should be capitalized. Check to be sure you have spelled names correctly.

THINK ABOUT TONE

Tone is the feeling you get while you read a story. A humorous tone makes you laugh. A serious tone makes you feel sad. One way to understand the tone of a story is to think about the events of the story. Decide if these were the kinds of events that make people happy or sad. Then think about the characters. Decide how they felt about the events of the story. This will help you decide how you as a reader is expected to feel.

1. How did you feel while you read this story?
2. Are the events of the story serious or light?
3. Do the characters seem serious or light-hearted?
4. What words gave you clues about the tone?
5. How would you describe the tone of this story?

DEVELOP YOUR VOCABULARY

The suffixes *-or, -er,* and *-ist* mean "one who ______." When you add one of these suffixes to a word, you make it into a noun naming a person who does the action of that verb.

direct + or = director
forecast + er = forecaster
violin + ist = violinist

Add one of the endings to each word below.

1. act
2. work
3. instruct
4. paint
5. employ
6. lobby
7. lead
8. council
9. harp
10. teach
11. special
12. organ
13. invent
14. conduct
15. solo
16. hunt

The Crib, Berthe Morisot. Musee d'Orsay, Paris. Art Resource.

Learn About

Character

A poem can be written from many points of view. Imagine a poem about a battle. How would the poem be written if the story were told by one of the winners—or losers?

Every poem has a point of view of a particular person. This person is called the **speaker.** Sometimes the poet is the speaker. However, the poet is not necessarily the speaker. The voice in the poem may just as easily belong to a sixty-year-old woman, a twenty-year-old soldier, a faithful dog, or even an old house.

Read the title of the poem. It will often indicate who the speaker is. Try to imagine the person whose feelings you are reading. Picture the speaker mentally. Try to put yourself in the speaker's place.

As you read these next three poems, ask yourself:

1. Who is the speaker in this poem?
2. What clues help me to picture the speaker?

Skill Builder

Imagine you are your mother, father, or another relative. Try to describe yourself as that person sees you and knows you. Remember you are not the speaker, your relative is.

Mother to Son

by Langston Hughes

Well, son, I'll tell you:
Life for me ain't been no crystal stair.
It's had tacks in it,
And splinters,
5 And boards torn up,
And places with no carpet on the floor—
Bare.

---

ain't (AYNT) contraction of has not; am not
crystal (KRIS tul) very fine and clear glass

But all the time
I'se been a-climbin' on,
10 And reachin' landin's,
And turnin' corners,
And sometimes goin' in the dark
Where there ain't been no light.
So boy, don't you turn back.
15 Don't set you down on the steps
'Cause you finds it's kinder hard.
Don't you fall now—
For I'se still goin', honey,
I'se still climbin',
20 And life for me ain't been no crystal stair.

Maid of the Douglas Family, Anonymous. Louisiana State Museum.

---

landing (LAND ing) a large flat area partway up a staircase
kinder (colloquial for "kind of") (KYN dur) rather; sort of

While I Slept

by Robert Francis

While I slept, while I slept and the night grew colder
She would come to my bedroom stepping softly
And draw a blanket about my shoulder
While I slept.

5 While I slept, while I slept in the dark still heat
She would come to my bedside stepping coolly
And smooth the twisted troubled sheet
While I slept.

Now she sleeps, sleeps under quiet rain
10 While nights grow warm or nights grow colder
And I wake and sleep and wake again
While she sleeps.

---

draw (DRAW) pull
still (STIL) peaceful; unmoving
troubled (TRUB uld) tangled; disturbed; worried; distressed

These Are the Gifts

by Gregory Djanikian

For my daughter, 2½

They are her signature:
Seashells in our boots and slippers,
Barrettes under each of our pillows,
Marbles and flecks of clay
5 In the deep mines of our pockets.

Some we find quickly, others
Are lost to us for weeks or months,
And when we come upon them
In our daily disorder, we are struck
10 By her industry, this extravagance
Which secretly replenishes
Our cupboards, baskets and drawers
With gifts from the heart.

O she ranges far and wide for her riches,
15 Returning with tales to astonish:
Of danger spilling like a jar of coins
Over the landing and down the stairs,
Of crabs in the graveled pathway,
Alligators in the flower beds,
20 And Mr. McGregor in all the gardens.

---

signature (SIG nuh chur) a person's name written by that person
barrette (buh RET) a small bar or clasp for holding hair in place
fleck (FLEK) small piece; fragment
disorder (dis OR dur) confusion; mix up
industry (IN dus tree) hard work
extravagance (ik STRAV uh guns) going beyond reasonable limits in conduct; speech; spending, etc.
replenish (rih PLEN ish) fill again; give more to

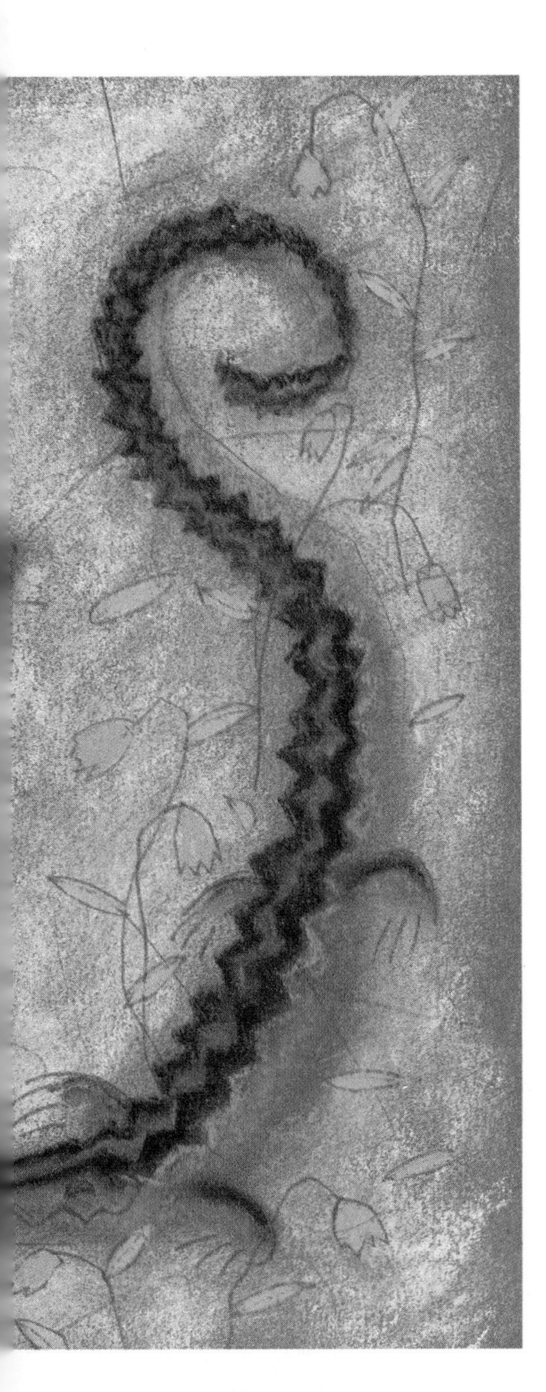

But she is undaunted, risking
Life and limb to retrieve for us
What the world mislays:
Surprise! she says, as she gives
25 Her mother a bouquet of sticks,
Happy birthday! she croons and squeaks
And pours into my hands a cupful
Of pebbles, gum wrappers, leaves.

What can I hope for her
30 As she slips into my lap full of play
And laughter, squiggling her toes
While I count them, this pig, that pig,
The one who goes to market,
The one who starves,
35 The one who has luck,
The one who hasn't any?

May she hold on to her courage always.
May she keep filling the world up
With the sweet presence of her mischief.
40 May she put her trinkets
In all the right shoes.

FOCUS ON THE SELECTION

UNDERSTAND THE SELECTION

Recall

1. Who is the speaker in Langston Hughes's poem "Mother to Son"?
2. Who is the subject of Robert Francis's poem "While I Sleep"?
3. Who is the speaker in Gregory Djanikian's poem "These are the Gifts"?

Infer

4. What kind of life is "a crystal stair"?
5. What is the mother in "Mother to Son" encouraging her son to do?
6. What does Robert Francis mean when he says his mother sleeps now?
7. What feelings does Djanikian have when he finds his daughter's treasures?

Apply

8. In Langston Hughes's poem, how do you think you would feel when you heard your mother's words?
9. Dramatize the events described in Robert Francis's poem.
10. Use details from the poem by Djanikian to show that the shells are treasures.

Respond to Literature

What kind of family relationship does each of the poems describe?

WRITE ABOUT THE SELECTION

Imagine that you are the son in the poem by Langston Hughes. What would you want to say to your mother? What feelings might you have? What would you say to make your mother understand that you knew what she was telling you? Write a poem that responds to Hughes's poem.

Prewriting: Make a list of the feelings the son might have in response to the poem. Add reasons for each of the feelings. Then make a second list. On this list, write words to use in your poem. You may wish to make use of the image of the "crystal stair." What might the son feel in response to this image. What is your response.

Writing: Write the first draft of your poem. Don't worry if your poem does not have rhyme or correct rhythm. It is important on the first draft to get your ideas down on paper. Use ten words on your list or think of new words that express your ideas. These words can be expanded into images. You might keep in mind that the strength of "Mother to Son" is partly due to the single strong image of the stair.

Revising: Reread your poem. Find words that can be changed to improve the rhythm and to make more powerful images.

Proofreading: You may capitalize the first letter of each line of your poem if you wish. Be sure to check internal punctuation. Sentences should end with periods, question marks, or exclamation marks.

THINK ABOUT CHARACTER

Understanding the speaker will help you get more from reading poetry. If you can imagine yourself in the place of the speaker, you will be better able to understand the thoughts and feelings expressed by the speaker. Remember, the poet is not necessarily the speaker. You have to think about the ideas of the poem to decide who is speaking.

1. How does the speaker feel in Langston Hughes' poem?
2. Who is the speaker in "While I Slept"?
3. What do you think the speaker in "While I Slept" might have done differently if he had it to do over again?
4. Who is the speaker talking about in "These Are the Gifts"?
5. What might the poem say if the speaker in "These Are the Gifts" were the daughter?

DEVELOP YOUR VOCABULARY

A **synonym** is a word that means the same as another word. An **antonym** is a word with an opposite meaning.

Write words from the vocabulary list to answer each question. Use a dictionary if you need it.

disorder	draw
fleck	industry
landing	replenish
still	crystal
barrette	extravagance
troubled	signature

1. Which word is a synonym for *waste?*
2. Which word is an antonym for *use up?*
3. Which word is an antonym for *laziness?*
4. Which word is an antonym for *calm and relaxed?*
5. Which word is a synonym for *mess?*
6. Which word is a synonym for *quiet?*

Learn About

Plot

Plot is what happens in a story. The arrangement of the incidents in a story makes up the plot.

Plot usually builds to one important event. This is called the **climax,** and it is the most important event in the story. Everything that happens after this event is caused by it.

Sometimes, authors give hints about this important event. They include story clues to tell you that the big event is coming and what might happen during the big event.

Watch for these story clues as you read. Think about story details. What might happen as a result of these clues? Will the ending be the one we expect?

Many authors write **surprise endings.** A surprise ending is not the ending we expect. All the story clues point to one ending, but the author finishes the story with an entirely different ending.

As you read "Charles," ask yourself:

1. What is the plot of this story?
2. What clues help me to guess the ending?

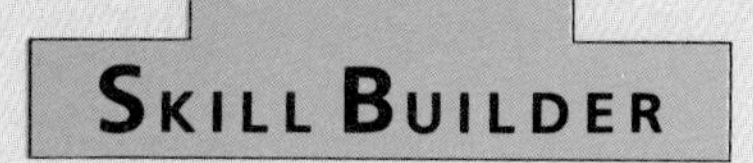

Skill Builder

Write the plot of a television show you have seen recently. Write your plot so that your readers will be surprised by the ending.

Charles

by Shirley Jackson

The day my son Laurie started kindergarten he renounced corduroy overalls with bibs and began wearing blue jeans with a belt. I watched him go off the first morning with the older girl next door, seeing clearly that an era of my life was ended, my sweet-voiced nursery-school tot replaced by a long-trousered, swaggering character who forgot to stop at the corner and wave good-bye to me.

He came home the same way, the front door slamming open, his cap on the floor, and the voice suddenly become raucous shouting, "Isn't anybody *here?*"

At lunch he spoke insolently to his father, spilled his baby sister's milk, and remarked that his teacher said we were not to take the name of the Lord in vain.

"How *was* school today?" I asked, elaborately casual.

"All right," he said.

"Did you learn anything?" his father asked.

Laurie regarded his father coldly. "I didn't learn nothing," he said.

"Anything," I said. "Didn't learn anything."

"The teacher spanked a boy, though," Laurie said, addressing his bread and butter. "For being fresh," he added, with his mouth full.

"What did he do?" I asked. "Who was it?"

Laurie thought. "It was Charles," he said. "He was fresh. The teacher spanked him and made him stand in a corner. He was awfully fresh."

"What did he do?" I asked again, but Laurie slid off his chair, took a cookie, and left, while his father was still saying,

---

renounce (rih NOUNS) give up; refuse
era (IR uh) a period of time marked from one important date to another
swagger (SWAG ur) walk or move the body in a tough, bullying way
raucous (RAW kus) loud; harsh; shouted
insolently (IN suh lunt lee) in an insulting and rude manner; disrespectfully
elaborately (ih LAB ur it lee) extremely carefully planned; with considerable detail
casual (KAZH oo ul) relaxed; unconcerned
fresh (FRESH) rude; disrespectful

"See here, young man."

The next day Laurie remarked at lunch, as soon as he sat down, "Well, Charles was bad again." He grinned enormously and said, "Today he hit the teacher."

"Good heavens," I said, mindful of the Lord's name, "I suppose he got spanked again?"

"He sure did," Laurie said. "Look up," he said to his father.

"What?" his father said, looking up.

"Look down," Laurie said. "Look at my thumb. Gee, you're dumb." He began to laugh insanely.

"Why did Charles hit the teacher?" I asked quickly.

"Because she tried to make him color with red crayons," Laurie said. "Charles wanted to color with green crayons so he hit the teacher and she spanked him and said nobody play with Charles but everybody did."

The third day—it was Wednesday of the first week—Charles bounced a see-saw onto the head of a little girl and made her bleed, and the teacher made him stay inside all during recess. Thursday Charles had to stand in a corner during story-time because he kept pounding his feet on the floor. Friday Charles was deprived of blackboard privileges because he threw chalk.

On Saturday I remarked to my husband, "Do you think kindergarten is too unsettling for Laurie? All this toughness, and bad grammar, and this Charles boy sounds like such a bad influence."

"It'll be all right," my husband said reassuringly. "Bound to be people like Charles in the world. Might as well meet them now as later."

On Monday Laurie came home late, full of news. "Charles," he shouted as he came up the hill. I was waiting anxiously on the front steps. "Charles," Laurie yelled all the way up the hill. "Charles was bad again."

"Come right in," I said, as soon as he came close enough. "Lunch is waiting."

"You know what Charles did?" he demanded, following me through the door. "Charles yelled so in school they sent a boy in from first grade to tell the teacher she had to make Charles keep quiet, and so Charles had to stay after school. And so all the children stayed to watch him."

"What did he do?" I asked.

"He just sat there," Laurie said, climbing into his chair at the table. "Hi, Pop, y'old dust mop."

"Charles had to stay after school today," I told my husband. "Everyone stayed with him."

"What does this Charles look like?" my husband asked Laurie. "What's his other name?"

"He's bigger than me," Laurie said. "And he doesn't have any rubbers and he doesn't ever wear a jacket."

Monday night was the first Parent-

---

insanely (in SAYN lee) in an uncontrolled, mentally unsound way; senselessly

privilege (PRIV uh lij) special right; opportunity

Teachers meeting, and only the fact that the baby had a cold kept me from going. I wanted passionately to meet Charles's mother. On Tuesday Laurie remarked suddenly, "Our teacher had a friend come to see her in school today."

"Charles's mother?" my husband and I asked simultaneously.

"Naaah," Laurie said scornfully. "It was a man who came and made us do exercises; we had to touch our toes. Look." He climbed down from his chair

---

passionately (PASH uh nit lee) in a very caring and emotional way

and squatted down and touched his toes. "Like this," he said. He got solemnly back into his chair and said, picking up his fork, "Charles didn't even do exercises."

"That's fine," I said heartily. "Didn't Charles want to do exercises?"

"Naaah," Laurie said. "Charles was so fresh to the teacher's friend he wasn't *let* do exercises."

"Fresh again?" I said.

"He kicked the teacher's friend," Laurie said. "The teacher's friend told Charles to touch his toes like I just did, and Charles kicked him."

"What are they going to do about Charles, you suppose?" Laurie's father asked him.

Laurie shrugged elaborately. "Throw him out of school, I guess," he said.

Wednesday and Thursday were routine. Charles yelled during story hour and hit a boy in the stomach and made him cry. On Friday Charles stayed after school and so did all the other children.

With the third week of kindergarten Charles was an institution in our family: The baby was being a Charles when she cried all afternoon. Laurie did a Charles when he filled his wagon full of mud and pulled it through the kitchen. Even my husband, when he caught his elbow in the telephone cord and pulled the telephone, ashtray, and a bowl of flowers off the table, said, after the first minute, "Looks like Charles."

During the third and fourth weeks it looked like a reformation in Charles. Laurie reported grimly at lunch on Thursday of the third week, "Charles was so good today the teacher gave him an apple."

"What?" I said, and my husband added warily, "You mean Charles?"

"Charles," Laurie said. "He gave the crayons around and he picked up the books afterward and the teacher said he was her helper."

"What happened?" I asked incredulously.

"He was her helper, that's all," Laurie said, and shrugged.

"Can this be true, about Charles?" I asked my husband that night. "Can something like this happen?"

"Wait and see," my husband said cynically. "When you've got a Charles to deal with, this may mean he's only plotting."

He seemed to be wrong. For over a week Charles was the teacher's helper. Each day he handed things out and he picked things up. No one had to stay after school.

"The P.T.A. meeting's next week again," I told my husband one evening.

---

routine (roo TEEN) ordinary; predictable
institution (in stih TOO shun) an established custom, practice or law; a regular part of something
reformation (ref ur MAY shun) a process of changing behavior for the better
incredulously (in KREJ uho lus lee) in a shocked and unbelieving way
cynically (SIN ik lee) in a manner that shows one doesn't really believe what one hears; distrustful

"I'm going to find Charles's mother there."

"Ask her what happened to Charles," my husband said. "I'd like to know."

"I'd like to know myself," I said.

On Friday of that week things were back to normal. "You know what Charles did today?" Laurie demanded at the lunch table, in a voice slightly awed. "He told a little girl to say a word and she said it and the teacher washed her mouth out with soap and Charles laughed."

---

awed (AWD) very impressed; extremely respectful

"What word?" his father asked quite unwisely, and Laurie said, "I'll whisper it to you, it's so bad." He got down off his chair and went around to his father. His father bent his head down and Laurie whispered joyfully. His father's eyes widened.

"Did Charles tell the little girl to say *that?"* he asked respectfully.

"She said it *twice,"* Laurie said. "Charles told her to say it *twice."*

"What happened to Charles?" my husband asked.

"Nothing," Laurie said. "He was passing out the crayons."

Monday morning Charles abandoned the little girl and said the evil word himself three or four times, getting his mouth washed out with soap each time. He also threw chalk.

My husband came to the door with me that evening as I set out for the P.T.A. meeting. "Invite her over for a cup of tea after the meeting," he said. "I want to get a look at her."

"If only she's there," I said prayerfully.

"She'll be there," my husband said. "I don't see how they could hold a P.T.A. meeting without Charles's mother."

At the meeting I sat restlessly, scanning each comfortable face, trying to determine which one hid the secret of Charles. None of them looked to me haggard enough. No one stood up in the meeting and apologized for the way her son had been acting. No one mentioned Charles.

After the meeting I identified and sought out Laurie's kindergarten teacher. She had a plate with a cup of tea and a piece of chocolate cake. I had a plate with a cup of tea and a piece of marshmallow cake. We maneuvered up to one another cautiously, and smiled.

"I've been so anxious to meet you," I said. "I'm Laurie's mother."

"We're all so interested in Laurie," she said.

"Well, he certainly likes kindergarten," I said. "He talks about it all the time."

"We had a little trouble adjusting the first week or so," she said primly, "but now he's a fine little helper. With occasional lapses, of course."

"Laurie adjusts very quickly," I said. "I suppose this time it's Charles's influence."

"Charles?"

"Yes," I said, laughing, "you must have your hands full in that kindergarten with Charles."

"Charles?" she said. "We don't have any Charles in the kindergarten."

---

haggard (HAG urd) worn out and tired looking
maneuver (muh NOO vur) move in a way that makes contact easiest
primly (PRIM lee) extremely properly and carefully
lapse (LAPS) failure; interruption

Shirley Jackson

(1919–1965)

During her brief but fertile career, Shirley Jackson became one of the most popular writers of her time. She made her readers laugh with warm, funny magazine articles about family life. She also thrilled them with haunting, suspenseful stories about the darker side of human nature.

Shirley Jackson was born in San Francisco, California and moved to New York at the age of fourteen. Throughout her childhood she kept diaries and wrote poems. Much of Jackson's early writing shows a lively interest in superstition and in the elements of magic.

Shirley Jackson recognized the importance of self-discipline. As a teenager, she trained herself to write at least 1,000 words a day. Her serious efforts paid off. At Syracuse University, she wrote many short stories and news articles for the campus magazine.

The year following her graduation was an exciting one for the young author. In 1940, Shirley Jackson got married and published her first short story. She also moved to the town of Bennington, Vermont, where she devoted herself to writing and raising a family of four children.

On June 28, 1948 Shirley Jackson's life changed dramatically. Her story, "The Lottery" was published, and it became an immediate literary "hit." Readers were fascinated by Jackson's ideas about superstition, prejudice, and fear. They were shocked to discover how people really behave when their own lives are threatened. They wanted to learn more about the author of this chilling story.

Shirley Jackson however, closely guarded her privacy. She refused to give interviews and rarely talked in public about her writing. She believed that a writer's only job was to catch the reader's attention and hold it by telling a good story. She wanted her work to "speak for itself." Shirley Jackson accomplished her goals in novels, short stories, humorous magazine articles, children's books, and in plays.

FOCUS ON THE SELECTION

UNDERSTAND THE SELECTION

Recall

1. Where does Laurie meet the character he calls Charles?
2. What were some things Charles did?
3. Who is the real Charles?

Infer

4. Describe the kind of person you think Charles is.
5. What do Laurie's family mean when they say someone is "a Charles"?
6. How did Charles's behavior change as time passed?
7. Why do you think Laurie invented the character named Charles?

Apply

8. Imagine you were Laurie's mother. How do you think she felt when she found out the truth about Charles?
9. Predict what will happen when Laurie's mother gets home after the PTA meeting.
10. What hints in the story point to the possibility that Charles is Laurie?

Respond to Literature

Laurie's mother has certain ideas about Charles's family. How might her ideas change when she finds out that Laurie is really Charles?

WRITE ABOUT THE SELECTION

Imagine that Laurie's mother had not been able to go to the PTA meeting. In the stories that Laurie tells, Charles most likely would have gone on misbehaving. Write another incident for "Charles." In your incident, explain what Charles has done to cause a new problem in school.

Prewriting: Decide what Charles has done. Make a brief, informal outline. Include events and details in your outline that lead up to Charles's behavior. It would add to the humor of the story to make the incident quite different from the earlier incidents. Use your imagination. Include a section that describes what happens to Charles after the incident.

Writing: Use your informal outline to write the incident. You may include ideas that occur to you as you write. Your outline is really a guide. When you are actually writing, you will have a better sense of what to add and what to leave out.

Revising: Remember how the author gave hints that Laurie and Charles were the same person? Reread your draft. Add a story clue that suggests that Laurie may be Charles. Be sure your clue does not give away the ending.

Proofreading: Each paragraph should contain one main idea. Include a strong topic sentence and indent the first word in each paragraph. Check internal punctuation. End each sentence with a period, a question mark, or an exclamation mark.

THINK ABOUT PLOT

Story clues can help you predict the events of the plot. These clues can be missed if you read too quickly or without thinking. A good reader watches for story clues and uses them to guess what will happen next in the plot.

1. What changes does the author observe in Laurie at the very beginning of the story?
2. How does Laurie act when he mentions Charles for the first time?
3. What story clue tells you that Laurie could be Charles when Charles has to stay after school?
4. What clue tells you Laurie might be Charles when Charles begins to reform?
5. What clue is there in the teacher's conversation that tells us Laurie is Charles?

DEVELOP YOUR VOCABULARY

Many adverbs can be recognized by their *-ly* endings. Write words from the vocabulary list to answer the questions below.

era	cynically
lapse	fresh
reformation	incredulously
insolently	institution
passionately	primly
renounce	routine

1. Which word is an adverb meaning "in a sneering, sarcastic way"?
2. Which word is an adverb meaning "in a doubtful or unbelieving way"?
3. Which word is an adverb meaning "in a stiff, formal way"?
4. Which word is an adverb meaning "in a rude, arrogant way"?
5. Which word is an adverb meaning "in a way that shows strong feelings"?

Learn About

Point of View

A story can be told from many positions. It might be told by someone who knows everything, or by someone who knows only a few useful facts. The position from which a story is told is called **point of view.**

In the **first-person** point of view, the author is one of the characters in the story. This character can tell its own thoughts and feelings, but it does not know the thoughts and feelings of other characters. This character is as surprised as the readers are by a plot twist at the end of the story.

Authors sometimes use the first-person point of view because they want us to share their surprise at the ways things turn out in a story. There would be no surprise if we knew the thoughts and feelings of every character.

As you read "Mother in Mannville," ask yourself:

1. From whose point of view is this story told?
2. Why did the author choose this point of view?

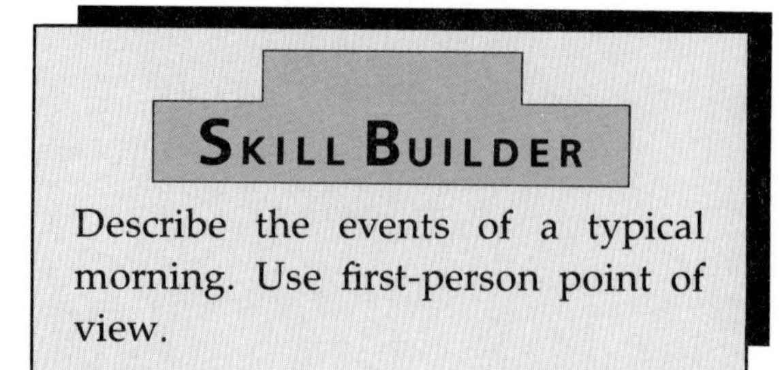

Skill Builder
Describe the events of a typical morning. Use first-person point of view.

A MOTHER IN MANNVILLE

by Marjorie Kinnan Rawlings

The orphanage is high in the Carolina mountains. Sometimes in winter the snowdrifts are so deep that the school and living quarters are cut off from the village below, from all the world. Fog hides the mountain peaks. The snow swirls down the valleys. And a wind blows so bitterly that the orphanage boys who take the milk twice daily to the baby cottage reach the door with fingers stiff in an agony of numbness.

"Or when we carry trays from the cookhouse for the ones that are sick," Jerry said, "we get our faces frostbit, because we can't put our hands over them. I have gloves," he added. "Some of the boys don't have any."

He liked the late spring, he said. The rhododendron was in bloom, a carpet of color, across the mountainsides, soft as the May winds. He called it laurel.

"It's pretty when the laurel blooms," he said. "Some of it's pink and some of it's white."

I was there in autumn. I wanted quiet, isolation, to do some troublesome writing. I was homesick, too, for the flaming of maples in October, and for corn shocks and pumpkins and black-walnut trees and the lift of hills. I found them all, living in a cabin that belonged to the orphanage, half a mile beyond the orphanage farm. When I took the cabin, I asked for a boy or man to come and chop wood for the fireplace. The first few days were warm. I found what wood I needed about the cabin. No one came, and I forgot the order.

I looked up from my typewriter one late afternoon, a little startled. A boy stood at the door, and my pointer dog, my companion, was at his side and had not barked to warn me. The boy was probably twelve years old, but undersized. He wore overalls and a torn shirt, and was barefooted.

He said, "I can chop some wood today."

---

agony (AG uh nee) great pain
isolation (eye suh LAY shun) being alone; away from others

I said, "But I have a boy coming from the orphanage."

"I'm the boy."

"You? But you're small."

"Size don't matter, chopping wood," he said. "Some of the big boys don't chop good. I've been chopping wood at the orphanage a long time."

I pictured a small pile of mangled branches for my fires. I was well into my work and not interested in conversation. I was a little plain spoken.

"Very well. There's the ax. Go ahead and see what you can do."

I went back to work, closing the door. At first the sound of the boy dragging brush annoyed me. Then he began to chop. The blows were rhythmic and steady. Shortly I had forgotten him, the sound no more of an interruption than a steady rain. I suppose an hour and a half passed, for when I stopped and stretched, and heard the boy's steps on the cabin stoop, the sun was dropping behind the farthest mountain.

The boy said, "I have to go to supper now. I can come again tomorrow evening."

I said, "I'll pay you now for what you've done," thinking I should probably have to insist on an older boy. "Ten cents an hour?"

"Anything is all right."

We went together back of the cabin. An astonishing amount of solid wood had been cut. There were cherry logs and heavy roots of rhododendron, and blocks from the waste pine and oak left from the building of the cabin.

"But you've done as much as a man," I said. "This is a splendid pile."

I looked at him, actually, for the first time. His hair was the color of the corn shocks, and his eyes, very direct, were like the mountain sky when rain is pending—gray, with a showing of that miraculous blue. As I spoke a light came over him, as though the setting sun had touched him with the same overspreading glory with which it touched the mountains. I gave him a quarter.

"You may come tomorrow," I said, "and thank you very much."

He looked at me, and at the coin, and seemed to want to speak, but could not, and turned away.

"I'll split the kindling tomorrow," he said over his thin ragged shoulder. "You'll need kindling and medium wood and logs and backlogs."

At daylight I was half awakened by the sound of chopping. Again it was so even in texture that I went back to sleep. When I left my bed in the cool morning, the boy had come and gone, and a stack of kindling was neat against the cabin wall. He came again after school in the afternoon and worked until time to return to the orphanage. His name was Jerry; he was twelve years old, and he had been at the orphanage since he was four. I could picture him at four, with the same grave gray-blue eyes and the same —independence? No, the word that

---

mangled (MANG guld) twisted
kindling (KIND ling) small pieces of wood used for starting a fire

comes to me is "integrity."

The word means something very special to me, and the quality for which I use it is a rare one. My father had it—but almost no one I know has it with the clarity, the purity, the simplicity of a mountain stream. But the boy Jerry had it. It is bedded on courage, but it is more than brave. It is honest, but it is more than honesty. The ax handle broke one day. Jerry said the woodshop at the orphanage would repair it. I brought money to pay for the job and he refused it.

"I'll pay for it," he said. "I broke it. I brought the ax down careless."

"But no one hits accurately every time," I told him. "The fault was in the wood of the handle. I'll see the man from whom I bought it."

It was only then that he would take the money. He was standing back of his own carelessness. He was a free-will agent and he chose to do careful work, and if he failed, he took the responsibility for it.

And he did for me the unnecessary thing, the kind and thoughtful thing, that we find done only by the great of heart. Things no training can teach, for they are done on the instant, and not based on experience. He found a cubbyhole beside the fireplace that I had not noticed. There, of his own accord, he put kindling and "medium" wood, so that I might always have dry fire material ready in case of sudden wet weather. A stone was loose in the rough walk to the cabin. He dug a deeper hole and steadied it, although he came, himself, by a shortcut over the bank. I found that when I tried to return his thoughtfulness with such things as candy and apples, he was wordless. "Thank you" was, perhaps, an expression for which he had had no use, for his courtesy was natural. He only looked at the gift and then at me, and a curtain lifted, so that I saw deep into the clear well of his eyes. Gratitude was there, and affection, soft over the firm rock of his character.

He made simple excuses to come and sit with me. I could no more have turned him away than if he had been physically hungry. I suggested once that the best time for us to visit was just before supper, when I left off my writing. After that, he waited always until my typewriter had been quiet for some time. One day I worked until nearly dark. I went outside the cabin, having forgotten him. I saw him going up over the hill in the twilight toward the orphanage. When I sat down on my stoop, a place was warm from his body where he had been sitting.

He became close, of course, with my pointer, Pat. There is a strange understanding between a boy and a dog. Perhaps they possess the same singleness of spirit, the same kind of wisdom. It is difficult to explain, but it exists. When I

---

integrity (in TEG rih tee) honesty; uprightness; wholeness of being
clarity (KLAR uh tee) clearness
accurately (AK yur it lee) perfectly on target
gratitude (GRAT ih tood) thankfulness
possess (puh ZES) have; own

went across the state for a weekend, I left the dog in Jerry's charge. I gave him the dog whistle and the key to the cabin, and left enough food. He was to come two or three times a day and let out the dog, and feed and exercise him. I should return Sunday night, and Jerry would take out the dog for the last time Sunday afternoon and then leave the key under an agreed hiding place.

My return was delayed and fog filled the mountain passes so that I dared not drive at night. The fog held the next morning, and it was Monday noon before I reached the cabin. The dog had been fed and cared for that morning. Jerry came early in the afternoon, anxious.

"The superintendent said nobody would drive in the fog," he said. "I came just before bedtime last night and you hadn't come. So I brought Pat some of my breakfast this morning. I wouldn't have let anything happen to him."

"I was sure of that. I didn't worry."

"When I heard about the fog, I thought you'd know."

He was needed for work at the orphanage and he had to return at once. I gave him a dollar in payment, and he looked at it and went away. But that night he came in the darkness and knocked at the door.

"Come in, Jerry," I said, "if you're allowed to be away this late."

"I told maybe a story," he said. "I told them I thought you would want to see me."

"That's true," I assured him, and I saw his relief. "I want to hear about how you managed with the dog."

He sat by the fire with me, with no other light, and told me of their two days together. The dog lay close to him, and found a comfort there that I did not have for him. And it seemed to me that being with my dog, and caring for him, had brought the boy and me, too, together, so that he felt that he belonged to me as well as to the animal.

"He stayed right with me," he told me, "except when he ran in the laurel. He likes the laurel. I took him up over the hill and we both ran fast. There was a place where the grass was high and I lay down in it and hid. I could hear Pat hunting for me. He found my trail and he barked. When he finally found me, he acted crazy, and he ran around and around me, in circles."

We watched the flames.

"That's an apple log," he said. "It burns the prettiest of any wood."

We were very close.

He suddenly needed to speak of things he had not spoken of before, nor had I cared to ask him.

"You look a little bit like my mother," he said, "Especially in the dark, by the fire."

"But you were only four, Jerry, when you came here. You have remembered how she looked, all these years?"

"My mother lives in Mannville," he said.

For a moment, finding that he had a mother shocked me as greatly as anything in my life has ever done. I did not know why it disturbed me. Then I understood my distress. I was filled with a passionate resentment that any woman should go away and leave her son. A fresh anger added itself. A son like this one. . . . The orphanage was a wholesome place, the officials were kind, good people, the food was more than adequate, the boys were healthy, a ragged shirt was no hardship, nor the doing of clean labor. Granted, perhaps, that the boy felt no lack, what about the mother? At four he would have looked the same as now. Nothing, I thought, nothing in life could change those eyes. His quality must be apparent to an idiot, a fool. I burned with questions I could not ask. In any of them, I was afraid, there would be pain.

"Have you seen her, Jerry—lately?"

"I see her every summer. She sends for me."

I wanted to cry out. "Why are you not with her? How can she let you go away again?"

He said, "She comes up here from Mannville whenever she can. She doesn't have a job now."

His face shone in the firelight.

"She wanted to give me a puppy, but they can't let any one boy keep a puppy. You remember the suit I had on last Sunday?" He was plainly proud. "She sent me that for Christmas. The Christmas before that"—he drew a long breath, enjoying the memory—"she sent me a pair of skates."

"Roller skates?"

My mind was busy, making pictures of her, trying to understand her. She had not, then, entirely deserted or forgotten him. But why, then. . . . I thought, "But I must not condemn her without knowing more."

"Roller skates. I let the other boys use them. They're always borrowing them. But they're careful of them."

What fact other than poverty. . . .

"I'm going to take the dollar you gave me for taking care of Pat," he said, "and buy her a pair of gloves."

I could only say, "That will be nice. Do you know her size?"

"I think it's eight and a half," he said.

He looked at my hands.

"Do you wear eight and a half?" he asked.

"No. I wear a smaller size, a six."

"Oh! Then I guess her hands are bigger than yours."

I hated her. Poverty or no, there was other food than bread, and the soul could starve as quickly as the body. He was taking his dollar to buy gloves for her big stupid hands, and she lived away from him, in Mannville, perfectly content with sending him skates.

"She likes white gloves," he said. "Do you think I can get them for a dollar?"

"I think so," I said.

I decided that I should not leave the

---

passionate (PASH uh nit) full of strong feeling
resentment (rih ZENT munt) feeling of being insulted or treated unfairly
adequate (AD ih kwit) enough
condemn (kun DEM) pronounce guilty; to convict

mountains without seeing her and knowing for myself why she had done this thing.

The human mind scatters its interests as though made of thistledown, and every wind stirs and moves it. I finished my work. It did not please me, and I gave my thoughts to another field. I should need some Mexican material.

I made arrangements to close my Florida place. Mexico immediately, and doing the writing there. Then, Alaska with my brother. After that, heaven knew what or where.

I did not take time to go to Mannville to see Jerry's mother, nor even to talk with the orphanage officials about her. My mind was busy with my work and my plans. And after my first fury at her—we did not speak of her again—his having a mother not far away, in Mannville, relieved me of the ache I had had about him. He did not question the odd relation. He was not lonely. It was none of my concern.

He came every day and cut my wood and did small helpful favors and stayed to talk. The days had become cold, and often I let him come inside the cabin. He would lie on the floor in front of the fire, with one arm across the pointer, and they would both doze and wait quietly for me. Other days they ran with a common ecstasy through the laurel, and since the asters were now gone, he brought me back red maple leaves, and chestnut boughs dripping with a grand yellow. I was ready to go.

I said to him, "You have been my good friend, Jerry. I shall often think of you and miss you. Pat will miss you too. I am leaving tomorrow."

He did not answer. When he went away, I remember that a new moon hung over the mountains, and I watched him go in silence up the hill. I expected him the next day, but he did not come. The details of packing my personal belongings, loading my car, arranging the bed over the seat, where the dog would ride, occupied me until late in the day. I closed the cabin and started the car, noticing that the sun was in the west and I should do well to be out of the mountains by nightfall. I stopped by the orphanage and left the cabin key and money for my light bill with Miss Clark.

"And will you call Jerry for me to say good-by to him?"

"I don't know where he is," she said. "I'm afraid he's not well. He didn't eat his dinner this noon. One of the boys saw him going over the hill into the laurel. He was supposed to fire the boiler this afternoon. It's not like him; he's unusually reliable."

I was almost relieved, for I knew I should never see him again, and it would be easier not to say good-by to him.

I said, "I wanted to talk with you about his mother—why he's here—but I'm in more of a hurry than I expected to be. It's out of the question for me to see her now. But here's some money I'd like to leave with you to buy things for him at Christmas and on his birthday. It will be better than for me to try to send him things. I could so easily duplicate—skates, for instance."

She blinked her honest eyes.

"There's not much use for skates here," she said.

Her stupidity annoyed me.

"What I mean," I said, "is that I don't want to duplicate things his mother sends him. I might have chosen skates if I didn't know she had already given them to him."

"I don't understand," she said. "He has no mother. He has no skates."

---

duplicate (DOO plih kayt) repeat; do the same thing

Marjorie Kinnan Rawlings

(1896-1953)

Marjorie Kinnan Rawlings was born in Washington, D.C., and educated at the University of Wisconsin. She worked for newspapers in Kentucky and New York while writing short stories.

Her newspaper career was successful, but her short stories were not. Finally, in 1928, she left her newspaper job and moved to the backwoods of Florida. There she found a place and people that moved her to write with understanding and deep sympathy. Her stories began to be accepted for publication. In 1938 her novel *The Yearling* appeared. It won a Pulitzer Prize and was turned into a movie. The novel's main character has been called "one of the most appealing boy characters since Huckleberry Finn."

FOCUS ON THE SELECTION

UNDERSTAND THE SELECTION

Recall

1. What does the author do in order to make a living?
2. Where does the author meet Jerry?
3. What are the author's feelings about Jerry's mother?

Infer

4. Why do you think the author needs Jerry's help?
5. How does the author feel when Jerry describes his mother?
6. Why do you think Jerry invents a mother in Mannville?
7. How does the author learn the truth about Jerry's mother?

Apply

8. Imagine you were Jerry. How do you suppose he felt about telling a lie?
9. Predict what the author might do now that she has learned the truth about Jerry.
10. Dramatize the scene between Jerry and the author at her fireside when he talks about his mother.

Respond to Literature

What kind of "family" does Jerry belong to?

WRITE ABOUT THE SELECTION

Imagine that the author wanted to write a letter to Jerry after she had arrived in Mexico. What might she have said to him? Based on what you know about the ending, write a letter that Rawlings might have sent.

Prewriting: It may be helpful to remember that the story tells you almost nothing about the author's background. You can guess that she admired her father, but nothing is said of her mother, or brothers and sisters. As you explore your thoughts about the story, try to imagine whether she has had children of her own. If not, how would this effect her thinking about Jerry? Before you begin, think about the events of the story. What might the author want to say to Jerry? What story details tell you topics the author might discuss? Make a list of topics Rawlings's letter might have included. Add details to your list to tell more about each topic. Put your topics in the order you will discuss them.

Writing: Use your list of topics and details to write your letter. You may choose to rearrange the order of the details or to add or eliminate ideas as you go along.

Revising: Each topic should have its own paragraph. Be sure you begin each paragraph with a topic sentence that states the main idea of the paragraph.

Proofreading: Does your letter contain the five parts of a friendly letter? Be sure to include the heading, greeting, body, closing, and signature.

THINK ABOUT POINT OF VIEW

First person point of view helps us see the events of a story through the eyes of one of the characters. We know and feel the same things this character knows and feels. There are clues to tell us whose point of view we are reading.

1. What pronouns does the author use in describing herself?
2. Does the story describe Jerry's feelings or thoughts?
3. How do we know anything about what Jerry thinks?
4. Do we know why Jerry disappears at the end of the story?
5. From whose point of view is the story told?

DEVELOP YOUR VOCABULARY

There are several suffixes that turn other parts of speech into nouns.

-ity as in *integrity*
-ion as in *isolation*
-ment as in *resentment*

Turn each of the words below into a noun by adding one of the noun suffixes from the list above.

1. resent
2. uniform
3. invent
4. collect
5. fatal
6. punish
7. enjoy
8. timid
9. enjoy
10. erupt
11. act
12. odd
13. content
14. connect
15. state
16. perfect

FOCUS ON...

Fiction means stories that are not true. A fictional story may contain characters who really existed or include events that actually happened, but the story itself is not a true story. Most of the selections in this book are fiction.

Fictional selections have four main characteristics: **plot, theme, setting,** and **characters.**

Plot. The plot is the series of planned incidents of the story. A plot tells what happened to the people in the story. A fictional plot may contain some events that actually happened. For example, a fictional story about the American Revolution might include the Battle of Bunker Hill. However, the main characters of the story did not exist, so the story itself is not true.

Theme. This is the basic meaning of the story. A theme is a main idea or even a "message." You have to think about the events of the story to understand the theme. Suppose the main character tells a lie and then finds that his friends and family are angry with him. The theme might be that being honest is the best way to live.

Most themes try to tell you some truth about life or about growing up. Think about some of the selections you have read in this book. What kinds of themes did these selections have?

Setting. The time and place of a story is its setting. The setting may be historical; perhaps the story takes place in Virginia during the American Civil War. A setting may be fantasy such as a magical island that floats above the earth. Stories can take place today, in the faraway past, or in the distant future. Usually stories that take place in the future are called **science fiction.** It is important to understand the setting of a story. You have to know *where* and *when* events take place in order to see their overall importance.

Characters. The characters are the people in the story. There will be a main character or characters who are most important in the story. The story tells what happens to these characters. There are other characters as well, but they are not as important. They may appear only in parts of the book, or they may appear in the whole book but not have a very important part in the events of the book. Who were the main characters in the selections in this unit?

Sometimes authors want to write about historical events, but they also want to write fiction. Such writers include real people in their stories. If they do this, they must be sure the real characters appear when they were alive and in places they actually lived. You could not have a story taking place in the 1920s with Julius Caesar as one of the characters. The details of these real characters' lives may be made up, but the actual facts of their lives cannot be changed. What stories have you read that contain real characters in fictional situations?

Why Read Fiction? Fiction helps you travel to other times and places. You can share adventures with people your own age or people who are in no way like you. Fiction helps you think about problem solving. You ask yourself as you read, "What would I do in this situation? Did this character behave the way I would behave?"

You can also learn from fiction. You can see what happens when people help each other or when they tell lies. You can see how people feel when they find a missing friend or when they steal from others. You can learn a lot about yourself and about life by reading fiction selections. Think about fiction you have read. What lessons did you learn from these stories?

SWEET POTATO PIE

by Eugenia Collier

From up here on the fourteenth floor, my brother Charley looks like an insect. A deep feeling of love surges through me. I watch him moving quickly down Fifth Avenue to his shabby taxicab. In a moment, he will be heading back uptown.

STUDY HINTS
Identify the setting of the story

I turn from the window and flop down on the bed. I think about the cheerful cleanliness of my hotel room. It is a world away from Charley's apartment in Harlem. It's a hundred worlds away from the shack where he and I grew up.

Who is the main character being described here?

As far as I know, Charley never had any childhood at all. The oldest children of sharecroppers never do. Mama and Pa were shadowy figures. I heard their voices in the morning when sleep was shallow. I glimpsed them as they left for the field before I

---

surge (SURJ) build up; fill
shabby (SHAB ee) run-down; beat-up
sharecropper (SHAIR krop ur) someone who farms land in return for a share of the harvest
glimpse (GLIMPS) to see for only a short time

was fully awake. I would glimpse them again at night. They would trudge wearily into the house when my lids were heavy.

They came into sharp focus only on special occasions. One such occasion was the day when the crops were in. That was the day the sharecroppers were paid. In our cabin, there was a lot of excitement on that day. Even I, the "baby," responded to it.

How has the setting changed?

For weeks we had been running out of things that we could neither grow nor get on credit. Now we would gather around the rough wooden table. I would be sitting on Lil's lap or clinging to Charley's neck. Little Alberta would be nervously tugging at her braid. Jamie would be crouched at Mama's elbow. For once, all seven of us were silent, waiting.

Pa would place the money on the table. He did it gently, for the money was made from the sweat of their bodies and from their children's tears. Mama would count it out in little piles.

"This for store bill," she would mutter, making a little pile. "This for church collection. This for piece of gingham." She stretched the money as tight over our needs as Jamie's outgrown pants stretched over my bottom.

How is the plot affected by the family's poverty?

"Well," she would say finally, "that's the crop." She would look up at Pa and add, "It'll do." Pa's face would relax. Then a general grin flitted from child to child. We would survive, at least for the present.

The other time my parents were more than dream figures was in church. On Sundays, we wore our threadbare Sunday-go-to-meeting clothes. We would tramp with the neighbors to the Tabernacle Baptist Church. It was a frail building of bare boards that was all my parents ever knew of a future promise.

Describe the author as a character in this part of the story.

In church, my father sat like a silhouette framed against the sunny window. My mother's face would change with her emo-

---

trudge (TRUJ) walk slowly and heavily
wearily (WIR uh lee) in a tired way
clinging (KLING ing) holding tightly
crouched (KROUCHT) bent low
mutter (MUT ur) speak softly and not clearly
gingham (GING um) a kind of printed cotton cloth
flit (FLIT) flutter; move lightly and quickly
threadbare (THRED bair) old and worn
frail (FRAYL) weak; fragile
silhouette (sil oo ET) outline drawing of a person or object, filled in with a dark color

tions. She would move from a quiet "amen" to a loud "Help me, Jesus." All of it was wrung from the depths of her gaunt frame.

These early memories of my parents are associated with special occasions. My everyday memories are of Lil and Charley, the oldest children. They kept the rest of us in line while Pa and Mama worked in fields they did not own. Not until years later did I realize that Lil and Charley were little more than children themselves.

Lil had the loudest voice in the county. She'd yell, "Boy, you better get yourself in here!" And you *got* yourself in there. It was Lil who caught and bathed us. She fed us and sent us to school. Her laughter was as loud as her voice. When she laughed, everybody laughed. And when Lil sang, everybody listened.

Charley was taller than anybody in the world. I spent a lot of

How would you describe Charley as a character?

---

gaunt (GAWNT) thin; worn

time on his shoulders in the earliest years. From that level, the world looked different. I looked down at tops of heads, instead of up at chins.

As I grew older, Charley became more of a father than a brother. I remember his slender dark hands whittling a toy from a chunk of wood. I can see his quick fingers guiding a charred stick over a bit of paper. A wondrous picture would take shape. It might be Jamie's face, or Alberta's rag doll, or our bony brown dog.

Some memories are more than fragmentary. I can still feel the *whap* of that wet dishrag across my mouth. I had developed a stutter, and Charley was determined to cure it. Someone had told him a slap with a wet rag was a good cure. Whenever I began, "Let's g-g-g—," *whap!* would come the rag.

Charley would always insist, "I don't want to hurt you none, Buddy." Then he'd *whap* me again.

I don't know when or why I stopped stuttering. But I stopped.

What part of the plot is explained in these paragraphs?

Ignorance and superstition hunted us like hawks. We sought education feverishly—and for most of us, futilely. All our energies had to go into survival. Each child had to leave school and carry his share of the eternal burden.

Eventually, the family's hopes for learning fastened on me. I remember one day when I was five years old. Pa sat on a rickety stool near the coal stove. He took me on his knee and studied me gravely.

"Well, boy," he said, "I hope you don't have to depend on looks for what you get in this world. If you do, you just as well quit right now." His hand was rough from the plow. But it was gentle as it touched my cheek. "Lucky for you, you got a *mind.* And that's something ain't everybody has got. You go to school,

---

charred (CHAHRD) burned
fragmentary (FRAG mun ter ee) in pieces; shattered
ignorance (IG nuh runs) lack of knowledge
superstition (soo pur STISH un) belief or attitude based on fear or ignorance
feverishly (FEE vur ish lee) hurriedly; excitedly
futilely (FYOOT ul ee) uselessly; with no effect
eternal (ih TUR nul) lasting forever
burden (BURD un) load to be carried
rickety (RIK it ee) weak; likely to fall apart
gravely (GRAYV lee) very seriously

boy. Get yourself some learning. Make something of yourself. Ain't nothing you can't do if you got learning."

Charley was determined that I would break the chain of poverty. He said I would "be somebody." As we worked the land, Charley would say, "You ain't gon be no poor farmer, Buddy. You gon be a teacher. Or maybe a doctor or a lawyer."

What do we learn about Charley's character in this paragraph?

I loved school with a passion. The feeling increased when I began to realize how my family struggled to keep me there. The cramped, dingy classroom became a battleground where I was the winner. I stayed on top of my class. I out-read, out-figured, and out-spelled the country boys who mocked my poverty.

What kind of character is the author?

As the years passed, the economic strain was eased enough for me to go to high school. There were fewer mouths to feed, for one thing. Alberta went North to find work at sixteen. Jamie died at twelve.

I finished high school at the head of my class. My graduation suit was the first suit that was all my own. On graduation night, our cabin was a collection of nerves. I thought Charley would drive me mad.

"Buddy, you ain't pressed them pants right. . . . Can't you get a better shine on them shoes? . . . Look how you done messed up that tie!"

The combination of Charley's nerves and my own made me explode. "Man, cut it out!" I yelled.

Charley relaxed a little. "Sure, Buddy," he said. "But you gotta look good. You *somebody.*"

What do you learn about Charley here?

I have forgotten the speech I made that night. But the sight of Mama and Pa and the rest is burned in my memory. Pa held his head high, his eyes loving and fierce. For Mama, I believe this moment was the high point of her life. And Charley looked as if he were in the presence of something sacred.

How would you describe Mama and Pa's characters at this point?

I gave the speech. But I felt as if part of me were standing outside watching the whole thing. I saw their proud faces. And I

---

poverty (POV ur tee) having little or no money; condition of being very poor
passion (PASH un) strong feeling
cramped (KRAMPT) small and crowded
dingy (DIN jee) dirty-colored; not bright or clean
mock (MOK) make fun of
economic (ek uh NOM ik) having to do with income and expenses
fierce (FIRS) strong; intense

thought of their own potential, all lost with their sweat in the fields. I realized at that moment that I wasn't necessarily the smartest. I was only the youngest.

What events helped the author to go to college?

And the luckiest. The war came along, and I exchanged three years of my life (and a good amount of blood) for the GI Bill. That led to a college education.

Now, the old house was empty. We were all scattered in different places. I got married, went to graduate school, and had kids. I became a professor, with a wider waistline and thinner hair.

My mind spins off those years. I am back to this afternoon and today's Charley. He's still long and lean, still gentle-eyed. And he's still my greatest fan.

How has the setting changed at this point?

I didn't tell Charley I would be in New York for a professional meeting. He and Bea would have spent days fixing up. I wanted to drop in before they had a chance to stiffen.

Yesterday and this morning were taken up with meetings in the fancy Fifth Avenue hotel. It was a place we could not have dreamed of in our childhood. Late this afternoon, I broke loose and headed for Harlem. Leaving the glitter of downtown, I entered the subway. When I emerged, I was in Harlem.

Whenever I come to Harlem, I feel as if I were coming home. There is something mysterious about the place. It is as if all black people began and ended there.

I joined the crowds on Lenox Avenue and headed for Charley's apartment. Along the way, I enjoyed the panorama of Harlem. Women trudging home with shopping bags. Little kids flitting through the crowds. Groups of adolescent boys striding boldly along—some noisy, some ominously silent. Tables of merchandise for sale spread on sidewalks. A blaring microphone sending forth words to draw people into a church. Defeated men

---

potential (puh TEN shul) something that can happen, but which has not happened yet; possibility
glitter (GLIT ur) bright sparkling light
emerge (ih MURJ) come out from something or someplace
panorama (pan uh RAM uh) full view; complete picture
adolescent (ad ul ES unt) teen-age
striding (STRYD ing) walking with long, quick steps
ominously (OM uh nus lee) threateningly
blaring (BLAIR ing) making loud and rough sounds

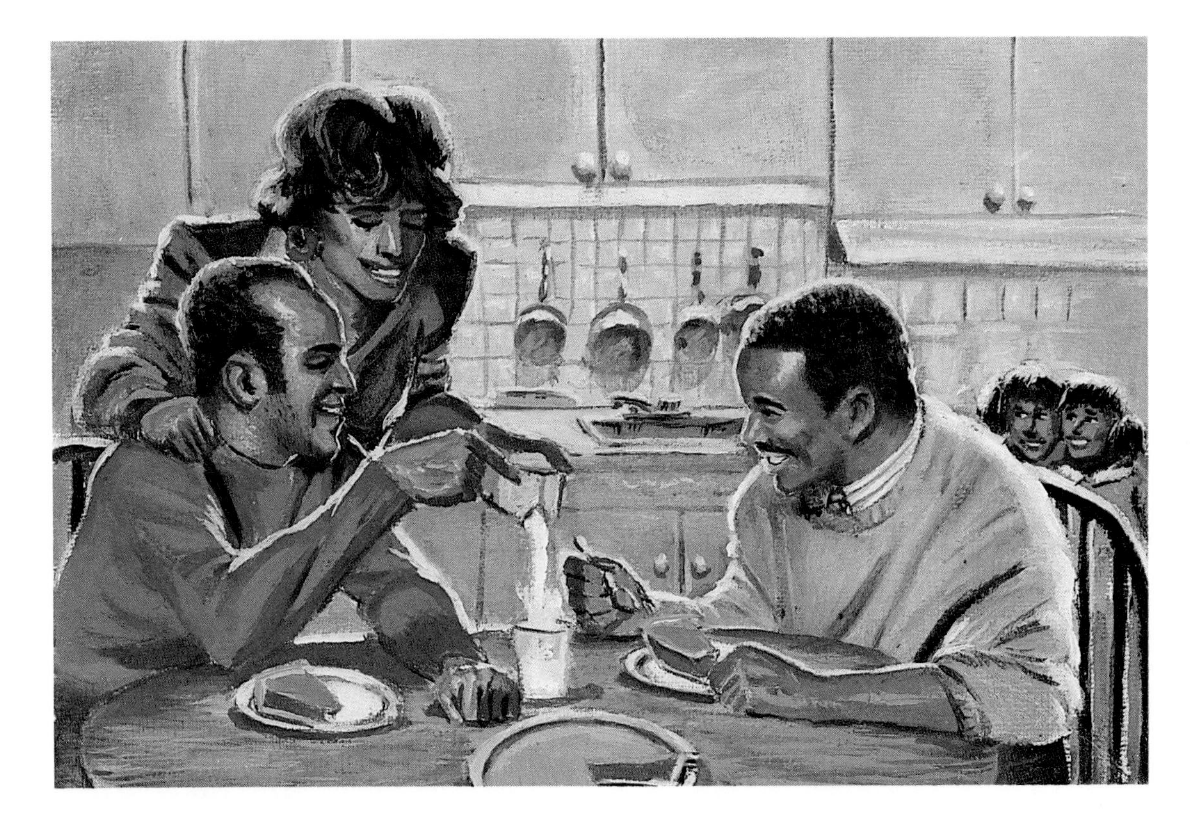

sitting on steps, heads down, hands idle. "Buy Black" stamped on pavements. Store windows bright with African products. Stores still boarded up, a livid scar from last year's rioting.

I climbed the steps of Charley's building. It was old and in need of paint, like all the rest. I pushed the button to his apartment. Charley's buzzer rang. I pushed open the door and climbed the stairs.

What has the author decided to do?

"Well, it's Buddy!" roared Charley, as I arrived on the third floor. "Bea! Come here, girl, it's Buddy!" They swept me from the hall into their dim apartment.

"The place look a mess!" said Bea. "Why didn't you let us know?"

What do you learn about Charley and Bea here?

"Looks fine to me, girl. And so do you!"

Their little girls came out to meet me. Uncle Buddy was something of a celebrity in this house. I hugged them heartily, much to their discomfort.

---

livid (LIV id) like a bruise; black-and-blue
dim (DIM) not bright
heartily (HAHRT ul ee) in a very warm and friendly way

What feeling do you get about the setting of these events?

We all sat in the warm kitchen, where Bea was preparing dinner. It felt good there. Beautiful odors mingled in the air. Charley sat in a chair near mine. The younger girl sat on my lap. Her sister darted here and there like a merry water bug. Bea bustled about, managing to keep up with both the conversation and the cooking.

I told them about the conference I was attending. I knew it would give them pleasure. I mentioned that I had spoken to the group that morning.

"You hear that, Bea?" Charley whispered. "Buddy done spoke in front of all them professors!"

"Sure, I hear," Bea answered. "I bet he weren't even scared. I bet them professors learnt something, too."

I sat there wondering. Could my world ever filter through to people who could never even dream of it? Could Charley and Bea hear me at all?

Why does the author decide to stay for dinner?

"Well, anyway," I said, "I hope they did."

We talked about a hundred different things after that. They insisted that I stay for dinner. I was easy to persuade. They promised fish fried golden, ham hocks and collard greens, and corn bread. Even if I'd wanted to leave, my feet wouldn't have taken me.

"Say, Buddy," Charley said, "a couple of months back I picked up a kid from your school in my cab. I asked him if he knew you. He say he was in your class last year."

"Did you get his name?"

What do you learn about Charley in this incident?

"No, I didn't ask him that. Man, he told me you were the best teacher he had. He said you were one smart cat!"

"He told you that cause you're my brother."

"Your *brother!* I didn't tell him I was your brother. I said you was a old friend of mine."

I put my fork down and leaned over. "What you tell him *that* for?"

Charley explained patiently. He talked as he did when I was a child and had missed some obvious truth. "I didn't want your students to know your brother was nothing but a cabdriver. You *somebody.*"

---

mingled (MING guld) mixed together
obvious (OB vee us) easy to see or understand

"You're a nut," I said gently. "You should've told that kid the truth." I wanted to say I'm proud of you. But he would have been embarrassed.

Bea brought in the dessert—homemade sweet potato pie! There's nothing in this world I like better than Bea's sweet potato pie! "Bea, how you expect me to eat all that?"

The slice she put before me was enormously big. I ate it all.

As we were finishing up, Charley said, "Buddy, you recollect when we was all at home? At Christmas time, when Mama always used to make us a sweet potato pie?"

"Sure, I do. I don't guess we had much. But when that good old pie came on, smelling like heaven, I thought we had us a feast."

What is the theme being stated here?

It was time to go. Charley went to get his cab from the garage several blocks away.

"Wait a minute, Buddy," Bea said. "I'm gon give you the rest of that pie to take with you."

"Great!" I said. I'd eaten all I could hold. But my *spirit* was still hungry for sweet potato pie.

Bea got out some waxed paper and wrapped up the rest of the pie. "That'll do you for a snack tonight." She slipped it into a brown paper bag.

In a minute, Charley's ancient cab limped to the curb. I plopped into the seat next to him, and we headed downtown. We chatted as Charley skillfully managed the heavy traffic. I looked at his long hands on the wheel. I wondered what they could have done with artists' brushes.

We stopped a bit down the street from my hotel. I invited him in. But he said he had to get on with his evening run. I opened the door to get out.

"Buddy, you wait!" he commanded in his old familiar voice.

"What's wrong?"

"What's that you got there?" he said.

I was bewildered. "You mean this bag? That's a piece of sweet potato pie. Bea fixed it for me."

What event occurs as they reach the author's hotel?

"You ain't going through the lobby of no big hotel carrying no

---

enormously (ih NAWR mus lee) much bigger than usual; hugely
recollect (rek uh LEKT) remember
ancient (AYN chunt) very old

brown paper bag."

"Man, you *crazy!* Of course I'm going. Look, Bea fixed it for me. *That's my pie!*"

Charley's eyes were miserable. "Folks in that hotel don't go through the lobby carrying no brown paper bags. That's a *country* thing to do. You *somebody,* Buddy. You got to be *right.* Now gimme that bag."

"I want that pie, Charley. I got nothing to prove to anybody."

I couldn't believe it. But there was no point in arguing. It seemed foolish to me. But it was important to him.

"You got to look *right,* Buddy. Can't nobody look dignified carrying a brown paper bag."

I thought of how tasty it would have been. I thought of how seldom I get a chance to eat anything that good. But finally, I handed over my bag of sweet potato pie. If it was that important to him—

I tried not to show my irritation. "Okay, man. Take care now."

I slammed the door harder than I had intended to. Then I walked rapidly into the hotel.

How does the author feel about Charley?

"That Charley!" I thought, walking through the bright, crowded lobby. I crossed the carpeted floor toward the elevator. I was still thinking of my lost snack. I looked at the herd of people who jostled each other in the lobby. I had to admit that not one of them was carrying a brown paper bag. Or anything but expensive briefcases or slick packages from exclusive stores.

I suppose we all operate according to the symbols that are important to us. To Charley, a brown paper bag symbolizes the humble life he thought I had left. I was *somebody.*

I don't know what made me glance back, but I did. And suddenly the tears and laughter of a lifetime exploded around me like fireworks in a night sky.

What is the theme of this selection?

For there was Charley. He was following a few steps behind me. And he was proudly carrying a brown paper bag full of sweet potato pie.

---

dignified (DIG nuh fyd) having proper pride and self-respect
herd (HURD) a large number of animals, or a group of people moving like a herd of animals
jostled (JOS uld) bumped and pushed, as in a crowd
slick (SLIK) smooth and shiny
symbol (SIM bul) an object that stands for an idea

Eugenia Collier (1928–Present)

In 1948, a gifted student from Baltimore, Maryland graduated at the top of her class from Howard University in Washington, D.C. She faced a difficult decision: whether to continue her education and become a teacher, or whether to devote herself to a writing career.

"Somewhere along the line you have a choice," says Eugenia Collier, the prize-winning English professor. "You can either be a teacher who writes or a writer who teaches. I chose to be a teacher."

Eugenia Collier has held a lifelong commitment to education. Her mother was an elementary school teacher in Washington, D.C. who raised two children, then completed her college degree. Her father was a doctor who read stories and poems to Eugenia and her brother every night.

"Education was very important in my family," she explains. "My mother and father set a great example for us."

Eugenia Collier worked hard to follow in her parents footsteps. She earned a Masters Degree in American Literature. She worked for five years at the Baltimore Department of Public Welfare, helping people who needed public assistance. She was awarded a Ph.D. and has twice been recognized as one of the "Outstanding Educators of America."

Yet, between all her studies and teaching responsibilities, Eugenia Collier has managed to devote time to her special interest: creative writing.

"I started writing when I was a child," she explains, "as soon as I could hold a pencil and first realized that people could make up poems and stories."

Eugenia Collier's first short story, "Marigolds," won the Gwendolyn Brooks Award for Fiction in 1969. Although she has published only a few other stories, each of her works has been praised for its wisdom, insight, and compassion toward all people. Eugenia Collier is now hard at work on her first novel, a story about a family like hers . . . or, perhaps, yours.

FOCUS ON THE SELECTION

UNDERSTAND THE SELECTION

Recall

1. Where was the narrator raised?
2. Who took care of the narrator as a child?
3. What does Charley insist on carrying himself?

Infer

4. Why was the narrator able to finish school?
5. Why was it important to Charley that the narrator finish school?
6. Why was it the apex of Mama's life when he finished high school?
7. Why couldn't the narrator carry the bag into the hotel himself?

Apply

8. Imagine you were the narrator. How would you feel about being the best-educated person in your family?
9. Predict what would have happened if the narrator had insisted on carrying the paper bag himself.
10. Predict what might happen if the narrator arranged a reunion for all his sisters and brothers.

Respond to Literature

Select details that show that the author came from a close family.

WRITE ABOUT THE SELECTION

Write a new ending for the story. Imagine that at the end, Charley drives away with the pie, leaving the author to struggle with his feelings about the event or imagine that Charles changes his mind and returns to bring the pie to his brother.

Prewriting: Make a brief summary of the events of the new ending. Think about the characters and how each might act in the situation. Add details that make the story seem more realistic and easier for your readers to imagine. Remember to think about what makes the characters act the way they do. Review parts of the story that tell about Charley's relationship with his brother when they were children.

Writing: Use your summary to write a new story ending. You may wish to include conversation between Charley and the author. Take out details that don't help your story. Add details to make your ideas clearer for your readers. Try to make Charley's return with the pie as much of a surprise as the original ending of the story.

Revising: Your story should flow easily from one event to the next. One way to do this is to use transition words such as *then* and *later.* Add transition words to make the flow of events easier to understand.

Proofreading: Put quotation marks around the exact words of each speaker. Put the correct punctuation around the other parts of any conversation you include in your story ending.

THINK ABOUT FICTION

We can learn a lot about ourselves and other people from fiction. Sharing the feelings of fictional characters helps us to think about events and problems in our own lives.

1. Who is the main character in this story?
2. What is the narrator's point of view about his brother Charley?
3. Compare and contrast the setting at the beginning and at the end of this story.
4. Why is the title of this story, "Sweet Potato Pie"?
5. What are the elements of fiction in this story?

DEVELOP YOUR VOCABULARY

Some of the language in this story is in **dialect.** It is not formal English, but is the kind of English spoken by people in one region of a country. Find the dialect in each sentence below. Rewrite the sentence using formal English.

1. "I axed him if he knew you."
2. "He said you were one smart cat."
3. "Can't nobody look dignified carrying a brown paper bag."

Learn About

Theme

The **theme** of a story is the story's message or main idea. It is what the author has to say about life. Some stories state the theme clearly; others ask you to figure it out for yourself.

Very often, the theme is what the main character learns during the course of the story. In a good story, the main character goes through certain experiences and is given a set of problems to overcome. By the end of the story, the character has gained a particular kind of knowledge, wisdom, or understanding. In a similar way, the theme of a story can also be *what* the reader learns as a result of reading the story.

As you read "Fifth Chinese Daughter," ask yourself:

1. What is the theme of this story?
2. What does Jade Snow learn as a result of her experiences?

Skill Builder

Feature stories in a newspaper or magazine usually have an important theme that appeals to readers. Sometimes, these stories are called "human interest stories." Read a human interest story from a newspaper or magazine, then state the theme of the story in one or two sentences.

FIFTH CHINESE DAUGHTER

by Jade Snow Wong

Of her college courses, Latin was the easiest. This was a surprise, for everyone had told her of its horrors. It was much more logical than French, almost mathematical in its orderliness and precision, and actually a snap after nine years of Chinese.

Chemistry, true to the instructor's promise, was difficult, although the classes were anything but dull. It turned out that he was a very nice person with a keen sense of humor and a gift for enlivening his lectures with stories of his own college days. There were only two girls in a class of more than fifty men—a tense blond girl from Germany, who always ranked first; and Jade Snow, who usually took second place.

But if Latin was the easiest course and chemistry the most difficult, sociology was the most stimulating. Jade Snow had chosen it without thought, simply to meet a requirement; but that casual decision completely revolutionized her thinking, shattering her Wong-constructed conception of the order of things. This was the way it happened:

After several uneventful weeks during which the class explored the historical origins of the family and examined such terms as "norms," "mores," "folkways," there came a day when the instructor stood before them to discuss the relationship of parents and children. It was a day like many others, with the students listening in varying attitudes of interest or indifference. The instructor was speaking casually of ideas to be accepted as standard. Then suddenly upon Jade Snow's astounded ears there fell this statement:

"There was a period in our American

---

enlivening (en LY vun ing) making lively
mores (MAWR ays) manners or moral customs of a social group

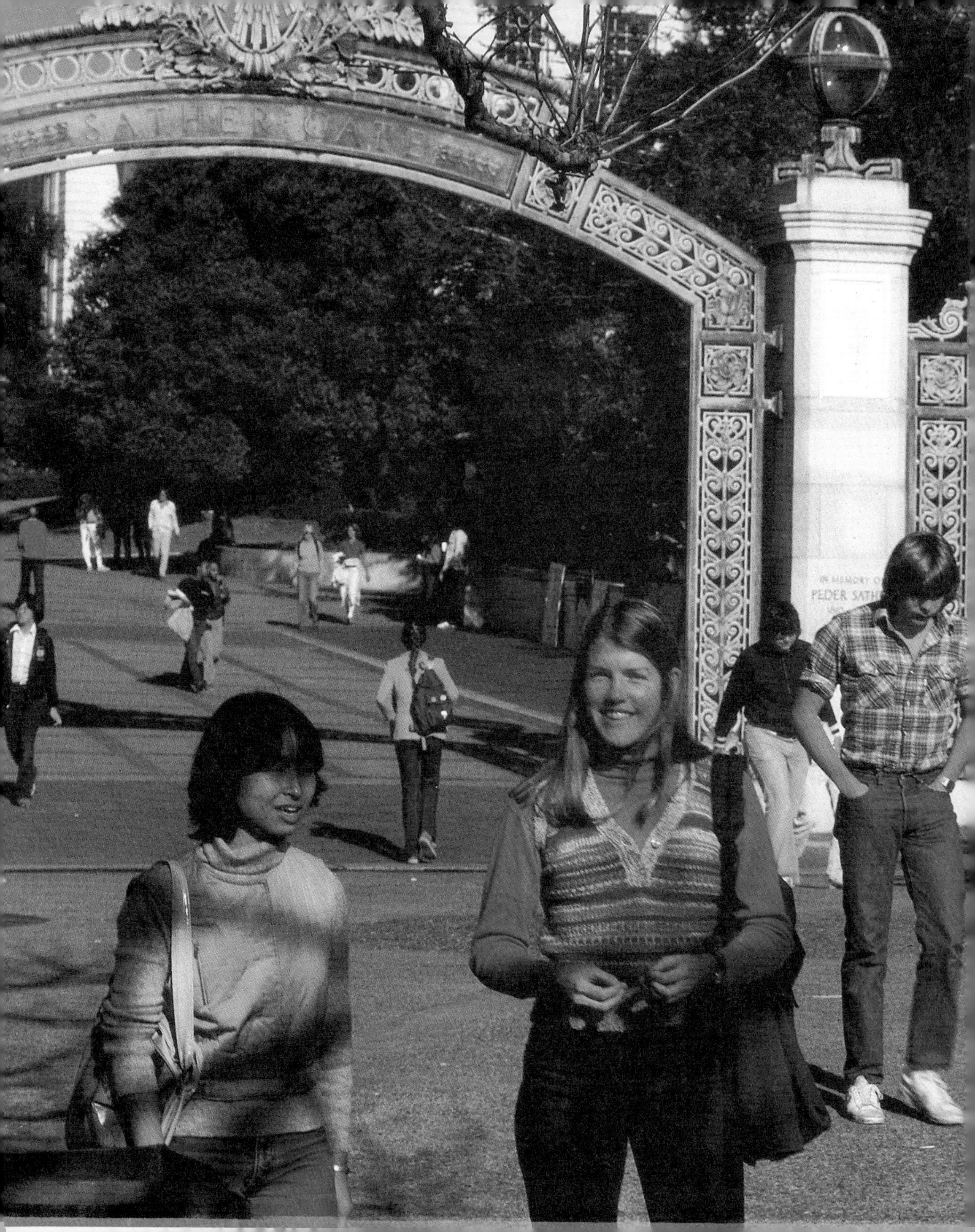
SATHER GATE
IN MEMORY O
PEDER SATH

history when parents had children for economic reasons, to put them to work as soon as possible, especially to have them help on the farm. But now we no longer regard children in this way. Today we recognize that children are individuals and that parents can no longer demand their unquestioning obedience. Parents should do their best to understand their children, because young people also have their rights."

The instructor went on talking, but Jade Snow heard no more, for her mind was echoing and re-echoing this startling thought. "Parents can no longer demand unquestioning obedience from their children. Children also have their rights." For the rest of that day, while she was doing her chores at the Simpsons, while she was standing in the streetcar going home, she was busy translating the idea into terms of her own experience.

"My parents demand unquestioning obedience. Older Brother demands unquestioning obedience. By what right? I am an individual besides being a Chinese daughter. I have rights too."

Could it be that Daddy and Mama, although they were living in San Francisco in the year 1938, actually had not left the Chinese world of thirty years ago? Could it be that they were forgetting that Jade Snow would soon become a woman in a new America, not a woman in old China? In short, was it possible that Daddy and Mama could be wrong?

For days Jade Snow gave thought to little but her devastating discovery that her parents might be subject to error. As it was her habit always to act after reaching a conclusion, she wondered what to do about it. Should she tell Daddy and Mama that they needed to change their ways? One moment she thought she should, the next she thought not. At last she decided to overcome her fear in the interests of education and better understanding. She would at least try to open their minds to modern truths. If she succeeded, good! If not, she was prepared to suffer the consequences.

In this spirit of patient martyrdom she waited for an opportunity to speak.

It came, surprisingly, one Saturday. Ordinarily that was a busy day at the Simpsons, a time for entertaining, so that Jade Snow was not free until too late to go anywhere even had she had a place to go. But on this particular Saturday the Simpsons were away for the weekend, and by three in the afternoon Jade Snow was ready to leave the apartment with unplanned hours ahead of her. She didn't want to spend these rare hours of freedom in any usual way. And she didn't want to spend them alone.

"Shall I call Joe?" she wondered. She had never telephoned a boy before, and she debated whether it would be too forward. But she felt too happy and carefree to worry, and she was confident that Joe would not misunderstand.

Even before reporting to Mama that she was home, she ran downstairs to the

---

devastating (DEV uh stayt ing) overwhelming
martyrdom (MAHR tur dum) ready to die or suffer for a cause or belief

telephone booth and gave the operator Joe's number. His mother answered and then went to call him while Jade Snow waited in embarrassment.

"Joe." She was suddenly tongue-tied. "Joe, I'm already home."

That wasn't at all what she wanted to say. What did she want to say?

"Hello! Hello!" Joe boomed back. "What's the matter with you? Are you all right?"

"Oh, yes, I'm fine. Only, only . . . well, I'm through working for the day." That was really all she had to say, but now it sounded rather pointless.

"Isn't that wonderful? It must have been unexpected." That was what was nice and different about Joe. He always seemed to know without a lot of words. But because his teasing was never far behind his understanding he added quickly, "I suppose you're going to study and go to bed early."

Jade Snow was still not used to teasing and didn't know how to take it. With an effort she swallowed her shyness and disappointment. "I thought we might go for a walk . . . that is, if you have nothing else to do . . . if you would care to . . . if. . . ."

Joe laughed. "I'll go you one better. Suppose I take you to a movie. I'll even get all dressed up for you, and you get dressed up, too."

Jade Snow was delighted. Her first movie with Joe! What a wonderful day! In happy anticipation she put on her long silk stockings, lipstick, and the nearest thing to a suit she owned—a hand-me-down jacket and a brown skirt she had made herself. Then with a bright ribbon typing back her long black hair she was ready.

Daddy didn't miss a detail of the preparations as she dashed from room to room. He waited until she was finished before he demanded, "Jade Snow, where are you going?"

"I am going out into the street," she answered.

"Did you ask my permission to go out into the street?"

"No, Daddy."

"Do you have your mother's permission to go out into the street?"

"No, Daddy."

A sudden silence from the kitchen indicated that Mama was listening.

Daddy went on: "Where and when did you learn to be so daring as to leave this house without permission of your parents? You did not learn it under my roof."

It was all very familiar. Jade Snow waited, knowing that Daddy had not finished. In a moment he came to the point.

"And with whom are you going out into the street?"

It took all the courage Jade Snow could muster, remembering her new thinking, to say nothing. It was certain that if she told Daddy that she was going out with a boy whom he did not know, without a chaperone, he would be convinced that she would lose her maidenly

---

chaperone (SHAP uh rohn) older person who supervises an unmarried couple

purity before the evening was over.

"Very well," Daddy said sharply. "If you will not tell me, I forbid you to go! You are now too old to whip."

That was the moment.

Suppressing all anger, and in a manner that would have done credit to her sociology instructor addressing his freshman class, Jade Snow carefully turned on her mentally rehearsed speech.

"That is something you should think more about. Yes, I am too old to whip. I am too old to be treated as a child. I can now think for myself, and you and Mama should not demand unquestioning obedience from me. You should understand me. There was a time in America when parents raised children to make them work, but now the foreigners regard them as individuals with rights of their own. I have worked too, but now I am an individual besides being your fifth daughter."

It was almost certain that Daddy blinked, but after the briefest pause he gathered himself together.

"Where," he demanded, "did you learn such an unfilial theory?"

Mama had come quietly into the room and slipped into a chair to listen.

"From my teacher," Jade Snow answered triumphantly, "who you taught me is supreme after you, and whose judgment I am not to question."

Daddy was feeling pushed. Thoroughly aroused, he shouted:

"A little learning has gone to your head! How can you permit a foreigner's theory to put aside the practical experience of the Chinese, who for thousands of years have preserved a most superior family pattern? Confucius[1] had already presented an organized philosophy of manners and conduct when the foreigners were unappreciatively persecuting Christ. Who brought you up? Who clothed you, fed you, sheltered you, nursed you? Do you think you were born aged sixteen? You owe honor to us before you satisfy your personal whims."

Daddy thundered on, while Jade Snow kept silent.

"What would happen to the order of this household if each of you four children started to behave like individuals? Would we have one peaceful moment if your personal desires came before your duty? How could we maintain our self-respect if we, your parents, did not know where you were at night and with whom you were keeping company?"

With difficulty Jade Snow kept herself from being swayed by fear and the old familiar arguments. "You can be bad in the daytime as well as at night," she said defensively. "What could happen after eleven that couldn't happen before?"

Daddy was growing more excited. "Do I have to justify my judgment to you? I do not want a daughter of mine to be known as one who walks the streets at night. Have you no thought for our reputations if not for your own? If you start going out with boys, no good man will

---

unfilial (un FIL ee ul) inappropriate for a son or daughter
[1]**Confucius** (551?-479? B.C.) a famous Chinese philosopher

want to ask you to be his wife. You just do not know as well as we do what is good for you."

Mama fanned Daddy's wrath, "Never having been a mother, you cannot know how much grief it is to bring up a daughter. Of course we will not permit you to run the risk of corrupting your purity before marriage."

"Oh, Mama!" Jade Snow retorted. "This is America, not China. Don't you think I have any judgment? How can you think I would go out with just any man?"

"Men!" Daddy roared. "You don't know a thing about them. I tell you, you can't trust any of them."

Now it was Jade Snow who felt pushed. She delivered the balance of her declaration of independence:

"Both of you should understand that I am growing up to be a woman in a society greatly different from the one you knew in China. You expect me to work my way through college—which would not have been possible in China. You expect me to exercise judgment in choosing my employers and my jobs and in spending my own money in the American world. Then why can't I choose my friends? Of course independence is not safe. But safety isn't the only consideration. You must give me the freedom to find some answers for myself."

Mama found her tongue first. "You think you are too good for us because you have a little foreign book knowledge."

"You will learn the error of your ways after it is too late," Daddy added darkly.

By this Jade Snow knew that her parents had conceded defeat. Hoping to soften the blow, she tried to explain: "If I am to earn my living, I must learn how to get along with many kinds of people, with foreigners as well as Chinese. I intend to start finding out about them now. You must have confidence that I shall remain true to the spirit of your teachings. I shall bring back to you the new knowledge of whatever I learn."

Daddy and Mama did not accept this offer graciously. "It is as useless for you to tell me such ideas as 'the wind blows across a deaf ear.' You have lost your sense of balance," Daddy told her bluntly. "You are shameless. Your skin is yellow. Your features are forever Chinese. We are content with our proven ways. Do not try to force foreign ideas into my home. Go. You will one day tell us sorrowfully that you have been mistaken."

After that there was no further discussion of the matter. Jade Snow came and went without any questions being asked. In spite of her parents' dark predictions, her new freedom in the choice of companions did not result in a rush of undesirables. As a matter of fact, the boys she met at school were more concerned with copying her lecture notes than with anything else.

As for Joe, he remained someone to walk with and talk with. On the evening of Jade Snow's seventeenth birthday he took her up Telegraph Hill and gave her as a remembrance a sparkling grown-up bracelet with a card which read: "Here's to your making Phi Beta Kappa."[2] And

[2]**Phi Beta Kappa:** an honorary scholastic society

there under the stars he gently tilted her face and gave her her first kiss.

Standing straight and awkward in her full-skirted red cotton dress, Jade Snow was caught by surprise and without words. She felt that something should stir and crash within her, in the way books and the movies described, but nothing did. Could it be that she wasn't in love with Joe, in spite of liking and admiring him? After all, he was twenty-three and probably too old for her anyway.

Still she had been kissed at seventeen, which was cause for rejoicing. Laughing happily, they continued their walk.

But while the open rebellion gave Jade Snow a measure of freedom she had not had before, and an outer show of assurance, she was deeply troubled within. It had been simple to have Daddy and Mama tell her what was right and wrong; it was not simple to decide for herself. No matter how critical she was of them, she could not discard all they stood for and accept as a substitute the philosophy of the foreigners. It took very little thought to discover that the foreign philosophy also was subject to criticism, and that for her there had to be a middle way.

In particular, she could not reject the fatalism that was at the core of all Chinese thinking and behavior, the belief that the broad pattern of an individual's life was ordained by fate although within that pattern he was capable of perfecting himself and accumulating a desirable store of good will. Should the individual not benefit by his good works, still the rewards would pass on to his children or his children's children. Epitomized by the proverbs: "I save your life, for your grandson might save mine," and "Heaven does not forget to follow the path a good man walks," this was a fundamental philosophy of Chinese life which Jade Snow found fully as acceptable as some of the so-called scientific reasoning expounded in the sociology class, where heredity and environment were assigned

ordained (awr DAYND) arranged

all the responsibility for personal success or failure.

There was good to be gained from both concepts if she could extract and retain her own personally applicable combination. She studied her neighbor in class, Stella Green, for clues. Stella had grown up reading Robert Louis Stevenson, learning to swim and play tennis, developing a taste for roast beef, mashed potatoes, sweets, aspirin tablets, and soda pop, and she looked upon her mother and father as friends. But it was very unlikely that she knew where her great-grandfather was born, or whether or not she was related to another strange Green she might chance to meet. Jade Snow had grown up reading Confucius, learning to embroider and cook rice, developing a taste for steamed fish and bean sprouts, tea, and herbs, and she thought of her parents as people to be obeyed. She not only knew where her ancestors were born but where they were buried, and how many chickens and roast pigs should be brought annually to their graves to feast their spirits. She knew all of the branches of the Wong family, the relation of each to the other, and understood why Daddy must help support the distant cousins in China who bore the sole responsibility of carrying on the family heritage by periodic visits to the burial grounds in Fragrant Mountains. She knew that one could purchase in a Chinese stationery store the printed record of her family tree relating their Wong line and other Wong lines back to the original Wong ancestors. In such a scheme the individual counted for little weighed against the family, and after sixteen years it was not easy to sever roots.

There were, alas, no books or advisers to guide Jade Snow in her search for balance between the pull from two cultures. If she chose neither to reject nor accept *in toto,*[3] she must sift both and make her decisions alone. It would not be an easy search. But pride and determination, which Daddy had given her, prevented any thought of turning back.

By the end of her first year of junior college, she had been so impressed by her sociology course that she changed her major to the social studies. Four years of college no longer seemed interminable. The highlight of her second year was an English course which used literature as a basis for stimulating individual expression through theme writing. At this time Jade Snow still thought in Chinese, although she was acquiring an English vocabulary. In consequence she was slower than her classmates, but her training in keeping a diary gave her an advantage in analyzing and recording personal experiences. She discovered very soon that her grades were consistently higher when she wrote about Chinatown and the people she had known all her life. For the first time she realized the joy of expressing herself in the written word. It surprised her and also stimulated her.

---

interminable (in TER muh nuh bul) endless
[3]***In toto:*** in the whole; entirely

She learned that good writing should improve upon the kind of factual reporting she had done in her diaries; it should be created in a spirit of artistry. After this course, if Jade Snow had not mastered these principles, at least she could never again write without remembering them and trying her best to apply them.

Hand in hand with a growing awareness of herself and her personal world, there was developing in her an awareness of and a feeling for the larger world beyond the familiar pattern. At eighteen, when Jade Snow compared herself with a diary record of herself at sixteen, she could see many points of difference. She was now an extremely serious young person, with a whole set of worries which she donned with her clothes each morning. The two years had made her a little wiser in the ways of the world, a little more realistic, less of a dreamer, and she hoped more of a personality.

In the interval she had put aside an earlier Americanized dream of a husband, a home, a garden, a dog, and children, and there had grown in its place a desire for more schooling in preparation for a career of service to those less fortunate than herself. Boys put her down as a snob and a bookworm. Well, let them. She was independent. She was also frank—much too frank for many people's liking. She had acquaintances, but no real friends who shared her interests. Even Joe had stopped seeing her, having left school to begin his career. Their friendship had given her many

---

donned (DOND) put on

things, including confidence in herself as a person at a time when she needed it. It had left with her the habit of walking, and in moments of loneliness she found comfort and sometimes the answers to problems by wandering through odd parts of San Francisco, a city she loved with an ever-increasing affection.

On this eighteenth birthday, instead of the birthday cake which Americans considered appropriate, Daddy brought home a fresh-killed chicken which Mama cooked their favorite way by plunging it into a covered pot of boiling water, moving it off the flame and letting it stand for one hour, turning it once. Brushed with oil and sprinkled with shredded fresh green onions, it retained its sweet flavor with all its juices, for it was barely cooked and never dry. Naturally, the birthday of a daughter did not call for the honor due a parent. There was a birthday tea ritual calling for elaborate preparation when Mama's and Daddy's anniversaries came around. Still, to be a girl and eighteen was exciting.

The rest of the year rushed to an end. The years at junior college had been rewarding. Now several happy surprises climaxed them. First there was the satisfaction of election to membership in Alpha Gamma Sigma, an honorary state scholastic organization. On the advice of her English instructor, this precipitated an exchange of letters with an executive of the society concerning a possible scholarship to the university.

In the meantime, overtiredness and overwork brought on recurring back pains which confined Jade Snow to bed for several days. Against her will because she could not afford it, she had been driven to see a doctor, who told her to put a board under her mattress for back support, and gave her two prescriptions to be filled for relief of pain. But there was no money for medicine. She asked Daddy and Mama, who said that they could not afford to pay for it either. So Jade Snow went miserably to bed to stay until the pain should end of its own accord.

She had been there two days when Older Brother entered casually and tossed a letter on her bed. It was from the scholarship chairman of Alpha Gamma Sigma, enclosing a check for fifty dollars. It was an award to her as the most outstanding woman student of the junior colleges in California. Jade Snow's emotions were mixed. What she had wanted and needed was a full scholarship. On the other hand, recognition was sweet —a proof that God had not forgotten her.

On the heels of this letter came another from her faculty adviser, inviting her as one of the ten top-ranking students to compete for the position as commencement speaker. "If you care to try out," it concluded, "appear at Room 312 on April 11 at ten o'clock."

Should she or should she not? She had never made a speech in public, and the thought was panic. But had she a right to refuse? Might not this be an

---

precipitated (prih SIP uh tayt id) brought about; caused

opportunity to answer effectively all the "Richards"[4] of the world who screamed "Chinky, Chinky, Chinaman" at her and other Chinese? Might it not be further evidence to offer her family that her decision had not been wrong?

It seemed obvious that the right thing to do was to try, and equally obvious that she should talk about what was most familiar to her: the values which she as an American-Chinese had found in two years of junior college.

At the try-out, in a dry voice, she coaxed out her prepared thesis and fled, not knowing whether she had been good or bad, and not caring. She was glad just to be done. A few days later came formal notification that she would be the salutatorian at graduation. She was terrified as she envisioned the stage at the elegant San Francisco War Memorial Opera House, with its tremendous sparkling chandelier and overpowering tiers of seats. Now she wished that she could escape.

The reality was as frightening as the anticipation when on June 7, 1940, she stood before the graduation audience, listening to her own voice coming over the loudspeaker. All her family were there among the neat rows of faces before her. What did they think, hearing her say, "The Junior College has developed our initiative, fair play, and self-expression, and has given us tools for thinking and analyzing. But it seems to me that the most effective application that American-Chinese can make of their education would be in China, which needs all the Chinese talent she can muster."

Thus Jade Snow—shaped by her father's and mother's unceasing loyalty toward their mother country, impressed with China's needs by speakers who visited Chinatown, revolutionized by American ideas, fired with enthusiasm for social service—thought that she had quite independently arrived at the perfect solution for the future of all thinking and conscientious young Chinese, including herself. Did her audience agree with her conclusion?

At last it was over, the speeches and applause, the weeping and excited exchange of congratulations. According to plan, Jade Snow met her family on the steps of the Opera House, where they were joined shortly by her faculty adviser and her English professor. Conversation proceeded haltingly, as Daddy and Mama spoke only Chinese.

Mama took the initiative: "Thank your teachers for me for all the kind assistance they have given you. Ask them to excuse my not being able to speak English."

"Yes, indeed," Daddy added. "A fine teacher is very rare."

---

salutatorian (suh loot uh TAWR ee un) second-ranking graduate in a class

initiative (ih NISH uh tiv) taking the first step in a plan of action

[4]**"Richards":** On one occasion, Jade Snow had been taunted about being Chinese by a malicious boy named Richard who attended the same school.

When Jade Snow had duly translated the remarks, she took advantage of a pause to inquire casually, "How was my speech?"

Mama was noncommittal. "I can't understand English."

"You talked too fast at first," was Older Brother's opinion.

Daddy was more encouraging: "It could be considered passable. For your first speech, that was about it."

The subject was closed. Daddy had spoken. But there was a surprise in store.

"Will you ask your teachers to join us for late supper at a Chinese restaurant?" Daddy suggested.

"What restaurant?" Jade Snow wanted to know, bewildered.

"Tao-Tao on Jackson Street. I have made reservations and ordered food."

Hardly able to credit her senses, Jade Snow trailed after the party. At first she was apprehensive, feeling it her responsibility to make the guests comfortable and at ease in the strange surroundings. But her fears were unfounded. The guests genuinely enjoyed the novel experience of breaking bread with the Wongs. It was a thoroughly happy and relaxed time for everyone as they sat feasting on delicious stuffed-melon soup, Peking duck, steamed thousand-layer buns, and tasty crisp greens.

The whole day had been remarkable, but most remarkable of all was the fact that for the first time since her break with her parents, Mama and Daddy had granted her a measure of recognition and acceptance. For the first time they had met on common ground with her American associates. It was a sign that they were at last tolerant of her effort to search for her own pattern of life.

---

noncommittal (non kuh MIT ul) not showing what one thinks

Jade Snow Wong (1922 - Present)

"The book I wrote not only emphasizes the specific and philosophic differences between the old world and the new. It tries also to tell that the greatest values are the same in both worlds. Honor, courage, honesty, uncompromise in the face of personal conviction, service to fellow man—these do not differ." So Jade Snow Wong describes her autobiographical novel, *Fifth Chinese Daughter.*

Born in San Francisco's Chinatown, Wong grew up in a strict Chinese home. She learned at an early age that parents were to be obeyed without question, and that boys were naturally superior to girls. Only when Jade Snow went to high school and college did she discover the clash that exists between Chinese and American values. She described this discovery as the "turning point" in her life, when she must answer the question, "Am I of my father's race or am I an American?"

Today Jade Snow Wong is a distinguished ceramist whose works are part of permanent museum collections. Wong describes her career as an artist, as well as her marriage and the raising of four children, in a sequel to *Fifth Chinese Daughter* entitled *No Chinese Stranger.*

FOCUS ON THE SELECTION

UNDERSTAND THE SELECTION

Recall

1. What nationality is Jade Snow?
2. Does she learn new ideas about the relationship of parent and child?
3. How does she rebel against her parents?

Infer

4. What can you infer about what Jade Snow and her parents do for a living?
5. What are Jade Snow's father's ideas about dating?
6. How can you tell that the Wongs have very little money?
7. Jade Snow's break with her parents is not as total as it appears at first. What periods in the story show this?

Apply

8. Why did Jade Snow refer to her new discovery as "devastating"?
9. How did her teachers feel about the conclusions Jade Snow had reached?
10. What might have happened if she had not taken sociology in college?

Respond to Literature

How is this story an example of the "generation gap"? What do both generations do to overcome it?

WRITE ABOUT THE SELECTION

Jade Snow finds that she must integrate traditional Chinese teachings with modern American values. Can you think of a similar process that you may have gone through or will be going through in your own life? For example, perhaps you find yourself questioning your parents' religious beliefs. Perhaps you disagree with your parents about what you should wear, or how you should spend money. Write a paragraph in which you react to Jade Snow's situation out of your own experience.

Prewriting: Take a few minutes to list the areas in which you disagree with your parents or other adults in your family. Under each topic, write "parents' view" and "my view." Then fill in each viewpoint.

Writing: Use your prewriting notes to write a paragraph in which you relate *Fifth Chinese Daughter* to your own experience. You may wish to write about just one area of disagreement with your parents, or you may wish to write about several. You can do this with other adult relatives as well.

Revising: As you relate your experiences to those of Jade Snow, it may be helpful to use words or phrases of comparison, such as "like," "in the same way," "unlike," "in a different way," and so on.

Proofreading: Read your paragraph and check to see that you have used commas correctly. Review the use of commas in your textbook, then add or remove commas where necessary in your paragraph.

THINK ABOUT THE THEME

A person writes a story because he or she has something important to say. The message of a story is the theme. In many cases, the theme is what the main character learns, or what the reader learns.

Some stories have more than one theme, although one of these is usually the main theme.

The theme of a story should not be confused with the **subject**. The subject of a story is simply what the story is about.

1. What is the theme of *Fifth Chinese Daughter?*
2. Is this theme important in the story? Why or why not?
3. In what places is the theme quite clearly stated in this story?
4. What does Jade Snow learn by the end of the story?
5. What experiences and problems bring Jade Snow to these conclusions?

DEVELOP YOUR VOCABULARY

A **root** is a word or word part that is used to form other words. For example, the word *forest* is used to form the word *forestry,* which is the science of agriculture that deals with the care of forests. Root words often help you to figure out the meanings of larger words.

On a separate sheet of paper, underline the root in each word below. Use that root to figure out the meaning of the larger word. Then write a definition of the larger word. Check each of your definitions in the dictionary.

1. enlivening
2. revolutionized
3. orderliness
4. devastating
5. discovery
6. conclusion
7. instructor
8. unquestioning
9. martyrdom
10. embarrassment
11. unplanned
12. anticipation
13. pointless
14. unfilial
15. foreigners
16. defensively
17. consideration
18. undesirables
19. applicable
20. noncommittal

Learn About

Ideas and Values

The ideas that authors express are closely tied to their values, the principles and standards that the writers hold. In Jade Snow Wong's autobiography, the idea of rebelling against traditional ways suggests that the values of independence are important to Americans, no matter what their ethnic backgrounds are.

To find ideas and values in literature, you must read carefully and consider the main characters, actions, tone, setting, and symbolism. Look for direct or dramatic statements, figurative language, characters who stand for ideas, and the total impression you get from reading as clues to the author's ideas and values.

As you read "The Circuit," ask:

1. What are the ideas and values expressed in this story?
2. What issues do you think the author feels strongly about?

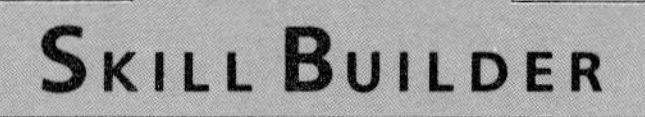

Think of an issue or human value that is important to you. For example, you may feel strongly that more should be done to help homeless people in the city. Decide what you would like to communicate to others about this issue. Then write a brief plot outline of a short story that could convey your message.

THE CIRCUIT

by Francisco Jimenez

It was that time of year again; Ito, the strawberry sharecropper, did not smile; it was natural. The peak of the strawberry season was over, and the last few days the workers, most of them *braceros,*[1] were not picking as many boxes as they had during the months of June and July.

As the last days of August disappeared, so did the number of braceros. Sunday, only one—the best picker—came to work; I liked him. Sometimes we talked during our half-hour lunch break; that is how I found out he was from Jalisco, the same state in Mexico my family was from. That Sunday was the last time I saw him.

When the sun had tired and sunk behind the mountains, Ito signaled us that it was time to go home. *"Ya esora,"*[2] he yelled in his broken Spanish. Those

---

sharecropper (SHAIR krop ur) a farmer who works land owned by another and receives part of the profits

[1]**bracero:** A Mexican farm worker.

[2]**Ya es hora:** "It's time."

were words I waited for twelve hours a day, every day, seven days a week, week after week; and the thought of not hearing them again saddened me.

As we drove home Papa did not say a word. With both hands on the wheel, he stared at the dirt road; my older brother, Roberto, was also silent. He leaned his head back and closed his eyes; once in a while he cleared from his throat the dust that blew in from the outside.

Yes, it was that time of year. When I opened the front door of our *casita,*[3] I stopped; everything we owned was neatly packed in cardboard boxes. Suddenly I felt even more the weight of hours, days, weeks, and months of work. I sat down on a box; the thought of having to move to Fresno, and knowing what was in store for me there, brought tears to my eyes.

That night I could not sleep; I lay in bed, thinking about how much I hated this move.

A little before five o'clock in the morning, Papa woke everyone up. A few minutes later, the yelling and screaming of my little brothers and sisters, for whom the move was a great adventure, broke the silence of dawn. Shortly, the barking of the dogs accompanied them.

While we packed the breakfast dishes, Papa went outside to start the *Carcanchita;* that was the name Papa gave his old '38 black Plymouth. He bought it in a used car lot in Santa Rosa in the winter of 1949. Papa was very proud of his car; *Mi Carcanchita,* my little jalopy, he called it; he had a right to be proud of it. He spent a lot of time looking at other cars before buying this one. When he finally chose the *Carcanchita,* he checked it thoroughly before driving it out of the car lot; he examined every inch of the car. He listened to the motor, tilting his head from side to side like a parrot, trying to detect any noises that spelled car trouble. After being satisfied with the looks and sounds of the car, Papa insisted on knowing who the original owner was. He never did find out from the car dealer, but he bought the car anyway. Papa figured the original owner must have been an important man, because behind the rear seat of the car he found a blue necktie.

Papa parked the car out in front and left the motor running; "*Listo,*"[4] he yelled. Without saying a word, Roberto and I began to carry the boxes out to the car. Roberto carried the two big boxes and I carried the two smaller ones; Papa threw the mattress on the top of the car roof and tied it with ropes to the front and rear bumpers.

Everything was packed except Mama's pot; it was an old, large pot she had picked up at the army surplus store in Santa Marie the year I was born. The pot was full of dents and nicks, and the more dents and nicks it had, the more Mama liked it. "*Mi olla,*"[5] she used to say

---

galvanized (GAL vuh nyzd) coated with rust-resistant zinc
surplus (SUR plus) amount left over when a need has been met
[3]**casita:** little house
[4]**listo:** ready
[5]**mi olla:** my kettle

proudly.

I held the front door open as Mama carefully carried out her pot by both handles, making sure not to spill the cooked beans. When she got to the car, Papa reached out to help her with it. Roberto opened the rear car door and Papa gently placed it on the floor behind the front seat. All of us climbed in; Papa sighed, wiped the sweat off his forehead with his sleeve, and said wearily, "*Es todo.*"[6]

As we drove away, I felt a lump in my throat; I turned around and looked at our *casita* for the last time.

At sunset we drove into a vineyard near Fresno. Since Papa did not speak English, Mama asked the boss if he needed any more workers; "We don't need any more," said the man, scratching his head. "Check with Sullivan, down the road; can't miss him; he lives in a big white house with a fence around it."

When we got there, Mama walked up to the house. She went through the white gate, past a row of rose bushes, up the stairs to the front door; she rang the doorbell. The porch light went on and a

[6]**Es todo:** That's everything.

tall, husky man came out; they exchanged a few words. After the man went in, Mama clapped her hands and hurried back to the car. "We have work! Mr. Sullivan said we can stay there the whole season," she said, gasping and pointing to an old garage near the stables.

The garage was worn out by the years. It had no windows; the walls, eaten by termites, strained to support the roof; the loose dirt floor looked like a gray road map.

That night, by the light of a kerosene lamp, we unpacked and cleaned our new home. Roberto swept away the loose dirt, leaving the hard ground; Papa plugged the holes in the walls; Mama fed my little brothers and sisters. Papa and Roberto then brought in the mattress and placed it in the far corner of the garage. "Mama, you and the little ones sleep on the mattress; Roberto, Panchito, and I will sleep outside, under the trees," Papa said.

Early next morning Mr. Sullivan showed us where his crop was, and, after breakfast, Papa, Roberto, and I headed for the vineyard to pick.

Around 9 a.m. the temperature had risen to almost one hundred degrees. I was completely soaked in sweat, and my mouth felt as if I had been chewing on a handkerchief. I walked over to the end of the row, picked up the jug of water we had brought, and began drinking. "Don't drink too much; you'll get sick," Roberto shouted. No sooner had he said that than I felt sick to my stomach; I dropped to my knees and let the jug roll off my hands; I remained motionless, with my eyes glued on the hot, sandy ground. All I could hear was the drone of insects. Slowly I began to recover; I poured water over my face and neck, and watched the black mud run down my arms and hit the ground.

I still felt a little dizzy when we took a break to eat lunch; it was past 2 p.m. and we sat underneath a large walnut tree that was on the side of the road. While we ate, Papa jotted down the number of boxes we had picked; Roberto drew designs on the ground with a stick. Suddenly I noticed Papa's face turn pale as he looked down the road; "Here comes the school bus," he whispered loudly in alarm. Instinctively, Roberto and I ran and hid in the vineyards. We did not want to get in trouble for not going to school. The yellow bus stopped in front of Mr. Sullivan's house; two neatly dressed boys my age got off. They carried books under their arms. After they crossed the street, the bus drove away. Roberto and I came out from hiding and joined Papa; *"Tienen que tener cuidado,"*[7] he warned us.

After lunch, we went back to work; the sun kept beating down; the buzzing insects, the wet sweat, and the hot, dry dust made the afternoon seem to last forever. Finally, the mountains around the valley reached out and swallowed the sun; within an hour, it was too dark to continue picking. The vines blanketed

[7]**tienen que tener cuidado:** You have to be careful.

the grapes, making it difficult to see the bunches; "*Vamanos*,[8]" said Papa, signaling to us that it was time to quit work. Papa then took out a pencil and began to figure out how much we had earned our first day. He wrote down numbers, crossed some out, wrote down some more; "*Quince*,[9]" he murmured.

When we arrived home, we took a cold shower underneath a waterhose. We then sat down to eat dinner around some wooden crates that served as a table. Mama had cooked a special meal for us. We had rice and tortillas with *carne con chile*,[10] my favorite dish.

The next morning I could hardly move; my body ached all over. I felt little control over my arms and legs. This feeling went on every morning until my muscles got used to the work.

It was Monday, the first week of November; the grape season was over, and I could now go to school. I woke up early that morning and lay in bed, looking at the stars and savoring the thought of not going to work and of starting school for the first time that year. Since I could not sleep, I decided to get up and join Papa and Roberto at breakfast. I sat at the table across from Roberto, but I kept my head

[8]**vamanos:** Let's go.
[9]**quince:** fifteen
[10]**carne con chile:** meat with chile peppers
savoring (SAY vur ing) enjoying

down. I did not want to look up and face him. I knew he was sad; he was not going to school today; he was not going tomorrow, or the next week, or next month. He would not go until the cotton season was over, and that was some time in February. I rubbed my hands together and watched the dry, acid-stained skin fall to the floor in little rolls.

When Papa and Roberto left for work, I felt relief. I walked to the top of a small grade next to the garage and watched the *Carcanchita* disappear in the distance in a cloud of dust.

Two hours later, around 8 A.M., I stood by the side of the road waiting for school bus number twenty. When it arrived, I climbed in. No one noticed me; everyone was busy either talking or yelling. I sat in an empty seat in the back.

When the bus stopped in front of the school, I felt very nervous; I looked out the bus window and saw students carrying books under their arms. I felt empty; I put my hands in my pants pockets and walked to the principal's office. When I entered I heard a woman's voice say, "May I help you?" I was startled; I had not heard English for months. For a few seconds I remained speechless; I looked at the woman who waited for an answer. My first instinct was to answer in Spanish, but I held back. Finally, after struggling for English words, I managed to tell her that I wanted to enroll in school. After answering many questions, I was led to the classroom.

Mr. Lema, the teacher, greeted me and assigned me a desk; he then introduced me to the class. I was so nervous and scared at that moment when everyone's eyes were on me that I wished I were with Papa and Roberto picking cotton. After taking roll, Mr. Lema gave the class the assignment for the first hour; "The first thing we have to do this morning is finish reading the story we began yesterday," he said enthusiastically. He walked up to me, handed me an English book, and asked me to read; "We are on page 125," he said politely. When I heard this, I felt my blood rush to my head; I felt dizzy. "Would you like to read?" he asked hesitantly. I opened the book to page 125. My mouth was dry; my eyes began to water; I could not begin. "You can read later," Mr. Lema said understandingly.

For the rest of the reading period I kept getting angrier and angrier with myself. I should have read, I thought to myself.

Between classes I went to the restroom and opened my English book to page 125. I began to read in a low voice, pretending I was in class. There were many words I did not know; I closed the book and headed back to the classroom.

Mr. Lema was sitting at his desk correcting papers. When I entered he looked up at me and smiled; I felt better. I walked up to him and asked if he could help me with the new words; "Gladly," he said.

---

hesitantly (HEZ ih tunt lee) pausing in doubt

The rest of the month I spent my lunch hours working on English with Mr. Lema, my best friend at school.

One Friday during lunch hour, Mr. Lema asked me to take a walk with him to the music room. "Do you like music?" he asked me as we entered the building.

"Yes, I like Mexican *corridos,*"[11] I answered. He then picked up a trumpet, blew on it, and handed it to me; the sound gave me goose bumps. I knew that sound; I had heard it in many Mexican *corridos.* "How would you like to learn to play it?" he asked. He must have read my face because before I could answer, he added: "I'll teach you how to play it during our lunch hours."

That day I could hardly wait to get home to tell Papa and Mama the great news. As I got off the bus, my little brothers and sisters ran up to meet me; they were yelling and screaming. I thought they were happy to see me, but when I opened the door to our *casita,* I saw that everything we owned was neatly packed in cardboard boxes.

---

[11]**corridos:** ballads, popular songs

FOCUS ON THE SELECTION

UNDERSTAND THE SELECTION

Recall

1. Who is the main character?
2. What do the storyteller and his family do for a living?
3. What does he do in November?

Infer

4. Why does the storyteller's father think that a blue necktie must be owned by someone important?
5. Why is the story entitled "The Circuit"?
6. Why does the storyteller's father tell him and Roberto to be careful when the school bus comes?
7. What does the storyteller realize when he comes home and sees everything packed?

Apply

8. What determined when and where the storyteller and his family would move?
9. Have you or one of your friends had to move many times? How did the moves make you feel?
10. Why was it difficult for the storyteller and his brother to get an education?

Respond to Literature

What influence can people from another generation have on a youth from another family?

WRITE ABOUT THE SELECTION

An important character in the story is Mr. Lema. How do you think he felt when Panchito did not return to school? Do you think that the boy had a chance to explain what was happening? Imagine that you are Mr. Lema. Write a letter to Panchito in which you express your feelings and give the boy whatever help you can.

Prewriting: Before starting your letter, decide what the circumstances will be. Does Mr. Lema know why Panchito has left, or is he writing to find out? Now jot down some notes about what you want to say in your letter.

Writing: Use your prewriting notes to write a letter from Mr. Lema to Panchito. Make sure that your letter stays "in character"—that is, that the letter is consistent with the way Mr. Lema is presented in the story. Take your cues from the details in the story.

Revising: If your letter has several paragraphs, try presenting the paragraphs in a different order. You may also want to try changing the order of sentences within a paragraph. Decide which version of the letter you like best.

Proofreading: Make sure that you have used the correct form for a friendly letter. Check to see that your address and the date are in the upper right corner; that the greeting is followed by a comma; and that the closing is also followed by a comma. Check all punctuation.

THINK ABOUT THEME

The meaning of a story is the theme. Some stories have more than one theme. Usually one theme is more important than the others, although the relative importance of each theme may depend on the reader. For example, in "Fifth Chinese Daughter," some readers may feel that the theme related to Chinese-American values is most important, while others may focus on the theme that relates to the generation gap.

1. What themes are present in the story, "The Circuit"?
2. Which of these themes do you think is most important? Why do you think so?
3. What theme in the story deals with personal human values?
4. What theme in the story deals with a social issue?
5. What theme in the story deals with the family and society?

DEVELOP YOUR VOCABULARY

A word that modifies, or adds meaning to, a verb is called an **adverb**. An adverb usually answers one of four questions: Where? When? How? To what extent? For example, in the sentence, "Everything was neatly packed in cardboard boxes," the word neatly is an adverb. It tells *how* the packing was done. Adverbs can also modify adjectives and other adverbs; for example, "I am very happy," and "I ran very quickly." In both sentences, *very* is an adverb telling to what extent.

Review the meanings of the following adverbs from "The Circuit." Then use each adverb in an original sentence. Underline the verb that the adverb modifies.

1. hesitantly
2. thoroughly
3. proudly
4. angrily
5. loudly
6. hardly
7. instinctively
8. early
9. understandingly
10. gladly
11. enthusiastically
12. politely

UNIT 6 REVIEW

LITERATURE-BASED WRITING

1. You read about many kinds of families in the selections in this unit. Imagine that you are a member of a committee to choose the "Family of the Year." The nominees are the families in this unit. Choose the family you feel should win. Write a recommendation for your first choice.

Prewriting: Select the family you will recommend. Make a list of reasons why this family should be chosen. Arrange your list from most important to least important reason. Add details that support each item on your list.

Writing: Use your list to write your recommendation. Begin with a statement of your main idea. List your supporting details in order of importance.

Revising: One way to make an effective recommendation is to use powerful words. Replace common or overused words in your recommendation with words that are powerful and persuasive.

Proofreading: Reread your recommendation. Whenever your main idea changes, begin a new paragraph. Be sure all punctuation is correct.

2. In this unit, you studied the elements of fiction. Choose one selection in this unit. You can choose what you think is a good example or a bad example of fiction writing. You will write a review of the story, using what you have learned about fiction as you write.

Prewriting: Select your story. Reread the section on elements of fiction. Make notes about the main ideas. Then reread the story. Jot down ideas you want to include in your review. Be sure you include each of the main elements discussed in the unit.

Writing: Use your notes to write your review. You may put your notes in any order you wish before you begin. Try to make your ideas clear and easily understood.

Revising: Be specific. Saying that a plot is "dumb" does not tell your readers why you feel as you do. Explain your opinion in clear, specific terms. Use story details and examples to illustrate your points.

Proofreading: Proper nouns are the names of specific people, places, and things. Be sure you have capitalized every proper noun in your review.

BUILDING LANGUAGE SKILLS

Sometimes you are reading and you come across a word you do not know. One way to find the part of speech of a word is to look at the word's ending. Here are four common adjective suffixes:

-ish   *-ous*   *-ic*   *-al*

Underline the adjective in each sentence below. Tell the meaning of the word you underlined.

1. The eternal flame is never allowed to go out.
2. Flag displays are ubiquitous on the Fourth of July.
3. We could not drink the brackish water although we were thirsty.
4. The money spent on the production of the show was monumental.
5. He wore a sheepish grin as he apologized for his clumsiness.
6. The boisterous children filled the halls with shouts and cries.
7. As dinner warmed, the kitchen filled with aromatic smells.

Use *subject* pronouns (*I, you, he, she, it, we, they*) for sentence subjects. Use *object* pronouns (*me, you, him, her, it, us, them*) as objects of verbs and prepositions. Use *possessive* pronouns (*my, your, his, her, its, our, their*) to show ownership.

If a pronoun appears in a compound subject or object, remove the other part to see what kind of pronoun to choose.

Example:

Give the ball to Mike and (*she her*). Give the ball to (*she her*). Give the ball to Mike and *her*.

Choose the correct pronoun to complete each sentence below.

1. Juno and (*Jupiter*) were Roman gods.
2. Brides brought gifts to (*Juno's*) temples.
3. Other people brought gifts to (*Jupiter and other gods).*
4. Apollo and (*Apollo's*) sister were twins.
5. People worshipped (*Apollo*) and (*Apollo's sister.*)

UNIT 6 REVIEW

SPEAKING AND LISTENING

In every story the main character is faced with conflict. As the main character acts to resolve the conflict, the plot unfolds.

There are three basic kinds of conflicts. There can be a conflict between persons. An example of this would be a story about characters who are in a physical, emotional or moral struggle between one another. There can be conflict between persons and things or forces. An example would be a story about a pioneer family that has to struggle to stay alive in the wilderness during the winter. Finally, there can be conflict within a person. An example would be a story in which a person who has committed a crime struggles to decide whether to turn himself in or let someone else be wrongfully punished for the crime.

Before you begin to talk about a main character from one of the selections in this unit and the conflicts that face him, practice the following steps:

1. Think about the character as a "real" person with a "real" problem. Try to relate your feelings to the character's feelings. As you become more familiar with the character, you will be able to identify his conflict or problem more easily.

2. As you read the selection be aware of the character and his reactions to people and things around him. Try to identify whether his struggle is taking place outside of him (external), or if it is taking place within him (internal).

3. Ask yourself what the character is struggling for and who or what may be opposing him. You'll want to determine what other characters or forces in the story seem to have the most effect upon him. Remember, the effect can be positive or negative. If it is negative, chances are there is a problem.
4. Think about how the character resolves his conflict. Determine if the main character was able to work out his problem on his own or if there was an event or a person who helped him.

Now, choose a main character from one of the selections in this unit. Let it be a character that left you with an impression. Prepare to introduce this character to your classmates as though they have never met him. Your introduction should take approximately three minutes. It should include information that describes the character, tells about the conflict that confronted him, and it should tell your audience how the conflict was resolved. Before you introduce your character, go back and review the steps above. They will help your introduction go smoothly.

CRITICAL THINKING

Predicting means making a guess about something that has not yet happened. You may have heard of predictions about the weather or sports events.

You can make predictions about things you read as well. A good reader is always thinking about the plot and making predictions about what will happen next.

You base these predictions on details in the story that you have read so far. You know what has happened and you form a pretty good idea of what will happen next. One unusual way to use predicting is the **surprise ending.** Stories with surprise endings do not end the way readers predicted they would end. The readers are surprised and entertained.

As you read, you should constantly be checking details in your mind: "This happened. What does that mean will happen next?" Then as you continue, you should check your prediction. Were you correct? Or were you surprised? If you were surprised, was there some way you could have made a more accurate prediction? Look for story details that clued you in to the surprising event.

Choose one selection in this unit and answer these questions about it.

1. Were you able to predict the ending of the story or was it a surprise? Was the ending a "complete surprise"? If not, why not?
2. What details in the story could you use to make a prediction about the outcome of the story?

EFFECTIVE STUDYING

Reference books are special books of information. There are several types of reference books. Common types are:

encyclopedia—detailed articles on many topics in alphabetical order

dictionary—a collection of word meanings and pronunciations in alphabetical order.

biographical dictionary—a collection of facts about famous people.

gazeteer—a dictionary of geographical place names.

almanac—a brief, up-to-date collection of facts.

atlas—a book of maps.

historical atlas—maps showing places as they were during various times in history.

Very few homes or classrooms have all of these reference books. So where do you find them? Any good-sized library will have all or most of these books. There is a special section of the library where you can find reference books. If you are not sure how to locate it, ask your librarian for help.

Dictionaries and encyclopedias are arranged alphabetically, so all you have to do is look up the word or topic you want. Almanacs and atlases have indexes. The indexes are in alphabetical order. Look up your topic in the index and then turn to the correct page to find the information you need.

GLOSSARY

GLOSSARY PRONUNCIATION KEY

Accent is the force or stress given to some words or syllables in speech. In this book, accent is indicated by the use of uppercase letters. Words of one syllable are always shown as accented. Thus, if the word *hand* were pronounced, the pronunciation would be printed *(HAND)*. In words of more than one syllable, the syllable that gets the main accent is printed in uppercase letters. The other syllable or syllables are printed in lowercase letters. If the word *handbag* were pronounced, the pronunciation would be printed *(HAND bag)*. The phonetic respellings are based on the pronunciations given in Webster's *New World Dictionary*.

Letter(s) in text words	*Letter(s) used in respelling*	*Sample words*	*Phonetic respelling*
a	**a**	hat bandit	(HAT) (BAN dit)
a	**ay**	ate makeup	(AYT) (MAYK up)
a	**air**	stare daring	(STAIR) (DAIR ing)
a	**ah**	dart farmhouse	(DAHRT) (FAHRM hous)
a	**u** *or* **uh**	about	(uh BOUT)
e	**e**	belt denim	(BELT) (DEN im)
e	**eh**	ingest	(in JEHST)
e	**ih**	delight result	(dih LYT) (rih ZULT)
e	**u** *or* **uh**	darken perhaps	(DAHR kun) (pur HAPS)
e	**ee**	he demon	(HEE) (DEE mun)
i	**i**	hit mitten	(HIT) (MIT un)
i	**ih**	distress gravity	(dih STRES) (GRAV ih tee)
i	**y**	dime idle	(DYM) (YD ul)
i	**eye**	idea	(eye DEE uh)
i	**ee**	medium	(MEE dee um)
i	**u** *or* **uh**	possible	(POS uh bul)
o	**o**	hot bottle	(HOT) (BOT ul)
o	**u** *or* **uh**	gallon	(GAL un)
o	**oh**	go open	(GOH) (OH pun)
o	**aw**	horn malt ballroom	(HAWRN) (MAWLT) (BAWL room)
oo	**uu**	book football	(BUUK) (FUUT bawl)
oo	**oo**	move pool ruler	(MOOV) (POOL) (ROO lur)
oi	**oi**	point boiler	(POINT) (BOI lur)
ou	**ou**	pout output	(POUT) (OUT put)
th	**th** *or* ***th***	thimble wither	(THIM bul) (WI*TH* ur)
u	**u**	up upshot	(UP) (UP shot)
u	**uh**	support	(suh PAWRT)
y	**i**	rhythm	(RITH um)
y	**ee**	lazy	(LAY zee)
y	**y**	thyme	(TYM)

abundant (uh BUN dunt) well supplied, very plentiful
accurately (AK yur it lee) perfectly on target
accusation (ak yoo ZAY shun) a charge of wrong-doing
acknowledge (ak NOL ij) admit that something is true
adequate (AD ih kwit) enough
advantage (ad VAN tij) something that gives a person a better chance, a more favorable position
alert (uh LERT) watchful and ready, as in facing danger; quick in thought or action
ambition (am BISH un) desire to do something
amiss (uh MIS) wrong; not correct
ancestors (AN ses turz) people from whom one is descended
ancient (AYN chunt) very old
anguished (ANG gwisht) in great pain, grief, or distress
anxious (ANK shus) worried; uneasy in mind
appropriately (uh PROH pree it lee) fitting the purpose, properly
architect (AHR kuh tekt) person who designs buildings
ascend (uh SEND) go up, rise
assent (uh SENT) agreement
astonished (uh STON isht) filled with sudden wonder or great surprise
astride (uh STRYD) with one leg on each side
attain (uh TAYN) reach; gain
automatic (awt uh MAT ik) done without thinking
aviator (AY vee ayt ur) person who pilots a plane
awed (AWD) full of respect or wonder

bankrupt (BANGK rupt) anyone unable to pay his or her debts
battered (BAT urd) beaten up; well-used
bearing (BAIR ing) way of carrying oneself
begrudge (bih GRUJ) feel angry at something another person has
bewilder (bih WIL dur) puzzle; confuse
billow (BIL oh) rise in waves, swell up
blaring (BLAIR ing) making loud and rough sounds
bluff (BLUF) cliff; high, steep land
bondage (BON dij) slavery
borders (BAWR durz) dividing lines between two countries, states, etc., or the land along it
bound (BOUND) leap; jump
brilliant (BRIL yunt) remarkably fine
burden (BURD un) load to be carried
burrow (BUR oh) to make a hole or tunnel by digging into the ground

calculate (KAL kyuh layt) figure out by reasoning; to determine by using mathematics
canteen (kan TEEN) a small container for carrying water and other liquids
casual (KAZH oo ul) relaxed; unconcerned
cautiously (KAW shus lee) carefully, trying to avoid danger
clarity (CLAR uh tee) the condition or state of being clear
clearing (KLIR ing) piece of land from which trees have been removed
clinging (KLING ing) holding tightly
clinking (KLINGK ing) making or causing to make a slight, sharp sound, as of glasses striking together
coincidence (koh IN suh duns) two or more things that happen at the same time, by accident
commotion (kuh MOH shun) noisy disturbance
compete (kum PEET) enter a contest and try to win
complexion (kum PLEK shun) color and texture of skin
comprehend (kom prih HEND) understand
compulsory (kum PUL suh ree) required
concentrate (KON sun trayt) give all one's attention to
condemn (kun DEM) pronounce guilty; to convict
confronted (kun FRUNT id) met face to face boldly
congregate (KONG gruh gayt) gather together, meet
conveniently (kun VEEN yunt lee) making it easy
converging (kun VUR jing) coming together
correspond (kawr uh SPOND) agree; match
countless (COUNT lis) too many to count
cramped (KRAMPT) small and crowded
crisis (KRY sis) dangerous time when an illness or other problem can either get better or worse
critical (KRIT ih kul) at an important moment
crouched (KROUCHT) bent low
cumbersome (KUM bur sum) clumsy; difficult to manage
cunning (KUN ing) cleverness; sly, clever behavior
curious (KYUUR ee us) very strange; odd
curiously (KYUUR ee us lee) carefully, arousing attention or interest because something is unusual or strange

cynically (SIN ik lee) in a manner that shows one doesn't really believe what one hears; distrustful

destined (DES tind) something that is bound to happen
determine (dih TUR mun) decide, make up one's mind
devour (dih VOUR) eat up quickly
diagnosis (dy ug NOH sis) a decision about the kind of illness a person has
diplomatic (dip luh MAT ik) careful and wise in dealing with people
disarray (dis uh RAY) disorder; confusion
disheveled (dih SHEV uld) messy, untidy, disordered
dismal (DIZ mul) dark and gloomy
dissect (dih SEKT) cut open and examine
distinct (dih STINGKT) not alike; different; separate; individual
distinction (dih STINGK shun) special quality
duplicate (DOO plih kayt) repeat; do the same thing

earnest (UR nist) serious; sincere
economic (ek uh NOM ik) having to do with income and expenses
eerie (IR ee) mysterious or weird in such a way as to frighten
elaborately (ih LAB ur it lee) extremely carefully planned; with considerable detail
embroidered (em BROI durd) decorated with fancy needlework
emerge (ih MURJ) come out from something or someplace
emitted (ih MIT id) sent out; gave forth; discharged
encounter (en KOUN tur) a meeting
encourage (en KUR ij) to give hope or confidence
endurance (en DUUR uns) the ability to withstand hardship, misfortune, or stress
engrossed (en GROHST) having all one's attention focused
enhanced (en HANST) made greater or more attractive
enlivening (en LY vun ing) making lively
enormously (ih NAWR mus lee) much bigger than usual; hugely
envelop (en VEL up) wrap; surround
envy (EN vee) feel jealous about
era (IR uh) a period of time marked from one important date to another
errand (ER und) a short trip to do some business, often for another person
eternal (ih TUR nul) lasting forever
expanses (ik SPANS iz) large open areas or unbroken surfaces
exultation (eg zul TAY shun) triumph or rejoicing

fatal (FAYT ul) resulting in death
favor (FAY vur) give special treatment
ferocious (fuh ROH shus) savage; vicious
feverishly (FEE vur ish lee) hurriedly; excitedly
fierce (FIRS) strong; intense
flank (FLANGK) side near the back leg; hip
flare (FLAIR) spread out
fleeting (FLEET ing) soon gone; fast disappearing
forbade (fur BAD) to prevent; a command against
fragment (FRAG munt) small piece
frail (FRAYL) weak; fragile
fraud (FRAWD) cheat
frivolous (FRIV uh lus) silly; not serious; just for fun
frustration (frus TRAY shun) disappointment people feel when they cannot get what they had hoped for
fugitive (FYOO jih tiv) runaway, one who escapes
furrow (FUR oh) long, narrow trench that a plow makes in the earth
futilely (FYOOT ul ee) uselessly; with no effect

gaunt (GAWNT) thin; worn
genteel (jen TEEL) polite; well-mannered
gesture (JES chur) motion, hand signal
giddy (GID ee) dizzy; excited with happiness
glare (GLAIR) angry look
glimpse (GLIMPS) to see for only a short time
glitter (GLIT ur) bright sparkling light
gnarled (NAHRLD) twisted
gnash (NASH) strike or grind the teeth together
grace (GRAYS) special beauty; ease of movement
gratitude (GRAT ih tood) thankfulness
gravely (GRAYV lee) very seriously
grisly (GRIZ lee) horrible
guarantee (gar un TEE) promise that something is true

haggard (HAG urd) worn out and tired looking
hallucination (huh loo suh NAY shun) seeing something that does not really exist
handicap (HAN dih kap) something that hampers a person; difficulty; disadvantage
harass (huh RAS) give trouble to; bother a lot
haughty (HAWT ee) overly proud of oneself

heartfelt (HAHRT felt) sincere, honest
herd (HURD) a large number of animals, or a group of people moving like a heard of animals
heritage (HER ih tij) things we inherit from our ancestors
hesitantly (HEZ ih tunt lee) pausing in doubt
hesitation (hez ih TAY shun) failure to act promptly
hideous (HID ee us) very ugly; horrible to look at
hoarded (HAWRD id) saved; stored up
host (HOHST) great number of people; army
hover (HUV ur) hang in the air

idiosyncracy (id ee oh SING kruh see) unusual trait, habit, or practice
ignorance (IG nuh runs) lack of knowledge
immaculate (ih MAK yuh lit) perfectly clean; without a spot or stain; unsoiled
impress (IM pres) mark; stamp
imprint (im PRINT) make a mark
incessant (in SES unt) without interruption
incisive (in SY siv) penetrating or sharp
inconvenient (in kun VEEN yunt) troublesome; not easy to do
incredible (in KRED uh bul) not believable
incredulously (in KREJ uh lus lee) in a shocked and unbelieving way
incriminate (in KRIM uh nayt) cause to appear guilty
indifference (n DIF ur uns) showing a lack of concern, interest, or feeling
industry (IN dus tree) hard work
infuriates (in FYUUR ee ayts) makes angry
inheritance (in HER ih tuns) money and belongings that are passed down from parent to child
initiative (ih NISH uh tiv) taking the first step in a plan of action
insanely (in SAYN lee) in an uncontrolled, mentally unsound way
insolently (IN suh lunt lee) in an insulting and rude manner
integrity (in TEG ruh tee) honesty
intently (in TENT lee) earnestly; firmly directed or fixed
interminable (in TER muh nuh bul) endless
intervals (IN tur vulz) time or space between
intricate (IN trih kit) having many parts, complicated
irresponsible (ir ih SPON suh bul) unreliable; lacking a sense of responsibility
isolation (eye suh LAY shun) being alone; away from others

jostled (JOS uld) bumped and pushed, as in a crowd

kindling (KIND ling) small pieces of wood used for starting a fire

lagging (LAG ing) falling, moving or staying behind
landing (LAND ing) a large flat area partway up a staircase
landscape (LAND skayp) a picture representing a section of natural, inland scenery, as of a prairie, woodland, mountain, etc.
languid (LANG gwid) lazy; weak; slow-moving
lapse (LAPS) failure; interruption
lavish (LAV ish) generous; having huge amounts
leisurely (LEE zhur lee) without hurry
lethal (LEE thul) causing or capable of causing death
liberator (LIB ur ayt ur) person who sets others free
lithe (LY*TH*) flexible; bendable
livery (LIV ur ee) stable where horses are kept for hire
loam (LOHM) rich soil

maneuver (muh NOO vur) move in a way that makes contact easiest
mangled (MANG guld) twisted
marked (MAHRKT) noticeable, easy to see
martyrdom (MAHR tur dum) ready to die or suffer for a cause or belief
marvel (MAHR vul) wonder; be astonished by
mingle (MING gul) mix together
miserly (MY zer lee) too careful with money
mishap (MIS hap) accident
mock (MOK) make fun of
momentary (MOH mun ter ee) lasting for only a moment; passing; transitory
monotonous (muh NOT un us) going on in the same tone without variation
moody (MOO dee) having many changes of feelings or mood
mores (MAWR ays) manners or moral customs of a social group
motivate (MOHT uh VAYT) cause to act
mournful (MAWRN ful) sad: sorrowful
multitude (MUL tuh tood) a large number of persons gathered together
mutter (MUT ur) speak softly and not clearly

noncommittal (non kuh MIT ul) not showing what one thinks
numb (NUM) weakened in or deprived of the power of feeling or moving

obsession (ub SESH un) overpowering desire or idea
obvious (OB vee us) easily seen; clear
omen (OH mun) sign of what is to come
ominously (OM uh nus lee) threateningly
ordained (awr DAYND) arranged

paddock (PAD uk) fenced-in area where horses are saddled and exercised
panorama (pan uh RAM uh) full view; complete picture
parched (PAHRCHT) dried out
passable (PAS uh bul) good enough
passion (PASH un) strong feeling
pasture (PAS chur) a grassy field or hillside
perplexing (pur PLEKS ing) confusing; puzzling
persuade (pur SWAYD) talk someone into doing something
pillage (PIL ij) rob and destroy
pitiless (PIT ih lis) without pity; unfeeling
plague (PLAYG) pester, give trouble to
planks (PLANGKS) long, broad, thick boards
possess (puh ZES) have; own
potential (puh TEN shul) something that can happen, but which has not happened yet; possibility
pounce (POUNS) spring or leap
poverty (POV ur tee) having little or no money; condition of being very poor
precious (PRESH us) most valuable
precipitated (prih SIP uh tayt id) brought about; caused
presently (PREZ unt lee) soon, before long
primly (PRIM lee) extremely properly and carefully
prominent (PROM uh nunt) standing out; easy to see
prophecy (PROF uh see) statement telling what will happen in the future
protozoa (proht uh ZOH uh) one-celled animals that can be seen only under a microscope
puny (PYOO nee) small and weak
pursue (pur SOO) chase, follow after

ransack (RAN sak) search through
raucous (RAW kus) loud; harsh; shouted
reckoning (REK un ing) way of thinking; calculated guessing
recollect (rek uh LEKT) remember
recommend (rek uh MEND) suggest someone who would be good for a job
refuse (REF yoos) things thrown away
regard (rih GAHRD) think about; consider
relic (REL ik) something that has survived from the past
renounce (rih NOUNS) give up; refuse
replenish (rih PLEN ish) fill again; give more to
resentment (rih ZENT munt) feeling of being insulted or treated unfairly
resolved (rih ZOLVD) firm and fixed in purpose
retrieve (rih TREEV) get something back
revered (rih VIRD) regarded with deep respect, love, and awe
revive (rih VYV) to bring back to health or life
routine (roo TEEN) ordinary; predictable

sauntered (SAWN turd) strolled or walked about idly
savoring (SAY vur ing) enjoying
scanty (SKAN tee) very small; hardly enough for what is needed
scattered (SKAT urd) thrown here and there or strewn loosely; sprinkled
scorn (SKAWRN) have a low opinion of
scrawny (SKRAW nee) thin; skinny
seeking (SEEK ing) tracing down, trying to find out; searching for
seemingly (SEEM ing lee) the way things appear to be
sentiment (SEN tuh munt) feeling, emotion
serpent (SUR punt) snake
shabby (SHAB ee) run-down; beat-up
shrill (SHRIL) high, sharp sound
shudder (SHUD ur) tremble, shake
signature (SIG nuh chur) a person's name written by that person
silhouette (sil oo ET) outline drawing of a person or object, filled in with a dark color
skimp (SKIMP) do without; stretch to cover
slick (SLIK) smooth and shiny
slither (SLI*TH* ur) slide and move as a snake does
slumbering (SLUM bur ing) sleeping
snag (SNAG) catch on something
snarl (SNAHRL) to growl fiercely, baring the teeth, as a threatening dog; to speak harshly or sharply
solemn (SOL um) very serious, not cheerful
sought (SAWT) searched for; looked for

spans (SPANZ) reaches from one side to the other
sphere (SFIR) ball
splendid (SPLEN did) grand; excellent; worthy of high praise
sprinter (SPRINT ur) one who runs quickly for a short distance
spur (SPUR) metal piece attached to a rider's shoe used to make the horse go faster
stagger (STAG ur) walk in an unsteady way
stamina (STAM uh nuh) strength and ability to last
stammering (STAM ur ing) speaking with involuntary stops and repetition
stance (STANS) way of standing
staunch (STAWNCH) steady and true
steep (STEEP) very expensive; costly
still (STIL) peaceful; unmoving
stout (STOUT) bold; strong
strain (STRAYN) cause to work as hard as possible; injure or weaken by force
stricken (STRIK un) affected by something painful or upsetting
striding (STRYD ing) walking with long, quick steps
strife (STRYF) contest; struggle
sublime (suh BLYM) grand; on a high level
subterranean (sub tuh RAY nee un) below the earth's surface
superstition (soo pur STISH un) belief or attitude based on fear or ignorance
swagger (SWAG ur) walk or move the body in a tough, bullying way
swiftness (SWIFT ness) moving or capable of moving with great speed
swindle (SWIN dul) cheat; to get money or property from another under false pretenses; defraud
symbol (SIM bul) an object that stands for an idea
symbolize (SIM bul yz) be a sign or symbol of

taper (TAY pur) make or become gradually smaller at one end
taunt (TAWNT) mock; laugh at
taut (TAWT) stretched tight
tempest (TEM pist) big storm
tendon (TEN dun) part of the body that connects a muscle to a bone
threadbare (THRED bair) old and worn
threshold (THRESH ohld) entrance to a house or building
thrifty (THRIF tee) carefully managing money
thumped (THUMPT) made a dull, heavy sound; pounded, throbbed
toil (TOIL) work; chores
traditional (truh DISH uh nul) according to customs passed on from parents to children
transfixed (trans FIKST) made motionless
treacherous (TRECH er us) unreliable; likely to betray trust; disloyal
tribute (TRIB yoot) words of praise
trickle (TRIK ul) to flow slowly in a thin stream or fall into drops
trudge (TRUJ) walk slowly and heavily
tumult (TOO mult) noisy uproar

unkempt (un KEMPT) neglected; untidy
urge (URJ) encourage; persuade someone to do something
utmost (UT mohst) greatest amount possible

venture (VEN chur) dare going; take a risk of going
visage (VIZ ij) face
visor (VY zur) front part of a cap that shades the eyes from sun

wardrobe (WAWR drohb) collection of clothes
wearily (WIR uh lee) in a tired way
whittle (HWIT ul) cut thin slices, or shavings, of wood using a knife
willful (WIL ful) wanting things one's own way
wisps (WISPS) thin, filmy strands
wretched (RECH id) very unhappy, miserable
wriggle (RIG ul) twist and turn; squirm
wrought (RAWT) worked, made

zeal (ZEEL) eager desire

INDEX OF FINE ART

xviii *The Block.* Romare Bearden
6 *Whale Dance.* Rie Muñoz
12 *The Overland Pony Express.* Engraving
24 *Susan B. Anthony and Elizabeth Cady Stanton.* Engraving
32 *The Misses Cooke's Schoolroom in the Freedman's Bureau, Richmond, Virginia.* Engraving
35 *Harriet Tubman.* Oil-painted photograph
44 *Frederick Douglass.* Attributed to E. Hammond
63 *West Bound Wagon Train on the Salt Lake Trail, 1840s.* O. E. Berninghaus
65 *I and the Village.* Marc Chagall
89 *The False Mirror.* René Magritte
108 *Street Light.* Giacomomo Balla
110 *The Cafe Royal.* Charles Ginner
194 *Ming dynasty noble's badge.* Anonymous
201 *Animals.* Rufino Tamayo
204 *Perseus Slaying Medusa.* Anonymous
207 *Medusa.* Caravaggio
210 Black-figured Greek Amphora
240 *Sea Serpent.* Hans Egidius
248 *The Kraken, detail.* The Granger Collection
252 *The Kraken, as Seen by the Eye of Imagination.* The Granger Collection
286 New School Mural. Thomas Hart Benton
319 *Mount Holyoke Female Seminary.* Engraving
326 *Henry Wadsworth Longfellow.* Engraving
329 *Woman in Green Dress.* Pablo Picasso
356 *The Starry Night.* Vincent Van Gogh
360 *Cruising for Stock.* Engraving
365 *Watering the Herd.* William M. Cary
368 *Head of a White Horse.* Théodore Géricault
369 *In with the Horse Herd.* Frederic Remington
387 *The Hollow of a Deep-Sea-Wave.* Hokusai
394 *Mt. Fuji in the Background.* Hiroshige
400 *View of Mt. Fuji.* Hokusai
408 *Landscape.* Sasahide
413 *Ferry Crossing.* Hiroshige
430 *Dolmen in the Snow.* J. C. C. Dahl
440 *Family Portrait.* Florine Stettheimer
446 *The Boch Family.* Edvard Munch
452 *Mrs. Eric Krans.* Olaf Krans
468 *The Crib.* Berthe Morisot
463 *Girls at the Piano.* Auguste Renoir
470 *Maid of the Douglas Family,* Anonymous

INDEX OF SKILLS

Abbreviations, 191
Action, character and, 108, 117
Adjectives, 85, 351
Adverbs, 485, 539
  formed from adjectives, 351
Alliteration, 140, 323
Antonyms, 427, 465
Apostrophe, 371
Articles, informational, 248, 257
Atlas, 543
Autobiography, 42–43, 51
Beginning rhyme, 462
Biography, 32, 41, 42–43
Characters, 98, 109, 198, 203, 304, 411, 450, 459
  actions of, 108, 117
  in drama, 392, 419
  in fiction, 234–235, 499
  lives of, 412
  major, 83
  minor, 83
  personality of, 354
  in poem, 468
  in short story, 424
Characterization, 70, 83, 117
Classification, 285
Climax, 98, 476
Conflict in plot, 107, 235, 290, 299
Connotations, 160, 189, 384, 391
Context clues, 97, 221, 343, 411, 437
  and foreign words, 461
Contractions, 371
Couplets, 216, 221
Critical thinking, 87, 192, 285, 355, 439, 469, 543
Denotations, 160, 189, 384
Description, 10, 15
Dialect, 513
Dictionary, 117, 139, 203, 257, 419, 449
  pronunciation symbols in, 435
Drama, 392–393, 419
Encyclopedia, 543
Fables
  compared with parables, 420
  morals of, 92, 97
Facts, and theory, 257
Fiction, 234–235, 424
  characteristics of, 498–499
  elements of, 234–235, 247
  reasons for reading, 499, 513
  setting in, 360, 371
Figurative expressions, 321
Figure of speech, 459
First person point of view, 52, 59, 150, 158, 486, 497
Flashbacks, 16, 425
Flat characters, 411
Foreign words, and context clues, 461
Free verse, 140, 216, 221, 323, 331
Gazeteer, 543
Humorous tone, 222, 233
Ideas, and values, 530
Imagery, 316, 321, 440, 444, 445, 449
Images, 428, 435
Internal rhyme, 462, 465
Irony, 332, 343, 372, 383
Jargon, 315
Language usage and mechanics, 85
Location, 412
Lyric poems, 4, 9
Metaphors, 353, 444
Meter, 140
Multiple-choice tests, 355
Myths, 204
Narration, 16, 23, 450, 461
Narrative pantomime, 192
Narrative poetry, 4, 9, 308, 315
Negative prefix, 445

Nonfiction
narration in, 450, 461
setting in, 360, 371
Notetaking, 87
Nouns, 85, 299
of direct address, 283
used as verbs, 391
Object pronouns, 541
One-dimensional character (See Flat character)
Onomatopoeia, 323, 445
Oral interpretation, 192, 284, 354, 438, 468, 542
Outlining, 285
Pantomime, narrative, 192
Parables, 420, 427
Paragraphs, 87
Persona, 323, 331
Personality, of character, 354
Plot, 98, 107, 476, 485, 498
in drama, 392–393, 419
in fiction, 235
Poems
meaning of, 331
point of view, 468
rhyme patterns, 216
symbolism in, 134, 139
Poetry
content of, 140–141, 149
denotations and connotations in, 384
essential parts, 322–323
forms of, 140
imagery in, 435, 440, 444, 445
meaning of, 284
purpose of, 141
rhyme in, 221
techniques of, 141
Point of view, 31, 159, 486, 497
first person, 52, 59, 150, 158, 486, 497
of poem, 468
of short story, 425
third person, 24, 344, 351
Possessive pronouns, 541
Predictions, 543
Prefixes, 149
Pronouns, 541
third person, 344
Pronunciation, 159, 233, 435
Punctuation
and nouns of direct address, 283
and quotation marks, 353
Quotation marks, 353
Reference books, 543
Resolution, 98, 107
Rhyme, 216, 221, 322, 331
Rhythm, 140, 149, 322, 331, 446, 449
Root of word, 449, 529
Root word, 149
Sentences, subject and verb of, 437
Setting, 98, 360, 371, 423
of drama, 392, 419
in fiction, 234, 247, 498
of narrative poem, 315
Short stories
elements of, 98, 424–425
forms of conflict in, 290
themes of, 300, 307, 439
Similes, 124, 133, 353, 444
Speaker of poem, 60, 69, 468, 475
Stanzas, 140
Studying, effective, 87, 193, 285, 355, 439, 469, 543
Subject, and theme, 529
Subject pronouns, 541
Subject of sentence, and verb, 437
Suffixes, 85, 283, 449, 467, 497
Surprise ending, 476
Syllables, 331
Symbolism, 134, 139, 425
Synonyms, 307, 393, 465, 475
Test taking, and multiple choice tests, 355
Theme, 118, 123, 281, 300, 307, 439
of drama, 392, 419
of fiction, 235, 498, 514, 529, 539
of poem, 140
of short story, 258
Theory, and fact, 257
Thinking (*See* Critical thinking)

Third person point of view, 24, 344, 351
Time or period of story, 412
Tone, 460, 467
  humorous, 222, 233
  of short story, 425
Topic sentence, 87
Values, and ideas, 530
Verbal skills (*See* Oral interpretation)
Verbs
  and subject of sentence, 437
  used as nouns, 391
Vocabulary development, 9, 15, 23, 31, 41, 51, 59, 69, 83, 85, 97, 107, 117, 123, 133, 139, 149, 159, 189, 191, 203, 215, 221, 233, 257, 281, 283, 299, 307, 315, 321, 331, 343, 351, 353, 371, 391, 393, 411, 419, 423, 427, 435, 437, 445, 449, 459, 449, 461, 465, 467, 467, 475, 485, 497, 513, 529, 539, 541
Word meanings
  clues to, 123
  and connotation, 160, 189
  and context clues, 97, 221, 343, 411, 437
  and denotation, 160, 189
  and part of speech of word, 541
  and suffix, 467
  use and, 189
  and use of dictionary, 419
Word usage and mechanics, 191, 283, 353, 437, 467, 541
Words
  pronunciation of, 159, 233, 435
  relationship to each other, 107, 215
  used as nouns and verbs, 391
Writing exercises, 84, 96, 106, 116, 122, 138, 148, 158, 188, 190, 202, 214, 220, 232, 246, 256, 280, 282, 298, 306, 320, 330, 342, 350, 352, 370, 372, 390, 392, 410, 418, 422, 426, 434, 436, 438, 444, 448, 448, 458, 460, 464, 466, 484, 496, 512, 528, 538, 540

INDEX OF TITLES AND AUTHORS

Advice to Travelers, 144
Aesop (adapter), 93
Amelia's Bloomers, 25
Aquí se habla español, 151
Aristotle, 357
Arthur, Robert, 223

Bare Tree, The, 431
Barron, Arthur, 161
Basho, Matsuo, 429, *430*
Bat, The, 218
Benet, Rosemary, 63
Benet, Stephen Vincent, 63
Bierce, Ambrose, 199
Big Wave, The, 395
Black Box, The, 421
Blind Sunday, 161
Boe, Deborah, 328
Bradbury, Ray, 237
Buck, Pearl, 395, *417*
Butterfly and the Caterpillar, The, 119

Carlson, James Aggrey, 119
Carlson, Natalie Savage, 99
Carr, Albert B., 421
Carr, Pat, 125
Casey at the Bat, 309
Charles, 477
Circuit, The, 531
Clouds, 388
Collier, Eugenia, 501, *511*
Confidence Game, The, 125
Cummings, E. E., 136, *137*

Day Millicent Found the World, The, 135
Dickinson, Emily, 317, 318, *319*
Disch, Tom, 217
Djanikian, Gregory, 66, 388, 472
Donkey Who Did Not Want to Be Himself, The, 93
Douglass, Frederick, 45
Dunbar, Paul Laurence, 291

Eskin, Eden Force (reteller), 205, 211

Factory Work, 328
Family Album, The, 445
Fifth Chinese Daughter, 515
Finish of Patsy Barnes, The, 291
First Day, The, 53
Fog Horn, The, 237
Forbes, Kathryn, 461
Francis, Robert, 471

Gibson, Walker, 144
Giovanni, Nikki, 146, 432, *433*
Grudnow, 64

Haiku, 429
Harriet Tubman, Liberator, 33
Henderson, Dion, 333
"Hope" Is the Thing with Feathers, 318
Hughes, Langston, 33, *39*, 474

I am an American, 61
If I Can Stop One Heart from Breaking, 318
Illinois at Night, Black Hawk's Statue Broods, 7
Inuit poem, 6

Jackson, Shirley, 477, *483*
Jimenez, Francisco, 531

Kick, The, 301
Kind of Man She Could Love, The, 109
Kjelgaard, Jim, 373

Last Words of My English Grandmother, The, 447
Lauren, Joseph, 119
Lawrence, D. H., 441
Lazarus, Emma, 67
Lesson in Sharing, A, 5

Lester, Julius, 361
Let Our Children Live and Be Happy, 6
Lieberman, Elias, 61
Lineage, 446
Longfellow, Henry Wadsworth, 324, 326*

maggie and milly and molly and may, 136
Mama and Papa, 461
Man Who Was a Horse, The, 361
Medusa at Her Vanity, 217
Merriam, Eve, 142, 147
Monsters Are Due on Maple Street, The, 259
Mother in Mannville, A, 487
Mother to Son, 469
Mr. Dexter's Dragon, 223

New Colossus, from *The,* 67
Nietzsche, 195

O. Henry, 109
O'John, Calvin, 327

Papashvily, George, 53
Papashvily, Helen, 53
Parable of the Eagle, The, 120
Pastan, Linda, 64
Pathway from Slavery to Freedom, The, 45
Perseus and Medusa, 205
Plato, 89
Pony Express, The, 11
Pot of Gold, The, 345
Prairie Fire, 17
Psalm of Life, A, 324

Rawlings, Marjorie Kinnan, 487, *495*
Rest of My Life, The, 145
Richer, the Poorer, The, 451
Rivers, J. W., 7
Roethke, Theodore, 218
Rossetti, Christina, *385*

Salazar Arrué, Salvador, 345
Schemenauer, Elma, 249
Serling, Rod, 259
Sia Indian poem, 5
Sokolow, Leslie Jill, 151
Speckled Hen's Egg, The, 99
Split Cherry Tree, 71
Stafford, William, 135
Staley Fleming's Hallucination, 199
Stevenson, Robert Louis, 287
Storm, The, 387
Stuart, Jesse, 71
Success, 317
Sweet Potato Pie, 501
Swenson, May, 145

Ten-Armed Monster of Newfoundland, The, 249
Thayer, Ernest L., 309
These Are the Gifts, 472
Theseus and the Minotaur, 211
This Day Is Over, 327
Thumbprint, 142
Tiger's Heart, The, 373
Tucker, Linda Schechet, 25
Twain, Mark, 11, *13*

Van Steenwyk, Elizabeth, 301

Walker, Margaret, 446
Wayne, Jane O., 445
West, Dorothy, 451
Western Wagons, 63
When I First Saw Snow, 66
While I Slept, 471
Who Has Seen the Wind?, 385
Wilder, Laura Ingalls, 17, *21*
Williams, William Carlos, 387, 431, 447
Winter, 432
Wolf of Thunder Mountain, The, 333
Wong, Jade Snow, 515

You, 146

ACKNOWLEDGMENTS

Unit 1: Education Development Center, Inc.—for "A Lesson in Sharing," from *Songs and Stories of the Netsilik Eskimos,* translated by Edward Field from text collected by Knud Rasmussen. Reprinted courtesy of Education Development Center, Inc., Newton, Massachusetts. James A. Houston—for "Let Our Children Live and Be Happy," from *Songs of the Dream People,* edited and illustrated by James A. Houston. Published by Atheneum Publishers. (A Margaret K. McElderry Book.) New York, 1972. Adapted by permission of the author. Poetry Magazine—for "Illinois: At Night, Black Hawk's Statue Broods" by J. W. Rivers. Copyright 1986 by J. W. Rivers. Reprinted by permission of the author. Harper and Row, Publishers, Inc.—for "The Pony Express," from *Roughing It* by Mark Twain. Adapted and reprinted by permission of Harper and Row Publishers. Harper and Row, Publishers, Inc.—for "Prairie Fire," adapted from *Little House on the Prairie* by Laura Ingalls Wilder. Copyright 1935 by Laura Ingalls Wilder; renewed 1963 by Roger L. MacBride. Linda Schechet Tucket—for "Amelia's Bloomers" by Linda Schechet Tucker. Adapted and reprinted by permission of the author. Dodd, Mead and Company, Inc.—for "Harriet Tubman, Liberator," adapted from *Famous Negro Heroes of America* by Langston Hughes. Copyright (c) 1958 by Langston Hughes. Reprinted by permission of Dodd, Mead and Company, Inc. St. Martin's Press—for "The First Day," from *Anything Can Happen* by George and Helen Papashvily. Copyright (c) 1945, 1973 by George and Helen Papashvily. Adapted by permission of St. Martin's Press, Inc., New York. Rose K. Lieberman—for "I Am An American" by Elias Lieberman. Reprinted by permission of Rose K. Lieberman, Executrix of the estate of Elias Lieberman. Brandt and Brandt Literary Agents, Inc.—for "Western Wagons" by Rosemary and Stephen Vincent Benet, from *A Book of Americans.* Copyright 1933 by Rosemary and Stephen Vincent Benet. Copyright renewed (c) 1961 by Rosemary Carr Benet. Reprinted by permission of Brandt and Brandt Literary Agents, Inc. Poetry Magazine—for "Grudnow" by Copyright 1986. Reprinted by permission of the author. Poetry Magazine—for "When I First Saw Snow" by Gregory Djanikian. Copyright 1987 by Gregory Djanikian. Reprinted by permission of the author. The Jesse Stuart Foundation—for "Split Cherry Tree," from *The Best-Loved Short Stories of Jesse Stuart,* published by McGraw Hill, New York, 1982. Reprinted with the permission of the Jesse Stuart Foundation, Judy B. Dailey, Chairman, P.O. Box 391, Ashland, Kentucky, 41114. **Unit 2:** Harper and Row, Publishers, Inc.—for "The Speckled Hen's Egg," abridged and adapted from *The Talking Cat: And Other Stories of French Canada* by Natalie Savage Carlson. Copyright (c) 1952 by Natalie Savage Carlson. Simon & Schuster, Inc.—for "The Butterfly and the Caterpillar" by Joseph Lauren. Copyright (c) 1957 by Pocket Books, Inc. Reprinted by permission of Pocket Books, a division of Simon & Schuster, Inc. Sheldon Press—for "The Parable of the Eagle" by James Aggrey, from *Aggrey Said,* compiled by C. Kingsley Williams. Adapted by permission of Sheldon Press, London. Young Miss Magazine—for "The Confidence Game," adapted from "The Confidence Game" by Pat Carr with permission of *Young Miss* Magazine. Copyright (c) 1977, Gruner & Jahr U.S.A. Publishing. Poetry Magazine—for "The Day Millicent Found the World" by William Stafford. Copyright 1987 by William Stafford. Reprinted by permission of the author. Harcourt Brace Jovanovich, Inc.—for "maggie and milly and molly and may" by E.E. Cummings. Copyright 1956 by e.e. cummings. Reprinted from his volume *Complete Poems 1913-1963.* William Morrow & Company—for "You Came, Too" from *Black Feeling, Black Talk, Black Judgement* by Nikki Giovanni. Copyright (c) 1972 by Nikki Giovanni. Reprinted as "You" by permission of William Morrow & Company. Eve Merriam—for "Thumbprint" from *It Doesn't Always Have to Rhyme* by Eve Merriam. Reprinted by permission of the author. Hastings House, Publishers, Inc.—for "Before Starting" from *Come As You Are* by Walker Gibson. Copyright (c) 1958 by Walker Gibson. Reprinted as "Advice to Travelers" courtesy of Hastings House, Publishers, Inc. Poetry Magazine—for "The Rest of My Life" by May Swenson. Copyright 1988 by May Swenson. Reprinted by permission of the author. American Broadcasting Companies—for permission to adapt "Blind Sunday" by Arthur Barron and Fred Pressburger. Copyright (c) 1976 by American Broadcasting Companies, Inc. Reprinted by permission of American Broadcasting Companies, Inc. **Unit 3:** Poetry Magazine—for "Medusa at Her Vanity" by Tom Disch. Copyright 1987 by Tom Disch. Reprinted by permission of the author. Doubleday & Company, Inc.—for "The Bat" by Theodore Roethke from *The Collected Poems of Theodore Roethke* by Theodore Roethke. Reprinted by permission of Doubleday & Company, Inc. Regents of the University of Michigan—for "Mr. Dexter's Dragon" by Robert Arthur. Copyright (c) 1943 by Renown Publishers, Inc., renewed 1970 by Robert Arthur. Reprinted by permission of the Regents of the University of Michigan. Harold Matson Company, Inc.—for "The Fog Horn" from *The Golden Apples of the Sun* by Ray Bradbury. Copyright (c) 1953 by Ray Bradbury. Adapted and reprinted by permission of Harold Matson Company, Inc. Globe/Modern Curriculum Press—for "The Ten-Armed Monster of Newfoundland" by Elma Schemenauer from *Yesterstories 2 (The Lost Lemon Mine).* Copyright (c) 1979. Adapted and reprinted by permission of Globe/Modern Curriculum Press. International Creative Management—for "The Monsters Are Due on Maple Street" by Rod Serling. Copyright (c) 1960 by Rod Serling. Reprinted by permission of International Creative Management. **Unit 4:** Dodd, Mead & Company, Inc.—for "The Finish of Patsy Barnes," from *The Strength of Gideon and Other Stories* by Paul Laurence Dunbar. Reprinted by permission of Dodd, Mead & Company, Inc. Walker & Company—for "The Kick" from Fly Like an Eagle by Elizabeth Van Steenwyk. Copyright (c) 1978. Adapted by permission of the publisher, Walker & Company. Harvard University Press—for "Success is Counted Sweetest" by Emily Dickinson. Reprinted by permission of the publishers and the Trustees of Amherst College from *The Poems of Emily Dickinson,* edited by Thomas H. Johnson, Cambridge, massachusetts: The Belknap Press of Harvard University Press, Copyright 1951, (c) 1955, 1979, 1983 by the President and Fellows of Harvard College. Doubleday & Company, Inc.—for "This Day Is Over" by Calvin O'John from *Whispering Wind,* edited by Terry Allen. Copyright (c) 1972 by The Institute of American Indian Arts. Poetry Magazine—for "Factory Work" by Deborah Boe. Copyright 1986 by Deborah Boe. Reprinted by permission of the author. Larry Sternig Literary Agency—for "The Wolf of Thunder Mountain" by Dion Henderson. Copyright 1959 by the Boy Scouts of America. Adapted and reprinted by permission of Larry Sternig Literary Agency. Random House—for "The Pot of Gold" by Salvador Salazar Arrué from *The Golden Land: An Anthology of American Folklore in Literature,* edited and translated by Harriet de Onis. Copyright 1948, 1976. Reprinted by permission of Random House. **Unit 5:** Julius Lester—for "The Man Who Was a Horse" by Julius Lester. Adapted and reprinted by permission of the author. Esquire Magazine—for "The Tiger's Heart" by Jim Kjelgaard. Copyright (c) 1951 by Esquire Magazine. Adapted and reprinted by permission of Esquire Magazine. Macmillan Publishing Company—for "Who Has Seen the Wind?" from *Sing-Song* by Christina G. Rossetti (New York: Macmillan, 1924). Reprinted by permission of Macmillan Publishing Company. New Directions Publishing Company, Inc.—for "The Storm" and "The Bare Tree" from *Selected Poems* by William Carlos Williams. Reprinted by permission of the publisher. Poetry Magazine—for "Clouds" by Gregory Djanikian. Copyright 1986 by Gregory Djanikian. Reprinted by permission of the author. Harold Ober Associates, Inc.—for the T.V. script of "The Big Wave" by Pearl S. Buck. Copyright 1947 by The Curtis Publishing Company. Copyright 1948 by Pearl S. Buck. Renewed. Copyright (c) 1958 by Pearl S. Buck. Adapted and reprinted by permission of Harold Ober Associates, Inc. Prentice-Hall, Inc.—for "The Black Box," adapted from *The Black Box* by Albert B. Carr. Copyright (c) 1969 by Albert B. Carr and William Brooks. Published by Prentice-Hall, Inc., Englewood Cliffs, NJ 07632. Reprinted by permission of Prentice-Hall, Inc. Peter Pauper Press—for "Three Haiku" by Matsuo Basho, from *Haiku Harvest,* translated by Peter Beilenson and Harry Behn. Copyright (c) 1962 by Peter Pauper Press. Reprinted by permission of Peter Pauper Press. William Morrow & Company—for "Winter" from *Cotton Candy on a Rainy Day* by Nikki Giovanni. Copyright (c) 1978 by Nikki Giovanni. Reprinted by permission of William Morrow & Company, Inc. **Unit 6:** Poetry Magazine—for "The Family Album" by Jane O. Wayne. Copyright 1984 by Jane O. Wayne. Reprinted by permission of the author. Margaret Walker—for "Lineage" from *For My People* by Margaret Walker. Copyright 1942. Published by Yale University Press. Reprinted by permission of the author. William Carlos Williams—for "The Last Words of My English Grandmother" from *Selected Poems* by William Carlos Williams. Copyright 1985. Reprinted by permission of New Directions Publishing Corporation. Dorothy West—for "The Richer, The Poorer." Adapted and reprinted by permission of the author's agent, Bertha Klausner International Literary Agency, Inc. Harcourt, Brace, Jovanovich, Inc.—for "Mama and Papa," adapted from "Mama's Bank Account," copyright 1943 by Kathryn Forbes. Renewed 1971 by Richard E. McLean and Robert M. McLean. Reprinted by permission of Harcourt, Brace, Jovanovich, Inc. Alfred A. Knopf, Inc.—for "Mother to Son" by Langston Hughes. Copyright 1926 and renewed 1954. From *Selected Poems of Langston Hughes.* Reprinted by permission of Alfred A. Knopf, Inc. University of Massachusetts Press—for "While I Slept" from *Come Out Into the Sun: New and Selected Poems* by Robert Francis. Copyright 1936, 1964 by Robert Francis. Reprinted by permission of University of Massachusetts Press. Poetry Magazine—for "These Are the Gifts" by Gregory Djanikian. Copyright 1985 by Gregory Djanikian. Reprinted by permission of the author. Farrar, Straus & Giroux—for "Charles" from *The Lottery* by Shirley Jackson. Copyright 1948, 1949 and renewed 1976. Reprinted by permission of Farrar, Straus & Giroux. Charles Scribner's Sons—for adaption of "A Mother in Mannville" from *When the Whippoorwill* by Marjorie Kinnan Rawlings. Copyright 1940 by Marjorie Kinnan Rawlings. Copyright renewed 1968 by Norton Baskin. Reprinted by permission of Charles Scribner's Sons. Eugenia Collier—for "Sweet Potato Pie." Adapted and reprinted by permission of Eugenia Collier and Howard University.

Note: Every effort has been made to locate the copyright owner of material reprinted in this book. Omissions brought to our attention will be corrected in subsequent editions.

ART CREDITS

Illustrations

Unit 1: 4/5: illustration p. 16: Richard Leonard/ Richard Martin; p. 52: Richard Loehle; pp. 60, 61: Richard Martin; pp. 71, 73, 76: Den Schofield; **Unit 2:** p. 90: Anthony Carnabuci/ HK Portfolio; pp. 92, 94: David Tamura; pp. 98, 99, 102,: Lane Yerkes; p. 114: Rodica Prato/ Richard Salzman; p. 119: Roz Schanzer; pp. 124, 127, 129, 130: Cindy Spencer; p. 135: Linda Y. Miyamoto; p. 136: Rubin Brickman; p. 143: Richard Elmer; p. 146: Paul Casale; pp. 150, 153, 156: Copie; **Unit 3:** p. 196, 197: Jean and Mou Sien Tseng/ HK Portfolio; p. 198: Maggier Zander; pp. 226, 230: Linda Draper; p. 244: Robert Parker/ Publisher's Graphics; p. 258: Rhana Janto/ William Giese; **Unit 4:** p. 288: Anthony Carnabuci/ HK Portfolio; p. 294, 296, 297: Diana Magnuson; p. 304: A. Hubrich/ H. Armstrong Roberts; p. 316: William Hunter Hicklin; pp. 318 Michael Garland; p. 332, 335, 337, 339: Pat and Robin Dewitt; p. 344, 347: Victor Valla; **Unit 5:** pp. 356, 358: Jack Stockman; pp. 377, 381: Angelo Franco; p. 384: Photo Researchers; p. 389: Marcel Durocher; pp. 420, 423: Michael Bryant; **Unit 6:** p. 442: Judith Joseph; p. 469 Pat Cummings; pp. 472, 473: Paul Biniasz; p. 476, 479, 481: Maggie Zander; pp. 490, 493: Jan Naimo Jones; pp. 500, 501, 503, 507: Sterling Brown; pp. 530, 531, 533, 535, 537: Dick Smolinski.

Photographs

Unit 1: p 7: James P. Rowan; p 10: Library of Congress; p 21: Laura Ingalls Wilder Home Association; p 21: Jim Brandenburg; p 35: The Granger Collection; p 39: The New York Public Library; p 67: Carter/The Image Bank; **Unit 2:** p 118: Bumgarner/Tony Stone Worldwide; p 121: Feulner/The Image Bank; p 134: Jean Marie Truchet/ Tony Stone Worldwide; p 137 (inset): AP/Wide World Photos; p 137: McLaren/Photo Researchers; p 144: SuperStock; p 147: Cain/Photo Researchers; p 147: (inset) Courtesy William Morrow Publishers; **Unit 3:** p 218: Melford/The Image Bank; p 219: Tony Stone Worldwide; p 222: Dixon/ The Photo Source; p 236: The Photo Source; **Unit 4:** p 300: Hamrick/The Image Bank; p 304: H. Armstrong Roberts; pp 308, 311, 316: North Wind Picture Archives; p 317: The Image Bank; p 318 top: Weller/ The Image Bank; p 318 bottom: Garland/The Image Bank; p 319 top: The Granger Collection; p 319 bottom: The Granger Collection; p 324: Parres/Photo Researchers; p 326 (inset): The Granger Collection; p 326: Armand/ Tony Stone Worldwide; p 332: North Wind Picture Archives; **Unit 5:** p 360: North Wind Picture Archives; p 384: Larson/ Photo Researchers; p 385: Color Library International; p 386: Courtesy Mr. Nicholas Rossetti; p 417: The Museum of Modern Art/Film Stills Archive; p 417 (inset): Ap/Wide World Photos; p 425: Video Graffiti/The Photo Source; p 428: North Wind Picture Archives; p 429: Schreiner/The Image Bank; p 431: Seitz/Photo Researchers; p 432: Clay/Tony Stone Worldwide; p 433: UPI/Bettmann Newsphotos; **Unit 6:** p 444, 456, 460: Culver Pictures; p 446: Three Lions; p 463: SEF/Art Resource; p 468: Art Resource; p 470: Louisiana State Museum; p. 483: AP/Wide World Photos; p 483: The Museum of Modern Art/Film Stills Archive; p 486: Jean Smolar; p 495: Museum of Modern Art/Film Stills Archive; p 511: Seitz/Photo Researchers; p 514: Pickerell/Tony Stone Worldwide; p 516: Streano/Tony Stone Worldwide; p 521: Frerck/Tony Stone Worldwide; p 523: Farmer/Tony Stone Worldwide: p 526: Pickerell/Tony Stone Worldwide; p 527: Cooper/H. Armstrong Roberts; p 527: AP/Wide World Photos.